ARMY of the
DRAGONBONDED
BOOK OF WATER

DRAGONBONDED®

THE DRAGONBONDED RETURN Series
Call of the Dragonbonded
Order of the Dragonbonded
Army of the Dragonbonded
Omen of the Dragonbonded

THE NEW CRONOAN CHRONICLES Series
Chronicles of Nartesis Shazarack: Father of
Necromancy
Chronicles of Alicia Farclave
Chronicles of Tatem Creeg

THE FIRST DRAGONBONDED Series

Visit **www.thedragonbonded.com** to get the latest information on these books and other works by JD Hart, to subscribe to the author's newsletter, or to contact the author.

ARMY OF THE DRAGONBONDED
BOOK OF WATER

Book 3: The Dragonbonded Return

JD Hart

Dragonbonded
Press

First Printing: November 2020

9 8 7 6 5 4 3 2 1

ISBN: 978-1-949101-02-7

All Artwork by J.D. Hart
Cover Design by Meg Cowley

Acknowledgments

This work, along with the entire Dragonbonded Return series, would not be possible without the support, encouragement, and suggestions of many people who have participated in making this work what it is. First, a very special appreciation goes to my amazing editor, Maya Myers (Maya Myers Books of Charlotte).

Also, special thanks go out to the members of the small, local writers' group in Charlotte, NC: Matt Myers, Andrea Reimers, and Amy Kuney, as well as those in the Asheville, NC writers' group: Diana Brewster, Chris Kuchar, and Melissa Rogers.

And finally, thanks to those who provided valuable feedback on this work, including Laura Hart, Suzanne Hart, Angel Haze, Carol Klingler, Amanda Wahula.

The HAR
REAL

ANTARIC SEA

Port Fount

Stronghold
of Aldemeer

Emb

D

Ashecombe
CASTLE

Moorestone
CASTLE

DARMASCUS

Shan-Grail
RUINS

Gri
(H

Mazer's Sanctuary

Blackmarke
CASTLE

Manor Caltarus

LAKE
LOCKS

GRAYSTONE

REALM OF
GRENETIA

Cleft
CASTLE

Stonewell
CASTLE

Moonslayer
CASTLE

REALM OF
ELVENSTEIN

CHAR

LEGEND

Royal Castle   Keep

Castle   Stronghold

City   Caverns

Town   Village/Outpost

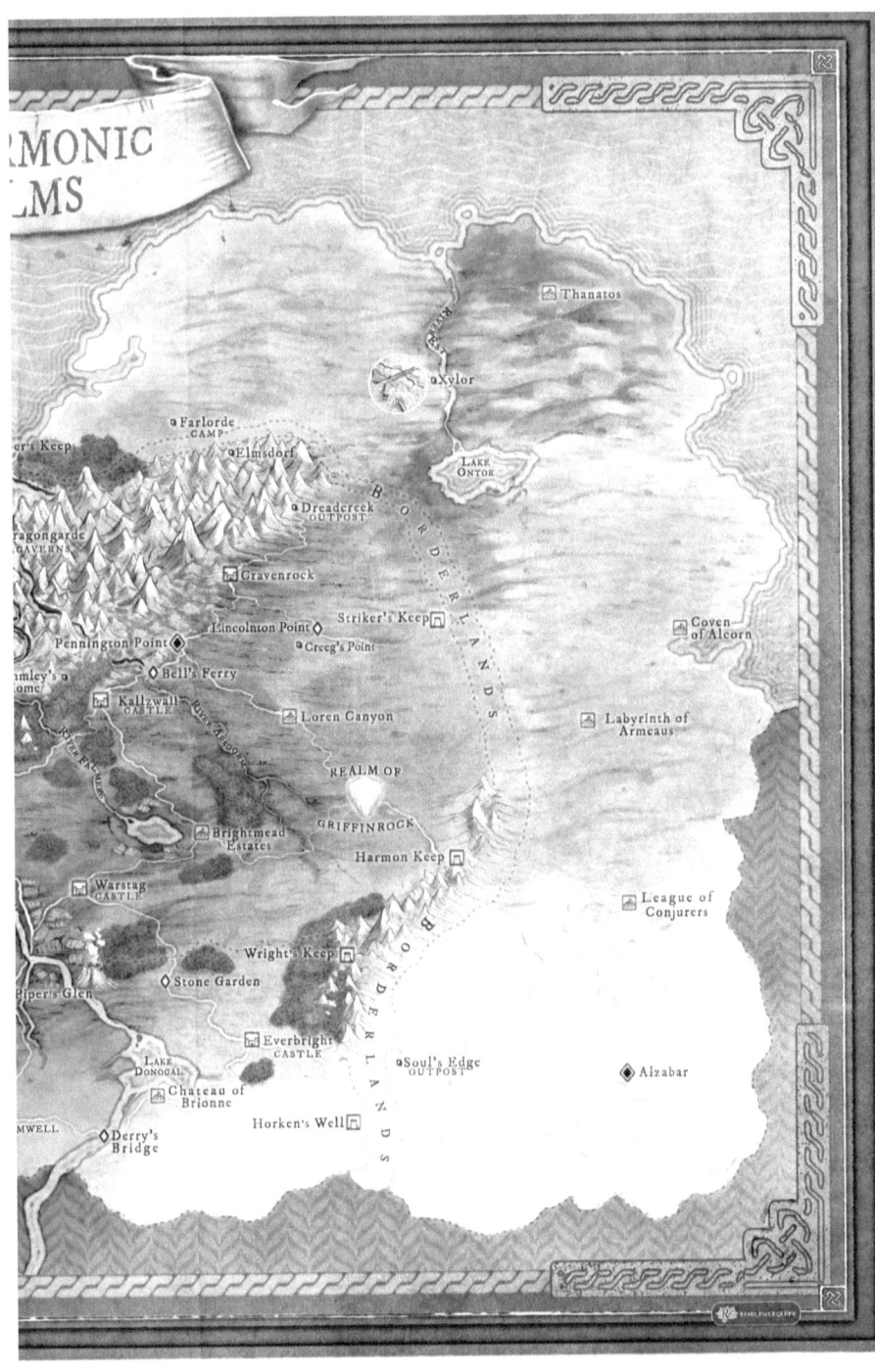

Contents

Biographer's Note

History books are filled with the names of transformative figures—kings, dictators, and despots of nation-states who swayed their masses by spouting visions of a brighter future. Yet in the end, nearly all those figures failed. And while the more interesting question might be why people let themselves be duped into believing that these so-called visionaries could lead them to paradise, I am left to ponder another question: Why were so many unsuccessful?

In pursuit of an answer, I have studied their failed promises and pledges to guide their subjects to a blessed land. And I have reached one conclusion: Having a vision does not make one visionary any more than being visionary means one has a vision. As the story in this binder unveils, a vision can be neither created nor owned by just one person. A true vision emerges from the collective soil like a flower, fertilized by the struggles of the downtrodden, watered by the tears of those unjustly punished, and warmed by the light of righteousness. All contribute to its creation.

Truly successful visionaries, those few transformative figures in our long history, have understood that a common vision is what binds us together. The responsibility of the visionary, therefore, is to draw upon the people's imagination of what can be, coalesce it into what should be, and compel others to transform it into what must be.

And that is why visionaries are so rare.

- JD Hart

Synopsis of Call of the Dragonbonded

(Book 1)

For over five hundred years, the Harmonic Realms have maintained relative peace with the Anarchists across the Borderlands. But a great planetary alignment signals that the Cosmic balance of power is shifting. With this new balance, two quite different sixteen-year-olds become entangled, and their actions will determine the fate of the known world.

Conner Stonefield is smart and idealistic. His sheltered life as the son of a freeman farmer makes him an unlikely hero. He dreams of becoming an honorable member of the Apothecaries Guild and, with this rise in social status, settling down with his arranged fiancée in their peaceful community. But the Cosmos has a different destiny for him. When he sets out on his trek to find his life-long animal bond (a coming-of-age rite inherent in each person's seventeenth year), it is soon clear that neither his limited experience nor his naive worldview has prepared him for what lies ahead.

Conner follows the physical pull of his bond's Calling, which first leads him to the city of Cravenrock. He is quickly swept into its criminal underworld, where he befriends a young Bandit and, much to his chagrin, becomes known as a thief and escape artist of great skill. When Bandit helps Conner escape from the clutches of the Thieves Guild, the Anarchist Assassin Lacerus sends a tracker, Morgas, to hunt him down. Morgas and his small team follow Conner as he continues on his quest into the heart of the Dragon's Back Mountains.

In Griffinrock's royal Graystone Castle, Princess Veressa is reluctant to accept her responsibilities as the next matriarch of her realm. She desires nothing more than to be a Ranger, fighting to protect the Harmonic Realms. So, when she receives her Calling, the strong-willed princess pressures her assigned protector, the master Ranger Annabelle Loris, to go on one last adventure. Posing as Annabelle's apprentice, Veressa escapes her protective parents to go in search of her animal bond. Annabelle begins to teach Veressa how to control the elementals that give Rangers their unique powers.

Meanwhile, Conner finds his bond: not the feathered or furry companion he had expected, but Skye, a young, two-legged dragon, a wyvern. When the scaly black creature attempts to convince Conner that the ancient stories of dragons and their bonded human riders, the Dragonbonded, are not just children's fables, Conner clings tenaciously to his rigid beliefs of the world. After much physical and emotional struggle, he suggests that the two seek out a great and powerful Shaman, Grimmley Rollingsworth, to break their bond. Skye, wanting nothing more to do with the ill-mannered and shallow human, heartily concurs.

Leaving the peevish dragon behind, Conner seeks the Shaman's whereabouts and stumbles headlong into a plot to kidnap and ransom a Ranger apprentice believed to be of noble birth; indeed, she is the princess Veressa. Conner aids Veressa and Annabelle in their escape. When a charlatan Sorcerer fumbles a binding spell, Conner becomes psychically linked to the ungrateful Veressa.

As Conner's and Veressa's paths intertwine, the Assassin Lacerus works in disguise to train Veressa's future Champion of the Realm, the incomparable Warrior Marcantos, as an unwitting aid to the Anarchists. When word of the first human-dragon bonding in half a millennium reaches Lacerus's ear, the Assassin reaches out to his Kindred Brothers in the Anarchic Lands. An Anarchic scouting party is dispatched to eliminate the duo before the dragon-bonded human discovers the power of the Dragonbonded who ended the great war long ago.

At the end of book 1, Conner and Skye reunite and begin their journey to the home of the powerful Grandmaster Shaman. Conner feels a renewed sense of urgency to break their bond. For behind the veil of Conner's fear of being forced to give up on his dream lies a greater terror: that he, a simple freeman Eastlander, may well be saddled to fulfill an ancient foretelling.

Synopsis of Order of the Dragonbonded

(Book 2)

Conner wants nothing more than to break his bond with Skye and get back to his simple Eastlander life. So when he and his dragon bond find the powerful but retired Shaman Grimmley Rollingsworth at his secluded home, Conner asks Grimmley to break their bond. Grimmley sends Conner and Skye on a quest to retrieve a silver box in hopes that the trial will help them learn to work together. The two find the box in a cave deep in the mountains, but in the process, Conner unknowingly awakens the dormant and very powerful Necromancer Nartesis Shazarack, thought to have died nearly a thousand years before with the destruction of the Necromancers' city, Thanatos.

Meanwhile, near Cravenrock, Princess Veressa finds her bond, a rare snow leopard named Antilles. During their bonding, Veressa falls and, near death, has a dream vision, where Ourea, vessel and spirit bearer of Earth elemental, tells her that she must prepare for an arduous future. The Ranger Annabelle Loris takes the unconscious Veressa to Cravenrock and reports the accident to Veressa's father, King Jonath. Angered, Jonath releases Annabelle from her service and assigns the Warrior Marcantos Evinfaire, who just happens to be in Cravenrock Keep, as the princess's new protector. Accompanied by his preceptor, the undercover Assassin Lacerus, Marcantos agrees to deliver the princess safely back to Graystone.

When news of Conner's bonding reaches the Anarchic Lands, the Anarchic councils dispatch a band of Barbarians led by the Necromancer Meera Asheborne, along with the Kindred Brother Groegan Briarmede, on a risky mission to find Conner and his dragon. While Meera is told she is an emissary to discuss a potential alliance with the Dragonbonded, Groegan's mission is to keep Conner from meddling in the Kindred's plans to install the Anarchic-trained Marcantos as Veressa's Champion.

After Conner returns the silver box to Grimmley, the Shaman informs Conner and Skye that there is no way to break their bond, sending the two into a fit of rage. Knowing Conner's secret of being bonded to a dragon cannot be contained for long, Grimmley offers to tutor the boy in manipulating elementals. When Conner finds himself incapable of casting any Shaman incantations, Grimmley calls upon Dragonbonded historian and grandmaster Sorceress Layna Newstone to assist. Unfortunately, Layna has no better success. In a desperate move to break through Conner's barriers, she takes Conner and Skye to Dragongarde, the ancient mountain-fortress home of the first Dragonbonded.

Veressa begins her long journey home under the watchful eye of her demanding protector, Marcantos. But she faces new challenges. Feeling strong urges to run free in the wild, she begins to question her sanity. The ever-observant Lacerus, recognizing that the conflict brewing inside Veressa is her strong connection with her new bond, takes advantage of her distress and covertly offers advice on how to adapt to these new emotions and impulses. Veressa reluctantly accepts.

While Conner and Skye are at Dragongarde, Layna is called away on an urgent matter, leaving the two to explore the ancient fortress alone. Conner discovers a trove of Dragonbonded armor, dragon saddles, tapestries, paintings, Modeic hieroglyphs, and food, all in pristine condition and protected by a powerful shield surrounding the fortress.

Released from her service as Veressa's protector, the disheartened Annabelle is reassigned to Dreadcreek, a Ranger outpost near the northeastern Borderlands. There, the station's commander, Lanchus Lendfeather, instructs her to assist the Alpslander guildsman Gertrum Smelterman and his band of Scouters in investigating reports of dragon sightings in the central mountains. In Elmsdorf, Annabelle acquires the bloodbond services of the Alpslander Morgas Terranus, and they set out for Dragongarde.

Veressa is visiting her aunt, Duchess Mariette, at Kallzwall Castle when Hector Dellrose, a former Harmonic Ranger, assassinates Veressa's mother, Queen Izadora. When the devastating news arrives, Veressa rushes home to tend to her father, who was wounded in the assassination. Plans begin to select the new Queen Imminent's personal life-long protector and Champion through a tournament of advocates chosen from each of the orders.

At Dragongarde, Conner and Skye are captured and detained by Meera and the band of Barbarians. It is while Conner is held captive that he pieces together the Anarchic plot to infiltrate Griffinrock by installing Marcantos Evinfaire as Veressa's Champion, putting the Assassin Lacerus one step away from the new queen.

When Annabelle and the Alpslanders arrive at Dragongarde, they battle with Meera and the Barbarians, and Conner and Skye are able to escape. Conner attempts to fly to Graystone to warn the king, but Skye grows ill. Just as the tournament begins, Conner is forced to leave Skye in a mountain cave and run to Grimmley's home, where he tells the Shaman everything he knows of the conspiracy.

Grimmley convinces Conner to go with him to Graystone to expose Marcantos. Appearing on the tourney grounds at the moment Marcantos is to be declared Veressa's Champion, Conner is forced to fight the Warrior in hopes that combat will reveal Marcantos as an Anarchist. Using elemental powers he didn't know he had, Conner defeats Marcantos, exposing the Warrior as Anarchic trained—and Conner himself becomes Veressa's new Champion. Unfortunately, he is rendered unconscious, giving Marcantos and Lacerus an opportunity to escape.

When Conner awakes, he recalls nothing of the contest nor of how he wielded the elemental forces he used to defeat Marcantos. Conner flies to Cravenrock and returns to Graystone with Kriston Heldcrest, the twelve-year-old thief known as Bandit, as his personal page.

Veressa's father, King Jonath, blames himself for the queen's death and suffers from agonizing remorse. Believing his love for the queen prevented him from saving her, Jonath privately convinces Conner to vow that he will not allow himself to get too close to Veressa, nor to let Veressa learn of his love for her.

The new Queen Veressa must deal with a realm demanding war against the Anarchists, with the full support of the six orders and the two other Harmonic crowns. She also struggles against powerful desires to be out in the wilderness. She feels a close emotional connection with Conner that she cannot explain, though she can trace it to their first meeting in Pennington Point, when he protected her from a Sorcerer's spell of binding.

Grimmley and Layna are certain that a network of Anarchic spies still exists in the Harmonic Realms. Grimmley convinces Conner that, until these other spies are uncovered, he must maintain the lie that he is in full command of the elemental forces he used to defeat the banished Marcantos. Conner begrudgingly agrees but worries that he may not be able to protect the queen should the occasion arise.

From Book 2: Epilogue

"The Dragonbonded?" asked Sovereign Prince Galan, head of the Necromancers Order. Annoyed, he studied the long faces of the other members of the council, then turned to his wife. "You said you could keep this young man out of the way, Breanen. Now he is the queen of Griffinrock's Champion?"

Lady Breanen shrugged, unconcerned by Galan's volatile temper. "You worry too much, my husband. The Cosmos shifts in our favor." But her recondite response did nothing to quell his storm. So she took a more direct approach. "Plans do not always go as expected. Even in the capable hands of someone like Meera, there will be setbacks."

Galan had considered sending a member of the council on the expedition to deal with the young Dragonbonded, but they were all needed in Thanatos at this critical juncture. It was Breanen who had pushed him to send the less-experienced Meera Asheborne. "You should have foreseen this!" Galan had known Breanen from the time they were both fledgling apprentices at the Necromancer academy a half century before. Even then, her powers of divination and innate skills of necromancy were incredible. She had even predicted Galan's rise to sovereign prince of the order. But she was not infallible. He shook his head at the unfathomable thought. "A Dragonbonded changes everything."

"The Dragonbonded changes nothing!" Breanen rose to her feet, her hand gripping the amulet hidden beneath her flowing gray hair. "Since the Great War, the Harmonics have refused to abide by the armistice, flagrantly building holds in the Borderlands and sending militia into our territories. Now, war boils in their hearts. The other orders still need our necro-army before spring is full if we are to successfully defend the Anarchic Lands. We cannot disrupt that process."

"And what of Meera Asheborne? She is more than just a loss to our order; as you well know, she holds many secrets. If she is forced to talk, the damage could be immeasurable."

"Wheels are already in motion to take care of that problem," Breanen stated flatly.

Before Galan could ask for her to elaborate, a hesitant rap at the council chamber door drew their attention. A young adept appeared and bowed low. "Sovereign Prince, Lady Breanen, apologies for bothering you at this hour, but you should come straightaway to the gates. There is a ... situation that demands your attention." ...

"Where is your master?" Galan demanded of the mob of undead clustered inside the fortress gates. Most were rotted beyond utility, with body parts and bits of armor dangling and swinging to and fro as they milled about aimlessly. The stench of dirt and decay was thick around them. He scanned but found no necromancer directing them.

One of the creatures near the ancient bronze likeness of their Supreme Lord Shazarack turned to inspect Galan with a lidless stare, half its face atrophied into a perpetual grin. Thin white hair hung in wisps over moldy, gray robes long since rotten. "You have rebuilt the fortress just as it once stood, and added to it as well!" The undead gave the prince a nod of satisfaction.

"Spirit, I asked where your master is!"

"Master?" The gray-hooded undead seemed shocked by the question. "I serve no master," it gasped.

"What kind of trickery is this? All undead serve a master. Who was your summoner?"

The undead shuffled closer. A gurgling sound escaped its dangling jaw, but it fell silent when it looked upon Breanen. Turning, it pitched toward her, raising a bony hand.

"What are you doing?" Breanen asked.

The undead drew on Earth and Fire elementals and rasped, *"Ourera ousia anypkosmima."* Breanen's amulet floated up from beneath her flowing gray hair.

Breanen inhaled and staggered back, but several undead lurched forward and gripped her fast in their sinewy arms. "Stop!" she screamed, her face contorting in uncontrolled terror as the undead caressed the amulet's thick gold chain. Her thin body jerked and twisted as she fought to break free from the vise-like grips.

Galan quickly cast a spell of protection: *"Ourera psychi prostatepsychi!"* Several others shouted and quickly began casting spells of command and protection against the undead intruders, but the creatures were immune to their efforts. Ignoring the mayhem and Lady Breanen's screams, the gray-robed undead lifted the amulet from about her neck. The onyx stone flashed a brilliant blue, and the old woman's violent convulsions stopped.

The undead studied the sparking blue flames in the onyx stone. With a flick of its hand, its undead companions released Lady Breanen. Her body tumbled to the dirt.

Prince Galan ran to her, cradling his love's still form. Turning his gaze upward, he whispered, "Who are you?"

Exalted, the undead held its bony arms wide to the sky in mimicry of the statue behind it. "I am Nartesis Shazarack, Supreme Lord of the Necromancers!" it declared in a hollow voice. "I have finally been awakened from my deep slumber in my mountain cave. At last, I am home!"

And the story continues ...

Part I

Nothing ever lasts. But neither is anything lost.

—The Modei Book of Earth (Fourth Book)

Fishing and Odd Fellows

Conner watched the cork tied to his fishing line spin and play in the swirling eddies just past a small outcrop in the swift River Tresdan. Hemera lit the thick, rich forest in the east, the tops of the trees sprinkled with the hint of autumn.

Pauli sighed deeply. "I could get used to this."

Conner peered over at his best friend, who had taken his ritual position under a willow. "Looks to me like you already have."

"Well, it's not going to last forever," Pauli said.

No it won't, Conner thought. But it was more than the changing colors of leaves and the cooler nights that gave him warning. Since leaving on his bonding trek, he had experienced enough change to last a lifetime, which was why their early-morning fishing excursions along the riverbank outside Graystone Castle had become so precious. The meager hours offered him a brief shelter from what evolved quickly into exhausting, hectic days. Besides having to deal with an importunate dragon who wanted nothing more than to fly away to his dragon home, Conner had to contend with two demanding preceptors secretively pushing him to rediscover his lost powers, a growing flock of tourists traveling to Graystone to get a glimpse of the famous "Dragonbonded Returned" and his bond like they were some carnival sideshow, and Queen Veressa's "requests" that he attend to her security on daily rides out of the castle.

Not that he was complaining about that last duty. The jaunts with Veressa improved her mood, which had been beleaguered by her continued struggles with the War Council over conditions for signing a proclamation of war against the Anarchists. Unfortunately, his affections for her grew with every moment he was around her. And with his solemn vow to Veressa's father, King Jonath, sworn on the Champion's amulet hanging around his neck, he was not about to let his fondness get in the way of protecting her.

Pauli interrupted his thoughts. "It's hard to believe your parents and Pattria have been here for nearly a fortnight. Seems like just yesterday you were introducing them to your dragon." Conner did not respond, so Pauli pressed on. "You know, I would have thought even the flappable Pattria would sooner or later come around to see that your bond is nothing more than an oversized windbag."

Conner furrowed his brow. It wasn't the first time Pauli had brought up the encounter between Skye and Conner's fiancée, Pattria. And, knowing Pauli, it would not be the last. When Conner had introduced Pattria to Skye, the dragon had gone through his usual ceremony of unfurling his wings and bowing to her. But Pattria, who was already frightened of him, had thought he meant to eat her and ran screaming. Since then, though Conner and Skye had attempted to correct the misunderstanding several times, Pattria had refused to get near Skye again. In fact, except for a brief appearance at a dinner banquet honoring the new Champion of Griffinrock, Pattria had spent most of her time alone in her castle bedchambers. Now she and Conner's parents would be heading back home to Creeg's Point the next morning.

Of course, all of this only scratched the surface of Conner's woes. While he had become the new queen's personal Champion by defeating Marcantos on the tourney field, he had since been unable to recreate the elemental powers that had brought him victory. And then there was the Barbarian, Groegan Briarmede, who, along with the Necromancer Meera Asheborne, had held him captive at Dragongarde. The Barbarian had raised doubts in Conner about Skye's true nature and whether the dragon could be happy living among Harmonics.

Conner had an idea who might offer some answers to these concerns. But he had no clue how he would ever get a chance to talk to her.

"Oh, look!" Pauli shouted, bringing his thoughts back. "Here comes your little thief."

"You mean *ex*-thief," Conner corrected. "I keep telling you, Kriston is my page now. He has no need for his old pilfering ways."

"He isn't an ex if he keeps stealing stuff from my room." Pauli puffed out his lower lip.

"Believe what you will, but he wouldn't take your things if you stopped calling him a thief. He only steals *your* items."

"That's because I have all the best stuff to steal. He just can't resist." Pauli glanced up as the thin twelve-year-old drew closer. "So, what did you steal from me today?"

Kriston started to respond, but shook his head, then stared at Conner with fists on bony hips. "From what I can translate, your dragon is in an especially testy mood this morning, Conner."

Pauli snorted. "From what you can translate? I've been around that irritable black creature long enough to know one thing: I don't need to speak a word of Dragon to know when he's cranky. And he's *always* cranky."

Conner sat up. "Yes, well right now, he is still incensed over the prying throng of spectators that collected outside the dungeon entrance yesterday. He gets annoyed when he feels trapped, even when he is confined in a place that he loves."

"Well, not all bonds are as irksome as yours, Conner," Pauli said. "I, for one, am excited to finally be bonded so I can start my Warrior apprenticeship."

"Skye keeps asking for you," Kriston added, undisturbed by Pauli's musings.

Conner rose and handed Kriston his fishing pole. "Here. Maybe you'll have better luck than I did. I might as well get this out of the way before the castle wakes up and I'm being whipped around six ways to nightfall." He trudged off toward the castle entrance, trying to ignore the argument erupting behind him about where Pauli's hunting knife might have gone.

On the castle grounds, Conner sensed people gawking at him, so he diverted his feet up one of the back alleys where there were far fewer people. There, the sounds and smells of breakfast cooking made his stomach grumble, so he picked up the pace. He rounded a corner and, entering a narrow lane, skirted around the street's only other occupant, a thin townsman who tipped his broad-brimmed hat Conner's way and gave

Conner a toothy grin. Conner skidded to a stop and turned back. "You!" he shouted at the townsman.

The townsman spun to face him. "Yes, sire?"

"I know you."

"Know me, sire?" The townsman gazed at the large ruby amulet dangling from Conner's neck, the one marking Conner as the queen's own Champion, then tilted forward at the waist, offering a humble bow with the wave of his hand, his other hand resting on a wooden cane he held wide to the side. "But we have not met before. Surely I would remember conversing with the great dragon rider and the queen's own Champion."

"I said I know you, not that we have met."

The man stared at Conner. "Ah, yes, I suppose there is a difference."

Conner poked a forefinger the townsman's way. "At the Champion's tourney; you were in the crowd. You tipped your hat at me."

"Ah! Why yes! I seem to recall being there, now that you mention it. I am truly humbled that you should remember me, with all the stress and noise and goings on at that moment—preparing to meet that disreputable Warrior what's-his-name on the Field of Contest." The man bowed again with an even greater flourish, then gave the bright skies above a contented sigh. His gray squirrel hung from his cane and chattered at Conner. "I must say! What a glorious day that was, disrupting the vile and treasonous acts of Anarchic spies right here in our own Graystone Castle, the very heart of Griffinrock! You do indeed bring me great honor by even recognizing my attendance."

Conner grunted. Something was off about the man, so it took more than a moment to put his mind to it. "That was not the first time I saw you."

Now the man looked surprised. "Oh? We have crossed paths before, then? How truly fortuitous for me!"

It came to Conner in a flash, and he stepped closer with a sudden keen interest in the man with a large proboscis. "Yes! In Pennington Point. It was you ... in Dorry's Alehouse. You sang 'Riders of the Order'!"

The man's face flashed from surprise to amazement, but in the wink of an eye, it was gone. He squared his shoulders before Conner. His back straightened, and for the first time, he looked Conner in the eye. "Amazing," he stated with a satisfied nod.

"Maybe it's amazing ... and maybe not. Two chance encounters hundreds of miles apart in a few fortnights? Somehow, I don't think it coincidence. Most townsmen don't do that much traveling in a lifetime."

This last sentence trailed from Conner's lips, losing energy with each uttered syllable as he realized he was standing in an empty street confronting (nay, accusing!) a man of having ulterior designs in their previous encounters. Suddenly, Conner felt vulnerable, and he shifted into a more defensive stance.

"Hmm," the townsman muttered as he sized up Conner with a probing eye. "Well, I suppose it was that kind of wherewithal that led you to crack the code of that sinister plot to get near the new queen."

This time it was Conner who was surprised. But his wariness receded as more unexpected memories bubbled to the surface. "Wait a minute. Pennington Point was not the first time we met either. Cravenrock!" Conner shouted. "You were there in the marketplace, among the crowd of faces the day I climbed the city wall!" Conner's mind reeled at the implications. And the man's steady expression set off a few alarms. What if this man was an Anarchic spy? Conner scanned the area. Would Skye come to his defense if the man attacked?

"Why there must have been three hundred people there." The townsman nodded with approval, never losing his pleasant smile. "Someone told me you were the whip's popper." He tapped his cane on the cobblestone. "Wallis Arkman, at your service."

Conner was not impressed with the man's sudden humble attitude, though it had defused his sense of alarm. The man seemed harmless enough. "My service? Why, you have been meddling in my affairs."

"Meddling? Why, I would never!" Wallis gasped at the suggestion, then threw his head back and exploded in a hearty laugh. Finally he tipped his head to the lanky teen. "Yes, I suppose it might seem that way."

"You deny my accusation, then?"

"No more than any other preceptor would deny meddling in a pupil's lessons."

Conner snorted at the man's audacity. "I don't recall making you my mentor any more than I recall you ever instructing me."

"Oh, is that true?" Wallis's eyebrows rose halfway up his forehead. "Lessons come in many forms, young man. At least thrice I have aided you along your journey from yon to hither. I will have you know it was I who cut the ropes of the bridge over the River Aradorm, forcing you to fly across the gorge on your bond for the first time." The statement washed clean Conner's skeptical expression, amusing Wallis all the more. A thin finger wiggled upward at the sky. "It is the Cosmos's blessing that one does not need to appoint a teacher for there to be one; otherwise we'd learn very little in life," he concluded with a knowing wink.

Conner would never forget that day. He and Skye had been bonded only a few days when they arrived to find the bridge across the gorge destroyed. It had taken the dragon hours to convince Conner they should fly across, and he had nearly died in the crossing. His cheeks burned, but he could not tell whether it was from embarrassment or anger. "So, you fancy yourself my teacher?"

Wallis pursed his lips while studying Conner from scalp to toe and back again. "Someday," he stated lightheartedly, then added with a more serious tone, "maybe. You have potential. And you are by far a quicker study than your previous incarnation."

Potential? Previous incarnation? Apparently, the man thought a few words of praise would garner him a position of advantage. Conner grunted. "I should tell you that I already have two preceptors. I don't think I could possibly take on another."

"Yes." Wallis chuckled again. "The Shaman and his dear friend, the Sorceress. Surely you know by now, they struggle as much as you do. They are not capable of illuminating your path. Where you must go, they have never trodden." Shaking his head, he raised his palm to hold back Conner's defense of Grimmley and Layna. "Understanding that they are not capable of showing you the way is the first lesson you must complete before you are ready for me to be your preceptor."

It was not so much what Wallis said as how he said it that put Conner on edge. How much did this man know about his continued struggles to call upon the elemental forces? He started to ask Wallis what he meant but decided the man was more likely fishing for information. It was best to let that sleeping dragon lie. Instead, he asked, "First?"

"There are several more before you will be ready to hear what must be said. Rain is wasted pouring on the sea." Noting Conner's confusion, Wallis came forward and placed his palm lightly on Conner's shoulder. "How can I put this in a way you will appreciate? ... Ah! As the son of a farmer, you know you cannot plant corn in the spring and expect to harvest peas in the summer."

"What does that have to do—?"

"Think of it this way: You carry a certain kind of seed. As you take your journey, the seeds drop from your hand, growing and flourishing along the path you tread. But they cannot yield the kind of nourishment that Gaia needs right now. You must let go of the seeds you hold before you can accept those I offer."

"That makes no sense."

"No, I suppose it doesn't." Wallis stepped back with a sigh, then gazed off as if admiring a sunset on the horizon. "The subconscious will refuse to speak as long as the mind is not ready to listen. Try to remember that most people cannot see further than where they have been taught to reach." Dropping his hat back on his head and giving the brim a strong tug, he concluded, "We shall meet again ... and far too soon, I fear."

And with that, Wallis angled up the main street, blended in with those busily on their way to wherever, and was gone.

For several minutes, Conner stood, hands on hips, in silent contemplation. *My! What an odd fellow!* he thought. Still, he could not help but feel unsettled and raw, as if the man had ripped him from soil he did not feel fully rooted in. Wallis's words had struck a nerve, making him doubt what he knew to be true—or hoped to be true. A part of him wanted to run after the man, to demand better answers to his questions, to shout at him for stirring up this restless uncertainty. But another part was afraid of what answers lay on the other side of those questions. When his feet failed to chase Wallis down, he understood what Wallis had meant. He was not ready.

Goodbye to the Past

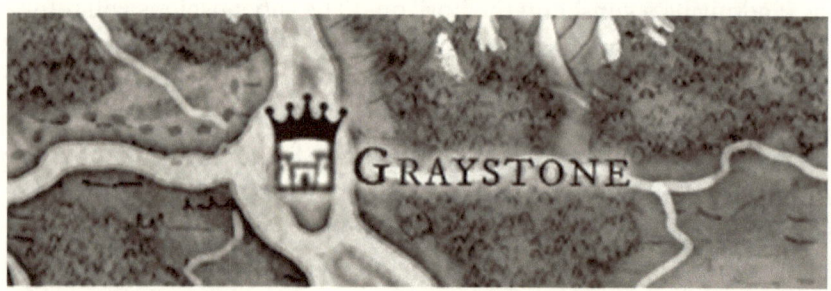

Oshan Stonefield pressed her palm to her son's cheek, looking up at him with caring eyes as blue as the morning sky. "Conner, you know we would stay longer if we could. But there are days of travel between here and home. And there is much to do in the fields with the shortening of Hemera's light."

Ignatius, Oshan's chipmunk bond, squeaked his concurrence from her shoulder.

It had been but a week since Conner's parents had arrived at Graystone, bringing their Eastlander starshine and warmth to the cold castle. But now, with their departure, Conner's dark world was closing in about him once more.

As if Oshan's words had invoked Gaia's star to appear, Hemera broke across the thick, rich forest to the east, lighting Graystone's upper towers and bathing the castle grounds in soft, muted reds. With their packed and harnessed wagon nearly ready, a dozen Queen's Defenders, including two ordermen officers, had gathered to accompany his parents on their long journey back to Creeg's Point.

"The late summer crops won't harvest themselves," Conner's father went on. Anton stepped closer and clapped Conner on the shoulder with a sinewy arm tanned to dark leather. "It was hard enough getting Anders Whiterock to agree to keep the weeds from owning the east fields the fortnight we've been away. If we don't get home soon, we may lose those crops as well."

Conner sensed his father's anxiousness to be on the road. He also knew the moistening in the man's eye was the real urgency—Anton thought it unseemly to be seen crying.

In the Eastlands, where words often failed, only actions held respect. Conner's gangly arms snared his mother and father. And in the silent embrace, Conner was carried back to that night two months before when they had told him he was to become an Apothecary guildsman's apprentice. Conner clung to his parents like frail ivy against a sturdy oak. He felt secure in their arms, and for the moment, his troubled mind was relieved of its burdens. A part of him ached to go with them, not so much for the life he had left there, but to return to that innocent world he'd once believed existed—to a time when Assassins and Necromancers were mere stories, when he believed he was the master of his fate, in command of his future. But such childhood fantasies only served those determined to bring harm to him—and to those he cared about. *Once your eyes are opened to the truth, there is no going back.*

Conner forced himself to pull away, salvaging enough courage to smile at his father. "I understand. I'm sure Miyra and Sayra are missing you. Besides, with everything going on of late, you should be there." Conner winked slyly his father. Through the summer, his sister Miyra had developed a keen interest in Tobi Cloverdale, Pauli's younger brother. Normally, that would not have been a concern. After all, Tobi and Miyra were fourteen, the typical age of betrothal among Eastlanders. Tobi was a good lad—generally. Unfortunately, he was a quick study, and that was a bit disconcerting when there was an older brother like Pauli around to mentor his every lesson.

"Well, the wagon won't drive itself." Anton shuffled off to check the hitches and straps for the fourth time.

Notorius, Anton's raccoon bond, sat on the wagon bench and chortled at Anton as if giving the man instructions on how to properly cinch the harnesses.

Oshan studied her son's troubled expression, then followed the boy's gaze to his father. "Your grandfather was fond of saying, 'It's better to say your goodbyes in moments of certainty than linger awkwardly in doubt.' Your father would never say it, but he is very proud of you. As am I." As if she read Conner's thoughts, she pressed on through the silence. "By now, there's not a single ear in Creeg's Point left wanting to hear of your deeds and what you have become. Once they hear Anton has returned, every Eastland well-wisher within a morning's stroll will want to have their say about how Eastlanders should not be involved in the affairs of the realms. He would rather return home and get all that behind him than have the rain cloud brewing over his head. Then he can focus on the urgent autumn chores ahead."

"At least I'm but a short day's flight to come visit," Conner quipped with a sideways smile.

Oshan shook her head. He knew she did not like envisioning her son speeding across the skies on the back of a dragon. Instead, she gazed past him toward Pattria, who fidgeted nearby, awaiting her own private moment with Conner. Oshan squeezed his hands. "Come home when you can."

Ignatius chirped his agreement from her shoulder, and Oshan and her chipmunk were off to offer Anton last-minute assistance.

"I wish you would stay longer," Conner said to Pattria a few minutes later, probing yet again to see if she had changed her mind about returning home with his parents. She did not reply, so he pressed harder. "Just a few more days? If it's your safety that worries you, Veressa would ..." He bit his lip and started again. "The queen would willingly command an entire regiment of Defenders to ensure your safe return."

"Yes, I am sure she would." Pattria's response bit with teeth of ice. She shook her head as if letting go of an unwanted thought. "Conner, there is something I must say before I go."

"Pattria, I know we haven't had much time together since your arrival. With me getting settled in here with Skye, my duties as the queen's Champion, my long hours of studies with Grimmley, and all the war preparations, things have been hectic."

"That is not what I meant—"

"Very well. If it is about my bond, you really have nothing to worry about. I know Skye is large and a bit blustery when he gets in a huff, but he would never harm you. That incident the other day—"

Pattria pressed her palm to his chest, lowering her gaze to the ruby amulet dangling around his neck. "That is not what I want to talk about either."

Conner squinted at her, noticing for the first time her pensive stance, her aloofness, her shaky voice. Her usual infectious smile was gone. He pursed his lips and waited.

"I think it best we call off our wedding."

Conner stiffened as her words wormed their way into him. He glanced over his shoulder at the wagon where his parents waited. He could see the pain and concern on their long faces. Of course they must have known what Pattria was saying. They had given their consent for the arranged marriage when he and Pattria were twelve; they would have to give their approval for its annulment. He swallowed hard and pulled away.

"Conner, I am sorry." Pattria searched his hazel eyes. "Please understand that I do not make this decision lightly. You know how much I care for you, how much I have always cared for you. But the Eastlands is my home, my life. This place ..." She gestured at the castle around them—with its busy keep of nobility and ordermen moving to and fro, its three grand towers reaching to the sky, and the formidable walls of enchanted glowing gray granite. It was the heart of the realm, the very center of Griffinrock. But it was also far removed from the thoughts and concerns of those in the Eastlands. "This is not the life I agreed to when we were betrothed. This place ... is too large for me, too complicated, too intimidating. I would not know how to even begin making a castle my home."

Conner wanted to argue but sighed instead. He did not blame her. It was not that long ago that he had spoken similar words to Skye, when he wanted their bond broken. Even with the dragon standing before her, Pattria had struggled to accept that Conner had bonded with a dragon. She had scoffed at his wild tale of encountering an Anarchic Assassin in Cravenrock's undercity. She had gasped in horror, fingers pressed to her puckered lips, as he told of his harrowing escape from a band of Anarchic Barbarians and a Necromancer at Dragongarde. He too had struggled to accept that such people existed. Could he fault her for having the same feelings?

Yet this question did not stem the flow of his pain. Other questions raced on the heels of his empathy for her. Yes, it had taken time, but he had accepted the change. Why couldn't she? Was he not important enough for her to find a path through this situation?

No. He had been ready to do anything, give up anything, to be free from the shackles of a bond he did not want. He had fought every step of the way along the journey the Cosmos had set for him. If he had been given a way out, if Grimmley had been powerful enough to break his bond with the dragon, he would not have hesitated a moment. No matter the cost, to himself or any of those near him, he would have taken it.

Conner bowed his head.

"You will do well in this new life of yours, Conner. You are astute, valiant, and unyielding in your commitment to helping others in need. Those are your strengths. Your Eastlander upbringing will take you far. Look at you in your new clothes—and a Dragonbonded like those tales of the old order." Pattria had heard the names bestowed upon him since that day he had thwarted the Anarchists' plans to infiltrate the Griffinrock monarchy. Many in Graystone believed Conner had single-handedly saved the entire realm.

"I do not think you realize it yet, but you are suited for this life." She ran her fingers over the ruby-studded amulet about his neck, marking him as the queen of Griffinrock's lifelong guardian and protector, as Champion of the Realm. "The queen needs protection, Conner. She needs *you*. And with war on the horizon, the realm needs you here. This is where you were meant to be."

She waited for him to say something, but nothing lucid came to his tongue.

Pattria broke the long silence at last. "I am proud of you." In an act of finality, she reached up and kissed him gently on the cheek. Turning with a sad smile, she walked away.

Within a few minutes, the wagon of precious cargo—his parents, their bonds, and Pattria—pulled away, ambling toward the eastern bridge that would take them to the Queen's Highway and to their home far beyond.

Conner found Pauli right where he'd expected—back in bed. With some effort, he was able to get Pauli up, and the two ascended a set of spiral stone steps to the top of the castle's high eastern parapet. Conner waited in reflective silence, staring out over the outer courtyard below and trying to ignore his brawny friend's squirming. Dark clouds were blowing in from the west, suggesting a dreary late-summer day.

"I'll never go back there," Pauli declared with a bored yawn.

Conner stared at Pauli's rare moment of honest contemplation. "Your dad wants you home? Even after learning of your acceptance into the

Warriors Order? Is that what my parents were chatting with you about last night?"

"Of course," Pauli huffed. "That's no real surprise. Dad knows better than to rely on Tobi to help get the harvest in on time." Pauli paused as if considering a new revelation, then added with a sad shake of his head, "For someone set on taking up the reins of farm life, Tobi is slow to learn the trade."

The corners of Conner's mouth tilted upward. Pauli had never had the patience to toil over plants that took an entire season to grow ... unless it involved thrashing them with a wooden sword.

The Stonefield wagon rolled into view in the distance, drawing Conner's thoughts as it ambled between the fields of thatched Graystone rooftops, encircled by a squad of Queen's Defenders.

"What's up with the Defender escort?" Pauli asked with another yawn.

"The queen wanted to be sure they got home safely."

Pauli snorted at the idea. "That's going to raise a few eyebrows in town."

"Yeah, I know. I tried to convince her they would be safe, but she would have none of it." Conner poked his head around to be sure no one was within earshot. "I've learned when she gets a notion in her head, a team of horses won't get it out."

Conner could not tear his eyes from the wagon as it rumbled over the bridge spanning the River Tresdan. The entourage of Defenders parted the bustling crowds before the wagon like the share of a plow.

"Like you, my future lies in a different meadow," Pauli said, as if convincing himself he would not get homesick. "I know that now. With each passing day, the Harmonic Realms draw closer to war with the Anarchists. Grandmaster Warrior Colonel Tollman visited me the other day. After I bond, he's going to put me through some kind of test to see if I have what it takes to be a Warrior. If so, I will be assigned to Cravenrock Keep. Then my apprenticeship *really* begins."

Pauli's words drudged up Conner's concerns about his friend's selection for the Warriors Order. Few who knew Pauli would dispute that the young man possessed the physical prowess of a Warrior. Still, watching firsthand how the Harmonic War Council interacted with Queen Veressa, Conner was learning how the orders really worked. Whatever had drawn the order's discriminating eyes to Pauli, the boy's size and strength were not their only considerations.

"Besides, home is only a few days from Cravenrock." Pauli elbowed Conner in the ribs, bringing him back with a pained grunt. It was Pauli's way of telling Conner he shared his melancholy mood.

Soon, the Stonefield wagon was lost amid castle folks bustling with morning chores. And the last remnant of Conner's prior life washed away.

The War Council

"**O**ut!" Queen Veressa of Griffinrock jumped from her throne and pointed at the thick wooden doors across the royal reception hall. None of those assembled before her moved. She stepped from the dais. "I said, *get out!*"

Antilles, Veressa's snow leopard bond, pressed against her thigh, making it clear his bond was not to be trifled with.

The two guards at the far end of the hall stared wide-eyed at each other, then leaped forward, yanking the doors wide. Never had they heard the queen, neither Veressa nor her mother Izadora before her, shout in the reception hall.

Master Ranger Annabelle Loris started to rise from the wooden chair she had occupied throughout the long hours of war negotiations. But Veressa flashed her a look that said, *Don't you dare move!* Annabelle eased back into the seat with a sigh, grimacing at the stiffness that spiked up her back.

Peron, Annabelle's falcon bond, ruffled his feathers on a perch nearby and shook away his own frustration. He too grew tired of these talks and longed to be back under the open skies.

General Grimwaldt of the Warriors Order stepped forward as the other members of the War Council shuffled across the gold-and-white-marble floor. "Majesty, if I may, I would like to—" But Veressa's intense stare forced the large man's jaw shut. "It can wait." He bowed with a tense smile, then followed the others, along with their bonds, through the door.

After the council members departed, the queen waved at the guards to wait outside, leaving Veressa in the chamber alone with the Ranger she'd known since she learned to walk.

"I don't believe they could be any more inconsiderate!" Veressa roared at the doors as they slammed. "They are more concerned about how to increase their status with the crown than they are with our people's safety!" The young queen began her ritual pacing across the large rug in front of the throne.

Antilles, forever vigilant for whatever might disturb his bond, paced at her side.

"Maybe," Annabelle suggested with a slight wave as her green eyes tracked the teen. "But getting emotional about their behavior will not work in your favor. Those on the War Council may be grandmasters of their orders, most even high-ranking officers in your Defenders service, but they don't have the authority to make any real decisions. They are but a front to the real power behind the orders."

"Oh, they are an affront, all right—an affront to everything civil, moral, and rational!" Veressa stopped pacing, noting the Ranger's wide eyes, then realized she had misheard Annabelle. She covered her mouth and chuckled. "I am not angry, Annabelle, just ... disappointed." She pushed at several strands of blond hair that had come loose during her gesticulations, then rubbed at her strained eyes. "In a time when we should be rallying behind a common purpose, I feel this War Council is pulling us asunder. And given that we are talking about invading the Anarchic Lands—something no one has attempted since the middle of the Anarchic War—I expected much more from them than arguments over who should direct our armies, which order should control the greatest number of forces, which fighting guilds should be left to defend our lands, and which should lead our assaults. They are capable of so much more. I will not let them denigrate our talks with such trifles as hurt feelings."

"That is partially why I have remained silent this past fortnight." Annabelle chuckled quietly. "To be honest, I've enjoyed watching you work these masters of negotiations over. You have your mother's tenacity and your father's shrewdness. The women and men on this War Council may have started out thinking they would manipulate a naive sixteen-year-old princess into agreeing to whatever demands they set before her. But you've dispelled those illusions."

"Your words are encouraging, Annabelle. I know I am delaying your grandmaster training, but I do so need your support right now."

Annabelle lowered her gaze and shook her head. "You have my support, my queen. But I must apologize, for I have not been adequately schooled in the refined arts of analytic deliberation ... nor do I care to be. And, to be truthful, you trap me in a tenuous position between your demands and those of my Rangers Council. Grandmaster Lendfeather believes I am conspiring against the Rangers Order by counseling you. He does not think you capable of such hard bargaining as he has witnessed here and believes I am behind it." The Ranger leaned forward, drawing the queen's eye. "I am not the one you should be looking to for guidance. I very much wish to remain truly objective, but I do struggle."

"There is no one else I can turn to." In a flash, Veressa's thoughts turned to her father, King Jonath, who spent most of his waking hours within the bowels of the castle, in Griffinrock's Tomb of Queens, filled with despair and remorse. A small entourage of Shamans had been assigned to look after him, but most had given up hope that his mind would return fully to the living. Without his guidance, Veressa needed someone she could confide in—someone she trusted with her darkest doubts and fears. Annabelle had always been there, like the older sister she'd never had. She smiled warmly at the master Ranger. "Besides, I would prefer someone I trust over someone with a polished tongue."

Annabelle finally rose from the wooden chair, groaning at the numbness in her back and rear. "I don't think I can take this chair for much longer, Majesty. You torture me with your delays. I'd suggest we conclude this business at hand, but somehow I doubt you'd listen to my advice."

Veressa thought the Ranger's distress amusing. She waved at the chair Annabelle had occupied. "Not that long ago, I entertained the idea of axing that dreadful chair to pieces and burning it in the banquet hall's fireplace." Veressa thought back to that day, how stifled she'd felt in this reception hall. "But I do believe mother's chair is much more unpleasant."

"It is *your* chair now, Majesty."

Veressa studied the dark mahogany throne, with its intricate patterns of bas-relief and gold leaf. "Yes," Veressa exhaled. "But I doubt I will ever lead our people as she did. I will never have such a commanding, regal presence."

Annabelle soothed Peron with a light stroke and sensed her brown falcon relaxing. "Perhaps you should have paid more attention to how your mother handled such situations."

Veressa sniffed at Annabelle's time-worn argument that Veressa had not taken her responsibilities as future queen seriously enough, a constant reminder of her mother's own apprehension. And she was not going to let the Ranger admonish her with another of her I-told-you-sos. "I don't think it would have helped me with *this* situation. In fact, it is quite possible that such knowledge would have worked against me."

Annabelle beamed her measured gaze at Veressa. "I'm afraid I don't follow, Majesty."

"My mother learned the ways of negotiating deals with the orders from her mother, as grandmother did from hers. After all, tradition is at the heart of the Harmonic way. That is how things have always been done, to the point that now no one sees any other way. But we haven't dealt with a situation like this in half a millennium. These discussions have to be broached differently, the problems viewed from new angles, even if it is not what these ordermen expect. Yes, I have caught them off guard. They struggle to figure out how to work with me. I am challenging them in ways they never thought possible. And I am starting to have an effect."

Veressa gestured toward the door. "General Grimwaldt, for example. The Warriors Order's standing with the crown was shattered when they unwittingly harbored an Anarchic spy at their highest level. Now, the Warriors Council believes war with the Anarchists is the only way out of the pit they have dug themselves into. The Warriors Council is most assuredly pushing Grimwaldt hard to get me to sign a proclamation of war. Yet he is showing signs of being swayed by my words. I sense he is losing his eagerness to push for war."

Veressa paused, noting Annabelle had not even blinked through her long discourse. Unable to contain her frustrations, she continued. "And if struggling to reach a compromise with the orders wasn't difficult enough, I have to deal with the kings of Grenetia and Elvenstein." She raised her arms and then let them drop to her sides. "Did you know that the king of Elvenstein actually suggested privately that an arranged marriage between me and his youngest son would make our plans for war more ... amiable with his realm?"

Finally, Annabelle responded. "It has, for centuries, been a common means of securing pacts between the crowns, Veressa. The blood pumping through your veins has a mix of all three realms—and the four other realms from a time before the Anarchic War."

"Well, I have no intent in sticking with any of the old ways just because they worked in the past. My responsibilities are to my people, not to the orders or the other two crowns."

Veressa watched Annabelle bite back a retort, no doubt a reminder that it would be nearly impossible to please her people without sating the demands of the order councils or the two kings. Instead, the Ranger asked, "So, what now?"

"We wait," Veressa replied, noting Hemera's position in the late-morning sky. "I have given the council enough to chew on for today. They will need time to bandage their wounded egos and consider their next line of attack in convincing me why we should rush into war."

"We are alone, Veressa. Why not say the real reason why you are holding out against a declaration of war?"

Veressa lifted her chin, trying to emulate her mother's regal appearance. "You think I am wrong to demand some kind of evidence as to the motives behind my mother's assassination? You don't think it a bit odd that the Anarchists sent Hector Dellrose to do this deed? Hector was once your preceptor, Annabelle. Doesn't it seem more likely this Ranger-turned-Assassin acted on his own? If we could confirm that, such knowledge could divert a war of epic proportions."

Annabelle looked troubled for a moment, then shook her head. "An Assassin, even Hector, would not take such a mark without the express approval of the Assassins Council. What seems more likely is that they sent Hector to make it *look* like he acted on his own volition." Annabelle opened her mouth, then hesitated, biting her lip.

Veressa held out her arms, urging Annabelle to continue.

"It has been a fortnight since you asked the orders to call upon their spies across the Anarchic Lands. And no verifiable evidence has come back regarding Anarchist motives. At some point, you will have to accept that nothing more can be obtained, no matter how hard you squeeze. Many Harmonic lives have been put at risk over this. I know this is hard for you, Veressa. I know having an answer would help bring closure to the trauma of losing your mother. But your indecision impedes war preparations. And who is to say that the Anarchists are not planning their own invasion? Further delays could jeopardize all our lives. At some point, you have to move on. Maybe it is time you resign yourself to the fact you have done everything you can."

Veressa smiled weakly, then squatted to run her fingers through Antilles's thick fur, staring into his emerald eyes. Her bond's deep purr softened her worried expression. "Yes. Of course, you are right, Annabelle. A few more days. I promise. Then I will have the proclamation of war drawn up." Summoning the elemental forces of Earth, Veressa stretched her palm toward the doors. *"Ora ousia kinothyra."* The massive doors groaned, then swung wide.

The two guards waiting outside snapped their heads around, eyes bulging when they realized the queen of Griffinrock had used an incantation to open the chamber doors from the other side of the long hall.

"Please summon my captain of the guard," Veressa called out to them. "Have his men prepare our horses for a ride out of the city." She hesitated, then commanded, "And send a message to my Champion that I will be requiring his protection this day." Veressa found herself eager for the diversions Conner would offer from her morning stress. Besides, she had something important to discuss with the young man.

Crutch

Conner tapped his foot on the stone floor as the sound of water dripping nearby reverberated off the dungeon's musty walls. If Conner had learned one thing about dragons, it was that they were, without a doubt, the most demanding creatures anywhere on Gaia. Conner knew his irritability was being fed by his bond's own frustrations. His parents' departure that morning was helping neither of their moods. And while Conner knew his position was untenable, he could not help but feel that the dragon shared some of the blame for Pattria's decision to return home. "You're not going to give up on this idea, are you?"

Skye's eyes narrowed to glowing blue slits. Iridescent deep sparks flowed and pulsed blue across the black dragon's scales. "Nope."

For the past fortnight, Skye had suggested flying home to show off his recent transformation from wyvern to full dragon ... and to seek out a potential mate. But of late, Skye's requests had reached a fevered pitch. Enduring the presence of "small, bipedal bores" made him ill-tempered even on his best days, to the point that his barrage of demands could neither be ignored nor diverted. After a long pause, Conner sighed in resignation. "Very well. However, the timing has to be right if this is going to happen. So, don't get your scales in a knot while I figure out when you can fly home."

"It is not possible for my scales to get knotted. Which reminds me of a revelation I had recently about your species."

"I'm surprised you have had time for any revelations given all your sleeping of late."

Skye ignored Conner's rebuke. "Our emotional link has given me an opportunity to understand your species in ways other Cloudbenders have lacked when encountering your kind. It's hard to understand a species when the only view you get is of their backsides as they are running away." The dragon snort-sniffed a slight chuckle. "Since then, I have reflected on why you all are so dishonest, and now I understand why. Your species uses deception to compensate for your lack of a tough outer skin."

"What in the name of Gaia are you talking about?"

Skye closed his brilliant blue eyes. When they opened again, they glowed with a new intensity. "Humans are deceptive as a means of protecting their egos. Dragons, on the other hand"—Skye scraped a steel-like claw across his forearm—"are physically well shielded, so we are not concerned about, nor do we have a need for such psychological armor."

"I'm sorry, Skye, but I am not following you."

"You should stop this pretense that everything is okay," Skye stated with a huff.

"I'm not pretending."

Skye grunted, then tilted his head, one eye an arm's reach from Conner's face. "You can pretend to be someone else if that is your desire. You can even continue to pretend with all of the bipedals around you. But you forget that I can sense your emotions, so do not pretend with me." The dragon's head wagged side to side. "It would help if we cleared the air about what you are feeling."

"Yes!" Conner erupted at his bond's persistent badgering. "I'm frustrated. I'm upset. I'm annoyed. This morning, Pattria ended our relationship and is returning home with my parents. *I too* would like to return home, Skye. But some of us don't get what we want." Conner sensed the flow of Skye's sadness and concern.

"I can sense your envy for what I ask, Conner," Skye said. "I am sorry. But you are ripping at the hide of your feelings when you should be gnawing on the bones of your emotions."

"I don't know what that means," Conner said.

"*Fear*, Conner. I can sense you are frightened. No. Even worse, you are pretending *not* to be afraid."

Conner had hoped Skye would not be so astute, especially given how much the creature slept. Like all dragons, Skye did not feel fear—that is, until he'd bonded with Conner. His shoulders sagging forward, Conner stared deep into a blazing blue eye. "Yes. I am afraid, Skye. And why shouldn't I be? After all, it is the queen's safety that's at risk with my charade of being a powerful orderman ... and one of the great Dragonbonded."

Grimmley and Layna had not been able to help him break through whatever was blocking access to his powers. And with each unsuccessful lesson, he doubted more that they ever would.

Conner took a deep breath to keep his next words from sounding like pleading. "That is why I need you here, Skye. Until I can work through my problem, I need you to help me protect the queen."

Skye's head bobbed with satisfaction, having finally broken through the crusty granite coating that surrounded Conner's ego. Then the dragon shifted with an annoyed grunt and glanced away. "I refuse to be a part of your charade any longer."

Conner growled at his bond, folding his arms across his chest while he revised his assessment of dragons. Even more than demanding, dragons were stubborn. Every step toward a reasonable compromise with the beast had to be fought for, leaving Conner in a perpetual state of exhaustion. "This is not a charade, Skye."

Skye snorted, his glowing eyes studying the puddle of water that had collected on the dungeon floor. "If you are pretending to be something you are not, then it is a charade. Besides, I am tired of you using me as an expedient to patch up your problems. As long as you rely on me to be your queen's protector, you will never break through this barrier you drag around with you. Which is yet another reason why I need to return home— so that you can work out your impediment without me."

"I said yes already," Conner huffed. "Besides, I could use a rest from your constant nagging. Surely there isn't anything more you could ask of me."

"There is," Skye replied.

"What now?"

"For one, to tell the queen how you feel about her."

Conner went cold with shock. "What?" he mumbled, mentally back-stepping.

"I have seen how the queen displays herself before you, Conner. It is clear to anyone attentive that she wants you to be her mate. It is time you tell her that you feel the same."

Conner nearly choked. "That's crazy. You don't know what you're talking about. Women don't show their affections that way."

"For many days now, I have been watching humans scurry about on this rock structure they built, and I can say with complete certainty that, besides being bores, humans are not that different from dragons." Skye sized up his human bond, then added, "At least not the females of our two species. Let me suggest you consider doing what you humans do to show affection. What is the word? ... *Kiss!*" Skye bobbed his head enthusiastically. "You should kiss her."

"What? Kiss the queen?" Conner shuffled back. "You've been spending too much time with Kriston. Clearly, I have not kept that lad busy enough with his studies. Let *me* suggest that you not rely on a twelve-year-old boy to be your only source of information when it comes to human behavior—unless it involves thieving or lying."

"I heard that." A thin voice echoed up the dungeon hall.

Conner spun to find Kriston stepping into the light of the dank room, coming to a halt with hands pressed firmly on his bony hips.

"I might be a thief, but at least I don't talk unkindly about others behind their backs."

"Obviously I wasn't talking behind your back, since *you* were behind *mine.*" Under his breath, he added, "And quite capable of hearing every word I utter." Kriston was a very quick study at picking up Dragon language and had already learned enough to catch the gist of conversations. Conner wondered how long Kriston had been there listening to the two of them argue. He shuddered at the notion Kriston might have understood him discussing his barrier to using elemental powers.

Kriston ignored Conner's words, choosing instead to convey a message. "The captain of the royal guard is looking for you. The queen demands your presence."

"See, Conner? She desires you. You should kiss her!" the dragon roared.

"Will you stop that?"

Kriston snickered.

Conner flashed the boy a scathing look. "No doubt, she wants to go for another ride to get out of the city—and away from that dreadful War

Council. Nothing more." He furrowed his brows at the dragon. "We'll finish our conversation later. I'll meet you outside the city gates," he said slowly, not wanting the statement to sound like the request it was.

Skye grunted his assent before the boys started back up the hall.

"Kriston, what ideas have you been feeding my dragon?" Conner whispered as they neared the stairwell that led to the castle bailey above.

"I've only been answering his incessant questions. You want me to stop talking to him?"

Conner hesitated, imagining being the only one the dragon spent his waking hours conversing with. "No," he said, though he wanted to say yes. "I honestly doubt anyone else is interested in talking to my bond."

Kriston snickered again. "You could teach Pauli how to speak Dragon. Imagine the mischief he could teach Skye to get into."

"Which is why I haven't tried teaching Pauli. Besides, Skye's scales would turn dull with age before Pauli uttered his first lucid sentence in Dragon tongue."

"Now who's talking behind someone's back?" Skye bellowed up the long hall.

Conner and Kriston stepped from the dungeon stairs to find the captain of the royal guard waiting at the far end of the court. When the captain saw them, he waved and started forward. Conner cocked his head toward his young page.

Kriston rolled his eyes. "Yes, I know. Back to my quarters and practice my calligraphy." Still, the ex-thief tended to get anxious whenever anyone with "guard" in their title was about, so the boy was off before Ballett was within hailing distance.

"Your horse is ready, my lord," Ballett announced as he approached. His gray possum, Scout, peered timidly at Conner from over the captain's shoulder.

The captain matched his stride to Conner's and the two started back toward the stables. In the little time Conner had been in Graystone, he had come to admire the captain, who prided himself on proper dress and the etiquette expected in a royal castle. He was a likable fellow, though he did not seem as confident as Conner had expected from someone commanding the royal guard. "Conner works fine, Ballett. Eastlanders don't have much use for titles."

"As you command. Conner it is." Ballett wagged his head. "I'm afraid my knowledge of freeman lifestyle is a bit murky. I've spent my entire life at Graystone, so I have not had an opportunity to see what lies beyond the city streets."

Conner surveyed the skies as the two marched toward the eastern castle gates. What remained of the morning had become all the drearier during his time in the dungeons arguing with Skye. Dark, brooding clouds were moving in, and a damp wind at his back made even the dungeon seem warm and dry.

"May I ask how long you have been in the service of the queen?" Conner asked.

"Eight years."

"And now, Captain of the Royal Guard." Conner shook his head. "I know as much of royal matters as you know of Eastlanders, but that seems like quite a rise."

Ballett sighed. "A long story, I'm afraid."

Conner was intrigued. He waved his hand at the long, narrow street leading back to the main entrance, eager to know more. "We have time, and there are but a few people about."

Ballett nodded. "I joined the royal guard shortly after completing my guild's apprenticeship. When Veressa was but a young princess, the king assigned me to watch over her. At first, it was an easy enough assignment. After all, she had a master Ranger charged with protecting her. But as the years progressed, the princess became quite a handful. The king was compelled to assign an ever-growing entourage of guards to watch over her—night as well as day." Ballett leaned closer. "And, since I know you are aware, once Master Ranger Loris began training the princess in Ranger skills some months back, even a full battalion was unmatched for her prowess." Ballett shook his head sadly. "I cannot count the number of times the princess has slipped past my watch, each time landing me before King Jonath to explain my failings—an especially challenging task given that I was sworn to secrecy regarding Veressa's Ranger training."

Conner laughed, envisioning Veressa handily doing whatever Rangers did to evade notice, even around well-trained guardsmen whose only job was to watch over her. "So, you got a promotion for your efforts?"

"In a manner of speaking, yes. Veressa chose me as her captain after she was crowned. Normally, royal assignments are the king's personal duties, but ..." Ballett's face clouded, then shook it away. "I tried to explain to her that there were more qualified members of the royal guard, but she would have none of it. She can be quite demanding."

Conner thought back to his first encounter with the queen in Pennington Point while she was on her bonding trek pretending to be a Ranger apprentice. "I see the queen hasn't changed much since her coronation."

"Actually ..." Ballett began, then fell silent.

"Yes?"

"I have been in the queen's service for some time now. With you as her new protector, and not knowing her well before she became queen, I feel compelled to mention"—Ballett's voice dropped to a whisper—"that she *has* changed of late, and I worry about her."

When Conner's eyes grew large, Ballett elaborated. "You must understand, this is not idle gossip. As captain of the guard, I get reports from my men—what they see and hear. Those close to the queen occasionally speak in the corners of secluded rooms when they think there are no ears about to catch their words. I know my guardsmen well enough to take what they report at face value, only I too have heard ordermen around the castle expressing their concerns for the new queen."

Anxiety clawed at Conner's chest. He swallowed hard. "And what do they say?"

"That the queen is inattentive, her eyes often lost amid the thick forest beyond the castle. And when she is not preoccupied with what is beyond these gray walls, she has the temperament of ... well, a feral cat. Many suspect it has to do with her new bond." Ballett's head drooped and he shook it slowly. "A powerful animal to be bonded to, for sure."

Conner did not hold much faith in such theories. After all, he was bonded to a dragon and he had not suddenly become demanding or bullheaded. He blinked. Or had he? He shook the thought away. "But you think there is more?"

Ballett pressed a finger to his lips, as if struggling how best to answer Conner's question. "I think that being so alone, especially at such a young age, thrust upon the throne and made responsible for so much must be a terrible burden. And not having a father there for proper guidance and support—well ..." He shrugged to fill in what he did not want to put into words.

Conner heard the tension in Ballett's tone. The captain's comments confirmed his own suspicions. Veressa had seemed more troubled of late.

He had sensed her wrestling with some potent, dark force—one her aid and constant shadow Master Ranger Loris was especially attuned to. The rides she took away from the castle seemed to be the only remedy to quell the storm raging within her. But the rides were too infrequent.

"You care for her," Conner said to Ballett.

"Just like I do my own two precious daughters. I suppose growing up in the Eastland fringes doesn't give you this perspective, but those central to Griffinrock carry a special love for their queen. I would do anything necessary to protect Veressa."

Conner thought about what Skye had said to him—about how he was using the dragon as a crutch for his own failures—and wondered if King Jonath's presence would have been more hindrance than aid to Veressa. And if Conner stepped in as Champion *and* guardian, and tried to fill her father's place? *No.* He shook his head. He couldn't muster enough elemental power to heal a plant. Grimmley was fond of saying, "You can't help another if you can't first stand on your own." Conner had his own problems to solve; Veressa would be better off not relying on him. Besides, he had made a promise to the king that he would not get too close to her, no matter how much he cared for her.

Conner clasped the captain on the shoulder with a firm grip. "As Veressa's Champion, that is useful. Thank you, Ballett, for sharing it with me. It seems we have something in common. We both will do everything in our power to ensure that our new queen can weather this troubling storm."

The two walked on in silence.

At the end of the street, they were flushed out onto a busy city causeway. Turning toward the bridge, they wove through the throngs of shoppers and merchants. Near the bridge, Conner caught sight of several dozen mounted royal guardsmen. The queen had not yet arrived.

Open Hearts

Veressa examined the young Dragonbonded riding beside her, noting how his long, dark hair swirled and played across his narrow shoulders in the cool breeze. Her Champion was being his usual sullen self, but he seemed even more preoccupied this day than most. It was not going to be easy to draw him into the conversation she wanted—no, *needed* to have with him. She would have to guide the discussion carefully. Unfortunately, she had too much of her father in her. His out-with-it way had been a thorn in her mother's heel.

"I heard your parents left this morning," she started. There was a long pause before she added, "And Pattria?"

"They all returned to the Eastlands this morning, Majesty. Under Defender protection, as you dictated."

Veressa nodded, though she doubted Conner noticed. His hazel eyes were frozen on the trail that wound along the banks of the River Tresdan. They rode on in silence, and she sensed an edginess to his heavy feelings. Her heart opened to his pain. "I imagine it must be hard living so far from home."

Conner gazed at her, looking as if she could not possibly understand what it meant to be homesick. "This is my home now, Majesty." Conner shifted his gaze over his shoulder. Fifty paces behind, Ballett waved a gauntleted hand to let him know the company of royal guard was not far away, if needed.

"I asked them to stay back so you and I could talk." Veressa answered what was certainly in his thoughts. "We have not spoken privately since the day of the Champion's tournament. I think it is time we do so."

Conner tensed. "What would you like to talk about, Majesty?"

"We can start with that night in Pennington Point," she blurted out, then kicked herself. *Oh well, too late now.*

"Majesty, I—"

"You are my Champion, Conner," the queen interrupted. "You were the one who prevented that chameleon Marcantos Evinfaire from being here today, riding as you are next to me. I think that if anyone has earned the right to call me Veressa, it is you." She smiled reassuringly. Calling up words her mother had often used on her father, she added, "In fact, as queen, I demand it."

"Of course, Veressa. But as I mentioned the day of the tourney, the things I said back in Pennington Point—"

"You did not mean them. I know," she said, then hammered the saddle's pommel in frustration. How was it that she could deal with the greatest negotiators across the realms, but couldn't seem to carry on a simple conversation with her Champion without constantly interrupting him? She decided instead to go straight into her prepared speech before she really botched things up. "There have been a few things on my mind for nearly three fortnights. I need to say them, so please—I would like to get this out."

Conner clenched his jaw in surprise. His eyes were full upon her now.

"I don't know what happened in Pennington Point, but something changed for me ... for us. From the moment that Sorcerer cast his spell and you wrapped your arms around—and you protected me, I have felt ..." She stared into Conner's eyes, and under his intense scrutiny, her confidence wilted. Words she had rehearsed many times the previous night scattered like pheasants flushed from the brush. Her heart raced; her damp palms made the leather reins slick. She recalled an "I feel safe around you, Conner," somewhere in that speech, but what came before and after were gone, shredded threads no longer holding the seams in place.

This was not like her. Suddenly, fear of never saying what she wanted countermanded all sense of propriety, and she forced the words up through her mouth. "I can sense your emotions." She held his stare and knew she had hit the target dead center. What's more, she knew he felt the same. And with that knowledge came sudden exhilaration. Eyes locked on his, she pushed on, slower, more certain now. "I know when you are distressed or worried. I felt your homesickness this morning though you were not near. I can even feel your doubts, your distress—like now. It is as if we are emotionally linked somehow, as if we are bonded. I know that makes no sense. The thought is completely insane, yet I can find no other explanation for what I feel. And I know you sense it too." But speaking the words made her feel strange, and she closed her mouth lest what came next made him think her demented.

She heard the clomp of Toran's hooves on the hard dirt path beneath her, the squeak of her saddle as she rocked to Toran's gentle gate, Antilles panting as he strolled at her side, the sound of swift waters rushing over exposed rocks in the river. Skye appeared on the crest of a hill not far away, looking at his human bond with … curiosity? The dragon's sea-blue eyes were aglow. He too must have sensed Conner's turmoil. The long silence cut deep into her heart.

Conner's words cut even deeper. "You must be imagining things, Majesty."

Veressa stiffened, then stared at him hard, cheeks hot in the damp air. "But that night when I was in Kallzwall Castle, the night my mother died, you came to my balcony riding your dragon. How did you know I was there?"

Conner hoisted his shoulders, then let them fall. "Well …" He glanced about as if searching for a way to escape. "Pure luck, I guess." There was another pause. "Skye was tired from his long flight … from Dragongarde to Grimmley's home. We were looking for a place he could rest. That was when we spied the lights from the castle's tower."

"So, you just went to investigate?" Veressa shook her head at the absurdity. "Conner, that makes no sense. You told me you were keeping the dragon's existence a secret back then. You wouldn't fly toward the lights of a castle or a city. Besides, where did you think you'd find a place for your dragon to rest and not be seen by someone?"

There was a long pause before Conner answered. "We fly over towns and villages at night all the time, and no one is the wiser for it."

"I don't believe you," Veressa declared. She knew Conner was lying. But why? "I remember that night you appeared on my balcony. I was struggling with my feelings. And suddenly you appeared." She gripped the front of her saddle until her fingers hurt. "I know you feel what I am feeling. I can sense angst in you even now."

"No, Veressa. I am concerned for your safety. That is all." But Conner would not return her gaze.

Veressa shook her head vigorously, not wanting to believe him. But doubt had returned, ripping through her feeble defenses. "I do not know what game you are playing—"

Conner snapped his head toward her.

"But nothing you say will make me dismiss this as some delusional fantasy." In truth, Veressa was beginning to believe it was. It would not be the first time she'd thought herself mad! First, Ourea, the Djinn of Earth had spoken to her in a dream vision; then came the uncontrollable urges to be in the wilderness, driving her to take night excursions hunting and running free with Antilles by her side; and now this? Suddenly, she felt ill. The wound she had received the day of her bonding throbbed, and she pressed her palm to her temple to ease the dizziness.

It began to drizzle, a slow and steady rain that promised to last for hours. It would serve as the perfect ruse to return to the castle without raising any alarms. Veressa yanked on Toran's reins. Her steed spun, and she heeled the gelding into a canter that would take her back to Ballett. She left Conner by the river to mull over his lies, his dragon bond watching from a hill nearby. Raindrops mixed with tears of sadness and humiliation. And she wondered if she would ever bare herself to him again.

Open Minds

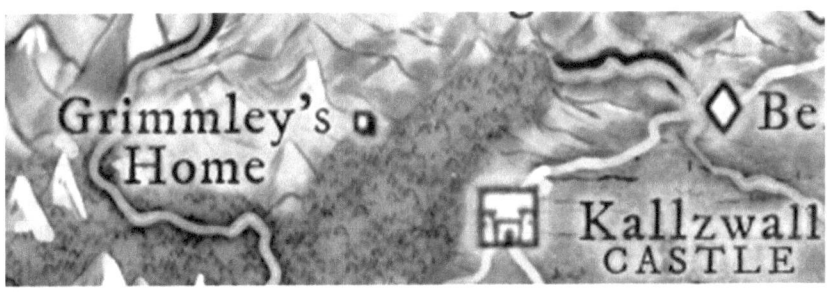

Conner stewed in despair for two days. During that time, Veressa had not spoken to him once; in fact, she refused to even recognize his existence. Unable to take her deafening silence any longer, the queen's Champion flew to Grimmley's home for a brief interlude to further his knowledge of elemental powers with his two preceptors. Unfortunately, his time there offered no reprieve from his frustrations.

Conner ran his fingers over the cryptic symbols splashed across the parchment on the dinner table, then mumbled to himself. This was his fifth lesson on Modeic hieroglyphs under the tutelage of the stoic grandmaster Sorceress Layna Newstone. And still the meaning of the symbols laid before him was as elusive as the first time he'd examined them. His ability to translate each symbol was improving—to some degree. But it would have been easier to glue a smashed teacup back together than to piece the images on the page into anything coherent.

"Try not to look for any order in rows or columns, Conner." Layna examined her pipe, appearing more concerned with keeping her tobac lit than her student's labors. "The pattern here is much more subtle, like petals on a sunflower or colored glass in a stained-glass window."

"I don't *see* any pattern, Layna." Conner whipped his arm over the paper.

The Sorceress furrowed her eyebrows, making it clear she would not have another emotional outburst from her pupil. "When you are reading a note, you don't see the letters that make up the words, do you? Similarly here, the harder you *look* for a pattern, the more difficult it will be to find it."

Conner was about to retort that her guidance made absolutely no sense. But as he glanced away from the parchment, something drew his eye back in. His gaze flowed over the parchment once more, connecting the swirling symbols in a seemingly random fashion. "The Cosmos's disapproval ... of those in power ... is reflected in who receives it."

Layna bobbed her head with delight. The fine gold chain threading through the rings down her left ear tinkled faintly. "Close. Very close." She stuck the stem of her pipe between her teeth, shoved the symbol-studded sleeves of her blue robe up her dark arms, and tapped a spot near the edge of the paper. "But these two images are juxtaposed for a reason." After a long draw on her pipe, she pushed straight coal-black hair behind her ear, eyes narrowing on Conner. "Try again," she demanded.

Finally, Conner spoke. "The Cosmos's disapproval of power is reflected in who it chooses to receive it."

"Very good, Conner." Layna clapped him hard on the back. "You're picking this up amazingly fast."

"Nice to know I can do *one* thing well."

"Don't be too hard on yourself, boy," Grimmley called from across his cottage. "You might find that a little enthusiasm, even when you aren't feeling it, can get you a long way down the road to success."

Barthox, Grimmley's barred owl bond, hooted her own encouragement from her worn perch near the fireplace.

"Okay, but don't you have something besides esoteric Modeic sayings to translate? Even in Cronoan tongue, these pages make my brain cramp."

Layna laughed. "Unfortunately, most of the artifacts that survived the massacre of the Modei were swallowed up by Tatem Creeg and his Bremenn, the forebears of the Paladins Order. Nearly everything containing hieroglyphs was snatched, cataloged, carted away, and stored in the underground vaults at Aldemeer. It took some time to convince those Modeic zealots to release copies of a few writings so the other early guilds could train their apprentices on how to read the language."

Conner brooded over the parchment. "Why is knowing how to read Modei so important to the orders? After all, it's a dead language."

Grimmley swiveled on his workbench stool, where he had been methodically labeling potions he had enchanted that morning. Peering over smudged wire-rimmed spectacles that had slipped down his nose, he gave Conner the kind of look that promised he was about to receive one of the Shaman's insightful lectures.

"Far from it, my boy. The chants you speak when you invoke incantations are in Modei." The old man gestured to Layna's gnarled battlestaff, with its metallic Modeic images, propped against the table, then to his own wood stave near the back door leading to his garden. "What's more, the symbols engraved on our focuses are Modeic hieroglyphs. Each order has its own type of focus—Warriors and Paladins have swords, Rangers have bows, Mystics and Sorcerers have staffs. The symbols on those devices are what give us access to the powerful elemental forces needed to cast incantations commensurate to our rank. Those images uniquely attune the device to the individual. That is why I could no more use Layna's focus than she could mine. And when an orderman is raised in rank, that person is charged with imbuing their focus by adding the right symbols at the right places and in the right order. They have but one chance to get it right or they will never be raised. Every orderman learns early that full command of Modeic hieroglyphs is a necessity if their focus is to function properly."

"So where is *my* focus?" Conner interjected, raising his arms before them. "And for that matter, why didn't I have to chant the incantations I used to defeat Evinfaire? You said I didn't speak any words like those you have taught me." Conner jammed the heel of his palm to his forehead, frustration returning. "I wish I could recall what I did on the tourney field. But my head is as blank now as it was that day nearly two fortnights ago."

Neither of his preceptors offered any answers beyond slight shrugs and uneasy glances.

"I thought so." Conner pulled the edges of his lips back with a nod. "At least help me understand why the Dragonbonded of old left behind nothing more than hieroglyphs painted all about Dragongarde's walls. Dragonbonded were Cronoan like us, not Modeic nomads. And only Dragonbonded can get through the elemental barrier protecting the fortress. Wouldn't those capable of slipping through need to know what had been written there? If so, why go to the trouble of putting everything in Modei? Were they hiding something? Did they think me unworthy of what is written on those walls? And why leave mysterious messages at all?"

Again, silence followed, so Conner trudged ahead. "Maybe what is written at Dragongarde is more meaningless proverbs and aphorisms." A dispirited laugh escaped his lips. "Or maybe all this is some dreadful joke devised by Erebus-struck humans wanting to have a good laugh from beyond the grave." Conner recalled the squalor, the gloomy living quarters at Dragongarde, and was reminded of old tales of Dragonbonded hermits. Was he destined for such madness? No matter where he poked his head for answers, all he ever found were more questions. And they were piling up like dry kindling.

Grimmley stepped closer, eyes clouded with concern. "Layna and I are working on getting answers to such questions, Conner. I wish we knew more, but we're going to need more time."

"Well, Grimmley," Conner said, summoning his courage. "Maybe it is time we try something completely different."

His two preceptors blinked back at him.

Like something insane, Conner thought. Right, Conner, just what someone going insane would say. "I've been thinking," he began.

Grimmley peered at his wistful student over his spectacles. "Too much of that is what gets in your way, boy."

"Maybe." Conner shrugged and took a deep breath. "Skye once said that the first dragons were created by a Shaman god named Shazarack." Conner paused. Neither offered any commentary, so he pushed on. "Through some research at Graystone, I found out that Shazarack was not a Shaman, but a Necromancer." Conner waited to see if they detected his half-truth but still got no reaction. They already *knew* about Shazarack, and they had kept it from him! He took a deep breath. "Maybe the Necromancer that was captured at Dragongarde knows something about Dragonbonded, something that could unlock the secrets to my powers."

Grimmley grunted. "You mean Meera Asheborne." After a long pause, he asked, "And why do you think that?"

"For one thing, she knows how to speak Dragon. If she knows that, maybe she knows something else about Dragonbonded that could help me through my problem."

The expressions on his two mentors turned from surprise to distress to something he had not expected—uncertainty. He glanced down to hide his alarm, trying to look nonchalant, picking at the dirt under his fingernails. "I've heard she is being held in the Shamans' temple at Graystone.

Grimmley, I know you have a lot of sway with the Shamans Council. I was thinking you could get me in to talk to her—alone."

Grimmley rubbed at his long, gray beard. "I don't think so."

"Why not? You've made it clear on more than a dozen occasions that members of your council owe you favors. I am certain you could get me in to speak to her. What could possibly be the harm in it?

"The danger is the same as the reason you *want* to talk to her. She is not just an Anarchist and Necromancer, Conner. She is a *grandmaster*. No, even more than that, she was first counselor to the wife of the sovereign prince himself." Grimmley crossed his arms and squared himself before the lad. "Someone doesn't rise to that level of importance at her age without having *very* powerful skills in persuasion and cunning. You would be a fool to listen to anything she might say ... about *any* topic. The moment she senses you need something from her, she will twist your questions to her advantage."

"What if you were there to watch over us? You would know if she were misleading me, and you could step in."

Grimmley shook his head slowly as Conner spoke. "It would be unwise to risk her picking up that you cannot use your powers. If she did, she would have you in a trap you would be unable to wiggle free from. I am sorry, but you cannot see her."

"She is shackled and surrounded by some of the most powerful Shamans from across the realms," Conner implored. "I don't understand why you are so resistant—"

"I said no, and I mean *no!*" Grimmley grumbled.

Conner stiffened. Grimmley had never spoken to him like that before, and he could think of many times he had said or done something more deserving of his temper. Even Barthox was giving her bond a startled look.

"You say that you want to help, but all you offer are platitudes of some happy future and suggestions that I wait. And when I suggest there might be someone who could know something useful, you refuse to even consider it. If I did not know you better, I would think you were afraid of losing control over this situation!" Conner shoved past his mentors and stormed across the cottage. He pushed the front door wide, then wheeled around. "I hate to break this to you, Grimmley, but you never had control." Without waiting for a response, he stepped out into the dead of night. "*None* of us are in control," he shouted behind him.

Skye, having sensed Conner's brewing frustration, descended out of the blackness above to settle a few paces from the porch.

"Conner," came Layna's voice from the door.

Conner skipped up Skye's front leg and leaped into the saddle.

Layna stepped out on the porch. "Don't you think you are being a little hard on Grimmley? He is doing everything in his powers to help you. If you can't see that, then you aren't looking hard enough. Don't be impatient with us."

"Layna, if this"—Conner held his arms out wide to her—"is the result of his best efforts, then it truly is a hopeless affair. I grow weary of being told to wait."

With a gentle nudge, Skye leaped into the sky. The two gained height with each powerful pulse of the dragon's leathery wings and were soon lost amid the stars to the west.

Conner pressed his cheek to the cool, iridescent scales near the dragon's withers. The wind roared in his ears and tugged at his hair. Erebus was full at his back to the east, lighting the forest below in eerie shades of grays. It would be beyond its zenith by the time he arrived back at Graystone, giving him time to consider what to do next.

Why had Grimmley been so adamant about not allowing him to talk to the Necromancer? Whatever the reason, he was certain it had nothing to do with the Shamans Council. When Grimmley had told the council that he had not only been hiding Conner out at his private sanctuary, but had been secretly training him on Shamanic skills, the ancient orderman had handled the council's fury with amazing expertise and fortitude. In the end, the council not only backed down from threats of banishing Grimmley from the order, they had given him approval to continue with Conner's training.

Yet when Conner had asked about seeing the Necromancer, his mentor had been unyielding. That was not like him. Yes, Grimmley could be headstrong, even infuriatingly obstinate, but his reaction had taken stubbornness to a level equaled only by that of a dragon. Conner had too many questions to just let this go.

Conner had kept things from Grimmley and Layna before, and he still did. He might not trust them with everything he knew. But he had never lied to them outright. In truth, it was Meera Asheborne, after capturing them at Dragongarde, who had told Skye that Shazarack, the creator of

dragons, had been a Necromancer. If she was right about that, what else could she be right about? But there was more to Conner's urgency than finding out what a dragon-speaking Necromancer knew about how to access his powers. Conner needed to understand what was going on with Skye.

With each passing day, the dragon grew more and more anxious about being among the Harmonics. The fact that Shazarack had been a Necromancer only dredged up memories Conner would have preferred to forget—of the Barbarian Groegan Briarmede standing before him, smiling confidently at Conner shackled to a cavern wall at Dragongarde. He recalled the Barbarian's words: *If you hold any notion of living out your life in the Harmonic Realms, you might find your dragon is of a different mind. Harmonic life is not in a dragon's nature.* Conner squeezed his eyes tight, wanting to shut out the world. How could Conner be Veressa's Champion if his bond did not want to live there? Even if he got his powers back, could he stay in Graystone without Skye? Would he want to?

Skye shook violently, nearly throwing Conner from his saddle. It was a habit the dragon had developed to get Conner's attention when he was wrestling with a perplexing problem. Glowing sea-blue eyes peered back. "Don't ask my advice."

Conner chuckled. "When did you ever wait for me to ask? Besides, I'm not looking for advice. I'm looking for answers."

"And where do you think you will find those?" Skye asked.

Conner heard the slow shift of air rippling over Skye's wings. Ahead, the glowing stones of Graystone Castle came into view, its brilliant reflection glistening off the wide, dark river. No matter what angle Conner viewed this maddening situation from, it always appeared the same. "There's only one place I know of."

By the time Skye glided through the dungeon entrance and floated to a gentle stop, Conner knew what he needed to do—even if he had no clue how he was going to pull it off.

The Long, Dark Road Ahead

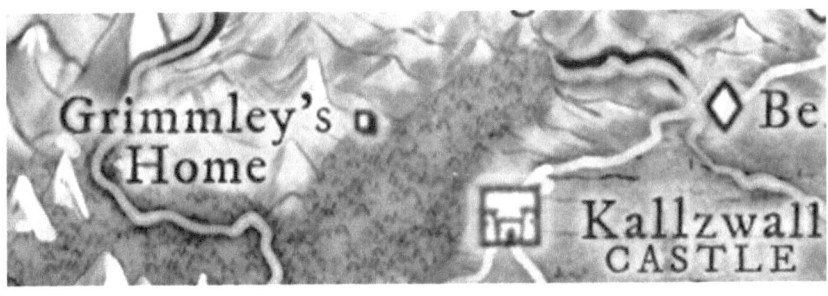

Back inside, Layna found Grimmley brooding in front of the fireplace. With the hectic schedule she and Grimmley had been handed, it had been nearly a fortnight since the two had spoken in private about the current state of affairs. And given Conner's outburst, it was time they put this opportunity to good use and shared their thoughts and questions.

"I don't understand why you leave Conner in the dark, Grimmley. Don't you think he has the right to know everything we are up against? After all, he is a key part of this adventure."

"*Hemea ousia fragidomatio.*" Grimmley spoke the ancient Fire-Earth incantation of protection, sealing his cottage from outside eyes and ears. "The boy needs our protection."

Layna's eyebrows rose. "I'm not sure I share that opinion, dear friend."

Grimmley's shoulders sagged as he exhaled long and slow. "Layna, Conner is already struggling with doubts that he will ever find the powers he needs to protect the new queen. It goes against every fiber of his Eastlander upbringing to hold such dark secrets close to his chest. What do you think would happen if he realized the queen might actually be in danger? We cannot predict how he would react if we tell him there may be more Anarchic spies in the highest ranks of the Harmonic orders—possibly close to the queen. The problem is that we don't have a clue what is obstructing the lad from calling upon the elemental forces we witnessed on the tourney field."

Layna gave a wry smile. "A wise old man taught me that withholding information only leads to more serious issues."

"Which only proves that you never did listen to anything I said. I also said that rule applies only under certain circumstances." Grimmley shuffled across the floor and took one of the two chairs at the three-tiered board of Crowns. He took a moment to study the game the two had been playing for many years.

"And this isn't one of those situations?" Layna took the chair on the far side of the game table. This would likely be a long evening, so she might as well get comfortable. "Conner looks up to you, Grimmley. He relies on you ... on us ... to help him. There is no one else he can trust with this." She snatched up her marshal of the realm and shifted the tall wooden piece down a tier and forward.

Grimmley frowned at the unexpected and bold assault.

Layna went on. "What do you think Conner will do when he discovers we have been withholding this information? His suspicions are growing with each day that we hide secrets from him. The way you handled his request to see that Necromancer no doubt notched his wariness up several levels."

Grimmley waved at a thick cloud of tobac smoke impeding his view of the board's lower tier. "I don't deny that what we are doing is risky." He leaned forward, bushy eyebrows furrowed. "What?"

"I've been pondering this ever since we last spoke of it. We can continue to offer Conner our encouragement and moral support, but unless we stumble upon some unexpected new facts, he is on his own to find his powers."

Grimmley could only nod.

The Sorceress thumbed her pipe bowl with fresh tobac. "But there are a few other things we can do, Grimmley. You and I need to discover whether there is still a threat to the queen. An attempt on her life—successful or otherwise—could spell disaster for the realms. That is where our priority lies. But make no mistake: the moment we have evidence that the queen or realm are in danger, we bring Conner in on this. He is her Champion. He deserves to know."

Grimmley's lips flapped against the stem of his pipe. At last, he grunted his consent.

Layna leaned back, releasing tension with a long exhale of smoke. "Besides, by now, you have a plan for how we can root out any remaining spies."

"Hmm, yes. Very well." Grimmley let his glance float to the ceiling as he leaned back. "I believe the Fettering Stones—or more precisely, the power these stones possess—hold the key to discovering whether there are more spies in the Harmonic Realms. Unfortunately, I have spent most of my life trying to obtain one of these stones to ascertain their true nature. And given my lack of success to date, I think any plan that includes garnering knowledge directly from a stone is foolhardy at best." The Shaman tapped the stem of his pipe against pursed lips. "That leaves us with just two threads to pull. The first involves me taking a trip to Moonslayer Monastery to see what I can learn about Alicia Farclave, the Shaman the Paladin Cardinals mentioned when I returned the silver box to them."

"And the second thread?"

Grimmley cleared his throat. "I am going to talk to the Necromancer Meera Asheborne."

Layna nearly choked on her pipe smoke. "Conner does not fully trust us. There is already much he is holding from us regarding the day he and Skye were captured by the Anarchists at Dragongarde. If he learns that you talked with the Necromancer after refusing him that same right ..."

"I know. *That* is why I was so troubled by the lad's request. He could not have asked at a worse time."

Layna nodded. "What knowledge might this Necromancer possess that is worth the risk of insulting Conner, or making him even more suspicious of us?"

"Well, given that Barbarians are averse to Necromancers, we can assume that the Anarchic troop was ordered to follow Meera Asheborne— they would never have done so by choice. That means someone gave the order to apprehend Conner, someone with enough influence to force a group of Barbarians on a perilous spy mission with a Necromancer." Grimmley refilled his pipe bowl and lit it. "And given Asheborne's position as personal aide to the sovereign prince's wife ..."

"You think it was the Necromancers Council?"

Grimmley grunted assent. "And likely the Barbarians Council as well. Who knows? Maybe other Anarchic order councils. It would be very enlightening if she were to corroborate this assertion."

Layna pursed her lips tightly. Anarchic orders did not mix company. It was commonly believed among the Harmonic orders that this was the primary reason why the Anarchists had never orchestrated an all-out invasion of the realms. But if the Anarchic orders were now talking among themselves, if they were negotiating, or worse, collaborating to find common ground and making pacts to work against the Harmonics ...

Grimmley wasn't finished. "We also have Conner's account that one of the Barbarians on this mission, Groegan Briarmede, was in possession of a Fettering Stone. We can assume the troop came from Farlorde, north of the Borderlands. That means Meera Asheborne traveled for several fortnights with this Briarmede. She most certainly learned something about him."

Layna filled in what she knew Grimmley had already surmised. "You believe Groegan Briarmede is connected to those who were pulling the strings to keep Conner out of the way while Evinfaire fought his way to becoming Queen Veressa's Champion."

Grimmley puffed out his lips. "That is why it is worth the risk of upsetting our young pupil."

"How will you get Asheborne to talk?"

"I haven't figured that out yet, and until I do, there is little more to say on this matter." After a long pause, he continued. "I think it's time we turn our focus on how we're going to gain more knowledge about the ancient Dragonbonded. So!" Grimmley slapped his thighs, eager to begin a new discussion. "Where do we start?"

"Well, let's start with a simple question."

"Such as?"

"When Conner faced down Evinfaire on the Field of Contest, how did he manipulate elementals without the use of any verbal incantations, focus, or hand gestures?"

Grimmley rose and stretched. "If that is your idea of simple, Layna, then this is going to be a long evening. Talk to me while I fix supper."

Layna trailed after Grimmley to his kitchen. "Do you recall the question you posed the night after you introduced me to the boy?"

"Remind me."

"How did Conner learn to speak Dragon?"

"Ah, yes!" Grimmley raised his voice over the clamor of metal pots. "That one did keep me awake for some nights."

"What if the two are related?"

"How do you mean?"

"What if Conner's use of elementals is as innate as his ability to speak Dragon?"

Grimmley grunted as he swirled melting butter in a saucepan. "But he's never suddenly forgotten how to talk to Skye. Whenever those two are together—and they are *always* together—they raise such a brawl my head thumps for hours." He shook a spatula her way. "We'd all be in a much happier state if he would remember more how he used elementals and less how to speak to his dragon!"

Layna chuckled with Grimmley. "The boy clearly used a different system than the one we—and all other ordermen—use to manipulate elementals. I think we can give up on the idea that teaching him our system will help him recall his. In fact, we may be doing more harm than good."

"That is why you've been pushing him on learning the hieroglyphs."

"He is by far the smartest lad I've ever worked with." She poked a finger at the parchment unfurled across Grimmley's dinner table. "It is like he already knows how to read Modeic, and I am just prodding him along, giving him reminders. When I take the time to roll these observations together—an innate ability to speak Dragon, a natural ability to learn Modei, and the use of a system of magic not known to exist—I am left struck in awe at the pure oddity of it all.

"And that leads me to the next question. Why are there no references that the Dragonbonded of old manipulated all four elementals? This is a profound revelation, Grimmley. I have read every parchment and artifact remaining in the realms that describe the Dragonbonded, so I am certain no such record exists. Yet any astute orderman around the Dragonbonded would have known right away what they were capable of doing. Why did no one ever make note of this insight?"

"I would say we have enough enigmas to chase down without adding *that* to the list," Grimmley suggested.

"I can't help but feel in my gut that this is somehow connected to everything else we are dealing with."

Grimmley stopped whisking eggs and winked at Layna. "You sure your gut isn't thinking about my supper?"

Layna let out a hearty laugh. "I can't deny that thoughts of your frittata are distracting." But she lost her cheery smile and heaved a deep sigh. "I need time to investigate."

Grimmley shoved the skillet into the oven, then straightened with a groan. "So, your goal is to uncover more knowledge about the ancient Dragonbonded; mine is to obtain evidence as to whether the realms are still infested with spies."

Layna nodded. "We have a plan."

Grimmley gazed through the back window, watching the stars reflected in the lake beyond his garden, seemingly unaware Barthox had returned. "Just when I was content with never leaving my quiet sanctuary, the Cosmos slaps me on the backside and tells me it's time to get moving again."

Barthox hooted an exhausted agreement.

The Shaman pulled his shoulders back and pursed his lips. "The lad needs another good quest to give us the freedom to move forward."

"Grimmley, I know this is not necessary, but I'm going to say it anyway. Tread cautiously on your path forward, my old friend. If there are more spies, poking at them may not be a wise move. Conner's display of powers on the tourney field may have deterred them, but at some point, they will become emboldened to test the waters once more. If they find Conner's abilities to be nothing more than smoke and mirrors ..."

The long silence that followed made Layna uneasy, so she stepped to the back door. "I should go check on Horasius for the night."

She stepped out, leaving Grimmley staring through the back window, lightly rubbing the ears of a raccoon who had appeared at the windowsill hoping for a taste of frittata.

box 48 so

Tales of Old

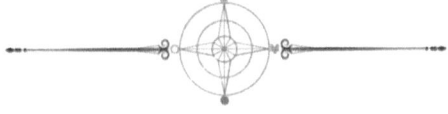

Nartesis Shazarack waited in the dark of the council's chamber, a withered, silent form dwarfed by the sovereign prince's massive throne, which he had taken as his own. Eight more chairs, reserved for the members of the Council of Necromantic Lords, arrayed in a semicircle on either side of him—empty. It had been nine nights since his triumphant return to his beloved city, Thanatos, and the only useful information he had acquired in that time was that it was now the year 1279.

Nartesis leaned his leathery head against the back of the throne. He would have closed his eyes—if he'd had eyelids. Nine hundred years had passed while he slept, entombed. He held his cadaverous hand to the light, twisting and flexing his gray, weedy fingers. Little life remained in this vessel. He could feel his life energy waning. Even the powerful stone he had embedded in his heart so long ago would not sustain this body much longer.

The crank of the door's handle drew his attention. The bolt popped free, and the thick door at the far end of the room swung wide. An elderly man shuffled into the chamber, stuttering to a pause amid the assembly of massive chairs. He carried a small hedgehog curled up in his palm. Occasionally, the man would glance at Nartesis's undead protectors standing guard.

Nartesis stirred and drew the man's eye. "Minister Barakin, finally we meet." Nartesis's reedy voice drifted across the room, void of any semblance of the living. "I have heard many good things about you."

The minister bowed low before the wraith-like figure. Barakin was wiry and tall, with a salt-and-pepper beard that covered most of his chest, though the thick gray hair on his head was cut short. "Supreme Lord Shazarack, it pleases me that there are those who find my service of value."

"Minister." Nartesis spoke the word as if speaking it for the first time. "It is an interesting title. Do tell me, what is it that you do?"

"I—I am head of the Academy of Necromancy, Supreme Lord." He paused, then added, "And I administer to the many assorted needs of our council, of course."

"Ah, yes, the Council of Necromantic Lords." Nartesis shifted in the immense chair. "And tell me, Minister, how do you find the strength and vision to keep the academy moving forward without the council's current guidance?"

"Guidance, Supreme Lord? I fail to understand—"

The Supreme Lord Necromancer leaned forward and gestured at the eight empty chairs. "The council has not met since my momentous return to Thanatos. I can only imagine the challenges you must be facing, keeping all those young minds at the academy focused on their studies. We know how ... inattentive ... youths can be."

"It was my understanding that you forbade the council—"

"To meet," Nartesis finished with a wave of his bony arm. "Yes, yes. I have forbidden them to assemble. But how does the academy fare?"

"The Academy of Necromancy is operating efficiently, as always, Supreme Lord," Barakin assured him.

"Which raises a most perplexing question, wouldn't you agree, Minister?"

The minister shifted, visibly uneasy. "What question would that be, Supreme Lord?"

"Why, the council's function, Minister Barakin. What is its purpose?" Nartesis read the minister's bewilderment. "If I severed the head of a snake from its body, the body would not continue as if nothing happened. Surely, you see my confusion."

"Supreme Lord, I— I—" It was clear the man had never been called to the council's defense.

"You may speak frankly, Minister Barakin."

The minister took a slow breath to steady his nerves. "Much has happened in the millennium since ... the destruction of Thanatos."

Nartesis ran a dry tongue over his cracked lips. After being awakened in his cavern two fortnights ago by a boy in the company of one of his creations, he had crossed the great mountain range to arrive back at his ancient home, amazed to find it completely rebuilt as it had been before its destruction. "Enlighten me," he rasped, then drew upon Earth elemental. *"Ora ousia kinothyra."* One of the chairs rumbled across the floor, coming to rest at the minister's thigh. "Take a seat," he commanded.

"My deepest apologies, Supreme Lord, but only council members are allowed to sit in this chamber." The minister's awkwardness grew in the silence that followed.

Fascinating, Nartesis mused with delight. "I don't think one transgression will matter." The minister still did not move. "I won't tell on you," Nartesis whispered.

The minister eased his torso into the chair, his face hot from the heretical act.

Nartesis nodded slightly to the undead creature at his side. The creature shuffled to a nearby table. Its rotted gray clothing dangled loose about its emaciated body. With considerable effort, it managed to pour a goblet of wine from a glass decanter, then lumbered to the minister's chair.

The minister took the offered glass with an unsteady hand.

"You're impressed, are you not, Ousel?" Nartesis asked, though the question was more a statement filled with self-confidence. "I hope you do not mind that I call you by your given name."

Barakin wiggled his head. He held up the hedgehog. "This is Helgish."

Nartesis needed someone he could rely on, a loyal follower, not a devout god-servant. That would not be easy to find, since Nartesis was the order's paragon. He tried to smile but was not sure the expression on what remained of his face had the desired effect. "Good. And you shall call me Lord."

Ousel drank deep from the goblet to steady his nerves. "Your servants do your bidding without instructions or verbal commands."

"I do not think of them as servants." An old memory clouded Nartesis's thoughts, of a servant he'd thought he could rely on. He shrugged it away. "I summoned this spirit into this female body a very long time ago. As you can see, it has little use of her arms, and it has lost most of her sight. But I cannot bring myself to release the spirit back to its plane." Nartesis waited while the minister examined the creature in the narrow light. "She was here, you know." Nartesis's grand motion encompassed the chamber. "She was with me that day when the Armies of the Seven Realms marched out on the plains below and laid siege to our illustrious fortress. She saved my life."

"Nearly a thousand years," Barakin whispered. "It is beyond belief that a spirit binding could last that long. The most powerful of our order can only summon spirits into vessels for months before the binding breaks down and the spirit is released. Periodic mooring incantations are needed to sustain the link longer." After a brief pause, he added, "The academy is alight with wonder at your extraordinary abilities. Those who once thought stories of your deeds were mere fables no longer challenge them."

Instead of being pleased, Nartesis grunted with disgust. "I have had time to inspect the undead those of this order bring to life, even those who call themselves grandmasters of Necromancy." Shazarack made a flamboyant gesture before his face contorted into a snarl. "They are but dismal remnants of what we once created in our grand order. Truly, it saddens me that there are no great wonders to behold. It is not what I expected to find after all this time. And to answer your unspoken question, that is why I dismissed this order's pathetic council."

Ousel lowered his eyes in shame. "Little remained after Thanatos burned, Lord Shazarack. And all those who practiced our arts were either killed during the siege or tortured before death released them to the planes beyond. The few who survived thought that you, along with all your knowledge, had perished with the city. Nearly everything had to be reconstructed." The minister hesitated. "I don't mean to justify our wretched attempts—"

"I can instruct you on how to summon such a spirit as this. To create an undead servant that would last until your last breath in the Physical plane."

Ousel's head snapped upward. "Me?" he asked, astonished at the thought. "I am not sure I am powerful enough—"

Nartesis waved Ousel to silence. "Limitations are merely a fabrication you have been told to believe, Ousel. Nothing more." The chair creaked as Nartesis leaned forward. "I assume you would like to learn."

"Of course, my lord. It would be an honor beyond measure to be chosen to receive such knowledge."

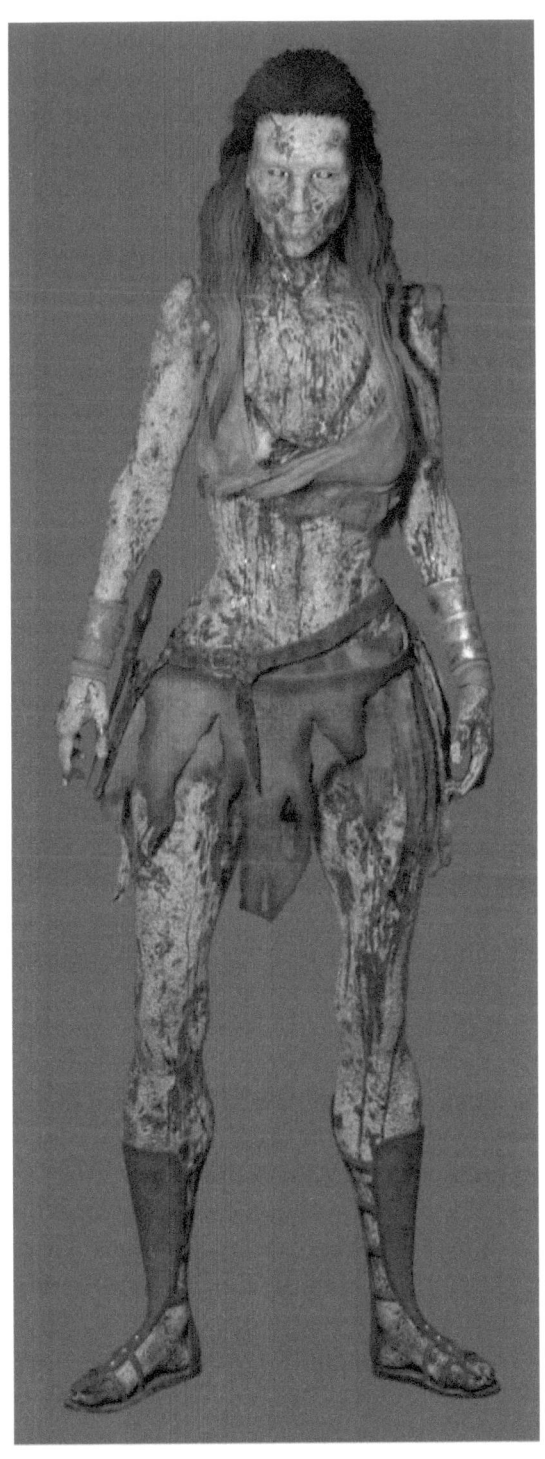

"Then it is settled." Nartesis pounded his palm on the chair's armrest as if striking a deal for the minister's soul. It was a meager first step toward taking complete control of the order. "We shall learn from each other. I shall teach you the old and powerful ways of necromancy, and you shall tell me about all the events these past thousand years." Nartesis settled back, a satisfying hiss escaping his narrow chest. "I shall let you go first."

Ousel's jaw worked involuntarily before words formed. "Where should I start, my lord? Perhaps with the War of the Orders that started a few years after Thanatos's destruction?"

Shazarack's hollow laugh echoed about the chamber. "No, Ousel, you can skip that tale. After all, it was I who sired that war." He chuckled at the minister's surprise. "It is a long and sordid account I care little to regale you with. I'd rather hear about how that war ended."

Through that evening and into the night, Nartesis listened as Ousel narrated the slow march of time since Thanatos's destruction nearly a millennium before. He mostly let the minister choose what was of significant historical importance for the Supreme Lord's ears, except for the occasional pointed question.

Nartesis's first disappointment came almost immediately in Ousel's tale. He had hoped that the twenty-year War of the Orders he had ignited would have forced all the early orders to unite behind a common cause, placing them at last on equal footing with the seven crowns. Sadly, that had not been the case. The realms and their armies had won that war, not because of greater might, but because those leading the orders could not get past their petty differences. Maybe he should have taken a more active role in the war instead of focusing on his pet project at the time. The early orders had learned nothing from his great city's demise. The rebellion Nartesis had fought to give life to had been snuffed out before its second breath. Thanatos, along with all those who had called that city home, close friends and colleagues alike, had died for nothing.

According to Ousel, under the Armistice of the Orders signed at the end of the War of the Orders, all those practicing the arts of combining two elementals were forced together into six orders, based on the six combinations of the four elementals. Further, under this armistice, the newly formed orders were no longer governed by individuals. Instead, councils of nine or more recognized grandmasters were appointed to oversee each order's operations. Selection to the councils was for life with consensus of the council members and approval by the seven crowns. This ensured the orders would remain loyal to monarchic demands. In addition, the orders agreed they would assist the Seven Realms in binding arbitration when there were disputes between the realms or their municipalities. In rare cases when war broke out between two realms, each order was given latitude to choose a side in the conflict. However, choosing a losing side would be devastating to an order's ranking among the crowns, so councils inevitably chose to abstain from messy affairs of state. Decisions and actions within the orders were determined more by the ebb and flow of crown politics than evolving elemental prowess. Nartesis quickly came to see that the order councils of the bygone day lacked anything resembling a spine, and that they were at the heart of why his once-great order of necromancers had stagnated over the past millennium.

Nartesis's vision, the one he had worked his entire life to see come to fruition—of the orders being out from under the boot of the seven crowns—slowly suffocated through Ousel's oration. That was, until the minister began the tale of the War of the Breaking.

Five and half centuries ago, factions within the six orders formed—between those who considered themselves of Harmonic and Anarchic influence. The distinction between the two camps seemed to Nartesis as superfluous as arguing over which shoe to put on first in the morning. But Ousel was quite adamant that the differences were central to the brewing conflict.

Nartesis was scheming over how he could use the ongoing struggles between the Harmonics and Anarchists to his advantage when he jerked forward in his chair. "What was that?"

"What was what, my lord?"

"What you just said—repeat it." Nartesis ran his fingers lightly over a small lump in his robe's breast pocket.

"Uh. I said that the Anarchists would have won the War of Breaking if not for the meddlesome band of Dragonbonded."

"I don't recall you mentioning Dragonbonded before. Who were they? Where did they come from?"

"I did not mention them before, Lord, because they are looked upon with such disapprobation. They were several score young men and women—nothing more than boys and girls, really—who had bonded with dragons during the time leading up to the war."

"Dragons? You mean like the mythological creatures from the old world?"

"It is unsure, Lord, from whence these creatures came. They were so named, as I have been told, because of their similarities to those described in folk tales from the old lands, before Cronoa's destruction. Only, these creatures were intelligent." After several silent moments, Ousel expanded on his response. "The murals and paintings that survive from that time portray them as rather large beasties, black and scaly, with wings like bats. But little more is known about them."

Nartesis pressed his spine into the chair, his mind reeling. Could his mighty creations have survived all this time? Several score, with their dragon bonds, defeated an entire army? "And now? Where are these ... Dragonbonded?"

"Gone, my lord. They all died in the final battle of the War of Breaking. They, like the creatures they had bonded with, have never been seen again." Ousel's lips moved as if deciding whether to say more.

"What? Speak!" Nartesis snapped.

"News arrived following your return about a young man who is reported to have recently bonded with a dragon, my lord, though few believe this tale holds any truth. It is said that he lives in the Harmonic lands of Griffinrock, as the queen's own protector and Champion. If it *is* true, he would be the first to bond with a dragon since the War of Breaking."

Nartesis thought back to the day a month ago when he had been awakened in his cavern laboratory. And then, it all made sense. He recalled the moment he awoke, the young lad squatting before him, gaping at his skeletal face. At the moment of his death, Nartesis had used a Fettering Stone to keep himself alive. But he'd never completed the incantation that would save him from reclamation. Instead, the incantation had enveloped him in stasis for a millennium, until the boy came along and somehow awakened him from his sleep. Nartesis had felt the boy's raw power to control elementals as life once more coursed through his decayed body.

And then there was the adolescent offspring of his creations, the one that had arrived just in time to save the boy from plummeting to his death down the cavern crevice. The creature's appearance had been the sign for Nartesis's triumphant return to his Thanatos. He knew the boy and beast had been connected somehow. But he had never thought a dragon might bond with a human. The Cosmos, it seemed, had a prophetic passion for the ironic.

Dragons. His errant creations had not only survived the past nine hundred years; they had propagated. And powerful as well! Just as he'd predicted. Old plans bubbled to the surface, taking new shape—visions of a rich and powerful world ruled by those capable of manipulating the elemental forces of nature rather than by descendants of an ancient ruling class. But many questions had to be laid to rest before he could enact those plans. Where had his creations been these past five hundred years? How many dragons now lived? And if he amassed the elemental power he would need to summon them, would they heed his call?

Ousel shifted in his chair, yanking Nartesis's attention back. "And how did this War of Breaking end?"

"The war did not so much end, my lord, as it was ... annulled. Leaders from the two sides met in 728 to sign the Treaty of Alignment, establishing a formal separation between the Anarchic and Harmonic lands. And those realms that had sided with the Anarchist faction—Dristonia, Gorgonia, Tanzanar, and Andorea—eliminated their ruling classes and became the Assembly of Anarchists. The treaty also established a twenty-mile ribbon of land separating the two regions, called the Borderlands, as neutral territory.

"It was also under that treaty that the six Anarchic orders formally split from their parent orders—Necromancers from the Shamans, Barbarians from the Warriors, Warlocks from the Sorcerers, Black Knights from the Paladins, Conjurors from the Mystics, Assassins from the Rangers. Under the leadership of the newly formed Necromancers Order council, Thanatos was rebuilt to the exact specifications of your original design. The city became our order's epicenter of necromantic studies and the arts, resurrecting what little knowledge remained of our ancient arts and traditions."

Nartesis was disappointed. So, the Necromancers Order had been born of the split from the Shamans. That was quite fitting. After all, Nartesis had created the first necromancer order from a shamans guild back before there were orders. At least some within the orders had broken free from the shackles of noble rule, toppling four of the seven monarchies in their wake. It was a start—and something Nartesis could build upon. But he could not get too far ahead of himself. He had a more immediate problem to contend with.

Moving forward with his plan would require that he seize decisive control of his rebuilt city and the Necromancers Order. But Sovereign Prince Galan would not go away quietly, and the man held sway over an influential portion of the order, including a majority of council members. Nartesis would have preferred an amicable resolution to this power struggle. Unfortunately, in addition to assuming the council's normal responsibilities, he had unintentionally killed the sovereign prince's wife, Breanen Sagamore, the day he'd arrived at Thanatos. Lord Galan was still furious. And angry people did irrational acts.

Breanen Sagamore. Nartesis shifted uneasily at the name, and its possible implications that she might be his assistant from long ago. Of course, it could be a coincidence, but he had not gotten where he was by ignoring seemingly random events. He would not let the idea go until he had pursued it to his satisfaction. Maybe great discoveries had been made during his absence.

Nartesis turned his milky eyes to the man before him, examining him with the first break of Hemera's light. He had chosen wisely in enlisting this minister as the first of many allies he would need for his cause. Head of the academy, Ousel was respected. His opinion held sway over the elders as well as the younger, more pliable students. And the man's clear devotion to rules would make him a modest and devoted follower. Yet even with all these qualities, Ousel's most valued talent was his keen mind for details and uncanny ability to recognize the historic threads that bound even seemingly insignificant events.

"Ousel, I am impressed with your knowledge of our history. Clearly, I have placed my trust in the right person."

Ousel tipped his head forward. "I am humbled by your words, Lord Shazarack."

"But I am exhausted and need time to consider all you have told me. When next we meet, we shall begin your studies in the old ways of Necromancy. Before you go, I have one more request. I assume the order keeps records of the names of all who have entered into this hallowed assemblage?"

"Meticulously so, Supreme Lord." Ousel puffed his chest with pride. "The Book of Census contains the entire history of our great order, beginning with those who entered following the restructuring under the treaty with the Harmonics."

"Good. I need you to bring that book to me ... without anyone knowing."

Ousel stiffened. "That will not be easy, my lord, even for me. The book is guarded closely, as you might expect. Even extreme diligence does not preclude the possibility of spies and traitors within our ranks."

"Spies do not concern me, Ousel. I need that book."

Ousel stood and bowed low before exiting the Lord Council's chamber. "As you command, my lord."

Clandestine Plans

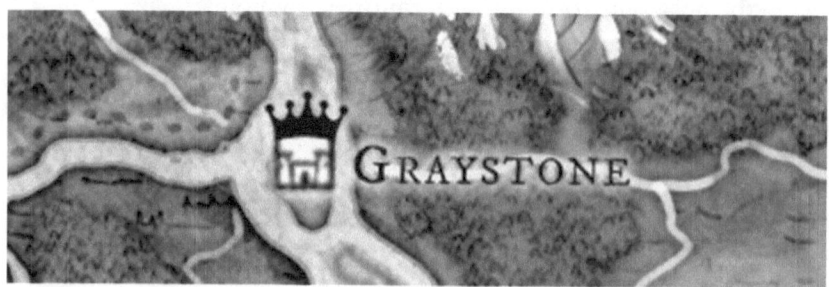

"**Y**ou want me to *what*?" Kriston shouted.

Skye snorted and twitched in his sleep at the far end of the dungeon.

Conner waited for his bond to settle. "I want you to help me break into the Shamans' temple so that I can talk to the Necromancer being held there," he whispered to Kriston.

"Conner, for a month now, you do be tellin' me—"

Conner furrowed his brow at his young page. Teaching Kriston how to speak properly was part of the boy's rehabilitation from stealing.

"Sorry." Kriston grinned. "You have been telling me that my thieving days are over. And now you want me to use my skills—all for some selfish gain?"

"I'm not asking you to steal anything," Conner clarified, though he knew he was drawing a thin line.

"You do know this is a bad idea," Pauli said while yawning, making his words barely intelligible.

Conner cocked his head in thought. "I'm not going to think about that. I have to talk to her."

"I've walked past that temple many times, Conner. *Fortress* is a better description than *temple*. The walls are at least a half dozen paces high. And the only gate in is guarded day and night. Just how do you expect to break in?"

"I'm working on that." Conner could not shake the feeling that he sounded too much like Grimmley.

"Maybe you could climb the wall like you did at Cravenrock," Kriston suggested.

Pauli huffed at the idea, reminding them both that he still did not believe their outlandish tale of Conner climbing the city walls using his hands and feet. "Yeah, I'd like to see that."

Conner ignored Pauli, not wanting to rehash that conversation. "I have been by the temple, too. No, the stones of Graystone's walls are enchanted, and built differently than those at Cravenrock. I'd never get a solid hold."

"I've heard Rangers have spells that make them climb like ants. You know any of those spells?" Pauli probed.

"No." Conner waved that idea away. "And even if I did, casting such an incantation near the temple would be like the town crier ringing his bell and shouting, 'Here I am!'"

"Hey! How about we climb on your dragon's back and he flies us over the wall?" Pauli offered.

Conner took in Pauli's considerable mass. "Even if Skye carried all three of us, landing on the temple grounds would whip up enough wind to wake the undead."

"Okay then," Pauli persisted, "Skye can hover from high above and we climb down on ropes."

Conner and Kriston glanced at each other. It was going to be a long night.

Pauli for once caught the exchange and puffed out his lips. Folding his arms, he fell silent.

"We have a problem that we'll need to solve even before we get near the wall," Conner began. "We will need—"

"A detailed layout of the temple," Kriston filled in.

The boy's eyes sparkled a little too much for Conner's liking. His former life as Bandit of the Cravenrock Thieves Guild was never far from the lad's quick reach.

The boy poked a finger at Conner's charcoal sketch. "This is a good start, but it's not going to be enough. I'll need to know exact dimensions, especially spacing between the buildings. I'll also need to know where there are lanterns so we can use the shadows right. And I'm going to need more information. Where is this Necromancer being held? Besides the guards at the gate, how many sentries might we encounter along the way? What kind of alarms do they have, and are the alarms enchanted?"

Conner shook his head slowly. "I'm afraid we're going to have to rely on some luck for this mission, Kriston."

"Then this is a bad idea."

Pauli elbowed Conner in the ribs. "Told ya."

Conner bit at his lower lip, doubts strengthening their grip on his gut. "We don't have time for all that. It's been nearly two fortnights since Asheborne was brought there. I've been hearing chatter of plans to move her to a real prison soon. I don't know how long we have."

"At least take another run of the place," Kriston suggested. "And I advise you do that before Hemera returns. You've got three hours at best."

"This drawing won't do?" Conner pointed at the parchment unrolled before them. "I've flown over the temple several times, so I'm pretty sure this map is close. For me to get a better view, Skye would have to fly low over the temple more than once. I don't think I'm willing to risk alerting anyone inside. If word got back to Grimmley, he'd be all over me wanting to know what I was about. He may be ancient, but he can still add one and one."

Kriston folded his arms, looking at the drawing as if it had bit him. "*Close* isn't good enough. Even a slight error in location or position of any number of details could be the difference between staying hidden in the shadows and getting caught out in the open. The map has to be *exact*." Kriston's eyes went wide with a thought. "I think Skye should have another flyover, just higher up, where he'll be lost against the backdrop of stars. Of course, at that height, we'll need someone with the keen eyes of a hawk. That really leaves us with one option." His gaze floated to the back of the large room where an iridescent black sleeping form grunted and snorted.

"As they say, 'dangerous days demand daring deeds.'" Pauli chuckled.

Just at that moment, Skye twitched at something invading his dreams, waking himself with a long belch. He opened glowing blue eyes to find the three boys sizing him up as if deciding whether he was tender enough to eat. His jaws locked wide, halfway through a smack. His head snapped up, eyes narrowing and shifting to Conner. "What?"

"Skyyyyeee." Conner's voice wafted across the dungeon room like the sweet smell of honeysuckle.

"No," the dragon grumbled back.

"You don't even know what I was going to ask."

Skye shook his head vigorously. "It doesn't matter. Whatever it is, *no*."

"Well, then. Fine. I thought you were getting bored in this dank dungeon all the time ... when you're not busy ferrying me about. We will just have to do this without you."

Skye's eyes narrowed. "What do you mean 'this'?"

"No, no. You're right." Conner patted his palm downward. "Go back to sleep. We've got this under control."

Pauli rubbed at his head. "Conner, I thought—"

Conner kicked Pauli in the shin.

In the time it takes a dragon to flick its tail, Skye lifted his bulk on four powerful legs, fully awake. "Got *what* under control?"

Conner waved dismissively. "We were talking about going to have a chat with Meera Asheborne, that Necromancer we met at Dragongarde."

Skye huffed at the name, sharp talons scraping across the stone floor. "That Necromancer holds no honor." A jolt of displeasure coursed through Conner's link with the dragon. Skye had not gotten over how Asheborne had detained him at Dragongarde under threat of Conner's life. After a moment, the dragon added, "Talking to her is a bad idea."

Pauli snorted a laugh, but cut it short under Conner's intense glare. "Yes, I've heard that."

Skye shifted closer. "There is something you need me to do."

"Since you asked—"

"That wasn't a question."

Conner pressed his palms to his hips. Skye had clearly not had enough sleep. "Are you going to help us or not?"

Journey into Anarchy

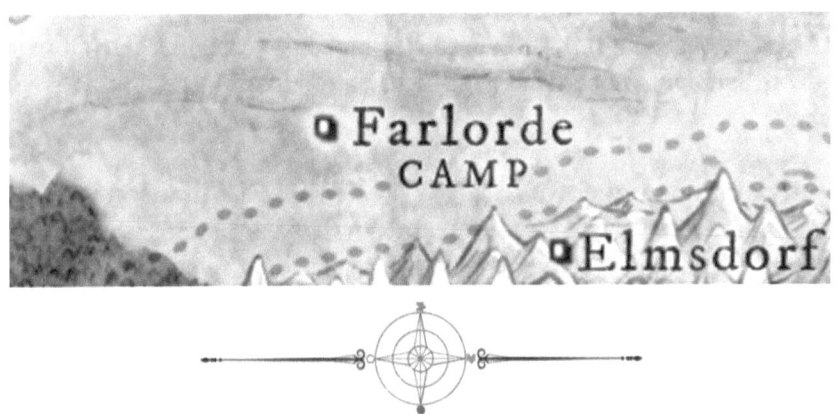

From the crest of a hill along the northern edge of the Dragon's Back Mountains, the defrocked ex-Warrior Marcantos Evinfaire drew to a stop and eyed the valley stretching for miles before him. A deep green from the long summer months sparkled with morning dew while the bluish haze of late morning chewed at the fringes of the northern horizon.

Grandmaster Assassin Lacerus sighed with relief, then offered Marcantos a rare smile. "It is good to be home." For nearly a month, the two had labored across the mountains, all while evading the many Harmonic patrols eager to apprehend them as Anarchic spies.

Marcantos sneered at the vast Anarchic grassland as if it were a blight over the face of Gaia. "Your home, not mine," he growled.

Lacerus gestured at the valley. "A sentiment you can no longer afford to sustain. I understand how being branded a traitor might affect you. But it has been a month since our hasty departure from Graystone, Marcantos. It is time you set aside the events of the Champion's tournament." The Assassin's expression darkened when Marcantos did not reply. Even Copious, Marcantos's brown bear bond, had taken to brooding at a distance. "We crossed the Borderlands yesterday. Your prideful self-image as a Harmonic grandmaster orderman will most certainly ensure your demise—and very quickly at that."

"I no longer fear death, Lacerus. If anything, I welcome it."

"You are a brilliant fighter," Lacerus said. "Even more, you have proven to be a natural with Anarchic powers, capable of—"

Copious growled irritably, cutting Lacerus short.

"I sense your story is far from complete, dear friend. I wish that I had not deceived you in your training. Only you can embrace your future." But the Assassin received only a fevered stare for his rare and heartfelt words of encouragement. Lacerus shrugged. "Live or die, Marcantos. It is your choice."

By early afternoon, the two travelers crested the last in a series of hills. There, Marcantos shuffled to a stop and surveyed a rolling sea of tan tents before him. They had survived their fording of the snow-peaked mountains at their backs, and soon they would reach the grassy shore of that canvas sea. On another hill beyond the tents, an ancient fortress rose high and gray in the late-afternoon mist, its mighty single tower like an aged lighthouse from a forgotten era. Citadel Farlorde had once been a majestic thriving fortress, an illustrious vestige of Warrior life. But that was before the Anarchic War, a time when this land had been called the Realm of Gorgonia, a time before it had fallen to the Anarchists. In the five centuries since, the citadel had been left on its own to weather the furies of Gaia and Cronus. The sight of the mossy castle, dilapidated and crumbling, made Marcantos's stomach knot in disgust.

The once-upon-a-time Warrior shifted his focus to the tents below. Of course he had heard of the infamous Farlorde camp, a swarming hive of Barbarians—dark Warriors—living in inglorious depravity and contempt at the footsteps of the great Farlorde, everything his order once held virtuous and sacred.

"It would be wise if you allowed me to bind your wrists before we proceed further, Marcantos," Lacerus suggested for the third time. "Your zealous Barbarian cousins may be unable to stay their swords once they have put their eyes upon your Harmonic armor."

Marcantos returned the man's glare. He frowned with disdain at Lacerus's black cloak and the long graying braids that marked him as a grandmaster Assassin. For four years Marcantos had studied under this man's fierce tutelage, believing him to be Blake Friarwood of the Warriors Order. Only after Marcantos's defeat at the Champion's tourney had he learned the truth: his preceptor was an Anarchic spy—everything he had been raised and trained to despise. At first, Marcantos had blamed Lacerus for the disgrace and misery that had befallen him, yet he burned with a shame that ravaged his soul. Several times in the first week after their escape, a delirious rage took him, and he drew upon Water and Air elementals and set upon the spy with angry sword. The mountains would echo with the sounds of clashing steel and guttural grunts until his outrage had been spent. Then, Marcantos would fall to the ground, exhausted, crying, and retching the meager contents of his stomach. In time, the cycle would repeat itself—disgrace, shame, anger, aggression, then sickness.

It took some time, but Marcantos came to see that he was blaming the wrong person. He was at fault for the nightmare his life had become. He had allowed himself to be duped by this man. Pride, arrogance, and his lust to win Queen Veressa's adulation had kept him from seeing through Lacerus's veil of lies. Defeat on the tourney field, a fugitive from High Law, a traitor to his homeland—he had defiled himself.

He glanced over his shoulder to the mountains walling him off from everything he had ever known. There would be no going back. But neither did he know how to move forward. No matter. He would not allow this Assassin to bind his hands any more than he would don clothing fitting ordermen of the Anarchic region. Marcantos pursed his lips and shook his head.

Lacerus turned his feet toward the sea of tents. "So it shall be."

When the two reached the edge of the Farlorde Barbarian camp, they passed a young woman practicing with her sword. A dark leather cuirass and leggings that fit tight along her torso hinted at a youthful, muscular figure beneath. Marcantos found the gleam of sweat on her light complexion alluring. Long golden hair with not even a touch of curl swirled as she spun and twisted, jabbed and parried, in a flowing form not that different from one used to teach Harmonic Warrior apprentices strong balance. Her movements revealed she lacked concentration. Still, Marcantos saw that her fighting prowess held potential. The young Barbarian's blue eyes met his mid-stroke, and she jolted to a stop, the tip of her sword sagging to the dirt.

A burly, middle-aged Barbarian man sat nearby drinking from a wooden mug. "Orianna! Focus! Or I will lift my sword to yours!" Then he followed his apprentice's gaze. The Barbarian rose stiff and alert from his log stump and reached for his sword, though he did not bare steel from sheath.

Marcantos would have liked to linger, to watch the apprentice despite her mentor's aggressive stance, but Lacerus drew his attention with a tilt of his braided head. A party of Barbarians had formed up near the center of camp and were making their way toward them. His feet spread wide in ready defiance to them, Marcantos prepared himself for his reclamation.

Copious sensed his bond's wariness and snarled as the group neared. Marcantos placed a palm upon the bear's muzzle.

"I am Master Barbarian Barcleave Tallenia, commander of the Farlorde forces," said the man at the head of the party. He was not a big man, but several gray scars adorned his round face and he walked with an assertive step. Barcleave ran a discerning eye over the black-cloaked man at Marcantos's side. "Why have you disrespected us by bringing this ... savage among us not bound and gagged as etiquette dictates, grandmaster Assassin?"

"My name is Lacerus," the Assassin declared as if his name carried weight, then studied the faces of those crowded around. "I have come seeking refuge for the night. I leave on the morrow to continue my journey to report to my order's council. This"—Lacerus gestured to his companion—"is Marcantos Evinfaire. He has come seeking to join your order."

Marcantos jerked his head at his ex-mentor, eyes widening. But he said nothing.

The commander made a slashing motion with his hand. "It is not my place to either offer or give honor to someone wishing to join our great order of fighters. I will not be an oath breaker, not even to a savage."

The throng of Barbarians about them laughed and cheered. Several began shouting "Cha Kohm!" and the words quickly became a chant.

"But it is your place to honor the will of your council," Lacerus shouted to be heard above the clamor, calling them all to silence.

The commander extended his hand toward Lacerus. "Then where is the parchment that so decrees this man's worthiness to be a member of our order? Show me the seal and I will make it so."

Again, the throng shouted their approval.

Lacerus rocked his head side to side, waiting until the din of jeers died away. "We have just arrived from across the Borderlands, so I do not have such a letter in my possession. However, send a dispatch to your Barbarians Council. Tell your runner to speak to councilman Erika Lacklander. She will confirm this man's enlistment with a letter."

Barcleave quieted the rowdy throng. "I know Lacklander. If she approves of this savage, then I cannot speak against it." The commander studied Marcantos for the first time, marking and weighing his powerful build, imposing stance, and cold hazel stare. "But if she does not give her approval, the savage dies."

"You speak clearly, Commander." Lacerus bowed. "Your words hold the force of oath and shall be."

The crowd began to disperse, though some lingered, disappointed there would be no combat.

A young Barbarian stepped forward. "Barcleave, I will arrange for their quarters."

"As you will, Groegan." The commander nodded, then pointed toward a hill to the south void of tents. "See to it the savage lays stakes on yon hill. I do not wish to spend any more time keeping our band from seeking honor with clash of sword against him. What is with him will be determined once we have received word from our council."

Groegan dipped at the waist. "It will be as you instruct."

Barcleave turned a jaundiced glare on Marcantos. "For now, you will go by the name Puppet. Now go." With everything sorted to his satisfaction, the commander returned to his tent at the epicenter of the camp.

Groegan did not speak but led Marcantos to a large hut to the west, where he was shown supplies and materials to throw his tent. Offering no further instructions, Groegan departed.

After rummaging through the hut, Marcantos proceeded to the southern hill with arms full of supplies. He labored through what remained of Hemera's light, and when that was gone, he built a large fire by which to complete the construction of his tent. While he worked, he thought about what had transpired since his arrival at Farlorde. Little made sense. He did not know why the commander would call him a savage or why he would be given the name Puppet. Whatever was meant by the name, he was certain the meaning was something slanderous.

And what was Lacerus up to? The two had spent a month traveling here, and not once had Lacerus mentioned the idea that Marcantos should consider becoming, or be given an opportunity to become, a dark Warrior—a Barbarian. Possibly Lacerus had not spoken of it because he knew what Marcantos's answer would be. For seventeen years, Marcantos had fought in the service of the Harmonic Realms. He had met Barbarians on the field of combat on multiple occasions along the Borderlands. And the outcome had always been the same—he was the only one who'd departed drawing breath. So why would the Barbarians Council approve a decorated grandmaster Warrior joining their order? Was Lacerus giving Marcantos a reprieve from execution, albeit a short one, to offer him time to reconsider his options, to sway him to the Anarchic side? Well, his eyes were open now to Lacerus's ability to deceive. One thing he could be sure of: whatever Lacerus's motives, he would not reveal anything substantive to Marcantos, even if asked.

At last, Marcantos stood cross-armed before his completed tent, then glanced north. The Farlorde camp was aglow with hundreds of fires. Sounds of laughter and singing, smells of food and burning wood, and the movement of people and bonds floated up from the glistening sea of tents. Beyond, the upper peaks of the ancient citadel's tower glowed dimly in Erebus's soft light. He had an affinity for that arcane structure, as if it represented the sum total of his life. *I am no longer a Warrior*, Marcantos thought. *But if I am not a Warrior, then what am I?*

Every Warrior needed a home, a place to belong. What was life's meaning if not tethered to some ideal, some cause worthy of fighting and dying for? Barcleave had used words like *respect, etiquette, honor, oath*, and *worthiness*. These were not words Marcantos had expected a Barbarian to understand, yet Barcleave had used them as if they held sacred meaning.

Then Lacerus's words earlier that day came to him: *You have proven to be a natural with Anarchic powers.* He recalled the day he'd fought the four master Warriors in Cravenrock, the exhilarating rush using the Anarchic eddies that ripped and played with him, pulling him into their alluring force of chaos and change. And he remembered the aching hunger when that rush was gone. Thoughts of the young female Barbarian with soft blue eyes and the jeering chants of Barbarians tugged at the fringes of his most sacred beliefs. None of what he'd experienced this day had matched his expectations.

Marcantos dropped his head forward, shaking it slowly. None of that mattered. His life was on borrowed time. Soon, reclamation would come to his tent. And while he welcomed an end to this tortured life, he would not let go easily. He would die with sword in hand, quenching some Barbarian's steel blade.

With that thought in mind, he stepped into his tent, leaving Copious snorting and twitching in his sleep beside the fire.

Lacerus stared out at the lone man on the hill south of the camp. The Kindred had placed too much of their hope upon Marcantos's performance on the tourney field. Now they were paying the price. Brother Sarmenion of the Conjurors' oracles had been certain Marcantos would be vital to their plans. How could Sarmenion have so horribly misinterpreted the signs? Of course, Lacerus had a theory, one founded in his ancient memories. Tonight, he would share that theory with his Brothers. None would like what he had postulated.

He sensed a man moving stealthily to his side, drawing him from his troubled reflections. He drew a slow, settling breath.

"Brother," Groegan acknowledged Lacerus, then mirrored his stance, studying Marcantos in the dark of night.

Lacerus only nodded. He sensed the animosity in his Brother's voice, but that was not his concern. Groegan would do what was best for the Kindred.

"I need you to look after Marcantos," Lacerus said.

Groegan rubbed his chin as he mulled over Lacerus's request. "Since he failed to secure a position at the new queen's side, I do not see that we have further need of his skills. His failure at Graystone was the result of a mind that snapped under the stress of your efforts to bend it. Besides, I have my own path, Brother. My failure to secure the young dragon at Dragongarde—as well as losing the Necromancer to the Harmonic scouting party—has Barcleave in a sour state. I believe it's pushed my advancement back several years."

Lacerus faced Groegan. "Patience, Brother. Rebuilding the Kindred's plan takes priority. Much needs to be rectified before we proceed with the final phase." His eyes shifted to the hill again. "And I sense Marcantos may still prove useful." Groegan did not reply, so Lacerus persisted. "Marcantos needs guidance along the path I have set for him. He would be distrustful of anything I suggest—with good reason." Lacerus did not try to hide his malicious grin. "You, on the other hand—"

Groegan shifted, tensing.

Lacerus continued. "I need to take care of something important before returning to the Labyrinth of Armeaus."

Finally, Groegan found his voice. "What of your Barbarian spy in Cravenrock? Was she not useful in this Warrior's transition to our cause?

If you truly believe Marcantos is worth keeping live, could she not be put to use?"

"Trista?" The Barbarians Council had planted Trista as a spy in Cravenrock. Lacerus had called upon her to help Marcantos adjust to using Anarchic Sight without him becoming suspicious. "Yes, she seemed adequately skilled at keeping Marcantos stable while he acclimated to his Anarchic ways. But he believes his affair with Trista was of his own volition. Bringing her back would only expose our treachery and drive him further from our reach. It would be unwise to risk sharing any more knowledge of our true plans with her. Besides, she developed actual affections for this Warrior." Lacerus scoffed at the woman's foolishness.

Carnia fluttered past and settled in a tree nearby, interrupting Lacerus's thoughts. The falcon held the remnants of a mourning dove clutched in her talons. With a precision only Lacerus could admire, she ripped away at the bird.

"In any case," Lacerus went on, "Brother Sarmenion suggested that Trista remain in Cravenrock for now. There is a chance she will be needed to assist in some future endeavor."

"So, what is it that you expect from me, Brother?" the Barbarian asked irritably. "Marcantos must choose his own destiny. I have neither time nor luxury to be handmaiden to a lost and forlorn Harmonic orderman."

Lacerus shrugged. "I have been with this man for several years, Groegan. You have not seen him in action. When he frees himself of his Harmonic restraints and embraces Anarchic Sight, he is truly a sight to behold. Besides, a challenging and worthy objective always involves some element of risk."

"Risk?" Groegan grumbled as he ground his teeth. "Must I remind you, Brother, what your failure to install Marcantos as the new queen's champion cost the Kindred?"

"Of course not." Lacerus had been forced to leave behind all he had built in the Harmonic Realms over thirty years—a high-ranking position of influence in the Warriors Order, preceptor to a Champion advocate that gave him status and access to untold secrets, an expansive network of informants and runners across the Narwalen Plains that had been the bedrock for the Kindred's plans and the Anarchists' hopes for invasion, and, of course, the Cravenrock Thieves Guild. No, Lacerus needed no one to tell him what he'd lost.

Lacerus went on. "If you are done admonishing me for my failures, Brother, I am exhausted and need sleep before I continue my journey."

Lacerus did not wait for Groegan's response. The Assassin left the Barbarian staring out across the plains in silent contemplation.

Herid the Heretic

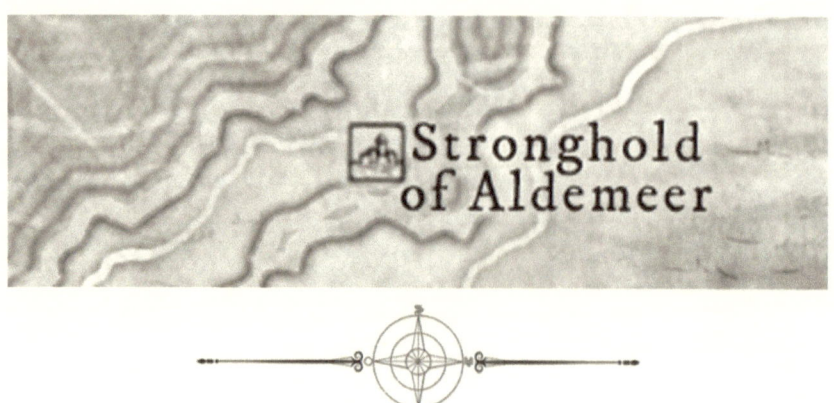

Stronghold of Aldemeer

"**A**re you sure of this, Archbishop?" asked Tierson Greenlace, Knight Exemplar and Supreme Cardinal of the Paladins Order. "That demented kook has been a danger to himself and everyone around him ever since he lost his bond three decades ago. The Yearning has taken him completely. Locking him away was the only means to ensure he didn't become a hazard—to us if not to our doctrines."

"I would agree that the ancient heretic is ... erratic, my Lord Greenlace." Archbishop Eladon tilted his head forward in a sign of respect. "However, you said you wanted answers regarding the empty box Grimmley Rollingsworth returned." Eladon gestured to the council members seated in a semicircle about him. "We all would like answers. What happened to the stones that were given to the Shaman Alicia Farclave long ago? How did Shaman Rollingsworth come by the box? And how did he know to bring the box here to us? Without answers to these fundamental questions, the story of the stones' fate cannot be reassembled. Besides, Tatem Creeg's instructions a millennium ago were quite explicit—our order was to protect the Fettering Stones *at any cost*. I do not see that we have a choice in this matter anymore." The Archbishop knew he was pressing his luck. But he needed the council to be unwavering in their commitment to his plan, and that meant they needed to see the urgency of the matter.

Supreme Cardinal Greenlace finally nodded, then held his left hand high. A gold ring with an embedded black stone blazing an azure blue from its heart adorned his index finger. Greenlace recited the ancient tale, though every council member could have done the same. "This ring, bequeathed by Torgameed, the first Paladin Knight, and worn on the hand of every Knight Exemplar since, is a reminder of the stones' importance to our faith. Many stones were lost in the time before the War of the Orders. And no stones have been returned in seven centuries of searching. If we don't unravel the mystery of what happened to them, this stone will be the last." Turning toward Eladon, his bushy brow low, Greenlace asked, "And you think Herid can bring us answers?"

"I do," Eladon lied emphatically. Brother Sarmenion had foreseen this path would eliminate several problems the Kindred were plagued with at once. Though he was losing faith in Sarmenion's oracular skills. "Herid and Grimmley are old friends, so the Shaman will not expect our deception. We *will* get the information we are looking for."

The supreme cardinal fell back into his chair, then summoned the guards by the chamber door. "The prisoner, Herid Osmonti. Bring him here."

Two guards tossed the old man to the floor at the feet of the council's seats. White, oily hair fell in tangles around his face, and a thin beard drooped to his waist. His ankle chains rattled across the marble.

"Herid," Greenlace called.

The shackled ragamuffin winced at the name. Turning his head to the side, he whispered, "Of course I know who that is! I'm no fool."

Eladon stepped forward. "Herid," he said softly, beckoning the man to him. He cradled the old face between his thick palms and lifted it up, waiting for Herid's eyes to settle on him. "We need you to listen to us. The council has a mission for you to perform."

Herid's mouth fell open, exposing two rows of honey-yellow teeth. "Mission?" he asked through scraggly lip hair.

"Yes. A very important mission."

Herid squeezed his eyes shut. "I want to go back to my cell," he whimpered.

"Listen to me, Herid. This is your opportunity to right a wrong. You want that, do you not? We can wipe the slate clean of your heretic brand— if you are successful." Herid's face contorted as he chewed on Eladon's words. "The Shaman Grimmley Rollingsworth came here two fortnights ago bearing a silver box."

Herid inhaled sharply. He reached out and gripped Eladon's sleeve. "A box of *Fettering Stones*," he whispered.

"Actually, Herid," Greenlace interrupted, "a box *for* Fettering Stones. The box was empty."

Herid's face grew cloudy.

Eladon glanced about at the assembled council, then, leaning closer, whispered so only Herid could hear. "Grimmley has been searching for a stone, Herid." He waited until recognition filled Herid's cloudy eyes. "Yes. You know of what I speak. Grimmley needs your help. Can you help him?"

"I—I—I suppose."

Eladon painted a kind smile across his face. "Excellent."

Herid's eyes widened, laced with some unspeakable fear. He pressed his lips to Eladon's ear. Eladon fought against pulling away. "But I cannot do the mission alone. Can I take Ezera with me?"

"Ezera? Your bond?"

Herid bobbed his head eagerly.

"Of course, Herid." Eladon lightly patted Herid's bony shoulder. *Poor deranged dolt*, he thought. "One must always take their bond with them."

The worn creases and lines around Herid's eyes melted. He gripped Eladon's hands in his. "Thank you, my liege."

"So, we have an agreement, then. You will take the mission?" But Eladon's question was more a directive.

Herid nodded, then let his chin fall to his chest.

"Good," Eladon beamed, rising before the old man. He flicked his fingers at the guards who had brought him before the council. "See that our new agent is properly bathed and shaved. And find something suitable for him to wear."

"Shh!" Herid waved at the musty air beside him. He had waited until nearly midnight before invading the cellars. His fortitude was wearing thin. "All that racket is going to draw someone's attention." He tipped forward into the dwindling light, then stumbled through the door he had chosen. He was not sure why this particular door looked appropriate, but something had drawn him here. After entering, he took one last peek up the silent hall before pressing the door closed. "What's that? No, Ezera, I don't see that we have a choice. Yes, I know we agreed to leave it be. But you heard Eladon. Our dear friend Grimmley needs our help."

Herid shuffled past a dozen long shelves of priceless Modeic artifacts as he continued to speak softly to the air. "Of course I know what the council is up to, you annoying creature. Stop berating me." Herid snickered. "I will outsmart them all, I will." He stopped and pressed his palm to his newly shaved forehead. "Now, where did we put it?" He looked around. "I think it was in this chamber. What's that? Down further? Well, if you know where the stone is, why don't you show me the way, you infuriating beast." He made shooing motions with his hands, then proceeded up a corridor separating two tall wooden racks of ancient metallic objects. Finally, he jerked to a halt, then moved to the shelf on the right. "Here?" Herid squatted. "Yes! I remember now."

He carefully picked up a green ceramic jar with spiraling leaves etched around its neck. Removing the lid, he tilted the jar up ... and out slid a small black stone into his waiting palm. Herid studied the flowing threads of blue light emanating from the stone. "It has been a long time, my friend," he whispered as he caressed its smooth surface. He slipped the stone into a small pocket of his new coat, returned the jar to the shelf, and crept out of the cellars.

Within the hour, Herid slunk through the dark fortress gates of Aldemeer unseen. Some part of him knew he did not need to lurk among the lamps' shadows. No one would challenge him dressed in his fetching new formal grandmaster clothing. But he would rather not take chances given the precious treasure he bore. Past the gates, he took a moment to straighten the finely stitched jacket. Then, turning south, he struck up a lighthearted conversation with his missing bond and let the wide dirt road to Darmascus take him on his merry way.

The Shamans' Temple

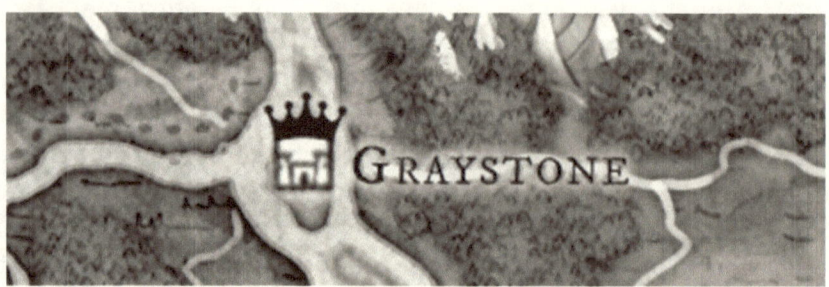

Conner held the tip of Skye's wing and tugged, stretching it wide across the dungeon chamber. "Will you please stop squirming?" he asked.

The dragon responded by tugging his wing free of Conner's grip. "I will when you explain to me what you are doing."

"I would have thought that was obvious, but I forgot—I'm conversing with a dragon!"

Skye puffed thin trails of sulfuric steam from his nostrils. "Well, as usual, you have an atrocious way of communicating. How would you like it if I tried pulling your arms off? Why don't you start by asking me nicely for what you want rather than trying to manipulate me into it?"

Down the long hall, Pauli and Kriston had apparently determined it was safer to remain at a distance while Conner worked out this problem with his bond. They would offer no support in this argument.

Conner backed away to get clear of the cloud of dragon steam, then folded his arms tight, giving Skye a seething look. Why did he always seem to end up on the losing side of every argument they had? He knew Skye's irritability was rubbing off on him. The fact his bond was correct didn't help. He wasn't just using Skye to protect the queen; he was using him to further his goal to see the Necromancer. He had not been forthright with Skye in what he was doing—or why. But he had good reason.

Conner would have preferred making Skye a part of the team. Bringing Skye in on their scheme to break into the Shamans' temple, however, would require spending precious time explaining human concepts the dragon was incapable of grasping. But that was not Conner's greatest concern. The instant Skye thought a different course was more suitable, the beast would abandon what they'd agreed to—and not think to inform Conner of his decision.

Grimmley continued to insist that Conner find a way to work with Skye as one. Maybe it was time to put the idea to a definitive test. And if that meant mopping up the mess of working with a headstrong, irritable dragon, then so be it. From this moment forward, Conner was going to make a concerted effort to get along with the beast. *Maybe I can begin by not thinking of him as a beast,* Conner grudgingly admitted to himself.

"Skye, I appreciate what you have done in helping us with our plan." Conner hesitated at his use of *plan*. It was not the word he would have preferred to describe the crazy scheme he and Kriston had concocted. In truth, he didn't have much confidence it would work, but he had simply run out of time. "This morning, I overheard several ordermen discussing plans to move Asheborne to a more secure site for powerful Anarchic prisoners. They'll be making the transfer at first light." Conner breathed deep to steady his nerves. "That leaves us this afternoon to finalize our preparations for the visit. And I am determined to talk to her no matter what."

Conner stepped closer and patted Skye's neck. "The details you have given us from scouting the temple have been incredibly valuable. But surely you can understand that measurements in wingspans and tail widths are of no real value if we can't convert them into something the three of us can use to construct a map of the compound."

Skye wriggled upward until the horns on his head bumped the ceiling, his glowing blue eyes mere slits. He stretched his wing out wide so Conner could get a decent measurement of its length. "Now that wasn't so hard, was it?"

Conner sensed his bond's appeasement, which helped considerably as he and his two human associates worked through what remained of Hemera's light finalizing the preparations for the break-in. But even that did not help Conner's waning confidence in their scheme. It was several hours after dark before the four left to put their plan into action.

The female Shaman shuffled to a stop, then compelled the body she'd been summoned into to turn and her eyes to scan the stone wall that extended into the dead of night. In the distance, near the edge of nearby streetlamps, shadows shifted like billowing night fog. But she discerned no imminent danger to her mission, so she lurched forward into the light emanating from lanterns hung above each side of the massive iron gate. "Seer Dilora Heldinger from the Charmwell region," she slurred to the two inattentive guards at the gate.

"You're a long way from home, Seer," the woman guard remarked, squinting at the apparition that had appeared like a phantom before them. With some work, she pushed away from the wall she had been propped against.

The second guard was less concerned. "Welcome back, Seer Heldinger. It has been a while since last you were here." The Shaman stepped forward, and he noted how the warm glow of the lantern flames reflected off her milky skin. "And you're not looking so well."

Calling forth memories, Dilora bobbed her head at the second guard. "Kearn, if I remember correctly. Yes, my master at Charmwell could not cure me of a sickness I acquired a fortnight ago." She approached with an uneven gait. "I am here in hopes one of the grandmasters can alleviate me of this illness."

The two guards shared a quick glance, then took a measured step back at the thought that a sickness could produce such manifestations. "I believe Grandmaster Markus is on the second level," Kearn offered. "I understand he is working late into the night preparing for the transfer of a prisoner in the morning. If anyone can assist you, I am sure it is he." The guard gestured vigorously at the seer to proceed inside.

Dilora grunted her thanks to the guards and stutter-stepped through the iron portal. She shuffled forward, directing the body to the center of the Shamans' temple grounds. The stiff limp she had developed over the past day caused the body to list to the right, so she was forced to pause occasionally and compensate. After considerable effort, she came to the base of the main temple structure, again calling up memories of Dilora's time here. One particular memory drew her thoughts, so she willed her gaze to the left, where the grounds were void of guards. *Good enough,* she thought with a jerk of the head. She ambled forward again, circumventing the large central structure, making her way toward a thick metal door riveted to the side of a small building.

Not far away from the Shamans' temple entrance, three young lads pressed their backs against the only section of the outer wall that offered sufficient shadow from the street lanterns beyond.

"I still think we should have brought a grappling hook," Pauli whispered as he patted the stone wall, his eyes focused on the top far above.

"We've been over that, Pauli," Kriston grumbled back. "Throwing a metal hook against this hard stone would attract attention. We stick to the plan as we discussed."

Conner, sandwiched between his two companions, squinted toward the lantern lights in the distance, where a robed figure limped toward the temple entrance. Only after the cloaked form disappeared through the iron gate did he follow Pauli's upward gaze. He sensed his bond soaring far overhead, lost among the blanket of brilliant stars. Skye had refused to stay behind in the dungeon, so Conner had assigned him sentry duty. He would send Conner an emotional warning if he noticed any changes in the patterns of activity within the temple grounds. The dragon's worry was feeding Conner's own wariness at what they were about to do, but they had come this far; he was not about to turn back now.

"Then let's see if all our planning paid off," Pauli said. Pressing his chest to the wall, his feet spread slightly, he placed his hands behind his back, palms up. Pauli winked at Conner. "I hope you can keep your balance better than that night you tried to sneak a look at Pattria."

Conner frowned at Pauli for dredging up such an unpleasant memory. The night Conner's parents had told him of his betrothal to Pattria, Conner had asked Pauli to help him steal a look at his future wife through a window. While standing on Pauli's shoulders, Conner had fallen and broken his wrist.

Conner stepped on Pauli's palms and scampered up his friend's back. His heart raced, but he was not sure whether it was from fear of getting caught or the thrill of finally having an opportunity—no matter how slim— to learn how he might break free from the mental boulder he was being crushed beneath.

Signaling he was ready, Kriston began his ascent, a coiled rope draped across his shoulder. Just as the ex-thief was about to crawl onto Conner's shoulders, he stopped. "This brings back fond memories," he whispered in Conner's ear.

"Fond?" Conner nearly gasped. He wanted to say more, but chose to wait for a time when Kriston was not dangling off his back. "Get up there!" he commanded.

"Okay. But you can't tell me you don't miss those nights thieving in Cravenrock."

With Kriston on his shoulders, Conner gripped the boy's ankles and hoisted them over his head. This was where their plan relied on a bit of luck. He waited for Kriston to signal that he had reached the wall's lip.

Instead, Kriston whispered down, "I'm still not there."

The tower of boys wobbled like a thin stalk of wheat in a brisk wind.

Conner peered down. "Okay, Pauli, time to show us that Warrior you've got pent up inside."

Pauli placed his palms beneath Conner's boots and, straightening his arms, pushed Conner farther up the wall. Conner fought to keep his own arms straight, his shoulders shaking as he pushed Kriston higher. He was relieved when his page vanished over the wall.

By the time Conner dropped from Pauli's shoulders, Kriston had tossed down one end of his rope. With Pauli gripping the dangling line, Kriston descended into the temple grounds. A few moments later, Pauli felt a tug, signaling the other end had been secured around a nearby tree.

Pauli grabbed the rope and climbed.

Conner pressed his palms to Pauli's underside and tried to offer whatever assistance he could muster. "I do believe you've put on a stone since I left home," he grunted.

Moving sluggishly, Pauli snorted and whispered down, "That's 'cause I'm not spending half my energy keeping you out of trouble."

When Pauli was on top, Conner joined him. Conner looped the rope around his arm several times, but hesitated before giving the signal that he was ready for Pauli to start his descent into the grounds. "Thanks, Pauli."

In the ambient glow of the streetlamps below, Conner caught Pauli's questioning look.

"You're risking a lot for me. I don't know what I would do—"

"You're not going to get all sappy on me, are you?" Pauli interrupted.

Conner's jaw went slack.

Pauli punched Conner in the gut. "Because I'm getting ready to climb off the top of this wall with only you keeping me from dropping like a rock."

Conner gripped the rope tight and leaned back to counter his best friend's weight.

Pauli threw Conner a mischievous grin, the type he reserved for when the two were mere moments away from trouble. "Let's go have a chat with your Necromancer."

Once Pauli was safely in the yard, Conner dropped his end of the rope to Kriston below. Dangling from the lip, Conner pushed out lightly and dropped. Pauli caught him as easily as he would a sack of grain.

Before Conner climbed out of his arms, Pauli gave him a quick wink. "Here I am, coming to your rescue again."

Conner ignored Pauli and jumped from his grip, tossed the rope behind a bush, and cleared away their footprints while Kriston scanned the dark area.

Pauli exhaled long and slow, his back sliding down the stone wall. "A Necromancer," he whispered, staring at nothing specific.

Conner leaned in. "What?"

Pauli stared back. "We're about to talk to a Necromancer."

Kriston reached over and rapped his knuckles on Pauli's thick skull. "That's what we've been talking about for nearly two days, Pauli. What did you think we were doing?"

Pauli blinked up at Kriston. "I know. But until this moment I thought this was all another one of those elaborate gags you two like to play on me. All your stories about Assassins and Barbarians were difficult enough to swallow. And I wouldn't have believed dragons existed if I hadn't seen Conner's with my own eyes. But people who can animate the dead ..." Pauli shook his head. "I thought it was all a big joke."

Conner shared a worried glance with Kriston, then squatted next to his friend. "Pauli, we need you here right now. You can chew on that thought once we're back on the other side of this wall."

It took a moment, but Pauli's eyes narrowed and his lips thinned with a determination that would make anyone in his path move out of his way. "You're right. Let's do this."

"Seer Heldinger?" The sentry glanced up the stairwell behind Dilora, taking a guarded stance when he realized the Shaman had come down the cellar entrance alone. "You aren't supposed to be down here. You need to leave."

"Is that you, Sidera?" Dilora stepped forward from the dark stairs, eagerly nodding beneath her hood. "Yes, I thought that was you. I remember you from when I was here as an apprentice. On occasion, you and I would have lunch on the veranda overlooking the gardens to the south." She was encouraged as the guard relaxed. Dilora drew forth memories of how the guard had seemed attracted to her, so she took a more alluring stance before him. But her body must have appeared as twisted and gnarled as it felt. The sentry's expression shifted from affable to wary. Maybe talking would have a more desired effect. "I am to be part of the entourage that will be escorting the Necromancer to the prison in Hemera's first light. Grandmaster Markus has sent me to check on the prisoner and to make sure everything is sorted for the transfer." She was making a number of guesses regarding Asheborne's transfer, but she needed the sentry to believe she was part of their entourage. Given how secretive Shamans were, it was a near certainty that the guard knew little more than to stand guard at this spot until morning.

Sidera kept his uneasy stance. "But I have been instructed not to allow anyone near the Necromancer."

Dilora sighed. "Then it seems we are at impasse. It would be truly unfortunate if something were to happen to the prisoner under your watch, especially so close to her transfer."

Sidera shuddered at Dilora's suggestion.

Feigning a sudden idea, Dilora wiggled a finger at the low ceiling. "Why don't you come with me? You can help me check the condition of the cell and make sure everything is in proper order for the transfer. Two would be much safer than one."

The guard hesitated, then relaxed. "Well, she is bound and gagged, so there is little she can do to put up a fight. I guess there's no harm in checking her condition one more time before dawn."

"That is good news." Dilora shifted closer. "I am certain Grandmaster Markus will be proud of your labors in this matter."

"Let's get this over with. I, for one, will be of a much better mind when this nasty creature is far gone from here." He waved up the dark hall for the Shaman to lead the way.

"I could not agree more, friend." When she stepped past the guard, Dilora sensed her opportunity and spun to strike with the speed of a coiled snake. She slammed her palm over the guard's mouth while her other hand moved to the back of his head. The Shaman held the guard in a vise-like grip, her forefinger and thumb closing about his nostrils.

But the guard had been well-trained for his job. As Dilora's body moved closer to maintain her leverage, he unsheathed a long knife he had at the ready. With a satisfying grunt, he plunged the sharp point deep into the Shaman's chest.

Dilora felt no pain, and responded by pressing down harder. The guard's narrow eyes widened when she did not fall away. She chuckled at his comical expression of fear.

The guard yanked the knife out and drove it in again, this time piercing the Shaman's heart.

Still, she held tight.

Realizing his blade had no effect, he began to struggle against her grip. He tried to scream, but it came out as a muffled howl. His greater size and muscular build were ineffective against her inhuman strength. He fell back against the wall, attempting to find some kind of leverage.

The guard's flailing was beginning to annoy Dilora. It was hard to find enjoyment in his death knowing someone might overhear the clamor of armor on stone. She could not risk exposing herself, not this close. She snarled and pressed her palms together, slowly rotating the guard's skull.

The guard began slapping his open palm against anything he could make contact with. His fingers clawed down her hand, peeling away ashy skin to reveal sinew, cartilage, and bone.

Finally, Dilora heard the satisfying pop of bones along the sentry's jaw, then at the base of his skull. The sentry's body quivered one last time.

The Shaman stepped back to admire her handiwork, then dragged the body down a dark side chamber. Stepping back into the hall, she pushed the skin of her hand back into place.

The struggle with the guard had taken too much energy. Dilora's corpse was failing the spirit that had been summoned into it. Rigor mortis made it hard to move, though the summoner's strength spells would hold long enough to finish the work. She needed to hurry. Still, it was hard not to revel in such delicious opportunities. With a gratifying twitch along the side of her clawed face, she shuffled down the hall.

At the far end of the hall, she came to a small cell with a facing made of thick metal. Inside sat a woman in black Necromantic robes, gagged, her wrists shackled to the floor by a long chain glowing with elementals.

Dilora sneered at the black-robed woman who peered questioningly up at her. "Meera Asheborne. My master, Breanen Sagamore, sends her fondest regards," she rasped at the muzzled and bound figure in the cell. "And her deepest regrets."

Meera's eyes narrowed at the clear meaning of Breanen's message.

Dilora wrapped her fingers tight around the cell door's bars and pulled. The door lock groaned and popped as the thick metal buckled under the inhuman strain of muscle and cartilage. At last, the latch gave way, clanging to the floor. The door swung wide. Dilora could not resist a chuckle as she stepped into the cell.

"You sure that's the building we're looking for?" Pauli squinted at the small structure ahead of them, its outline lit up by Erebus floating high in the east. Gaia's moon had been low while the three clambered over the temple's wall. But now, it filled the temple grounds with soft light. "It looks more like my ma's kitchen pantry than a prison."

Kriston rolled his eyes. "The most treasured items are found in the smallest places, Pauli."

Pauli puffed up his face in confusion.

Conner placed a hand on Kriston's shoulder to soothe his impatient page. The lad was still annoyed that Conner had not discerned where the Necromancer was being kept. At least they weren't at the end of some blind alley.

Conner gestured at the building. "You see that metal door on the side, Pauli? Can you think of any reason why those living at a guarded temple would need such a barrier just to stop people from stealing food? And given the building's size, it's not much of a stretch that room leads to an underground cellar—a cellar capable of holding very valuable items."

Pauli blinked.

"Like *prisoners*," Kriston filled in. Not waiting around to see if Pauli understood, the boy sprinted across a narrow alley toward the building.

On Kriston's signal, Conner skirted the shadowed side of a wall with Pauli on his heels while Kriston worked on the metal door's lock. Finally, Pauli grinned with delight and prodded Conner with an elbow. "Oh, you think she's in here?"

A few minutes later, Kriston pulled up short and raised his palm back toward Conner.

"What is it now?" Conner whispered. The three crouched at the bottom of a stairwell that opened into a long hall.

"It's a little too quiet for my liking," Kriston replied. "I would have expected at least one guard down here."

"Sounds more like a blessing to me," Pauli offered near Conner's ear. "Or maybe this isn't the right place after all."

But Conner's time in the Cravenrock Thieves Guild had taught him to rely on Kriston's uncanny senses in such matters. If Kriston's intuition sensed danger, they should be concerned.

With few choices available, Kriston pressed on, but stopped when he came to what appeared to be a chamber to one side. It was too dark to tell more. "Should we investigate?" he whispered to Conner behind him.

"I suggest we investigate any lit sections first. I can't imagine they'd put a prisoner somewhere *that* dark."

Kriston had not taken more than three steps when he lifted his hand.

"What now?" Conner asked.

"I thought I heard something—like metal striking the floor."

Conner cranked his ear forward, leaning over Kriston's crouched body. A moment later, he caught the sound of a muffled struggle ahead. Quick as a wink, Kriston dashed on up the hall. Conner and Pauli had no option but to follow at a run. At the end of the hall on their left was a small cell. In the meager torchlight, a gray-cloaked Shaman stood with her hands around Meera Asheborne's neck, choking the life from her. Conner was stunned, trying to make sense out of what he beheld. Before he reacted, Pauli let out a bellow like when they'd played warrior as children. A great force slammed into Conner's back, sending him spinning into the cell door. By the time he staggered back to his feet, Pauli was in the cell, behind the Shaman, his arms wrapped tight around her chest.

Pauli roared as he squeezed, lifting the scrawny Shaman into the air and breaking her hold on Meera.

The Necromancer fell back onto her bench, coughing and gasping for breath.

Conner found his legs and he ran to stand in front of Meera Asheborne. She was gagged, and her wrists were bound and chained to a ring bolted to the stone floor. A black otter-looking animal appeared over her shoulder.

"I've got the Shaman, Conner," Pauli proclaimed triumphantly.

"Pauli—" Kriston started.

"Can't you see I'm a bit busy?" Pauli began dragging the Shaman away from Meera.

"Pauli, I don't think you understand. That—"

"I've got her! I'll hold her back while you and Conner—"

Before Pauli finished, the Shaman raised her arms, forcing Pauli's locked fingers apart. Pauli's eyes bulged as he gripped harder. "What the ..." Muscles constricting beneath his shirt, he groaned with the sudden exertion he needed to keep his arms locked around the Shaman.

The Shaman was unconcerned by Pauli's efforts. She snapped her arms up high, breaking Pauli's grip, then drove her elbow back, connecting with Pauli's temple with a resounding crack.

Pauli tumbled backward, slamming into the iron bars at the side of the cell.

The Shaman never glanced back. She stepped forward again, sweeping Conner to the side with her arm and grabbing Meera by the front of her robes.

"I'll help Pauli keep that thing busy," Kriston shouted at Conner. "*You* need to figure out how to get the prisoner out of here!" While the Shaman throttled Meera, Kriston scampered up the Shaman's back. Twisting, he straddled her shoulders, then yanked her hood down over her eyes.

The Shaman released Meera, her arms flailing in an attempt to snatch the boy riding on her shoulders.

Pauli rubbed at his temple, trying to stand. "What are you doing?"

"I was trying to tell you—this thing isn't human!" Kriston shouted, holding the hood down over the Shaman's face as she spun. He waited until the Shaman made another revolution before adding with a grin, "Undead need sight. Take that away and they get all discombobulated."

"Undead? You mean a zombie?" Pauli asked.

Conner recalled an incantation Grimmley had tried to teach him once, one that sent ghosts back to the Mental plane. Making several gestures with his hands, Conner incanted, "*Ourera psychi entharprosopo.*" But just as it had at Grimmley's gazebo, the incantation failed.

"Will you stop playing around?" Kriston shouted at Conner as the Shaman spun around the cell like a spinning top, crashing into the bars. "There is only one person in this room capable of sending this atrocity back." He turned to Pauli. "Grab her legs and let's see if we can topple her!"

Meera stared up at him, shackled and gagged. She had an inquisitive look in her eyes, as if she was wondering what he planned to do. Well, he was wondering too! Conner removed the gag from her mouth.

Still, Meera goggled at him with that same questioning expression.

"Get rid of it!" Conner waved his arm at the apparition.

"To cast an incantation, I need these shackles off. They are preventing me from accessing elementals." She held her wrists up, her expression one of urgency.

Conner faltered as something dreadful had occurred to him. If Meera was going to survive this night, he might have to break her free. He had come here to talk to her, not help her escape. He heard Kriston cry out. Looking over his shoulder, he watched the undead toss the boy across the cell like a rag doll.

Pauli bellowed in rage. Jamming his thick shoulder into the Shaman's midsection, he lifted her and spun her around.

"Your friends are brave, but they cannot stop this creature. They'll only get themselves killed."

Conner placed his palms against the metal rings around Meera's wrists and closed his eyes, trying to shut out the shouts and groans coming from behind as Kriston leaped back into the fight. Immediately, Conner sensed the elementals. The weave was only slightly more complicated than the one Meera had used on him in Dragongarde's antechamber. Drawing on Air and Fire, he felt along their threads and pushed them together. The threads evanesced. And beneath those was another weave—one of Water and Earth. He called Water and Earth to him, but before he could destroy the weave, the undead struck him from behind. He reeled and stumbled forward as intense pain flashed like lightning down his spine. Pauli and Kriston lay in a motionless heap in the middle of the cell, a mass of arms and legs.

The undead stepped into view, grabbing Meera around the neck with one hand while she snatched Conner's neck with the other. The creature's clutch was incredible as Conner fought to break free. His feet lifted from the stone floor. The undead's hold intensified as the blood rushing in his ears drowned out the choking gurgles coming from Meera next to him.

Conner forced himself to concentrate, ignoring the fear screaming at him, the throbbing down his back, the rattle of Meera's chains pulled taut by the Shaman's inhuman grip, the groans from Pauli and Kriston. He closed his eyes, and the world receded. Gently, he called on Water and Earth again. Releasing his grip on the undead's arm, he reached out and touched Meera's shackles.

The metal rings popped free, Meera's body snapped up, and the Shaman staggered forward.

The undead flung Conner to the side and grabbed Meera with both hands. "You will not escape," the Shaman sneered.

Meera pressed her back to the wall and kicked out, shoving the Shaman away. Flicking her hands forward, Meera croaked, *"Ourera energi kinoprosopo."* A blinding flash blasted the undead across the cell.

Conner too was thrown back. He sensed Skye's intense emotional signal high above. People were coming! He watched in awe as Meera drew deep on Fire and Earth. *Conner, you fool. You let her free. Now you're going to die.*

The undead Shaman crawled to her feet. "You know Breanen will not stop as long as you remain a prisoner of the Harmonics. She will not allow you to divulge Necromantic secrets."

Meera thrust her hand out. *"Ourera psychi apostelpsychi."* The creature slumped forward, never to rise again.

Conner heard the sounds of shouting and boots running down the long, dark hall. He fell back against the cell door, the cool metal bars offering stability that his quivering legs no longer provided.

Meera gazed up at Conner. Her features softened, her black, furry bond trembling at her neck. From the flickering light, Conner caught the despair in her eyes. He understood what the undead had meant—that she would not be the last undead sent to kill Meera Asheborne.

Slowly, Meera slid down on her bench, silently rubbing the raw sores on her wrists, her eyes on the broken shackles splayed on the stone floor.

Grimmley's Reprimand

Grimmley paced across the small chamber in front of the three boys, his arms taut behind his back. The first rays of morning were breaking over the temple walls. Occasionally, he would stop and mumble to himself, flailing his arms, then after falling silent, he'd resume his pacing. Smoke from his pipe swirled about him. It did not take a town crier for Conner to realize his preceptor was livid. The old man's cheeks had bloomed into a shade of beet red Conner had not believed possible on a human face.

Kriston stifled back a yawn while Pauli rubbed at the knot on the side of his head. Between the stress of breaking in to the temple and fighting an undead, all three were well past exhaustion.

Grimmley finally rounded on the boys and released his full fury. "Do you three have any clue what you have done? You have broken half of the High Laws ever written, completely annihilated the Orderman's Code, and caused a realm-wide incident that is sure to be an embarrassment to the queen! All in a single night!" He paused, disappointed in their reaction, then pointed at the door. "There are two Shaman Dons down this hall right now wanting ... no, *demanding* to know why the queen's Champion was found uninvited deep within their temple. So, what am I supposed to tell them? Hmm? That the young man they reluctantly agreed to allow me to tutor took it upon himself to break into their edifice because he wanted to have a chat with a powerful Anarchic prisoner?"

"We did stop the prisoner from being murdered," Conner offered.

"Oh, I suggest you do not attempt to defend your actions, young man! There is no way to sugarcoat this fiasco. The Dons will never believe your intention was to protect her. It is more likely they will deny me the right to continue your training. What will you do then?"

Conner bit his tongue. Grimmley's training had been ineffective at helping him rediscover his powers. Losing the Shaman as a preceptor would give him more time to work it out on his own. He shrugged while the other two sat in indifferent silence.

The boys' nonresponse only inflamed Grimmley more. "Him!" He jabbed a gnarled, ink-smudged finger at Kriston. "Him, I would expect this from!"

Kriston's jaw fell open and his eyes widened.

Pauli snickered at finally having proof there was no hope of rehabilitating Bandit's thieving ways.

"And you!" Grimmley's finger shifted to Pauli, choking off the lad's raspy chuckle. "I have a good mind to take this whole affair to the Warriors Order. If they discover you were involved in this insult, you'll be lucky to get a job guarding a doghouse!"

Pauli pulled back with a start, tears pooling in his eyes.

Crying? Pauli is crying! Conner had never seen Pauli cry. "That's enough!" He slapped his thigh and stood. "I will not sit here while you threaten my friends, Grimmley."

Pauli and Kriston shifted their bulging eyes to Conner. No doubt they had never imagined anyone would actually *shout* at an orderman ... and a grandmaster at that!

Grimmley was just as surprised. He rocked back on his heels, looking like Conner had just popped into the room.

Conner stepped closer. "*I* was the one who talked them into this. They came along because *they* are my friends, and *they* are willing to do whatever it takes to help me." Grimmley couldn't have missed Conner's reference to his own refusal to assist in the matter. "I am the only one to blame for what happened. So, if you feel the need to lay blame on someone, then point that finger toward me!"

Grimmley only stared back, unblinking.

Conner continued, "Now that we have that out of the way, let's get down to what is *really* going to happen next—or should I say, *not* happen. First of all, the Shaman Dons are not going to say anything to anyone outside this temple about what transpired last night, so you can stop with your threats."

Grimmley tensed. "And what makes you think that?"

"Because exposing us as uninvited guests in the temple would force the Dons to reveal the attempt on Asheborne's life—one, I might add, that would have succeeded if it hadn't been for us." Conner knew he had struck a chord. "Oh, wouldn't that be embarrassing, the Dons having to tell the queen of Griffinrock they allowed a prisoner in their charge to be murdered—by an undead Shaman?"

Grimmley rocked side to side, mumbling under his breath.

"Second, the Dons are not going to demand you stop training me. The queen knows they approved it, and she would ask too many questions if you cut me off—questions they would rather not be forced to answer."

Grimmley removed the stem of his pipe from his lips and grunted. "You are too smart for your own good, boy."

"Yes. Compliments of observing how the orders *really* work. So, isn't this a fine mess of tangled webbing we all weave?"

"You two"—Grimmley eyed Conner's compatriots and pointed to the iron door—"get out. And no more foolery from either of you. We will *not* have this conversation again. Is that clear?"

Pauli and Kriston nodded vigorously, slid from their chairs, and vanished through the door.

Grimmley pursed his lips at Conner, tilting his head back to get a clear view through his spectacles. "It seems it is time we had a serious chat." His eyebrows sank as he leaned in, and he lowered his voice to a whisper. "But even thick walls can have ears. I suggest we suspend these discussions until we're back home."

Conner nodded, his lips pressed tight. He wanted to tell Grimmley that he and Layna were not helping him. He had hoped that being thrust into a life-or-death situation would have been the inspiration he needed to access his powers. It had worked on the Champion's tourney field when he was forced to face Marcantos. But the incantation he'd tried had failed last night ... completely. Even more importantly, he wanted to tell Grimmley he knew the two of them were withholding information. They had way too many conversations when he was not around, and private glances when he was. It was past time to air their dirty laundry. At least there was one subject he could put to rest right away. "I want to talk with her."

Grimmley rolled his eyes and threw up his arms in defeat. "Let's assume for a moment I go along with this idea. Just how do you plan to arrange that? Any opportunity you might have had convincing the Dons to give you access to Meera Asheborne evaporated with last night's debacle. If you're expecting to break through that wall—"

"I know how to deal with the Dons."

"Deal with them? You are talking about the most stubborn, infuriating ordermen across all the realms, Conner. No one has ever *dealt* with the Shaman Dons—and I know, because I taught most of them."

"Then it's about time someone did. I don't know why this didn't occur to me earlier." Conner rubbed his throbbing shoulder, then grimaced as he rotated it. "It would have saved us all a lot of pain and frustration." Grimmley opened his mouth, but before he could usher forth his first syllable, Conner cut him off. "You might as well save your energy if you're planning on talking me out of this." Stepping to the door, he waved his preceptor to follow. "We had better go see them before I need to return to the castle."

"We're going to do what?" Gerrett, one of the Dons, rocked forward in his chair. He cocked his head to the side as if he had not heard Conner correctly.

"You're going to hand the Necromancer over to me," Conner stated for the second time.

Gerrett turned his stunned gaze to Tara, the other Don in the room, then to Grimmley, who stood next to Conner with an unsettled expression. "Are you going to rein in your pupil, Grimmley, or is your infamous stubbornness part of the curriculum now?"

Grimmley shrugged. "Don't look at me. This is all his doing."

"And why would we hand her over, Conner?" Tara asked, her annoyance brewing.

"Am I not recognized as a member of the Order of the Dragonbonded, one of the Harmonic orders?" Conner asked.

Tara pruned up her aged face at the question. "Of course. All that was settled the morning of the Tournament of Champions."

"And the Necromancer attacked me, did she not?"

"Yes, but what—"

"And she was captured at Dragongarde, which is recognized as my order's holding, is it not?"

The Dons appeared even more confused, shrugged, then nodded.

"Let me refer you to section fifteen, article four of the Orderman's Code, which states, 'Whensoever a recognized enemy of the realms has inflicted a grievance, be the infliction physical, emotional, or spiritual, upon members of an order at one of that order's own estates, that order shall have full rights and privileges of custody over that enemy assailant.' According to your own laws, the Necromancer is *my* prisoner."

Tara erupted out of her chair. "That is ridiculous. You have no way of holding a grandmaster Necromancer. If—no, *when* she escapes, she would be an endangerment to the entire realm. We cannot take that chance. We will not turn her over."

Conner held her intense stare. "When I am finished with her, she will no longer be a trouble to the realm."

Grimmley snatched his pipe from his mouth before it fell to the floor. "Conner, if you're suggesting—"

"Meera Asheborne orchestrated our capture," Conner interrupted. "Her actions led me to believe she had poisoned Skye. That was not just a frightening experience. It was ... humiliating. I will make sure she never has an opportunity like that again. Besides, my bond has a particular dislike for the woman. It is time the two ... work out their differences."

Grimmley's expression grew darker with each word from Conner. "If I understand what you are suggesting, that is not the Harmonic way. You can't just—"

"No, Grimmley," Conner stated sternly. "As I said, Meera Asheborne is my responsibility. Skye and I will take care of her."

"I won't allow it," Grimmley stiffened and shook his bearded head firmly. "We are not Anarchists, Conner. Every life is precious. If you do not understand that by now, then ... well, I have failed as your preceptor."

"Grimmley, I appreciate the virtues you espouse." Conner's gaze shifted out the narrow window. "Layna once told me that sometimes I must set aside my lofty ideals and do what is necessary if a fairer world is to flourish one day. Today is one of those days."

Grimmley puffed out his lips. "I know Layna better than anyone, and I am certain she did not mean that the way you interpreted it."

"It doesn't matter."

"Well, I will not be a party to this. Clearly, you have already decided what to do, no matter how vehemently I disagree ... or how wrong it is." Grimmley snatched up his staff and shuffled to the door. He waited only long enough for Barthox to flutter through the portal before slamming the door behind him.

Conner hated driving a wedge between himself and Grimmley, but he saw no other way.

Gerrett spoke up. "Young man, I cannot go against the Orderman's Code. However, please ... I implore you to reconsider this action. Maybe we can come up with some kind of mutual arrangement, one that does not threaten this realm. How about we agree to keep the Necromancer here at this temple? You could come visit her when you wish."

Conner shook his head.

"This Necromancer is very powerful!" Tara erupted again. "You do not have the facilities to contain her!"

Conner did not reply.

Gerrett rubbed his palms over his face, then raised them. "Since your preceptor was unsuccessful in convincing you of the error in your ways, I somehow doubt council members of his order will have any better luck. However, young man, be advised. The Shamans Order will assume *no* responsibility for any ramifications of your action. Once we have remanded the prisoner into your care, she is fully and solely your responsibility. Is that understood?"

Conner took a deep breath. "I understand."

Gerrett rose next to Tara, who nodded reluctantly at him. "Very well, then. We cannot defy the Orderman's Code. We have no recourse but to release the Necromancer into your custody. We will need the morning to prepare the proper papers for our records and ready the prisoner for transfer. Return to the temple gates early this afternoon, and we shall yield her to your custody." The Dons stormed out.

Conner hated what he was doing, what he felt compelled to do. He was taking a big chance. Worse, he saw the disappointment reflected in his preceptor's eyes for disobeying him. But he had played it safe too long, and that strategy had produced no fruit. He swallowed hard, pushing the uneasiness down. Grimmley may not have taught him how to cast incantations, but he had schooled him well in the sordid art of telling half-truths. And they were stacking up, like bricks in a wall he was building between them. He would have a candid conversation with his two preceptors, to clear the air of the chaff borne from all their threshing. Just as soon as this episode with the Necromancer was behind him.

A Shocking Revelation

Nartesis closed the Necromancers' Book of Census with a resounding thump and pushed the massive volume across the table.

Ousel stood at Nartesis's bedchamber door wringing his hands, his hedgehog bond's head hanging out of his chest pocket.

Nartesis waved at the man. "You may take the book back now." He fought back his annoyance at the man's panic-stricken appearance before turning his attention to the brown parchment on the table.

With a gratified sigh, the minister snatched up the thick volume and swept through the chamber door, the tome cradled to his bosom.

Nartesis drummed his bone fingers on the chair's arms as he skimmed the list of names he had scrawled down the brown parchment, his new minion forgotten.

Briean
BreeAnna
Bria
Brianne
BryAnn
BrieAnna

The list went on. Twenty-two given names in all, ending with the name he had expected to find—Breanen Sagamore, the sovereign prince's wife. But it was not just the names' resemblance that made him pause. It was the timing of each name's appearance in the Book of Census. Each woman, most rising to the level of grandmaster, had entered the Necromancers Order as a teen between five and ten years after the death of the previous incarnation on the list. The pattern was too predictable to be a coincidence.

So why has no one paid notice to this before me? Nartesis pondered as he stroked the small lump in his breast pocket. He shook his head, then pushed the parchment away with a frustrated sigh. "Don't be a fool, Nartesis. Only someone looking for the pattern would see it." Which was, in itself, ingenious. Too much time passed between each successive name for anyone to recognize the lineage for what it was.

Old memories flared to life, dancing visions of the years following his escape from Thanatos's destruction to a time when he had been gripped by an obsession to own all the powerful Fettering Stones. He'd needed an able-bodied assistant, a thief of sorts, to achieve his objective, and BrieAnn had been a thief like no other. Of course, BrieAnn had not been her real name. Spirits from the Psychic planes had no name—at least not names they shared. This spirit had adopted the name BrieAnn from one of the first vessels he had summoned the spirit into. A fiery young Bremenn priestess, as he recalled, who had met a most untimely demise—a death most deserving for the atrocities the woman had committed against him and his fledgling order. And the perfect vessel for the work Nartesis had needed done.

Nartesis rose and let his fingers glide down the parchment, reading each name again in the flickering light of his fireplace, coming to rest on the last. "My dear BrieAnn," he mumbled as he tapped the parchment. "What have you been up to all these centuries?"

Naturally, that was not the most critical question. Nartesis stretched, groaning at the snapping of wizened muscles as they expanded. He had devised the method of using Fettering Stones to summon spirits to the Physical plane and give them life, a technique he had never shared with anyone. So then who else had gained the knowledge to summon this being that called itself BrieAnn? From the pathetic examples of undead he had observed around Thanatos, it appeared no one had the keen skills necessary for such a necromantic feat. The notion that there might be powerful Necromancers hiding in the dark gave him chills ... and a sense of excitement.

BrieAnn had been brought back ... what? Twenty-two times at least, over five centuries. So, who had passed this knowledge down through the centuries? And how had it been kept secret? What was the purpose of bringing this one spirit back over and over again? And had BrieAnn repeatedly returned to the Necromancers Order of her own volition, or had she been commanded to do so?

And, of course, there was the question of this rare Fettering Stone. Shazarack slipped the amulet from the pouch at his waist—the one he had removed from around Breanen Sagamore's neck—and held it to the light. The brilliant bands of blue swirled and sparked from the onyx stone, casting dancing shadows of his meager, hunched frame along the walls. Nartesis had gathered and used every stone not locked away deep in the dark vaults of Aldemeer, under the protection of Bremenn priests ... or, as he had learned from Ousel, protected now by the Paladins Order. Where had *this* stone come from?

And finally, if the spirit he had come to know as BrieAnn had been summoned to the Physical plane as he suspected, what was the chance others were summoned as well? Were other spirits from her plane walking the firm terra of Gaia, living and breathing as if they had been born into Gaia?

He shoved the amulet back into his pouch. He had no doubt his BrieAnn had spent much of the past five hundred years right here in Thanatos.

Nartesis contemplated taking this information to Galan, the sovereign prince of the Necromancers. Perhaps this would help smooth out the tension growing between them. But Lord Galan stewed over Breanen Sagamore's death. It would be a while before the man was amiable to being swayed to believe any story other than that Nartesis had murdered his wife. Besides, how does one go about telling another that the woman he'd loved his entire life had been—well, not really alive? Living, yes. But something else. Nartesis chuckled at the thought. But no. Sharing such knowledge would only cause more havoc.

Nartesis shuffled to the fireplace, the parchment with the list of names rolled tight in his fist, and tossed the paper onto the fire. His thoughts flickered like the flames greedily eating the parchment as he arranged the steps ahead. A smile that looked more like a wince crossed his lips. *Nothing like a good mystery to occupy my interest!*

Perhaps Lord Galan would even serve him better as angry adversary than as comrade-in-arms.

A Secret Meeting

Grimmley used his staff to balance his old bones as he inched down the narrow stone steps. The cellar air smelled musty and felt cold and moist on his skin. But he was on a mission—a mission vital, he was certain, to the survival of his young apprentice, to his great order, to Griffinrock's new queen, maybe even to the Harmonic Realms themselves. He had called in a number of debts owed him over many years just to get this meeting. He hoped that this conversation would lift at least a corner of the veil shrouding what he needed to understand. He slowed as he reached the end of the hall. Turning left, he stepped into the dim light. Before him was a thin woman in black on a stool, chained and gagged.

Grimmley gestured to the grandmaster Mystic standing guard before the cobbled prisoner. With a grim tip of her head, the Mystic whispered, *"Aethra energi afairosyndeta,"* then slipped the glowing gag from the prisoner's mouth. The Mystic exited the cell, then disappeared up the dark hall without a word.

Grimmley eased forward and settled on a stool he set before Meera Asheborne, watching as she worked the stiffness from her jaw.

At last, she spoke. "I never imagined I would one day be sitting with the great Grimmley Rollingsworth."

"You know of me?" Grimmley asked with a hint of surprise.

"I could rightfully argue that every living Necromancer knows of you—by name if not by deed."

Grimmley's bushy brows furrowed. "How so?"

"The only grandmaster Shaman to ever turn down a seat on the Shamans Council?" Her upturned lips betrayed a smugness as his eyes narrowed. "Our network of spies is as adept as yours are in our lands."

Grimmley grunted at her claim. *Maybe more*, he thought. "Which is a good lead-in to the conversation I was hoping we could have—"

Meera cut him short. "If you are hoping to learn more about the mission I was on, you will be disappointed. Surely, you aren't expecting my tongue to loosen from being enamored by your presence." Her gaze shifted to the door. "Nor will being distant cousins through our old order get you anywhere."

Grimmley pressed his lips tight. It was the response he'd expected. But, given what the Ranger Annabelle Loris had shared about the Anarchic band's actions at Dragongarde, it had not been hard to discern the band's purpose—to ensnare Conner and his dragon bond and ensure that the two stayed clear of Graystone and the Tournament of Champions while Marcantos and his Anarchic preceptor infiltrated Griffinrock Realm's royalty.

Grimmley removed a pipe from his robes, bit down on the stem, and lit the tobac with a match. "And what if I were to say that I really don't care about your mission?" The Shaman waited as his words settled upon her, until the creases of surprise around her eyes softened. He had to tread carefully if he hoped to eke out any useful—and reliable—information. After her mouth closed, he pressed on. "I understand you are as bound to your order's laws as I am to mine. However, I had hoped as ... distant cousins in the arts, we could find some common ground for an open conversation—one built on mutual respect in our shared trade."

Meera grunted, then leaned back against the stone cellar wall, her eyes closed. A black mink crawled out from behind and snuggled in around her neck. "I have heard of your insatiable thirst for knowledge. But I am far beyond being interested in quenching your desires, Rollingsworth. My fate is sealed. My preceptor was the one who sent the undead assassin. I know too many secrets, and she will not stop until my life is forfeited." She paused, relenting to the inevitability of her bleak future. "The only satisfaction left to me is that more Harmonics will perish at the hands of my assassin."

Grimmley had reached the same conclusion. Now, to exploit that weakness. "In a way, your undead assassin has changed your fate."

"How so?"

Grimmley gestured grandly at the dank cell about them. "This was never intended to be a permanent prison for someone of your abilities, Grandmaster Asheborne. You were mere hours from being transported to a more secure location, one quite suitable for constraining someone with your means."

Meera dropped her back against the wall. "You could drop me in a hole a hundred paces deep and it would not help. My mentor will not stop sending assassins until I am dead."

"And what if there was a different way through this? One that does not end with you dead?"

Meera glared back, but did not move. "I'm listening."

"According to our laws, the rights to you as a prisoner do not reside with the Shamans Order ... or with any of the five other orders for that matter. You are a prisoner of the Dragonbonded."

"And of what use is such trivia to me? It changes nothing."

"The young man who is bonded to the dragon, the young man you detained, is my apprentice."

"Apprentice?" Meera snorted. "You cannot teach the boy—" And then she clamped her jaw shut.

"Maybe, maybe not. In either case, I do have some sway over how he sees the world. It is possible I might convince him to have leniency in his ruling." Grimmley was teetering on the edge of truth, but truth could often be bent before it broke. Besides, negotiating with an Anarchic orderman violated half a dozen laws of the Orderman's Code he had spent a lifetime defending and protecting. But ever since Conner and his wayward dragon had stumbled into his life, breaking those rules had become part of the game.

Meera tried to rub at the shackles chafing her wrists. "I am sure the boy—and his dragon, for that matter—would like nothing better than to see me dead."

"Compared to the fate you face in the hands of the other orders . . ." Grimmley shrugged. "With my assistance, you at least have a chance at life."

Meera dropped her hands into her lap. "Well, I am intrigued to hear what knowledge you think I possess that is worth all this effort."

"Let's start with something simple. Have you ever heard of Fettering Stones?"

"No," she replied flatly.

"I have never seen one myself, but I can describe them. They are black onyx stones rich with Earth and Fire elementals. Their signature trait is a flickering web of blue light that emanates from its depths. I've read that this is impossible to miss." As Grimmley spoke, Meera's expression changed. She had seen at least one of these stones. "The master Barbarian who traveled with you—Briarmede, I believe is his name?" Conner had told Grimmley that Briarmede wore one of the stones. Grimmley puffed vigorously on his pipe. "Do you know how this particular Barbarian came into your service?"

"No. The commander at Farlorde assigned him to be in charge of the band that accompanied me."

Grimmley stroked his beard. "But you found his ... abilities useful." It was more a statement than question.

Meera hesitated, tilting her head forward before answering. "Yes."

Grimmley knew he had struck a chord. Meera seemed startled by his line of inquiry. He waited.

"At first, I found his behaviors odd for a Barbarian," she said. "Few of his order are fond of Necromancers or the undead we often acquire for our personal service. But Groegan never looked bothered by either. More, unlike other Barbarians, he seemed attuned to what was going on around him, even beyond his senses. He was the one who rightly directed us to Dragongarde even though the clues we had gathered were sending us south." Meera's eyes narrowed. Her black-eyed bond studied him from under her chin. "I am wondering whether your interest lies in these stones or in those who are in possession of them."

Grimmley waved away the accusation with a flick of his hand. "Think of it as an old fool's hobby. I spent most of my adulthood curious about these stones. Then recently, I heard of a few in possession of these stones. Naturally, my interest was piqued." His attempt to defuse her troubled expression was not working. Maybe a different approach would help. "I am looking for someone who might know something about them ... or might have one that I could study."

Meera pursed her lips, her brows low. "Grandmaster, you are a Shaman of great renown. But I would bet the Dons know nothing of our little chat. And keeping this conversation a secret had to cost you dearly. So, don't try to fool me into thinking your interests are purely academic or the ravings of an addled old man. The only person who could have told you about Briarmede and his Fettering Stone was that astute *apprentice* of yours. You are here because you want what I know about him."

Grimmley chuckled. "Now I see how such a young person rose to the highest ranks of your order." He cleared his throat and leaned forward. "Honestly, I don't care about the Barbarian. It is the stones I am trailing. Yes, Conner was the one who told me about the Barbarian and his stone. He also told me about another man, an Assassin as discovered later, also in possession of one of these stones—the same Assassin who attempted to place the Warrior Evinfaire as the queen's own Champion. Two missions. Two ordermen. One objective." Grimmley studied Meera's stunned expression. His intuition had told him she was not part of the network of spies. Judging by her reaction, he had been right. "No matter what you think, neither fortune nor fate landed this Briarmede in your camp. It was planned and executed with a precision that defies simple explanation."

Meera sat wide-eyed. "You say these stones are rare. Yet here are two."

"Yes," Grimmley tried to keep his voice from sounding ominous. "There were fewer than fifty such stones recovered by Tatem Creeg and his disciples when they excavated Shan-Grail." Grimmley rose and ground his knuckles into his lower back with a groan. He was way too old for such skullduggery. But he was willing to go all the way to the end of this riddle, even if it took the rest of his days.

He signaled to the Mystic waiting outside the cell. "Grandmaster Asheborne, I thank you for your time."

"Grandmaster Rollingsworth." Meera's eyes pleaded with Grimmley as the Mystic shoved the gag back in her mouth.

"As I said, I will talk to Conner and express the need for leniency." Grimmley moved back up the hall. Meera had not been as helpful as he had hoped. He still had no idea who was in possession of the stones. But he now knew the Barbarian had directed the Anarchic band to Dragongarde before Annabelle and her force of Scouters got there. Now he was certain the stones had helped facilitate the Anarchists' awareness of Conner and Skye. And that led him to the answer to another question that had nagged him for years.

Harmonics had various means of communicating through the Physical plane—Shamans had Transit Stones, Rangers used enchanted emeralds, and royalty dispensed commands throughout the realms with Scrying

Chambers built by the Mystics. But these all had limitations, and only worked over short distances. If what Meera had said was true, then the network of spies had coordinated with Anarchists as far away as Thanatos—thrice the distance capable by known methods. If Fettering Stones were being used to communicate, then they were very powerful indeed.

He needed to get his hands on one of those stones. And soon.

Open Channels

$\mathbf{C}$onner arrived outside the Shamans' temple just as Hemera slipped beyond the outer wall. It was a cool afternoon, the air heavy with the smell of smoke from evening home fires. Hemera's afternoon rays felt good on his face. Skye stood silently next to him while they waited. Within minutes, the double gates clanged and swung wide. Tara, the Don he had met early that morning, looking quite haggard, led a procession of Shamans into the city street. Amid the group, astride a gray horse, was Meera, bound and gagged as she had been in the dungeon, her thick-furred bond draped over her shoulder.

As they neared, Conner imagined raking his powerful claws from Meera's gullet to her hips, her viscera spilling out over— Conner shook his head, then awarded his bond with a scathing look.

Skye only snort-sniffed his amusement.

"I have an obligation to make my case one last time," Tara urged as she neared Conner's horse. "Let the other orders take care of this woman. She is *extremely* dangerous."

Conner gestured toward Skye. "Thank you for your concern. But I think the two of us can handle her."

Pressing her lips together, the Don dropped the end of the gray's reins into Conner's outstretched hand. "You were warned."

Conner turned his sorrel mare and moved east. Skye walked beside him, his wings lifted high over his back to keep from bumping into the many busy people crowding the morning street, though the mere sight of a dragon ambling along the thoroughfare was enough to clear a generous berth down the middle. Townsfolk stared and pointed, whispering softly as the procession of two horses and dragon passed. Since Conner usually flew in and out of the castle, it was rare to see them in the city. Conner acknowledged the stares with frequent waves and greetings, though no one spoke back.

Once they cleared the buildings of Graystone, Conner reined his horse north on the wide dirt towpath that ran along the eastern edge of River Tresdan. Skye took up a position behind Meera's horse, close enough that Conner was sure she felt the dragon's breath down her neck. He did not speak to Meera, nor even acknowledge her presence as they traveled through the afternoon.

Near dusk, they reached the north base of the river. He rode east down a narrow path that led to a campsite. He had seen the site several times during their flights into the mountains, a secluded spot just south of where the river fell and broke over rocks in a grand waterfall a thousand paces high. Mist rose on the cooling air, revealing a magnificent rainbow as Hemera dipped low in the west.

After dismounting and securing his sorrel to a tree, Conner assisted Meera off her gray. He directed her to a log that had been split in half, the two parts placed perpendicular near a fire pit encircled by large rocks. Conner tied the gray next to his own horse and gathered kindling and dead branches from underbrush nearby. It was well past dusk by the time he had a small fire going. As he had in the temple dungeon, Conner removed the shackles on Meera's wrists. "I have a few questions," he said as she pulled the gag from her mouth.

"Seems common among you Harmonics." She snorted as she tossed the gag to the side. If she was frightened or worried, she did not show it. If anything, she looked relaxed. "Why should I answer any questions if you are going to kill me? Or do you mean to torture me for the information?"

"Who said I was going to kill you?"

Meera looked confused, then glanced over at the large, black form near the fringes of the camp. "Ah. You're going to have your bond do the dirty work."

Conner chuckled at the idea, then realized she was serious. "I can't deny Skye would like nothing more than to shred you into thin strips of loincloth. He's very angry about our encounter at Dragongarde."

Meera's head dipped forward. Her bond gave a high-pitched squeak. "I am not proud of the subterfuge. But then again, your dragon would not have listened to me otherwise."

"No. I suppose not." Conner pushed away the irritability pulsing up through his link with Skye. It had taken time, but he was learning how to shield his own feelings from his bond's spirited emotions. "I plan to let you go."

Meera worked her jaw with her hands. "Let me go? Just, 'No worries about the offense, Meera. All's well. Now go on back home.'?"

"Well, it's not that simple," Conner corrected. "I can't exactly release you in the heart of the realms, now, can I?"

Meera blinked. "No. But then—"

"It took a lot of hard negotiating with my bond for us to settle on a compromise, but Skye has agreed to fly you to the Borderlands."

Meera scratched the back of her bond's head. "Why would you do that? After all that I did?"

"The order councils claim that you came to Dragongarde to kill me. But if that had been the case, I doubt I would have survived our encounter. And Grimmley believes you were part of some Anarchic conspiracy to embed Warrior Evinfaire as Queen Veressa's new Champion. But in fact, now that I have had time to reflect on our encounter, I think your mission was to tell me something." Conner tilted his head toward his bond. "Or tell *us* something. So I suggest an amicable exchange. You get to complete your mission and return home, and in so doing, be free from any more undead attempts on your life. In return, I get answers to a few questions."

Meera straightened, but her eyes narrowed his way. "Even if I took you at your word, how can I be sure your bond won't drop me from the clouds?"

Skye, who had taken up residence on the far side of the fire, gazed north to where the falls sparkled in Erebus's bright glow.

Conner could not argue with the notion. "There are days when I can't trust Skye any farther than I could toss him. But the information you possess is more valuable than appeasing my bond's sensibilities. On this matter, he won't oppose me."

Meera rubbed her bond's back in thought. "That is an offer I did not expect." She stared into the fire for a few minutes. "Very well. My mentor, wife to the sovereign prince of the Necromancers, Galan Martesian, sent me in hopes of convincing you two to join our side in the brewing conflict. Or at least to stay out of it. I was to be the first of several emissaries sent to negotiate an equitable arrangement. Regrettably, we were ... interrupted ... before we had an opportunity to talk."

"The first of several?" Conner repeated. He was determined not be drawn into any war, but he saw no need to share that with her yet. Her explanation was consistent with what the Barbarian Groegan Briarmede had said. But Groegan had gone further. He had tried to convince Conner to return with him to the Anarchic Lands, to learn about Anarchic life. Of course, Conner had flatly refused. "And how did constraining us help your cause?"

"It was a calculated risk," she continued. "Neither of you would have been harmed. Eastlander or not, you are from the realms. We had to assume that announcing ourselves upfront as Anarchists would have resulted in a confrontation that none in my group wanted to have with an irritable, adolescent dragon and his Harmonic bond. Once we had been certain you would not fight us, we would have released you. As for your dragon, I was the only one who could explain the situation before he scorched us all into ash."

"Where did you learn to speak Dragon? My preceptor, the Sorcerer Newstone, is the only one other person I know of in all the realms who can speak to Skye."

"Five hundred years ago, in the early days of the War of Breaking, both the Anarchic and Harmonic factions within the orders dispatched emissaries to Dragongarde to woo those bonded with dragons to their side. Learning to speak Dragon was essential to that process. As an apprentice, I had a natural curiosity of those days. I happened upon several books in Thanatos about the language. That is why I volunteered for the first mission to Dragongarde ... to meet you and your dragon."

Conner had heard that the Harmonics had sent diplomats to Dragongarde during the Anarchic War. But the Anarchists? "What made the Anarchists think they could sway the old Dragonbonded to their side?"

"Actually, the Anarchic emissaries believed they held the upper hand in the negotiations."

"Why?"

"Because, according to the book I read, dragons are Anarchic."

Conner pulled his knees up and hugged them tight to his chest, staring into the flames. Groegan Briarmede had told him something similar: *If you hold any notion of living out your life in the Harmonic Realms, you might find your dragon is of a different mind. Harmonic life is not in a dragon's nature. That is why, during the War of Breaking, the Harmonic Realms struggled for so many years to establish a pact with the Dragonbonded.* But Conner didn't want to believe there was any truth to that claim, or anything else the Barbarian had said. Could everything Conner knew about Anarchic life be merely tall tales and half-truths? "Briarmede asked me if I knew what I was bonded to. Do you know what he meant?"

Meera grunted. "I have no clue what a Barbarian would know about dragons. However, I can say this. One of the books I read asserted that Anarchic spirits inhabit the body of dragons, spirits not from our Physical planes of existence, but the planes far beyond. Of course, it was not written by a Necromancer, so I do not know what to make of such wild accusations."

Conner squeezed his knees. *Could dragons be Anarchic?* he asked himself. He had no idea what to do if they were. He could not afford to be distracted. He had too many other knots to untie. And none of what she had told him helped unravel any of them.

"I can sense you are hesitating. There is something else you want to ask me."

Well, he *had* been putting it off. "You heard that I defeated the Warrior Marcantos Evinfaire?" After she nodded, he went on. "Well, I don't recall how I did it. I don't know how to access the powers I used that day."

"I was wondering if you would get around to that." Meera laughed at Conner's surprise. "In the Shamans' temple, you struggled with the incantation to turn the undead assassin. You spoke the invocation correctly. You made all the right gestures. You drew upon a substantial amount of Earth and Fire. All the right ingredients. Still, it failed."

Conner gnawed on his lower lip, unable to tear his gaze from the flickering flames.

"Yet you had no problem deciphering the seals on my shackles, seals placed there by two grandmaster ordermen wielding different combinations of the four elementals. You unraveled those locks without uttering a single word."

Meera reached out and touched Conner's arm lightly, drawing his worried eye. "Conner, I have no doubt Grandmaster Rollingsworth is a very powerful Shaman. And having been offered a seat on the Shamans council, I am sure he has proven himself many times to be as great a preceptor. Logically, you should have been able to cast that incantation. So only one conclusion can be drawn from this: no orderman can help you. Controlling your powers is something you are going to have to work out on your own."

Conner had reached the same destination, only via a different route. But vindication did not lead one down the road to happiness. There were limits to what his preceptors could provide. He rose, and together, they cleared the camp, repacking what remained of the supplies Conner had brought. While strapping the leather bags to the gray Meera had ridden, he heard her voice. He glanced back.

Meera was on the far side of the fire, bowing low before the dragon. "I am Meera-Antala of the family Asheborne, Necromancer of Thanatos," she said reverently.

Lifting up on his legs, Skye glanced away. Meera did not rise or move. Finally, his head swiveled toward her and he bowed formally in return. "I am Skye-Anyar-Bello of the family Cloudbender."

"Truly, you are an exquisite dragon," Meera said, "Skye-Anyar-Bello of the family Cloudbender, with talons as sharp as daggers, teeth as big as branches, and wings as powerful as the wind. Your days and deeds shall surely be among the greatest of the Cloudbenders, and you shall add honorable verses to your family's dragonsong." They were words similar to those Layna had used when she first met Skye. "I would be most honored and ever so grateful if you afforded me transportation to my homeland."

Skye's head craned upward as Meera spoke. His eyes were glowing slits.

Through their mental link, Conner sensed the anger and humiliation that had boiled in the dragon's belly through most of the day slowly evaporating. Conner rolled his eyes at Skye's gullibility. Dragons were as quick to congeniality as they were to anger. He was struck with a sudden idea. In fact, he was not sure why he had not thought of it before. "Skye," he said softly as he walked around the fire, "did you know that Necromancers originally came from the same order as Shamans?"

The dragon snorted in surprise. "Then it would be my privilege to attend to your needs, Shaman Asheborne. Did you know that dragons were created by a great Shaman?"

"No, I did not," Meera stated with her own surprise as she stepped to Skye's shoulder.

Conner pressed back a smile. At least he felt better about Meera riding on Skye's back. Conner patted Skye's shoulder.

The Necromancer stuffed her boot toe through the left stirrup of Skye's saddle, then hesitated. "Don't be disheartened, Conner. It's going to take time, but you will figure out how to access your powers."

"Yes, *time*. Grimmley keeps telling me that time is the enemy of an orderman."

Meera climbed into the saddle and settled. "The Shaman is a wise man."

Grimmley was wise. But wisdom wasn't helping get Conner through his logjam.

"One more question," Conner said.

"Yes?"

"What kind of bond is that?"

"Morgana is a black mink." Meera slid her fingers around the grips in the front of the saddle. "I will not forget what you have done for me. I am in your debt. And Conner ... I hope it would not be too brazen of me to report back that channels are still open for further dialogue?"

Conner only nodded. He would not commit to anything at this point. But as his father often said, nothing bad happens with a mended fence. Conner stepped back as Skye leaped into the air, then climbed above the oaks with a single powerful stroke of his leathery wings. Banking to the right, Skye glided east and disappeared above the rustling treetops silhouetted against the brilliant night sky.

Conner swung his leg over the sorrel's back. Gripping the gray horse's reins, he took one last glance to the east. Skye was well beyond sight, but Conner sensed the dragon's contentment. The cry of a lone wolf along the mountains to the north drew his eye. A chill came over him and he tightened the coat around his chest. Heading south, Conner let the sounds of water roaring down the great Tresdan guide him home.

Slightly past midnight, he reined in his sorrel before Graystone's Shamans' temple gates, where two guards stood watch. One of the guards stepped forward, and Conner caught the accusation in her eyes. He had ridden away with the Necromancer straddling the gray, but he had returned the same day with the horse riderless. The guard's judgment of him could not have been more apparent if Conner had returned the gray splattered with Meera's blood. But he was too exhausted and full of his own concerns to care.

He tossed the gray's reins to the guard, then urged his sorrel forward in search of his warm bed.

A Spy's Mission

Conner did not get the rest he'd anticipated. Past first light, someone pounded on his bedchamber's door. He tried to ignore the noise by wrapping his pillow over his head. But the drumming was unrelenting. "Yes!" came the muffled sound from under his pillow. With a groan, he slid from between the sheets and staggered to the door. Kriston.

"Don't you have something important to study?" Conner grumbled as he fell back on his mattress, snatching his pillow back over his head.

"There's not a moment when I don't have a dozen unfinished assignments to work on," Kriston huffed as he tailed Conner into the room and plopped on the foot of the bed. "You must have really kicked a hornet's nest yesterday."

Conner lifted his pillow and squinted up at his page. "Why do you say that?"

"Before first light, I was called to the queen's reception hall. And I didn't sleep well last night, seeing's how you got dragged away before the Shaman Dons and I didn't see you all day—"

"Kriston. Get to the point."

"I will. It just seems that if they wanted to talk to you, why not come and get you?"

The morning rays flooding through the narrow slit of his north-tower bedroom made Conner's head throb. He dropped the pillow back over his eyes. "Because we are Harmonics, and adhering to rules and procedures is precious to us. Royal etiquette is to call the page, who then scurries off to get his liege." Conner flicked his hand left-to-right as he wiggled his fingers, mimicking someone running.

"That makes no sense."

"Can we skip past that and move on to where you tell me what's happening?"

"I would if I knew. But judging by all the long faces in the queen's hall—"

"Whose long faces?" Conner jerked upright, rubbing his eyes. Running through all the mischief he'd made in the last few days, he could imagine half a dozen deeds that would have raised the queen's ire. As if his footing with her since their ride in the rain hadn't been precarious enough.

"The queen, her father, your two preceptors, the master Ranger who seems to live attached to the queen's dress train, and that husky old Warrior."

"General Grimwaldt?"

"That's him." Kriston squinted at Conner, who had lost all color in his face. "You okay, Conner?"

"I don't know," he swallowed hard. "I suppose I'd better go find out."

Conner paused before the queen's reception hall doors and composed himself. Taking a deep breath, he stepped past the four guards and pushed the doors wide, but slowed as he walked in the chamber. He had been in this room only once before—the day King Jonath called a meeting of the Tournament Council, where Conner was declared to be of the Order of the Dragonbonded, fit to challenge the Warrior Evinfaire to become the queen's Champion. It was a small room, designed for intimate conversations while sharing a private meal. A mahogany table stretched end to end, a half dozen chairs spaced evenly along each side. Queen Veressa was seated at the far end of the table looking as cross as she had for some days, while Antilles paced behind her. King Jonath was standing near one of the few windows, staring out at the royal forest to the west, unaware of Conner's arrival. General Grimwaldt sat next to the queen with his back to Conner. The general's red-tailed hawk ruffled her feathers, and the general turned his way. Ranger Loris, wearing her usual blank expression, sat to Veressa's left, looking like someone had strapped an oak plank to her back. Conner's two preceptors were farther down, their faces drawn with expressions of worry.

The walls of the chamber sparkled with an incredible weave of Water and Fire elemental that he recognized immediately. It was the same weave Layna had used to seal this very chamber from unwanted ears the morning of the tourney. Whatever they were discussing, it was meant to be private.

"If this is about the other night, I can explain," Conner began.

Grimmley furrowed his bushy brows at him and pointed at the chair across from Layna. "Conner, sit down, and will you please, for once, listen."

Conner slid into the chair while Layna pulled at a loose thread on her sleeve. His mouth watered as he reviewed the feast of breads, fruits, meats, and sliced vegetables lining the center of the table. The plates were untouched. None seemed even aware the food was there.

Veressa cleared her throat. "You should bring our Champion up to date on what we've discussed so far." She nodded to Grimmley.

Grimmley propped his elbows on the table. "Conner, this morning, my order's council received word that there has been another."

"Another ...?"

"Another human-dragon bonding," Layna filled in.

It took a moment for the announcement to seep in. Then Conner beamed, a toothy smile filling his face. At last! Someone he could commiserate with, to share all his troubles and worries. Another mind to work out what to do. He imagined showing this person around Dragongarde, talking about all the ancient wonders he had uncovered—the grand hall big enough to fly around in, racks of black Dragonbonded armor, tapestries and paintings of the old Dragonbonded order, Modeic hieroglyphs to decipher, a kitchen filled with food that never went bad, the device he had used to train on how to draw upon the elementals. And another dragon! Skye would stop his incessant grumbling over having to deal with bipedal creatures. "This is great news, Layna!"

"Not so quick, Conner," Grimmley reached a gnarled hand across the table and patted Conner's arm. "The bonding took place in the old Dristonian region of the Anarchic Lands."

Conner slumped back in his chair. He could not find his breath. "Anarchic Lands?"

"Yes," Grimmley confirmed, pipe smoke swirling about his head.

"Which is why this conversation will only involve us seven, Conner," Grimwaldt announced. "Nothing said here leaves this room. With calls of war against the Anarchists, if a story of this import were to leak, we would have fear and anxiety rippling across the realms, if it didn't start widespread panic."

Conner nodded vigorously.

"Actually, your timing is perfect, Conner," Annabelle inserted. "We've just started discussing whom we should send into the Anarchic Lands on a fact-finding expedition, and if possible, to convince this person to come back here. You should know that Grandmaster Newstone has volunteered for the mission."

"Layna?"

"Yes." Layna answered with a formal nod, though she made it sound like she was talking to a three-year-old. "No one in the realms has more knowledge of dragon bonds. And if need be, I can speak with the dragon. I am also a trained diplomat."

An odd feeling flowed through Conner. He wondered if a number of Anarchic ordermen had, not so long ago, sat around the table and talked about him this way. And if Meera had similarly volunteered to be "the first of several emissaries." Would Layna encounter the same fate? Would she have better luck getting this person to come to the realms than Meera had had getting Conner to go there? He scanned the faces around him. They doubted Layna could succeed. But someone had to try. "I'm sorry, Layna, but I think I have more knowledge of the Dragonbonded and dragons than you. I should be the one who goes." The words surprised him nearly as much as they did everyone else.

The room fell silent for a heartbeat before erupting into total mayhem, everyone shouting at him. Only the queen sat quietly watching him, gently stroking Antilles's hackles.

Conner rose and rapped the table with his knuckles to silence them all. "I am the obvious choice for this mission. You all know it." He turned to Layna. "Nothing against you, Layna, but once you discover this report is real, what then? Return here for another debate about what to do next? We don't have time for that. Once this other dragon-bonded human figures out how to wield elementals, he could reshape the balance of power. What if he sides with the Anarchic orders?" He took in each solemn face. "No. You have only one chance at convincing whomever this is to not be sucked into the Anarchic spiderweb. I am the only one here—or anywhere else—who has a chance of persuading them to return here ... or at least to Dragongarde."

"He has a point," General Grimwaldt stated after a weighty pause, sizing Conner up as if seeing him for the first time.

"You cannot be seriously considering letting him go." Annabelle flicked her wide gaze from Grimwaldt to Conner. "Conner, you do not know anything about Anarchic ways. And what would you do with your dragon? Besides, you are the queen's Champion. Your responsibility is here, protecting the queen."

"I'm a quick study. And I can get there a whole lot faster than anyone else at this table. I could get there and back—"

"Wait!" General Grimwaldt shouted. "Before we jump into a plan, we need to think a few things through. I agree that Conner is the perfect choice"—he raised his big hands before anyone argued—"which is why this smells all wrong. Grimmley, how do you know this is not a trap set by the Anarchists to lure Conner there?"

Grimmley scratched at his beard. "While there is no way to be certain, let me explain why I believe the message to be authentic." He settled back, ready to dive into one of his stories. "Shortly after I achieved the rank of master, I was given a young man by the name of Fenagal to be my first pupil. Fenagal was a bright lad—nearly as bright as you, Conner." Grimmley wore a distant smile. "One day, a Scouter returned from a mission into the northern Anarchic Lands, having heard about a strange phenomenon in an expanse southwest of Thanatos involving several Necromancers from that province. Eager to make a name for himself, Shaman Fenagal volunteered to go on a fact-finding mission. I can still recall the morning he rode away. That was nearly fifty years ago." He closed his eyes. "That was the last time I saw Fenagal. Several fortnights after his departure, the Shamans Council received a message from him that he was onto something. And then all contact with him went dark."

"Until now?" Annabelle inferred from Grimmley's tale.

"Exactly. Without going into details, we settled upon how Fenagal was to sign his reports so we knew them to be genuine. The message that arrived this morning came bearing that signature. I believe this message came from Fenagal."

"Unless your young pupil-turned-spy was captured and tortured for the information," the general suggested.

"That does not seem likely. If what you say is true, there have been many occasions since Fenagal's disappearance that the Anarchists could have used to their advantage—spreading disinformation to misdirect our spying efforts, for example. Why risk using an outdated means of communication to lure Conner to the Anarchic Lands?"

"Grimmley is right," Annabelle said. "The dark orders would not risk it. I believe it safe to assume the message is real."

Grimwaldt placed his palms on the table, his thick fingers spread wide. "Then that brings us to who to send on this dicey mission."

"I am not right with Conner going on this assignment," Grimmley blurted out. "If something were to happen to him ..." The old Shaman choked back the thought and stiffened his back. "Well, the queen would lose her Champion! And what if he is captured and used to extort us toward some Anarchic purpose? Or what if he is tortured for information? The lad knows even more harmful secrets than he thinks he does. No," Grimmley shook his head emphatically. "Conner is too valuable to risk for some uncertain gain."

Despite Grimmley's pessimism, Conner could not help but note the numerous upsides to taking this mission: to get away from the castle, that constant reminder of everything he had lost, to find some relief from the irksome queen he was becoming too fond of, and to fulfill his promise to Skye and let him fly home. And though another dragon-bonded human would bring a world of new issues to the table, Conner knew this revelation could lead him to find answers to a lot of questions.

As Grimmley spoke, Conner recalled the Barbarian's proposition at Dragongarde. Groegan had wanted him and Skye to return to the Anarchic Lands, for Conner to learn about Anarchic life. Two fortnights later, Groegan's words still echoed in his dreams: *Eastlander, there is so much you do not yet understand. Nothing is as it appears, and much of what you have been taught is wrong. Come with us, and I promise you will not regret it.* Conner shook the echoes away. Yesterday, Meera said she had come as an envoy, not to capture or kill him. Maybe the Anarchists thought him too valuable for torture or ransom. More likely, they wanted to sway him to their cause. But he had made up his mind. He would not participate in any agenda involving death or destruction. He surveyed those in the room ... those he considered his close friends and more. Of course, he mentioned none of this to them. More secrets to hold close to his chest.

"Conner should go," Veressa announced as if the statement were a royal decree. With all eyes on her, she explained. "Is there anyone here who believes that my life would be in less danger if this new dragon-bonded human fell into the hands of the Anarchic orders?" She took in their silent consent. "A Champion's service to protect his queen does not require him to dote over her every move. My fate, like that of everyone else in the realms, may well rest on the success of this mission."

Conner caught Ranger Loris rubbing her hand over her lips in an attempt to cover a smile.

"So," Veressa went on, "if there are no more disagreements about who should go on this quest, let us put our eyes toward a plan that will succeed."

"I have a few ideas that will alleviate some concerns," Conner offered. "First, I won't be taking Skye into the Anarchic Lands. He has been asking to return to his home since his … transformation. This seems the perfect time for that. And it gets him out of the way."

Annabelle tipped forward, a finger in the air. "That may work, Conner. It is very rare for Anarchists to travel outside their clans' domain. The Calling is one reason they might. You could pose as an Anarchist from the Gorgonian region on an easterly trek into Dristonia in search for your bond. Few in the Dristonian clans know much of the customs and dialects of the Gorgonians. With your farming upbringing, it is possible you could get by."

Layna carried the idea further. "It is customary that young Anarchists traveling between regions on their trek are accompanied by a guide. Conner will need someone to go with him. Someone who knows those northern regions, their customs, dress, and dialects."

"You mean someone to keep him out of trouble," Grimmley grumbled as he bit on his pipe. He was clearly still struggling with this plan.

"I know just the person to be his guide," Annabelle suggested. "There is an Alpslander named Morgas Terranus, the leader of a village near the Borderlands. He was trained by the dark orders and has spent many years with the Anarchic peoples."

"Can he be trusted?" Grimwaldt asked, his face darkening.

Annabelle chewed on her lip for a moment. "Yes. He served as guide for the troop of Scouters I was with in search of Conner's dragon. He is neither orderman nor guildsman, but he is one of the most valiant fighters I have ever met. He also assisted in the capture of Meera Asheborne at Dragongarde. So yes, I trust him completely. However, it will not be easy to convince him to take Conner on this mission. His people are freemen."

"I don't know." Grimwaldt rubbed at his beard. "We're hanging a lot on a freeman's choice."

"I am willing to listen to any other options you would like to offer." Annabelle panned her eyes over the quiet room. "It seems to me we had best come up with a way to ensure this Alpslander does not refuse our request."

Conner sat back and observed the others as they polished their plans. But his mind raced elsewhere. Unlike Pauli, he had never been keen on taking risks. The day he left home on his bonding trek had changed all that. And now, here he sat in the queen's chamber, having volunteered to take on a spy mission into the Anarchic Lands. Worse, he had made that decision as if he had been choosing what to have for lunch.

The memory of the first time he rode on Skye's back to cross the wide gorge crossed his mind. He smiled fondly, remembering what he had said to his bond. *Sometimes I wish I could be fearless, even for a day.* He peered down at his hands, calloused from hours spent gripping the Dragonbonded saddle. Now that he thought about it, he had not felt real fear since the day he'd confronted Evinfaire on the tourney field. Had Skye changed him in some subtle way? Had he gone through his own transformation, like Skye's from wyvern to drake? He had not seen this coming. Another thought came to him, one that made him shiver. What if there were more changes to come? What would he transform into? Conner did not have a chance to pursue the notion as the tone of the conversation changed.

Veressa glared at Grimwaldt. "Let me make one final point. General, this puts me in a very fine pickle. As you are the only member of the War Council privy to this plan, let me state this unequivocally. I will not sign any declaration of war against the Anarchists while my Champion is in the Anarchic Lands. Until he has returned safely, you need to suppress the council's constant demands for war. Are we in agreement?"

Those around the table appeared troubled by the queen's request. Annabelle squirmed uncomfortably in her chair.

General Grimwaldt cast his eyes on his hands. "Majesty. What you ask is for me to work surreptitiously against my council's wishes. That will require that I break the Orderman's Code. By asking me before four other ordermen, you make them co-conspirators in this plot."

Veressa inhaled sharply.

"However," Grimwaldt continued, his gaze frozen on the table, "we live in exceptional times. I will do as you bid if the others at this table are of the same mind."

The queen's pleading eyes swept those at the table. Each silently signaled their consent, then glanced away. "Very well. We are in this conspiracy as one. We need a break, or there will be talk about why we are meeting privately. Let us reconvene this afternoon." Veressa stiffened as she looked at her Champion. "Conner, I wish for you to stay a few minutes."

"Yes, Majesty." Conner bowed.

After everyone else had departed, Veressa did not move or speak. She just stared at him.

He fidgeted, looking around for something to draw his attention from her scrutiny. "That really was quite ingenious."

Veressa rumpled her forehead. "What on Gaia are you talking about?"

"I know you do not want to sign the declaration of war. Sending me on this mission was an excellent ploy, Majesty, giving you more time to consider your options."

"That is not why I decided you should go. And I told you, stop calling me that when we are alone," she snapped.

She is still angry at me. She wants me away from her. That is why she wants me to go. Maybe some time apart is a good idea. He needed to hear her say it. "Then what reason do you have that you could not share with the others?"

"Because I believe and trust in you, Conner." She rolled her eyes at her Champion's doe-eyed goggle. "Do you recall our conversation right before you strode out onto the Field of Contest to face the Warrior Evinfaire?"

Conner bobbed his head. How could he forget? He remembered everything—up to the moment he stepped onto the tourney field.

Veressa stepped forward, a faint smile parting her full lips. "You came to my rescue, even though I did not know I needed it. You were right. How you knew Evinfaire to be a traitor is still a mystery to me ... to everyone, for that matter." She stared deeper into his eyes, searching for an answer.

Conner glanced away. He felt a sharp pain in his heart. He hated keeping so many secrets. More, he hated what it was doing to their relationship. Grimmley had made Conner promise not to divulge to anyone that he had deduced from the man's ring that Evinfaire's preceptor, Friarwood, was actually the Assassin spy Conner had met in Cravenrock.

"No matter," she went on. "Your courage saved our realm that day. I told you then, and I will repeat this every time you step into danger for me: you have won my lifelong trust and friendship."

Her words felt like a stab to his gut. *Friendship.*

"If you say you are the right one for this mission, then I will do whatever it takes to make that happen." Veressa lost her smile. "Wait." The fury he held seen in her eyes the day they had gone riding in the rain returned. "How did you know I have been struggling with signing the declaration?"

Conner opened his mouth, but his mind froze.

"Annabelle was the only one who knew that, and she would die before that fact escaped her tongue. How did you know?"

Conner shrugged. He was running out of excuses. "Good guess?"

The queen folded her arms tight, her perfect lips pressed together. "Not working."

Conner waved his arms in surrender. "All right. You were right the other day on our ride. There is some kind of connection between us. I can't explain it either, but I can sense your emotions, can feel when you are sad or worried or struggling with a decision."

"Ugh!" She exclaimed. "Why didn't you say that then? I thought I was going mad."

Conner wanted to explain his actions that day, but could not find the words that would keep him within the bounds of his promise to King Jonath.

"My father has something to do with this, doesn't he?"

Conner cast his eyes at her feet. His stoic shield was weakening under her constant bombardment. What if he did not return from this dangerous mission? Part of him did not want to leave without telling her how he felt. *No*, he thought. *Not that.* He had sworn on the Champion's amulet that he would never divulge his true feelings for Veressa. But he hadn't sworn to keep that promise itself a secret. He straightened his shoulders and looked into her blue eyes. "I promised King Jonath that I would keep you safe ... no matter the cost." That was the closest to the truth he could go and keep his pledge to her father. Yet again, he was taking a page from Grimmley's book on twisting the truth into what he wanted others to believe. Still, even that much was liberating.

Veressa stomped her foot. "I should have seen his handprints all over this. I am the queen of Griffinrock," she declared, as if stating it would give her new powers, "and still he tries to control my life. I won't have it!" Veressa shook her finger under Conner's nose. "I will not allow him to decide how I will live *my* life based on what happened in *his*."

"Veressa. He is right."

"What?"

"King Jonath is right." Conner reached out and gently wrapped his hands around hers. For a moment, her warm, soft skin distracted him. "I— I am a lightning rod. And everyone close to me lives in peril of getting struck by a stray bolt of energy."

She did not pull away, but leaned closer. "Is that his idea of keeping me safe at any cost? For you to be wary of getting too close to me so that I won't be hurt? You cannot keep your distance *and* be my protector." Her eyes narrowed. "There's more you're not telling me."

Conner opened and closed his mouth several times before clamping it shut. He had yielded enough ground. He needed to make a stand somewhere if he was to keep his oath to Jonath. His last line of defense was to not tell her that he loved her. Through their connection, she knew it, even if she refused to believe it. He would leave it there. He pasted a broad smile across his face, hoping she'd accept his flag of truce. Veressa's stern expression told him otherwise. "You did say you trust me," he reminded her.

"Oh! You are so infuriatingly secretive. Fine, then. I will let this go ... for now. But let me be clear. We are far from done with this conversation. And while you are away, I am going to have a long talk with my father."

Conner swallowed hard. Once again, even with all his best intentions, he had stirred up a glorious mess.

"You had better come back to me," she said, then stepped back, slipping free of his hold on her hand. Her anger had been replaced with a warm smile. "So we can finish this conversation, of course."

Conner did not want to break their gaze. His heart raced. He felt dizzy, spent from the exertion of keeping his love in check. But his life was about to go topsy-turvy again. And why not? It happened every time he thought he was getting his legs under him.

"May the will of the Cosmos guide your step," Veressa whispered, and swept through the door.

He stood alone in silence, wondering if he could ever mend the gaping hole in his heart.

ARMY OF THE DRAGONBONDED

Part II

True changes happen with the dull subtleties of life—the sense of wonder in Hemera's rise, a soft kiss and gentle hug, a rainbow after a spring shower. Do not be distracted by a thunderclap, an avalanche, or a rainstorm. Listen instead to the wind in the trees and the water along a stream, and let it move your spirit.

—The Modei Book of Water (Third Book)

Departure

Conner stifled back a yawn he could have shoved his entire fist into. He rattled his head, hoping to clear away fog as thick as the morning mist that often blanketed the forest east of the castle. The previous afternoon had been long, followed by a longer evening, while Annabelle, Grimwaldt, and Layna had stuffed his head with as much knowledge as he could retain about the Anarchic Lands. By midnight, he understood why, according to Grimwaldt, spies spent years preparing for Anarchic missions. By the time he fell into bed, he was determined to succeed at this mission.

"You should not dawdle any longer," came a deep feminine voice at his back.

Conner spun in surprise. Layna was standing beside him, her arms folded as she sized up his haggard appearance.

The Sorceress cleared her throat, glancing toward Hemera peeking between the thick trees in the east. "The plan was for you to slip away under the cloak of darkness."

Conner peered over her shoulder. "I was hoping to talk to Grimmley before I left."

Her dark eyes took in Conner's troubled expression. "I am sorry, Conner. Grimmley has been at the Shamans' temple since yesterday afternoon brewing up a batch of potions for a sickness that has taken root in Moorestone." Layna watched Conner's chest deflate. "Is there something you would like me to relay to him?"

Conner's shoulders sagged further. Ever since Grimmley had elected to stay in Graystone so he could work with Conner more, his preceptor had been drawn into Shaman operations at the temple. "No. It's nothing critical. It can wait until I return." In truth, what he wanted to say to Grimmley was nearly critical. He did not like the thought of leaving with his preceptor thinking he had killed Meera. Conner needed to tell him what he had done. "Just ... tell him I will come back. And that I still need his guidance."

Layna pressed her palm to his arm. "I will tell him you said so. He knows that. It is just that sometimes he gets busy and forgets." She started to say more but shook it away. He already knew the old Shaman would fret until Conner returned safely.

Conner tilted his head toward Kriston, who was checking the cinch around Skye's chest while the dragon complained that the strap pinched scales behind his front legs. "Look after the lad while I am away?"

"I talked to Ballett. He promised he would check in on the boy every day to make sure he keeps up his studies."

And keep him out of trouble, Conner hoped. The edges of his lips curled upward. Having the captain of the royal guard nearby should help keep the boy's itchy palms in check. He signaled his appreciation and strode over to his bond. "Ballett is going to check in on your schooling while I am away," he said to his page while he inspected the boy's handiwork.

"The captain of the guard?" Kriston rolled his eyes. "Isn't leaving me here alone with boring studies torture enough?"

"I wouldn't be much of a liege if I didn't spend my evenings thinking up innovative ways to torment you." Conner winked. He had left crafting a plausible story of where he had gone to Veressa and his preceptors. They knew best how to handle such matters. He placed his hand on Kriston's bony shoulder. "Don't tell anyone that I have left or how long I may be away—especially Pauli. You might as well paint the news on the castle walls as tell him."

"And if he keeps asking where you've gone?"

Conner thought about how to answer the question. That was precisely why Kriston had been kept in the dark about his mission until now. "I cannot have Pauli running around stirring up more trouble searching for me. If he persists, get a message to General Grimwaldt. He will take care of the problem."

Conner's suggestion put a big smile on Kriston's face.

"And try to get along with Pauli. At least one of you needs to act like an adult."

"I'm only twelve."

"Age has little to do with maturity, especially when Pauli is around. I know better than to expect much from him." Conner clambered up Skye's shoulder and plopped into the saddle. "You ready?" he asked the dragon.

"Do I have a choice?" Skye grumbled back.

Conner sensed his bond's exhaustion. Skye had spent most of the night before last flying Meera to the Borderlands and returning. But Conner was not about to let on that he empathized. If he did, the dragon would not let up with the complaints. "Two days ago, you were all in a huff about getting home. Now that it's time, you want to dawdle?"

"No. Just for once, I would like to be the one who decides."

Conner rapped Skye's scaly withers with his knuckles. "Once we clear the castle and are deep in the mountains, you can decide how fast to fly. How's that?" Conner waved farewell to Layna and Kriston.

"So much better." Skye catapulted into the air. With each powerful stroke of the dragon's wings, Conner's body jerked upward, then back down. His stomach lurched, his knuckles white on the saddle grips. Skye was being cantankerous, but the dragon wasn't going to have the upper hand. Conner swallowed hard and closed his eyes, mustering the perseverance to get to Elmsdorf without losing his breakfast.

A Discussion of Marriage

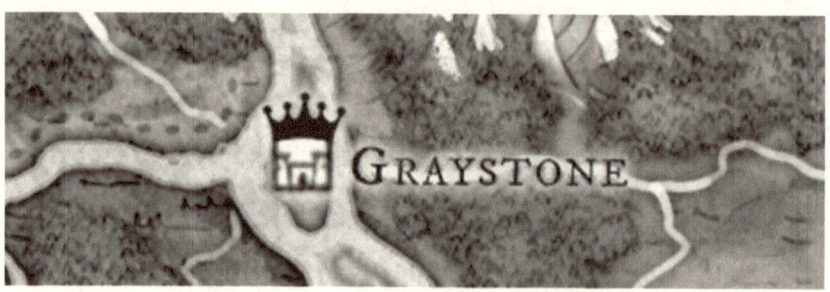

Veressa took a slow breath, releasing some of her stewing tension. She had received word from General Grimwaldt that he had urgent news he needed to share with her and the others who had planned Conner's mission. It had been nearly impossible getting Grimmley, Layna, and her father in the queen's reception hall on such short notice without it looking like another planned meeting of conspirators. Annabelle was away, in a discussion with Lady Kyles about starting her grandmaster studies.

"I hate all this chicanery in my own castle," Veressa growled slightly above a whisper. "I am the queen, for Cosmos's sake!"

Grimmley, who had been quietly puffing on his pipe since his arrival, lifted his head to say something when the door to the chamber swung wide. General Grimwaldt strode in.

Veressa waited for the general to close the door. "Please, General Grimwaldt, for all our sakes, make this quick."

"I will do my best, Majesty." Grimwaldt took a breath, then dove in. "Last night, I was called to attend an unscheduled meeting of the War Council."

"Unscheduled?" Veressa asked.

"I was not told the purpose of the meeting prior to my arrival. It appears there is a growing minority on the council who do not appreciate the time you are taking to deliberate the matter of the proclamation of war."

"Is that so?" Veressa's cheeks burn. Antilles gently rubbed his side along the back of her leg, purring loudly, and she relaxed. "And what reason did these council members offer for calling such a surreptitious meeting?"

"Reason?" Grimwaldt nearly snorted the word, then waved a thick hand as if to rid himself of the absurdity. "They offered nothing new, Majesty, just a rehashing of the same tired worries. Fear that Anarchists are amassing forces along the Borderlands for an all-out invasion of the realms—"

"Even though our reliable spies have reported no evidence of this?" Layna asked.

"I argued that point," Grimwaldt said. "But they do not want to be distracted by trivial things like facts. They also reiterated the need for time to prepare for war. Apparently, they have the support of the duchess in this endeavor."

"Mariette?" Although Veressa's aunt Mariette was next in line for the throne of Griffinrock, she had never shown much interest in affairs of the realm. In the wake of Izadora's assassination, Mariette had made it clear that she expected Veressa to declare war on the Anarchists. "She has no business talking with the War Council. What kind of support could she offer?"

"That I can't say, Majesty." Grimwaldt moved his bulky frame about the room, becoming more agitated with each word. "Of course, I reminded them that the queen has given the orders substantial leeway to begin preparations without a formal proclamation. They even had the insolence to suggest that the people might lose interest in supporting a war if we do not act quickly enough."

"I assume that you are telling us this because you were unsuccessful in diverting their charge," Veressa stated, her eyes tracking the large man around the small room. Her own worries knotted the center of her stomach.

The general grunted. "I reiterated to them that the mission of the War Council is to offer the queen guidance, not pressure, and that only the queen can make the proclamation. I would say that I bought you a little more time, but not much. Once they have a majority of the council on their side ..."

"I have a good mind to call them all here—" Veressa started, her fists at her side.

"Thank you, General, for doing what you could," Layna said clearly over the queen.

Veressa flexed her hands, then pressed a clammy palm to her forehead. She was shaking, but whether from anger or doubt in her ability to rule she could not tell. She hated that all this was coming down on her right after the two she relied on most in all of Gaia had left her to deal with it. "Yes, General, I appreciate all you are doing, especially given the circumstances we have placed you in."

"It will always be my honor to serve you, my queen," Grimwaldt bowed low.

Grimmley cleared his throat. "General, can you at least share with us who seems to be leading this effort to coerce the queen into action?"

Grimwaldt pressed his lips together for a moment, then responded. "Grandmaster Ranger Lanchus Lendfeather."

Layna sat up at this. "Now that is interesting. There is something I have found puzzling about that man's presence on the War Council. Lendfeather is infamous for his self-serving ruthlessness and cunning ways, even among those high in my own order. That is a very dangerous personality to have on a War Council. Lady Kyles prefers situations she can control ... or at least predict. So why risk personal embarrassment in choosing a man who offers her neither as a representative of the order?"

Grimmley grunted, bobbing his head as he listened to Layna. "Rangers have their own form of currency. They call them debts and marks. It is possible that a Ranger of high standing could be given a seat on the War Council if he were to call in a mark."

"A very expensive mark," Layna amended.

"But why?" Veressa asked. "What does he have to gain?" While those around the table mulled over the question, Veressa recalled how Lady Kyles, council chair of the Rangers Order, had given Annabelle permission to covertly continue Veressa's training into advanced Ranger skills. *Debts and marks*, she thought. She swallowed hard. Annabelle had tried to warn her that one day Kyles might come calling for payment on that debt. But she had ignored her dear friend and protector's warning, abandoning prudence for the opportunity to learn the skills of a Ranger. Now, as she thought back on that day not long ago, the demands she had placed on Annabelle seemed ... rash.

Jonath's voice drew Veressa back to the conversation. "I think I have a partial answer to Lendfeather's motives."

"Father?" Veressa asked.

"On the morning of Midsummer's Night, I received an urgent request from the College of Mystics to attend the observance of a 'momentous event' that was to take place later that day. And while the Mystic Oracles did not know what that event was, they were able to divine its location—just west of Dreadcreek and north of Cravenrock. When I dismissed Annabelle as your protector, Veressa, I was told she would be reassigned to Dreadcreek. So I took advantage of the opportunity to dispatch with her a letter to Dreadcreek's commander, Lendfeather, in which I requested his assistance in uncovering any information he could turn up regarding this event."

Conner gasped. "That is about where and when I bonded with Skye."

Jonath stared back. "Yes, Conner. Your bonding was that momentous event." He turned his gaze on those around the table. "I needed the petition to be private, so I offered Lendfeather my *personal* debt of gratitude if he were able to uncover any news."

Grimmley grumbled under his breath as he bit on his pipe. "Well, as I said, Rangers trade in debts. It would seem Lendfeather has set his sights on a very valuable prize. And it seems that prize can only be obtained with a declaration of war."

Jonath's chin drooped to his chest as he wrung his hands. "I am sorry I made such a mess of things."

"On the contrary, my king," Layna argued. "Your personal letter inspired Lendfeather to organize a scouting party, led by our very own Ranger Annabelle Loris—a party that ultimately arrived at Dragongarde just in time to assist in Conner's escape so that he could fly here to Graystone and save your daughter from being forever bound to an Anarchist Champion spy. I would say in the grander scheme, you did what was needed."

Jonath gave Layna a kind smile.

"There is one more thing about Lendfeather," Grimwaldt interjected. "When it became clear that I was backing him into a corner, he suggested that he had a backup strategy if he was unsuccessful in convincing the queen to sign the proclamation in quick order."

Layna exchanged a troubled glance with Grimmley. "Well, that sounds ominous. Of course, it might be only bluster from an angry, cornered brute."

"Maybe," Grimwaldt shot back. "However, he does not strike me as someone who deals in idle threats."

Veressa did not doubt the general's troubling insight that Lendfeather had a backup plan. Her mind worked feverishly to find some way through the tangled maze.

Grimmley's scratchy voice drew her back. "I would say it is time our new queen had another parley with the king of Elvenstein to ... shore up that crown's dithering support for war."

Layna glanced sidelong at Grimmley. "What are you talking about? King Friedrick has given his complete backing ..." Catching herself, she rocked forward, her eyes brightening. "That's brilliant, Grimmley! It would be truly unfortunate if the king were to reconsider his position on the proclamation since Queen Veressa has shown no real interest in a marriage with his son, Prince Camion."

Veressa was starting to restate her lack of interest in an arranged marriage when she caught on. The War Council could not pressure her if she was away on an errand vital to the war efforts.

Grimwaldt drummed thick fingers on the table, his eyes rolling to the ceiling. "It is a three-day journey to Charmwell. You would, of course, need several days to deliberate with Friedrick over his position before returning home. That would give your young Champion a week to complete his quest. That may not be enough, but at this point, every day gained is important."

Veressa did not like the thought of another summit with King Friedrick. She was not fond of his attitude toward women. But, then again, it could not be worse than having to deal with the War Council. "Well, father, you *have* been pushing me to consider an arranged marriage with the king of Elvenstein's youngest son."

The king pursed his lips. But he also grew in stature as he squared his shoulders. For perhaps the first time since Izadora's death, the old wily sparkle returned to his eyes. With a nod, he replied, "We leave tonight under the cloak of darkness. Lendfeather can storm about for a few days trying to uncover where you disappeared to."

Shortly after departing the queen's reception hall, Layna found Grimmley in his temporary quarters at Graystone. She had come to him to share a decision she had reached. But she wanted to cover a few other things first.

"I must say I was a bit surprised our young pupil took this quest," she started as she slipped into the wooden chair next to his unkempt bed. "I was fully prepared to set aside my own investigation and take up the mantle. The thought that there is another ..." She let Grimmley fill in the rest. "Some part of me really wanted to go talk to this dragon."

Grimmley sighed from his chair, where he had been scribing potion labels. An array of glass vials filled the table under the narrow window where midday light streamed through. "Well, I, for one, am glad he stepped forward."

Layna snorted her surprise. "Then why did you argue against it?"

"I needed to be sure he understood the danger he was stepping into."

Layna could still see Conner standing tall in the queen's chamber demanding he be the one to go on the quest, an unfettered glint of independence in his eye. She had never seen him so ... decisive. "He is changing, Grimmley. Not that long ago, he would have looked to you for guidance. And then taken it. He is seeking his own path now."

The Shaman sighed. "I know." He rubbed at the ink smudge along his index finger. Then he glanced over, his lips arching upward at the ends. "You should have seen how he handled those two Dons, demanding they hand over the Necromancer," he said with a twinkle in his eyes. "I worry he will return even more changed."

Layna cocked her head forward, looking at Grimmley below furrowed brow. "We agreed that was what he needed."

Grimmley pressed his lower lip firmly to the other. "It doesn't make it easier. I have trained a lot of students, Layna, and cared for them all. But this lad is special."

The barred owl agreed with a quick hoot, then winked at her Shaman bond.

Layna reached out and lightly placed her hand on his thin shoulder. "I know, Grimmley. All the more reason we should let him go."

After an awkward pause, she rose and stepped to the door. "Well, I plan to use this time while Conner and the queen are away. Horasius needs to stretch his legs. I will be departing within the hour for Darmascus. If I reach the city day after tomorrow, I should have enough time to find some answers to the questions we discussed."

Grimmley took a deep breath. "And I have been thinking it has been too many years since I visited Moonslayer Monastery. Maybe I will uncover something at the monastery about our old Shaman friend ... assuming those crotchety old Paladinian Clerics let me sift through their library."

"Okay, Grimmley, but don't go digging where you might find more than you intend."

Grimmley waved his arm her way. "I'll be cautious, Layna."

"Then let's meet back at your home, then, in ten days' time. Hopefully, by then we will have something meaningful to share.

Bloodbond

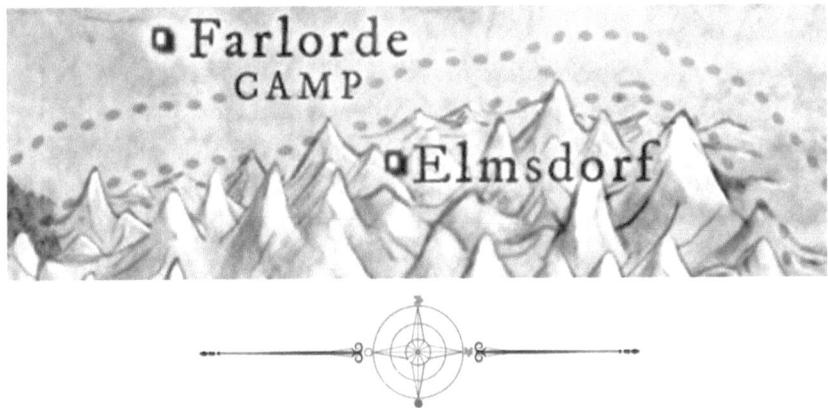

Skye was passing over the snow-capped mountains before Conner broke the long silence. "You are noticeably quiet considering I may be returning with another dragon-bonded human," he shouted over the wind. He needed a diversion from the incessant gale chilling him to the bone. Hemera was nearly overhead, and by Conner's best guess, they were due south of Dragongarde, which put them halfway to Elmsdorf. "I expected more enthusiasm from you."

Skye snorted back.

"At least you will have another of your kind to commiserate with while dealing with all us 'small bipedal bores.'"

"If the dragon you seek is a Cloudbender, then I will likely know him. If he is of another family ... well, nothing of interest there."

Conner searched Skye's flowing spectrum of emotions, which covered about everything except curiosity. Conner had accepted the stunning revelation that there was another dragon-bonded human. Now, questions bubbled to the surface in an incessant stream—questions that demanded answers. Was this dragon-bonded person anything like him? Did he also struggle with being bonded with a dragon? Did he constantly argue with his dragon bond? And, maybe more than anything, what might it mean that this bonded pair was from the Anarchic Lands? "I don't get it. Why wouldn't you be intrigued by a dragon from one of the other families?"

"According to our dragonsongs, when the Ancients escaped the Shaman god Shazarack, the four families fled in different directions. Since then, the dragon families have never mixed—except for the time of your first Dragonbonded." A few powerful flaps of his wings later, Skye added, "It seems that is about to change again. With our luck, it will be a dinky and feeble wyvern."

"Okay, but he is still another of your kind."

"Bipeds called us all dragons, but it is said we have more differences than we are alike. It really is quite simple. If he is not a Cloudbender, then he is not another of my kind." Skye must have sensed that his explanation did not help, so he tried again. "Our early dragonsongs say that each family came from a different creature. Cloudbenders were created from pythons. Mountainshakers from rattlesnakes. And so on. Maybe that has something to do with it."

Late that afternoon, Conner spied a rocky, double-peaked mountain along the northern fringe of the mountain range. The snow-covered western peak rose high above the rocky eastern peak, the shape Ranger Loris had described to look for. He heeled Skye to take a closer look. Skye dipped lower and wove over a narrow trail snaking north toward the mountain. They drew nearer, and Conner made out a large oval ledge along the upper region of the mountain's southern section. In the very center of the rocky ledge rose a tall, thin monolith like a massive spike. "That's Elmsdorf!" he shouted, excitement competing with the howling wind.

Just as Ranger Loris had recounted, long bridges to the south and east spanned a great chasm shrouded in afternoon mist and thick, green vegetation. The trail they had followed north continued past the eastern bridge, carving a meandering path farther to the east before vanishing over the next rise. A hundred or more round hollows pock-marked the smooth rock surface above the terrace, connected by a series of stairs and cascading waterfalls. Bushy plants with late-summer blooms and colorful fruits filled the rocky gaps. The caverns were reminiscent of the labyrinth of exit points along the northern vertical face of Dragongarde, those carved by the bonds of the first Dragonbonded.

"Do you suppose those were made by dragons?" Conner asked, pointing toward the cavern entrances.

"The shapes of the holes have similarities to a dragon home. But these were sculpted long before dragons existed. However, I sense a number of dragon-hewn caves off to the east. Dragons lived near here once."

Conner was not sure how Skye would know this. But his bond knew things that could not easily be explained. "Cloudbenders?" Conner asked, his interest piqued.

Skye craned his head around to eye Conner. "No," he said flatly.

Village Alpslanders spilled out from the hollows along the face of the mountain, shouting and pointing up as Skye spiraled over the large, rocky terrace. Looking for a safe place to land, Skye banked hard to the right and dropped like a stone. With a quick twist of his wings, he settled between the tall spike and the bridge extending over the deep ravine to the east.

Conner did not want the villagers to interpret any action he took as aggression, so he climbed down and waited next to Skye. A group of men and women gathered near the lower cave entrances and came toward him. Each was well-built, layered in pelts, leather, and roughly hewn steel. And each wore a thick sword strapped to their back. He sensed his bond's sudden inquisitiveness and glanced back to find Skye's snout nearly touching the stone spike at the center of the terraced yard. "Why are you looking at that?"

"Because this structure is very similar to one at the top of my island home," Skye replied with a touch of irritation.

Conner gave the obelisk his brief attention. Eerie faces of scowling men and women had been carved and painted over the entire structure extending over twenty paces into the sky. The obelisk looked incongruous with the beauty of the village gardens and landscaping. "You mean there is more than one of these?" he asked, repulsed by the ugly stone pillar.

Before Conner added any further critique, a deep voice drew his attention. "I am Morgas Terranus, tomal of Elmsdorf," said a big, burly man with a large nose and long, flowing brown hair. He waved at the large, white wolf pressed against his thigh. "This is Valmer."

"May the mountains always be the bedrock of your strength," Conner said as Ranger Loris had instructed. "And I am—"

"Conner Stonefield of the Eastlands region," the tomal completed, then smiled at Conner's surprised expression. "I am sure you do not recall our first meeting."

Movement drew Conner's eye to a tall woman with braided blond hair and a husky gray wolf. He stood in shock. He doubted he would ever forget the woman who had captured and bound him the night after his bonding—on Midsummer's Night. "Pallia Aldmar and Galven," he said hesitantly, unsure where this would go. He placed his forearm across his chest and tipped forward in a greeting of deep respect among Alpslanders. "I am sorry that our first parting was not on the best of terms." He studied the big man beside her, and the pieces fell into place. "The day I escaped Cravenrock. You were the leader of the group tasked with bringing me back." More memories came to him, fitting the pieces together. "And you were the one at the top of Dragongarde who called to me before I flew away for Graystone. As I recall, you needed to tell me something?"

A deep baritone chuckle sprouted from the big tomal's chest. "You do recall!"

The ends of Pallia's lips turned up as her gaze tilted up to the large man. "I told you he was a smart knabe."

Morgas folded his thick arms over his chest, his bulky legs spread wide. "Yes, I wanted to warn you about Lacerus, the Assassin in Cravenrock, and his continued desires to apprehend you." Morgas pointed toward the black dragon still sniffing the obelisk. "Now I understand why."

The tomal's words were not the complete tale. Lacerus had sent Morgas and his small band after Conner the day *before* he'd bonded with Skye. How could Lacerus have known what he would bond with? Or was there some other reason, one that put him ... and maybe the queen ... in grave peril? Another memory came to him, one he would never forget, of the nightmare he'd had about Lacerus. Shortly after bonding, he and Skye had embarked on their journey to find Grimmley, to have him break their bond. Conner had imagined being one of the great Dragonbonded when, in that dream, he spied the hooded Assassin riding toward him on an ebony warhorse. He had tried to run in terror from the black-cloaked Anarchist. Had the dream been a forewarning of something still coming for him? He shivered, a chill slithering down his spine.

"Is that why you have come here? If so, then I cannot say more about it." The tomal's expression darkened. "The Assassin Lacerus prefers keeping his secrets exceptionally close."

Conner swallowed hard at the words. *Great*, he thought, pushing the angst away. He needed to focus if his mission was to be successful. "No, Tomal. I have come seeking your assistance in a critical matter."

Morgas diverted his eyes to the villagers gathered behind him. "You wish to enter into a bloodbond?"

Conner held his breath, then nodded stiffly, unsure what would happen next. As Annabelle had explained, a bloodbond was the foundation for all relationships between Alpslanders. An acceptance of mutual kinship, a bloodbond was not entered into without thorough deliberation and exhaustive bargaining between the parties.

"Very well, Conner Stonefield of the Eastlands. Let us retire to my home so that we can parley this agreement in private."

Conner returned to Skye and popped the buckle that held the saddle's girth. "I will talk to this man while you hunt," he said as he slid the saddle from Skye's back. "Will you fly home tonight?"

"I will stay close until morning. My home is a long flight over the Antaric Sea."

Suddenly, Conner felt light-headed. If negotiations with the village tomal did not go well, he would have to return to Graystone. It would take many days before he could report that his mission to the Anarchic Lands had failed.

Conner patted Skye's shoulder, then, taking a deep breath, trailed the tomal and his wife toward one of the cavern entrances.

Conner waited, seated at the table, while Pallia brought out a clay pitcher of water and a bowl of colorful cut fruit gleaming with sweet nectar. He had not eaten since breakfast, so the freshly cut produce looked like a banquet. He gestured at her round midsection. "Your first?"

Pallia brushed her fingers across her stomach. "She is." Pallia said softly. "Conner, I wish to apologize for the way I treated you the first time we met. I ..."

Conner shrugged. "There is nothing to apologize for, Pallia. You were doing what you thought right."

Morgas, who sat across from Conner, sizing him up since they had entered, waved at the bowl. "Help yourself, Conner Stonefield. You look like you have traveled far."

Conner forced his hand to move slowly so it did not look like he was snatching the food. "We left Graystone at first light," he said before biting into the most delicious pear he had ever tasted.

Amazement passed over Morgas's face and then was gone. He poured water into three clay cups. "Tell me of this critical matter with which you need assistance."

Annabelle had instructed Conner that he should share everything with Morgas if he had any hope of gaining his assistance. The art, she insisted, was knowing when to share things. "I need someone to guide me deep into the Anarchic Lands."

Morgas rocked back. "Conner, I was raised and trained to be a spy by the Anarchic orders. The fact that you are here looking for a guide to take you into their lands means you knew that already. However, my days of spying ended when I betrayed my liege, the Assassin Lacerus, and refused to bring you back to Cravenrock." The big man reached over and placed his large hand on Pallia's stomach. "My responsibilities are here, as village tomal, husband, and father."

Conner shook his head while he chewed, then swallowed. "I am not going there to spy. At least, it is not one of the usual missions."

The skin around Morgas's eyes crinkled. "Then why do you wish to travel there?"

"As you may know, the Harmonic Realms are likely to declare war on the Anarchic Lands soon. The balance of power between the two sides will sway the outcome." Conner waited until Morgas gestured for him to go on. "There is another like me living near a village called Xylor. I must find this person ... and his dragon ... and convince them to return with me to Dragongarde before the Anarchic orders find them."

Pallia's eyes widened. Tensing, she slid her hand on top of Morgas's, pressing it tight against her belly. "May I ask how you heard of this?"

"My preceptor received a message yesterday from a Harmonic spy living in the Anarchic region. Both he and the king swear to the message's authenticity."

Morgas and Pallia exchanged anxious glances.

"Tomal," Conner said. "I would prefer not to fight this human and his dragon. Yet I fear it may come to that if the Anarchic orders get to him before I do. Speed is of the essence. That is why I convinced my new queen that I am the one for this mission."

Morgas took a deep breath. "And you have a plan for how to extract them?"

"We devised a story that I am a Gorgonian heading east on my bonding trek. Ranger Loris suggested you pose as my minder while guiding me to Xylor, where this other dragon-bonded human lives. Once I find him, I will convince him to come back with me." Conner chewed on his lower lip for a moment. He sensed Morgas was not impressed by the scheme. "But this plan only works with your assistance. That is why I seek a bloodbond."

A long pause followed. Finally, Morgas stared at Pallia, who tilted her head forward. "I will be your … minder," he said.

Conner jerked his head back. Layna and Annabelle had spent hours drilling him on how to properly conduct bloodbond negotiations with Alpslanders. And out of the many simulations the two ordermen had made him practice, outright agreement was not one of them. What was he to think of this? Was Morgas's response some kind of ploy to throw him off his objective? Maybe to encourage him to give away more about the mission than he intended? He opened his mouth several times, then finally clamped it shut before Morgas thought him daft.

Morgas smiled. "Not what you expected?"

"No," Conner said cautiously. "May I ask why you are agreeing?"

"It would be easier to understand if we showed you." Morgas took a deep breath as if a great undertaking was about to begin. "Tonight, we celebrate the dragons' return."

That night, Conner sat cross-legged before an enormous bonfire that eradicated the cold that had seeped into his bones during his long flight to Elmsdorf. His stomach was full of elk meat, vegetables, and a pudding made with the paste of a sweet orange fruit. He watched as a woman danced and spun around the fire to the pulsing beat of several large wooden drums. A shiny black cloak covered her hunched back. "The dance is amazing," he shouted above the throbbing noise.

Morgas leaned closer so that he could be heard. "She is telling a story, Conner," he shouted back, then noted Conner's inquisitive expression. "A century before the Great War, our village ancestors saw strange phenomena. At night, the mountains pulsed with an eerie blue light. At times, the strobing lights were so radiant, they drowned out the blanket of stars. Scouts were sent to unearth the source of this aberration. But none returned to share what they learned. So, the tomal decreed that all were to stay clear of any mountains glowing thus. Shortly after this, villagers began sighting large, winged creatures. They were named dragons from myths born from another place and era. It took a long time, but Alpslanders and dragons learned to live here in peace."

"Skye told me there are caves near the village carved by dragons. But they are now uninhabited?"

"Yes," Morgas answered. "The dragons simply vanished at the end of the Great War. Nighttime skies returned to darkness. It was the last time Elmsdorf saw a dragon. That is, until you arrived this afternoon." Morgas held his hands before him, then rubbed them together. "Alpslanders are a people steeped in symbolism and auguries. For five hundred years, our ancestors passed down the foreshadowing that dragons would return one day. And when that happened, we would be given a chance to atone for our past."

"I don't understand. What do you have to atone for?"

The firelight blazed in Morgas's eyes. "This is no time to exhume such past deeds. This is a celebration for what lies ahead."

"And what exactly is ahead?"

Morgas studied the bright stars sprinkled between the white summits that ate most of the horizon, then turned Conner with an intensity that made him draw back. "A correction of sorts. Much needs to be righted. My bloodbond with you this day is a solatium of sorts, the first of many, I fear." Conner hoped Morgas would say more, but the tomal rose and dusted himself off. "Let us not speak more of this tonight, Dragonbonded. Enjoy this evening." He signaled a redheaded girl who had been eying Conner at a distance all evening. "Dance with Helda," Morgas commanded as the girl ran forward and snatched Conner by the arm, pulling him from his cushioned seat. "With Hemera's first glow, we begin our journey into the Anarchic Lands."

Conner gave in to Helda's persistence, letting her drag him toward the fire, where youths swirled and shouted. In a far recess of his mind, he sensed Skye to the east, sleeping in one of the dragon caves, his belly stuffed with the catch from his evening hunt. Yes, tomorrow, Skye would fly away, and Conner would be without his guardian, his crutch. But tonight, he let go and rode on the back of the dragon's contentment. They danced, the mingling of gyrating bodies casting ghostly silhouettes across the vertical rocky face of Elmsdorf. The rhythmic pounding of the drums, with their seductive call, drew him deeper.

Conner joined in on the villagers' celebrations. He had not felt so free since the day he'd left home on his Calling. And for the first time in a very long while, he was content.

Into the Anarchic Lands

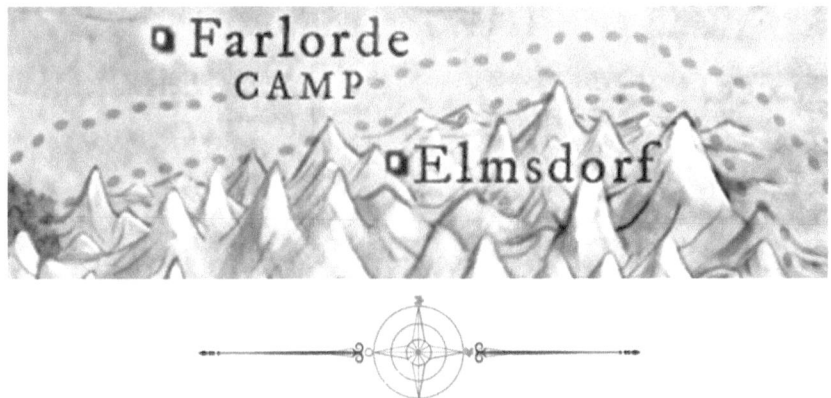

Conner awoke sore from his long flight to Elmsdorf the previous day and the long night he'd spent dancing. Still, he surprised himself when he rolled from his bedroll with an energy he had not felt in a fortnight. Though his quest would be highly dangerous, he felt a great sense of excitement about the days ahead. Gone were the pressures of protecting a queen, learning under his preceptors' fierce tutelage, and, most of all, having to keep secrets from everyone. With beams of morning light flooding past the crevices of the hide draped over his small bedchamber's portal, he dressed in the tawny skins and summer furs that had been left at the entrance sometime during the night. The clothes were not that different from those the Elmsdorf villagers wore, just thinner hides and furs. Conner then stowed his Graystone clothing, Champion's amulet, and Skye's saddle in the back corner of the room as Morgas had suggested, assuring him that the villagers would protect his items with their lives if they must.

Conner flipped back the hide and stepped out into the cool morning breeze. The smell of smoke and boiled vegetables assailed his nostrils.

Skye was back from his flight into the mountains nearby, sniffing the tall monolith again.

"Well, don't you look as fresh as a sprouting pansy," Conner said as he crossed the large, flat ledge to the structure.

Skye bobbed his head. "I forgot how much better I sleep in the mountains. The cave I found offered the perfect habitat for listening to the sounds of Gaia. And you? Are you ready for your frolic into the Anarchic Lands?"

Conner wanted to quibble over his bond's choice of words—there was nothing playful in what he was about to do—but knew Skye would not understand. He raised his arms and turned. "Just another Gorgonian clansman on his Calling trek across the northern plains."

Skye snort-sniffed. "I would have thought one Calling was enough, especially considering what we endured those first few days after bonding."

Conner folded his arms across his chest and inspected his bond. "Yes, well, given how my first trek turned out, I thought I would have another go at it."

"So, you are still wishing you had a small, fur-shedding creature for a bond?"

Conner chuckled. The day he told Grimmley that he should have a small, friendly bond felt like a lifetime ago. "No, Skye. You're stuck with me now."

Skye's head levitated upward as it wiggled side to side. "Well, not for several days anyway." Then, just as quick, his head dropped back down. The dragon glared at Conner with one blazing blue eye. "Conner, if you ever need me, you remember how to send a signal?"

If Conner got himself into so much danger that he needed a dragon's assistance, he doubted Skye would reach him in time. But no need to tell the dragon that. He patted Skye's scaly chin, mindful of a few spikes sprouting along his jawline. "Yes, Skye. Just like we agreed at the Shamans' temple."

Skye continued to stare at him.

"Go ahead. My guide will keep me safe until we reach Xylor. Besides, he looks impatient enough to bite a chunk from his longsword."

Skye snorted. "Soon, then." The dragon did not wait for a reply. In one graceful motion, he leaped into the sky, glided over the ridge to the west, and was gone.

The tromp of heavy-soled boots drew Conner's attention. He turned to find Morgas beside him.

Morgas inspected Conner's dress, then adjusted the sword straps across his shoulders. "We will need most of Hemera's light if we are to reach the foot of the mountains before day's end."

Conner said nothing. He was already accustomed to the tomal's directness, which he found refreshing after dealing with all the high-ranking ordermen slinking about Graystone Castle. He followed the tomal to one of the fires, where the two ate their fill of root vegetables in thick stew. Morgas did not speak, and when he was finished, he rose and slid his massive sword into the sheath strapped to his back. The tomal led the way east where a small crowd of villagers had gathered at the base of the bridge. As Morgas passed, each reached out and brushed their fingers across Morgas's bare arms. "May the mountains guide your step, Tomal," many whispered. Occasionally, Morgas returned their touch.

Conner was not sure what to expect, but the villagers repeated the same ritual of wishing him safe travels as he stepped through. He nodded back. Helda, the redhead he had danced with through the evening, waited at the foot of the bridge. "May the mountains guide your step, Dragonbonded," she said with a smile, lightly touching his shoulder.

From the other side of the bridge, Conner glanced behind. The villagers had dispersed, returning to their gardening and preparations for the day.

The rest of the morning he jogged behind Morgas in contemplative silence. The trail his guide had chosen took them toward the mountain east of Elmsdorf. Near the summit, they entered a narrow pass that shrouded the bright sky above. The air was light and cold. Overhead, ice hung like carrots, sparkling like crystals from a narrow shaft of light ahead. Conner pulled his light clothing around his shoulders and chest.

Under Morgas's blistering pace, the two conquered their second summit by noon. They soon reached a crossroads, where they stopped for a midday meal. Conner's clothes were soaked with sweat, but his spirits were anything but dampened. His worries from his life back in Graystone were receding. He pressed his back against the side of the pass wall and chewed his rations, giving him time to contemplate what Annabelle and Layna had told him of the Anarchic people. Some of what they'd said did not seem possible. "Do you know anything about this village we are looking for?" Conner asked between bites.

"Xylor?" Morgas asked, then shrugged. "I know of it. Like most Dristonians, they are a peaceful band living near the River Est. They are known to many as the Tree People."

"Why is that?"

"They attend to the last remaining forest within their clan's domain. It is said that there are ancient oaks a thousand paces tall and then some. Those I have met who have seen it say they will never forget such a wondrous sight."

After the two finished their hasty meal, Morgas stuffed the remains of his food into his backpack and pointed down the trail that would take them over their third mountain. "We will pick up the pace from here. I would prefer we are out of the mountains before we set up camp."

Conner gazed at the other trail veering downhill to the north. "Why not head out of the mountains from here? Wouldn't we be faster crossing the plains from there?"

"We could, but I want to stay away from Gorgonian territories." Morgas sized up Conner, then adjusted the boy's sword for the third time that day. "You might pass as Gorgonian to those in Dristonia, but I would prefer not testing your skills if we were to happen upon a Gorgonian hunting party." Morgas darted up the eastern trail, ending any further debate Conner might offer.

Through the afternoon, Morgas showed no signs of slowing, nor any desire to converse. Conner had always thought himself a fast runner. But as he ran, he thought back to the night after fleeing Cravenrock. Morgas and his crew had chased him, and, no matter how fast Conner ran, he could not shake them. In fact, Morgas and Pallia had caught up with him in a day and a half!

Morgas stopped so abruptly that Conner nearly ran into the back of the big man.

"We are near the eastern border of Gorgonian territory. This trail," Morgas jabbed his left arm to the north, "will drop us out onto the Dristonian plains." With legs spread and arms folded, Morgas stared down at him. "Conner, I say this here because I want you to be sure you understand. Within an hour, we cross the Borderlands and into the Anarchic Lands. From here on, you must keep your wits about you. A single mistake is all that is needed to put *both* our lives in jeopardy. Is that clear?"

"Yes."

Morgas grinned, a glimmer of excitement in his eye. "Then let us go into the Anarchic Lands."

That night, Conner huddled before a modest fire, watching Morgas stir the soup he had made in a small tin pot. The meager warmth offered little relief from the cramps in his legs.

"Where did you learn about Anarchists?" Morgas asked as he bent forward to taste the green liquid.

"At Graystone. Ranger Loris spent the better part of an evening telling me about Gorgonian lifestyle."

"An entire evening, eh?" Morgas asked, peering at him over the flames. "Whatever she told you about the Anarchic Lands, and anything else you think you know, throw it out. Half of what the Harmonic ordermen think they know of Anarchists is wrong, and the other half is inaccurate enough to get us both killed. This is not about what you know. It is about what you *believe*. You must think and act like a Gorgonian. Does that make sense?"

"Yes."

"Good." He poured some of the steaming liquid into a tin cup and handed it to Conner. "Then tell me, what is the greatest sin?"

Conner buried his nose in the cup and inhaled deep. The aroma of onions and garlic reminded him of his mother's cooking. "Murder," Conner answered.

"Wrong." Morgas sat back and waved his arm at the vast plains to their north. "We have crossed the Borderlands."

Conner pressed his lips together. "Layna told me that breaking a promise is an Anarchist's most heinous act. But she couldn't tell me how breaking a promise was possibly worse than murder. At least, not in a way that made any sense."

Morgas exhaled slowly, turning his eyes away, then glared back. "In your Harmonic land, you have guards and chancellor courts in the cities, Defenders along the roads and byways, sheriffs in the Eastland villages. Here, there is no government, no laws, no regulators. Yet people do not live lawlessly, nor in disorder. They live their lives in mutual respect for one another because their hearts are bound to the Anarchic code."

Conner pulled the half-empty cup of soup from his lips and gulped. "Anarchic code? What is that?"

"It is not a thing that can be described, nor can it be taught, because the code is not about what is known, nor even what is felt." Morgas thumped his chest hard with his fist. "It is what is written on every Anarchist's heart from the time they are born."

Conner gazed deep into the dancing flames. *How does he expect me to act like an Anarchist if I don't know how they live?* He snapped a twig in half and tossed the pieces into the fire.

Morgas broke the silence. "I have been told Eastlanders have little interest in what happens outside their homelands. But your world is no longer of the Eastlands, young Dragonbonded. You should know more about the world in which you live. I will do my best to help you. But I have never been a preceptor."

A moment later, Morgas set his empty cup down and continued. "The Anarchic code is founded on a sacred belief that no one has the right to rule over another. Or maybe better to the point, nature is the authority in life. So Anarchists have an acute disgust for any man's attempt to override such authority. That is why breaking a promise, to be an *oathbreaker*, is to place one's own self-interest above that of another. An oathbreaker is not a sin against another person, but a sin against everything natural, a sin against the Cosmos that created the worlds and set them into motion." Morgas rose and tossed another limb onto the fire. "That is enough for you to consider this night. Sleep on what I have said. Tomorrow, we will pick up from there."

"Then how about a different kind of lesson?" Conner asked.

"What did you have in mind?"

"My best friend was fond of teasing me about needing to learn how to fight. Until I touched Skye, I did not hold much conviction that such skills were needed."

"Your friend is a smart lad."

Conner bit his lower lip, not wanting to say anything ill of Pauli. "I suppose being around Dristonians, we are not likely to get into a fight. But I should at least know how to hold a sword properly if I am to look the part of a Gorgonian."

Morgas chuckled. "I fear if you had to call upon your blade for protection, it would not be a pretty sight. I will instruct you on the basics of Anarchic sword fighting."

"You will?" Conner blinked back. A moment ago, he'd had to twist Morgas's arm to get him to talk about Anarchists. Now, he seemed a little *too* eager to cross blades with him. And given the man's size and build, that was alarming.

"It would be an honor." Morgas reached over his broad shoulder and slid his monstrous sword from its scabbard. "Maybe while you are learning how to deflect the stroke of my steel, we can discuss how you can become a faster runner and better tracker."

Conner slid his own sword from his sheath and mirrored Morgas's stance. "Oh! *That* was Alpslander banter!"

Morgas's gritty smile could be seen in the flicker of firelight. The big man raised his blade before him. "Yes. Now let us see if you are as quick with a sword as you are with your wit." He stepped forward. "Let us begin."

Later that night, Conner lay on his blanket staring up at the stars. Every joint in his legs and arms was stiff. Several blisters along his thumb and palm throbbed. Living at Graystone had made him soft.

But Conner was grateful. Morgas's instructions on Anarchic life had been extremely useful in helping him knit together the pieces of knowledge he had gathered from Annabelle and Layna. For instance, he learned that coppers and other coins were valuable to Harmonics only because they were smithed and backed by the crowns. With no form of government nor rule of law as in the Harmonic Realms, Anarchists had no currency. Not that it mattered. Money would have conflicted with Anarchists' classless society. Anarchists bartered with what they called the "force of oath," which was surprisingly similar to the Alpslanders' bloodbond. He was beginning to see why Anarchists lived in total opposition to Harmonics and their government, currency, and caste society. Even the Anarchic force of oath was antithetical to the web of lies Harmonics liked to spin. No wonder there had been a war, and the two sides remained split half a millennium later.

Conner rolled to his side and stared into the flickering embers of the dying fire, his eyes growing heavy. By the time they reached Xylor, he would be ready, assuming Morgas didn't lose patience with Conner's incessant questions.

The next morning, while they broke down their camp and packed their supplies, Morgas instructed Conner on how to run. As Conner listened to Morgas's coaching about proper posture, arm swing, balance, pushing off with the balls of his feet, even how high to lift his legs, he realized that he had always relied on his strength to run fast. As Morgas explained, his strength had become his weakness. This was a revelation to Conner. He had a lot to learn about many subjects. By the time his pack and sword were strapped to his back, he was excited to put what Morgas had taught him to use.

"Today," Morgas said as he adjusted Conner's sword strap, "we will travel northeast for the better part of Hemera's light. Once we are due west of Xylor, a full day's run maybe, we will cut east, which is the path a Gorgonian on his trek would travel." And with that, they were off.

They had traveled no more than an hour across the grasslands when Morgas came to an abrupt stop. Reaching back, he placed his large palm on Conner's shoulder and dropped to a crouch, pulling Conner down into the tall grass with him.

"What is it?" Conner whispered, craning his head to see around Morgas squatting in front of him. He peeked cautiously over the waving field of brown stalks. Three hundred paces to their left, a black-robed figure rode a speckled gray, cantering along a path intersecting theirs fifty paces ahead. A falcon perched on his extended arm.

"Lacerus," Morgas growled as the rider drew near. His hand involuntarily reached back to grip his sword.

As the black rider neared, his hood bunched about his shoulders, Conner recognized him. The Assassin from Cravenrock. The man in his nightmares riding a black warhorse. Conner ducked back down. Just as it had that night in the catacombs beneath Cravenrock, when he'd stood before Lacerus, his heart raced in his chest. His hands trembled.

A hundred paces from them, the rider reined his horse to a stop.

Conner had heard stories that Assassins could hear a beating heart a mile away. He wiped at sweat burning his eyes. *Please, keep moving. Just ride on,* Conner wished desperately, his eyes squeezed tight. He waited to hear the horse's pounding hooves once more, but the sound never came. *He knows we're here!* He wanted to shout at Morgas to run. But the big man did not move.

In desperation, Conner searched his mind for something, *anything* he could do. In one of his lessons, Layna had tried to teach him how to cast a shielding incantation, similar to the one she used in the queen's reception hall. Of course, the incantation had failed, like all the others he tried. He drew on Water and Fire, and they came to him. Lacerus, like the Ranger Annabelle, used Air and Earth, so the Assassin would not detect the ones Conner held. He recalled the feel of Layna's weave of elementals, the mix of Fire as she bent it about Water, like cloth, interlocking the two into a tight fit. He pushed the elementals outward, imagining that weave forming a blanket over him and Morgas.

Conner peeked up. The black rider, shimmering through the veil of his weave, flicked his left arm high. His falcon bond took flight, rising twenty paces into the air. Spinning in a flurry of feathers, the falcon fanned its wings wide and flew toward them.

Morgas began to draw his sword.

Conner reached up and held his guide's wrist, shaking his head as Morgas stared back.

A moment later, the falcon fluttered past overhead before circling back and returning to the Assassin's arm.

The Assassin cast his eyes about one last time, then heeled his gray forward, riding hard until he disappeared over the horizon to the southeast.

Morgas slid his sword back into its sheath. "I assume I have you to thank for this outcome." He rose, scanning their surroundings. "How did you do that?"

Conner shrugged, as surprised as Morgas. "Something I learned from my preceptor."

Shazarack's Plan

Ousel stepped into Shazarack's dark chamber. "My lord, four ordermen have arrived at the gates requesting an audience with Lord Galan," he announced, gently stroking Helgish's prickly forehead. "It appears the other orders have not yet received word that you have returned to Thanatos or that you have assumed command of the Necromancers Order."

Nartesis rose stiffly from his chair, his fingers pressed against the bump in his breast pocket. "Which orders are in attendance?"

"There are members from the Warlocks, Barbarians, Assassins, and Conjurors Orders, my lord. The Black Knights would not be among them, as they have little interest in the mundane affairs of the orders. Their work is only for the greater glory of the Cosmos."

"Together? You told me ordermen are averse to speaking with those from other orders."

"That *has* been true, my lord. But that changed when the six orders signed the pact."

"What pact? Why have you not told me of this?"

"My Lord. I am only the minister of the academy. Those are matters for the council. Galan told me he would brief you on the inner workings of this agreement."

"Yet he did not. But I cannot be distracted by thoughts of how to solve that problem. And how does our great order contribute to this agreement?"

"We are to build and command a large army of undead for the purpose of protecting our lands in case the Harmonics decide to invade." Ousel hesitated with his finger pressed to his lips. "Maybe these ordermen are here to receive an update on our progress toward that objective."

"So, this is what our Necromancer colleagues have been busy with every night—building a necro-army?" An upcoming Harmonic invasion? Nartesis grew more irritated as he considered that Galan had been keeping all this from him. The divested lord of the order was clearly hoping to be rid of Nartesis before the situation blossomed into a problem.

"How would you like to proceed, my lord?"

Nartesis took a hollow breath. "Escort our guests to the reception chamber." The spark of an idea came to him, and he raised his withered hand before Ousel departed. "And ask Galan and the council members to join us there."

Ousel opened his mouth with surprise, then swept the look away. "As you command, my lord."

Nartesis shuffled into the reception hall on the heels of several undead guardians. Galan and the Necromancers Council were already there, intermingling and speaking in low tones with the newly arrived guests assembled in the middle of the grand hall.

Nartesis stopped before his guests, a commanding presence despite his bent, shriveled form. He spoke forcefully to all those gathered. "Good day to you all. I am Nartesis Shazarack."

The black-cloaked female Assassin eyed him up and down. "So, reports of the great Lord Shazarack's return hold a ring of truth." She bowed. "I am Master Ozan Bezrah of the Assassins Order. With me are Master Warlock Jakob Gerrick, Master Barbarian Petra Zool, and Master Conjuror Akeem Belameed."

Nartesis nodded to each. "Have you come all this distance to verify reports of my return? Or is there something more you wish to discuss?"

The Barbarian Zool chuckled. "It is so refreshing to meet another orderman who prefers to dispense with formalities. Word of your ... resurrection ... is only the tip of the spear."

"Then maybe this conversation would be best suited while we fill our stomachs?"

"A most excellent idea!" The Warlock Gerrick rubbed his palms together, his bulbous eyes on the display—plates of steaming food and crystal goblets filled with wine, set meticulously along the long, cloth-covered banquet table.

Nartesis stepped to the head of the table before Galan could, then directed the visitors to seats along the far end.

Nartesis sat, impatiently playing with his food until the meal's third course was being brought in. With plates set, he began in earnest, as etiquette dictated. "Given your earlier comments, I assume that you are here to look into the state of our order since my return." He gazed sternly at Galan. "Especially given the pact that our orders have drawn up and sealed with signatures."

Galan shot daggers at Nartesis with his eyes.

"First, Lord Shazarack," Warlock Gerrick declared as he patted his bulging midsection, "please understand that under normal circumstances, we would never impose on the affairs of your order. We are Anarchists. Change is inevitable and thus should be neither constrained nor influenced by those outside. When the Anarchic faction split from the Harmonic orders, our orders agreed that each was responsible for charting its own course ... and for deciding how best to manage its own house." Gerrick took in the Necromancers seated around him. "How you Necromancers decide to tidy your house is not our affair."

"Music to our ears, Gerrick," Nartesis responded with a stiff smile.

Zool cleared his throat. "However, when the fitness of one house directly impacts that of another, concessions must be reached that might force us to do what we would not otherwise do."

Assassin Bezrah smiled thinly. "We realize that you are not from this time, Lord Shazarack, so you may not yet fully appreciate the importance all Anarchists place on pacts struck between parties—guidelines that have bound our society together for five hundred years." She picked up the sharp dinner knife by her plate and absently twirled the blade between her fingers. "To make an oath to another—to promise an act, an item of value, even one's heart in love—is the most sacred of all actions."

The Conjuror Belameed leaned forward. "Breaking an oath is the worst possible offense—worse than lying, stealing, even murder. An oath requires the greatest care and forethought. It is extremely rare that even two orders enter into a pact, and they might labor for years to get it just right."

Zool exhaled hard, fidgeting in his chair. "The point is, each of our councils, including Galan and the Necromancers Council, entered into this pact only after doing our individual due diligence."

Nartesis nodded, then spoke. "All of this helps me understand the society that has blossomed since the expulsion of the crowns from these lands. And I do applaud your ancestors' accomplishments in building a viable society in the vacuum of regal governance." His bony shoulders rose. "However, I was not raised as an Anarchist. No such doctrine or tradition binds me, willingly or otherwise, to honor your ways."

Bezrah placed a hand on Zool's arm before the Barbarian responded. "Do you not value freedom from the tyranny of royalty?"

Belameed finally found a moment his mouth was not stuffed with food to offer his own thoughts. "We are entering into a new age, Lord Shazarack—an age that requires we reassess how the six orders interact. The Harmonics have been relentless in their flagrant violations of the Borderlands, and the chances of a Harmonic invasion grow greater by the day."

Nartesis gazed out the large window to the south, to the hills beyond, fighting off a brewing impatience. Hadn't there always been the likelihood of a Harmonic invasion? He raised a sinewy arm before the Conjuror. "Ordermen, you have had more than enough time to create a glorious world, where skilled ordermen practice their powerful arts, living in sanctuaries filled with students eager to learn, all focused on the betterment of a society for the advancement of all. Imagine my disappointment upon my arrival at what I beheld."

Shazarack took in the silent faces around him, then went on. "As I see it, your orders have had five hundred years to advance your elemental skills and learn how to work together. If the thrill of discovering new powers and abilities has not inspired you to reach greater heights, then the threat of incursion by the remaining realms should have. Now you come to our order's sanctuary, our institute, and tell me that, after all this time, you are ill-prepared to protect your lands without Necromantic assistance?" He scowled at the pathetic lot of delegates. "The orders have become pitifully insipid, driven more by petty, selfish greed than by a common vision. I care no more about protecting those who squander their time and talent than I do about shielding the myopic, weak, or helpless."

The Warlock Gerrick erupted. "We are neither weak nor helpless! Every generation of ordermen has added ever-greater incantations to our pool of knowledge. After fifty generations, we now have at our fingertips an extraordinary repertoire of invocations. My glorious order has acquired the knowledge of more incantations than a single orderman can learn in their entire life."

"Power is not defined by how many conjurations you can chant," Nartesis interrupted. "And power has no value if it is not directed with visionary purpose."

"Our orders are more powerful than they have ever been," Barbarian Zool declared.

"Prove it!" Nartesis barked back. "If there was a weight of truth in your statement, you would not be here, groveling at our feet, threatening to hold me to a promise our order made to protect your institutions. If you truly believe in what you argue, then let us rip up this pact and be done with these talks. Now *that*, Zool, would truly impress me!"

Their silence and downcast eyes would have made him vomit if he'd had anything in his stomach.

Galan, who had been sitting in silence, chimed in. "Ordermen of the Anarchic way. As you can see, your arrival has preempted our internal discourse regarding the pact. However, I assure you that the Necromancers Council speaks as one voice for the order. And we continue to stand behind the pact each of us put to ink. I believe that in time, Lord Shazarack will see the importance of this relationship."

Nartesis slammed his fist on the table. "And I am sure I will not. My position on this matter is final."

Galan's mouth fell open.

Nartesis sat back in his chair, savoring the pleasure of defying a dethroned ruler, especially in open court. "Let me tell you a story. When I was a young man, shortly after I assumed command of my new necromancers order, a group of emissaries was sent by the monarchs of the Seven Realms to find evidence that a secret pact had been drawn up between a number of the fledgling orders of our time. They sat at a table not unlike the one we sit at now. They ate the food I had set before them, and drank the wine we offer you." Nartesis rose, leaned forward, and placed his fisted knuckles on the table. "And when I made it clear I would not bend to their demands, the sanctimonious fools threatened me and my order. Threatened *me*!"

Gerrick sat with his mouth full, no longer chewing. Only Bezrah looked immune to Nartesis's stance, eyebrows raised, a chunk of steak speared to the tip of her knife.

"Do you know what I did?" he asked.

"Do tell, Lord Shazarack," Bezrah said.

"I poisoned them all right where they sat."

The Warlock spat the food he had been chewing back onto his plate. His eyes flashed wild at Nartesis.

In the silence, Bezrah threw back her head and laughed heartily, then, giving Nartesis a knowing wink, bit deep into the steak. "That tale has been told to every Assassin apprentice for half a millennium, Lord Shazarack," she nearly shouted with enthusiasm, blood running down her chin. "I heard it during the first year of my apprenticeship. And I recall thinking, 'Now *that* is a true assassin.'"

Nartesis rocked back on his heels at her words. Of all the things he had done during his life, he wondered if that was the only event he was remembered for. He had never considered himself an assassin, though he'd had many people murdered. He turned his focus on the Necromancers about him. Astonishment painted their faces. "Those of our order care little for killing of any kind. Our interests lie with the vessels that remain behind."

"As I recall," Bezrah said, "after they were poisoned, you returned those emissaries back to the crowns who had sent them ... as undead." She took in the surprise of the delegates around her. "I would say we know now not to make any *impotent* threats."

Nartesis closed his eyes, recalling how his rash actions that day ultimately sparked a war that led to the deaths of thousands, toppling entire orders of his time. "I think you misunderstand the purpose of my tale, Bezrah. I sent them back not as a threat, but as a message to the crowns that they were to leave us alone. Unfortunately, I miscalculated the crowns' response." He straightened and lumbered to one of the windows, then waved those at the table to follow him. He held his arm out to the green valley below. "The crowns of the Seven Realms gathered their entire military might, one great army intent on bringing our rebellious order to heel, and if that was not possible, to rain down total devastation upon us."

"The Army of the Seven Realms," one of the Necromancer council members whispered.

"Yes," Nartesis answered. "The army of ten thousand amassed there, along the far edge of that open field, while here, a hundred men and women stood in defiance, necromancers who had never known combat, who had never killed another human." He gazed on the field below. "For eight nights, the Army of the Seven Realms charged that field. Night churned into day and back to night. And when it became clear the army could not break through our defenses, they called upon your ancestors—rangers and sorcerers, mystics and warriors—all brought to heel like chained, muzzled dogs to do the crown's bidding."

"Now why do I tell you this?" Nartesis asked. But no one spoke. "Because the ordermen who marched alongside the crowns' army, the fledgling sorcerers, rangers, mystics, and other ordermen, had, just a few years before, been the ones who'd signed a pact of cooperation and protection not unlike the one you now argue I am bound to uphold."

He rounded on the assembled delegates. "So do not come *here*," Nartesis shouted, "on this hallowed ground, and lecture *me* about the importance of pacts ... or about the consequences of breaking with them. I lost everything that day—my order, my friends and colleagues ... even my love." It took a moment for him to push back the groundswell of emotions he'd forgotten he had. "As I see it, the pact you speak of was struck before my return. I am not bound to it. Get back on your horses and ride from here. Go back to your orders and tell your councils they will find neither sanctuary nor support within these halls."

Nartesis shambled from the room.

"Shazarack!" Galan shouted behind Nartesis.

Nartesis pivoted on his heel to face the sovereign prince and two other council members moving up the narrow hall. All three wore brooding faces.

"You cannot do this," Galan growled as he stepped forward, his face bright red. "The pact was made between our orders, not between men. It is as unbreakable as steel."

"I've lived long enough to know that everything breaks sooner or later, Galan. Even steel."

Galan pressed closer with a snarl. Nartesis's undead guards seized him by his arms and dragged him back, nearly toppling the two councilmen behind.

"When the other councils hear that you have turned your back on them, our entire order will be ostracized. Without the supplies and materials the other orders provide, we won't survive the winter."

Nartesis snorted. "Then it seems we had better learn how to be self-sufficient. Our order will no longer bow to others for their supplies if it means being forced into agreements that do not benefit us."

One of the councilmen peered over Galan's shoulder. "What will happen when the Anarchic people hear that we are oath breakers? Few will join our ranks."

"Good!" Their pathetic doom-mongering was grating on Nartesis's nerves. "Our ordermen should be driven by a desire for self-fulfillment. If they are not drawn here inspired to do great necromantic works, then they have no business in this place. I don't want such ingrates crowding our halls and eating our food any more than I want them distracting our preceptors from those truly motivated to learn."

"Our people need protection," whimpered the other councilman.

Nartesis glared. "Then go protect them. I will not hold you back. I am sure there are many within these walls who would enjoy sleeping in your cozy chambers, eating the fine foods and wine prepared for you each night." He waited, but when they had nothing to say, he went on. "I didn't think so. Always content to let others do your work, as long as you don't have to get your hands dirty. Now, gentlemen, I am tired, and your feeble arguments are irritating me. As we may no longer be trading with the other orders, I suggest you find something useful to do—weed a garden, tend the goats, pull carts of vegetables to the kitchens. Or return to your rooms and stay out of the way."

Nartesis proceeded to the far end of the hall. As he was stepping into his personal chambers, Galan called out, "Your undead will not protect you forever. Do you hear me? We are not done with this!"

By the time Nartesis arrived at the council chambers, Ousel was there, pacing and wringing his hands. "Confronting Galan in front of the entire council and members of the other orders is very serious, my lord." The minister paused. "And dangerous."

"I do not care at this point if I offend Galan or his incompetent band of acolytes." Still, Nartesis pondered Ousel's warning. Nartesis had successfully deflected the council's incantations at the gates the day he arrived, but he had prepared for that possibility. If Galan and his supporters were to challenge him unprepared, his decrepit body might not withstand drawing upon the elemental forces he would need for his defense. One thing was certain: Galan would continue to get in his way, questioning and undermining his authority, authority he needed to see his vision through.

"I understand that my lord is not from this time and may not fully appreciate the political dynamics at play. But please consider that Galan would never have become sovereign prince without an extensive network of influential people at his side."

"Duly noted. I do appreciate all you do for me, Ousel. Your counsel serves me well. However, meaningful change requires risk. Walls need to come down before I can show our order what resides on the other side. I will not bring a hammer to the job when a wrecking ball is needed."

Ousel nodded. "What about the army we have been assembling? What do you wish to do?"

Nartesis tapped his forefinger on his chair. "Keep adding to the undead ranks, but slow the pace to something more sustainable. I am sure we will find a useful purpose for it soon enough."

Later that night, Ousel led Nartesis down a long series of stairs and to a vault below ground, to a cellar mockingly dubbed the Birthing Chamber. As it turned out, it was the same chamber he and his necromantic colleagues had used to create their order's first necro-army long ago. However, as Nartesis entered the huge cellar, he noted that this arrangement was quite different.

A series of large cages with thick steel bars ran along either side. In the center of each cage, thirty or more in total, stood a waist-high marble slab. Shrouded cadavers lay on many of the slabs, while black-robed Necromancers toiled in various stages of completion to birth a new undead.

"Where do the cadavers come from?" Nartesis asked.

"Thanatos has trade agreements with most of the neighboring villages and towns," Ousel responded as he tucked Helgish in his cloak pocket. "We provide food and certain health services in exchange for their freshly dead."

"Interesting." Nartesis ran his fingers through his thin beard. "In the time after I usurped control of Abbey Newdowns, when Thanatos was a mere dream, we were forced to steal bodies from morgues and graveyards in order to conduct our experiments and advance our knowledge."

"I should mention, my lord, that many of the towns have received news that our order has broken the pact with the other orders. Some now refuse to provide the cadavers we need. Our supplies are running low."

"In time, Ousel, we will be looked upon with great reverence." Nartesis stopped before one of the cells where a young Necromancer named Jesseph stood over the body of an old woman, sprawled across the slab.

Inside the cage, Jesseph inhaled deep, eyes closed, and began. First came a series of incantations to prepare the old woman's body for the summoned spirit, charms that would toughen the skin to steel and endow the old muscles with superhuman strength. Intermixed were a few more that would slow decay and arrest rigor mortis. Once those castings were in place, Jesseph proceeded to the next phase, combining Earth and Fire in a series of atmospheric enchantments that would weaken the barrier between the Physical and Mental planes, then create and sustain a portal through it.

Nartesis watched in silence. While the general process Jesseph used was similar to the one he had developed, the nuances were strikingly different. Already, he noted a number of suggestions he could recommend to enhance the essence of the undead.

With the portal to the Mental plane secured, Jesseph cast several incantations to locate and ensnare a worthy spirit, drew the spirit through the portal into the waiting vessel, and cast several binding incantations to adhere the spirit to the vessel.

Memory spell, Nartesis thought. Do not forget the memory spell.

"*Hemea psychi stereosyndeta,*" Jesseph uttered, then took a step back to examine his work.

Instantly, the woman's eyes snapped open. Her head jerked toward Jesseph. With the speed of an adder, her arms shot out. The creature lifted the poor man, then sent him cartwheeling across the cage. Jesseph's back smashed into the steel rods. He crumpled to the floor and did not move. In a heartbeat, the old woman leaped from the slab and slammed into the cage door, snarling and baying at Nartesis a pace away. The bars groaned and popped as the undead bent her might on breaking through the door.

Sheardra, one of the order's council members, ran across the hallway. She began to send the spirit back to its plane. "*Ourera psychi—*"

"Stop!" Nartesis shouted. "There is no need to waste a perfectly fine body." Gripping his staff hard, he invoked, "*Aerora ousia pagomapsychi.*"

The old woman froze. Calmly, he unbolted and opened the door. Stepping around the unmoving undead, he crouched beside Jesseph.

Jesseph groaned and tried to move, then grimaced, his radius jutting from his forearm. "What happened?"

"Get a stretcher!" Nartesis called to Sheardra, his bony hand pressed against Jesseph's arm. "You forgot a very important ingredient, young man—a memory enchantment. The spirit cannot understand your commands if you do not first link it to the old woman's memories." He chuckled at the young man. "I suspect you will not forget that again."

"No, Supreme Lord."

Nartesis moved to the side as several others assisted Jesseph onto a stretcher. "It appears you are done for the night. After you have mended, Jesseph, come see me. I have a few suggestions on how you can improve your skills."

"Of course, Supreme Lord. I would be honored."

Being a Human's Conscience

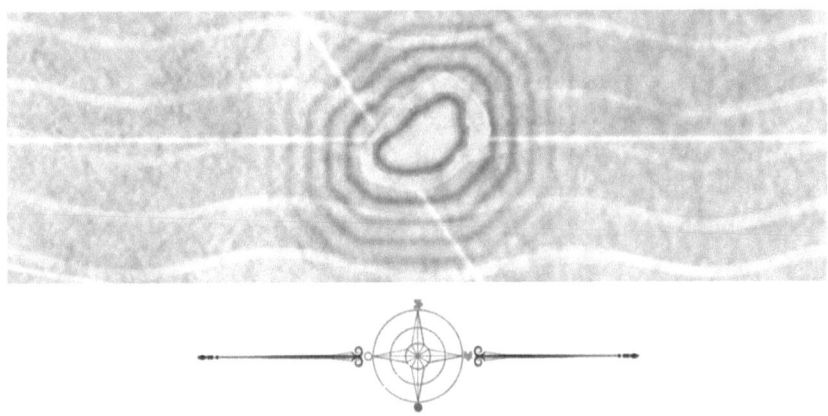

The female dragon snaked past Skye, her blazing blue-green eyes trained on him. "So you are the one who bonded with a human."

Skye's head wiggled higher to get a better look at her over the thick sulfuric steam venting through the shafts to his left. The chamber was hot, filling him with the wonderful sense of home. "I am," he stated, quite proud of himself. He had arrived that morning, and already attracted the attention of several possible mates. He had refused the advances of two younger females desiring his notice because he had become a dragon of some renown, having bonded with a human. An experienced mate was more to his liking—and for sure, would involve less drama. So a female three decades his elder did not bother him.

"Fascinating," she hissed, eyes widening. "And you have spent time around more of these creatures since you bonded?"

Skye released an audible growl before he could put any thoughts to words. "Unfortunately, I have been around too many for far too long. They are lured by living inside rock structures they build, to the point that it is nearly impossible to walk about without stepping on a few."

"Truly fascinating. I never thought there might be so many," she added with a smack. "I suppose with that many, none would notice if a few ... disappeared." She snort-sniffed a hearty laugh. "Have you ever tried one?"

"You mean, *eat* one?" Skye hawked reflexively, unable to embrace the thought of ingesting one of the foul-smelling creatures. "I am not dragork, if that is your concern." *Dragork,* or "two-human-eater," was the name given to an insane dragon—for a dragon would have to be insane to try eating more than one.

"No. Nothing about you concerns me." The female paused long enough to let her sea-blue eyes slip over Skye's sleek form. "But any Cloudbender with half a wit would be highly interested in humans. And not just because of our dragonsong."

The claw along the edge of the female's wing grazed the scales along Skye's haunches, and he inhaled sharply at the prickly sensation spiking up his back.

"I know a few who have attempted to learn more about these creatures," the female went on. "But every time they get close, the creatures scurry away like molerats from a flame."

Skye snorted. "Your friends should consider themselves lucky. The critters are insincere, selfish, and deceitful." Skye realized he had used Conner's tongue to describe the human proclivity to lie and cheat. The dragon tongue had no word for *deceit.* Surprisingly, the female took it all in, likely saving such details for a later conversation. Skye recalled his first encounter with Conner's fiancée, how she ran screaming when he fanned his wings wide in a show of respect. If *deceit* was not challenging enough to explain, he doubted he could ever describe *fear.* "I find nothing interesting about them," he concluded, hoping they could shift to a more appealing topic. Maybe it was time to introduce himself. She was definitely an alluring prospect—intelligent, inquisitive, experienced. He was enjoying her attention.

She swiveled her rear toward him and swished her tail in his face. "And what of this human you have bonded with? What is it like?"

It took Skye a moment to realize she had asked him another question. "It is a male of their kind. I did not like him at first." He considered all that he had endured following their bonding, then snort-sniffed. "But surprisingly, I have grown fond of him. He is intelligent and cares for others of his species." He decided to not discuss Conner's many imperfections until he had addressed *deceit* and *fear.*

The female glanced over her shoulder at him, eyes ablaze with fascination. "They do not all have such qualities?"

"They are all as different as the wildflowers growing along the eastern ridge of our island. Why do you have such a curiosity for these creatures?" She pulled her wings tight to her body and curled up, lounging seductively before him. "My first mate once flew to the lands to the south looking for a new delicacy. While on the hunt, he was assaulted by a flock of these creatures and forced to scorch them all. The effort left him famished, so he ate one. When he returned, he told me of his adventure. He said that if you burn them until they are crispy black on the outside, their insides are quite delicious."

A sudden burst of sickness washed over Skye, and then a deep, rumbling breath drew his attention. Near the entrance, staring at him, was his grandmother, the Ancient Iridescus. Her massive head swiveled on a black neck as thick as Skye's waist. Her eyes were so bright they lit the entire cavern. Unable to fit her body through the portal, she pressed her shoulders against the entrance walls.

Dwarfed by her sheer size, Skye humbled himself before the Ancient, pressing his chest and chin to the rocky floor. "Iridescus."

"Skye-Anyar-Bello. You are to come with me," she commanded, then backed out of the chamber.

Skye shadowed Iridescus back up the long tunnel, where she took one of the larger ventilation shafts leading to the top of their volcanic island home. As he ascended, the rock around him quivered and cracked as Iridescus's massive claws dug into the passage walls. Though Iridescus was huge, she made the climb look easy.

Finally, he emerged from the shaft onto the island's plateau and into Hemera's bright midday light, where Iridescus was waiting for him. The air was fresh here, and already Skye missed the dark caverns beneath, the pungent smell of sulfur and the warm drafts of steam rising from the volcanic pools deep beneath the island. Far below, the strong Antaric winds whipped over the surface of the sea, churning up white foam and surf. Waves, relentless in their assault, crashed and sprayed the island tower's craggy cliffs. Heated by the fissures of molten lava honeycombed deep within the volcanic pillar of stone, steam and ash rose on columns of air up the sheer rocky face. Overhead, wyverns dove and spun through the clouds in a manic game of tag. And in the distance, drakes skimmed the clear blue-green waters, expertly floating over breakers in the hunt for a succulent meal of porpoise.

Skye pointed his snout at the family's sacred totem at the center of their island. "Ancient one, did you know there is a similar totem to the southeast, deep in the mountains?"

Iridescus tilted her head forward. "Only a few Cloudbenders have ever seen any of the other totems."

"There are more?"

"There are four sacred totems, one for each family of dragon. But they were constructed long before the great Shaman Shazarack created us." As if to answer Skye's next question, Iridescus went on. "When we escaped the great Shaman god, each family flew off in different directions, called to their new homes by the sacred totems. This is the totem of Water. The one in the mountains is of Earth."

"That explains why there were dragon caverns near the totem."

"Yes," Iridescus said. "None of that is in our dragonsong. I tell you this because, as one honored with a bond, like your father before you, there may be a time this knowledge will be useful. It is for you alone."

"Of course, Ancient one." Skye bowed.

"I normally do not involve myself in the carnal needs of my offspring, but I would suggest a little prudence around Ormedi-Collius-Azelda."

"The female I was with?"

Iridescus cranked her head sideways in a show of concern. "She is dragork, Skye-Anyar-Bello. It would be hard to imagine a romance with such a female working given your situation."

Skye's wings sagged at the news. "I suppose her fascination is more for my bond than for me."

"Not exactly. It is more for what your bond may know." The Ancient studied Skye's reaction. "Ormedi-Collius-Azelda is part of a small band who occasionally fly south to the coastline to hunt for human meat. She may be hoping you know where a good hunting ground might be."

Well, if there was anything worse than dragon drama, that would be it. Skye had had no clue finding a good mate would be so hard.

Iridescus snort-sniffed. "Do not take it so hard, Skye-Anyar-Bello. You are very young. Mistakes are the foundation for wisdom. Revel in making them. You will find a mate, as your father did when he chose my daughter." She stretched her wings twice the length of Skye's and flapped them several times. "I forget how much I enjoy sunning myself. But that is not why I wanted you here." The great drake curled herself into a ball, her wings spread out wide. "Tell me about your relationship with your bond."

Skye was surprised by her interest. Ancients never showed much interest in anything. "It did not start well. He was not happy being bonded to me. And though we grow closer with each passing day, he can still be infuriatingly headstrong and demanding. And he seldom asks my advice or heeds my warnings in matters that affect us both. I try to assist him in his struggles, but he does not always accept my assistance."

Iridescus snort-sniffed again. "So like the words I heard from your father. I believe you describe the very nature of being human."

Skye did not see the humor. "What did Anyar-Bello do?"

"He gave it time. But"—she extended her neck his way—"he had nearly a century with his bond before the second dragon-human bonding. You do not have that time."

"No. There is already a second bonding."

Iridescus's eyes narrowed. "That news is foreboding. It has only been fifty days since the celestial alignment past. You and your bond need to learn to work together. You both must be prepared."

"Prepared for what?" Skye asked. A flash of hope coursed through him that she might have insights.

Iridescus drew her head in. "For whatever comes."

Skye glanced away, not wanting the Ancient to see his irritation.

"Do you know the purpose of our dragonsongs?" she asked.

"Dragonsongs are our history, our heritage as a family."

"They are much more than that. I am in my nine-hundred-fifteenth cycle. My memories of my early life, especially those before we escaped Shazarack, are hazy now. Even worse, my memories of who I was before being summoned into this Physical form have faded. As a young amphithere still molding to the skin our Shaman god gave me, I knew who I was before. And who I will be again someday. But now, only fragments remain, shadows of what was. Memories fade, dragons die, but our dragonsongs live on. They connect us to our long past. Only four of the eight Ancient Cloudbenders still breathe. Dragonsongs keep our history fresh; they ground and link us to who we are, which shapes who we will become. Past, present, and future are all bound together."

After a deep breath, she continued. "I wish I could offer you something more. But I can at least provide what I gave your father, something he and his bond never fully grasped. The powers of a dragon do not come from our fierceness, nor our ability to resist elementals or expel fire. They come from something much deeper, more primal than such superficial things. We are not of this plane. But from where we came, I remember not. The Shaman god created us so that we could aid his kind. Do you sense that?"

Skye recalled how he felt when Conner first rode on his back. It had felt ... natural. "Yes."

"Good. Do not lose that feeling. Let it guide you in the days ahead." Iridescus scraped long talons over the rock. "Skye-Anyar-Bello, the Cosmos chose you for a reason, as it chose your bond. You must make a choice about your relationship, as your father made his choice. He chose a path that led us to this moment. Become your human's conscience, guide him toward decisions he would not make by himself. That is the purpose of your bonding. I tell you these things so you can make wise decisions. Now it is time I rest." And she slipped back down one of the shafts, leaving Skye alone on the plateau to watch the wyverns pinwheel through the clouds above.

An Arduous Assignment

Meera had not seen such a wondrous sight in a very long time. Even Morgana trembled with excitement as the mink sat up tall on the saddle horn. *Thanatos*. Meera reined in the mare she had acquired near the Borderlands, taking a moment halfway up the gently sloping hill to survey the dark-walled fortress, its ringed ramparts encircling the hill like a summer garland. A light breeze played with the grass blanketing the rise. The smell of smoke from the all-night fires filled the air. It was early morning, so many would be heading to bed by now. Excitement of the familiar, nearly forgotten, took her and she heeled her mare to a trot, directing her toward the tall outer gates swung wide, as if those inside had been awaiting her return. Alas, her excitement was short-lived.

Inside the gates, the people appeared subdued, their shoulders gathered up under their thick, black cloaks. Some wore their hoods pulled forward, which was unusual within the city proper. Groups of Necromancers congregated near doorways and shadowed overhangs, hunched and speaking in hushed tones, their eyes darting to those meandering by. No one took notice of her arrival. Or if they did, they did not care. An eerie sense that something was amiss permeated the city. For a moment, she thought she glimpsed the minister of the academy, Ousel Barakin, at the entrance of the central building, near the bronze statue of their supreme lord and paragon, Nartesis Shazarack. But when she glanced again, he was gone.

As she entered the stables, someone grabbed her from behind and shoved her hard into the dark recesses behind the stable doors. Morgana let out a sharp cry.

"What—" Meera fought to break free from the figure's grip. The tall figure flipped his hood back. "Galan?"

Wild, brown eyes gleamed, reflecting the morning light beyond the darkened door. "I saw you ride in from my chambers. I don't have long, so you must listen. There have been changes since you departed on your mission to the Harmonic Realms, and I would prefer you hear about them from me first."

"Changes?"

"Breanen is dead," Galan stated flatly.

"Dead?" *My mentor—*

"There's more. A ... man ... arrived at the gates a fortnight ago proclaiming himself to be Nartesis Shazarack."

"Shazarack?" Meera scoffed. He'd died a thousand years before. She struggled to make sense of what Galan was saying.

Galan gripped her shoulders, shaking her lightly. "Listen to me, Meera. When they discover that I've left my chambers ..." He shook his head. "This creature has taken control of our order. Now he is making plans to revoke our pact with the other orders!"

"Taken command? What?" She was exhausted. It was all too much.

"I have the backing of a majority of the council," Galan went on. "But with the passing of each day, more are swayed by this fiend. We must act decisively, and soon, if we are to win back control." Galan shook her again—it was becoming quite vexing. "Meera, can we count on your support?"

"I—I don't know. I've traveled across half of the realms and most of the Anarchic Lands. I need time to rest before I can think through—"

"I cannot linger any longer to debate with you." Galan flipped up his hood. He hunched forward to leave, but hesitated. "There is one more bit of news you need to be aware of. This man, this undead who calls himself Shazarack? *He* murdered Breanen." Galan stepped into Hemera's morning light, zigzagging through the shadows back to the central building.

Meera stayed in the shadow, replaying what had just happened. *Breanen is dead, Breanen is dead. Murdered by ... Nartesis Shazarack?*

She was relieved, of course, to know there would be no more undead assassins sent after her. But Breanen had been her mentor.

She was not sure how long she stood there. Her mare nuzzling her shoulder brought her around. Numb, she slipped stealthily into the stables. After feeding her horse, she pulled her hood forward to mirror those around her, then took the path Galan had used. She spoke to no one along the way.

Nartesis leaned forward as Ousel entered the room. "What did you find out?"

Ousel bowed humbly. "Your intuition on this matter was correct, my lord. I have spent the better part of the past two nights walking the halls and chatting with those within our order. The pact that the council signed with the other orders was never well received. I would estimate seven out of every ten opposed the pact."

"So, your great sovereign prince of the Necromancers lied," Nartesis drummed his fingernails in irritation. "Galan claimed the council had engaged most of the senior members of our order during the negotiations, when really he only sought to subdue anyone who might object."

"That does seem to be the case. When the council announced that they had negotiated the pact, they said a majority of the senior staff had been included in the conference. I was not asked for my opinion in the matter; I would not have supported it. Building a necro-army for the other orders in the timeframe demanded has left us with few resources to do anything else. Every Necromancer in the city has been sapped of energy and power since Midsummer's Night. Still, I had no reason to doubt their claim that most supported the pact. Who am I to go against the common will of those in the order?"

"How do you feel about having been manipulated in such a manner?"

Ousel peered down at Helgish in a tight ball in his palm, her spikes out. "Irritated, my lord." After a moment, he amended it. "No. I feel betrayed."

"As would I, dear friend." Nartesis rose. Sinew popped and snapped from muscles unaccustomed to use. "That is a situation left for later mentation," he suggested, though he had already chosen the path that would remedy that malady. "And regarding the other matter I asked about?"

ARMY OF THE DRAGONBONDED

"The story you told in the reception chamber about Thanatos's final days has been recounted dozens of times through the halls of the academy, each time embellished and shared with ever greater vivacity and fervor. It is the only thing discussed when ordermen are not busy raising undead for the army." Ousel pressed his forefinger to his pursed lips. "You have to understand, my lord, the destruction of Thanatos has been an indelible part of our order's psyche since the city was rebuilt. Details of its destruction did not survive. Thanatos is not just a city or academy. It has always been the symbol of what our order once represented."

After a brief pause, Ousel went further. "Few Anarchists appreciate what we Necromancers do. Fewer still value the services we provide to those in the lands. We are ostracized by most, tolerated by some, but outcasts in our society. So it is not hard to understand why few Necromancers support building a necro-army, given its mental and physical toll. Your story of that fateful night and the events leading up to it have become an inspiration."

Ousel's words were like cut stones, building blocks for the vision Nartesis wanted to resurrect, one he hoped would breathe new life into the order and give them a renewed sense of purpose. Nartesis thought back to a time when he had directed the creation of a great necro-army, recalling how the work strained those about him. He grunted his understanding. Thanatos was like a vessel that needed a worthy spirit. Nartesis would be the one to summon that spirit. Too many powerful Necromancers were sitting on the fence, waiting to see what happened next, biding their time while he and Galan wrestled for control. Nartesis had usurped Galan's position of power only because of his stature as paragon. But reputation alone would not sustain him for long. If Galan discovered his mastery of elementals was not what it once was ... Nartesis shook his head. Given that he had just called an end to the pact, he needed something substantial to tip the scales his way. Otherwise, he could not proceed with his plans.

Nartesis studied the man standing pensively before him, waiting to be given his next task. Ousel had become his first valuable asset, a companion he could trust to carry out his every wish. Further, Nartesis had realized the man was quite powerful in manipulating Earth and Fire elementals. Apparently, it had not been aptitude or potential that kept the man from taking a seat at the council's table; it had been his meek demeanor. But regrettably, Ousel suffered from the same illness afflicting all those on the order's council—lack of vision. Nartesis needed another powerful

Necromancer. One he could not only trust with his life, but who had the ability to see his vision.

"My lord." Ousel interrupted his thoughts. "There is another matter of importance you should be aware of. Grandmaster Meera Asheborne has returned from her mission into the Harmonic Realms."

"Asheborne?"

"Grandmaster Asheborne was Breanen Sagamore's personal assistant and long-time pupil, and has been a close adviser to Galan and his council for some time. I bring this to your attention, my lord, because Meera Asheborne carries significant weight within the order. Her opinion has, on several occasions, swayed outcomes being studied by the council."

If Nartesis had had a beating heart, it would have fluttered right then. "Breanen had a pupil?"

"Yes, my lord. Returned today from her mission in the Harmonic Realms," Ousel reiterated.

Despite Ousel's insistence that it was unwise to expose himself unnecessarily given Galan's earlier threats, Nartesis chose to go directly to Meera Asheborne's quarters instead of summoning her to his. It was not long before Nartesis and Ousel were outside her chamber door, his undead guards looming close behind.

Ousel rapped a small metal ball hinged against the thick oak door.

"Who is it?"

"It is Ousel Barakin, Meera. There is someone here who wishes to meet you."

A moment later, the door swung wide to reveal a handsome woman of dark complexion. She was tall, with hair as black as ink that hung long and unkempt about her shoulders. Her hazel eyes were intense, dark, and sunken.

"Grandmaster Meera Asheborne, Supreme Lord Nartesis Shazarack," Ousel announced with flamboyant pride and a wave of his arm. Helgish held on tight to his pocket so she would not fall out while he bobbed about.

Nartesis examined the robed woman bowing before him. He estimated her to be mid-thirties. "You are younger than I expected for a grandmaster."

"I had excellent preceptors through the years ... my lord."

Nartesis laughed. "And modest." He strolled through the entrance, not waiting to be invited. The unpretentious room was large and sparingly furnished. Hemera's late-morning light streamed through slits in the outer wall, narrow rays lighting up dust that swirled about the musty chamber. A mink was chasing a ball around the room.

At the center of the room, Nartesis drew upon Fire elemental and directed it at a candle nearby. The wick sparked and flared. "Show me what your talented preceptors have taught you. Extinguish the candle flame, but do so without harming either melted wax or wick." Eons ago, he had used this same exercise to determine his students' mental capacity to focus. Great precision and control were needed to smother a flame by incanting without hardening the wax or shriveling the burning wick.

Uncertainty flickered across Meera's face. "I will try, my lord. I am quite exhausted." Meera's lips twitched upward.

"I cast my most challenging incantations when I had nothing left inside, Meera. Mastery is not about how much strength you have in reserve, or how much Fire and Earth you can draw upon. Determination and sensitivity are needed to create a delicate weave and a tight fold of the elementals."

Meera focused on the flame.

Nartesis sensed her drawing upon the elementals. He closed his eyes, letting his mind slip into the state of Sight.

"*Ora energi pnigofotia,*" Meera murmured.

Nartesis sensed Meera's gentle flow drift across the chamber. Several moments passed. The candle snuffed out.

Meera let out a weary breath.

"Very well done." Nartesis studied the candle, then reached out with Fire and lit the candle again. "But I'd like you to do it again. This time, I want you to take the time to feel the Earth in the wick, to feel the Fire in the flame, before you weave the elementals. Only after you have done this do I want you to will the flame to die."

Meera repeated the incantation.

Nartesis again sensed Meera guiding the elemental flow outward, slower this time, more intent. The raw power of her will delighted him. The flame dimmed, then flickered, dwindling to a faint point of light. Then, even that vanished. A stream of smoke curled upward. "Well done. How did that feel?"

"Amazing, my lord. I was able to fold the elementals more easily. My weave was much finer." Meera tilted her head forward. "Thank you for your guidance."

"Of course." Nartesis moved to one of two chairs in the room and sat, taking in the two grandmasters before him. "I see why Breanen chose you as her second, and why she chose you for the mission you were sent on."

"You know of my mission, my lord?"

"Only sparingly." Nartesis casually ran his fingers over the serpentine carvings along the armchair. Though he no longer had the sensation of touch, he needed to appear disinterested. "I am curious about a few details. What you learned may impact future order decisions."

Meera settled into the chair next to Nartesis. Her mink bond bounded into her lap, then curled up in a tight ball. "My mission was to meet a young man and his dragon bond ... and to begin dialogue, to find common ground for building an alliance."

Again, the boy and his dragon, Nartesis thought as he tilted back. "Alone?" he probed.

"No, my lord. I was accompanied by a band of Barbarians."

"How unusual. I keep hearing how arrangements between the orders are so rare, yet you convinced a company of Barbarians to go on a dangerous mission into the realms with you?"

"I was given a signed agreement, sealed by the Conjuror, Necromancer, and Barbarian councils, authorizing the mission. Farlorde's Barbarian commander could not refuse such a directive."

"No. I suppose not. And this was only one of several missions being conducted?"

"I am aware of three, my lord. But I know nothing about the other two missions' objectives."

Multiple, simultaneous affairs of intrigue coordinated at the highest levels of the orders, each possibly contingent on the other? Nartesis glanced at Ousel, who shrugged. So they had been conducted in isolation and secrecy. How deep did this gopher hole go? And why compartmentalize these missions so? He filed these questions away for later. Nartesis pinwheeled his forefinger for Meera to move on.

"We arrived at Dragongarde, then captured and used the boy to subdue his dragon."

Nartesis pruned his face in confusion. "But Ousel told me this ... boy ... is the young Griffinrock queen's new Champion. Or is this a different boy?"

Meera hung her head. "No, my lord. Before we could start discussions, we were attacked by a small pack of Harmonic scouts. In the confusion of battle, the boy broke free. Without being able to threaten the boy's life, we had no way to restrain the dragon."

Nartesis exploded in laughter. "A grandmaster Necromancer and a band of Barbarians couldn't handle a newly bonded boy?"

Meera's cheeks bloomed a bright red.

"I do not mean to offend you, Meera," Nartesis chuckled. "But it seems this young man has been worming his way into everybody's business. You'd think there were three of him." Nartesis tilted forward. "But tell me, what did you think of his bond?"

Meera's lips moved before words came to her. "Magnificent, my lord. Incredibly intelligent. And powerful. He was beyond description. Beyond anything I had read in the old books."

"Oh? Describe this creature to me."

Meera fidgeted with her black robes. "With two powerful legs, it had a squamous black hide, like a snake, with beautiful iridescent scales and eyes a brilliant blue. Two magnificent horns spiraled upward from its crown with several more, smaller and thorny, protruding from its snout and jaw. I cannot account for the creature's wingspan or its true height as I encountered it in a tight tunnel. Still, it was easily twice the height of a man, and each wing was longer still."

"Hmm," Nartesis nodded with satisfaction. "A male. With bluish eyes?" He licked his leathery lips, eager to know more. "Did you notice any pattern to his hide? Maybe down his spine or tail?"

"As I said, he was black. ... But now that you ask, yes. I had not thought of it before, as the pattern was very faint."

"The pattern—was it rows of small dots or large, more cornered and elongated?"

"Of the second type, my lord. How did you know?"

Nartesis had not heard Meera's question. He was recalling the day in his laboratory cavern when he was awakened from his long sleep by a lad. Meera's description confirmed the dragon she had met was the same as the adolescent dragon that had accompanied the boy. "So, our scaly friend is of the Water family. And based on your description, he was nearing his final transformation. By now, he is surely a drake. Small in comparison to what he will become, and far more powerful than when you met him."

"My lord? How is it you know this?" Meera asked.

Nartesis realized he had been thinking aloud. *Never mind.* He would have needed to expose the truth at some point. It was one he could use to his advantage here. He caught Meera's and Ousel's confused stares. "It was *I* who created the first dragons."

Meera and Ousel stared blankly at him.

"But that was a long time ago. A tale that I will reserve for another conversation." Nartesis had primed the pump; now, he would draw from the well. "I am in need of two powerful Necromancers, two I can count on for a very difficult … a rather arduous assignment vital to the very future of our order. You two are precisely what I am looking for."

He had their full attention. "However, what I will ask of you is beyond your current capabilities. Before you can perform this assignment, I will teach you to hone your powers, to control them with a precision that will incite envy in even the most formidable Necromancers. We will be on a tight schedule. The pace will leave your spirits spent, your nerves fried. There will be moments you'll wish you'd never started. There will be days when you have given your all, yet I will demand more. But if you have the will and fortitude to see this through, I promise, when you reach the other side of my teaching, your skills will be unmatched. And when you have completed this assignment"—Nartesis wagged a bone finger in the air—"then, my dear friends, I will gift you my most precious possessions: fifty years of research and the most powerful Necromantic incantations ever known and long forgotten." He let them reflect for a moment. "Think of it. The knowledge and power to create dragons. So, what do you say? Are you with me?"

Too stunned to speak, eager as hungry youngsters in a confectionery, they jiggled their heads up and down.

Rising to the creak and pop of joints, he shuffled toward the door and his waiting guards. "Then rest. We begin in a few days."

Harmonic Balance

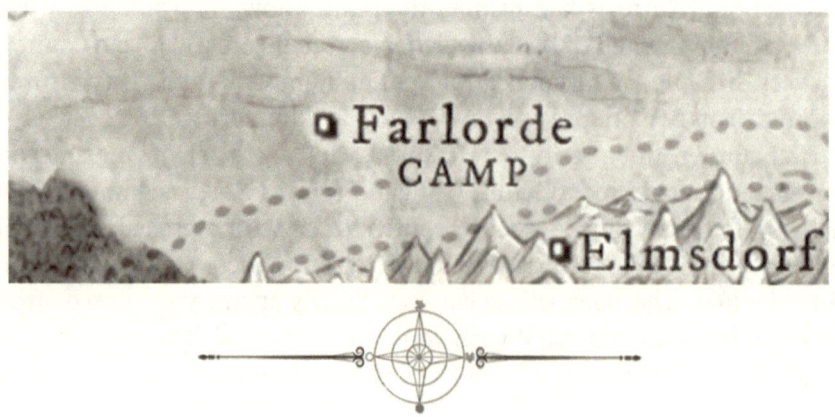

Marcantos rolled from his blankets and staggered from his tent into the early-morning light. Copious was nowhere to be seen. He closed his eyes and sensed his bond off to the west, likely foraging for a morning meal of nuts and berries. To the east, Hemera was breaking over a hill, lighting the ancient ruins of Farlorde with golden rays. Smoke from morning fires was thick on the air. The ancient citadel, in the morning haze, appeared to quiver at the sight of the Anarchic tents blanketing the hills about it. There, as Marcantos had witnessed the six previous mornings, Barbarian life stirred.

He observed their activities with a calculating stare. He had already committed to memory the layout of tents; little had changed since his arrival. His gaze shifted south to where a company of Anarchic soldiers was forming up, their black steel-studded armor gleaming. Each morning, the soldiers would marshal under several Barbarian leaders, then march south toward the mountains and the Borderlands. Sometimes, they would split in two—one group turning west, the other east; other times they would disband into smaller groups. Sometime later in the day, another company of soldiers would return from their night patrol, their leaders reporting in to the commander any chance encounters with Harmonic forces.

For centuries, the Harmonic Realms had tried to infiltrate Farlorde with spies. But each attempt had failed miserably. What Marcantos had learned about the size and movement of Anarchic forces in the area would be worth his weight in gold. He licked his lips considering a plan to get such information to the realms. Would the crowns rescind the kill order on him? Maybe they would reinstate him as a citizen? His heart pounded harder with excitement.

No, Marcantos. He clenched his hands into fists until they shook. They would kill you on sight, fool. You would never get the chance to parley for your life. He scanned the snow-peaked mountain range far to the south. Assuming you could reach the Borderlands before the Barbarians caught you and dragged you back. Turning his back on citadel and camp with a sigh, he tossed away the thought and returned to his tent. He retrieved his sword, throwing his scabbard on his cot.

Near his tent, he began his morning ritual. For all the years he thought he had been training under Blake Friarwood, Lacerus had actually been training him in the use of Anarchic Sight. Now that he knew the truth, he was driven to rid himself of the malady. *Exercise the body to exorcise the mind*, he thought with a touch of humor as he crouched and thrusted. Each stroke of his sword, each step and turn of his feet, each spin of his supple wrist was a mastery in precision, balance, and control. The hours wore on, and though the rigor of his workout would not end the tortured life he lived, the insanity that had gripped him for so long slowly ebbed.

Just before noon, Marcantos stowed his sword in his tent. Retrieving the tin plate and cup he had been allotted the day he arrived, he trudged down the hill. Turning north, he skirted the edge of the massive camp to where several cooks busied themselves about a large fire. There, he ladled a large helping of porridge and covered it with thick gravy. Yet another daily ritual. As he turned, a large Barbarian shoved him in the chest, nearly sending him tumbling into the fire.

"ShoKohm," the Barbarian sneered at him.

It was a name Marcantos had been called many times the past few days, though no one had bothered to tell him what it meant. His previous name, Puppet, had been short-lived. Marcantos did not look the Barbarian in the eye but stepped around him, ignoring the snickers and jeers at his back.

Soon, Marcantos reminded himself, a few more days and a ruling will come from their council. Then this will be over.

That evening, as Marcantos ate dinner by his campfire, he pulled a second bowl from the small stack of supplies he had brought with him from

Graystone, scraped out the remnants of his breakfast with his fingernails, and ladled a serving of rabbit stew and root vegetables from the small kettle on his fire. Setting the bowl on a rock next to him, he spoke softly over his shoulder. "You should step into the light. It is dangerous to loiter in the shadows thus."

A few moments passed before a young woman moved forward into the firelight. She was dressed in Barbarian summer clothing, which included light leather armor from shoulders to knees secured with buckled leather straps, dark leather leggings. "My name is Orianna," she said softly.

"You are the one I passed the morning I arrived. Yes. I recall." Marcantos started to introduce himself, but was unsure what name to use for himself—Puppet, ShoKohm? Instead, he wanted to see what she called him. He motioned to the bowl of food he had prepared, then waited for Orianna to sit on the rock.

"Is it true what they say about you?" she asked as she ate hungrily, never taking her eyes from him.

Marcantos gestured to the open range around his tent, and to the distant voices and laughter near the top of the hill beyond. "I am not privy to what anyone says—about anything. Frankly, I am surprised anyone has ever noticed me."

Orianna laughed, showing bits of rabbit between her teeth. Her eyes widened. "Oh, they notice," she mumbled before returning to shoveling stew into her mouth.

"And what is it they say of me?"

"For one, that you were once a grandmaster among the dark Barbarians."

"Dark Barbarians?" Marcantos blinked. "Oh. You mean Warriors."

Orianna lost her smile. Her head turtled toward her shoulders. "Do not speak that word too loudly, Marcantos. It is offensive to all who would hear it."

Dark Barbarian, Marcantos thought. He had never considered the reference before, but it was fitting since Harmonics called the Anarchic orders "dark."

Orianna interrupted his thoughts. "There is news in the camp that a boy has bonded with a dragon and lives at the heart of the Harmonic lands. Do you know of this?"

Marcantos was struck with the image of young Conner Stonefield on the Field of Contest. And flowing with that image came the heinous act of treachery he had attempted to become Queen Veressa's Champion—to the young boy, to his order, and to the realms. He swallowed back the bile burning in his throat.

Orianna must have caught the expression on his contorted face. "I am sorry. My mother used to say that I had a knack for prying into places I do not belong. I meant no offense."

Marcantos covered up his snarl with a smile. "It is all right. Yes, I know of him."

"I did not believe it possible. I heard stories of the Dragonbonded and the omen when I was a little girl, of men and women who would return someday. Do you think the prophecy is true, then?"

"I fear it is."

The two sat in silence for some time before Marcantos decided Orianna might answer a few questions he had. "What does ShoKohm mean?"

"It means 'without honor.'"

Marcantos flinched. "Why do they call me that?"

"Because you refused Cha Kohm with Engert."

"The big man who stomps around like he rules over the camp?" The morning after his arrival, Marcantos had gone to get breakfast when Engert accosted him, crowding him and shouting names at him. Marcantos's eyes barely broke over Engert's wide shoulders. A number of Barbarians had gathered and started chanting "Cha Kohm" while Engert strutted about him like a male peacock. Marcantos had interpreted the gesture as being told not enter the camp wearing his sword. After that, the only time he removed his sword from his tent was when he practiced. Engert had not bothered him since. And that is when the Barbarians started calling him ShoKohm.

"He is Commander Barcleave's closest lieutenant."

Marcantos grinned. "I don't think he likes me much."

"He is an arrogant bully. His closeness to Barcleave makes him highly influential with many in the camp. He expects all those who lay stakes near his tent to behave as he does, and demands extreme loyalty, something not valued by most Anarchists. He especially enjoys toying with those who are the least skilled, and believes Cha Kohm is the only means of becoming a master Barbarian. Cha Kohm is supposed to be a trial by combat to test students' abilities. But Engert perverts the ritual. He has killed several apprentices just in the past few years."

"Has he challenged you in Cha Kohm?"

Orianna diverted her gaze, hesitating, then shook her head. "I have stayed clear of his disgraceful attention so far."

"What does the commander say about this?"

"Barcleave is a busy man and has delegated much of the Barbarians' training to Engert. There are a few who do not like his style—such as young Groegan, whom you met on your arrival. Groegan has recently become Barcleave's personal pupil but does not yet have the influence to change current conditions." She stared directly at Marcantos. "I understand that you have been trained in the arts of the Barbarian."

The end of Marcantos's mouth twitched. He was unsure how to respond to such a question.

"Will you train me?" Orianna asked.

Marcantos winced at the unexpected question. Why would she want someone branded as being without honor to train her? He started to refuse, but, for some reason, he loathed snuffing out the eagerness in her wide eyes. He had worked hard the past week to exorcise the Anarchic demon that had stolen his sanity and left him in such a sorrowful state. "I don't think that is a good idea," he mumbled.

He was surprised when his rejection did not temper Orianna's fervor. She leaned closer. "I cannot learn from those who believe and behave as Engert does."

"You misunderstand me, Orianna." His eyes flicked to the center of the Farlorde camp, where the commander's tall tent was aglow. "I doubt that I have long remaining on Gaia. I doubt we would have enough time to—"

Orianna snorted. "You should have faith the order will rule in your favor."

In my favor, Marcantos thought. He did have faith. Only the outcome he hoped for was not the one she suggested.

"Marcantos, I am Dristonian. We are a simple, gentle people. I cannot rely on anger as the seed to draw on the elementals. I have been in the Barbarians Order for nearly a year, living here. I have studied under the tutelage of four preceptors. In time, they all gave up on me. They say I cannot learn, that I am not worth their time. And I had come to believe them. That is, until the morning following your arrival."

Marcantos furrowed his brow and waited for her to continue.

"I watched you practicing that morning. And I could not help noticing that your skills are different. The basics of footing and stroke are similar, the forms you practiced akin to those taught to me by my preceptors. But your movements were efficient, precise ... careful. I was mesmerized by your dance. And that is when I understood. That is the technique I need to learn. I will do anything you wish ... if you will teach me."

Orianna was desperate if she was coming to him for help. He had trained a lot of Warriors, and he had never had much empathy or patience for students who could not keep pace with his regimen. So he understood the frustrations her preceptors must have felt. His eyes traced along her narrow shoulders and sinewy arms and legs. He recalled watching her the afternoon he arrived, how he had assessed her potential, even if she was inattentive. "I will need to sleep on this. I cannot make an oath with you without first considering the implications."

Orianna stood. "Until first light, then." She vanished into the darkness beyond his camp.

Nightmares of being sucked into the swirling eddies of anarchy kept Marcantos awake through most of the night. He woke with a start, dreaming of being helplessly spun about. As he had on previous mornings, he slipped from his blankets. He yanked his sword from his scabbard and started to toss the leather and steel sheath on his bed, but a new idea came to him. He strapped his scabbard to his waist and stepped outside. The morning was chill and overcast. Hints of rain hung in the west. Orianna sat on a rock beside the remnants of his evening fire, fidgeting with her sword and gnawing on her lower lip. She got to her feet as Marcantos approached. "Before I agree to train you, I need you to understand something."

Orianna took a deep breath and blew it out. "Okay."

"There was a time ... once," he began, "when I was one of the greatest swordsmen in my order. I had hopes and visions of using my talents to protect my people. Last night, you asked if I had been trained in the arts of the Barbarian. I was, but it was not of my own volition. To be more precise, I was duped into it by a long-time preceptor, someone I had placed my trust in. He deceived me, using my craving for recognition and status against me."

"I am sorry," Orianna whispered.

"Don't be," he barked. "I deserve what I received." He took a deep breath and held his hand up as a sign of apology. "But I suffered greatly from his deception. I did not understand the battle raging inside me between being raised Harmonic and my craving for Anarchic Sight, to the point that it became my bane. It took my sanity." Marcantos's cheeks warmed at being open thus with a stranger, a Barbarian at that. "I tell you my secret because you must understand that I have made a vow never to use Anarchic Sight again. I will not train you to become a Barbarian. If I take you as a student, it must be on my terms."

"Teach me. I want to learn what you know."

"You do understand the risk? I doubt anyone at Farlorde would take kindly to my ... unique training."

"I have suffered their abuse for nearly a year. They can do little more to me."

"Very well. I think a simple demonstration is in order." Marcantos walked to where Copious had piled a variety of nuts he had collected from the small forest to the north. He rummaged through the pile, retrieved a walnut, and returned to the campfire. He placed the walnut on a log the thickness of his forearm, then stepped back and drew his sword. He let his mind relax, taking a slow calming breath. The gentle caress of the Harmonic weave surrounded him, the elemental energies sparking from the surfaces of the objects nearby—his clothes, the ground, Orianna, the log, the walnut. He focused his thoughts, sensing the thick lattice structure of the hard walnut shell, the damp fruit inside.

In a flash like lightning, Marcantos whipped his sword in a spin to his left, arcing his blade back, over his head and down. Just as the blade touched the walnut, he snapped his arm and sword back. Letting the momentum of his sword carry his arm, he flicked his wrist and returned his sword to its scabbard. The walnut fell open as the cross-guard snapped against the scabbard's locket.

Orianna stepped forward and picked up the two halves. Her mouth fell open as she ran her fingertip over the smoothly sliced edge. Then she began to laugh. "When a Barbarian wants to eat a walnut, he crushes it with the side of his sword, then grumbles about having to pick the meat from around the broken shell. And you never drew upon the elementals."

"Anarchic Sight relies on the destructive forces to manipulate the elementals; Harmonic Sight relies on the forces of harmony and symmetry. Accessing elementals through Harmonic Sight is about precision and balance."

"But is it as powerful?" Orianna asked.

"Don't confuse destruction with power. Great power can be achieved when one's mind is in a state of rest. Do you understand?"

Orianna goggled at him. "The thought of the Harmonic weave frightens me, Marcantos."

"That is only because you have been taught to fear it, as I was raised to fear Anarchic Sight." But her eyes were still as large as the walnut halves she held. "Fear will prevent you from being calm. And that will work against your interests. So, we will ignore Harmonic Sight for now and instead you will work on learning to center yourself, to being at peace." After a thought, he added, "As will I. Do you agree?"

Orianna shuddered, then nodded.

"Then let us begin."

A Callow Child's Wooden Sword

A snap of wind, heavy with the promise of rain, whipped across Veressa's back. She pinched Toran's withers to calm her gelding, then glanced over her shoulder. A dark line of storm clouds churned fiercely at their backs, casting the road ahead in an ominous gloom.

Jonath gestured at the split in the King's Road. To the left, the road led to Derry's Bridge, a small town along the river south of Lake Donogal. They would take the road to the right and west from here. "Good thing we're only an hour out of Charmwell," her father commented at her side. "A few hours ago, I wasn't sure we'd arrive before those clouds broke loose."

Veressa squinted up, but Hemera was lost in the dark grayness. "I don't know how you can tell what time it is."

"You forget, daughter," Jonath smiled. Wiggling his fingers before his face, he whispered ominously, "I am a grandmaster Mystic!"

Veressa could not hold back a lighthearted chuckle, which helped her relax for the first time since they'd left the small city of Piper's Glen that morning. "I am sorry, father. I know I have not been good company these past three days of travel. It seems I cannot get far enough away from my burdens."

Jonath started to comment, then glanced at the large force of Elvenstein royal guardsmen encircling them before thinking better of it. The force had been dispatched by King Friedrick of Elvenstein as

Harmonic protocol dictated to protect royalty from another realm. The Elvensteinian escort had met them at the border the previous morning, informing them that Veressa's personal protection of Queen's Defenders was not allowed in Elvenstein. It was all highly unusual. If not for Jonath's quick decision to agree to King Friedrick's terms, there surely would have been an incident between the two unyielding ordermen commanders. Her father leaned closer. "I know a great deal about the burdens of leadership, daughter. No apologies are necessary."

Veressa gave a quick tick of her head in silent agreement. "Commander," Veressa said to the officer riding nearby.

"Yes, Majesty?"

"Before we arrive at Charmwell, my father and I have several personal matters to attend to. I hope you are not offended ..." She drew out the words and waited.

The commander's eyes narrowed with a hint of suspicion. Finally, with a terse hand signal, he led those near the queen farther up the road at a brisk cantor.

"There. That is better," Veressa said with a sigh.

"But let us be sure." Jonath pulled up his sleeves and gestured with his hands. Veressa felt the strong pull of Air elemental and knew her father called upon Fire as well. *"Aethra energi plattosfaira,"* he invoked, and a sphere of air enveloped the two and their mounts. "That will keep us safe from any prying ears. Now! I know you are not truly interested in marrying Prince Camion. But do not fret. I will play my part in acting the role of a concerned and doting father." Jonath winked. "Your mother relied on me to help when ruling over our people, you know." He chuckled lightly, as if being told the punchline to a joke. "Once King Friedrick realized the only way to strike a deal with Iza was through me, he and I kindled a close working relationship. I think I know how to work that grizzly old coot."

"That is all good to know, but not the topic I had in mind."

"Then what did you wish to discuss?"

"First, I wanted you to know how happy I am that you came with me. And I say that not because of the protection and experienced guidance you offer. Over the last several days, I have sensed a great weight being lifted from your heart. And the farther we get from Graystone, the lighter your heart becomes." She pointed at the spotted owl flying circles in the dark skies above. "I can see Beggar is also grateful."

"She is," Jonath said. "And yes, this trip has helped me immensely. Maybe I needed to focus my mind on helping solve something vital to the realms' survival."

"It pleases me that you see that you are dearly needed, father. And I don't mean just to me."

The two rode in silence for several minutes.

"You said there were several personal matters," Jonath prodded. The shield he had created would not last forever.

"It is, in fact, because of your improved spirit that I now feel compelled to bring up the other matter, something that has been eating at me for some days now—ever since my Champion left on his mission."

"I see. This sounds serious." Still, he could not keep a smile from his face.

"I would most sincerely appreciate it if you would stay out of my affairs when they deal with the heart."

Her father puffed out his lips at her. "I don't know what on Gaia you are talking about."

"Don't play coy with me. I know of the arrangement between you and Conner. You made him swear not to get close to me."

Jonath looked incensed at her accusation. "I made the boy do nothing."

Veressa leaned closer and shook her finger his way. "I know how you work, Father," she whispered. "You have a way of bending people to your will and then making them believe you had nothing to do with their action."

"Honestly, I merely told the lad he needed to be careful around you. He was the one who swore on the Champion's amulet never to divulge his feelings."

"Feelings? For me?" Veressa nearly yelled with surprise.

"Oh, now look what you've gone and made me do! I'm not saying another word, Veressa. Every time we have a conversation, I end up saying more than I intended. As your mother's Champion, I was trained to undergo the most extreme torture at the hands of the most ruthless Anarchists you could imagine. I do declare you are so like your mother."

Veressa sat numb with shock, not really listening to her father as he chattered on about how Mystics could withstand all kinds of physical pain. She had been right. She could sense Conner's feelings for her. Even though he had conceded they shared a bond, she'd found it hard to believe what she sensed from him was real. But now she had no doubts. Conner ... *loved* her!

By the time the tan walls of Charmwell came into view, the black clouds flickering with lightning were nearly overhead. Thunder rumbled across the prairie, each clap louder than the previous. Antilles grew anxious, his eyes constantly searching the open terrain for cover to wait out the storm, forcing Veressa to send her bond continued sensations of safety to soothe his nerves.

Ahead, the castle rose a hundred paces above the top of the only hill on the Elvensteinian plains. Eight tall cylindrical towers, connected by a thick outer curtain wall, encircled the crown of the hill. Within, the main keep extended skyward nearly another hundred paces. Charmwell Castle was a feat of true mastery by the greatest stonemasons of the early days of the guilds. A dozen armies had attempted to breach the walls during the Anarchic War. All of them had failed. In twelve hundred years, the castle had never fallen into enemy hands.

North of the castle, Veressa, Jonath, and the royal guard reined their mounts southward and took the meandering dirt road leading to the castle's only gate. As they rode through the gate opening, Veressa glanced up where the black iron portcullis hung suspended from within the transom. She had only read about such systems of gears, pulleys, and chains that raised and lowered the gate heavier than a dozen warhorses. Graystone had no need for gates or doors, never had. Griffinrock's royal castle was always open. Its citizens freely entered and departed via two wide bridges connecting the great castle to the city that grew along both sides of the River Tresdan. But that was because Graystone was safe in the heart of the realm. The outland wilderness was just a day's easy ride south from Charmwell.

The royal guard escort led the way across the bailey, a spacious and well-groomed gravel yard with scattered patches of grass, and up to the main keep, where King Friedrick, a stocky man with a round face and a knobby nose, stood grandly at the front of a small gathering of noblemen. The little hair that remained on his head had long since turned gray, as had his chest-length beard graced with an occasional streak of flaming red. As a young man, the king had been called Friedrick the Red; a recent jest he be called Friedrick the Gray had not been well received. The king's Champion, a male grandmaster Sorcerer of some renown named Xenor Walbright, waited under the branches of a great oak in the ward, where he could observe everything.

"Jonath, it is good to lay eyes on you again." The king rounded on Veressa, smiling broadly as he whipped his hand around in little circles. "And Queen Veressa, I cannot express how happy I am that you accepted my invitation to visit."

Veressa bristled. *Invitation to visit?* When he had met with her the day after her coronation, he'd made it quite clear that a discussion of marriage was a compulsory precondition for Elvenstein's support in the realms' war preparations. She was so looking forward to watching his eyes bulge and veins pop when she conveyed the demands she expected to be met before she would even consider an arranged marriage. "Thank you, King Friedrick. I am sure that I will thoroughly enjoy my stay."

Friedrick lifted his arm and swung it back toward the tall and silent man standing near the keep's entrance. "Of course, you remember my oldest, Crown Prince Tanner."

Tanner tilted his head forward slightly, making it seem like even that was exhausting. He said nothing, which suited Veressa perfectly. She remembered his visit to Graystone five years before. At fifteen, he had already been a crafty and conniving schemer of unsavory activities. The smartest of the brood of boys, he had learned at a young age that steering outside the boundaries of Friedrick's sense of morality would ensure he earned the king's explosive fury. The crown prince's personal guardian, a master Ranger named Godwin Gellastandt, stood at his side. Annabelle had told plenty of unpleasant stories about Godwin.

"And Prince Oakes," the king proceeded with a wave and furrowed brow. Heavier built than Tanner, Oakes leaned against one of the keep's portico columns, his right heel hooked over the column's base, scraping dirt from his fingernails with a hunting knife. Veressa had never met Oakes, and given what she'd heard of the man's behavior, she was glad of it. Oakes was infamous for rabble-rousing. And whether as a means to draw his father's eye or because he lacked any mental capacities between his large ears, he remained in perpetual trouble with the king.

Friedrick placed his thick hand on the shoulder of the red-headed lad standing beside him and shoved him forward. "And last, Prince Camion. Don't just stand there. Say something, boy!"

"It is good to see you again, Majesty," Camion mumbled.

Well, not the best introduction, but a far cry better than his brothers in comparison. "It has been a few years." The only thing Veressa recalled about Camion during their visit to Graystone was that he was a shy thirteen-year-old. Apparently, he had not yet grown out of his awkwardness.

"I am glad you remember." Camion's green eyes darted between her and the ground at his feet.

Friedrick rolled his eyes. "Well, I am sure you two are exhausted from your long journey. Besides, the sky will be dumping buckets on us soon enough. Let us get you inside."

Veressa could not help but note that there were no women in the courtyard—family of the king, royal guard, or protector. *So like Elvensteinians.*

"Oakes!" Friedrick shouted. "Don't stand there holding up the keep. We paid good coin for pillars to do that. Summon a few manservants to take care of their horses."

Oakes made no effort to do as instructed, so one of the royal guardsmen came forward and collected Jonath's and Veressa's rides.

The king did not seem to notice, and he led the way into the keep. Camion faltered for a moment as if unsure where etiquette dictated he should be, then trailed on Veressa's heels.

Friedrick stopped in the keep's entrance. "I have assigned you both a handmaiden who will show you to your quarters and help you freshen up. I see no need to rush into discussing the terms of our … arrangement. We have time for that tomorrow. Maybe we can also take the time to fit in some negotiations regarding the upcoming war. But no more talk about such topics now!" He waved at several young women in brightly colored dresses. "Tonight, Queen Veressa, my wife has arranged the most magnificent banquet in honor of your arrival. I hope you and your father are not too exhausted."

Veressa hooked her arm around her father's sleeve. "I am sure it will be enchanting. We look forward to the affair." *At least then I can meet some of the ladies of the home.*

Veressa drummed her fingers on the hard table with one hand while lightly stroking Antilles's forehead with the other. The food on her pewter plate— three kinds of meat and a serving of boiled potatoes—had long since grown cold. She glanced up and down the long table. Not a green or fruit in sight. Hardly four hours at Charmwell, and already she was ready to head home. Even riding through a rainstorm and confronting the War Council were more to her liking than dealing with a room full of boring Elvensteinian noblemen. A bright flash of lightning drew her attention from the unappetizing meal. Bored, she looked around the large dining hall for the fourth time.

She had been seated near the center of the head table, which, at least, gave her a decent vantage point to observe Elvenstein dining at its finest. To her left sat her father, next to King Friedrick. The two were locked in an animated discussion on an unknown matter for which Veressa was sure she did not care a trifle. To her right, Prince Camion. Beyond that, the table was filled with a litany of the king's male brothers and cousins. Two rows of tables ran longways down either side of the hall, where noblemen dressed in silks made rude noises and gestures as they jostled, jeered, and laughed with one another. The air was thick with the smell of meat, spices, and hops all mingled with smoke, testosterone, and sweat. The women, wives and companions of the men in attendance, sat at a separate table at the far end of the hall. None made any attempt to look like they were enjoying the evening. Beyond that, near the doors, a small ensemble of musicians worked to be heard over the roar of masculine laughter and the occasional rumble of thunder. A colorfully dressed young man with a mandolin bobbed his head to keep the ensemble's tempo even, making the troupe look like a comical act of jesters. Not that anyone noticed.

"It would seem your arrival was impeccably timed," Prince Camion shouted into her ear, making Veressa jump. He had been using the rising clamor in the hall as an excuse to get ever closer. When she looked at him, he pointed at a window as if she might have missed the rain falling in torrents outside. The prince's comment would have been obvious to the most oblivious dullard. She glanced away without a response, making it clear that his third attempt to strike up a conversation had failed as miserably as his previous two.

"I guess I have you to thank for the evening's entertainment," Camion tried again, this time with a smile.

Veressa glanced up to find his green eyes upon her. At least he scored a point for perseverance. "Why is that?" she asked. *Let's see if you can hold my interest for three minutes.*

"If not for you, *I* would be the one sitting near the end of the table." Camion gestured toward the far edge, where his two older brothers sat with brewing scowls. They were clearly used to being the center of attention. They glanced his way, so Camion raised his stein, then drank deep of the bitter warm mead. His brothers' expressions darkened.

So, the queen of Griffinrock is nothing more than a wooden sword for a callow child to brandish about, she thought as she smirked. "I don't think you are engendering any amity."

"My brothers and I learned some years ago not to waste amity on each other. But no worries." The prince's eyebrows bounced up and down with delight before he tilted his head back and emptied his stein. "They will most certainly exact some form of punishment upon me tomorrow morning on our hunt. But they can do nothing tonight."

Veressa bolted upright. Finally, a topic worthy of discussion! "You are going on a hunt? What are you hunting?"

Antilles's head popped up over the table beside her.

"Boars," Camion responded with bravado, then released a rumbling belch.

Growing weary of the man's discourtesy, Veressa waved her hand at the tables of men about her. "I would have thought there were enough of those already in this hall."

Camion squinted in confusion for a moment, then burst into thunderous laughter as if trying to compete with all the other obnoxious noblemen in the room. "Oh, boors! I see you have not lost your wit since our last encounter."

Veressa hummed. *Wit? Is that what you call it? Then you haven't been paying attention.* Still, she refused to let him dampen her spirit for the opportunity to escape this tedium. "May I come?"

Camion's eyes widened, his face stretching long. "You? On a hunt?"

Veressa's eyes narrowed slightly, daring him to doubt her.

Camion scratched at his chin. "Well, it is highly unusual. Elvensteinian women—"

"I am not Elvensteinian, now, am I?"

"No." Camion's eyes, sparkling like two emeralds in the dim candlelight, flicked to his brothers. "Yes. I think you should come. Let's make a fun adventure of it."

"Very well, then." Veressa laid her fork and knife across the rim of her plate, signifying she was done. She stood. "I will take my leave."

"You are retiring already? The evening is still young." Camion pushed out his lower lip.

"I am exhausted from the road and would like to be rested by morning. I am sure you understand."

Camion rose, his eyes darting to his brothers, who had their mouths covered to hide their snickers. "I—I personally checked your chambers before I came to supper. I wanted to be sure they were ready when you were ready to retire."

"And who said chivalry was dead?" she snipped.

"I am always at your service." Camion bowed.

"Then I will see you at first light." Veressa swept from the room, not bothering to disturb her father, who was busy arguing with King Friedrick.

The Dragonbonded's First Army

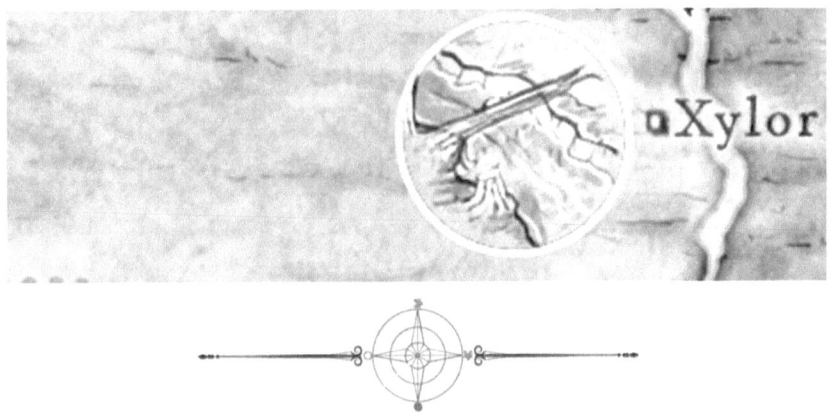

At the end of the third day out of Elmsdorf, Conner crouched before the evening fire. The wind across the plains had picked up, and the air was cold. He shivered in his sweaty clothes. Turning, he studied the dark path they had taken. Billowy white clouds were rolling in, reflecting the timid glow of the sliver of Erebus low in the west. The two had traveled well into the dark to reach this point. Morgas moved about the camp, grumbling under his breath that he had hoped to put more distance behind them. Valmer, Morgas's wolf bond, had left the camp for his evening hunt.

They were nearing Xylor, and with every stride that day, Conner's anxiety had grown. Would he blunder and expose them? What would the people of Xylor do if the truth was revealed? And yet, out of all the thoughts sprouting like weeds in his head, one in particular had taken root.

"There is something heavy on your mind, young Dragonbonded." Morgas broke the deep silence as he settled by the fire.

"The night I arrived in Elmsdorf, you mentioned something about Alpslanders and the need to atone for your ancestors' past."

"And you want to know what I meant?"

"I don't want to pry, but you made reference to dragons. Anything you could share ..." Conner shrugged, his cheeks blooming red. "Besides, you said I needed to know more about the world."

Morgas chuckled. "I did say that. Very well, then." He cleared his throat and adjusted his position near the fire. "That night in Elmsdorf, I told you how dragons came to our region of the mountains. But the tale of Alpslanders began much later.

"From the time our common ancestors rode the waves of the Antaric Sea to the shores to the north, Elmsdorf remained sheltered from the affairs of the old Seven Realms. So, it took many years for the stories of young men and women bonding with dragons to reach our village. And while such tales were intriguing, even entertaining, Elmsdorf life continued; that is, until a hundred years later, when conflict broke out within the orders, and the Seven Realms descended into chaos and destruction. Life for my people continued peacefully for several more decades. But even mountains could not shield my forefathers from the ferocity of the war that spread across the lands.

"It is said that one day, a young girl arrived at our village riding her dragon bond. She had come seeking a bloodbond with Elmsdorf's tomal. She told of how the Dragonbonded had made a pact with the realms to protect their lands, but that the Dragonbonded were few, spread thin while they safeguarded the many castles and fortresses."

Morgas took in Conner's stare. "For some reason, the tomal struck a bloodbond with the girl. Maybe it was because she said she was from our region before she bonded, though none in Elmsdorf recognized her. Or maybe it was because the dragons made their home nearby. Or maybe it was because the dragons were such magnificent creatures. Regardless, everyone who could wield a sword, nearly the entire village, packed their belongings, and headed west to join a regiment of ordermen and guildsmen who had volunteered to assist the Dragonbonded in protecting the realms. In time, that regiment would be called the Army of the Dragonbonded."

Conner rocked forward. "Your forebears fought alongside the Dragonbonded during the Anarchic War?"

"They did. For more than forty years. Near the end of the war, a massive Anarchic army was assembled on these plains, not far from here, rallied together for a daring, all-out assault upon the northern Harmonics. The army marched across Gorgonia north of the mountains, then crossed the border into Grenetia, which was unprepared for such an audacious attack. The night before the army laid siege to a beleaguered Ember's Keep, a battalion of my forefathers, in an act of desperation, descended from the mountains east of Dragongarde and engaged the army camped at the foot of the keep. Outnumbered five hundred to one, they held the Anarchists at bay for several days while the Dragonbonded rallied their small cadre across the realms to come to their aid."

Conner recalled the night he and Layna had arrived at Dragongarde, and the Sorceress's account of what had happened during that battle. "But I was told the Anarchists laid siege on Dragongarde, that the Anarchic army had to destroy the home of the Dragonbonded if they had any hope of securing their supply lines here to the east."

Morgas pulled up his shoulders. "That is the history Harmonics choose to tell. The Dragonbonded did muster their forces, and, along with the entire Army of the Dragonbonded, engaged the Anarchic forces in one of the most valiant military engagements ever waged. At the end of that bloody battle, the Army of the Dragonbonded had been decimated and the Dragonbonded slaughtered, along with half the Anarchic army. That is why the valley north of Dragongarde was renamed Valley of Souls."

Morgas waited as Valmer's howl echoed across the plain to the south. "With the Dragonbonded gone, the few survivors of the Dragonbonded's army tried to return to their former orders and guilds. They should have been heroes. Instead, they were summarily turned away, shamed and humiliated, branded as renegades and deserters by their societies, and cast out by those they had fought valiantly and died for. With the signing of the Treaty of Alignment at the foot of Dragongarde, the three crowns of the Harmonic Realms gave the eastern mountain region to my ancestors as recompense for their service to the Order of the Dragonbonded."

Conner recalled what Groegan had said to him at Dragongarde, words that continued to haunt him. "I was told the Treaty of Alignment also gave the Eastlands to my family's ancestors, to live free from noble rule."

"Our stories say the same. Living the way of a freeman offers one a certain perspective on freedom that others neither understand nor appreciate. Would you not agree?"

Conner stared back, Groegan's words echoing in his head: Your Eastland ancestors fought alongside the Anarchists against the oppression of Harmonic feudal lords.

"Yes," Conner said with little energy.

"Those from my village fought for nearly half a century in the Army of the Dragonbonded. The ordermen and guildsmen who'd marched and battled next to them had become like brothers. So my ancestors invited the other survivors, homeless and abandoned by their communities, to return with them to Elmsdorf and leave their Harmonic ways behind. That was when Alpslanders were born. Conner, *I* am a descendant of those survivors. My Alpslander forebears fought for your Dragonbonded forebears."

Conner straightened and took a deep breath. "That is why you struck a bloodbond with me so readily."

"You would have preferred I bartered harder for my services?"

"Something tells me I would not have fared so well. I would probably be carrying all the gear, building the campfires, cooking the meals ... even fluffing your bedroll at night."

Morgas let out a deep belly laugh. "Maybe I should have held out for more!"

Morgas's story helped explain why Alpslanders generally did not favor either side. It also showed Conner that the world was much more complex than he had ever been taught to believe. His Eastlander ancestors had fought with the Anarchists, yet the first Dragonbonded fought for the Harmonics. If he was drawn into the war, how was he supposed to know which side was right? It seemed whichever side he chose, he was likely to feel he was betraying someone. He would have to ruminate on some third way through this maze.

"There is something I don't understand," Conner said. "You said those who returned with the Elmsdorf villagers were ordermen and guildsmen."

"Many of them masters and grandmasters."

"Yet none in your village use elementals?" Conner asked.

Before he answered, Valmer ambled into the camp, panting. The wolf nuzzled Morgas's arm, and the big man lavished his bond's pelt with a vigorous rub. "When those who'd fought with the Dragonbonded returned to Elmsdorf, they vowed never to use elementals again. Those skills were lost."

"Why did they stop using them?"

"I cannot answer such questions for certain, but our stories point to the Dragonbonded."

"But the Dragonbonded were dead."

"Yes. Which brings me to the end of my long tale. It is said that all those in the Army of the Dragonbonded swore an oath to protect those bonded with dragons. The humiliation they bore for having failed to keep their oath haunted them through their remaining days. Perhaps that is why they never used elementals again."

Morgas stretched. "This account has been recited to every Alpslander youth, handed down mouth-to-ear for five hundred years. And each time, the youth is reminded that just as Hemera rises in spring to burn away the heavy snows of a long winter, so too will the dragons return to our homelands. And when they do, Alpslanders will be granted the opportunity to atone for the failures of our forefathers."

Conner awoke the next morning exhausted. He had not slept well. As much as he tried to deny it, he was already feeling his separation from Skye. He rubbed his eyes hard, Hemera a bright ball in the east. His guide had made a point every evening before going to sleep to remind Conner that he was to be packed and ready each morning before the stars winked out. Why had Morgas let him sleep so late? Alarm bloomed into fear. He staggered from his bedroll in a panic.

Morgas was near the far end of their small camp, his eyes cast toward Hemera, Valmer by his side. "Look there." Morgas commanded, pointing to the east.

Conner blinked, then followed Morgas's finger. "Trees," he muttered as he squinted. "I have not seen a living tree since we crossed the Borderlands."

"There are other forests in the Anarchic Lands to the south. But none like that one. We are a mile away."

Conner squinted at the horizon. "Those trees are massive. The stories of a forest a thousand paces high were not an exaggeration." The sight thrilled him, and he quickly gathered his gear.

Morgas had stamped out the smoldering embers of the fire and was staring at Conner with an odd expression.

"What is it?" Conner asked.

"Today we reach Xylor. Let us have one last practice session." Morgas reached back and drew his sword.

Conner jerked his head back and blinked. Letting him sleep late, not criticizing the condition and position of every garment he wore, and not fussing about needing to break camp early? It was all so out of character. "If you think it will help." He shrugged off his backpack and slid his sword from its scabbard. He took a defensive stance. He could never tell the precise moment Morgas would start a lesson, so he had learned to be prepared early. "Maybe I'll get lucky and get past your defenses."

Still, Morgas did not move. "I want to tell you that I have been impressed with how swiftly you are learning to use a sword. You would make a Gorgonian preceptor proud."

Conner considered the first time someone had tossed him a sword—Marcantos in Cravenrock. It had not gone well for him that day. "I have never been keen on fighting. But, as you said, I am not just an Eastlander any longer."

Morgas came at him fast, bringing his sword around for a stroke to Conner's midsection.

Conner parried the stroke, then jumped back. Something was different about Morgas—his aggressive stance, a determined gleam in his eye. Conner took a ready stance again, watching for Morgas's signal. But none came.

Morgas came at him again, faster. He spun his sword around and delivered a backstroke that would have caught Conner in the right thigh if he had been a hair slower with his blade. The swords rang out harshly.

"Morgas! What—?" But Conner was too busy parrying each stroke of Morgas's sword to say more. He danced and stepped to keep time with Morgas's spinning blade.

Morgas changed the tempo of his attack. Faking a shift to Conner's left, Morgas brought his blade down hard on Conner's sword, deflecting it outward. Spinning, Morgas slammed the flat of his blade into Conner's right temple.

The blunt-force strike snapped Conner's head to the left. His body followed. He struck the ground hard, air expelled from his lungs with an *oof*. Except for the gravel biting his cheek, he felt nothing. He opened tearing eyes. Everything wheeled.

Morgas shimmered like a reflection on a trough of water. Drifting nearer, he stared down at him.

Confusion washed over Conner. He worked his jaw. "Why?" he croaked, then slipped into darkness.

The Hunt

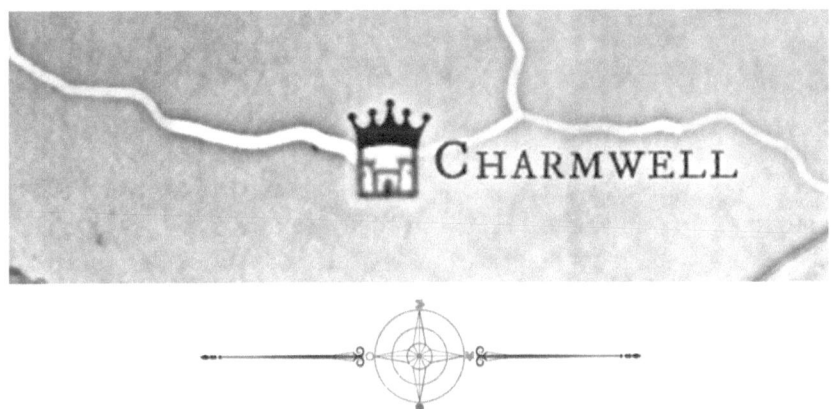

Veressa had not slept well, despite retiring early for the night. Unfortunately, it was not from too much excitement over going on a hunt. Images of Conner being injured haunted her dreams, images of him running, wounded and staggering through a giant forest, images of him trying to escape a band of Anarchic ordermen. Given their unique connection, she worried her visions were more than projections of her fears for his safety. The thought that they might be real, or at least a portent of his future, troubled her still. But she could not do anything for him here. She would have to trust he would find his way back home.

She pushed back a yawn as she descended the marble stairs of Charmwell's main keep. The predawn fog was as thick as soup. She stepped into the bailey, navigating her way around large puddles from the night's hard rain, letting the snorts of horses, muffled chatter, and shifting shadows near the haloed glow of lantern light guide her steps. Just inside the open drawbridge, she came upon Toran, saddled and ready. Camion was checking his legs for bone spurs.

Camion looked up. "So you were serious about joining us. Good! I had my manservant prepare your ride. I also had him pack the supplies you will need for the day. Some hunts can last well into the night." Veressa did not respond, so he gifted Toran with a friendly pat on the neck. "Your gelding seems to be in fine shape given your long ride from Graystone." When

Camion's eyes fell upon her green cloak and hood, the stocky bow in Veressa's hand and bulging quiver of arrows strapped to her back, he nearly choked. "I thought you were riding along to get out of the castle. I didn't know you wanted to actually *shoot* at something."

"You did use the word *hunt*. I heard somewhere that is what you do on them. Or did I get that wrong?" she asked with a teasing smirk.

"Yes. Just please warn me before you notch an arrow. I want to be sure I am standing on the backside of wherever you point that."

Veressa started to laugh, then realized he was deadly serious. Before she could give the young prince a satisfying retort, Tanner and Oakes appeared, slicing through the mist on their mounts. Gellastandt, in dark Ranger dress, emerged a few paces behind. All three wore the same tetchy scowls.

"If you two are done flirting," Tanner grumbled without looking down, "maybe we can get on our way? Since we are getting a later start than usual, we will need to ride hard." He gave his brother a quick wink as if sharing something amusing. "Once the dogs have the scent, we will start the hunt, whether you are there or not." He spurred his stallion into a canter across the drawbridge and vanished into the fog.

Camion leaned closer as Oakes and Gellastandt rode past. "Don't mind Tanner. He's never happy before lunchtime. Would you like some assistance mounting?" he asked eagerly, cupping his hands next to her saddle.

"I think I can handle it, thank you." She stuffed her foot into the stirrup and swung into the saddle, then took a deep breath. She was determined to make a good time of this adventure despite the pitiful weather, Camion's coddling, and his brothers' irascible demeanors. She urged Toran ahead with a quick heel.

On the other side of the drawbridge, the royal party was met by a half dozen mounted guildsmen with hounds on leashes. After a brief discussion, Tanner and Oakes kicked their mounts into a thundering canter, heading north across the open plains blanketed in thick gloom. Not liking being left behind, Toran bolted forward before Veressa could signal him. She sensed Antilles's excitement at being in the natural element. The white cat sprinted along beside her, and she laughed with glee. *Yes, my dear friend, me too!*

After a few minutes, Camion caught up. He kept glancing over at her as if he expected her to tumble from her saddle at any moment. "We will ride north off-road for about an hour until we come to an outcrop of trees," he shouted over the pounding of hooves across the wet earth.

Veressa considered saying that the horses and dogs would not keep their current pace for an hour. But, of course, the men all knew that. Camion's brothers were hoping to leave her behind. She motioned her understanding. Hunching down, she gave Toran more rein, and he responded to the gesture by picking up speed. Well-trained, he would know when to let up.

An hour from the castle, in the middle of a large grassy meadow, the men reined their horses in. Tanner glanced over his shoulder with a grin, but lost it as Veressa came riding in hard. When she lifted her reins slightly, Toran dropped his head and tucked his haunches, going into a long paddle slide on his hind legs over the slick grass, coming to rest a few paces away from the pack of men.

"Well! That was fun," Veressa said, brandishing her teeth at them all. "Can we do that on the way home, too?"

None of the men responded. With a flick of his wrist, Tanner sent the guildsmen and dogs on ahead.

As they waited, Veressa chewed on her lower lip to keep from suggesting they should have left their dogs in the kennels; she and Antilles could have flushed out a quarry in far less time. Having hounds do all the work defeated the sporting aspect of a hunt.

After some time, the three brothers conversed among themselves. What started as anemic chatter about the storm the previous night and details about how to properly roast a pig on a spit devolved into a game of trying to best one another in whatever exploits they could imagine themselves doing.

Veressa grew bored. She slipped an arrow from her quiver and cleaned her nails of the mud she had collected that morning.

This went on for nearly an hour before the baying of hounds floated across the grassy meadow from the northwest. From their sounds, the dogs were moving west along the tree ridge line.

"Camion, take Veressa north to the edge of the woods, then cut west to flush him out into the open," Tanner commanded. "If the swine retreats into the thicket, we will lose him. Oakes and I will go west and take him as he comes at us." The two older brothers did not wait for debate as they urged their mounts ahead once more.

Veressa stowed the arrow and clenched the reins until her palms hurt. *Well, isn't this fun!* Not budging from her current spot crossed her mind, but the thought that she might miss out on any action was way worse than having to deal with the three dimwitted princes. With a low growl that made Antilles's ears perk, she reined Toran ahead.

The sounds of the dogs grew louder off to the west. Still, Camion did not sway from Tanner's command, pulling up only once they reached the edge of the woods. He reined his horse around to face her. "We will wait here for the signal."

What? That the hunt is over? "Which is...?"

"Hunting horns," Camion answered, then glanced over his shoulder to the west. "Anytime now."

Veressa's anticipation grew as the baying of the hounds continued, but still, no signal came. She flexed her hand on the reins while her other hand fidgeted with the bow hanging from her saddle latch. Antilles paced in circles around Toran. She needed something to distract her from her growing restlessness. "Tell me something about the boar we hunt. I hear they can grow to be quite large."

Camion grinned smugly. "Oh, yes! Their size is outmatched only by their aggression. They can grow to be twice as tall as a Carpathian boar and thrice the weight. Generally, they stay clear of settlements, though they have been known on occasion to gore an experienced hunter." Then his eyes popped open wide, and he raised his hand defensively. "I am sorry, Veressa. I did not mean to scare you. Rest assured, you have many able-bodied men about to secure your safety."

Veressa snorted softly, pushing down the annoyance that sprouted once more like a marigold in wet soil. And then, all too quickly, the world about them went crazy. Even before she heard the light snap of a twig or caught the musty scent on the shifting breeze, Veressa sensed Antilles's alarm. Her head snapped around to eye a tall patch of grass to the west. And there, in a small thicket, it stood—nearly the height of a pony and twice the girth. Two long, yellow tusks as thick as Veressa's wrist angled up from the sides of its gaping mouth. The gray boar must have doubled back, eluding the dogs still baying and chasing its track to the west. With ears forward and head down, it held its two black eyes fully on Camion's horse.

"Camion!" Veressa shouted, pointing behind him.

The prince twisted in his saddle just as the boar charged. He never saw the gray blur. The beast plowed into Camion's mare from behind. The mare shrieked in startled agony, and her hindquarters buckled from the force of the impact. Thrown off-balance, she reared upward. And the trio—horse, rider, and boar—vanished in a fury of tangled legs, fur, and screams.

In one smooth motion, Veressa snatched her Grenetian bow and notched an arrow. Drawing it back, she leaned forward for better balance, waiting for a chance to take the shot. But before she could, the boar bolted away, leaving Camion on the ground, his legs splayed wide, his back pressed against the rump of his dead horse.

Coming out of the skirmish the apparent victor, the boar must have decided to have another go at the creature hapless enough to get in its path. It spun and dropped its head, long tusks pointed directly at the prince. After churning a patch of mud with its front feet, it charged.

Veressa pivoted to her right only to realize she had waited too long to take the shot. Even if her aim were true and she brought the boar down, its forward momentum would kill Camion. She had no time to think. So she reacted. *"Aerora energi stereoproaspi!"* she shouted. The air in front of Camion shimmered as Air and Earth interacted.

The boar slammed headlong into her shield. Blue light sparked; air sizzled and popped. But the barrier held, and the boar went down hard, sliding to a rest with its snout between Camion's ankles.

Veressa dismounted and staggered forward, dizzy from the chant. The boar lay twitching and grunting. Blood oozed from its snout and one eye. One of its tusks had snapped off. But the impact had only stunned it. As much as she hated to, she needed to put it down before it came to. It tried to rise, legs quivering violently. It snorted and shook its head. Stepping forward, Veressa straddled the boar's wide girth. And with a quick pull on the bowstring, she drove an arrow deep into the base of the animal's skull. It dropped once more, and did not move again.

"Are you all right?" she asked.

Camion stared up at her wild-eyed, his crotch soaked in his own urine.

"Camion, are you hurt?"

He wagged his head, unable to speak. Or to close his mouth. He began to sob and shake uncontrollably.

"Camion?" The rhythmic pounding of running horses drew Veressa's eye. Tanner, Oakes, and Gellastandt were riding in hard. She stretched her hand down to Camion. "Your brothers are coming. Stand and get a hold of yourself before they get here."

Camion swept tears from his cheeks and, taking her offered hand, rose up on wobbly legs.

"Camion!" Oakes shouted as they neared. Reining his mount around Camion's dead horse, he circled the boar. "You killed your first boar, little brother. Most excellent!"

"I was not the one who killed it," Camion snapped, pointing at the arrow in the back of its skull. He refused to look any of them in the eye as he stalked past them all and started the long hike home.

Veressa noted Ranger Gellastandt's odd expression. *What is that?* she wondered. *Surprise? Outrage? Did he sense me drawing on Air and Earth?* She flipped her bow over her shoulder. No use worrying about that now. She could hardly have stood there and let the boar gore Camion. She climbed into her saddle, ignoring the brothers still staring at the boar, and reined Toran about. She would leave it to his brothers to figure out how to get Camion back to the castle.

Dissolution

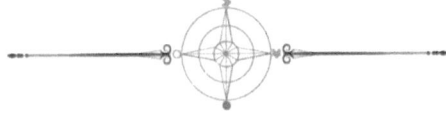

The evening after he'd informed Meera and Ousel that he would instruct them for an important task, Nartesis called Ousel to his chamber. "I have important news to share with the order, Ousel, and want you to be the first to know. I assuredly will need your thoughts on how to proceed."

Ousel groveled before him, looking remarkably like his hedgehog bond. "Yes, my lord. How can I serve?"

Nartesis handed Ousel a parchment, then sat back, stroking the bulge in his breast pocket.

Ousel read then reread the parchment, biting his lower lip and shifting from foot to foot. Finally, the minister spoke. "My lord, I have until now refrained from stating my opinion regarding decisions you have made, though you have encouraged me on multiple occasions to do otherwise." Ousel waved his hand over the parchment. "But I must question your instructions written here."

"You disagree with my decision to disband the council?"

"I do, my lord. Wholeheartedly."

"Go on."

"For every large wheel and knob turned at the top, there are many little wheels that must spin."

Nartesis forced down a sneer at the idea that the order was some cold mechanical timepiece. "Ousel, our order does not lack people making decisions about which wheels to turn when and by whom. What this order lacks is a clear vision—a direction to guide all those working so diligently within these walls. Those around us work very hard, faithfully believing that those in command know which direction we are heading. Yet, since my return, I have yet to hear any councilman state a clear purpose or mission for the order. They have become lost while everyone busily turns this wheel and then that wheel." His argument was not alleviating Ousel's worried expression, so he elaborated. "A vision no more grows from a committee than a massive oak grows from a pile of acorns. *I* am the seed this order needs to set its course. And I cannot do that as long as others question and debate my every decision."

"My lord, this is a bold move—one that will surely draw intense scrutiny, not only from the council, but many others who are ... less inclined to accept changes in how the order has functioned for half a millennium."

"And you? Where do you stand on this matter? After all, you are next in line to be given a seat on the council."

Ousel stiffened. "A position on the council never interested me, Lord Shazarack. I have been quite content in my position as Minister of the Academy of Necromancy. I am, and will continue to be, a humble servant of the order. However, others do not operate that way. Many will want a justification for this abrupt change."

"And I will provide one. Let me be frank, Ousel. I have never been fluent in the ways of politics or affairs of intrigue. I will need assistance to navigate the tumultuous waters we will be sailing through in the coming nights, or we will run aground. I need people I can trust. What's more, I need your eyes and ears to help root out any who would have designs to undermine my authority as their Supreme Lord. I know that I can count on you."

"Of course you can, my lord. I believe completely that our order has much to gain under your leadership and guidance. I am your faithful servant. And I will do what I can to keep you apprised of ... undercurrents that may force us to run adrift."

Nartesis slapped his palm on the table before him. "Excellent!" He rose, confident he had what he needed. "Then call a conference of all the senior ordermen. It is time we set a new course, in search of a new destination."

"As you command, my lord."

Nartesis entered the great chamber hall on the heels of several undead protectors. As his guards parted, he stepped forward. Suddenly, he was transported back to another day, another time, when Thanatos was nothing more than a paltry abbey struggling to survive, and he a young, bright-eyed shaman student struggling to pave his own path. It was here, in this room, that he had usurped control of Abbey Newdowns from the man who had exacted so much abuse and cruelty upon him for years. Odd, he could not recall the old abbot's name, that crusty old fool he'd killed. It was in this very hall, while he sat among the rows of chairs, that the spirit he had summoned into the old abbot's body—the one who would later adopt the name BrieAnn—set everything in motion, leading up to this very moment. An endless stream of faces, friends, and comrades who had filled this great hall paraded past his mind's eye. So many people lost in the vastness that time had forgotten, dead and buried. *Does anything we do really matter?* he mused. *Perhaps it is time to see.*

Nartesis shambled to the podium. "I have called you here to inform you that, as of today, the Necromancers Council is dissolved of all its duties. From this point forward, *I* will assume all council responsibilities and governance over our order. I have provided Ousel with an official proclamation that elaborates how decisions henceforth shall be made, as well as which decisions require my approval."

"This is insanity!" Galan erupted out of his chair.

Nartesis rounded on him. "Galan, I take it you disapprove of my decree?"

Galan glanced about to bolster his stance. "As I am certain every other Necromancer in this room does! You can't disband the entire council."

"Then I will see that you receive the first copy of my proclamation so that you know how to present your grievance to me."

"I do not need a piece of paper to tell me how to state my grievance. I will do that here and now!"

Nartesis stepped around the podium and shifted forward, several of his guards closing around him. "Very well, Galan. For this one time, I shall allow you to argue your case."

"Allow me ..." Galan choked on the words. He raised his fist in the air and shook it at Nartesis. "I am the sovereign prince of the Necromancers. No one *allows me* to say what I wish to say."

"Except the order's anointed paragon," Nartesis retorted. He waited to let those words settle.

Galan's cheeks reddened. "Your assertion that you are the great Shazarack has never been proven."

"Already another grievance?" Nartesis laughed. "If you wish to question the legitimacy of my claim to being Nartesis Shazarack, then take it up with Ousel. He will happily record your complaint in the registry, and it shall be arbitrated in due process. Now, let's not be diverted. I wish to hear your case regarding the *sanity* of my decree."

Several moments ticked by while Galan wrestled to gain control of his emotions. "Very well, then. First, the Necromancers Order ... like all the orders ... has had a council since its inception. For nearly a millennium, the council has been to the order as the spirit is to the body. A council is essential for the efficient operations of the order. To exorcise the council from the order would render the corporeal institution ... well, dead."

A number of others in the room bobbed their heads as murmurs blossomed about the chamber.

It was time to stem that flow. "The council has not met since my return over a fortnight ago, so whatever services the council provided have stopped. Yet, in that time, I have not observed any disruptions in the daily operations of the order. Apprentices attend their classes, while students and novices see to the planting, harvesting, and storage of food for the coming winter. Proselytes maintain our buildings. And at night, all busy themselves in adding to our burgeoning necro-army. Our order is by no means 'dead.'"

"It takes months for the effects of council inaction to bubble to the surface," Galan grumbled.

"We do not have the luxury of waiting months. And folklore is not a sound argument for why a council should exist. We need cogent and competent decisions." Nartesis paused to let them consider whether he was suggesting council decisions had been otherwise, but Galan had no retort. "Answer this, Galan. Under what authority does the council exist?"

Galan squared his shoulders. "Order councils were mandated under the Armistice of the Orders set nearly nine hundred years ago. That has been the foundation for our organization."

"So, your argument hinges on an agreement struck and signed by monarchies from a bygone era." Nartesis let the murmur die down before continuing. "And since the Treaty of Alignment signed at the end of the

War of Breaking eliminated the ruling class within the Anarchic Lands, I would say that foundation has been invalid for half a millennium. Frankly, I am surprised no one thought of this before now. If anything, the notion of a ruling council runs counter to being Anarchic. You never did rid yourselves of royalty; you simply replaced it with a new ruling class." Nartesis's eyes swept the sea of stunned faces. "I tire of this debate. My decision on this matter stands and is final. The council is hereby disbanded. And I hereby assume all their responsibilities. Any other grievances shall be funneled through Ousel, and I will address them in due order."

Nartesis lumbered from the hall, his left foot grating along the stone floor.

Nervous energy gnawed at Sovereign Prince Galan through the night, his heels grinding away at the threadbare rug splayed across his bedchamber's hearth. He was often afflicted with uncertainties, more so since Breanen's death. But the time for thinking and scheming was over. He was relieved when a narrow red shaft of Hemera's early light pierced his window, calling him to action.

It was common knowledge in the order that Thanatos had been constructed to the exact specifications of the original city before its destruction. But several key buildings held new secrets, passed down and shared only among those on the Necromancers Council—secrets added as an afterthought for occasions just such as the one Galan now faced. His fingers slid along the wall to the right of his fireplace. A complex succession of pressure points resulted in a gratifying audible click. The sovereign prince stepped through the portal that opened before him. At the end of a dark, narrow alcove, he took stairs that led to a chamber far below the city's main structure, a room shielded from any prying ears above, even those elementally enhanced.

Within moments, three of the eight other council members had gathered around him. They knew why he had summoned them; his own doubts were reflected in their wild, anxious stares. They waited.

"No more are coming? Then let us begin. We must make our move, before this narrow window of opportunity is lost forever."

Sheardra, the tall, thin woman next to Galan fidgeted. "We need more time, Galan, if we are to be certain who sides with us. If Shazarack—"

"Do not blaspheme the name of our great and exalted Supreme Lord before me!" Galan ground his teeth. "That creature is *not* the long-dead paragon of our order."

"And what if you are wrong, Galan?" Baltor, Galan's life-long adviser and friend, pulled at his thick, white beard. "You are asking us to put a lot of faith into your claim."

Galan considered the statement. Even those he held in highest esteem were becoming tainted by the fantasy that the Necromancers' paragon had returned home from the dead. They had all heard the whispers—that it was not a coincidence that this creature's arrival followed on the heels of the great Cosmic alignment. They were all being ensnared by the creature's spell. "You are all so easily swayed by this beast's words."

"He does not sway those around him with his words alone," Sheardra was quick to retort. "We have seen the undead he commands. I have had an opportunity to inspect one up close. They are very real, as is the power used to summon them to the Physical plane. And have you forgotten the day of his arrival? Our combined powers had no effect—"

"Do not speak to me about that day! It was my wife that ... *thing* ... took!" Galan shook his fist at Sheardra. "The creature succeeded merely because it caught us off guard. There is something more going on here than what floats on the surface. Our incantations were not so much ineffective as they were ... deflected. There is a powerful enchantment protecting the creature's life force."

"Which is precisely my argument that we wait until we know more," Baltor added.

Galan shook his head. "If we are to act, we must not tarry. This creature's hold over those in our order grows each night, making it harder—and much more dangerous—to root him out. And don't forget the pact with the other orders," Galan persisted, taking in the three with a long glance. "What do you think will happen when the other councils receive news that we abandoned our pact in defense of our homelands? I would rather be wrong about this creature than break our oath with the councils. We cannot fail to protect the Anarchic way of life."

Sheardra opened her mouth, but Baltor placed a gnarled hand on her shoulder. They did not need to be dragged back into the argument of the previous day after the creature had declared the pact void.

Baltor asked, "What do you propose, Galan?"

"Our first course of action should be to find more council members to sway to our side. It is possible they are hesitating until we reach out with an offer. Once we secure a majority, many within the order will fall in line. Even those who don't will be less likely to oppose us."

"And if we cannot find even one more to join us?" Baltor inquired. "I ask because even a majority is no guarantee that the other grandmasters will stand behind what they perceive as an insurrection. We have made enemies of some of them to get where we are ... or were. And few Necromancers have a stomach for violence. A majority is not a quorum. We had better have a backup plan ready to handle such a contingency."

"If this approach fails, we will have no recourse but a more direct and confrontational strategy. We already know much more about this creature and its undead compatriots than we did when they arrived."

None pressed Galan further on his plan, so he continued. "I will probe to see where the other five council members stand. You three must work to undermine, or at least arrest, this creature's influence on the other grandmasters. Lay seeds of doubt where there is fertile soil, keep those under its influence from congregating and spreading their opinions, and see if you can discover more about the limits of his guards' powers. Any information could prove valuable to our success."

"And if it is not enough?"

"Then let us pray that we have the Cosmos on our side. Remember that the order's survival, even that of the Anarchic Lands, hinges on our success."

The Way of Harmonics

After returning to Charmwell, Veressa went immediately to the royal guest chambers and yanked on a gold cord dangling beside her bed. While she waited for a response, she splashed water over her face from a ceramic basin and rubbed away thick, dark mud speckling her face and arms. Antilles made a few tight circles on a brightly patterned rug in the middle of the room, then flopped down, panting.

Moira, Veressa's assigned handmaiden, appeared at the door with her robin bond sitting on her shoulder. She curtsied, her head bowed. "Yes, Queen Veressa?"

Veressa removed her mucky riding boots. "Can you prepare a bath for me, please, Moira? It seems fall hunting in Elvenstein is a dreadfully dirty business."

"Of course, Majesty," the handmaiden replied with a titter. Curtsying again, she pulled the door closed behind her.

Veressa had no more than wrestled her boots to the floor when there was a hard rap on her door. "Enter!"

The door swung wide to reveal her father. His brow was bent low, and the edges of his lips were pulled down.

"Father? What is it?"

Antilles perked his ears at Jonath.

"King Friedrick has directed our immediate attendance in the Charmwell royal hall."

"My, but the man is impatient to begin deliberations of terms for a marriage. Last night, he suggested having a summit this evening after supper." She had accepted his suggestion to delay the discussion since she had no real desire to marry the prince. Further, she had hoped an opportunity to share her intentions with Camion might arise while on their hunt. Sadly, that hadn't happened before the incident, and she doubted he'd have had the mental capacity after. "I cannot properly attend any negotiations dressed like this. The odor alone would be offensive." She chortled and flicked her hand at her father. "Return a message to the king that I must have my bath before talks can begin."

"Normally, I would do as you request, daughter. Unfortunately, the messenger was quite specific. The king emphasized the words *directed* and *immediate*."

Veressa's breath caught. "That sounds ominous. Very well." Taking a deep breath, she brushed globs of caked mud from her riding garments and cloak, and pulled her boots back on. "But he had better not comment about my state or I will give him my mind."

As they proceeded down the long hallway, Jonath leaned over and whispered near her ear, "You want to tell me what I can expect we are walking into?"

"How would I know?"

Jonath's eyebrows rose on his forehead. "Nothing happened during your hunt that you would like to share?"

Veressa pulled to a stop and glared at her father. "Why is it that every time something dire happens, you immediately jump to the conclusion that I had something to do with it?"

"Hmm." Jonath's eyes floated to the ceiling. "Maybe because I speak from experience?"

Veressa tucked her arm under his and drew him along, Antilles and Beggar right behind. "Then I must make a more concerted effort to prove you wrong."

The two took the grand staircase at the end of the hall down to the main level, then proceeded toward the central part of the main keep. At the end of another wide hallway, they came to a set of guarded double doors. The guards pulled the doors wide and they entered the royal hall.

While the three realms shared many aspects of lifestyle, language, and culture, they were not without their distinct differences. What each realm considered extravagant was the perfect example. And nothing, as Veressa took in the great room, exemplified Elvensteinian ideal of lavishness like Charmwell's royal hall. While granites and hardwoods like oak and hickory were abundant in Griffinrock and therefore relatively inexpensive, the Realm of Elvenstein—comprised primarily of prairies, marshes, and desert—had to rely heavily on their extensive trading with outlanders beyond its southern borders to provide all the stone and wood needed for their lavish lifestyle. And given the immoderate use of these resources about the room, construction must have cost the realm dearly.

The walls and ceiling of the large royal hall were flush with thick panels of darkly stained woods meticulously cut in bas-relief. Each panel depicted various images of Elvensteinian life—hunting, fishing, and other sports and games, all intermixed with occasional scenes of famous battles with Anarchic forces along their share of the Borderlands to the east. The panels were framed in lighter woods inlaid with red and white crystalline stone. The flooring was painstakingly cut and laid in hexagonal slabs of quartz and mica polished to reflect Hemera's afternoon rays streaming through the windows to their right.

Camion sat in a chair behind a long cherry table at the far end of the room, with Tanner and Oakes behind him like matching bookends to help prop him up, their arms folded tight across their chests. All three looked as if the king had just decreed they would be tortured later that afternoon. King Friedrick stood before the table, staring at his sons with hands on hips, while Gellastandt waited at the dark end of the table.

"Here as requested, Majesty." Jonath tilted forward slightly.

With a jerk, Friedrick spun about, his face a livid red. "Tell me, Jonath, is this how you raise queens in Griffinrock?"

Jonath twitched as if pinched. "I don't understand, Majesty. I am sure whatever grievance you may have suffered is the result of some cultural misunderstanding. Griffinrock is a matriarchy and—"

"You misconstrue my meaning, sir," Friedrick snapped, then waved toward Camion. "My son tells me your daughter used a ... a *spell* to kill the boar they hunted this morning."

"Spell?" Jonath blinked. The word *spell* was often used by Elvensteinians to describe elemental invocations performed by heathens and charlatans—those not properly trained in the arts. "You mean an incantation." His eyes shifted to Veressa. "Is this true?"

Veressa swallowed hard. Some time ago, she had made a solemn promise to keep Annabelle's training a secret. This was not how she'd wanted her father to discover the truth! Maybe there was still a way out of this. "It is not true. An arrow from my bow is what did the boar in."

Friedrick's face darkened. "Do not quibble over details with me, Queen Veressa. Did you use a spell or did you not?"

Veressa squared her shoulders and pushed her chin out. "I did."

Friedrick turned his ire back to Jonath, whose jaw had gone slack. "Ranger Gellastandt, tell King Jonath what you know of this."

Gellastandt stepped forward and cleared his throat. "I felt the queen draw upon Air and Earth as the princes and I rode in to find the two with the dead boar." His green eyes were fully on Jonath. "It was a very powerful spell."

"Air *and* Earth, Jonath!" Friedrick shouted. He threw his arm into the air. "As if a member of your royal family casting a spell were not offensive enough, I discover it is something an *orderman* would cast. Now do you see the meaning of my question?"

Veressa was reaching the end of her patience. It was time to take control. Antilles brushed against her leg and she relaxed. "I think you are all failing to see the bigger story here."

"And what story is that?" asked Friedrick, whose face was displaying deepening shades of purple.

"That I saved Camion's life." She took in the somber faces behind the table. Clearly, those who had been there needed their memories jogged. "If I had not done what I had, you would be mourning his loss instead of attacking me for coming to his defense!"

Friedrick's eyes narrowed. "My sons do not need rescuing."

Veressa stared at the seated prince. She could not even tell whether he was breathing. "Tell them, Camion. Explain to your father what happened."

Camion gave no expression as everyone turned their eyes upon him. Finally, he shrugged. Tanner and Oakes made no attempt to speak either.

Veressa's mouth fell open. So, the three weasels would rather their father not believe the sovereign queen of Griffinrock saved the prince's life. "I am through standing here while you cast indictments at me. I am not on trial." She turned her fury on the three statues behind the table, the blood fully drained from their faces. "You should be thanking me. In case there is any semblance of morality in there wishing to express appreciation, you are welcome!"

Friedrick's face had gone from purple to violet. "I think we can consider any plans for a wedding off."

"Good! The boy is better suited to wed an ewe or a sow!" Veressa turned her back on the lot of them. "Come, Father. We have clearly overstayed our welcome."

Several hours later, Jonath and Veressa were on the mud-packed road, riding north toward Griffinrock. A troop of royal guard rode far behind. When they had been escorted upon their arrival, it had felt like protection. But this armed force made Veressa feel like she was being driven out of the realm. *Such childish behavior,* she thought.

Jonath, who had forgotten the guardsmen were behind them, distracted her with a hearty chuckle.

"What?" Veressa snapped.

"Better suited to wed an ewe or a sow?" Jonath shook his head. "I suppose we should not expect much support from Friedrick in any declaration of war."

Veressa snorted. "Friedrick is charged with defending the southern section of the Borderlands. I think he has forgotten it is *I* who negotiates with the orders over how a war would be conducted. If the realms go to war, I will make sure he pays dearly for treating me like one of his concubines."

Jonath smiled at her. "You are so much like your mother."

"You're not mad at me?"

"I never said that. But when is that anything new?" he asked. Noting Veressa's astonished expression, he winked. His eyes darted to the left, where Beggar perched in an anemic shrub. "There is, however, the issue of what Tanner's protector called 'a very powerful spell.' Air and Earth? It doesn't take an oracle to divine who might have taught you how to cast the incantations of a Ranger." They rode for a full minute before he broke the silence. "Well, so much for proving me wrong."

Veressa balked. "I had nothing to do with that mess back there. Friedrick left his garden untended long before we rode in. His sons are not just callow and spoiled; there's not a spine in the entire clutch." *Why couldn't Tanner's guardian have been of any other order? Someone who could not sense both Air and Earth?*

"If the Rangers Council find out Annabelle was training you in advanced skills ..."

He did not have to finish the sentence. Veressa looked away. In any normal situations such an offense of the Ordermen's Code would have resulted in Annabelle's banishment from the order. "Actually, Lady Kyles gave her consent for Annabelle to train me."

"What?" Jonath gripped the reins until his hand shook. It was several moments before he could speak. "I thought I had taught you better than that. Do you recall what Shaman Rollingsworth mentioned about Rangers dealing with debts and marks? Well, it is too late now. But you had better remember this warning, daughter. When the timing is the least convenient, Lady Kyles will come knocking to request payment on that debt."

Veressa dropped her head. "Annabelle did try to persuade me not to continue. But the chance to learn Ranger skills was just too alluring."

"It seems I also failed to tend my garden."

Her father was nothing like Friedrick! "I don't understand what is so offensive about someone of royalty using elementals. After all, you are of both royalty and the orders."

"An orderman, yes. It was my honor as well as my duty to protect your mother. But royalty?" Jonath shook his head. "If I hadn't had Iza's ear, Friedrick would have treated me like he treats all ordermen—with disdain. It is also why your Aunt Mariette never accepted me into the family."

"Because you are a Mystic? You told me it was because of your serfdom heritage."

"That was only a small part of it. A greater sin in their eyes was that they saw me as someone who cast ... *spells*. To them, I will always be an underling." Jonath held up his arms. "Robes of nobility cannot hide the person within."

Veressa huffed. "You have more nobility in your pinkie than the entire Elvenstein royal menage. Besides, those who rise in class are celebrated by the people, not frowned upon."

"Yes, Veressa, there are occasional situations where a freeman is brought into a guild, like your young Champion who was to become an Apothecary. Or, like Annabelle, an assiduous yeoman becomes an orderman. These stories give people aspirations that even they might rise above the masses. But, in truth, these are rare exceptions to rules long established in our society. Rules can be bent, but they can never be broken. That is the way of Harmonics."

"Well, if I learned anything today, it is that I have had enough of rules that make no sense. And when I get home, the War Council will discover what I am truly capable of."

Jonath laughed lightheartedly. "From the day the Griffinrock crown was set upon your head, you have been a very sharp rock in the sandals of the War Council. But try as you might, dear daughter, you cannot call yourself Harmonic and rail against the very structures that hold us together."

For some time, they rode in silence while Veressa chewed on her father's words. Everyone she had ever known had tried to teach her that lesson—her mother, her father, her early teachers, even Annabelle. But she had always refused to accept it, even fought against it, as a basic truth. Why was she so defiant? So determined to forge her own way? Did she have some unconscious wish for self-destruction? Or did she just have a desire to prove her doubters wrong?

"At least we don't need to devise an excuse for not accepting an arranged marriage with Camion."

Veressa shivered at the thought that some hapless woman might someday marry that prince.

"But," Jonath went on, "we will be returning home sooner than either of us had planned. I hope your Champion completes his mission in short order."

Xylor

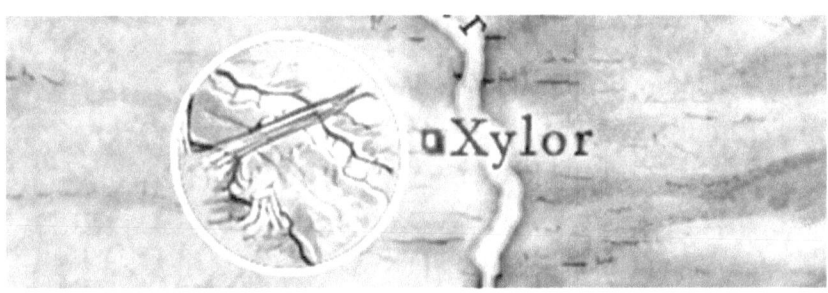

Conner's eyes fluttered open to find a young girl, fourteen or fifteen, inches from his face. She had light blue eyes, high cheekbones, and a small nose. Flaxen hair hung freely about her round face, bobbed to follow a sharp jawline.

"Grandfather?" the girl yelled out.

Conner winced at the piercing sound, his head throbbing.

"Yes?" a deep voice answered back from another room.

"He is awake."

A moment later, an elderly man with facial features like a much older version of the girl appeared beside her. Straight, gray hair, cut short on the sides but long in the back made him appear thin. "Get out of his face, Wren." He fluttered his hand her way. "My apologies, young sir. She is not accustomed to being around people from different bands, much less from a different clan."

Wren crinkled her nose at Conner, leaning in close enough to count the stubble growing over his upper lip. "He is not what I expected from a Gorgonian."

"Leave him be, child," the man scolded.

"I will go tell grandmother he is awake," she said, seemingly unconcerned for her grandfather's rebuke.

"Yes, please do that." The man waved at the door, and the girl vanished from view.

"Hello, young man." The man assumed the girl's place, then peered into Conner's eyes with the bearing of a Physician. "My name is Azarah Amadeer." He pointed to a mourning dove pacing about on a windowsill. "That is Jitters. You will have to forgive my granddaughter, Wren, for her lack of etiquette." Azarah nodded at the open doorway where late-morning light flooded through. "She is a bit of a free spirit."

As Conner tried to sit up, Azarah pressed him back to the mattress. "You have only been here an hour. I suggest you let that head heal more before you go dashing about." Azarah placed his palm to Conner's temple. The touch was light and soothing, and Conner relaxed. He sensed the man drawing Earth elemental. Azarah mumbled something, and a moment later, Conner's forehead warmed. Heat radiated from his temple outward, to the back of his head and down his neck. With the warmth, the throbbing receded. "Better?"

"Much, thank you."

"Good," Azarah nodded with a satisfied smile.

Motion at the door drew Conner's eye. Morgas's imposing frame filled the doorway.

"Well, now that your minder is here ..." Azarah started.

Conner drew himself up, pulling the bed sheets tight over his chest. His desperate eye fell on his sword and sheath dangling from a post at the foot of his bed, just out of reach.

Azarah's gaze flipped between the big man in the door and the lad in the bed. "Far be it for me to demand anything from a Gorgonian, but I would strongly urge you wait a few days before continuing your endeavor. It would be unfortunate if you keeled over; all my healing energy wasted on some rash decisions." Azarah caught the silent glares between the two, and cleared his throat. "Well, I will take my leave so that you two can discuss your plans."

Morgas waited inside the doorway long after Azarah and Jitters departed. "Truly, I am sorry for causing your injury, Conner. However, it needed to be done."

"Needed?" Conner started, but he choked back the rest of his response as the throbbing returned. He sat, jaw slack, staring at his deceitful guide.

Morgas stepped to the side of the bed, ignoring Conner's defensive posture. "Maybe you have not thought through this exploit as well as I had hoped. That is disconcerting."

"I'm sorry. What exactly did I miss ... besides you trying to kill me?"

"You are on your *endeavor.*" Morgas spoke the word slowly—the word Anarchists called their bonding trek. "Without a good reason, entering Xylor would have drawn undesired attention, making our stay for more than a few hours impossible. I chose to give you that wound because we could explain it away as an accident, one that would require a week to heal." The big man's shoulders sagged. "I did not expect Xylor to have such an able healer."

"You planned on hurting me all along?" Conner asked, struggling to keep his voice low. "And you didn't tell me?"

Morgas shrugged. "Would it have made what had to be done any easier?"

"Well ... no." The thought of knowing the imposing tomal would purposely wound him made his forehead bead with sweat.

"Conner," Morgas said firmly, drawing Conner back. "We have but a few days to find what you seek. This morning, I introduced myself to some of the villagers."

Conner took a deep breath and blew it out. "And what did you find so far?"

"This band is small for Dristonia—no more than one hundred twenty people, which should make your task easier. But that is the only good news. No one has been on their endeavor the past three fortnights, except for one yoot who is still away. And he has been away for over a week, which is an unusually long time."

Yoot, Conner thought—what Anarchists called someone before they bonded. "Sounds like he could be the one we are looking for. The timing is right."

"Could be," Morgas repeated, though he did not seem convinced. "How would whoever sent your preceptor the message know of the bonding if the teen has yet to return?" After thinking for a moment, Morgas suggested, "It is possible this dragon-bonded yoot is blending in with the other village yoots."

Conner pondered the idea for a moment. "That would make our work much harder."

"Yes. And as I said, we only have a few days." Morgas leaned in to inspect the knot on Conner's temple, then grimaced. "How does it feel?"

"Like a very big man ripped my head from my neck and then stuffed it back on." Conner waved off Morgas's frown. "I will be fine. As soon as I can convince the healer I am better, I will come out."

Morgas bobbed his head. "Then I will continue to ask around. But try not to raise any alarms with too many questions. People are already on edge having Gorgonians in their midst."

Azarah returned an hour later with a handful of leaves from a plant Conner did not recognize. The old man darted into the next room, where he clanged around for several minutes before returning with a colorful ceramic bowl. "Drink this." Before Conner could react, he shoved the edge of the bowl to Conner's lips and tilted it.

Conner took a cautious sip and swallowed. The hot brew was thick and rich with flavors that made his jaw ache and his stomach feel hollowed out. He placed his hands on Azarah's and tipped the bowl further. The fluid flooded into his mouth.

"Slowly, please." Azarah pulled the bowl back gently. "This elixir is potent. Your body needs energy to heal, but let us not overwhelm it."

With the bowl drained, Conner rested back. The tingling in his stomach spread outward, soothing his body. For the first time since leaving Elmsdorf, he felt calm. The pleasurable feeling continued. A sudden light-headedness overtook him, his head lolling to the side. He tried to move, but his arms were too heavy. Alarmed, he forced his eyes open. He tried to say something, wanted to shout for Morgas, but his tongue no longer worked.

Azarah patted Conner's shoulder. "Relax, Conner." The old man's voice seemed to drift from the far side of the room. "You are safe here, but your body needs rest. You will feel much better when you wake in a few hours."

Unable to fight the numbness consuming him, Conner gently slipped away.

"Well, there is a fine yoot!" came a jubilant voice.

Conner opened his eyes cautiously to find Azarah standing over him. Jitters sat on his footboard, poking its head one way then another, occasionally cooing. "How long did I sleep?" Conner grumbled back, annoyed that he had been duped yet again by someone he trusted.

"Well, let me see." Azarah pried Conner's eyes wide and leaned in. "It appears you have slept long enough. I think it is safe for you to be up and about now. But I would like you to take it slow at first, okay?"

"Okay." Conner let the old healer help him sit up.

Azarah continued to dote over him until he was certain Conner could move about on his own. Finally, fully dressed and sword slung over his back, Conner was ushered outside.

Whatever Conner had expected for a village when he stepped through the healer's door, the reality that hit him sent his head into a tailspin. Luckily, there was a railing. Conner grabbed on tight. A long boardwalk continued two hundred paces from the doorway, connecting to another boardwalk that spiraled about the most massive tree trunk Conner had ever seen ... or imagined. Along the way, rope bridges, as plentiful as stems on a branch, sprouted from the boardwalk, some sloping upward, others down, each connecting to more boardwalks that fanned out from the same trunk. Conner's eyes followed the tree trunk upward. Overhead, a web of boardwalks and rope bridges spidered everywhere. And intermixed in that web, nestled among the colossal branches, were hundreds of small cylindrical buildings.

"Like our village?" came a voice from behind.

Conner turned to find Wren smiling at him. "I must admit, it is not what I expected." He tilted his eyes over the railing. The same webbing of wood planks and ropes fanned out beneath as well, reaching all the way down to the shadowed forest below. *How high up are we?* Growing up, Conner had had a fear of heights. But he'd thought his time riding Skye through the clouds had fixed that. He swallowed hard, knuckles tightening on the railing. Apparently not.

"Come along, then. I'll take you to the savants."

Savants. The name given to the eldest women in a band. They were the villagers' only leaders, though leadership had little to do with how people lived in the Anarchic Lands. According to Morgas, Anarchists followed no laws, and were completely free to determine their own fate. However, because of their age and experience, savants had a unique perspective on the social fabric of the community and were often consulted for guidance. Despite Conner's continued questioning, he still found Anarchic ways very confusing. Why they wanted to see him was beyond him. The more he was scrutinized, the more likely he would mess something up. Conner took a deep breath and nodded for Wren to lead the way.

Conner tried to memorize the path Wren took him along, but it was pointless. Even with his keen memory, he lost all sense of direction. After twenty turns of first taking this boardwalk and then that rope bridge, he was hopelessly disoriented. Instead, he focused on keeping to the center of the wood planks and not looking down. How was he going to gather the information he needed to find this dragon-bonded teen if he could not navigate his way around the village?

"Here we are!" Wren finally exclaimed, holding her arm out before a small round cottage with a short, closed door. She rapped once. A muffled voice inside called for them to enter. Wren pushed the door wide, then stepped back.

Conner dipped his head through the door and inched his way into the cottage, comprised of a single, cozy room. In the center, a very large iron pot hung above a pit with a slow-burning fire, the source of the thick smell of spices and wood smoke that wafted up toward circular vents at the apex of the conical roof. Bubbles popped and burped along the surface of whatever thick liquid filled the pot. A dozen elderly women sat in a ring around the pot, intently crocheting various colored swathes of fabric. Each wore simple drab clothing, and sat cross-legged on a thick pillow. On the far side of the room, several young men were cutting up what appeared to be very large mushrooms into a wicker basket.

None of the savants glanced up, nor indicated that they knew Conner and Wren were there.

"Grandmother?" Wren asked softly.

"Thank you, Wren." A thin woman to the side waved her hand. "Wait outside." After Wren left, the woman leaned over and gently patted an empty pillow beside her, then returned to her crocheting. A small, fluffy white feline with bright, emerald eyes next to her squinted at Conner, swishing its tail in contentment.

Conner stepped closer, then waited to see if she would say something. In the awkward silence, he eased his hind end into the pillow, crossed his legs, and waited.

"And what did she say to her husband?" Wren's grandmother asked.

Another savant on the far side of the circle answered, "She said he could live in the storage shack for a week, and maybe that would soften him enough to be courteous."

A few of the other savants chuckled lightly.

"Erin!" Wren's grandmother called out. "You need to get those mushrooms stewing or we will be serving supper late. If that happens, I will let you deal with the wrath surely to befall us from a hungry mob. Is that understood?"

"Yes, Elda." The young man came forward and held the wicker basket containing the mushrooms before Elda, who leaned forward to inspect his handiwork. "Not as precise as I expected from you, but it will have to do." She nodded toward the pot and returned to her crocheting.

The young man poured the contents of the basket into the pot, then stirred the thick stew with a wooden spoon before quietly departing.

A number of minutes passed in silence. *Are the savants expecting me to start the conversation?* Conner thought.

At last, Elda spoke. "Is my husband taking good care of you?"

Conner nearly jumped. "Azarah? He has been more than kind. I am feeling much better because of his healing."

Satisfied, Elda nodded, never looking up from her work. "Tell us of your family, Conner."

His heart leaped into his throat. He swallowed hard. He had spent a great deal of time with Annabelle and Layna debating which parts of his past would pass as Gorgonian if he were interrogated. They both knew he possessed no skills in lying and were afraid veering too far astray would reveal him. This was one of the few areas that were safe. "My father is a farmer, and my mother makes baskets for those in our village."

"Reputable professions," Elda replied, bobbing her head.

Several savants in the circle made *mmm* sounds and nodded but did not look up.

"And siblings?" Elda probed.

"I have two younger sisters."

"The eldest, then." Elda bobbed her head again. "Strong and independent, the eldest are."

Several more *mmm*s and nods around the circle of women.

"And what are your plans once you have bonded?" Elda asked.

It was not a question Conner had planned for, and he was not completely sure how to respond. He called forth the hopes and dreams he'd had the day he left home on his trek. "I have thought of becoming a healer, if the Cosmos wills it."

Even louder *mmm*s and emphatic nods. Several exchanged glances with raised eyebrows.

Conner had no idea what their reactions meant, but at least none looked alarmed by his responses.

After some time, Elda set her crocheting to the side and glared at Conner. "In the rare occasions a yoot visits our village, we do not ask them to be anyone other than themselves. However, you are not Dristonian, so I feel obliged to ask one request of you during your stay. I know your clan values the swank of a strong blade, so I won't ask to leave your sword in your room. However, we are not accustomed to flaunting power. So I ask that you and your minder not, under any circumstance, draw your swords while you are among us. Do I have your oath to this?"

"Of course, Elda." Conner tipped forward slightly.

Elda smiled as she rubbed her feline bond's ear. "I still recall the urgency of my bond's call. I am sure that if you abide by my husband's instructions, you will be on your endeavor soon enough." Turning to the door, she called out. "Wren, I know you are listening. Come in here."

The door creaked open. Wren poked her head in, her cheeks rosy.

"Wren, you are to look after Conner while he is here," Elda announced.

"Of course, Grandmother."

"And please do not get him injured any more than he already is."

Wren slipped forward and wrapped her arm around Conner's, tugging him off his cushion. Turning her sky-blue eyes up at him, she grinned. "I will try my best," she said, dragging him out of the savants' lodge. "Follow me," she said when they were outside, and ran off.

Conner did his best to keep up, which required ignoring how high he was above the ground.

Wren turned and skipped backward up a narrow causeway. "She likes you, you know."

"Your grandmother?"

Wren giggled. "Yes."

"How can you tell?"

"She asked you about what you want to become. She does not ask that unless she has an interest in you."

"And you? What do you want to become?"

Wren pulled to a stop. Staring over his shoulder, she replied, "I have not decided yet." Then turning, she dashed ahead, calling back, "But definitely not a healer!"

For the rest of that day, Wren took Conner on a whirlwind tour of their tree village. For a small band of one hundred, the village had an amazing number of cottages, storage sheds filled with supplies and food, and common centers. Wren led him on a spiraling journey over the vast network of boardwalks and bridges. By the time Hemera dipped into the west, the two clambered onto an open wooden terrace at the very top of the forest canopy.

Wren chuckled as Conner staggered across the terrace, while he focused on forgetting how the platform gently swayed side to side. "How did the trees grow so tall?" he asked.

Wren winked back. "It is a secret among our village."

Before Conner asked more, a young girl, no more than ten, appeared at the opening in the center of the platform's floor. "Wren! Come quick! Squirrel has returned with his bond!"

"Squirrel?" Conner asked.

"He left a week ago on his endeavor," Wren said with a beaming smile. "Some of us thought him lost." She placed her hand on his arm. "This is special, Conner. Tonight, Squirrel gets his name!"

"His name?"

"Oh, Conner," Wren laughed at him. "You are such a fledgling! Dristonian yoots are given animal names until they have their bonds." She pointed at the little girl peeking through the opening. "That is Little Robin. Tonight, you get to witness a celebration of adulthood."

Wren took Conner on another spiraling romp back through the village, introducing him to yet more buildings, cabins, and sheds along the way. It was dusk by the time she came to a halt at a boardwalk spiraling the tree trunk. Beside her, a rope ladder dropped from a wooden building above containing a complex series of rope pulleys and metal gears, and disappeared through a hole in the boardwalk.

"What is this?" he asked.

"The village lift, you mooncalf. It is how we get down and up." Without taking her eyes from him, she leaped sideways, her hand deftly snagging one of the ladder rungs. Several metallic clicks followed by a whirring sound emanated from the gear box above, and Wren sank through the hole. Conner was not sure how the lift worked, but Wren's confidence was enough to bolster his courage. He clambered onto one of the rungs passing by, and he descended into darkening forest.

After reaching the forest floor, Conner shadowed Wren to where the other village yoots gathered about the young man just returned. Nearby, a roaring bonfire silhouetted a throng of people. He inched closer, listening to the yoots' banter and chatter, hoping to catch a clue that would guide him to the one he was looking for. Out the corner of his eye, he caught Morgas at the edge of the fire's light. Conner drew close.

"Any progress?" Morgas asked in a deep, low voice.

"Not much." Conner gestured toward the small gaggle of yoots. "There can't be more than four old enough for bonding. It has to be one of them."

"There is another possibility, one looking all the more likely." Morgas looked around, then dipped closer. "Whenever conversations turn to recent bondings, the villagers change the subject. I sense that many, if not all of them, know of the dragon bonding. What if the person you seek is no longer marked as a yoot, but instead is among the village adults?" Morgas pointed to the large crowd dancing and singing around the fire. "It could take a long time to find someone of the right age who does not have a bond with them—more time than we have."

So many, Conner thought, his shoulders drooping.

"Squirrel! Come forward!" Elda cried out near the fire, waving to the young man in the midst of the yoots.

The young man bounded to Elda, then sank on bended knee. He carefully pulled his field mouse bond from his pocket and held it up for the savant to see.

Elda placed her palms on Squirrel's shoulders, but gazed on those gathered around her. "He has bonded!" She waited for the whooping and yelling to stop. "When the Cosmos gives the village a child to raise in the ways of our ancestors, we must take great care in fostering them to find their way. Just as our bonds connect us with Gaia, so our children connect us to the future. But when the Cosmos gives a yoot their bond, they are no longer of the future. They are of the present. Thus, they have earned the right of responsibility to care for themselves, and in so doing, to care for the others. This time is marked by a naming, a true name that denotes duty and virtue for all we are today. In that time-honored tradition, as savant of Xylor, it has been my joy to give many of you your names." Elda looked at Squirrel. "Just as it is my honor to give you yours. From now on, you are called Hanstel. Welcome to Xylor!"

Hanstel rose and, turning with a beaming smile, gave a double fist pump in the air. The gathering of yoots whooped and hollered in response, then rushed to encircle Hanstel. Within minutes, the entire village was shouting and dancing around the fire.

Conner glanced up at Morgas. "I guess we're going to have to work faster."

Plans Revealed

Thanatos

"**I**t is time for your first lesson," Nartesis declared as his two new pupils entered his study. He moved unsteadily to the table in the middle of the room. "I hope you are ready for what lies ahead. Before we begin, I have asked my staff to prepare a meal before you undertake this task. You will need all the energy you can muster this day, so please sit and eat." He waved at the food splayed before them.

"That is most gracious, Lord Shazarack," Ousel bowed low before his paragon, his eyes frozen on the savory dishes.

Nartesis took a chair at one end of the table. "Meera," he called after the two had joined him. "While you eat, tell me a little about your preceptor. I am very impressed by how well she trained you. She clearly knew what she was doing."

"Breanen Sagamore was exceptional, my lord." Meera waited while the undead servant filled her goblet. She raised the goblet and took a deep quaff of the wine. "I met her when I was but eighteen, barely bonded and a first-year apprentice. She was already studying to become a master. She walked past me one evening while I was practicing my first ignition incantation. For whatever reason, she stopped and offered me a few pointed instructions, then waited while I attempted the incantation again. After several successful castings, she departed without further remark."

Rubbing her mink draped over her shoulder, Meera continued. "I didn't think much of the encounter until that winter when I was summoned to her personal study. I remember it was a very cold night." Meera giggled. "The thick doors rattling on their hinges hid the sound of my knees rapping together as I stood before her, and I can honestly say that it was not from the chill in the air. Breanen explained to me that as a new master, she had been given the right to choose whichever pupil she wished to personally instruct. She recounted to me that day we met in the field and told me that she had been very impressed with how quickly I had learned the incantation. And that she had chosen me to be her first student."

"Highly unorthodox," Nartesis remarked, his palms pressed together as he listened. "She should have chosen a proselyte as her pupil."

"Yes, my lord. I mentioned that to her. She told me that I had exceptional skills and she foresaw that I would go far within the order."

At the far end of the table, Ousel cleared his throat.

Nartesis's head snapped up. He had nearly forgotten the minister was there.

"The Lady Sagamore made a reputation early in her career with her uncanny powers to know things others could not divine," Ousel added.

Nartesis rocked forward. "Such as?"

Ousel took a deep breath, his eyes locked on the ceiling. "Such as what was going on elsewhere within the Anarchic Lands ... and beyond."

"Yes," Meera agreed. "The day of the Cosmic alignment, for example. She not only knew that it was approaching but predicted the precise moment of its occurrence."

Ousel's face grew cloudy. "No one ever uncovered how she acquired this knowledge. I doubt even Galan, who knew her for most of his life, ever learned the secret to her divinations. And ... in all the years she offered prophetic advice, she was never wrong."

"Intriguing." Nartesis pressed the desiccated tips of his fingers together.

Ousel set his silver spoon to the side, then handed Helgish a piece of bread. "I can personally recall five occasions when she warned the council of events happening elsewhere. One of those was when she announced that the other orders had gathered to propose the pact recently presented and signed. She explained the pact to the council, and our order's obligations under the agreement. She even knew when the committee would arrive with their proposal. Then she worked privately with Galan to prepare the terms of our negotiation."

"I see." Nartesis grinned. "Yet another unorthodox choice." He turned to Meera. "Breanen was married to Galan, was she not? I understand that it is very rare for council members to marry, as such emotional relationships can be a distraction to our work."

"Yes, my lord," Meera said. "Breanen and Galan were inseparable from the time they were apprentices. They married after Galan was named to the council. He advanced to the top in short order, and, with the untimely death of the previous sovereign prince, assumed head of the council."

"Interesting." *But what is more interesting is that no one grasped what was right before them,* Nartesis thought. Breanen had been the true power behind Galan. "If this Breanen was as powerful as you two suggest, then why was she never named to the council?"

"I cannot say, my lord," Ousel said. "She was offered the position ... several times."

"I asked Breanen once why she'd turned down the appointment," Meera added. "She told me that she could best serve the order working in a supporting role, using her talents where needed. She never enjoyed engaging in the council's endless debates. Council politics irritated her to no end."

Now that Meera mentioned it, none of the twenty-two women Nartesis had found in the Book of Census had risen to the council, though many had been quite powerful. Yet another trait consistent with the spirit he had known as BrieAnn. "Yes. I have seen firsthand how politics can dampen one's spirit. Besides, I suppose being married to the great sovereign prince comes with its perks."

One of Nartesis's undead placed a thick slice of cake on the plate before Ousel, who licked his lips and rubbed his hands together. Helgish waddled over to have a closer look at the cake.

"I heard many times from other council members," Ousel said, "that she was the real power behind the duo, that she influenced and guided Galan in his decisions, especially with respect to the pact. But it is possible they were speaking out of jealousy."

"So Breanen supported the pact?"

"Oh, absolutely, my lord," Ousel replied. "She pushed the council into negotiations from the start. I had never seen such a passion in her before; she was even willing to jump into the fray of council debate. I recall she fought a few council members on several key points in the pact to ensure our commitment was as it was scripted."

"Again, interesting," Nartesis said flatly, wanting to not look too interested. But he strained to bottle up his excitement at this further proof. BrieAnn had always preferred working from behind the scenes. That way, she could never be held responsible when things went sour and Nartesis erupted into one of his rants. But he still needed to understand what she had to gain from the pact with the other orders.

"It's odd," Meera stated softly. Her gaze shifted, distant and aloof. "Now that you ask these questions, and I reflect back on how she behaved, it all was so very ... peculiar."

Nartesis could not agree more. But he did not need his line of inquiries to stir up anything he could not handle. He needed a solid plan for how to deal with Galan first. Then he could dig further into Breanen's life. "*Peculiar* seems an appropriate description of a Necromancer conducting herself in such a manner. Wouldn't you agree, Ousel?"

Ousel looked up, his fork halfway to his lips, then pinched his shoulders upward. "Such is the way of our vocation, my lord. I never cared much about what those from other orders thought of us."

Nartesis slid his fingers over the lump in his pocket. He had heard enough. He was almost certain this woman Breanen was indeed his servant BrieAnn. With their meal nearly complete, it was time to redirect the conversation. "Enough small talk. There are more important things to grapple with, so I think we can begin. However, before we do, let me be clear about this. What I am about to tell you is to remain our little secret. You are not to share a single word of what we discuss with anyone. Are we clear on this?"

After each had marked their oath with a solemn nod, he leaned forward. "Your task is to get me a new body."

Meera was stunned. Had she heard Shazarack correctly? Get him a new body? Like all Necromancers, she had spent her career learning how to summon spirits from the other planes into human receptors—animating human vessels, as this work was much more gratifying than simply calling incorporeal spirits to the Physical plane to do one's bidding. But Shazarack was asking for something far beyond this, beyond the conceivable. Countless Necromancers had spent their lives chasing the ever-elusive path to immortality. Some had been the most brilliant minds in the order. And all of them had reached the same indisputable conclusion. Physical immortality was not possible. Too many formidable barriers were in the way, such as knowing how to summon a human spirit into the vessel, how to draw upon the immense power necessary to permanently and safely bind a human spirit to the vessel, and how to prevent the summoner's consciousness from being sucked through the vortex created while summoning the spirit. Even if the enchanter solved all these problems ... and none ever did ... incantations of resurrection had a brief lifespan. At some point, binding incantations break down, and the spirit is drawn back into the plane from whence it was called, even human spirits. There were just too many aspects that could go terribly awry, and the amount of elemental power needed to overcome them all was far beyond anyone's reach.

"Come again?" Ousel asked.

Shazarack chuckled. "I expected just such a reaction. And rightfully so! No doubt, you have been told that such a feat is impossible. And there was a time when I was young that I would have agreed with you. However, with the right aids, it can be done. After all, I once brought my dear love, Arna Grey, back to life."

"And you believe we have the power to do this?" Meera asked, still struggling to accept that what Shazarack asked was possible.

"Alone? No. Not even with my training. But together?" Shazarack shrugged. "Maybe. Part of the reason you have been incapable of this feat is that you have not been taught how to properly direct and weave the flow of the necessary elementals. That was the purpose of our little exercise with the flame the other day, Meera. I needed to see if you have the potential— and you do. And that is why we are going to focus on honing your skills in Fire and Earth in the days to come."

"You said this is only part of the reason?" Meera asked.

"Yes." A row of tawny teeth appeared behind Shazarack's mangy white beard. "But we have a much bigger problem that we must address before anything else. For your entire Necromantic life, you have been told that there are limits to what you can achieve. That is utterly false."

Shazarack settled back as she processed his statement. "I'll be honest with you," he went on. "I would have preferred selecting apprentices for this task, as Breanen did with you, Meera. Apprentices have not been prejudiced by the beliefs and attitudes of their preceptors. Sadly, I don't have the luxury of the years it would take to properly prepare them."

Shazarack flexed his fingers as he spoke, working the sinew in his hands. "Let me be clear about what I am asking you to undertake. Once we begin the procedure to call my spirit into a new body, I will be completely powerless to assist. You will have but one chance at this. A miscue, a misspoken chant, the wrong elemental weave, and I will be sucked into the Mental plane. Once I am there, you will not be able to retrieve me. In turn, you lose your chance to acquire the knowledge I will share once I have a fresh body. There is no room for error. And that is why, before I place my future in your hands, I am going to take you to the very periphery of your souls. We will seek out your every limitation—in what you do, in what you believe, even in who you are. And only when you have broken free of those limits will you be ready."

Ousel dropped his chin to his chest. "My lord, I don't know if I can do what you ask. If I were to make a mistake, or if I could not find the strength needed, I would be responsible for losing you. I—I don't think I could bear such a burden, nor the shame of failing you."

"The task is not as onerous as you may believe, Ousel, so take heart. I made mention of an aid." Shazarack reached into his cloak pocket. "This will guide us in this endeavor, help you weave the Fire and Earth that you will call forth, and most importantly, keep my spirit bound to the body into which you summon me." He removed a medallion from a tattered piece of gray cloth and placed it reverently in the center of the table.

Meera shifted closer to inspect the piece of metal—a golden amulet in the shape of the Cosmic Star attached to a thick chain—while Morgana sniffed it. A small, black stone was fastened to the center of the gold star. Meera had spent several years working under a gemologist, so she recognized the stone—a black onyx. It had been masterfully cut and polished, though the surface reflected no light from the candles set about the table. She leaned closer. Not just a black onyx. Bright, thin ribbons of blue light sparked and rippled within the stone. "Breanen had an amulet exactly like this."

A troubled expression darkened Shazarack's face, but it vanished a moment later. "Yes." He waved as if dismissing Meera's observation as insignificant. "It was hers. She had no further need for it."

So, Galan was right, Meera thought. *Shazarack did kill Breanen. He killed her for this stone.* Shazarack drew her back before she could ponder the revelation's significance further.

"It is a Fettering Stone. Take a few minutes to study it. You cannot damage it, so use whatever incantations you wish. Once you have completed your examination, tell me what your inspection reveals."

Meera cast a series of invocations on the stone while Nartesis sat observing. She felt like a fish in a glass bowl. Being measured, weighed, and judged by one's paragon was pressure greater than anything she had experienced under Breanen's critical tutelage. Finally, she sat back, light-headed more from what she had gleaned than from exhaustion.

"Well?" Shazarack asked once Ousel's analysis was complete.

"The stone is a doorway to the other planes," Ousel whispered. His gaze was transfixed by the blue sparks and swirls buried within the onyx.

"I agree. But there is more," Meera amended. "The stone is also a pathway *into* the other planes."

"Say more," Shazarack encouraged, his dull eyes brightening.

Meera stared at the amulet as she wrestled with putting her thoughts into words. "There is Earth elemental, interlaced with faint traces of Fire, emanating from the stone—thin as a thread yet seemingly unbreakable. It winds and spirals to the very edges of the Physical plane, slipping into the Mental plane beyond."

"Actually, the thread traces all the way to the Astral planes." Shazarack's jaw clamped shut. Meera sensed that in his eagerness to share his own revelations about the stone, he had said more than he'd intended.

The thread traces all the way to the Astral planes. The words reverberated across her mind. A pathway to the very core of the Cosmos? Could it be? The significance of the statement was unfathomable.

Shazarack brought her back, breaking the death-like silence. "That is enough about the stone for now." He swept the amulet away and placed it in his hip purse. "There are aspects of the stone's powers you will need to understand before you can perform the task." Shazarack ran a leathery tongue across his gray lips. "Let us begin your training."

Meera fell into her cot, her body numb from the long night of strenuous mental activities. And yet her mind would not stop racing. She pressed her face into her pillow, trying to will the nagging thoughts to let her rest. But they were relentless, and soon she realized she would get no sleep until she had chased them all back into the dark recesses of her mind. With a sigh, she rose and heated water for some Camellian tea. Morgana squeaked her disappointment at not being able to snuggle against Meera.

Shortly, Meera sat huddled on her couch, eyes closed, hands lightly cradling the warm porcelain cup, inhaling the intense aromatic steam that soothed her restive spirit. She let the night's discussions with Shazarack swirl about her, undirected. She picked at each thought and drew them together, revealing new insights and forming deeper questions with each revelation.

Grimmley's questions about the Fettering Stones had nagged at her ever since the day the two had spoken in the cellars of the Shamans' temple. The old Shaman stated he had never laid eyes on one of the stones, declaring he knew almost nothing about them. If that were true, how did he know their name and appearance? And why had he been so keen on learning more from her about what these stones could do ... and about those who possessed them?

Based on what she had learned last night, answers were beginning to surface. First, the stones were imbued with Fire and Earth elementals, so they would only be important to Necromancers and their antithesis— Shamans. Further, she now had a reasonable explanation for the name Grimmley and Shazarack had used—the stones were used to fetter a spirit to a body. Grimmley, like Shazarack, was withholding secrets about these stones—their history and their extraordinary powers. The thought of learning more about the stones gave her chills. *I don't blame you, Grimmley, for wanting to keep this a secret.* But had Grimmley simply been probing because he was Conner's preceptor? Or had he received word of Shazarack's return and the stone he possessed, and wanted to know more? The answers swirled around a boy, his dragon bond, his Shaman preceptor, and the resurrected creator of dragons. Something was drawing Conner, Grimmley, and Shazarack together, and she was confident that Conner's dragon sat at the center of that triad.

And what about Shazarack? Any doubts she might have entertained that the withered old man was not who he claimed to be had shriveled up and died. Still, while the legendary tales of Shazarack's elemental prowess seemed genuine, she also knew the husk of a man who now schooled her was not that powerful. If anything, Shazarack's powers were feeble.

That brought her to Breanen. The dinner conversation the previous night had been too awkward and contrived to be just a fireside chat to pass the time. Shazarack might have deceived Ousel, who was too distracted by the excellent meal to notice, but she recognized the conversation for what it was—an inquisition. Shazarack had been fishing for specific information about Breanen. But to what end?

Meera might never be able to prove it, but Shazarack had killed Breanen. His possession of Breanen's rare and powerful amulet, a requirement if Shazarack was to have a new body, offered plenty of motive. But how had he done it? Breanen might have been old, but when it came to wielding elementals, she'd been in her prime. Yet, according to Ousel, Nartesis had dispatched her in a matter of moments. How could a feeble old half-dead man dispatch a powerful Necromancer so quickly?

Meera took a long draw from the cup, feeling the warm tea gently caress her throat. Already, her eyelids were beginning to droop. Too exhausted to think through this further, she set her cup down. And with an eager Morgana bounding toward the bed, she went to get some well-deserved sleep.

A few hours later, with Morgana quivering on her shoulder, Meera crept stealthily into the barn and waited near her horse's stall to let her eyes adjust to the dark. She squinted, the message she had found under her door crushed in her sweaty palm, looking for signs of human life. The late afternoon rays seeping between the barn wall slats offered little help in her search. She did not have long. The urgency was frustrating. She had told Ousel she wanted to check on her horse, but she was certain the minister had seen through the half-truth. She moved toward the back. An icy grip snatched her arm and spun her around. She stifled a shout.

A tall man in black cloak and hood flowed out of the shadows, hunched and thin, pressing closer.

"Galan." She exhaled hard.

"I am glad you found my message," he whispered. "Meera, I cannot afford to be out too long, so we must speak quickly."

"What—?"

"I now have a majority of the council's backing. We are making our move tonight to take back the order." She did not reply, so he clarified. "We need you with us. I know you have spent time with him. Your knowledge of the creature would be invaluable to our cause."

"Galan ... don't do this. Please, I beg you."

The hooded man staggered back as if he had been pushed. A long moment of silence followed. "You don't believe that we can defeat this creature. That is why you don't want me to try."

"No, Galan." She stepped closer, keeping her voice low. "It is because I think you *can* defeat him—"

"So you felt it too," Galan interrupted.

Meera diverted her eyes from his intense stare. He always saw straight into her. But maybe he was speaking of something different. "Felt what?" she mumbled.

"The creature is weak. Fragile. His undead guards are the only real power he possesses. The rest is an illusion."

Meera's breath caught. She was on the verge of acquiring a whole new world of necromantic power. How could she explain to Galan her craving for more knowledge? Could she even explain it to herself? The oath she had sworn prevented her from saying anything about the amazing secrets Shazarack was sharing with her.

Galan's eyes narrowed. "It is true! I was right about him." He straightened, seeming to grow in height before her. "He's somehow seduced you. You know his promises of power are empty, right? We move on him tonight. You must choose a side. Are you with us, or with him?"

"Galan, even if you don't believe that he is our Supreme Lord, you must realize that he possesses profound knowledge. We could learn so much from him." She was dancing near the edge of her oath to Shazarack, but she needed to convince Galan to back down. Or at least give her more time.

"And what price will you pay for that knowledge? No. Whatever the cost, our order cannot afford it. He is uprooting our entire culture. Breaking our pact with the other orders is only the first transgression against Anarchism and the security of our order. He will demand more, each demand taking us further down the path of peril and destruction. If we do not stop him, and now ..." Galan shook his head vehemently. "I should not have to convince you of what we must do." Galan's eyes darted to the stable door as if he expected Shazarack to burst in. "Breanen chose you as her very own protege. She guided you, molded you to become the woman you are. She taught you everything about necromancy."

"Breanen sent an assassin to dispose of me like I was refuse. Did you know that?"

Galan inhaled sharply. "No. Breanen said she was taking care of your situation. Clearly I misunderstood her meaning."

Meera could not look him in the eye. *What allegiance do you owe those who would see you dead?* asked a tiny voice in her head. *Shazarack needs you. He offers you immortality. What did Galan ever offer you?*

She scowled at Galan, anger boiling just below the surface. "You do not need me," she hissed.

Galan shook her harder. "You were the daughter Breanen never had! The daughter she could never conceive. I am sure it broke her heart to dispatch an assassin. But you cannot fault her for enacting the laws intended to keep our order safe."

Meera twisted free of his grip, rubbing at the pain shooting down her arms. Morgana squealed in anger. "I know that!" *Do you?* the tiny voice whispered. *Breanen had no heart!* "She was the closest I ever had to a mother ... and you, a father." *Yet Breanen cared more for the Code than for you,* the voice berated.

"Yet you choose to help the creature that murdered her?"

Meera wiped the tears pooling under her eyes. She felt like she was being ripped apart. She was so close to discovering how to tap into an unlimited wealth of elemental power. Under Shazarack's tutelage, she was standing on the shore of a raging sea. Immortality beckoned to her. Now, Galan had the audacity to ask her to give that up. "Choices are seldom as clear as you would like them to be."

"No, Meera. The choice could not be clearer. Whatever this creature is, it comes from another time. Its beliefs are obsolete. The world it lived in no longer exists. It cannot simply leapfrog a millennium of painstaking progress that our ancestors clawed their way through. No one has that right. It goes against more than our orders' code, Meera. It goes against nature itself!"

"Just because Shazarack comes from a different time does not make him, or his beliefs, obsolete. If anything, Shazarack has opened my eyes to how dogmatic and self-absorbed our world has become. He comes from a time when the world was filled with the thrill of exploration for new knowledge, when every orderman shared the discoveries they made, before the orders split. Unlike the ordermen of today, they grasped an essential truth—that we stand on the shoulders of those intrepid souls who came before us. That is why the ordermen of old had capabilities far greater than those we possess, greater than anything we dare dream of." *Like immortality.* The tiny voice laughed gleefully. "That world can live again, Galan. His beliefs are not obsolete; they have just been ... dormant. And maybe, possibly, we will restore the power and wisdom of the Thanatos of old."

"It seems you have made your choice. As have I." Galan slipped past her and tromped to the stable door.

"Galan."

The once-sovereign prince paused but would not meet her gaze. In the afternoon light, he appeared haggard, gray hair tangled, shoulders hunched, eyes bloodshot and puffy.

Meera felt a pang in her chest, as a hundred things came to her—things she should have said long ago. She sensed his urgency, his unwavering resolve, the same determination she witnessed whenever he faced a formidable task. "Be careful," she whispered.

He did not respond, but turned away, and was gone.

An Unexpected Guest

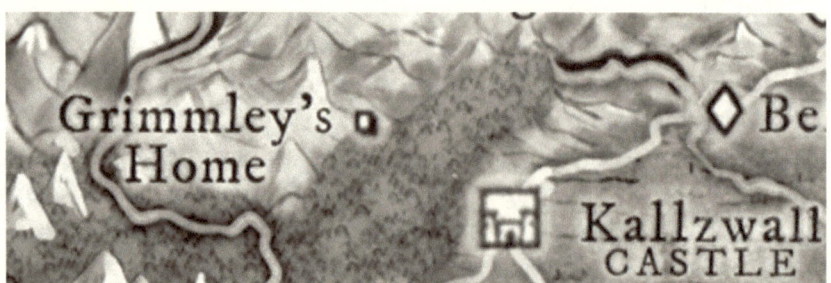

Grimmley set down his quill pen and straightened his back with a painful groan. It had been a long night of labeling vials in preparation for the next day's potions. And he had hardly rested since his return from Moonslayer, where he'd gone in search of information on the Shaman Alicia Farclave. He was thinking about how wonderful bed would feel when there was a hard rap on his front door. "Now, who do you think that might be?" he asked as he shuffled past his fireplace and his owl bond on her perch.

Barthox winked wearily at Grimmley.

He retrieved his staff propped near the back door, then shuffled back by his bond, slowing long enough to give a grunt of displeasure. "It is so like you to offer up no help after you've had dinner." He pulled his front door wide to get a good look at his unexpected caller.

In the dark doorway, an old man in rumpled brown clothing raised his arm, blinking at the light in his eyes. His head and face sported week-old thin, gray hair. "Grimmley?"

Grimmley leaned forward and squinted at the man. His features seemed familiar, but the man was scruffy and gaunt.

The man dropped his hand. "It is I, Herid."

"Herid? Herid!" Grimmley reached through the doorway, snatched the man around the shoulders, and pulled him in close for a big hug. "What are you doing here, old friend? It has been, what … more than thirty years since I saw you last?" Grimmley waved his arm with sudden energy and drew Herid inside, then poked his head through the doorway again and checked his small porch. "Where is your bond, Ezera?"

Herid waved at the air at his side. "She's right here, you blind old loon," he grumbled. "I keep telling her to stop hovering about in the shadows." He leaned closer, placing his hand to the side of his mouth, and whispered, "But I'm sure you understand fully how bonds are prone to ignore you."

Grimmley's brow dropped as he closed the door. In the better light, he took a long, hard look at Herid. More than time had kept Grimmley from recognizing his dear old ally and friend. Though Herid was younger than Grimmley by twenty years, he could have easily passed as Grimmley's older brother. The man was thin as a fencepost, with sunken brown eyes and milky skin that sagged and jiggled as he moved. The Cosmic Star tattooed on his forehead had grayed. He stood with a bowed back and walked with a pronounced limp. And most concerning were Herid's manifestations of the Yearning, such as the wildness in his eyes, which never settled on anything for more than a few seconds.

"It looks like you haven't eaten or slept in days. Come on in here and let me fix you a hot meal while you fill me in on what you've been up to all these years." He guided Herid across the room and helped him into a chair at his dining room table. After heating the stove, he poured Herid a cup of herbal tea, then kept it filled while he whipped up a meal of lake bass, nuts, grains, and leafy greens to help reduce Herid's anxiety.

As Grimmley cooked, he had Herid recount his story of the past thirty years, which took a lot of guided questions and patience. Herid was incapable of focusing for more than a few minutes, often diverting into side discussions with his dead bond, claiming Black Knights—dark Paladins— were after his mind, and asserting he, not Tierson Greenlace, was the rightful Knight Exemplar and Supreme Cardinal of the Paladins Order. Herid's schizophrenic state disheartened Grimmley greatly. As a young Paladin, Herid had been brilliant, a rising star in his order, which was why the two of them had struck up such a close friendship.

It was not until Herid was licking the last crumbs from his dinner plate that Grimmley had extracted the essential points of his tale. Shortly after the last time Grimmley saw him, Herid had been branded a heretic and deemed harmful to the order and their beliefs, sentenced to imprisonment in Aldemeer for life. Grimmley tried to coax out of him what he had done that was blasphemous, but got only conspiracy theories jumbled with elaborate fantasies for his efforts. Whatever had happened, Grimmley was confident that the Yearning was partially to blame. Unfortunately, Paladins were religious zealots and had no qualms brutalizing those within their order that they deemed unworthy or nonconformist.

Grimmley handed Herid a cup of warm herbal tea, this one laced with a few drops of a mild potion that would help him sleep through the night … and on into the next day. After Herid gulped it down, Grimmley helped him to the far corner of his cottage and eased him onto the soft cot he kept out for the occasional night Conner stayed over. "I am going to help you through this, my old friend. I will be here, at your side, until your spirit is settled."

Herid reached over and patted Grimmley's arm. "Thank you, Grimmley. You are truly a good friend." Herid puffed out his lips and glanced over Grimmley's shoulder. "Of course, I haven't forgotten our mission. I was just waiting for the right time to say something." Herid waved his hand at the air. "I'll get on with it when I am ready, so leave me be!"

Grimmley shifted into Herid's line of sight. "Mission? What mission?"

"Mission? I don't know of any—" Herid's hollow eyes got round. "Oh yes. I brought you something." He reached into his vest pocket and removed something small and shiny. He carefully gripped Grimmley's hand and with his other pressed a black gem into Grimmley's outstretched palm. "I never forgot that you said you wanted this. And I never told them where I hid it. I kept it safe until I could get it to you." As if a great weight had been lifted from Herid's shoulders, he closed his eyes and was instantly asleep.

Grimmley stared at the well-cut onyx in his hand. Something drew his eye, and he leaned closer. Inside the core of the stone, small bands of blue light swirled and danced, like waves lapping along a shoreline. He gasped. Excitement exploded in him, to the point he wanted to cheer, and to dance a spry jig. At long last, he held a Fettering Stone. He rose and clenched the stone tight and shook his fist at the ceiling in victory.

And then he froze.

The timing of this was wrong. And on the tail of that thought came a sobering string of questions. Why would the Paladins Council free a branded heretic from a life sentence? Paladins were as fanatical about protecting their prisoners as they were about protecting the Modeic treasures they kept locked away. And how had Herid come by a Fettering Stone? The last time they'd parted, Herid had mentioned he would keep an ear out for any clues where a stone might be. And maybe most chilling of all, did the council know Herid had a stone ... and where he would go with it?

Grimmley opened his hand with pursed lips and stared at the flickering stone. "Well, Grimmley, like your mentor Emery liked to say, 'Don't ask for something you aren't equipped to handle, because the Cosmos will be sure you get it.'" He returned to his workbench, where he withdrew a blank leaf of paper and a quill. Swallowing hard, he began to write. He could have written more, but when he had run out of space on the sheet, he carefully stuffed the paper in an envelope and sealed it with wax. On the envelope, he wrote:

To Conner

He went to his mantel and slid the envelope into his secret compartment. "Come along, Barthox. We're going to need a lot of rest if we are going to make it through the coming days." He left the stone on his bench, climbed the ladder to his small loft, and went to bed. With Barthox taking her usual sentry duty on his bedpost, he lay in bed, watching the blue bands of light dance across his ceiling.

The next morning, Grimmley checked on Herid, who was still sleeping deeply. Then he performed a series of tests on the stone. It was nearly noon before Grimmley was satisfied with what he'd found. He dropped his spectacles on the workbench with a thud and rubbed at tired eyes, then leaned his head back. He had to admit the incantations he had cast on the stone had yielded results far more interesting than anything he'd thought possible. The stone emitted a thread of energy, not quite Fire or Earth elementals, but not too different, either. It was as if Earth and Fire had been fused together to create a fifth elemental. Even more fascinating, the thread was a gateway to the other planes. While these discoveries were all quite fascinating, none of them explained why the stones were deemed powerful.

Fettering Stones. Grimmley drummed his fingers on the armrest as he contemplated the meaning of the words. Why that name? Did fettering mean to shackle, as with manacles? To what or whom was something being shackled? And what was being shackled? And why? Or did it mean to compel someone? He stared at the stone, which stubbornly refused to give up its secrets. He had gone as far as facts would lead him. Now began the arduous labor of devising a plausible theory.

He needed to start somewhere. Given that the stone was somehow linked to the Cosmic planes beyond, it made sense to assume those in possession of the stones could communicate over vast distances. That would explain how the nest of Anarchic spies could coordinate simultaneous missions across the realms. Grimmley would start there and see where it took him.

He exhaled long and slow. His excitement had long since burned away through the morning labors, leaving him exhausted and exasperated. He dropped the stone into a small, hidden drawer on his bench, then went to prepare a wondrous lunch. Herid would be waking soon, hopefully more rested, and likely famished from his long sleep. Then he would have a long talk with his friend. He had decided Herid should stay, so Grimmley could keep his friend safe until he had recuperated ... well, as much as someone with the Yearning could recover. Then, maybe Herid could explain just what was going on.

Shame to Bear

Galan studied the four drawn faces huddled about him in the dark chamber. "And you are sure the incantation will disable the undead guards?" he asked Sheardra.

"I am certain," she replied with a sly grin. "I could not believe the luck I had being in the Birthing Chamber when the creature used the enchantment to freeze an undead. Just to be sure, I tested it on one of his sentries while it retrieved his dinner the other night. The chant froze it for several minutes. It was completely unaware of what I had done."

Galan nodded with an eager snarl. Everything was coming together perfectly.

"He eats his evening meal alone in his study," Baltor offered. "During that time, only a few guards are near him. And there are seldom more than two outside his chamber door. That seems the best time to strike."

"I agree." Galan waited to see if someone offered a better suggestion. "Then let us disperse and reconvene outside his study in an hour, and finally put an end to this charade."

"Wait. Anyone near his study will know when we have disabled the guards," Sheardra said. "And Shaz ... the creature will certainly sense it. Once we have impaired the guards outside his door, he will know."

Galan grinned. "That is why this night is particularly suited for us. I have made sure the few night watchmen in the vicinity of his chamber are loyal to our cause. They have been instructed to ignore anything they hear or sense. Even if someone were to raise an alarm, they wouldn't be able to respond quickly enough to save the creature. With its death, the remaining council members and grandmasters will have no choice but to fall back in line."

Baltor looked about. "And Meera?"

"She has chosen not to participate in our rectification." Galan noted the concern in their eyes. "She is loyal to the order and will not betray us. She may not agree with our action, but she would never assist the one who murdered her mentor."

A few hesitated before nodding at the grim news.

"Do not look so concerned, dear friends. The creature does not possess enough power to challenge even one of us unaided. Tomorrow, we will be in control of the order once more."

Nartesis sipped his cool glass of wine, imagining delicate flavors that he could no longer taste. He swirled the glass before the lone candle flame on his desk, watching the purplish glint of light dance through the cut crystal. He was not even sure food and drink provided any sustenance. After all, he had slept nearly a thousand years in his cavern laboratory without eating. Still, the act of consuming offered some semblance of routine, a meager offering of normalcy to keep insanity at bay. He closed his eyes and took a large gulp. *There it is,* he thought as the cold liquid tingled down his gullet. At least some sensation remained in this decrepit relic of a body.

The strong pulse of elementals washed over him. *That* sensation had not died.

His study door burst wide and five robed figures coursed through the portal, only to vanish into the dark recesses of his room.

"Who is there?" Nartesis called as the door slammed shut. He squinted into the darkness beyond his candlelight, at the sound of sandaled feet approaching. "Speak now or you will surely draw my anger."

"It is I, creature." Galan stepped into the dim light.

The grotesque snarl on Galan's face nearly made Nartesis laugh. "How dare you enter my chambers unannounced? Leave this moment—"

Before Nartesis finished his command, Galan whispered an incantation and something like heavy weights dragged Nartesis's hands down. His body whipped forward. Incredulous, he could not lift his forearms from the table. Sparking iron rings encircled his wrists, shackling him to the table. "You impudent—"

"I have had enough of your feeble threats to bully me." Taking a deep breath, Galan pushed up his sleeves. Four more council members stepped into the light, their grim visages pale and sweaty. "By decree of a majority of the Necromancers Council, we have found you guilty of murder. Prepare to be sent back to whatever horrific place you came from, foul creature."

Nartesis yanked on the shackles. They did not budge. "You would kill me thus? Am I not offered the honor of a defense?"

Galan leaned in, pressing his palms on the table. "Did you offer my wife any honor when you took her from me?"

"So this is how the council does its dirty deeds? You prowl the dark halls, holding secret meetings in cellars to plot your acts of revenge?" Nartesis noted a few astonished faces in the flickering light. "Then you slink into private chambers to carry them out?" Nartesis opened his fists. "Will you not allow me the right to defend myself as our great order's laws dictate? Does not every member of our order have the right to confront his accusers in the light of fair trial by a court of one's peers—"

"You are not of *this* order, creature!" Galan hissed, then cleared his throat. The dark figures raised their arms in unison. They began the incantation that would sever Nartesis's spirit from his body. "*Ourera energi syncho—.*"

Nartesis roared, straining against the unmovable iron rings and startling those around him from their chant. "This is not justice; this is revenge! You are violating everything our order stands for!"

"Yes!" Galan shouted. "We are! And laws be damned. I will have vengeance for what you did!" Galan's eyes flicked to the closed door. "Let us get this done, quickly."

Before Galan began the first syllable of the incantation, a deep, hollow laughter rumbled up from Nartesis's emaciated chest. "Ousel!" he shouted. "You heard that?"

"I did, my lord," echoed a voice from a dark corner of the room. The minister stepped forward, along with a dozen more Necromancers encircling the five interlopers.

"My dear Galan." Nartesis chuckled as Ousel waved a hand over his shackles. The rings on his wrists flashed and fell apart. "Did you really think I would not find out?" Rubbing his throbbing wrists, he jerked his head at the Necromancers surrounding the councilmen. "Shackle them all and drag them to the chamber hall. Then call an emergency tribunal of the senior order members. We end this tonight."

Meera huddled in a dark corner of Shazarack's study, Morgana nestled about her neck, and watched in numbed silence as Galan and his co-conspirators were dragged away in chains. Their pitiful shouts and clanking irons were like daggers in her ears. After they had been removed, she stepped forward into the light. "Lord Shazarack, it would be prudent to wait before calling for a trial. Cooler minds must prevail in such matters."

Shazarack hesitated before stepping into the hallway. "No, Meera, I think not." Turning right, he followed the heavy thud of boots and clanging irons reverberating down the stone hall, Meera like a shadow at his back. "Ridding ourselves of dead weight from our past is essential if we are to voyage into a new future. We must put this entire episode behind us. Our order will be unable to get past this terrible ordeal until Galan and his confederates have been dealt with conclusively."

Meera wanted to respond, but she could not defend Galan's odious act. She had pleaded with him not to do this. She trailed Shazarack and Ousel to the end of the hall, then down the spiral stairs that led to the order's main hall. By the time she arrived at the auditorium, members of the tribunal were already filing in. Some crowded at the entrances, stretching to see Galan and the four other council members bound and gagged in the middle of the stage. Meera staked out a dark corner near the back curtains, hoping to remain unseen. It took some time before a quorum of the grandmasters of the order filled the chairs in the hall.

"My fellow ordermen," Shazarack began, "you have been called here tonight to stand witness to the accusations placed upon these usurpers and to determine their fate." He made a motion with his hand and waited while one of the undead ripped the gag from Galan's mouth. "Galan, you and your cohorts stand accused of high treason and attempted murder against the recognized head of this order. Do you have anything to say before the tribunal passes judgment?"

Galan spit on the floor before Shazarack. "You call *us* usurpers? I do not recall a vote ever being taken that would secure you as head of the order. It is you who has usurped all standards of propriety held by our great order!"

"Ousel," Nartesis waved the minister forward on the stage. "Tell me, how was the name of Nartesis Shazarack selected as this order's paragon?"

Ousel oozed forward in meager steps, his eyes glued to the floor. "The year that reconstruction of Thanatos was completed, a tribunal of the order's senior members held a vote to select our order's exemplar. As scribed in the books, the vote unanimously named you as our paragon."

"Then it stands to reason, does it not, that as the order's paragon, I have the right to assume the position of head of the Necromancers Order if that is what is required for the success and security of the order?" Shazarack waited for the murmurs to die down. "Is there anyone on the tribunal who finds fault with this logic?"

Galan snorted. "No sane person can support your baseless and unfounded claim that you are Nartesis Shazarack."

Shazarack stared out on the sea of faces. "You do not have a say in this matter, Galan. I told you before that if you had a grievance regarding my identity, you were to take it to Ousel so that it could be recorded in the registry. You did not do that."

Galan rattled his chains. "Look at you all!" he shouted at the assembly. "Can you not see what this *thing* is doing to the order?" In the ensuing silence, Galan's shoulders slumped. "What I did, I did for you!"

Shazarack cackled. "So, you claim your motive in attempting to murder me was to defend all these fine people?"

Galan bit at his lip. "I do."

Shazarack laughed even louder. "How compassionate of you, Galan! How virtuous! How ... deceitful. Ousel, please tell the tribunal what you and the others overheard Galan say in my chamber, as he prepared to murder me."

"It was for revenge, my lord," Ousel muttered at the floor.

"Revenge!" Shazarack proclaimed. He faced the Necromancers assembled on the stage behind the council members, the ones who had waited in the dark with Ousel. "And did any of you bear witness to anything different?" After a moment of silence, he continued. "There you have it. Galan lies to you about his intentions, yet his own words reveal his true motive." Shazarack rounded on the man on the stage, his back bent under heavy iron chains and shackles. "And Galan is an expert liar. Isn't that so, Galan?"

"I am not a liar," Galan declared.

"Hmm. Then we should discuss the circumstances by which you convinced the order to adopt the pact—the one that required these gentlemen and ladies to labor long hours through the night to create an army … to defend the other orders."

Galan's eyes bulged. His lips moved but produced no sound. He straightened his back and staggered forward. "I demand the Right of Exacting!"

After a tense moment, shouts erupted around the hall, and the tribunal descended into total chaos.

Ousel stepped forward and raised his arms. Helgish clambered out of his pocket and climbed on Ousel's shoulder. "Hear! Hear! Decorum, please!" he bellowed over their clamor, bringing the entire assemblage to stunned silence. "Galan, in five hundred years of our order, that law has never been invoked."

Galan lifted his jaw. "That in no way voids my demand."

"That statute was written for a different purpose than this!" Ousel squawked back. Meera had never before seen Ousel stand up against the man he had once admired. The minister had changed so much.

Galan's face reddened. "Our books state no conditions necessary to invoke the law. I will have my absolution. I demand my rights under the Code."

"What is this law?" Shazarack interjected.

Ousel settled back on his heels and snapped his jaw closed. After a deep breath, he answered, "Lord Shazarack, the Right of Exacting exists for all of the order. It states that anyone of sufficient mastery may challenge the recognized head of council for that title through combat. But no Necromancer has ever invoked that law because we are a civil society, not one founded on barbarous martial skills. Necromancers bicker and argue, we even shout and berate one another, but we do not … *battle*. Especially not to the death."

"So, you wish to fight me to the death?" Shazarack surveyed the avid faces of those in the hall. "Very well."

"My lord!" Ousel yelled.

Shazarack cut the minister short with a chopping motion. "Ousel, remove the man's shackles and give him his staff."

Galan's fiery stare grew into a snarl as several ordermen removed the chains binding him. Before the irons struck the floor, Galan snatched his staff from Ousel's grip. "Let us be done with this madness! *Ourera energi synchosyndeta,*" he chanted, whipping his staff forward and down. A bloom of Earth energy gushed from the tip of his staff, arcing up and over Shazarack's head, then extending downward. Simultaneously, Fire elemental sparked and roared from its base, surging across the stone floor. "*Ourera energi apostelfotia,*" Galan shouted. Flames leaped forward and rose, engulfing Shazarack while spikes of metal nails rained down from above. Galan howled with rapture as the glowing fire feasted on Shazarack's flailing body. Churning black smoke billowed forth, wrapping around funnels of heat growing ever hotter and brighter. Galan cackled with delight, pouring more energy into the incantation until his staff glowed red.

The incantation ended as quickly as it had begun. And with no elemental force to feed the flames, the fire flickered out. Those who had been standing near Shazarack staggered back, their hands covering mouths and eyes, gagging and tearing at the noxious fumes that blanketed the stage like black smoke. Those in the audience stretched upward, craning their necks to gape at the charred remains of the creature who had called himself their paragon. Slowly, the smoke dissipated. Shazarack's body, silhouetted in the swirling vapor, was but a blackened hunched, smoldering form, motionless.

Galan crowed with glee—then choked. A loud crack reverberated through the hall. With a quake, Shazarack's scorched shell crumbled away. To a stunned, silent audience, Shazarack rose and stepped from the rubble, unscathed.

"Is that the best you can do?" Shazarack asked. Raising his arm, he whispered something and flicked his wrist as if turning a doorknob.

With a gut-wrenching snap of bones, Galan's left hand twisted up and back until it touched his elbow. He screamed, his face convulsing in horror. His smoldering staff clattered to the floor, and he cradled his grotesquely injured arm.

Shazarack flicked his wrist the other way and Galan's right femur splintered with a loud snap. Galan's leg splayed at an odd angle and, with a scream, he went down hard on his side.

Galan lifted himself with his good arm and leg, and lurched toward his staff.

Shazarack kicked the staff away. Then he clenched his fingers. Galan's back buckled and he sagged to the floor.

From Galan's mouth came an ear-piercing shriek. His right hand clawed at the floor, reaching for his staff, but his body no longer did his bidding.

Shazarack stood over Galan as if examining a wounded insect he had picked the wings from. Shazarack made a downward motion with his arm. There was a succession of pops as more bones splintered, and Galan's good arm bent like rubber. Galan opened his mouth, and his jaw twisted to the left and snapped. He emitted a guttural gurgle. Galan's broken limbs flopped as he tried to roll onto his back, but his legs and hips did not follow. Broken teeth spewed from his bloody mouth.

"Enough of this," Shazarack growled and clapped his palms together. There was a sound like a heavy boot crunching gravel, and Galan shuddered and collapsed. The once-great sovereign prince of the Necromancers Order grew still. Bright blood oozed from his mouth, nose, eyes, and ears. His body twitched and quivered one last time.

"Meera," Shazarack called out, waving her out of the shadows. He straightened his cuffs.

Meera shuffled forward, her hands pressed tight against her gut. She gazed down in disgust as Galan's body jiggled and sank into a boneless carcass. His cheekbones and jawline recessed, his chest and hips flattened, his forehead sank. She no longer recognized what remained; no one would. "Yes, my lord?" she murmured. Her mouth was dry; her stomach, hard knots.

"What you did this evening will be remembered for a long time in our order."

"It was my duty." *Was it?* asked that tiny voice in her head. Reflexively, she pushed the voice away. Meera recoiled from the crowd of onlookers surging forward to examine Galan's gelatinous remains. Several prodded and jiggled the dead flesh with their feet.

"You have proven your dedication to my cause, to my vision," Shazarack said with the snarling grin she had come to know so well. "That is why I will name *you* as my second, and the first member of our new council. That is, once you and Ousel provide me with a new body."

"And Ousel?" Meera gestured toward the man on the far side of the stage debating how to remove Galan's body without making a bloody mess of it. She wondered if the minister would feel slighted by Shazarack's gesture. Ousel had handed his life over completely to their new preceptor. *And you haven't?* the intrusive voice asked.

Shazarack gazed at Ousel, as if he had just remembered others were nearby. "The man is powerful, I will admit. But he lacks certain ... elements of character that our new council members must have if we are to forge a strong order for the future. Do you not agree?"

Meera had to admit that Ousel's meekness was what had kept him from taking one of the council's chairs. Still, the minister had displayed something unexpected on the stage when he'd thought Shazarack was in peril. "If I may ask ..."

"Yes?" Shazarack waved for her to follow, then started toward the back of the stage, where his undead guards crowded around him. He stepped through the door they had entered and proceeded back up the long hall.

Meera followed close behind, gently stroking Morgana's soft fur. "Why would you lead me to believe you were weak in powers?"

Shazarack snorted. "I would have thought that obvious."

Meera waited quietly for her new preceptor to say more. She needed Shazarack to state the reason, but feared pressing him on the matter.

Finally, he answered her. "When it became clear that Galan could not be reasoned with, that his feelings for Breanen would keep him from getting over his anger toward me, I capitulated on the hope he would become an ally. That presented me with a rather unique problem. Disbanding the council hadn't stopped him from fomenting strife within the order. Galan and his followers continued to undermine my efforts to solidify my power. He had to be eliminated. He just needed a little incentive to stage a coup ... and to believe he would succeed."

Meera swallowed hard. "You knew I would tell him I thought you ... weak."

"No, but I hoped you would."

"You're not angry that I did?"

"Why would I be angry? You came to me and revealed what Galan was planning and when to expect it."

"So, it was all a test." A coldness seeped into Meera's gut, seizing her soul and squeezing it hard.

Shazarack rounded on her outside his private study. "Meera, if I am going to hand my life over to someone, I need to trust them completely. So, yes, it was a test. Now, what else? I can see your mind is unsettled."

"I don't understand how a failed coup would ensure his elimination. If he had not challenged you back there, he would have just as well become a martyr. It was quite a gamble on your part."

Shazarack chuckled. "I like how you think, Meera. Yes. I could not rely on the tribunal to rid us of the scourge. Galan needed to decide his own fate."

Suddenly, the pieces fell into place for Meera. "Galan *did* lie about the pact to the council and tribunal. He manipulated them to get their endorsement, and you knew it. If they found out that he'd lied, he would have lost whatever support he had left ... and his ability to influence them. You forced Galan to challenge you."

"I knew of the Right of Exacting. There could be no more fitting end to Galan's life than for him to die a traitor." Shazarack opened the door and stepped through, his guards posting themselves at intervals along the hall. "But it really didn't matter. Either decision he made would have worked against him. I could not allow a martyr for some righteous cause to stand in my way." With a sneering grin, he closed the door behind him.

Meera waited outside Shazarack's office for a few minutes, replaying the few options Galan had had.

She staggered back up the hall. *Keep it together, Meera*, the tiny voice advised. She found her way outside, where she fell to her knees and retched up what was left of her supper. She wiped chunks of vomit from her lips, and spat green bile from her mouth. It was some small relief.

She went to the bath house. As she disrobed, she thought over the night's events. A coup had been put down, a sovereign prince of their order defrocked and killed, and a law never intended to be invoked had resulted in a Necromantic duel to the death. She kept hearing Galan's warning: *He is uprooting our entire culture. Breaking our pact with the other orders is only the first transgression against Anarchism and the security of our order. He will demand more, each one taking us further down the path of peril and destruction.* Shazarack had used her as a tool to help eliminate a problem, while simultaneously ensuring she was committed to him.

She dipped into the hot pool and scrubbed her body with fragrant soap and a hard-bristled brush. She scoured her skin until it bled. But she could not wash away the lingering stench in her nostrils of Galan's pulverized body.

Morgana lay stretched out on the side of the pool as Meera soaked in the hot water, Shazarack's words of approval repeating in her head. "What you did this evening will be remembered for a long time in our order."

That is the shame you must now bear, Meera, the voice sniggered. All will know you traded Galan and the other council members for a chance at more power.

The icy coldness that had taken root in her soul spread through her core. She held her breath, sinking below the surface. The searing water on skin rubbed raw distracted her from the all-consuming numbness that was overtaking her.

When at last she resurfaced, Meera pressed her shaking palms to her cheeks, bowed her head low, and cried.

With Fates Sealed

Lacerus waited in the dark, marking off the hours before daybreak, listening, watching, making note of every sound, every motion. As he loitered outside the hole in the side of a hill, he contemplated the many Assassins he had known through the centuries. A thin smile crossed his lips as he recalled all those who'd spent their lives honing and mastering their skills with a sword, a knife, a spear, a bow. He had personally witnessed ordermen performing many astounding feats with those tools. And yet none of them grasped a fundamental truth of their great order—that these were not the real weapons of an Assassin. They were merely agents of an outcome, aids for a desired effect. Patience was an Assassin's only weapon. And this Lacerus had mastered with great zeal. A waning Erebus was just breaking in the east. It would be light soon. He had memorized every dip and rise of dirt, every blade of grass unnaturally tilted or stiff, every pebble between his location and the opening ahead. It was time to make his move.

He slipped across the open field, Carnia winging stealthily behind. His feet, silent as a passing cloud, were like dry leaves rolling over the terrain in an autumn breeze. A moment later, he reached the entrance to the lair. He dipped into the mouth of the hole and stopped, his eyes gliding over the wooden door.

A few heartbeats were all he needed to disable the trap. He reached for the door handle but hesitated. *That was a little too easy.* Stepping into the lair of another Assassin unexpected, especially of a grandmaster, was particularly dangerous. Lacerus searched the entrance once more, and found two more traps—one near the handle, another near the top hinge. As he worked, he recalled one of his Assassin preceptors from a century ago, a woman named Arkimedes. He could still hear her grating old voice. "The Assassin who enters another's lair is the walking dead," she would say. "Only his legs have not been told yet." He sneered at the fond memory. Arkimedes had been brilliant, though sometimes wrong. She used to say he was not cruel enough, and thus was unworthy of her tutelage. He'd proved her mistaken the night he plunged a thin blade into her heart. She never saw it coming.

Certain there were no more traps, he rotated the handle. The door swung inward, revealing a dark, musty antechamber. No darts or arrows came at him. No explosions. He took a moment to close his eyes. Concentrating, he called Air and Earth to him. Just a trickle. Not enough for anyone to detect. He slipped inside. And the door blew shut behind him, sealing him in the antechamber.

He surveyed his surroundings. The room was large and busy, one he would describe as cluttered, with creaky plank flooring. Dusty old books and yellowed parchments covered many of the tables and shelves that lined the dark wood paneled walls. The smell of mold, mildew, and earth was thick.

"Lacerus," a voice spoke through the walls. "You are a fool to enter my home uninvited. I would have thought you wiser than that."

Lacerus set his staff against the wall by the door and raised his arms high, fingers out wide. "Any motive not understood is often perceived as foolish."

"Then state why you are here," the voice growled.

"To parley. That is what Assassins do." Any sudden or suspicious move would end his life. He scanned the room for more traps but detected none. The fact he was still breathing gave him some small hope. "Why don't you come out so we can chat?"

There was a snorting sound. "I know better than to make myself vulnerable."

"Even in your own home? Surely, you have a dozen devices trained on me right now. I know any sudden moves or incantations I might cast would spell my doom. Is that not protection enough? Or perhaps you fear your Assassin's training was inadequate? Maybe it was presumptuous for the council to give you the rank of grandmaster?" Lacerus was taking a chance. Badgering an Assassin was a sure way to make a situation deadly. But he was relying on the fact this man had not been raised as an Assassin.

A long silence was followed by an abrupt clack of metal that made Lacerus jump. A black-cloaked form stepped into the room.

"Ah, Hector," Lacerus cooed with pleasure. "See? You have nothing to fear from me." During the long pause that followed, Lacerus unclenched his jaw, homing in on Hector's every movement, every breath.

"Why are you here? I will not ask you a third time." Hector's gaze shifted to the staff at Lacerus's back.

It was the cue Lacerus had waited for. *"Aerora eftos tachyepith,"* he incanted quickly. He blurred like black lightning across the room, re-materializing in front of Hector, one hand a vise around his wrist, the other clutching the man's throat. Lacerus squeezed on his larynx until Hector made a gurgling sound. Running his hand up Hector's arm, he removed Hector's blade. In one quick motion, he lifted Hector into the air and slammed his back into the wall. He pressed the pilfered blade against Hector's neck. "Now I think we can have that chat."

Hector gripped Lacerus's arm tight with both hands, trying to loosen his grip enough to breathe. "How did you ..."

Lacerus choked him off. "How did I what? Bring elementals to bear before you could react? That is a nice little trick I mastered a very long time ago." A quick snap of his wrist slammed Hector's back on a nearby table. Books skittered everywhere. "Now to answer your question, I am here to enjoy the opportunity to listen to you beg for your life." He brandished the blade he had taken before Hector's eyes, then placed the tip against his rapidly pulsing jugular. "If your begging and cowing pleases me, then maybe, just maybe, I will let you live." He drew his lips back tight, hoping it looked something like a smile. "Or maybe I will take your territory. Whichever way this goes, I *will* have some gratification tonight."

Hector shook his head, loosening Lacerus's grip on his throat. "You cannot! These lands were given to me by the Assassins Council. Only they—"

Lacerus flicked the knife upward, slicing off the tip of Hector's earlobe. The man jolted and shook from the pain.

"Oops," Lacerus murmured. "I am sorry about that, Hector. But I don't recall asking you a question."

Hector seethed but said nothing.

"Now. As I was saying, you disobeyed the council's wishes. And I am here to correct that wrongdoing."

"Correct *my* wrongdoing?" Hector laughed in Lacerus's face. "Coming to my home and threatening me! You are in deeper trouble than I ever will be. The council knows of *your* failures as well, Lacerus. When they discover that you attacked another orderman unsanctioned, they will have your head."

"Then you do not know the council members as well as I. You were given specific instructions to kill both the queen of Griffinrock *and* her husband, King Jonath. Yet you left the king breathing." Lacerus moved in close. "Do you think the council made their decision without thinking through all possible ramifications?" Lacerus ran the tip of the blade along the side of Hector's neck. Blood trickled down his clavicle. "By not fulfilling your mission, you have placed the entire Anarchic Lands in danger. So tell me: why did you not complete your mission?" Lacerus showed Hector the bloody blade. "And keep in mind your life hangs on the words that next come from your tongue."

"A dead man suffers no wounds," Hector snarled. "Jonath needed to be tormented, knowing that, in the end, he failed his queen. I wanted to prove to Jonath that *I* was his better, that *I* should have been Izadora's Champion."

Lacerus sneered at the man trembling beneath him. Hector reeked of fear, sweat, and bitterness. Raised as a Harmonic and trained as a Ranger, he had been chosen as the Rangers' Advocate, ultimately fighting Jonath for the right to become Queen Izadora's Champion. And though Hector lost, he vehemently held to the belief that Jonath had cheated. Ridiculed by his order and scorned by the crown, he'd defected to the Anarchic side. Lacerus had hoped the ex-Ranger's deep-seated and powerful emotions, manifested from his encounter with Jonath, would make him the perfect choice for the queen's assassination. He had never thought Hector's personal grudge would get in the way.

"You swore to the Assassins Council that you ceded all ties to your previous life as a Harmonic Ranger, including any emotional attachments you might have had. That was a precondition for the council to adopt you. Anarchists are not fond of traitors ... from either side." Lacerus shook him hard. "I vouched for you! Now, your dereliction of duty has weakened my standing in the order." He breathed deep and straightened. "In fact, I am willing to wager they have determined that you have outlived your usefulness. Now that I think about it, you are going to be my way back into the council's good graces. I am hedging my bet that all my mistakes will be forgiven once I dump a rogue Assassin's head at their feet." His eyes grew wide with glee as another idea came to him. "Maybe I will convince the council that, during my time in the realms, I found out you never did switch sides, that you were working as a double agent. Yes!"

Terror blossomed in Hector's eyes. His breath came in quick starts and jerks. "Don't kill me."

Lacerus guffawed. "Good, Hector! That's the spirit! But try harder! You can beg a lot better than that! After all, we are talking about your life."

"Let's make a deal," Hector suggested, nearly stumbling over his words.

"Deal?" Lacerus blinked. This was not what he expected. *How delightful! Finally, some fun!*

"Yes. A deal. I have information ... useful information ... that I—I—I received just yes— yesterday. Swear you will let—let me live, and I will share it with you."

Lacerus was not convinced. He placed the knife to Hector's throat, eyes narrowing. "You are trying to delay the inevitable."

"No. No! I am not," Hector quavered.

Lacerus flicked the knife again. Another sliver of Hector's earlobe fell away.

Hector cried out, shaking violently.

"If you waste my time, I promise to make the pain last all night." He pressed his face closer to Hector's. "And if I alarm you now, just wait until you really make me angry."

"There has been a second dragon bonding—in our lands," Hector blurted out.

Lacerus bolted upright. His grip slackened. *A second dragon bonding? It could not be. Not yet!* Brother Sarmenion would have foreseen it. "I don't believe you. You're fishing for a way to keep me from killing you."

"No, no! The bonding is real." Hector jiggled his head up and down.

"Where? Where is this person?"

"I cannot share that with you. This information is my leverage to quell the council's anger."

Lacerus waved the blade before Hector. "Knowing there is another bonding is useless without the location. If you do not tell me where, then I am done with you." He pointed the blade down, moving the tip over Hector's eye.

"Xylor!" Hector shouted. "He is in Xylor."

"Xylor? The tree people of Dristonia?"

"Yes!" Hector sobbed. "Yes."

Lacerus shoved Hector down on the table. The ex-Ranger sickened him. It took every last bit of discipline not to plunge the blade through the miserable coward's heart. "You are not to share this with anyone else ... especially with the council. I will take care of this dragon bond."

"No. Please! What about my standing with the council?"

"Aerora ousia pagomaprosopo." Lacerus froze Hector to prevent him from tripping any deadly devices before Lacerus could scamper free. Besides, he'd tired of listening to the sniffling buffoon. "That is not my concern. You sealed your fate the day you let King Jonath live."

Lacerus found Carnia waiting outside, her peregrine feathers fluffed with excitement. He closed the door behind him and jogged across the open field, picking up speed as he entered the woods. Hemera was rising, peeking through dark, angry clouds churning low in the east. His mind reeled with anticipation as he ran. *Another human-dragon bonding.* This was surely a chance for redemption after his failure to ensnare the Eastlander boy. *But why had Sarmenion not foreseen this?* There was no way of knowing who else might have received the information, so he would need to act swiftly. His current plans would have to wait. A mile from the lair, he retrieved his mare. He would report this to his Kindred brothers; then, with a quick diversion to enlist the assistance of a few more Assassins in case the dragon got feisty, and he would be on his way to Xylor.

Becoming Aware

Marcantos watched Orianna work her way through the eight forms of Anvil. He had selected this series to be the first for her training because it was designed to develop a Warrior's core strength. His first preceptor had made him work the series for six months straight, refusing to teach Marcantos any other forms until he had fully mastered Anvil's objective.

"Stop," he commanded.

Orianna stuttered to a halt, her arm extended in a low thrust.

Walking up behind her, he pressed his palms down on her shoulders, pushing her hips lower, until her legs quivered from her weight. "Remember what I said about your root. Keep your feet planted at all times. You don't step through the forms, you slide. You must be prepared for an attack at any moment, even midstride. During battle, a Barbarian relies on moving from unstable position to another; a ... dark Barbarian always seeks balance, which relies on root. No root, no balance. Understand?" It was the same message he had given her a dozen times a day, just conveyed in different ways. He was determined to find the right combinations that would break past the year of Barbarian indoctrination that had been inflicted upon her. She had made incredible strides in the four days he had been instructing her.

Orianna gulped air through Marcantos's instructions. Wide-eyed, she bobbed her head.

"Then show me," he said, stepping back. "Start with the third form."

Orianna took the ready stance, but instead of starting the form, her head snapped around. She stared intensely at Marcantos. "Did you fight many Barbarians?"

It was one of many subjects Marcantos would have preferred to avoid. But she would remain distracted and would plague him with the question until he answered. "I fought quite a few Anarchic ordermen—fifty or more. Half were Barbarians."

Marcantos expected her to revile him, but to his surprise, Orianna grinned. "Then I am blessed to be tutored by such an accomplished instructor." Closing her eyes, she blew out a long breath. When she moved, Orianna was pure grace in motion. Each stroke precise, each step unerring, each turn serene.

After she completed the forms, Marcantos stood mesmerized. "I do not know where that came from, but I do believe you have mastery over the Anvil forms."

"That time was different." After a moment of concentration, she added, "I know I am a slow learner, but that felt true."

"Orianna," Marcantos stepped closer. "You are the most gifted student I have ever had. You are a natural at Harmonic Sight."

But Orianna winced. Her beliefs and fears about Harmonic Sight were deeply ingrained. *Were you any different, Marcantos? How did you react when Lacerus said you were a natural Anarchist?* "Believe in yourself. If it felt true, then it was."

Orianna peered at him with a twinkle in her eye. "Then I have something I wish to show you." She picked through Copious's pile of nuts, then returned brandishing a walnut.

"You think you are ready?" Marcantos chuckled. "You think you have the mastery to repeat what I did?"

"No." Orianna winked as she bent over and balanced the walnut on a limb. "I think I can do one better." Gripping her sword, she stepped back and closed her eyes.

Marcantos folded his arms, a smirk plastered across his face, but keen to see what she could do.

Orianna spun her sword as Marcantos had done in his demonstration, then brought the blade overhead and down. But instead of striking the walnut, she twisted her wrist. The side of her sword slapped the limb beside the nut. Walnut and sword rebounded off the limb. She let the blade's momentum continue upward, then whipped the sword in a backward arc and flicked it up in an underhand swing. The edge of her blade struck the walnut at the peak of its trajectory, cleaving the nut in two and sending the pieces spinning to the ground.

"How ...?" Marcantos could not find the words to finish his question.

"Something came to me last night while I lay in bed recalling your day's lessons. And I thought about Harmonic Sight. And I asked myself, why is it necessary that one must embrace either Anarchic or Harmonic Sight? Does it really have to be either/or? And I wondered, what if there is only one sight?" She held up her blade. "What if Anarchic and Harmonic Sight are really just different sides of the same blade, and you need both sides to have an edge?"

Different sides of the same blade, Marcantos repeated to himself. He involuntarily stepped forward, an eagerness to know more exploding inside him. A part of him was confused by the thought, yet he could sense the supposition's veracity. "Tell me more."

Orianna smiled. "Anarchic Sight focuses on chaos, Harmonic Sight on stasis. But there is a point between motion and stillness where both are present. A kind of ... dynamic balance, like dancing and walking. That was the point where I struck the walnut. When it was neither in motion nor in stasis."

"Show me," he demanded. "I want to learn what you know." He sounded like Orianna the day they'd met. He could feel the chaos swirling in him, his mind in motion.

With a glint in her eye, Orianna repeated Marcantos's words back to him. "Then let us begin."

Through the day, Marcantos and Orianna worked to discover how to simultaneously embrace both sights.

Marcantos could not recall a time since his early days in the Warriors Order when he'd felt so alive, so intense, so excited—about anything. The two would begin by discussing and working out a hypothesis, then how they could test it. Many experiments failed. And after each failure, the two would have a good laugh, discuss the experience, then try something different.

By late afternoon, small advancements became big ones, and Orianna said she could consistently become *Aware*—the word they had adopted for using the combined sights. Marcantos was not so blessed. His long-time training, first in Harmonic Sight, then in Anarchic Sight under Lacerus's tutelage, was a barrier to his learning, something Orianna did not have to deal with. Marcantos could not bring himself to embrace Anarchic Sight.

"I suffered the same fear with Harmonic Sight," Orianna explained.

"It is not Anarchic Sight that I fear. It is the desire, the hunger, the exhilaration of taking Anarchic Sight. Or maybe it is the madness that follows soon after it."

Orianna shook her head. "Embracing one sight then the other will not work. They must be taken together. Let the Harmonic weave be your anchor." She stepped up behind Marcantos and placed her palm lightly on his shoulder. "To embrace both, you have to *see* both as one. Do not think of them as separate. Do you not see how they are intertwined, Marcantos? See how the swirling Anarchic eddies of destruction feed off the Harmonic weave? Yet the weave directs the eddies with its stable patterns. Anarchy is the essence of change; harmony is the essence of stasis. Separately, they are out of balance with life. Together, they work in a dance of dynamic balance. One does not exist without the other."

Marcantos tried again. After several minutes, he shook his head. "I cannot do this."

Orianna stepped in front of him. "You can, Marcantos. It is there for anyone who wishes to take it." Her eyes turned to the west, where the sky was darkening. The two had been so focused that they had not noticed Hemera slipping beyond the horizon. "I think we should stop for today," she suggested. "Sometimes pounding on a wall only makes it stronger. I am hungry. You?"

"Very," Marcantos replied.

"I will get our meals."

Marcantos reached out and gripped her shoulder. "Thank you, Orianna."

"No need for excess gratitude. It's just food."

"No. Thank you for ... showing me." He nearly said *saving me*, but he was too embarrassed to open up to a Barbarian, even one who had befriended him. "Thank you," he repeated.

Orianna started to say something, then closed her mouth. She turned and jogged off toward camp, tin bowls in hand.

The night was coming on swiftly, so Marcantos busied himself with starting a fire. While he worked, he considered whether he might turn Orianna to work for the Harmonic Realms. She would be a valuable asset. But he filed the notion away. He would look for clues in her behavior before pitching such an idea with her. Then again, it was his eleventh day at Farlorde. He was certain a decision from the Barbarian council would arrive any day now. That led him to another decision. After she returned with their meal, he would prepare her for the inevitability of his death.

The kindling was just catching when a frenzied chant floated up the hill. "Cha Kohm! Cha Kohm!" He rose and squinted toward the camp, and caught a seething mass of Barbarians near one of the large bonfires. He could make out Engert prancing around the fire like a peacock, his arms out wide, sword in hand. Marcantos shook his head. Another night of Barbarian madness and turpitude. Some poor fool was about to get a thrashing. He started to turn away when something caught his eye.

Engert took a lazy swing at a thin figure also in the center of the circle. The figure deftly deflected the attack, stepping in sideways and sliding the edge of their sword along Engert's extended arm. Engert howled with rage, driving the wreath of jeering Barbarians into a tumult. Something about the figure's movement was familiar. The stance was one he would have taken, one he'd taught. "Orianna," he whispered, then sprinted down the hill at a dead run.

Marcantos reached the back of the ring and began wedging his way through the forest of Barbarians as they jumped, hooted, and tussled with each other. He nearly missed the piercing sound of high-pitched rings of steel on steel over the deafening roar of excitement and exaltation from the crowd. On he fought until, finally, he burst through the front line.

Orianna was crouched near the fire, holding her sword low with both hands while Engert swaggered about. Blood seeped from several red lines along his arms.

Helpless, Marcantos could only watch.

Engert turned his back on Orianna, shouting at the frenzied horde, then spinning and rushing at her with a roar, his blade positioned high over his head. The maneuver was sloppy, not one Marcantos would expect from a master swordsman. That meant ... it was a trap! Marcantos shouted, but his voice was drowned out by the clamor of the crowd.

Orianna fell for the ruse. She raised her sword before her to block Engert's downward stroke that never came. At the last moment, Engert dropped low and went into a reverse spin on his back heel. His sword followed. He torqued the hilt toward him, his blade slipped beneath her defensive stance, and the tip glided deep between her ribs.

Orianna's eyes went wide with astonishment. She gawked at the thick sword protruding from her chest, her blood flowing freely down Engert's blade. Her own sword sagged, then dropped from her hand. She staggered back, a sadness filling her eyes as she glanced about. Then, like a felled tree, she pitched backward and did not move.

Marcantos's memories of the next few moments would be forever dark to him. He would only recall standing over Orianna, her cold blue eyes staring up at him. She had made an apprentice mistake, one any trainee would make. Overconfidence had cost her everything.

"Cha Kohm," the mass of Barbarians whispered.

Marcantos took in the eager faces of those along the inner ring lit by the bright firelight. He had not recalled stepping inside the ring.

"Looks like someone found some spirit!" Engert nearly spat the words at the horde. If he was hoping to stir them up again, he was disappointed. They gazed at Marcantos.

Marcantos peered down at Orianna's body. How could Barbarians be so callous? So free in tossing away life? What was the lesson here? What was Engert expecting his students to learn from this? To take advantage of the weak? This was not Anarchic life; it was ruthless immorality.

Engert took a step toward Marcantos, brandishing his bloody sword at him. "She will not come to your rescue, ShoKohm." Another step closer. "Tell me, did she teach you how to fight? Did she fill you with courage to stand here now? Come. Show us." Engert ran his palm down his bloody sword, then held his red hand up to show the crowd. "Let me mix your blood with hers."

Marcantos ignored the taunt. In the stillness of the moment, he crouched and drew Orianna's eyelids down, then invoked a Warriors' prayer to honor her life. "May the Cosmos's gentle embrace reclaim your spirit. May you find peace in the planes beyond."

The horde looked on in silence.

Their response was not what Engert had expected ... nor did he like it. His expression turned from troubled to angry, looking almost inhuman in the flickering fire glow. "Get up, ShoKohm! Let our blades dance and sing in the traditions of Barbarian glory!"

Marcantos rose. Engert was goading him into combat, but he did not move a muscle. "Glory can only be found in the oneness of everything," he whispered.

Five steps away, Engert lifted his blade high and took a ready stance. "Challenge me, ShoKohm!" A thick stream of Orianna's blood dripped from Engert's sword.

"I will not fight you," Marcantos stated. But his words lacked conviction. In truth, he wanted to fight. A distant part of him hungered to embrace Anarchic Sight, to draw his sword, to finally set the animal inside him free. He knew that creature well. *Take Anarchic Sight, Marcantos! Release me! Let me end his miserable life!*

But Marcantos clamped his eyes closed, walling off the voice. Fingers twitched greedily as the memories of endless battles marched before his eyes. All those deaths. And what had any of them achieved? His life's work—meaningless. And on the winds of that futility, he felt spent. *Why wait for the Barbarian council's decision, Marcantos? Let it all come to a glorious end here!*

In the silent void of support by those encircling them, Engert's anger exploded. With a mighty Barbarian roar, he came at Marcantos.

Marcantos raised his chin high, watching, as if in slow motion, his deliverance from this life at Engert's hand.

But a voice, Orianna's voice, whispered in Marcantos's head. "No, Marcantos. These are the signs that the time is nigh. Prepare yourself!"

Something rushed at Marcantos's mind, surrounding him, gripping him, possessing him completely. And the world opened up to a glorious vision. No words could have expressed the exaltation that filled him. It was beyond beauty and awe. He gasped at the Sight that overtook him as he perceived the interconnectedness of everything. He wanted to weep at the wondrous sensation, to shout its magnificent glory. It was not Harmonic Sight, nor was it Anarchic Sight. He was ... Aware.

Marcantos's eyes flicked toward Engert, watching the man charge at him. Air and Water elementals sprang like a well from the Barbarian. Engert's sword flickered with the speed of lightning and struck like thunder. Marcantos dodged the first cut, which would have cleaved him in two, then ducked beneath the second, meant to remove his head.

Engert bellowed with rage and came on at Marcantos again. A third, fourth, and fifth swing of the massive blade blurred past.

Marcantos let the gentle weave and violent eddies direct him as he danced around the Barbarian, effortlessly staying just out of reach.

Engert grew more desperate, his swings wilder and wider, hoping to catch the nimble Marcantos off guard. The big man pivoted to his left, but reversed his unbalanced momentum and spun to his right. Engert's blade snapped forward, leveled at Marcantos's chest. Even before the blade struck, Engert's eyes went wide with delight, and he grunted his satisfaction, ready to be bathed in the shower of Marcantos's blood.

Marcantos didn't see the moment coming, didn't feel its arrival. But when it arrived, he knew it for what it was—that point of dynamic balance, like the moment Orianna's walnut had reached the peak of its journey. Marcantos dipped underneath the stroke. As Engert's sword made a swooshing sound, he popped back up, his feet springing from the ground. His arm shot back in a wide arc behind him.

There was a sound, like something soft striking the hard ground.

Marcantos noted for the first time that he held his bloodstained sword in his hand. He spun, ready for Engert's next assault. But blood spurted like a geyser from where Engert's head should have been, spraying the astonished faces of those at the front of the circle. Marcantos watched in amazement as Engert's body continued to dance about, as if it refused to accept its own demise. Arms flailed in lazy circles as if mimicking a novice swordsman. After a moment, the body jolted to a stop, quivered violently, then toppled forward into the dirt.

Everyone watched, stunned as shiny, red ooze continued to jet from the wound between Engert's shoulders. For a full minute, the only sounds were the pops and hiss of burning logs.

And then the circle erupted in a storm of fury. Marcantos was buried under the weight of a dozen Barbarians descending upon him, all wanting to exact their anger. He was crushed beneath an avalanche of fists and boots. He tried to protect his head, but he was pummeled everywhere his arms were not. Someone was shouting, but the beating continued.

Then, as abruptly as it had begun, the pounding stopped. Marcantos continued to flail his arms, his body and face battered.

"Back off!" someone shouted over him.

Marcantos squinted up, peeking between upheld arms, unable to see who was standing over him.

"What is the meaning of this?" the man shouted. "Where is your honor?"

A young Barbarian nearby jerked a finger toward Marcantos. "This ShoKohm killed Engert!"

The man standing over Marcantos pointed at Orianna. "You are incensed over one Barbarian's death, yet not over another?"

"Orianna died at the hands of our kind," the young Barbarian yelled. "Engert was killed by a heathen!"

"A death is a death, at any hand. Now go!" the man commanded. "All of you. Disperse!"

"We will have Cha Kohm with him." The young Barbarian shook his fist toward Marcantos.

"Not tonight," the man over Marcantos warned. As the group disbanded, the man extended his hand to Marcantos.

Marcantos took it. "Thank you, Groegan," he said as steadied himself. He wiggled his jaw to make sure it was not broken.

"The young are hotheaded," Groegan offered as an apology. He gave Marcantos a toothy grin, seemingly pleased about the situation. "They will see more clearly in the morning. Until then, it would be in everyone's best interest if you stayed on your hill."

Marcantos nodded his thanks. Stumbling over to Orianna's body, he lifted her gently into his arms and started back toward his tent and his waiting fire.

Marcantos shuffled to a small patch of trees to the west and collected as much wood as he could find in the dead of a new moon's night. Even Copious helped by dragging a few heavy branches up the hill. It was well past midnight by the time he completed stacking the dry logs and branches. He lifted Orianna's body on top of the pyre, adjusting her straight hair to hang over her shoulders. Then he placed her sword down her body, her hands on the hilt, and stepped away.

"I have labored under the scrutiny of many self-proclaimed experts in all forms of martial arts. And the only thing I truly learned from them was how to be a narcissistic fool. They filled my head with refuse, until I believed I knew what path the Cosmos had set me on. I was told I would do great things for the realms, and for my order. All I really learned is that no greater torture can be exacted upon someone than to be shown a great and desirable goal, only to have it taken away before being given a chance to achieve it."

He bent down and lifted a burning branch from his fire. "Your wisdom was beyond their understanding, Orianna. What you could have realized if given the opportunity . . ." He jammed the end of the branch into the pyre, letting the flames lick the dry wood. Stepping back, he watched as the fire blossomed into a raging inferno. "I will miss you."

He stood at rest, an honorary guard of one, as the pyre rose higher into the black sky, until the entire hill was lit up like a warning beacon. Maybe those in Farlorde would not miss her, but he would not let them forget her passing.

As he looked on, the memory of Orianna's voice rang in his head. *These are the signs that the time is nigh. Prepare yourself!* The words rang with familiarity. He had heard them before ... or read them somewhere. But where defied his best efforts to recollect. It would come to him. In time, the words' meaning would become clear.

The next morning, Marcantos rose and splashed water over his puffy face. One eye was nearly swollen shut, a purplish ring along his jaw, and his cheekbone sported a welt the size of a walnut. He strapped on his scabbard, flipped back his tent flap, and stepped outside. Copious met him with an upside-down morning yawn and an itchy belly. Marcantos scratched the bear's stomach as he surveyed his surroundings.

A dozen Barbarians waited at the base of the hill, looking up at him.

With a sigh, Marcantos trudged toward them. As he neared, he drew his sword and tested his stiff wrist with a swirl of the blade. He would make sure this day would be talked about for years to come. "If you have come for Cha Kohm, I am ready. But I do not have the strength to fight you one at a time. Might I suggest we all take the dance together and be done with it?"

A middle-aged woman at the front crunched up her face, then glanced back at those gathered behind. A few shrugged, then drew their swords. The woman turned back to Marcantos, unsheathing her two-handed blade. "I think you misunderstand our intent, Marcantos. We are not here for Cha Kohm. Last night, Orianna fought magnificently. And you honored her with a great funeral none below can deny." She knelt, lifting her blade horizontally toward Marcantos. "We are here because we wish to lay stakes near your tent. We are here because we wish to learn what you taught her."

In unison, the others bent down on their knees and lifted their swords. They looked expectantly at Marcantos.

Marcantos relaxed. Placing the tip of his blade to his scabbard, he slid his sword home again. It was certainly not what he'd expected. It seemed the Cosmos had given him a chance to ensure that what Orianna had gifted him, the understanding of how to become Aware, would not be extinguished with his death. *So little time,* he thought. With an urgency nearly palpable, he spoke. "Then let us begin."

When Everything Changes

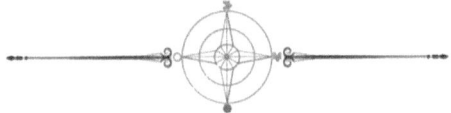

Nartesis stirred from a deep slumber, his mind foggy and dull. Darkness filled the void around him. He tried to rise, but something held him fast. He tugged against the formidable restraints across his chest, ankles, and wrists. Confusion rose in him as he strained to break free. "Is anyone there?" he called out. His voice was oddly deep and raspy.

"Who are you?" someone asked, drawing Nartesis from the border of his consciousness.

Nartesis started to answer, but the name that came to his thick tongue was not what he'd expected. *Carnon Gallowman.* The name felt familiar, but he did not know why. He held back from saying it. Instead, he asked, "Why am I being restrained?"

"Answer me, spirit," the urgent voice came again.

"Nartesis Shazarack." But that name did not feel completely right either.

"And what is the signal?" asked the voice.

"Signal?" Nartesis labored to understand the question. He heard the sound of thin steel being drawn from its sheath. "No, wait." His mind's mist was slowly solidifying. Misshapen impressions formed into memories—his own memories. "Peeps." It was the name of his bond, and the signal he had given Ousel to be sure that it was *he* whom they had called into this body.

He opened new eyes, squinting and blinking in the intense light and bright colors.

Meera and Ousel hunched over him, their faces drawn and haggard. They unbuckled the straps on his wrists.

Nartesis raised his arm and flexed new fingers, noting the muscular tone, the dark complexion. "You did well."

Ousel bowed. "Thank you, Lord Shazarack. I was concerned ..." His voice trailed off.

"No, Ousel. You called the right spirit." Nartesis waited as his two pupils removed the restraints around his ankles. He tried to shift the legs over the edge of the cold slab, but he found them difficult to move. "Help me." With their help, Nartesis slid off the cold slab, noting that his new body was dressed as he had dictated. He pushed away, his knees wobbling for a moment.

Ousel hovered next to him, ready to catch him if he fell. "My lord, prudence—"

Nartesis slapped Ousel's hand away. "Stop being a mother hen." He pushed his right foot forward, control of his new body already improving. Left leg, then right, he crossed the narrow chasm to the next slab, where a withered cadaver lay. Willing his shaking hands forward, he reached inside the cadaver's robes and gently removed the remains of a small gray animal. A leathery skin encased tiny, desiccated bones. He caressed the little nose, careful not to disturb the delicate whiskers, sliding his finger between the shriveled gray ears and down its bony back.

"What is that?"

Nartesis directed his new eyes to Ousel. "My bond, Peeps," he said as he slipped the carcass inside his new jacket pocket. How he missed his dear little friend. "One day, I will find a way to bring back dead bonds. Leave me," he commanded the two shadows hanging over his shoulder. "Now! I wish to be alone with my old body." What he had to do required privacy.

After Meera and Ousel departed, he unsheathed the gemmed knife at his waist. Turning to the cadaver, he drove the sharp tip down hard into the corpse's abdomen just below the ribcage, slicing the gut open with one powerful jerk. He flexed his bloody hand in the light, then laughed. He had forgotten the feel of strength, and this body's brawn was thrice what his previous body's had ever been. Tossing the viscid knife to the side, he rolled up his sleeve and jammed his arm into the crevice. The stench forced him to turn his head and fight back nausea. A moment later, with a sucking sound, he yanked his arm out. In his hand was a pallid heart. An inky, oily seepage coating the heart slid down his forearm, dripping in pasty globs to the marble floor. Nartesis set the heart on the slab and, with his fingernails, pried it open. Carefully, he removed a black onyx stone, a mate to the one he now wore around his neck.

Nartesis wiped the stone clean with a kerchief and held it reverently to the light. He recalled the day he had driven this particular stone into his own heart, the stone that had kept him alive all this time, the stone he had ripped from BrieAnn's neck. He slipped the thumbnail-sized gem into a pouch on his belt. If his efforts continued to evolve as planned, much would be revealed in the coming days.

Nartesis bent over the woman's body. Like an expectant lover, he watched anxiously as color blossomed on her ashen cheeks. Finally, the body inhaled sharply and stirred. Her eyes fluttered open.

Her forehead crinkled as she studied his face. "Carnon?"

"No, Arna," he whispered, relieved. Long ago, when he was young and he coveted power, Nartesis had killed Arna, his love, for personal gain. In so doing, he had trapped her spirit in the Physical plane. After he brought her back, she had forgiven him and taught him how to love. Now she was back with him once more. And everything felt right again.

"It is I. It is your Narty."

"Narty?" she asked hesitantly.

"Yes, my love," Nartesis said softly, brushing his fingertips lightly over her cheek.

Slowly, her face brightened. "Narty. You look nothing as I remember." She pressed her palm to her forehead. "I feel like I have been sleeping a long time."

"Yes, my dear. A very long time." Nartesis reached down and embraced her.

"I remember. A wooden beam collapsed across me. You appeared. I ... begged for you to leave me. We said goodbye before ..." She grasped the amulet around her neck and studied the stone. It was the one he had pulled from his old heart, the same one he had used to bring Arna back the first time, so very long ago. She noted her thinner arm, her porcelain skin. "This woman was in love with the man Carnon Gallowman."

"Yes. It was their own way to be together." Nartesis smiled at her. "Never mind that, my dear. You are back now, back with me. We are together now." Nartesis hugged her again, tighter. Her scent called up memories that were not his, the passion Carnon had had for this woman; memories of being with her swirled through him.

"What is wrong with her?" Meera interrupted from behind.

Nartesis stiffened. He had forgotten that Meera and Ousel were there to offer assistance in Arna's resurrection. "She is fine, Meera. Being brought back can be extremely disorienting. It will pass in time."

"That is not what I meant, my lord. I—"

Nartesis turned on Meera. "Do not concern yourself with Arna. I know what I am doing." In truth, he did not want to hear Meera confirm what some part of him already knew. He had worked too hard to get to this point to change course now. "Why are you two still here? We have a lot yet to accomplish in the days ahead. Go focus on your studies."

He had nearly everything he needed to make his designs complete—a powerful and young body, his love by his side, command over the Necromancers Order, and a burgeoning army of undead. Just one more ingredient to tie it all together. Only that one would seal their fate forever.

Nartesis helped Arna from the table and guided her to the bed. He was too attentive of Arna to notice Meera and Ousel leave. "I have you, my love. You are with me once more. This time, I will set everything right. No one will harm us again. We will have eternity to be happy together."

Nartesis pressed his back into a dark corner of the stage. There, in the shadows, he watched with a calculating eye as Ousel stepped forward and raised his arms before the burgeoning crowd filling every seat in the great hall, Helgish proudly riding on Ousel's shoulder. Every Necromancer living in and around Thanatos had been rallied for this special occasion. His heart raced with excitement at the thought of resurrecting his life-long dream. He wiped his sweaty palms down his robes, having forgotten the sensation. It was wonderful to be alive again!

"Colleagues of the corporeal!" Ousel shouted the mass to silence. "You have been summoned here this day to behold the most extraordinary event to have taken place since before the time our great order broke from the Shamans." If Ousel's reference to "the most extraordinary event" did not catch the assembly's attention, his reference to the Shamans did. "It has been my honor to have borne witness to the greatest wonder ever achieved by man. Comrades, it is with reverence that I introduce ... Nartesis Shazarack, Supreme Lord of Necromancy. Our great paragon!"

The silence in the large hall was heavy as Nartesis stepped forward into the light. He took a few moments to revel in their shock. "I can see the reticence in the sea of faces before me from Ousel's introduction. Nay, I should say disbelief. 'How can this young man,' you are thinking, 'not even twenty years of age, be the great Shazarack, the quintessential standard of our order?' Some of you may recognize this face as that belonging to Carnon Gallowman, a young acolyte and apprentice of this city." At the sound of that name, memories bubbled to the surface of his mind. He forced them back into the recesses where they belonged. "This is no hoax. I *am* Nartesis Shazarack."

Once the crowd quieted, he continued. "Word has reached me that some of you marvel at my magnificent works." He pointed to the undead near the edge of light. "Of my guards ... and my battle with the traitor to our order, Galan Martesian." Nartesis raised his arms and turned, showing off his new body. "What if I told you that such feats were nothing special in my day? That many in that early order possessed powers that you would today call *miraculous*?" He took in their wide, silent stares. "Oh, yes, there were great wonders in my time. So why, some of you are asking, is it that, since my return, I have not spoken more of those marvels? Let me answer that question now. When you think of Thanatos, the old city that stood on this spot a millennium ago, what words come to mind?" He waved for them to speak.

"Preeminence!" someone called out. "Greatness!" shouted someone in the back. "Transcendence," came a quiet response from someone in the front.

"Yes!" Nartesis shouted back. "Transcendence!" His new voice resonated and rebounded throughout the large hall. How he liked this new body! "Take a moment to look around you. Behold this great hall that your necromantic predecessors built for you—to conference, to study, to advance your skills in our order's fine arts. They did not build just *any* city, not just *any* institute of learning, not just *any* center of command for one of the greatest elemental accomplishments ever achieved. They named it *Thanatos* because they believed in what I and my followers achieved long ago. They recreated our city to the exact specifications of the one we raised, because they wanted to reclaim what my order had realized before its destruction.

"History tells us that the crowns of my time sent their Army of the Seven Realms out of fear to crush a treasonous uprising." Nartesis wagged his finger before them. "That is a false narrative perpetrated by those who twisted the truth into something sinister, something wicked. The crowns' army was sent here to crush an *idea*, to destroy the belief that people could make their own destiny, to annihilate the notion that we could live without being ground beneath the heavy suede boot of royalty. Their heinous act was executed out of hatred, ruthless intolerance, bigotry, and a desire to sustain a regime of hereditary-based sovereignty!

"Do you not see?" Nartesis shifted his tone, now calling softly to them. "It is not the powers we had uncovered in those early days that echo down the halls of time in defiance of their historians. It is the legacy of how we *used* those powers. Thanatos was more than a city; it was an inspiration, a shining beacon of hope in a world that had gone dark with small-minded people and the petty tactics of nobility. The very name Thanatos inspired our early ordermen to rebuild this magnificent city. In so doing, they rebuilt the heart and soul of necromancy." Nartesis let those words wash over them.

"Listen," he whispered. The crowd leaned forward, straining to hear. "Can you *hear* the city calling you?" he asked. "Like a potent Necromancer summoning your spirit into its corporeal existence, giving it life? ... *Thanatos*." Then he called out, his baritone voice bold and resonant, "Do you *feel* the old city surging with the energy of our past?" He bent forward and dropped his voice once more to a whisper. "*Thanatos*."

Nartesis straightened his shoulders. "Most of you have heard my tale. Right here, on the hill where our beautiful city stands, I and a small band of intrepid souls, mostly young men and women, had the audacity to dream of building a true marvel to our society. That is why the other day I corrected one glaring error in our city's reconstruction. I had words carved over the city gates just as they were scribed long ago. 'Of what use are all the greatest powers on Gaia if they are not directed toward a purpose of benefit to all?' It was for that dream ... and to share that dream with others ... that our modest order of explorers chose to defy the rulers of the lands.

"Imagine my elation when I returned to find our order thriving, free of suppression. Truly, I delighted in what had been restored. However, brothers and sisters"—he shook his head slowly—"our task is far from complete. Others are in desperate need of the freedom that we take for granted every day—those living in the Harmonic Realms. I know, I know." He raised his palms to calm the growing murmurs. "You hold no love for those on the other side of the Borderlands. But are they truly so different?

They come from the same stock as those sitting in this grand chamber. Imagine for a moment if we could bring all the people of both lands together—Harmonics and Anarchists—one social body, everyone liberated, free to study the use of elementals without fear of restrictions, reprisals, or oppression. Imagine adding more to our numbers, eager to pave the way to a daring, new future."

"We are Necromancers, not Barbarians or Warlocks," someone grumbled from the middle of the hall.

"And who better to be called to correct a travesty than those who understand the true nature of life? Who more justified to rectify the deeds of the past than those who understand death? But let me address the question hiding behind your criticism. How could we who are not trained in martial arts achieve such a feat, one that has defied resolution for five hundred years?"

Nartesis stepped to the edge of the stage. "Look at me. I am a thousand years old. Who else can say that? Who else has ever said that? You have seen my guards, undead who have been with me all this time. What if I were to tell you that what we created in those early days, powers that you are only now beginning to comprehend, were but a fraction of what is out there, ready to be taken? What society might we build in this free land, *all* Cronoans, working together, if we only were bold enough to dream of such a world?

"Now I have heard, as you all have, that war is brewing between the two lands. I have survived a few wars, so I can state with certainty that when it comes, the remarkable order you have built here will be sucked into it. You will be asked to fight against your cousins, against those whom, in a different future, you might have called comrades. In truth, you have already been dragged into it, working diligently each night to create a great army.

"But what if we found a different path, one to a brighter future? What if we created a better future for all Cronoans *and* put an end to the conflict before it begins?" Nartesis jabbed a long forefinger into the air, toward the city gates. "If our goal is not to build a better world, then what is our purpose? Are you building a city that will last a thousand years? I ask you now, 'Of what use are the greatest powers on Gaia if they are not directed toward a purpose of benefit to all?' Young Carnon Gallowman believed in those words. He gave the greatest commitment he could to this cause."

"Our necro-army is not enough to defeat the Harmonics, Lord," a woman called back from the assembly. "And we cannot rely on the other orders for help."

"I would not ask you to do this if there were any chance of failure. I know the necro-army will not be enough."

"Then—" she began.

"Another army awaits my call," Nartesis interrupted the woman. "And not just any army, comrades. One so powerful that no force *anywhere* can defeat it." He waited for the murmuring to settle. "So, I ask you now, are you with me in this adventure? Are you ready to seize this moment, and create a destiny that will withstand the ravages of time itself, one that will be exalted as the greatest civilization ever built? Thanatos!" he shouted.

"Thanatos!" The crowd roared in response, thrusting their fists high into the air.

"Thanatos!" he shouted.

"Thanatos!" they responded.

"We will reignite that beacon of hope for all, and it will be a light across these lands!"

"Thanatos!" The crowd leaped to their feet, chanting, growing to a fever pitch.

"I call on you. Help me finish what I started long ago. Let us go forward together and create a future for all!"

Meera and Morgana watched Ousel march back and forth across Meera's study. He had been gripped with excitement ever since Shazarack had addressed the assembly the previous night. Even Helgish on his shoulder bristled with enthusiasm. Hemera was peeking over the hills in the east, and he was still restless. "Did you hear him, Meera?" he asked for the fourth time, nearly shouting. "My, what a speaker! Since his speech, I have paced the halls of the academy and seen their excitement. What they are saying is beyond what I thought possible. He has lit a flame of righteousness that burns bright throughout the city."

Indeed, Meera thought, her eyes tracking as Ousel stomped here and there. This was not the reaction she'd expected from the ordermen. She found it all so unbelievable. Shazarack had worked the crowd into a frenzy. She too had felt the seductive pull of Shazarack's words, drawing her into his bewitching dream. *How did he do that?* Necromancers were logical, rational thinkers, methodical in their practices, not prone to emotional outbursts like what she'd witnessed in the auditorium.

Had he invoked some incantation? But she discarded the thought just as quickly. Everyone would have noticed if he had manipulated Earth or Fire. *Or would they?* came the annoying voice. She had watched in awe as a youthful Shazarack secured Arna's spirit to her new vessel. He had channeled more Fire and Earth than she and Ousel combined had drawn when they summoned Shazarack's spirit into his new body. The man was far more powerful than she had ever imagined. And that frightened her.

Another vision filled her thoughts—of Galan lying prone on the stage, his quivering gray body nothing more than a blood sac. Four nights since Galan's death, and still, she could not exorcise that image from her mind. She squeezed her eyes shut, but that did not stop the echo of Galan's death rattle, his eyes searching as if asking, *How?* How had Shazarack survived Galan's attack? And what kind of Necromantic incantation turned every bone in a human body to pulp? She shivered.

"I have never seen students so impatient to learn, adepts so eager to bring Shazarack's vision to bear. What army do you think he was referring to?" Ousel stopped pacing, his face drawn up tight. "Meera, are you all right?"

"I am fine." *Don't lie, Meera. You are not fine,* the voice scolded. "But I think I need rest."

"Of course," Ousel raised his palms to her. "How inconsiderate of me. I will take my leave."

After ushering Ousel from her chambers, Meera made tea. She sat on her couch, knees pulled to her chest, and laboriously reviewed all she had experienced since her return. Morgana lay next to her, trembling. Everything had changed; everyone she knew had changed; she had changed. Those she had considered close were gone. *And those who are new?* There was something ... repulsive about Arna Grey. Whatever had lured Meera back, the Thanatos she'd called home was no more.

She got up and started packing everything essential. By the time Hemera was high in the sky, she was riding through the city gates, Morgana pressed under her collar, keeping her neck warm. Glancing above her, she read the newly painted words along the arch: *Of what use are all the greatest powers on Gaia if they are not directed toward a purpose of benefit to all?*

ARMY OF THE DRAGONBONDED

Yes, she thought. *It is time I find my purpose.* With her hood pulled low, Meera heeled her mare forward, cantering past the gnarled, petrified trees, heading north.

A Slight Change in Plans

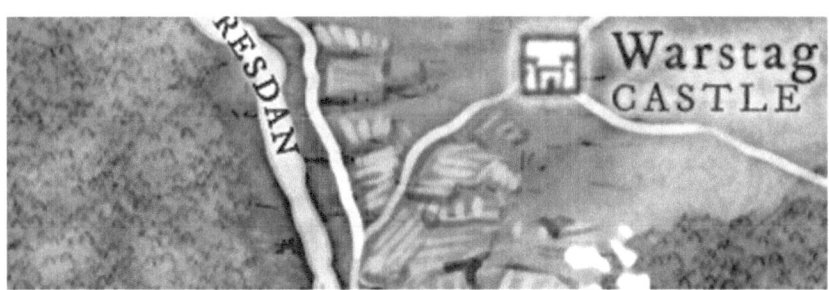

Late morning on the third day out of Charmwell, Veressa, Jonath, and a full battalion of Queen's Defenders came to a fork in the road. Veressa reined Toran to a stop. "Colonel," she said to the battalion commander. "Could you and your Defenders give me and my father a moment of privacy?"

"Of course, Majesty." With a quick signal, the battalion cantered south to a ridge to wait.

"What is it?" Jonath asked.

"When we were heading to Charmwell, I mentioned that I could tell a great weight had lifted from your heart. And the farther we were from Graystone, the lighter your heart."

Jonath glanced away. "I recall that conversation."

"Now, as we near Graystone, your heart grows heavier once more." Veressa waited for a response, but Jonath said nothing. "If I can see it, I know you can feel it as well."

"What do you suggest?"

Veressa pointed down the road angling off eastward. "We could make Warstag Castle by nightfall."

"Warstag?" Jonath's eyes lost focus as they searched the horizon to the east. He had told Veressa many stories of growing up a serf, romping through the fields his parents toiled in until he was strong enough to help

work off their debts. Veressa thought it a brutal life, but Jonath had nothing but fond memories: of loving parents, caring neighbors, and a close-knit community that struggled together. He often told her that the lessons of responsibility, fortitude, endurance, and tenacity had paid him back later in life many times over.

"I think returning to your old home would be good for you," Veressa suggested.

Jonath rose in his stirrups as if he could get a better view a hand higher. "No. You need to get back to Graystone. I promised to protect you until Conner returns. Besides, who else can you rely upon for guidance? The War Council will be well rehearsed for their next assault."

"Then how about I go with you? That way we don't have to decide right away. We will stay through tomorrow, and the morning after, we can discuss whether you should stay or return with me to Graystone." She leaned over and placed her hand on his arm. "I don't want you to think I am trying to rid myself of you. You were invaluable to me during our ... *visit* to Charmwell. But I still worry for your health. And I will need you healthy in the months ahead if we do go to war."

"Warstag," Jonath whispered the name again as he chewed on her suggestion. "I have not been home since before you were born."

"Then it is settled." Veressa slapped her thigh and signaled for the commander to return. "Now, no more discussion until the morning after tomorrow." Veressa waited until the battalion had reformed about them. "Commander, there has been a slight change in plans. We ride for Warstag. I want to be there before dark."

"Of course, Majesty."

Garden of the Pixies

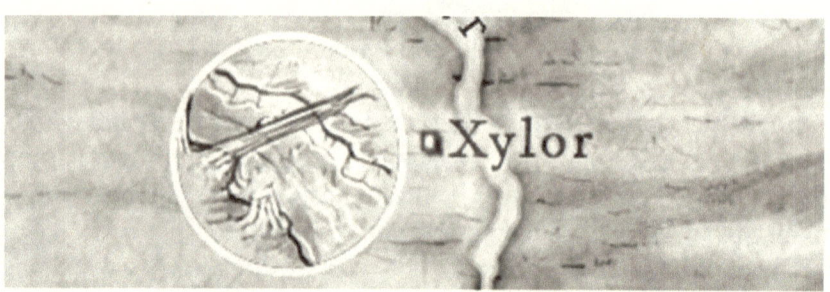

Crows wheeled overhead, cawing and spiraling around a hawk that had gotten too close to their nests. Leaves with flecks of autumn brown rustled on the soft breeze. The earthy scent of rich forest dirt and the bright smell of oak wafted upward. Conner inhaled deep and closed his eyes. It reminded him of fall on his parents' farm. He had nearly forgotten the feeling that came with those sounds and smells, so long had it been since he'd felt this rested.

"I thought I would find you here." Morgas's deep voice came from behind.

From the edge of the large platform, Conner glanced up. "This has become my favorite spot."

Morgas scanned the secluded deck high above the village, then sat next to Conner. "Not that long ago, you could not sit here without getting ill."

"Not that long ago, I saw the world much differently." Morgas did not comment, so Conner asked, "Why would anyone want to war with these people?"

"You speak of the Harmonics? Killing is always easier when the opponent is misunderstood. It is hard to hate when we understand the other's view on life. And hatred is essential to allow us to sleep at night after we have eradicated our enemy."

In the silence that followed, Morgas grew more troubled and fidgeted with his sword hilt. "Conner, we are nearly out of time. The healer is beginning to sense your disinterest in continuing your endeavor. Anyone with the Calling could not resist it this long."

"I know," Conner said, recalling the urgency he'd felt when he was trapped in Cravenrock's undercity. "Yet, we are no closer. And I have seen no sign of Grimmley's longtime apprentice. I am wondering again if this whole adventure was some elaborate deception, that there is no dragon-bonded human here."

"To what end? We have been here four days and I have neither seen nor heard anyone raise an alarm or make a move to capture us. What other reason would someone have to bring you here?"

"To get me away from the queen."

Morgas grunted. "If there is any chance the queen is in peril, then you need to decide swiftly what to do. If we do not find this person tomorrow, we must start back the next morning."

Conner bobbed his head. "One more day, then."

That night, Conner tossed in his bed. During one nightmarish dream, he and Skye were being chased through thick clouds by an unseen force. He awoke with a hand pressing down firmly over his mouth. Before he cried out, he felt someone's breath near his ear.

"Shh!" came the intruder's harsh voice.

Conner had fallen from Skye's back, looking up as he dropped from the skies, the wind roaring in his ears. His bond had disappeared in Hemera's late bright beams over the ocean. *Wait. No, that was a dream.* "Wren?" he mumbled.

The girl slid her hand from his mouth.

"What is it? What's wrong?" Conner sat up in alarm.

"The other day, you asked how the trees in our forest grow so big. Would you like to see how?"

Conner bolted out of bed. "Sure!"

"Then we must go now ... before it gets any later. Grab your traveling clothes, but be quiet! It won't do if grandfather finds out we are gone."

With clothes and sword in hand, Conner followed Wren into the dead of night, where he quickly dressed. He was stuffing his shirt inside his pants when he noticed Wren watching him, a smile across her face. "Focus," he whispered to Wren, buckling his sword strap over his shoulder, then tilting his blade's hilt to be within reach. It was becoming second nature to him.

"Come on, then." She sprinted away.

Conner tailed Wren to the village lift, where they descended to the forest floor.

They had gone no more than twenty paces from the lift when Wren pulled up short and squatted next to a thick bush with thorny leaves. Chatter and laughter filled the night air ahead. She indicated a campfire nearby, where a few villagers and bonds sat around the dying embers. Their animated motions could be seen with the muted red and orange glow from the fire against the rustling trees nearby. She pressed her palm downward for Conner to be quiet, then slipped off to the right, away from the camp.

Conner's next step was on a twig that snapped. He froze. The noises around the fire faded.

Wren scowled at him. And she mouthed the words, "Do you know nothing, you buffoon?"

Conner shrugged helplessly, mouthing back, "I'm not a woodsman."

Wren rolled her eyes and slipped away, silent as a shadow.

Conner found her waiting at the edge of the village tree, watching him in the light of Erebus as he pulled his vest over his shoulders. His cheeks burned under her intense scrutiny. "Are you going to tell me where we're going?" he asked, hoping a conversation might divert whatever thoughts she was having.

She grinned, a sudden glimmer of Erebus's light in her eyes. "Any attempt to describe the place would be pointless."

"Uh-huh." Most of what Conner had seen in the Anarchic Lands had been that way. The idea that Wren had something to show him that could not be sketched with words excited him. Not that long ago, such a mystery would have aroused fear or dread, not exhilaration. He shadowed her.

Wren's laugh was light and airy as she skipped along, leading him away from the village along a trail that carved its way through the thick forest. After a few minutes, they came to a massive gorge. Conner could not tell how deep it went, but judging by the sound of the waters raging below, it measured hundreds of paces. Turning, he caught Wren scrambling up a huge root staircase to the right. He followed and found her at the top, where a toppled tree, larger than the one Xylor was built upon, extended across the gorge. The bark and a good third of the trunk had been planed smooth to form a wide bridge with thick railings along either side. Conner thought the bridge was what Wren wanted to show him. But she sprinted across. Conner took up the chase once more.

On the other side of the gorge, they descended another root staircase and picked up speed. They ran for half an hour, jostling and laughing in a game of tag, until Wren pulled up at the top of a gentle hill. Ahead, the trees thinned. Beyond that, a bright glow, nearly as brilliant as Hemera's rise, emanated from a small clearing.

Wren moved forward again, but her demeanor had changed. Instead of her usual heedless abandon, her steps were measured and cautious. She had said Azarah would not like them here. Conner could not help but wonder just what she had dragged him into. But his curiosity called to him and he followed.

"What is this place?" he muttered as they stepped into the clearing.

Ferns, coleus, daylilies, forget-me-nots, hostas, and a variety of other plants Conner did not know filled the small glade. Each radiated an unearthly luminescence of reds, greens, and yellows. Even the bark and leaves on the oaks and poplars nearby glowed. A half dozen moths with glowing wings the length of his arm fluttered around brightly lit flowers. At the edge of the clearing stood the scant rubble of a small cottage. Little remained but large toppled blocks of stone. A cherry tree grew near an opening in the wall, and a huge oak grew inside the foundation.

"It is old," Wren said, "so old that no one in the village knows its origin. That is why grandfather does not want us here." She squatted and lightly stroked an oak sapling sprouting at her feet. "The plants that grow here are very powerful, as are their seeds. The trees we nurture in our forest come from this glade."

"That explains their supernatural size." Conner stepped past Wren to the middle of the open space. "But I sense there is something more happening here." Two huge, colorful butterflies fluttered before him. He raised his arms to shade his eyes from their intense glow. To his surprise, a butterfly landed on each hand. He held very still as their wings twitched up and down.

Wren gasped next to him. "I have never seen them do that before."

A moment later, they flew away.

Conner crossed the glade. As he neared the cottage, pressure began to build in his head. "Something terrible happened here. It is like the very fabric of Gaia was ripped wide."

A thought sprang to Conner. No, a memory—the moment he'd stepped out onto the tourney field. It was the first time he'd had any recollection of that event. He seized the memory thread with his mind, gripping it tight, afraid that if it slipped away, his memory of the contest would be forever lost. He slid along that thread. Marcantos Evinfaire had offered him his sword, but he had refused it as he stepped onto the field. Evinfaire had attacked him, slicing open his side. Conner grabbed his side and groaned from the memory of the pain. The Warrior had been so smug and certain. He said he would let no one stand in his way of becoming Veressa's Champion. And in that desperate moment, Conner had stepped into the stream of energy that was his bond with Skye.

Now, just as he had done that day in Graystone, he reached inside himself and found that conduit of energy. And just as he had done that day, he embraced it. The rush of power jolted him, the shifting patterns of the Cosmos opened before his eyes, and his spirit drifted upward along that bright beam of energy. This was how he had accessed his powers! Traveling along the energy beam, his spirit rose over the remains of the small cottage, passing through a tear across the Physical plane. The gnarled edges of the gash rippled as he soared past. Just as on the tourney field, sights became sounds, smells became tastes, a jumbled confusion of senses that blended and mingled. But through his newly empowered senses, Conner discerned someone at the border of his awareness ... no, some*thing*. It shifted in the vastness of the Psychic planes. It was aware of his presence. There was more movement, like a thousand leaves quivering on a summer breeze. For a moment, everything grew still. Then the leaves exploded at him in a frenzied chaos of motion, like dark forms of Anarchic energy, rushing at him.

Conner recoiled, his spirit tracing back along his bond's conduit. Creatures, buzzing like angry hornets, closed in on him. Faster he fled, zipping back through the rip in the Physical plane. His consciousness slammed into his body, and Conner cried out. He bent forward, wanting to alleviate the sudden throbbing in his head. He pressed his palms to his temples, trying to keep his skull from cracking open. But the pressure continued to grow.

A horde of small black creatures burst through the tear above him. They swept across the open glade, laughing with glee as they spun and dove playfully on gossamer wings. No larger than the size of his hand, they reminded Conner of pixies from old mythology. They were of human shape, with gleaming skin, pointed ears, and cat-like eyes that glowed against the night sky. Their oval wings were translucent and beat at the speed of a hummingbird's.

Wren screamed, trying to shoo them away as they swarmed her. But the little brutes continued to buzz around her like a plague of locusts, giggling and jeering.

Just as on the tourney field, Conner drew upon all four elementals, compressing them between his palms and molding them into a bright ball of light. He cast the light out, striking the thickest mass of the pixies, scattering them about the glade. The pixies turned their feline eyes upon him. They had lost their frolicking spirit. They zipped and dove at him, screaming indignation and pelting him with tiny fists. Conner flailed his arms to deflect the assault, weaving the elementals together again. He reached up with his mind and stitched together the edges of the tear in Physical space. His efforts worked the pixies into a frenzy. The ferocity of the attack grew to a crescendo of high-pitched screams and pummeling.

Lacing the last stitch, he pulled hard on his link with the elementals. The pixies vanished.

As did the pounding in his head.

Conner crawled forward on hands and knees, panting and trembling. His stitch would not hold for long. Still, he hoped it would be enough to keep the pixies out of the Physical plane.

Wren was next to him, helping him to stand. "Conner? Are you okay?" She was trembling.

"I remember," Conner mumbled, wiping away tears of relief.

"Remember?" she asked, brushing back his hair and checking his bruised face. "Remember what?"

Conner searched Wren's worried stare and laughed. "Everything."

The Cost of Truth

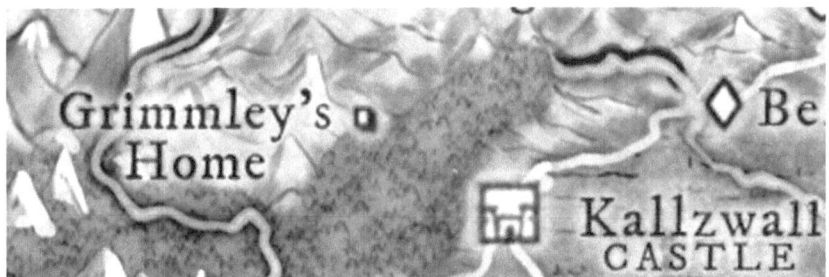

Grimmley rested his chin on his palm, drumming his fingers on his chair while keeping time with Herid's snoring in the far corner of his cottage. For two days, every waking moment that he had not been tending to Herid's condition he'd spent obsessing over the Fettering Stone. But this latest experiment had given him insights he had not expected, insights that poked huge holes in his earlier theory that the stones were used to communicate across vast distances. The stones were so much more.

It seemed unfathomable that the stones were powerful enough to fetter or shackle a spirit from another plane to a Physical body. Not like the undead Necromancers used as slaves. But something powerful enough to give that spirit life, living and breathing life. To a Necromancer with the right skills, such a device would be ... well, invaluable. That would explain why Shazarack had scarfed up all the stones he could steal or kill for. But to what end? Grimmley was about to make a few notes when he sensed the sudden and massive draw of Earth and Fire elementals. The ground beneath the cottage shook and rumbled. China rattled in his cupboard. An iron skillet clattered across the stove. Even the empty vials on his workbench danced.

"What's that?" Herid shouted, jumping from his bed and blinking.

"One minute, old friend." Grimmley had half expected an attack of some kind, but not one like this. And not so soon. He was not prepared! He grabbed his staff, which he had kept within reach since Herid's arrival, and shuffled through his back door and out into his garden. There, the lake water swirled and pulsed with an eerie green light. The trees encircling his home swayed and creaked in a breeze whipped up around the white gazebo, where his Transit Stone pulsed a deep brown light. Grimmley's robes snapped in the sudden spirited wind. Gripping his staff in both hands, he planted his slippered feet firmly and drove the base of his staff into the dirt. *"Hemea ousia fragiaspida!"* he shouted. Earth and Fire sparked, then swirled about him. He closed his eyes, putting all his mental focus into forging the elemental sphere that descended around his cottage. The sounds of wind and rustling trees subsided.

With the barrier set, Grimmley moved back inside and closed the back door. Bending over his desk, he snatched a label from a narrow slot along the back panel and plucked his quill pen from its inkwell. He began to scribble.

I need you. Now!

Grimmley shambled over to his bond, perched near the fireplace, rolling the note into a thin cylinder. Another, more powerful quake shook the windows in their sills. "Barthox, my dear old girl. We're out of time." He waved the furled parchment before the owl. "I am counting on you to get this to Layna. In Graystone. Do you understand me?"

"Hoot-da-hoot!" Barthox snatched the rolled paper in her beak.

Grimmley shuffled to the front door and flung it wide. The ground shook again as a flash of bright white light lit up the yard beyond. *They are here!* "Stay low until you have cleared the hill." He squatted low, then flapped his arms to display his intent. He had designed the barrier so that matter could go out, but not come in.

The barred owl lifted her wings and bobbed on aged legs. Adjusting her weight, she swooped through the open door, pierced his shield, and vanished into the dead of night.

Grimmley chewed on the tip of his pipe. He was not sure Barthox would return with Layna before his barrier dissolved. But he had no other option. He felt a sharp tug on his sleeve.

Herid was beside him, trembling. "What—what is it?"

Grimmley returned to the back window overlooking his garden, Herid clinging to his robes. He peeped a quick glance out the back, where two dark forms were crossing the wooden walkway that connected his gazebo to the banks of the lake. He returned his gaze to Herid. "I should have been prepared for this, my friend. It seems we have a couple of uninvited guests at our back door."

Herid started to say something, but Grimmley pressed his fingers over Herid's lips.

The two forms stopped at Grimmley's shield. A deep, raspy voice spoke. "It seems the old man was expecting us." There was a long delay as the two studied the barrier. "We don't have time for this, Brother."

"Shh, Brother! He can hear you!" the other voice whispered back. There was a pause. "Grimmley," the voice called out.

"Yes?" Grimmley shouted back.

"It is Karmenian."

Grimmley slumped against his staff. One of the Shaman Dons. Well, if someone had suggested there was an Anarchic spy on the Shamans Council, Karmenian would have been his guess. The man was why Grimmley had refused a seat on the Shamans Council. To say there was no friendship lost between them was an understatement. "Just dropping by for a friendly chat, are you? After all these years?"

"In a way, yes. We have come for something you have."

"Oh?" Grimmley tried to sound surprised. *So, you wish to forgo any decorum? A little pressed for time, are you?* A faint smile crossed Grimmley's face. "I would have thought you knew me well enough to know I am a man of little means. For the life of me, I can't imagine what I might have that you need."

"He is stalling," the man with the raspy voice whispered to Karmenian.

Grimmley peeked through the window. In the faint glimmer of Erebus waxing in the west, just past his barrier, he caught the form of a bald man standing next to Karmenian, features warped and blurred by the shield. Still, he could not miss the dark Cosmic Star tattooed on the man's forehead. *A Paladin?* He bit down hard on his pipe stem and puffed. Realizing his tobac had gone out, he stuffed his pipe into his pocket. So, he *had* kicked a hornet's nest when he took the empty silver box to Aldemeer. He poked his head up. "Who did you bring with you, Karmenian? Anyone I know?"

"We have not met before, Rollingsworth," came the gravelly voice. "Come out and let me introduce myself."

Herid's eyes bulged, and he shivered. "I know that voice," he whimpered, wringing his hands.

Grimmley placed a palm lightly on Herid's trembling shoulder. "It's all right, Herid. They cannot get through my protection. You are safe here." *For now,* he thought. He glanced out into the garden, then leaned toward the window. "Karmenian, surely you did not forget how much I despise rudeness. Neither of you was invited to my home, so you will have to forgive me for staying right where I am." He doubted Karmenian would ever forget the day Grimmley had embarrassed him by calling him the rudest Shaman he had ever met. *Never too late to get a little dig in while passing the time.*

"Safe," Herid repeated Grimmley's word, his eyes darting about him. "He told me you needed my help. Why is he here?" Herid hummed and squinted his eyes, then his head snapped to his phantom bond. "I know, you foul beast! It was *my* mission to help Grimmley, not Eladon's!"

Grimmley gripped Herid's shoulder firmer. "Mission? Who is that Paladin, Herid?"

"Eladon Enfearson." Herid's eyes went wide at speaking the man's name, then he sank back. "Archbishop of the Paladins Order."

A Shaman Don and the keeper of the Paladins Council, Grimmley thought. *Oh Grimmley, you kicked a very nasty hornet's nest!* He needed to stall. He leaned toward the window. "If you are here for Herid, you should know that I have claimed charge of him. He suffers greatly from the Yearning, so it would not be wise to take him—"

"We didn't come all this way for the old heretic, you idiot!" the Paladin rasped.

Grimmley laughed loudly for his visitors. "Thank you, sir Paladin, for proving the old saying about bad-mannered people seeking solace with shameless compatriots."

The Paladin's silhouette drew his sword and raked the edge of his blade over Grimmley's shield, drawing a stern look from Karmenian.

Herid craned his head up like a tortoise deciding it safe to come out of its shell. His eyes were as large as goose eggs. "Yes, Ezera," he chortled. "We are safe here. Grimmley told us we had nothing to fret over. Don't you see? He was right all along!"

Grimmley's bushy eyebrows furrowed at Herid. "Actually, Herid—" But Karmenian interrupted him before he could say more.

"None of us is looking for a confrontation, Grimmley."

"That is good news, Karmenian," Grimmley remarked. "Very good news. There is no need for a fight. Besides, you should know, there is a squad of Queen's Defenders on their way here now."

Eladon growled. "You're stalling, Rollingsworth. Bring us the stone and we will be on our way."

"Stone?" Grimmley asked, feigning ignorance.

"Stop playing games, Grimmley," Karmenian said. "My colleague is not in the mood. Bring us the Fettering Stone. And be quick about it."

"Ah, *that* stone." Grimmley stroked his beard. "It may take some time for me to recall where I put it. My mind is not as sharp as it used to be, you know. Maybe while I am remembering where it is, you can answer a question for me."

Karmenian dropped his head, stabbing the sandy bank with the base of his staff. "What, Grimmley?"

"There were only three Shamans who ever knew how to operate my Transit Stone." The three elder Shamans who had helped Grimmley construct his device decades before had all sworn to secrecy the pattern to unlock the Stone. Karmenian could not have been more than an apprentice when the last of the three Shamans died. Who had told him how to use it?

There was another question nagging Grimmley, one his friend might be able to answer. "Herid," he whispered. "Where did you find the stone? And how did you get out of Aldemeer with it?"

Herid flinched at the question. "I—I stole it. I found it in the cellars a long time ago and hid it so that I could bring it to you." Herid covered his mouth. "Oh, Grimmley. The stone. That is why they are here—to get the stone back." Water pooled in his eyes. "I brought them here."

"It is all right, Herid. You did nothing wrong."

Herid whipped his head around. "What's that, Ezera?" He ran shaky hand over his bald head. "Not safe? Why of course we are safe, you eccentric old creature. Delusions, Grimmley says they are ... No, they aren't real."

Grimmley placed his hand on Herid's shoulder. His medication was wearing off. "Let me get you something to help soothe your spirit. He started toward his bench.

"It's okay, Grimmley," Herid said, laughing. He opened the back door. "Come, Ezera! I'll show you!"

Grimmley reached for Herid's cloak, but the old Paladin ripped free, running and cackling out into the garden. "Herid! Come back!"

"See, Ezera? They're illusions. That's all they are!" Herid started to dance about in the middle of the garden. "See how they shimmer like the pale night shadows of trees in the wind?" He cackled and spun. "There is nothing to fear! That's what Grimmley said. I'm free, Ezera! I don't have to be afraid anymore!"

Grimmley grabbed his staff but bolted to a stop at the doorway.

Herid ran down the path, howling with delight, rushing through Grimmley's shield ... and straight into the Paladin.

Eladon gripped Herid by the shoulders, then pushed him toward Karmenian and kicked him to his knees.

Karmenian placed his palm on Herid's head. *"Hemea energi kaumafotia."* His hand ignited in flames.

Herid shrieked, his body convulsing, as fire scorched the top of his skull.

"Stop! Please stop!" Grimmley cried out.

"I am weary of your delays, Rollingsworth." Eladon shouted. "No more excuses! Bring us the stone!"

He knew Karmenian well enough to not trust anything he said. And he had no faith in any Paladins he had ever met.

"Promise me," Grimmley called out in desperation. "Give me your Anarchic oath that you will not harm Herid or me, and I will bring you the stone."

"Fine, Grimmley," Eladon said. "You have my oath. Neither of you will be harmed. We have no desire to hurt you. Just bring us the stone and we will be on our way."

Grimmley stepped outside, then released the energy holding his barrier. He moved to the three figures, stopping before Eladon with arm extended. With a sigh, Grimmley placed the stone gently in the Paladin's palm.

Eladon's other arm blurred—motion so swift, Grimmley thought he had been mistaken. There was a sound, like steel slicing through muscle and gristle.

Grimmley looked down and blinked at the bejeweled hilt of a blade jutting from his side. He recognized the knife Herid kept sheathed at his waist.

"It is a technique I learned from an old preceptor. A very long time ago," Eladon added. "It will be a painless death."

Death? Grimmley thought as he ran his fingers over the glistening hilt. He did not want to believe the blade was real. There was no pain. *No, no. I have too much yet to do.* He wrapped his fingers tight around the handle.

"I would suggest you don't remove the blade, or you'll bleed out much faster."

Grimmley examined the hilt closer. From the angle and location of the blade, Eladon had likely severed his abdominal aorta and sliced through several nerves down the right side of his body, possibly his femoral nerve. A ripple of dizziness flooded over him, and he collapsed to his knees. Falling back on his haunches, Grimmley peered into Eladon's dark eyes, eyes void of compassion. "You swore ... an oath. Anarchists ... keep their oaths."

Eladon squatted and leaned in close, eyebrows raised. The expression on the Paladin's face reminded Grimmley of a time when he was a young Shaman, traveling through the impoverished villages of the southern outlands, performing sock puppet shows for the young children. They would sit in wonder, motionless, astonished. That was how Eladon looked. Eladon held the small gem Grimmley had given him up to Erebus's light, then slipped the stone into a pocket at his waist. "We never said we were Anarchists."

Not Anarchists? Grimmley blinked. But no Harmonic orderman would commit such an act. "If you're not Anarchic or Harmonic, who ..."

Eladon carefully reached inside his collar and fumbled with a chain around his neck, then slid his hand forward. Dangling on the chain was a golden amulet in the shape of the Cosmic Star. Secured to the center was a small black onyx, finely cut, a twin to the stone Grimmley had just given him.

Of course. The stones ...

"Brother," Eladon said, "I do believe the old Shaman is finally catching on."

Karmenian crouched next to Eladon. It was the first time Grimmley had ever seen the Shaman smile.

Numbness made its way across Grimmley's chest. Breathing became labored. He slumped forward, eyes cast down at Eladon's feet. He had not seen this. For the first time he could recall, he had been wrong, dead wrong. They were not spies. No. His new theory was the answer, that the stones were being used to tether interloping spirits to human bodies. Karmenian, Eladon, the Assassin Lacerus, even the Barbarian Groegan. They were all spirits from a plane beyond! Herid had been but a means to acquire another stone.

Grimmley's vision began to narrow. He fought to keep a clear head. In the distance, there was a long horrific scream, the sound of someone in immense pain and suffering. With little feeling left in his body, Grimmley slowly listed, then tumbled to his side. Herid lay next to him, looking back at him with pleading eyes. A portion of his face was scorched, still smoldering, from an intense Earth-Fire incantation. Grimmley had not been able to keep his promise to Herid after all. In the end, he had failed everyone.

Eladon rose, and the two spirits stepped over Grimmley, moving toward his secluded home, his once-peaceful cottage.

Far in the distance, Grimmley could make out a deep, scratchy voice. "BrieAnn will be pleased. Now we just need to find her a new body."

"Good. Then she will stop harassing us about it," Karmenian said, his voice fading into the distance. "You ravage the cottage while I do a thorough search for anything else useful."

Grimmley inched his arm toward Herid's until he held his friend's cold fingers with his. "It's okay, my friend," he said softly. "You are safe now. There will be no more suffering." Grimmley lay there holding Herid's hand tight, numbness washing over his body in colossal waves. "Be at peace, my dear friend." A slow smile crossed Herid's face, and his worry wrinkles softened. Grimmley stayed, gripping Herid's hand until the light went out of his old friend's eyes.

A Savant's Offer

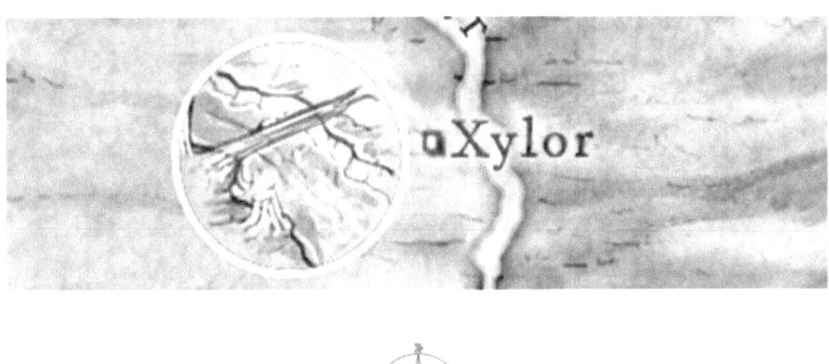

Conner awoke the morning after the misadventure at the ancient garden with a throbbing headache that turned his stomach. Yet that did little to temper his excitement. He had his memories back! And with them, his powers. The thought of returning to Graystone and telling Grimmley and Layna filled him with exhilaration. *And now I can protect Veressa without having to lie or pretend!* He was done with lies and deceit. After he got back, he would clear the air with everyone. And that promise felt liberating.

He started to rise but cried out with a stabbing pain in his palms. He held his hands up and studied them in the early light. His palms were raw and swollen. The heels and several fingers sported large, bulbous blisters, the result of calling elementals last night in the garden. Seeing them scorched reminded him of waking up two days after his fight with Marcantos, wondering why his palms were burned and blistered. *Well, now I know.*

But something else extraordinary had happened last night. He strained to recall details. Some of his recollections made no sense. When he'd returned to his body from traveling to another plane, dark spirits had followed him back, swirling and diving at him, like playing some kind of frolicking game, and ... His breath caught. "Wren," he whispered. She had been dazed and confused on their hike back from the garden, rambling on about what she had seen. If she were to say something to her grandparents ... He needed to find her, to make sure she did not tell anyone about what happened.

Conner jumped from his bed, ignoring the throb in the side of his head and his hands. In a few moments, he was dressed and running down the long causeway.

Conner found Wren an hour later standing near the edge of the village's top platform in the upper branches of their massive tree home. She was facing away from him as he climbed up the stairs and through the hatch. "Good morning," he said, painting on a friendly smile.

Wren tensed as he approached, but did not turn to look at him. "You slept late," she said flatly.

He came up next to her. "I woke up with a terrible throbbing in my head." He started to mention the pain in his palms, but decided not to go there.

Wren said nothing.

He stepped closer. "Are you okay?"

It took a few moments for Wren to look at him. When she did, he could see fear in her eyes. "Those creatures ... last night ... What were they?"

Is she afraid of what happened last night or is she afraid of ... me? He swallowed hard and glanced away. "I don't know." He had to work at forcing the words over his tongue. The truth was he knew *what* they were—spirits from another plane—he was just not sure how they'd gotten there. "But they remind me of creatures from stories I was told when I was younger. We called them pixies."

Wren trembled. "I have been to that field many times. That never happened before."

"You should not go back there, Wren." Maybe Conner could not explain everything, but at least he could warn her. Azarah had been right to make the garden off-limits. "There is something wrong about that place. I cannot say how I know, but something terrible happened there once, a very long time ago."

"How do you know that?" She glared at him with such intensity that he flinched.

He wanted to tell her what had happened, to explain that he had traveled through a rip in the Physical plane, a rip that allowed dark spirits to come back through with him. But if he said such things, Wren would ask more questions he was not prepared to answer. Whatever truth he said, she would not understand ... or believe.

"At least explain what you did. I was helpless against them. But a ball of light appeared in your hands, brighter than a thousand candles. And—and you threw the ball at those ... pixies. And they scattered. How did you do that? How did you make them disappear?"

"I cannot tell you." Conner reached to place his hand on her arm, but she pulled away. "Wren, please don't tell anyone else about last night."

She stared at his blistered hands. "Why not? What are you hiding? Who are you?"

There it was. The question he could never answer. *Yes, Conner, who are you?* He was so tired of his deceptions, so tired of all the lies. He shook his head. He hardly recognized himself anymore. He stepped closer, trying hard to come up with some answer, any answer that would mend this fence.

She drew back farther, staying out of reach of his swollen hands. "You are not telling me everything."

"There are things I cannot tell you. Please don't tell your grandparents about last night," he implored. He took a deep breath. "If you tell them, you'll be exposing yourself for taking me to a forbidden place. Your grandfather—"

Wren's eyes went wide, and she started to turn away.

Conner grabbed her arm. "I am no threat to you, Wren. Or to your village. Believe me. I want to tell you more. But I—I can't."

Wren wrenched her arm free and ran.

Conner let her go. He would not be able to catch her anyway. He stood there, alone, stunned not at Wren's behavior, but at his own. *Conner, what are you doing? An hour ago, you were joyous for freeing yourself from lies and deceit. And now you just threatened one of your few friends?* Embarrassed at himself, he sat down hard and pressed his aching palms to his eyes. He wanted so much to cry.

For most of the morning, Conner stayed to himself, walking mindlessly around the village, mumbling greetings to those he passed. Some part of him nagged about needing to focus on his mission, but self-pity kept him from caring enough to do anything about it. He was trudging along a narrow causeway leading back to the main trunk of the village tree when Little Robin popped up in front of him.

"Conner, there you are!" she nearly shouted. "I have been looking for you since breakfast."

"What is it?"

"The savants council. They want to speak to you. Now."

Conner's gut wrenched at the sound of Little Robin's last word. Why would the savants want to talk to him? Since he'd first met them five days ago, the savants had paid him no attention. But whatever the reason, he could not refuse them. He looked around. "I think I am lost. Would you mind taking me to their cottage?"

On the short walk, Conner tried to think of reasons they would want to see him. But it always circled back around to one possibility: that Wren had told her grandmother what had happened last night. He waited at the cottage entrance for several dozen heartbeats before he gathered the courage to rap on the door, as Wren had the first time he was there. Hearing Elda's call to enter, he pushed the door wide and ducked inside. The one-room hut had not changed much since his first time there. The same dozen elderly women sat in a ring around the fire with Elda to his right, her cat bond Moggie sitting beside her. The smell of smoke was thick. And a small fire burned in the middle, except there was no iron pot this time.

As Conner stepped in, the savants put down their crochet hooks and set their eyes upon him. Elda patted the cushion beside her, then patiently waited as Conner crossed the room. There was a hardness in Elda's eyes, like a shopper deciding whether some bauble was worth a stubborn seller's price.

The savants all sat staring at him. That was something new.

Conner eased into the pillow and waited. With each passing moment, his uneasiness grew. His heart raced. The blisters on his palm itched with sweat. *Easy, Conner*, he admonished himself. *Deep breaths*.

"Have you seen Wren this morning?" Elda asked.

Conner grappled with the sudden urge to run from the room, so it took several moments to finally pin the impulse to the ground. He glanced around at the women glaring at him, his face flushed. Were they toying with him? Seeing what he might give up on his own? "Shortly after I awoke," he answered breathlessly.

"I sent for her hours ago, but she is nowhere to be seen. I assumed she was with you."

"We spoke briefly, but I have not seen her since."

Elda leaned closer and winked. "Trouble in Idyll?" she asked.

The question made several savants titter.

Conner did not know where Idyll was, so he sat frozen to his cushion.

Elda waved the question away. "I spoke with Azarah this morning. He said you are healthy enough to continue your endeavor. Yet you are still here."

Conner chewed on his lip for a moment, frustrated with Elda's circuitous conversation. Was she pressuring him, or telling him in her own savant manner that it was time to be on his way? If so, then he had run out of time to find the other dragon-bonded. "I was planning to leave tomorrow morning," he said.

Elda's brow sank and her eyes narrowed.

"At first light, of course," he amended with a faint smile. Hopefully, that would satisfy her urging and still give him and Morgas the remainder of the day to continue their search.

Elda stared back at him, unblinking, sizing him up, measuring him with her gaze. "Did you know Azarah was not originally from Xylor?"

Where is she going with this? Conner was finding it hard to remain patient when all he wanted to know was whether his true intentions here had been exposed. "No, mistress."

"He was traveling through our region when I met him and invited him to visit Xylor. I was young then, having just received my bond and name. But we both knew right away that we were meant to be together."

Conner felt uncomfortable with where he thought this might be going. Did Elda think his intentions with Wren were romantic? They had been spending a lot of time together, so he could see how it might appear that way. Should he correct her? Or would she take offense, or find him impolite?

"It does not happen often, but occasionally, when the savants council sees value outsiders might bring to our band, they can invite them to become part of our family. That is what happened with Azarah. He had already studied to be a healer. And no one else was qualified to replace our aging healer. He accepted our invitation." Elda was back to studying Conner again. "You like our village?" But it did not sound like a question.

Finally, Conner thought, *something I can answer truthfully.* "I like it here ... a lot. It is very peaceful."

A few of the savants around the fire nodded and made *mmm* sounds.

"Peaceful?" Elda asked. "That is not a word I expected a Gorgonian to use."

Conner nearly choked. Ten minutes here and already he was stumbling over his tongue. "Not all Gorgonians are alike."

"No, I guess not. No more than we Dristonians." Elda stroked her bond's fur. "When you have completed your endeavor, the council would like to offer you a home here in Xylor."

Conner sat dazed. He blinked several times. "A home? Here?" He had not seen that coming. "But I don't have anything of value—"

"Azarah mentioned you have a knack for healing, and that you already have some training. He is looking for someone to whom he can pass along the responsibility as village healer. He would be excited if you were to accept the offer." Elda reached out and placed her warm hand lightly on Conner's arm, breaking him from his thoughts. She wore a gentle smile. "I do not know how anyone raised as a Gorgonian could have such a modest and kindhearted spirit, but I sense a great struggle inside you, Conner. I can sense you do not wish to leave."

Of course he did not want to go. He had a mission to finish. But that thought did not feel complete. Was there more? All at once, he knew she was right. A part of him *did* want to stay here. Under Azarah's instruction, he imagined becoming a healer, something he had always wanted.

"You do not need to decide now. Once you have bonded, if you wish, return here to us. Be part of our family."

How does one respond to such an offer? Conner wondered. The few words that floated to the surface of his mind felt woefully inadequate to express his astonishment and gratitude for the honor they'd bestowed upon him. Humbled, he rose and bowed, then took his leave.

Signs

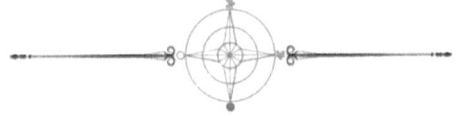

The training regimen Marcantos had set for his new Barbarian pupils was blistering. But no matter how hard he pressed them, none of the dozen who'd rallied around him complained. And though he had spent much of his life loathing Barbarians, he had to give them credit for their fervor and tenacity when it came to intense practice. But he would push them even harder this day. It had been a fortnight since he had arrived at Farlorde. The Barbarian council's decision would be arriving at any time. He could feel the hours of his life slipping away. He did not have many remaining to pass along the torch of knowledge he had acquired from Orianna about embracing both Harmonic and Anarchic Sights. He would have preferred other conduits for what he knew, but none had made themselves available.

On the third morning of training, Groegan appeared at the foot of Marcantos's small camp of tents, watching his students with growing interest.

Marcantos instructed the assembly to continue their exercises, then went to see what Groegan wanted.

Groegan pointed toward the group, who looked like they were choreographing a synchronized dance. "I have never seen that style of combat before," he said as Marcantos drew near. "What is its purpose?"

Marcantos hesitated. Since Engert's death, Groegan had become the commander's lieutenant. Groegan was likely there for surveillance. Unsure how the leaders at Farlorde would react to him training Barbarians in Harmonic Sight, Marcantos said, "I am instructing them on how to access greater power."

"Greater power?" Groegan studied the muster on Marcantos's hill.

The Barbarian's reaction was not what he'd hoped for. The challenge was how to defuse Groegan's interest without lying. "Orianna and I discovered that ... by expanding Anarchic Sight, there are ways to access greater elemental forces."

Groegan's face darkened. "Like your demonstration the other night with Engert? Is that how Orianna was able to stand toe to toe against him?"

Marcantos folded his arms over his chest. "Have you come to disrupt my instruction, or is there something more urgent on your mind?"

One side of Groegan's mouth twitched. "Barcleave has requested your attention to his tent."

"He received an answer from the Barbarians Council, then?"

Groegan shrugged. "It would seem so. A messenger arrived from the east just past dawn."

Marcantos glanced toward the large tent in the center of the great camp. Could this have been the meaning of the voice's words? *These are the signs that the time is nigh. Prepare yourself!* He fiddled with the hilt of his sword.

"All of us are here on borrowed time, Marcantos. Some never see reclamation coming until it is too late, and even more do not want to see it. You have been given a very special gift."

"Interesting way to look at death." Marcantos spied Copious meandering out of a patch of woods to the west. "Tell Barcleave I will come shortly." He waited until Groegan departed, then went into his tent. He removed the clothes he had stolen from a farmer's clothesline the day he and Lacerus had fled Graystone. Then, in ceremonial style, he shaved and dressed in the Warrior clothing he had kept neatly folded behind his cot and strapped his scabbard to his waist. Returning outside, he called his black bear bond to him, and the two started the long walk to the canvas sea.

"Come in, Marcantos."

Marcantos stepped through the tent flaps with Copious at his side. He surveyed the space with the eye of an experienced commander. The tent was similar to many command centers he had tenanted during his many campaigns. A number of small strips of paper were tacked to a large board hung to his left—reports organized by topic and area from the garrison that was scouting near the Borderlands. Before the board, a colorful map of the known lands stretched across a wood table. Ancient books anchored the map. To his right was the commander's sparse living space—a disheveled cot, two simple chairs, a dining table with the morning's remains, and several stacked wooden lockers to hold the commander's possessions.

Barcleave sat behind a large desk at the center of the tent, his fingers entwined across his chest, closely observing Marcantos. He wore a friendly smile—too friendly for Marcantos's liking. "I forgot you have never been in my tent before ... nor anywhere in the central ring of Farlorde for that matter."

Marcantos continued committing everything to memory out of habit, then shrugged. "No one has ever invited me before today."

The commander guffawed. "No." He drew the word out as if he held some misgiving. "Though of late, the idea has crossed my mind." He leaned forward and waved Marcantos closer for better inspection.

Marcantos stepped to the desk. "I at least expected a summons after I dispatched your lieutenant."

Barcleave waved his hand dismissively. "I never liked Engert or his command style, though he did keep the rowdier apprentices in line. Anarchists have faith that the Cosmos has a way of righting itself without letting our egos get in the way. We do not believe in directing the course of history down a path the Cosmos has not intended. Engert was more interested in building his own fiefdom. He let his vanity get the better of him that night when Orianna faced him. In so doing, he forgot a key tenet. Anarchists thrive on change, not stability. It was clear his time on Gaia had run its course."

Marcantos grunted. "Not even the oracles of the Mystics Order would say they know the path the Cosmos intends for us."

Barcleave laughed. "While I would thoroughly enjoy an intellectual conversation on the merits of Harmonic living, I would prefer our conversation go in a different direction."

"You want to know why I am training your Barbarians?" Marcantos guessed.

"Bah." Barcleave waved again. "You training Barbarians does not concern me. I am glad that you have found purpose once more." His eyes slipped over Marcantos's Harmonic military dress, commanding stance, and clean-shaven face. "It suits you better than being a miserable lout. Besides, if you can drill skills of easy dispatch into their thick skulls, then we all stand to gain, would you not agree?"

"It would be wrong to argue," Marcantos said.

"However, I hope that you appreciate that your presence here has added a layer of complexity to camp life."

Marcantos liked the idea he was giving the commander some discomfort. "Your situation is unique to say the least." He moved to the map table, curiosity getting the better of him. In the realms, those in the Cartographers Guild, overseen by the Sorcerers Order, were trained to meticulously reproduce the maps used during the signing of the armistice five hundred years ago. But at the end of the Anarchic War, all guilds in the four realms that fell to Anarchic control had disbanded. Like others in the realms, he had always wondered about the maps Anarchists used to carry out their incursions into the realms. He stooped over the table to examine the map's artwork. To his surprise, it was incredibly detailed and well scripted. He studied the stamps along the lower fringe. Then something peculiar drew his eye. He bent lower and squinted. In the middle of the open plains southeast of the Dragon's Back Mountains was a mark labeled *Alanon's Refuge.* Its location, given other landmarks to the north and south, coincided with Striker's Keep. Having been stationed at the keep for several years early in his career, Marcantos knew that region very well. He ran his finger along the thin ribbon of the Borderlands that marked the eastern section of Griffinrock. *Wait a minute,* Marcantos thought. *That is not right.*

The commander drew his attention back. "I called you here because I received word from our council regarding your situation."

Marcantos stiffened. Straightening his back, he centered his shoulders on the commander. Copious, who had been rolling on his back near the tent entrance, sat next to him and snorted. How would this unfold? Would the commander draw his sword and run him through? Would he be dragged outside so one of his lieutenants could remove his head with a Barbarian blade before the entire camp? Whatever the commander had planned, Marcantos would not make it easy. And maybe he would take a few more Barbarians with him. "So?"

Barcleave rifled through a drawer in his desk and extracted a parchment. "It seems the Assassin Lacerus spoke true. Councilwoman Lacklander confirmed that you are to be given all rights and privileges of our order." He noted Marcantos's expression. "It seems I am not the only one surprised by the news."

But Marcantos did not hear the commander. His attention had shifted inward. *Why would an Anarchic council sanction my entry into their order?* Orianna's voice echoed in his head again. *These are the signs that the time is nigh. Prepare yourself!* "Signs. Yes, signs," he whispered to himself.

"What?" Barcleave snapped.

Marcantos took a deep breath. "Am I to remain here in Farlorde? Will I have to move my tent? Must I ... lay my stake near another's tent to show my allegiance?"

Barcleave scowled at Marcantos. "You are not a prisoner. But you have a following now, and that means you have responsibilities, and must show your lineage of respect. Only those on the Barbarians Council are free of fidelity to another."

"And if I choose not to select a superior?"

"Then I shall force you to leave."

"I can go?" It was not something Marcantos had even considered possible.

The commander grunted. "Once you swear an oath to renounce your home, never to return there, you will be an orphan, like all Anarchic ordermen. Then, you will be accepted and bequeathed all the freedoms that come with this privilege."

"I have no home," Marcantos grumbled.

"Then your oath shall be quick. We will have the ceremony this afternoon," Barcleave declared with finality. He held out the parchment.

Marcantos took the papers. "I shall return to my tent and prepare myself."

Barcleave's eyes ran up and down Marcantos. "That would be wise," he said, then gave him a quick flick of his fingers.

As Marcantos strode up his hill, Copious grumbling at his side, he pondered the changes in his life since he'd fled Graystone—arriving at Farlorde and learning firsthand about the Barbarian lifestyle; befriending Orianna, who changed everything he thought he knew about Anarchists; helplessly watching her die; being forced to fight Engert; learning how to become Aware; discovering the secret of the map on the commander's table; and then being given a new lease on life. *These are the signs that the time is nigh. Prepare yourself!* the voice whispered again. Marcantos bolted to a tense stop. Now he recalled where he had heard those words before. Yes! Signs! Signs leading him to his true destiny! He picked up his pace, then drew up before the assembly of Barbarians on his hill. "This afternoon, I will renounce my allegiance to the Harmonic Realms."

The small crowd of Barbarians looked relieved with his decision.

"And with morrow's first light, I am leaving for the Borderlands to the west."

Their smiles turned to confusion.

"These are the signs that the time is nigh. The dawn of a new age is upon us. And I have been called to help usher in that era. If you wish to be a distinguished part of something truly magnificent, if you want to learn how to become Aware, as Orianna taught me, then I offer you this one chance to glory. Come with me, and I promise you will not regret it."

The Barbarians drew their swords. And stepping before Marcantos's tent, they ceremoniously drove the points of their blades into the dirt, marking their allegiance to him. When they were done, he nodded. "Good. Be prepared at daybreak." He stepped into his tent and began removing his Warrior armor for the last time, the uniform he had worn on his hasty departure from Graystone. Then, he donned the Barbarian clothing given to him on his first day at Farlorde.

For the first time since the morning he'd stepped onto Graystone's Field of Contest to fight for the honor of becoming Veressa's Champion, resolve roared within him. *These are the signs that the time is nigh. Prepare yourself!* Orianna's voice repeated in reverence and joy at his new appearance. The words, he now knew, came from the preamble to the Omen of the Dragonbonded.

Escape

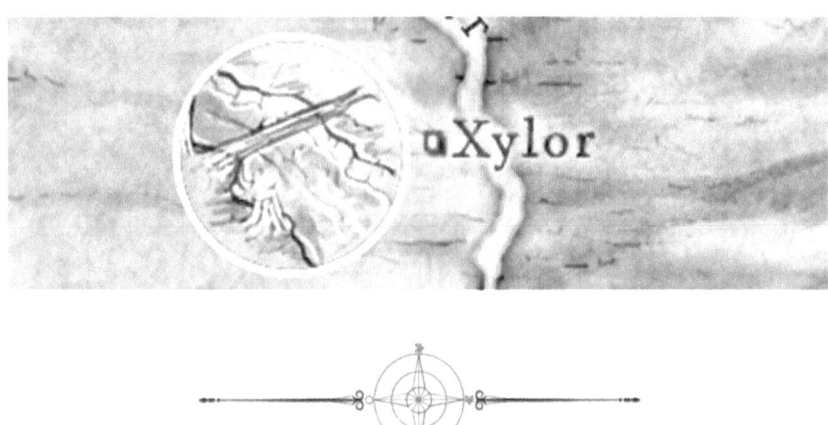

Just after Hemera set, Morgas found Conner where he had been the evening before—alone, on the high platform above Xylor. The day had gone as the previous four—having yielded nothing substantive. Their time at Xylor had run out.

Conner could not look his guide in the eye. "I am sorry, Morgas. More than failing my mission, I dragged you into this and put your life in peril."

"I am disappointed as well, young Dragonbonded. It has been my honor to guide you, to watch your eyes open to the ways of the Anarchists. I am confident that what you have seen, and what you have felt, will guide you in what is yet to come."

"I'm not sure I want to go back." Conner held his guide's fierce gaze. "The savant Elda said that after my bonding, the village would accept me back, to be a part of the village."

"It is common among some tribes to adopt outsiders they think will fit in. It speaks well of you."

"And Azarah said he would teach me to be a healer. Morgas, that is all I ever wanted to be. Well, an Apothecary."

Morgas rocked back. "It pleases me that you are finding the Anarchic ways valuable. But if you wish to honor the Anarchic way of life, you must not ignore your duties. You have oaths to keep."

Conner considered the path Morgas was suggesting for him. Regardless of any affinity he might feel for these people, he would keep his oaths and return to Graystone. Conner rubbed his palms over his face.

"Do not forget that we are interlopers in their world." Morgas leaned closer so that Conner heard his whisper. "Do you think they would want you here once they knew where you are from? Or why you have come to their village? And what will you do when the dragon returns for you? And he will. He must. You cannot keep your dragon a secret."

"Okay. Okay, Morgas." Conner slapped his palms against his thighs. "Sometimes, it's nice to dream, even if briefly." But his guts twisted into a knot. He had been telling lies for so long that it had become second nature, even when he was lying to himself.

"There is nothing wrong with a dream, as long as you do not try to live in it."

Still, Conner did not feel ready for what he had to do. As custom dictated, they would say their goodbyes tonight so that they could slip away before Hemera's light. Conner rose and led Morgas back to the trap door, and along the winding path to Azarah and Elda's home.

When Conner and Morgas arrived, they found the couple in the main room with Wren. But before Conner could say anything, a young woman appeared at their door. Waving Elda and Azarah near, the woman whispered something, then vanished into the dark of night.

Elda placed her hand on Azarah's chest. "I will try to delay them." Glancing at Conner, she added, "Be quick, husband." She hugged Wren, swept Moggie into her arms, and departed.

"What is it?" Conner asked.

Azarah's face paled. "I fear angering you, young man, but we have run out of time, and I must ask. Are you truly Gorgonian?"

Morgas stepped forward, but Conner held him back. "No."

Azarah exhaled, closing his eyes as Jitters pranced about nervously on the windowsill. Opening his eyes again, he chuckled. "You had me fooled."

Morgas's eyes widened in surprise. "How did you know? And why are you not angry?"

"All good questions. And I wish there were time for me to answer. But I will leave it at this. I was the one who sent the message to Grimmley Rollingsworth."

"You?" Conner asked. Then, it all made sense. Why had he not seen it before? Azarah had more than healing skills. He had been trained as a Shaman! "You are Shaman Fenagal!"

"Grandfather?" Wren stepped forward. "What is this about? What message?"

"Wren, do you recall when I said you would need to make a decision someday, and that you needed to be ready?"

Wren's eyes went wide, and she flung her arms around Azarah. "No," she cried. "I will not go."

"Go? Go where?" Conner asked, more confused than ever.

Azarah held Wren tight, tears on his cheeks. "Conner, Wren is the one you have come in search of."

"Wren? But ..." Conner started to say she was too young. But that had been his assumption—and apparently a bad one. All this time they'd spent searching the village, with Wren right there, assisting him. He chuckled at the irony.

"Now, no more questions from any of you. Three Assassins have come looking for Wren. Elda and I will give you time to escape."

Morgas growled. "I would bet Lacerus leads them." He reached for his sword.

Conner needed time to think through what to do next. Images of the nightmare he'd had on his way to find Grimmley came at him—of Lacerus riding a black warhorse toward him. Everything was happening too quickly. He reached up and steadied Morgas's hand. "No, Morgas. I made an oath with Elda we would not draw our swords. *I* will face them." Maybe it was time he tested his newfound skills, to see if he could repeat what he had done on the tourney field. Then another thought came to him. Lacerus had witnessed Conner's decisive victory over Marcantos on the Field of Contest. Maybe Conner just needed Lacerus to *believe* Conner could best him as well.

Azarah stepped between Conner and the door. "Do not be foolish and squander this brief opportunity my wife has offered you. You need to be thinking of my granddaughter, not how to get into a spat with three trained killers." Azarah's mannerisms, his forcefulness, even his bedside style, reminded Conner so much of Grimmley, he wondered why he had not seen it before. Azarah pulled Wren away. "You remember what I said?"

Wren jiggled her head and sniffed.

Azarah looked to Conner. "You must give your oath that you will look after her."

"You have my oath, Azarah."

The healer squared his shoulders at Wren. "Then just like you practiced. Take Conner and Morgas. You can trust them. Do as they say. Conner will explain everything once you are away."

Wren flicked a glance at Conner, her lips pressed tight. She snatched his arm and yanked him toward the door.

"Conner," Azarah called out. "When you see Grimmley ..." He hesitated. "Tell him that I am sorry. Tell him that sometimes love is more powerful than any Harmonic loyalty."

Conner placed his hand on Azarah's arm. "I will let him know."

Conner and Morgas hurried to keep up with Wren as she wound along a tangle of causeways, darting up and down ladders. Erebus's half face, low in the west, offered Conner enough light to keep his footing secure. As they ran, he wondered how they would slip past the Assassins at the entrance below. From what he knew of the dark Rangers, nothing slipped past their notice. Before he could form a plan, Wren stopped hard in her tracks. The boardwalk ahead ended abruptly. She looked back, her face glistening with tears.

They had crossed into a section of the village unfamiliar to Conner.

Wren pointed at a rope bridge ahead, its far end disappearing into the murky forest. "From here, we cross over to the next tree. We will drop to the ground from there."

"That will not be enough to secure our escape," Morgas interjected. "Assassins are trained to hear any sound, to anticipate any trickery. They will be expecting you to run."

"I think I can help with that." Conner stepped closer.

"Something else your Sorceress preceptor taught you?"

Conner licked his lips nervously. "It worked for us before." Concentrating, he drew on the elementals Assassins could not detect—Fire and Water—and wove a new pattern around their bodies. "That should muffle any noise we make."

Wren gawked at herself. "I can see what you did," she said, but her voice was muted and deep. She giggled at the sound, then covered her mouth. Turning, she sprinted across the bridge.

Conner was right behind her. He worked to keep his footing as the bridge bucked and swayed to the pounding of their feet.

They slid down a rope to the forest floor and headed east toward the gorge. Valmer appeared out of the darkness, sprinting beside Morgas. Within a few minutes, they reached the root stairs leading to the log bridge Wren and Conner had taken the night before. At the top of the stairs, instead of crossing over, Wren ducked down the other side of the landing.

Morgas pulled to a stop. Reaching forward, he gripped Conner's sword strap, pulling him up short.

Conner faced him.

"This is where we part ways, young Dragonbonded," Morgas whispered. Conner opened his mouth, but Morgas threw up his hand. His eyes flicked down the long bridge across the gorge. "I sense Lacerus is not far behind. I, too, will do what I can to slow them." Away from the village, Conner was free from his oath. Morgas reached back and drew his sword. "Do not forget what you have learned this week."

There were many things Conner wanted to say, but he had no time. "I will never forget, ever."

Morgas and Valmer dashed across the bridge and vanished from sight.

At the far end of the tree bridge, Morgas spun, gripping his sword in both hands, just as the three Assassins materialized out of darkness. He roared. With Valmer at his side, man and wolf charged.

The lead Assassin raised a hand and whispered, *"Aerora ousia pagomaprosopo."* Morgas and Valmer froze midstride.

The black-cloaked man stepped forward and flipped back his hood, his eyes glowing from his Night Vision spell. "Well, look who we have snared." He raised two fingers and flicked them forward. The other two Assassins dashed past like shadows.

Morgas grunted from the pressure holding his body. He fought to inhale, to speak. "You ... cannot ... have them, Lacerus," he rasped.

The Assassin chuckled. "A big man making empty threats." His smile dropped. "It's a pity that the enchantress and horde of soldiers I sent to your village failed to rid me of your traitorous ways."

Morgas spat blood from the pressure increasing on his body. "My blade skewered her to a tree outside my village."

Lacerus's two assistants returned. "There are two sets of tracks ahead. The girl's and a young man's. But they are nearly a day old."

Lacerus snarled. "It is time our relationship came to an end, old friend. You have troubled me for the last time." He raised his hand, hooked fingers spread. Slowly, he drew his fingertips together.

Morgas' throat constricted. Blood hammered in his forehead and ears. He fought against the strangling pressure. Valmer whined and yelped, the bond's distress adding to Morgas's own. Rage pounded in his heart and he howled. Muscles shaking, lungs burning, he raised the tip of his quivering blade toward Lacerus's chest.

Lacerus drew closer, until Morgas's sword pressed against his sternum. His callous face inches away, Lacerus licked his dry lips in anticipation of the inevitable, as Morgas battled for his life. "I have not seen such determination in you before, Morgas. Certainly more tenacity than I ever beat into you. What invocation has this young dragon-bonded Anarchist put on you?"

Morgas fought against the might of the Assassin's incantation. His sweaty body convulsed, breath coming in hammered gasps. A stream of blood oozed from his nostrils, wetting his lips.

The Assassin's breath caught, eyes widening. "Or maybe it is not an invocation." He glanced at his two comrades. "You said two sets of tracks?"

The Assassins nodded.

Lacerus released his incantation. Morgas tumbled to the ground, quivering and spent. Valmer fell forward and lay prone beside him. "This man was nothing more than a distraction." He signaled to one of them. "Go back to the other end of the bridge and find which way the girl scampered off. Quick now!" Lacerus's glowing eyes shifted to Morgas. "Well, Morgas. If I were to pull on your chain, who might I find on the other side? Who told you to come here? Or ... better yet, who did you bring with you?" Lacerus chuckled. "Tell me you did not bring the boy here, the one I sent you to retrieve?" Lacerus caught the flash of anger in the big man's eyes. "This is so precious!"

Morgas pulled himself up to his knees and sat back on his heels. "As I said, you cannot have them."

Lacerus squatted before him. "Oh, but I will have them. I will have them both. It seems I've found a purpose for you after all, old friend." He rose. "Bind him," he barked to the remaining Assassin, then darted back across the bridge.

Wren led Conner along a steep and rocky path to a narrow ledge below the top of the gorge. The waters roared far below, but as with the previous night, he could not see to the bottom. They had hardly gone two hundred paces along the ledge when Wren called back, "The cave is just ahead."

"Just a minute." Conner twisted around, his heels pressed tight against the gorge's wall, and summoned the four elementals. He was taking a chance the Assassins would not detect his casting, but he was ready to try something bold. Recalling the elemental shield surrounding Dragongarde, he wove the elementals together. The barrier he constructed felt amateurish in comparison, but he hoped the shield would hold long enough for them to get away.

Twenty paces on, he stepped into a small cavern pulsating with a deep blue light. *Dragonfire*, Conner thought. A huge dark form in the back of the cavity drew his eye. And while the black creature was clearly a drake, it was quite different from Skye. This dragon was thinner, with a more sculpted body and harder angles along his head and shoulders. And it sported more horns and thorns along its back. But the most telling difference was that this dragon's eyes shone an earthy brown.

The dragon lowered its chest to the floor, wings spread wide. "I am Valkere-Troya-Recko of the family Mountainshaker."

It had taken time, but Conner now understood that such dragon behavior was about more than manners. It was about respect. He would not make the same mistake he made when Skye introduced himself. Besides, dragons had no fear, so Wren's bond would not understand the urgency of their situation. Bowing, he responded, "And I am Conner of the family Stonefield. May your days and deeds add honorable verses to your family's dragonsong, Valkere-Troya-Recko of the family Mountainshaker."

"Wren!" the dragon boomed. "I like this human! Can we keep him?"

"You can speak to my dragon?" Wren's mouth was agape.

"I guess that is the first of several secrets I have kept from you. I am also bonded with a dragon."

"Another human bond!" Valkere bawled, making the cavern tremble. Small rocks cascaded from the walls nearby. "I like this Stonefield even more!"

"Conner," a deep voice called softly from outside the cavern. "Are you there?"

Valkere's glowing brown eyes widened. "Oooh! Another human!"

Conner stepped out onto the ledge. Wren pressed against his back, peeking over his shoulder, clutching tight to his jacket.

Lacerus loomed just past Conner's woven barrier, eyes glowing with Night Vision. His black cloak rustled in the wind rushing up from the depths of the ravine. "Ah! There you are! I thought you would be snuggling up with that new queen of yours by now."

Conner sneered. Drawing himself up, shoulders taut, he started to step forward.

Wren's firm grip held him back. "Conner, your oath," she whispered, her voice quivering.

The Assassin raked fingernails across the barrier, sparks trailing. "Very impressive. Your skills have improved since that day you bested my pupil."

"Do not underestimate me, Lacerus. I am taking Wren and her dragon bond with me," Conner declared, fists at his side.

"To where, boy?" Lacerus shouted. "To Graystone? By now you know that is useless. The two of you should come with me. Besides, I have your guide," he called out. "Yes, boy. I have Morgas with me. I think I will keep him safe until you come to get him."

Conner opened his mouth to reply, but he faltered.

A dark blur of motion against the bright stars made him jump. Wren screamed, her grip ripped free from Conner's jacket as she was yanked backward.

An Assassin stood behind her, an arm wrapped tight around her waist. He must have climbed down from above. The thin tip of his blade was pressed against Wren's chest, just above her heart.

"What is this?" Valkere bellowed. The dragon started forward, but the Assassin pressed the tip in. Wren cried out, and Valkere froze. A thin red stain spread across her tan shirt.

Conner raised his hands, palms out. "I suggest you put that knife away, sir Assassin. Dragons get jumpy when someone threatens their bond."

The Assassin dipped his head toward Lacerus, and raised the sharp edge of his blade to Wren's throat. Wren gasped and stiffened. "I will put the knife away when you dismantle the shield."

"Valkere." Conner said, suspecting the Assassin did not understand Dragon. "Did you know that you cannot kill your bond?"

"What a silly question." Valkere's brown eyes blazed bright. "All dragons know—" There was a long pause. When the dragon's strike came, it was sudden and swift. Valkere spun, whipping his spiny tail at the Assassin. Wren leaped away from the knife and rolled. Valkere's tail whistled past, striking the Assassin in the chest. The man sailed out over the gorge, vanishing into the darkness beyond.

"I suggest we leave before more Assassins drop from the skies," Conner said as he guided Wren toward the dragon.

"Where are we going?" she asked as she climbed on Valkere's back. "Not to Graystone," she added with round eyes.

"No. To Dragongarde," Conner answered.

"Dragongarde?" Valkere quaked with excitement. "Many Mountainshaker dragonsongs refer to that great fortress."

"Valkere, can you handle our combined weight?" Conner asked.

The dragon snorted. "I am very strong. Besides, I am ready to leave this place. Show me Dragongarde!" he bellowed.

Conner clambered onto the dragon's withers behind Wren.

Wren pressed her back to Conner's chest. Gripping his wrists, she pulled his arms around her waist. "Hold on tight," she said as Valkere trotted to the cavern entrance.

Conner closed his eyes and relayed the emotional signal he had worked out with Skye. "We have one place to stop on the way. We will meet my dragon there."

"Is he a Mountainshaker as well?" the dragon asked.

"I'm afraid not, Valkere. He is a Cloudbender."

"Oh." Valkere's wings deflated as he trudged to the entrance. "Then let us get on with it."

As Valkere stepped to the ledge, Conner glanced to his left. Lacerus was still there behind his elemental shield.

"You cannot escape, boy," Lacerus called out calmly. "We will find you."

Conner started to say something when Wren let out a jubilant whoop, flinging her arms in the air. Valkere leaped from the ledge.

Despite the heart-stopping bound and gut-wrenching dip, Conner kept his eyes on Lacerus on the ledge, his black cloak flapping in the wind.

Part III

In the maddening rush of the day, pummeled with hectic plans and mundane pressures, remember to carve out moments for yourself, to pause, and to dip your spirit into the fullness of what is. Rejoice in quiet contemplation that everything is right. Let your spirit be lifted, knowing you are where you need to be, that this moment was designed to further your awakening. Be in that moment, and in the silence of its gift, breathe.

—The Modei Book of Water (Third Book)

Dragongarde

$\mathbf{V}$alkere strained as he climbed higher into the sky, the Dragon's Back Mountains looming ahead of them, their snowy tips reddish in the glow of Hemera's early morning light. Not long after entering the mountains, Conner spotted the east-west trail he and Morgas had taken out of Elmsdorf. Wren directed Valkere along its winding path. Not that Conner needed the path to get them to the village. Skye was there waiting, a mental beacon guiding him. Conner felt a sudden rush of excitement. Still, he had to wait another hour before the three crested the mountain east of the village.

Conner jabbed a finger over Wren's shoulder. "There!" he shouted into the wind. With a few hand gestures from Wren, Valkere tilted left and glided toward the large oval terrace along the mountain's southern face.

The dragon settled on the plateau twenty paces from Skye, curled up and sunning himself near the stone monolith. Valkere had hardly folded his wings to his sides when Wren flipped her leg over the dragon's neck and slid down his scaly front leg, landing on the rocky surface with a resounding crunch.

"Skye!" Conner shouted as he clambered down.

Instead of acknowledging Conner, Skye sidestepped around Valkere, giving the other dragon a sidelong look through blazing blue eyes.

"Skye?" Conner called out.

Valkere took a similar motion around Skye, and the two slowly circled each other. Occasionally, they would growl, swish their tails, and scrape their claws across the rocky surface.

Conner took Wren by the arm and pulled her out of the way.

"What a puny dragon," Skye grumbled, then snorted. "I am surprised you can fly with such petite wings."

Valkere grunted. "Your claws look dull, Cloudbender. I had no clue your family was so lazy. You should spend less time sleeping and more time sharpening those talons."

Skye's nostrils puffed steam. "Your muted scales are truly uninspiring, Mountainshaker. I have seen amphitheres with more attractive hides than yours."

Valkere snapped his jaw. "Tell me, Cloudbender. Were you the runt of your litter?"

"Any idea what this is about?" Conner asked Wren.

Wren smiled up at him. "I don't know, but they are so cute!"

"Cute?" Conner was surprised that Wren seemed thoroughly entertained by their bonds' menacing behavior. "Ducklings and kittens are cute. That's not the word I would use to describe those two."

"Conner, you bonehead. Let them be who they are." Wren walked away.

Conner started. He was acting like a Harmonic parent, wanting to step in and supervise the two. Of course Wren would have a completely different perspective. Through his bond's emotional link, he knew Skye held no real animosity toward Valkere. He relaxed. "How long do you think this will go on?" he asked, following Wren toward the caverns where villagers were beginning to gather.

Wren shrugged. "As long as it takes, I guess."

Conner was about to suggest it might take hours when motion to his right drew his eye. A tall woman with braided golden hair drew close, her timber wolf at her side. Conner pressed his arm across his chest. "Pallia." He nodded toward Wren. "This is Wren of the Dristonian village Xylor."

"Conner. Wren." Pallia looked past the two dragons still circling each other and spouting steam. She pressed her palms to her bulging belly, her fingers wide. "Where is Morgas?"

Conner had spent the hours on their long flight from Xylor working on the right words to break the news to Pallia, but there was nothing *right* about any of it. Besides, Alpslanders preferred the direct approach. He looked down. "He was taken prisoner."

Pallia's eyes darted to the east, searching the brightening sky. Tears pooled as she chewed on her lip.

"I am truly sorry. Last night, three Assassins arrived at the village looking for Wren. Morgas was captured helping Wren and me escape. We would all have been caught if not for his heroism." He hesitated, hating having to say the next words. "Lacerus was one of the three."

Pallia gasped and stiffened.

Conner rushed to reassure her. "But he wasn't after Morgas. He was after us—Wren and me. He still is. He's using Morgas as bait. Lacerus won't kill him."

"Lacerus is an unhinged sadist capable of things far worse than death."

Conner had not thought of that. "It's my fault. Maybe I should have confronted him." He straightened his shoulders before her. "I will bring Morgas back to you ... alive. He will be here for his daughter's birth. That is my oath to you."

Pallia turned her fiery gaze on him, her cheeks blooming red. "Conner, do not say such words. Such words carry weight—"

"I know the weight, Pallia. I say it, and I mean it." Conner stepped in front of her. "I give you my oath—I will return Morgas to you. I cannot say when. But the first chance I have, I will get him back. This is my bloodbond to you."

"I also make this oath," Wren declared, stepping forward.

"Wren—" Conner started.

Wren waved her arm at him. "No, Conner. Morgas gave up his freedom to ensure ours. This is also my choice to make. We must return that freedom to him. I will help."

Pallia's shoulders dropped with relief. "Thank you both."

"Thank you for allowing Morgas to take the bloodbond with me."

"You do not know Morgas like I do. He believes in our Alpslander tales, and that one day, we will have an opportunity to correct our deeds of the past. Besides, when he sets his mind on something, it is easier to hold an avalanche back than to change his mind."

Conner chuckled. "Truer words were never spoken by an Alpslander." He looked back at the two dragons spiraling each other, then rolled his eyes. "Pallia, I am sorry, but we must go. I will gather my gear, and we must say our goodbyes."

After a brief bow, Conner strode to the alcove where he had slept.

Wren trailed after him. "How did you know Valkere would not hurt me back in the cave?"

Conner recalled the morning after Skye had plucked him from the clutches of Pallia and the two Narkain brothers. He had spent hours debating whether Skye was truly a dragon. "Skye showed me shortly after we bonded. He tried to attack me just to prove that he couldn't. Until then, I wasn't sure he really was my bond."

"It sounds like your bonding experience did not go so well."

Conner cleared his throat. "Our relationship was ... problematic for a while."

"Really? Valkere and I hit it off from the moment I touched his snout."

Conner flipped back the animal pelt drapes and stepped inside the small dark room. Wren followed him into the chamber, so he took her by the shoulders, spun her around, and guided her back through the drapes. "Wait *outside*."

Wren chuckled at his modesty.

Conner changed back into the clothes he had worn from Graystone, then slipped on the Champion's amulet. He bent over to grab the saddle but stopped. The amulet swung from his neck, its polished gold and finely cut ruby sparkling in the dim light. He had not yet told Wren of his sworn duty to protect a Harmonic queen. He was not sure how she would handle that. He stuffed the amulet beneath his shirt. *That can wait,* he thought. He swung the saddle over his shoulder.

Conner found Wren just outside the chamber, her back pressed against the rock, arms folded.

"What is that?" Wren asked, pointing at the black saddle.

"It's a saddle."

Wren stared back at him.

"For me to ride Skye," he added.

Wren giggled. "Why do you need such a thing? Did you not just say that your bond cannot kill you?"

Conner stuttered to a stop. That was something he had not thought of. "I'd rather not take too much for granted." His cheeks reddened when Wren snickered again, shaking her head slowly. "Come on, then. We have a lot to do before dusk."

Back at the monolith, they found their dragons resting next to each other. Still, they were refusing to look at each other.

"Our dragonsongs tell that dragons of the four families made the great fortress Dragongarde." Valkere's deep voice boomed as Conner strapped the saddle to Skye. "Is that true?"

Conner climbed into the saddle, noting that Wren had already mounted. "That is what I was told as well."

"Then let us go see Dragongarde!" Valkere bellowed, and leaped into the air.

Wren threw her arms up high and let out a whoop that echoed off the mountain.

Skye craned his head and stared at Conner. "Really?"

Conner patted Skye's withers. "I know. But we'll get through this."

Conner directed Wren and Valkere to the plateau west of Dragongarde where Layna had taken him the first time he was there. "We'll need to enter Dragongarde the first time on foot," he stated as the dragons landed, pointing up the steep stairs to the east. "There is a shield surrounding the fortress. You will need to dismantle it before you can enter. Skye and Valkere can use the main entrance along the northern face." Noting an odd expression on her face, he asked, "What is it?"

"Trees," she said, her lips pushed out as she looked around. "There are no trees."

Conner might have argued that the few scraggly saplings fighting for survival along the rocky cliff were trees, but that would have been a waste of time with Wren. He waved for her to follow. Skye and Valkere had vanished from view by the time they were climbing the old, broken stairs leading to the fortress's entrance. Inside the small antechamber, Conner stepped past the clutter of rotted furniture. It was his first time here since the day Meera had shackled him to the back wall. With nothing but bad memories in the place, he proceeded up the long hall that would take them into the fortress. About halfway, he came to a halt where he had encountered the elemental shield.

"I see a field of energy," Wren said before he could warn her. She inched forward with her hands extended. "It looks just like the one you made along the ledge near Valkere's cavern. The one that held the Assassin back."

"The first time I came upon the shield, I struggled for a bit before I figured out how to dismantle it. You will need to—"

"Got it!" Wren declared, then stepped through the shield.

"How ...?"

Wren winked. "Grandfather instructed me on Anarchic Sight."

"Okay. But how did you know how to break through?"

Wren shrugged. Leading the way, she picked up the pace down the long hallway. "I am not sure. It just *felt* like the right thing to do. How did you get in?"

Conner followed on her heels. "Skye guided me through how to dissolve the threads. I fought with it for a bit because I was just starting to use elementals. I just assumed you would have similar struggles."

"When did you first notice you could use elementals?"

Conner scratched at his stubble. "Not sure exactly. Sometime right before arriving here with my preceptor."

"From what you said, it was right after you accepted Skye as your bond."

Conner stuttered to a stop. That was it. His ability to access elementals was tethered to when he'd stopped fighting Skye and accepted his bond. Grimmley had alluded to that possibility when he first started giving Conner lessons. But Wren's simple observation cleared away the fog.

Within a few minutes, they arrived in the main chamber. Conner found Skye curled up in a dark corner, snoring contentedly. But Valkere bounded about the hall, too excited to rest.

"Wren!" Valkere shouted, causing Skye to snort and twitch. "Look at the size of this chamber! And look at these. He pointed with his snout at one of the many tapestries hanging from the stone walls. It showed a young girl clutched in the claws of her flying dragon bond, dangling beneath while shooting a bow at a target. "We should try that!"

Conner tried to imagine himself in such a precarious posture under Skye, then shook the horrific idea from his mind. "Come on, Wren. Let me show you the rest of Dragongarde before it gets dark."

With Wren and Valkere in tow, Conner started with the armory, with its long rows of Dragonbonded armor and black leather saddles. Conner handed Wren a suit. "The first time I held one of these, I knew the myth of the old Dragonbonded was a reality."

Wren did not look impressed.

"I have heard Anarchists do not have fond stories of the Dragonbonded," Conner probed. He needed to know her thoughts before asking her to return with him to Graystone.

Wren returned the suit to the rack. "Xylor has few tales that mention the Dragonbonded. Those that do describe them as wicked people, even more wicked than the Harmonic orders."

That's troubling, Conner thought. "But you have accepted the idea that you might become one of them?"

Wren drew back from Conner as if he had slapped her. "Just because I bonded with a dragon does not mean I have to become a Dragonbonded."

"No," he said. "I suppose not."

Before he could say more, Valkere called out from an adjacent room. "Wren! Come look at this!"

Valkere had located a chamber filled with sets of massive metal plates the size of shields stitched together with leather straps and buckles. Each set, ten paces long or more, had been meticulously assembled for easy access.

"Full body armor for dragons," Conner declared as he ran his fingers lightly over the engraved designs on one of the shiny plates. He sensed the metal's resistance to elemental forces. The straps were adjustable to fit various sizes of drakes, even wyverns. The mail had clearly been crafted by a true master of metallurgy and tailoring.

Wren walked past, trailing her hand over a set of plates. "They look heavy. Let us hope we never need to use these." With that, she disappeared back through the entryway.

Conner crossed his arms, body taut. Frustration over Wren's reaction was wrestling for dominance with disappointment—and winning. He'd nearly burst with excitement when Grimmley had told him someone else had bonded with a dragon. Now—

"You coming?" Wren called from the hall.

"Yep."

Next, Conner took them to the chamber he called the game room. It was a small cavity at the end of a long hall containing a table and two chairs. Upon the table sat a golden wheel with swirling patterns around an engraved Cosmic Star. Four small polished gems—ruby, diamond, sapphire, and emerald—were set at the tip of each point on the star.

"This is a practice wheel for improving your ability to draw upon the elementals," Conner explained, pointing at the murals of Dragonbonded hung around them. "When you call upon an elemental, the wheel rotates until one of the points on the star is near you. The idea is to learn to switch elementals, getting the wheel to turn, at first slow, but in time, faster. This was how I learned to use my elemental powers."

"That ball of light you formed between your hands ... the night we were at the ancient cottage?" Wren asked, wiggling into the seat and studying the wheel.

"Yes. This wheel helped me learn how to form that ball." Conner watched Wren's eyes grow round. Finally, he had her attention. "Come on," he offered, excitement returning. "One more room to show you." He led the way back up the hall.

"And all this food has been here since the days of the first Dragonbonded?" Wren asked as she poked around the galley, more amazed that the food was still fresh than that they could eat there for years. She picked up an apple and bit into it with a sharp crunch.

"Over five hundred years ago."

"So, what are you fixing for dinner?" Wren asked, her mouth bulging with hunks of apple.

Later that night, the two sat with their legs dangling over the ledge to the main chamber's entrance.

"Not bad," Wren said, chewing on a steaming chunk of potato. "I'm glad one of us knows how to cook."

"Thanks. It's good to be needed for something."

The two sat and watched Hemera slip behind the mountains to the west. Dragon snores echoed across the large room behind.

Conner was thinking about Veressa. He was not sure what was happening, but he sensed the queen's anguish over something. All he knew was that he needed to fly to Graystone in the morning. And he wanted Wren to go with him. The problem was how to broach the topic with her.

"Conner? What is that?" Wren pointed to the north past Lake Arastone. The distant glow of campfires lit up the sparse trees in the Valley of Souls beyond.

Conner squinted to where she pointed. Five, maybe ten fires. "I don't know. I don't recall seeing them the last time I was here. I think that region is part of the Borderlands. There shouldn't be anyone camping there."

"Should we investigate?" Wren asked.

Conner rose, then yawned. It had been a long day, and listening to the dragons snore at the other end of the chamber was making him sleepy. "I'm sure it is nothing we need to be concerned about. Besides, we should let our bonds rest. Let's find you a bedchamber."

Conner woke in the middle of the night. He thought he had heard something in his room, but it was too dark to see anything. Then he heard a sniff.

"Wren?" Conner called from his bedroll. Using the incantation he had observed Grimmley and Layna using to light their pipes, he drew upon Fire and created a small flame nearby.

Wren was standing in the middle of his bedchamber, her arms folded over her chest. She was shaking.

"What is it?" he asked, rubbing sleep from his eyes.

She ran to him and slipped under his blanket. Curling up, she pressed her back to his chest. Her shoulders quivered violently.

Unsure what to do, he wrapped his arms about her.

After a while, she spoke. "I was looking forward to Grandmother giving me a name," she sniffled. "But I had to keep my bonding a secret from the village. She never had a chance to name me. I will spend the rest of my life as a yoot. I will always be Wren."

Not sure what to say or do, Conner held her tight until she finally fell asleep.

As Hemera broke over the mountains to the east, Conner slipped from beneath the covers, still exhausted. Wren had slept fitfully through most of the night. But as he crept away, Wren pulled her knees to her chest and rested peacefully. Several hours passed before she woke. Skye and Valkere had departed for a morning hunt to the south.

Wren staggered into the main chamber and settled on the ledge, eyes red and swollen. Conner set a steaming plate of eggs and sliced apple before her. She looked untroubled by having slept in his bed, which made him feel even more awkward. Banishing the thorny thought from his mind, he said, "There is something I need to tell you." He reached inside his shirt and pulled out the Champion's amulet. It swung on its gold chain, an emblem of official obligation. Holding it close for her to inspect, he went on. "I am Champion to the queen of Griffinrock."

"Champion?" Wren asked, brushing her fingers over the surface of the ruby. "What does that mean?"

"It means I am the queen's personal guardian."

Wren snatched her hand away as if the cool stone had burned her fingers.

"Wren, I need to return to Graystone." She did not respond, so he continued. "I want you to come with me."

"To the center of the Harmonic Realms?" Eyebrows raised and lips pressed tight, Wren shook her head vigorously.

"There is nothing to be afraid of."

Wren pulled her knees up, wrapping her arms around her legs. "Kings living in villages made of rock enslaving their people to toil their lives away for disks of round metal? Children forced to think and act the same? No freedom to do, to think, to feel what you want? I will *never* go there."

"I was raised to believe all Anarchists were wicked. When I agreed to find you and Valkere, I was frightened at the thought of going into the Anarchic Lands. But when I arrived at your village and saw how your people lived, all those false stories were dispelled. I saw their lives as honorable and good. I want to show you that the same is true for Harmonics. No one will harm you. I give you my word."

"Do not go back there, Conner. They beguile and ensnare with false tongues. Stay here with me. We can play in the clouds."

He slipped the Champion's amulet under his shirt. "I must keep my oath to the queen."

Wren shied away.

Conner was considering what angle he could approach this that would yield a better response when, on outstretched wings, Skye and Valkere glided through the entrance to land in the middle of the chamber. The two were arguing about who had been the first to see the elk they'd killed. Out of ideas on how to change her mind, Conner went to strap the saddle on Skye. He was about to stick his foot into the stirrup when he hesitated, looking over his shoulder. "Is there no way I can convince you to come with me?" he asked.

Wren waited nearby, her eyes still round with fear. She rattled her head side to side.

"Conner, are you ready?" Skye asked. "The sooner we leave, the sooner we get back."

Conner patted Skye's shoulder, then hesitated. At last, he climbed into the saddle. "I will return as soon as I can. Until then, maybe you can practice on the wheel."

"Yeah." Wren rolled her eyes. "I'll get right on that."

Skye strode across the main chamber and leaped from the edge.

Mourning News

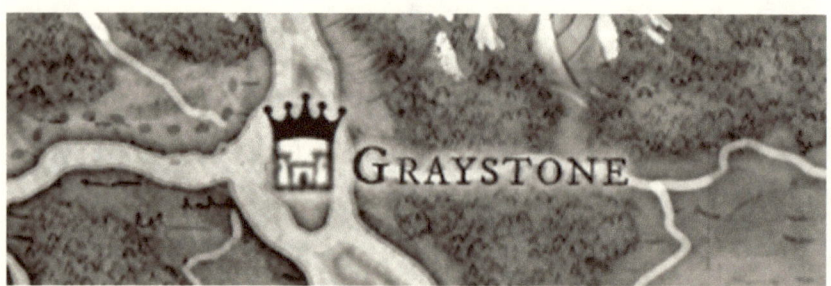

The flight from Dragongarde to Graystone had never felt so long. Conner's growing respect for the people of the Anarchic Lands, combined with his new understanding of elementals, gave him restored hope for the future. He had discovered how honesty cleansed and renewed the spirit. He was eager to share everything with his two preceptors, and with Veressa. He could only hope that when he was open and honest, they would be likewise. He hunched over Skye's withers, enduring the monotonous flight. At last, Skye glided gently through Graystone's underground entrance and settled in the middle of the dungeon's central chamber. Conner was just pulling the saddle from Skye's withers when he heard Kriston's light footfalls coming down the dungeon steps.

"Well, aren't you a dutiful page," Conner jested with a wink and smile as Kriston drew near. But as his page stepped into the dim light, he caught the boy's drawn face. "I thought you would be happy to see me back. Or have you grown to like having the captain of the royal guard's attention?"

Kriston glanced about, seemingly unaffected by Conner's quip. "When I saw you flying in, I sent a message to your Sorceress preceptor of your return. It would be best if you talked to her."

"Okay." Conner paused, still holding the saddle. "I'll find her just as soon as I report to the queen."

"The queen is not in the castle. She left for Charmwell the day after you departed ... to wherever you went. No one knows just when she will return."

"Charmwell? Why would the queen go to Elvenstein?"

Kriston stared at his feet. "Not that anyone tells me, but word is she went to discuss an arrangement of marriage with one of the princes."

Conner nearly dropped the saddle. "Marriage?" He swallowed hard.

With lips pressed tight, Kriston bobbed his head.

"Conner, are you okay?" Skye asked, sensing his bond's shift into despondency.

Conner patted the dragon's jaw, then stowed the leather saddle in the only dry place in the chamber. "I'm fine, Skye. You should rest. We will need to return to Dragongarde soon enough."

Skye yawned, his jaw nearly coming unhinged. He trudged over to the back corner and curled up.

Kriston waited until Skye was settled. "Ballett instructed me to tell you in secret that the queen is expected back tomorrow sometime."

Conner was not sure he was ready for that encounter. What if she carried with her news of an imminent wedding? He shook the thought away, his heart quivering. He had more pressing issues to address and did not need the distraction. He draped his arm over Kriston's shoulder and the two headed to the stairwell. "And Pauli? Has he been causing any trouble?"

"Pauli received the Calling a few days ago. He headed west yesterday morning on his trek."

"Well, I am certain there will be no end to the tall tales once he returns, tales that will no doubt become legendary while he apprentices in the Warriors Order. Now, let's go see if I can draw out of Layna what you seem incapable of saying."

Conner sat in his private chambers drumming his fingers on the table. After long hours of the roaring wind in his ears, exhaustion and the stillness took him, and he nodded off. He had no idea how long he'd slept, but he awoke at a light touch on his arm.

Layna sat in the chair next to him. "You look drained," she said.

Conner arched his back with a long groan and sat up. "The last several days have been very long. Layna, the mission was a success ... mostly. I found the other dragon-bonded. Her name is Wren. She and her Mountainshaker dragon, Valkere, are at Dragongarde."

"That is good news." But her smile did not touch the deep sadness around her eyes.

"Okay, what's going on?" Conner asked. "What's with all the melancholy? I have never known Kriston to hold back, and he was tight-lipped the whole way here. And now, I tell you my mission was a success, and you act like ... well, like I just said Hemera is going to rise in the morning."

"Grimmley is gone, Conner. His spirit has been reclaimed."

Conner sat dazed for a moment. "Reclaimed?" He spoke the word, hoping it would make Layna's news more real. It took him a while to find his voice. "How?"

"Before I left for Darmascus, I told Grimmley we would meet up in ten days at his home. While I was away, he received a visit from a very dear old friend—a grandmaster Paladin named Herid. I returned two days ago and stopped off at Graystone for the night. Late that night, Barthox came to my chamber carrying a note from Grimmley saying he needed me right away. Alas, I did not make it there in time. Early yesterday morning, I found their bodies outside Grimmley's home. If I had returned just a day sooner ..."

The Sorceress took a deep breath and went on. "As required by the Orderman's Code, the Shamans and Paladins Councils conducted a bilateral investigation. Their report concluded that Grimmley and Herid killed each other. Herid lost his bond many years ago and suffered greatly with the Yearning. To the Paladins, he was a deranged heretic—a danger to society. Along with the report, the Paladins Council released an official apology for allowing Herid to escape their care."

Conner was numb, his eyes tracing a long scratch running the edge of the table. Grimmley was gone. Beyond the veil of the Physical plane. "He shouldered so much for me. And look what I did to him." King Jonath's haunting warning came back to him. "It is true. I am a lightning rod to everyone who gets near. I should have seen this. Done something!"

Layna tilted forward to get in his line of sight. "You are *not* responsible for his death. If anything, you gave him life."

Conner looked into her dark gaze, suddenly adrift, hoping to latch on to something she might offer, words to make sense of this insanity. "Life?"

"I knew Grimmley from the time I was a willful and angry fourteen-year-old outlander. He was always a man on a quest. But by the time you arrived at his doorstep, he had long since given up on the world. Maybe too many years battling the Shaman Dons who refused to listen to his sharp wisdom. But that day I arrived at Grimmley's home, the day I met you, he had a spring in his step, a light in his eyes I thought had been snuffed out. Conner, you gave that salty old Shaman a renewed sense of purpose. And though he never said it, I know in my heart that he was grateful the Cosmos saddled him with being your preceptor. For him, there was no greater blessing or honor."

"But he died thinking I killed Meera Asheborne."

Layna sat back and folder her arms. "That is what you wanted to tell him the morning you departed on your mission?"

"Yes," Conner said.

"Regret is a fierce demon to fight. But you should know, Grimmley never believed for a moment you, or your dragon, were capable of such a heinous act. We assumed you let her go. It was a very dangerous decision on your part, but *you* had to be the one to make it."

"Skye flew her to the Borderlands." Something Layna had said was gnawing at him and he realized what it was. "You said they killed each other? Layna, Grimmley would die before he harmed another soul. The councils had to be mistaken."

Layna leaned closer. "Their investigation was a cover-up," she whispered. "Grimmley died at the hands of someone else."

Conner's eyes narrowed. "Why do you think that? And who would want to kill Grimmley?"

Layna drew a deep breath and sealed the room. *"Hetos ousia fragidomatio.* I am taking a risk using elementals here. But it is time I let you in on several secrets before I answer that question. Details and more questions are for later. Okay?"

Finally, Conner thought. "Okay."

"First is regarding the quest that Grimmley sent you and your dragon on shortly after you arrived at his home, the one to recover the silver box. Grimmley told you that he sent you on the quest to work out your differences. But that was only half the story. The box, and the lair you retrieved it from, belonged to the Necromancer Shazarack."

"The creator of dragons," Conner whispered.

"Well, we have yet to prove that, but it seems plausible."

Images Conner wanted to forget came back to him—of partially decomposed bodies strewn throughout hastily constructed buildings in a massive cavern, the gray-hooded corpse he found in a chair, the spark of elemental energy that jolted him when he touched the knife buried in its chest, the dead animating and coming at him ... and Skye bowing to the cloaked figure. In some insane nightmare, all of that made sense. The cloaked figure had been Shazarack. He was still ... *alive.*

Layna drew him back. "The box you recovered was empty. But once, according to Grimmley, it contained nine very rare gems called Fettering Stones—black onyxes with brilliant blue light."

"Like the one in the Cravenrock Assassin's ring."

"Yes. And the one worn by the Barbarian you met at Dragongarde." Layna removed her pipe from a pocket and lit it with a match. "The conspiracy you uncovered, the one attempting to make the Warrior Evinfaire Veressa's Champion, was just the veneer for a much more insidious plot, one that involved assassinating Veressa's mother. Grimmley and I were convinced more Anarchic spies reside in or around Griffinrock."

"That explains why Grimmley became deathly pale the morning of the tournament when I told him about Evinfaire being a spy," Conner said. "And why he had me fight Evinfaire rather than reveal to the Tournament Council how I knew. He didn't want anyone to know what he had unraveled. But why keep all this from me?"

"The night you stormed out of Grimmley's home, he and I agreed to bring you in on this mystery. But Grimmley thought the time was not right, and I learned a long time ago to rely on his intuition. He believed that if he told you, you would believe the new queen could be in danger. And the burden of that knowledge would hinder you in finding your powers. We were to bring you in when we had something more definitive."

"I wish I had known. I was so hard on him."

"Which is no reason to now be hard on yourself. You don't have the time or energy for that kind of thinking. Now let me finish." Layna puffed vigorously on her pipe for a moment. "Grimmley was certain these stones were the key to exposing the full conspiracy, and would lead us to the remaining spies. So he set himself to the task of finding out more about them, but grew frustrated because he had no stone to study. That is, not until Herid showed up carrying one of them."

"How do you know Herid brought him a stone?"

"Grimmley always took meticulous notes in his research. I just happen to be the only one he ever confided in about where he kept those notes. When I found him ..." Layna swallowed, taking a slow breath. "I retrieved his notebooks and read through his last entries. He described how his dear old friend Herid had appeared at his door one night carrying one of the stones. Grimmley knew something was amiss. The only hornet's nest he had poked was the Paladins Council. So, someone on the council must have released Herid, knowing he would go straight to Grimmley. But why they would allow one of these powerful stones fall into Grimmley's hands is another mystery."

"And the stone? Where is it now?"

"Well, after reading his notes, I rummaged about the cottage and checked both bodies. The stone was gone. And that is how I know Grimmley and Herid did not kill each other. The investigators concluded that the incantations used were by those two orders. How better to cover the tracks of the true murderer? There were also a few oddities about the situation. The report said the attack was sudden because Grimmley's home was a disaster with furniture upturned and stuff flung about his home. If that were so, then why would Grimmley have sent me a note saying he needed me? Also, I found their bodies in the garden. Grimmley was wearing his house slippers."

"Grimmley would never wear his favorite slippers outside! Did you tell the investigators this?"

"Yes, I explained all of that to the lead investigator, a Shaman Don named Karmenian. He waved it off as ... circumstantial."

Conner's hands closed into fists at the thought that Grimmley's murderers were still at large. "How do you plan to expose these spies?"

"Right now? By doing nothing."

Conner snapped upright. "Layna, I will not let them get away with this. I will find them. And I will make them pay."

"Revenge is not the Harmonic way," Layna admonished. "These spies will be brought to justice. And now we know there are at least two very powerful spies in the realms—a Shaman and a Paladin. But that is not enough. Until I know more, we cannot tip our hand. The best course of action is to let these spies to believe they have prevailed. And to be ready when they show themselves again."

For a moment, Conner was lost in musings of what he would do if he found out who had killed such a gentle soul. He imagined putting his hands around their necks and squeezing until ... His fingers coiled tight at the seductive thought. He closed his eyes, and the image of the Harmonic pattern lay before him. But in his new savage desire for revenge, he saw something he had not noticed before—eddies that churned along the pattern's fringes, grinding the pattern's edges into dust.

"What will you do now?" Layna asked.

Conner pulled himself from his reverie and breathed deep. "I need to return to Dragongarde. Whatever happens next, Skye and I will most certainly need Wren and Valkere's help. I fear that it is going to get rough soon. And they need to be prepared for the rocky road ahead." Conner rubbed his eyes. "Layna, you should know. While I was at Xylor, I regained my memories of the day on the tourney field. I remember how I defeated Evinfaire."

"That is good news, Conner," Layna said kindly. "Let's save that conversation for when we have time. For now, you need rest. But I have one more thing to tell you. There may be more in Grimmley's notes that would prove vital to uncovering the nest of spies. I did not have time to read through them all."

"Where are his notebooks now?"

"I put them back. In case something happens to me as well, there is a metal knob under the left side of the fireplace mantel that looks like a bolt. Turn the knob, then pull it out." She placed a hand lightly on his shoulder. "I also found a sealed letter there, a letter addressed to you."

"To me?"

"I guess having Herid appear at his door carrying a rare stone was enough to warn Grimmley his life was in danger. He must have had a few things he wanted you to know in case ..." Layna let her hand slip from his shoulder. "Go have the head cook prepare you a hot meal. I have already sent for the chambermaid to prepare your bedchamber."

Conner thanked her and departed.

The next morning, Conner packed a few sets of clothing for his flight back to Dragongarde. On his way to the dungeon, he met up with Layna, who agreed to keep an eye on Kriston. When Layna suggested that Conner might make a good preceptor for Wren, he balked. He was barely a stride ahead of her in skills, and given how quickly she picked things up, that could change at any moment.

"Tell the queen I will return as soon as I can," he said as he climbed into Skye's saddle, ducking to keep his head from banging into the low ceiling. Being sandwiched between his responsibilities to Veressa and Wren were proving to be a real challenge. But if the queen was safe enough to globetrot after a potential husband, she surely could go a few more days without him around to get in the way.

"I am sure that once I explain your predicament, the queen will understand. And Conner?" Layna waited for Conner's eyes to settle on her. "I made a few new discoveries on my trip to Darmascus about the old Dragonbonded. Yet another topic we can add to our list when the dust settles."

"You mean *if* it ever settles."

Skye trotted to the dungeon's entrance and launched himself into the air.

Duchess Mariette's Purpose

Veressa rode through the city of Graystone hunched forward to hide her height and gender, her green hood pulled forward to shade her face. It was a common enough occurrence for a small unit of Queen's Defenders to be escorting people through the city with faces concealed. Not that she was concerned about being recognized. With Antilles strolling along side Toran, anonymity was a near impossibility. Still, none noticed her, or if they did, they didn't care.

The late morning was like most, the city teeming with life as citizens bustled about, living their hectic lives. Busy shop owners haggled with shoppers filling the streets, while workers rushed to load and unload wooden carts filled with myriad foods, supplies, and materials needed to create the wares most in demand. A group of barefoot children sprinted past and disappeared amid a crowd enthralled with a play being performed by a troupe of actors. Several performers were inside the black costume of a dragon, complete with shiny scales and gaping mouth shooting fire. Veressa caught a few words from a player next to the dragon with a sword raised high in the air.

"The Dragonbonded have returned! I will rid the realms of the foul stench of wicked Anarchists!" he shouted, bringing on a roaring cheer from the crowd.

Veressa smiled. The tale had become a favorite among the visitors to the city hoping to catch a glimpse of Conner and his dragon. She heeled Toran on along the cobblestone byway, turning west and passing under the castle entrance arches. Within a few minutes, she came to a stop outside the Graystone keep.

Her captain of the royal guard was there waiting. "Welcome home, Majesty," Ballett said, bowing low with a flourish.

"Thank you, Ballett. It is good to be home. And I am relieved to know you received my message." After arriving at Warstag, Veressa had sent a message to Ballett, letting him know where she was and when she would be arriving. She also instructed him that if anyone asked of her whereabouts, he could pass along that she would be at Warstag, seeing to her father. She dismounted, handing Toran's reins to a stable hand.

Ballett rose up on the balls of his feet and peered over Toran's withers. "And will King Jonath be arriving as well?"

"He will be staying on a while at Warstag. It seems country food and air are the medicine he has been needing. He is doing much better, thank the Cosmos. Several Shaman masters are seeing to him as well."

"Excellent news, Majesty. I will be sure to pass that along to the royal physicians."

Veressa had been hoping Conner would be there to greet her. After days of mulling over their relationship, she had a hundred things to say. And a fortnight after his departure, he should have returned. "Any word from Conner?"

"You just missed your Champion, Majesty."

"He is back from"—Veressa glanced about, then tilted closer to Ballett—"his mission?"

"He arrived yesterday, but he left again earlier this morning."

Veressa's shoulders sagged. She wished she had told Ballett the truth before she'd left, that her trip was to get away from the War Council. If Conner had heard what everyone else had, that she'd gone to Elvenstein to negotiate an arranged marriage with Prince Camion ... Her stomach twisted into knots. She needed to correct any misunderstandings he might have as soon as possible. "Did he not get the message that I would be returning?"

"He did, Majesty. From Kriston," Ballett clarified. "But once he heard that Grandmaster Rollingsworth ..." His voice trailed off.

"What about Rollingsworth?"

Ballett cleared his throat. "Grandmaster Rollingsworth is dead, Majesty."

"Grimmley? Oh no." The spirit of a very influential figure and Conner's preceptor reclaimed? The timing was ominous. She would need a full report—*later*. "And did you hear whether Conner was successful?"

"If he was, he did not say anything to me, Majesty. He did speak briefly to Grandmaster Newstone in private yesterday."

"Send an urgent message to Sorceress Newstone that I need to speak to her. I would like to see her before the War Council learns of my return."

"Yes, Majesty. There is another matter I should make you aware of." The warning in Ballett's voice was unmistakable.

"What?"

"Your aunt, Duchess Mariette, arrived a few hours ago."

Veressa's cheeks bloomed red. "What is she doing here? I sent her no invitation." People of nobility just did not drop in unannounced at the royal castle. Such a move was audacious, if not shameless.

"I cannot say why she is here, Majesty."

Veressa glared at Ballett. She could feel her anger rising. "Hold off sending the message to Newstone. This takes priority. Take me to my aunt."

Ballett dipped low and led the way into the keep.

As they walked, Veressa tried to conjure up some rational explanation for Mariette to come to Graystone without Veressa's invitation. None was comforting. Veressa was certain this had something to do with the War Council. She swallowed hard. Suddenly, she wished she had not convinced her father to stay in Warstag. But maybe it was better this way. Her aunt would erupt at the sight of her father, and he would be no less irate to see his sister-in-law. And then Veressa would never get to the real reason for Mariette's unexpected appearance.

Veressa did not hesitate as the doors to the royal reception hall swung wide. At the far end, near her throne, a crowd of a half-dozen members of the War Council huddled in some animated conversation. In the middle, towering over them all was her dear aunt, Duchess Mariette, turning her head this way and that as those around her spoke in hushed tones. General Grimwaldt, along with several other members, waited nearby, his thick arms folded over his chest and his gray brows drawn in a disapproving glare.

"Queen Veressa!" a startled guard shouted.

The crowd of faces turned her way. All seemed shocked by her sudden appearance, and several ducked their heads and tightened their shoulders, as if they had been caught in some improper act. They all bowed stiffly.

"Why Veressa," Mariette declared. "There you are."

The council members cleared a path between the queen and her aunt.

Veressa bristled at her aunt's informality and impertinence before the War Council.

Mariette must have caught Veressa's frozen glare, for her beaming smile vanished. "My apologies, Majesty," she said with a hesitant dip of her head. "The War Council was just going over the plans—"

"Everyone out," Veressa commanded. "I wish to speak privately with the duchess." She noted Grandmaster Ranger Lendfeather's troubled glance toward the duchess before Mariette nodded. The Ranger stepped back, acquiescing to the queen's demand, and silently departed with the other council members.

"Why are you here?" Veressa snapped when she was alone with her aunt.

Mariette stiffened. Her upper lip quivered slightly. Corsazia, her red fox bond, trotted over to Mariette and sat, giving Veressa a cunning stare. "Well, nothing like skipping all good manners and getting straight to the point." Mariette lifted her chin. "So like your dear father. How is he, by the way?"

"Do not attempt to steer the conversation at your leisure. I asked you a simple question. I expect an answer."

"Simple questions don't always have simple answers." Mariette's smile was anything but warm.

Veressa gave her aunt a look that made it quite clear she was seething.

"Very well," Mariette said. "I have come to find out why you have not yet signed the proclamation of war."

"When or whether I sign the proclamation is *not* your concern."

"It is every bit my concern. As it is the concern of every man and woman across the realms, dear girl. You need to stop thinking as if this is all about you. It is not." Mariette took a long breath, then tugged at her dress below the waist seams. "We are both undoubtedly exhausted from our trips, which surely is making us irritable. Perhaps this conversation will be better visited tomorrow once we have rested." She gave the queen a curtsy. "Majesty," she added, then stalked from the hall.

Antilles paced in figure eights in front of Veressa, purring and rubbing against her leg. She recalled the morning before her departure for Charmwell, when Grimwaldt reported news that there were some on the War Council who did not appreciate the time she was taking to decide, and how Lendfeather was marshaling support to force Veressa into signing the proclamation. Had the council "invited" Mariette to Graystone?

She sat on the thick rug before the dais and began rubbing Antilles's short ears. The cat closed his eyes, his purring growing louder, soothing her own spirit. "Antilles, my dear friend. It seems that more than just the council need to learn that I am not an instrument to be played at someone's pleasure. I think we will need to be prepared for a fight in the days to come."

Antilles rolled on his back, opening his giant maw, and tugged on Veressa's arms, a sign he wanted to play. Instantly the two were romping across the floor, laughing and playing tag. And for a few minutes, she was just a sixteen-year-old girl frolicking with her playful bond, free from the burdens of deciding the fate of three realms.

Changes Are Coming

After they entered the mountain range, Conner decided to use the time to reconnect with Skye. "What's going on with you of late?" Conner shouted over the wind.

"What do you mean?" Skye asked back.

"You are being incredibly patient with me. I would have thought your improved mood was the result of traveling home, but I can feel there is something deeper at work." Conner sensed a thread of aggravation through their link. "It's about time you realized this connection runs both ways, my bonded friend. You can't go around reflecting on my feelings and not expect me to do the same."

Skye snorted back, then flew another mile before responding. "While I was home, the Ancient Iridescus, Bello's mate, spoke to me. She reminded me that the Cosmos chose us for a reason ... and that we must work together if we are to be prepared for what lies ahead."

"Okay. But what else? You're still not being completely forthright."

Skye hawked, a sound Conner had learned the dragon used as laughter when he was flying. "And *you* are?"

"Fair enough. And what is ahead for us?"

Skye peered back, sizing up the human on his back. "I do not know. But she made it clear we are running out of time."

Conner chewed on Skye's warning for the remainder of their flight back. He sensed a change was coming, like a storm on the horizon, or an Eastlander song building to its finale. Grimmley murdered, Layna working to uncover spies in the realms, Veressa pushed to the edge of declaring war. *Yes,* he thought. *We* are *running out of time.*

As they neared Dragongarde, Skye pointed to a small dark blur skimming along a billowy cloud overhead. "There they are." Stroking his wings harder, Skye flew higher, until the black dot, dipping and turning in lazy figure eights, started to take shape. Finally, Skye glided up alongside Valkere.

Wren was laughing gleefully.

"I thought you were going to practice with the gold wheel," Conner shouted. He tried to tamp down his suspicion that she was not taking her studies seriously enough.

"This is *much* more fun!" Wren yelled back. "Watch this!" Pulling her legs up under her, she slowly rose until she was standing on Valkere's back, her clothes thrashing wildly in the gale. She gave a victorious whoop and threw her arms up high just as a strong blast of wind blew her off Valkere's back.

"Wren!" Conner shouted in horror as she disappeared in a pinwheel of motion through the thick clouds below.

Valkere snort-sniffed, then jabbed his head downward. Folding his wings to his body, the dragon shot like a slender black arrow in pursuit of his bond.

Conner dropped his head and closed his eyes. There was so much she needed to master ... if she survived long enough to learn.

Dusk found Conner and Wren sitting at the entrance of the main cavern, their feet dangling over the edge, watching Hemera dip below the mountains in the west.

"That was delicious!" Wren exclaimed, patting her bulging belly.

Conner peered down at the bowl she had scraped clean—twice—and set to the side. "What have you been eating while I was away?" Conner asked.

"Leftovers mostly. I finished the large pot of food you made before you left." She smacked her mouth in a way that reminded him of Skye after consuming a particularly tasty catch. Conner had nearly forgotten that nothing ever spoiled or rotted inside Dragongarde's protective shield. "Still, it is nice to have a little variety again."

"So glad you missed me," Conner teased. Just as twilight was coming on, he caught the glow of the fires north of Lake Arastone. *Something else I nearly forgot.* Too many things occupied his mind of late. "I think there are a few more fires down there than there were before."

Wren nodded as she rubbed her full stomach. "I resisted going down to check it out."

"Maybe it's time we see who has taken up camping in the Borderlands. I would prefer not to be surprised." *Or to worry about you going on your own and saddle me with having to pull you out of some mess*, he thought.

Despite Wren's impatience, Conner waited until it was fully dark before leaving Dragongarde. At last, Skye and Valkere glided in, stealthily landing near the lake shore several hundred paces southwest of the fires. More than half full, Erebus hung in the west, shrouded by clouds.

"Skye," Conner whispered. "Stay vigilant. If you get my signal, come in quick and hot."

Skye snort-sniffed. "I can do both of those easy enough."

Wren slid down Valkere's leg, then hooked her arm over Conner's shoulder. "I hope you have learned to be quieter than you were at home."

Conner repeated the elemental weave he had used to evade the Assassins at Xylor. "That should help."

Wren glanced down at her body. "You really need to show me how you do that," her voice warbled through the protective weave.

"Once you learn to make the wheel in the practice room spin, this will be the first weave I show you."

The two crept north, skirting several dark-dressed sentries along the way, snaking toward the warm glow of campfires ahead. Squatting behind a thick bush, they waited and listened. But there was nothing beyond normal fireside mumbles and movement.

"What do you make of this?" Conner whispered in Wren's ear.

"It looks more like an outpost or settlement than a makeshift camp. There are a few foundations for buildings over there. Some of those by the fire are Barbarians."

Conner craned his neck over the bush. The only Barbarians he had seen were those who'd come to Dragongarde, and they had been disguised as Alpslanders. "Why would Barbarians be sitting around fires in the

Borderlands chatting?" He pointed at a man sitting on a stump in the middle of the camp. "And he's not wearing Anarchic clothing."

Wren rose. "Maybe that is a question we can ask them."

Conner gripped her wrist. "Wait! We don't know how they will respond."

"I am not worried. Valkere is a mere minute away." Wren wrenched free of Conner's grip. Slipping around the bush, she started forward.

Conner had no choice but to follow.

They were twenty paces from the nearest fire when Wren shouted, "Hello, there!"

The ordermen around the fire jumped to the ready, turning and drawing their blades.

The man on the stump swiveled, holding a bowl and spoon, his face lit by a nearby fire.

"You!" Conner bellowed and drew upon the four elementals.

Marcantos Evinfaire set down his bowl, rose, and held his arms out to his side. "Well, I wondered how long it would take to get your attention." He raised his arm, then swept his hand to the side. Those around him relaxed and sheathed their swords. He waved to Conner. "Come, Conner, sit by the fire. We have a great deal to talk about."

"You know this man?" Wren asked.

Conner growled. "It has been my displeasure to have crossed paths with him several times."

Marcantos burst into a hearty laugh, then stood and bowed low to Wren. "I am Marcantos Evinfaire, once grandmaster Warrior of the Harmonic Realms."

Conner inched forward, wary of the dozen well-armed Barbarians around him. "Yes, *once*."

A few Barbarians nearby chuckled, releasing tension around the fire.

Marcantos, unaffected by Conner's rebuke, returned to the stump he had taken. "Please relax, young Dragonbonded. I have no doubt your bond is nearby. None of these good men and women are foolish enough to try anything against you, even if they wanted to. And they don't. Consider us friends."

Conner stepped close to the fire, Wren by his side. "Friends? That is not how we parted at our last encounter. Has something changed that I'm not aware of?"

"A great deal has changed, Dragonbonded." Marcantos ladled a thick stew into a wooden bowl and offered it to Wren. She took the offered bowl, sat, and started shoveling stew into her mouth. "Judging by your clothes, you are Anarchic. Dristonian clan?"

Wren grunted, her mouth full of stew, "Xylor."

Conner wondered where Wren was putting all that food.

"Indeed!" Marcantos said. Slapping his thigh, he jumped from his stump. "Allisor! Where are you?" he bellowed. A moment later, a female Barbarian strolled toward the fire.

When the woman saw Wren, she ran forward. "Wren?"

Wren dropped her bowl of stew and jumped up. "Allisor? Is that you?" Laughing, the two women embraced in a tight hug.

Marcantos looked at Conner, eyebrows raised. "It seems she *is* from Xylor. Now, why would the queen's own Champion be traveling with an Anarchist?" His eyes flicked toward Dragongarde, then flew wide. "Ah! Compatriots!" he bellowed. "The Cosmos has advanced our cause! We have a second Dragonbonded among us!"

A clamoring roar rose from those gathered around the fire. Any remaining tension evaporated as they drew closer, though Conner sensed a formality as Marcantos presented each of the twenty or so Anarchic ordermen. Still, he was surprised at just how amiable the Anarchists were toward him given their ardent hatred for both Harmonics and Dragonbonded. Wren introduced Allisor, who said she had come from Xylor before she was adopted by the Barbarians Order. She went on to explain to Conner how those conscripted into the Anarchic orders relinquished all duties to their clan before they were accepted. And that was why Anarchic ordermen were called orphans, even by those who raised them.

After Wren took Allisor to meet her dragon bond, Marcantos gestured to his people. "They may not look like much, and we are not yet many, but they are the seeds of what will become a mighty army, right here at the foot of Dragongarde." He reached past Copious snoring loudly by the fire to rummage through a dark leather rucksack. "And not just any army, Conner." He removed a black cloth and unfurled it before the firelight. Larger than a full-length cape, the swirling, blood-red image of a dragon was stitched over the middle. "*Your* army."

Conner stared at what could only be described as a poorly fashioned flag. "*My* army?"

"Yes. Just like the days of old!" Marcantos caught Conner's goggling stare and followed his eyes to the flag. "I know it does not look like much. Not yet! But soon, the light from a thousand fires will shine on the lake, creating a glow that will be seen all the way to Graystone."

He's mad! Conner thought, and swallowed hard.

"But I am just the army's general. It needs a true leader, Conner. Someone to give us purpose, to give us meaning." He gazed at Wren. "Only the leader of the Dragonbonded can command the Army of the Dragonbonded."

"I don't need an army." Conner studied the solemn faces gathered about him. "What would I do with an army? I am not at war with anyone, and I certainly don't plan to start any wars."

"Conner, war is coming. The Omen of the Dragonbonded makes it clear—"

"I don't believe in omens or prophecies," Conner struggled to keep from shouting. "I am the master of my own path, not some ancient dribble from a bygone era."

Marcantos tensed. A savage look passed over his face like a storm cloud, reminding Conner of the day they'd met on the tourney field. But in the blink of an eye, it dissipated.

Conner straightened his shoulders. Why are you yelling at these people? he asked himself. Didn't Skye just warn you that you are running out of time, and that you need to be ready for something unexpected? Like it or not, changes are coming.

"I understand." Marcantos glanced about as if seeing the ragtag cluster of Barbarians for the first time. "We have work to do before we are ready for your leadership." He folded the flag and stuffed it away. "But that will change, young Dragonbonded. I have seen the signs of the Omen. Try if you wish, but you cannot run from destiny."

Marcantos waved his arm at his troops in training. "I am teaching them a new way to fight, a more powerful means of using elementals." He held his hands up and interlaced his fingers. "One neither Harmonic nor Anarchic, but melded together into one. They will be ready when they are called. You should know that I have dispatched messengers across the Harmonic Realms, into the mountains, and to all regions of the Anarchic Lands. More will come, young Dragonbonded. Ordermen, guildsmen, freemen. Just wait. Many believe in the Omen, even Anarchists. You will see. And I will prepare them all for what lies ahead." Marcantos gestured behind him as a figure in necromantic robes moved through the camp toward them. "In fact, our latest recruit arrived just hours ago. She was sleeping, but I sent for her when you arrived."

As the Necromancer stepped into the light, a sleek black bond on her shoulder, she pushed back her hood.

With mouth agape, Conner stood in shock. "Meera?"

Meera's Story

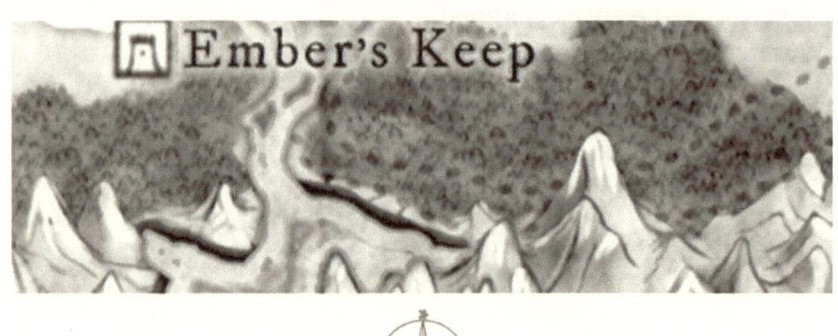

Ember's Keep

"**H**ello, Conner," Meera said with a broad smile.

"Why—why are you here?" Conner asked.

"That is a very long story."

Marcantos chuckled from his stump. "A story I have yet to draw from her, young Dragonbonded. Maybe you will have better luck."

Meera frowned at Marcantos. "I told you earlier. What I have to say is for Conner alone."

Conner shrugged. "I refuse to keep any more secrets, Meera. In the strangeness of our times, secrets are getting good people killed."

Meera nodded, then took a deep breath. "I suppose you are right. Maybe Marcantos should hear this." She and Conner settled on stumps near Marcantos. "I returned to Thanatos as promised. But in the fortnights of my absence, everything had changed. My mentor's spirit was reclaimed, and control of the Necromancers Order usurped by a very old and powerful Necromancer named Nartesis Shazarack."

Conner stiffened. There it was—the name Skye had used as the creator of dragons, the name Layna had mentioned when she'd told of Grimmley's murder. Now, Meera appeared speaking it? This could not be coincidence.

"Shazarack is building a dictatorship," Meera went on, "with himself in the seat of power. Suffice it to say that as an Anarchist, I no longer fit into this sudden governance. When it became clear that Thanatos was no longer my home, I left. I reached the northern shores of the sea just as word arrived of an army being assembled for the coming war, an army to support the Dragonbonded. That was my cue to seek a new calling. If I could not be an emissary from the Necromancers Order to you, maybe I could be your emissary to the Anarchic orders."

Marcantos raised his arms high, looking starward. "The fall of a great order shall be the presage of the times."

"What is that?" Conner asked.

"It is from the preamble to the Omen of the Dragonbonded," Marcantos answered with a hint of reverence.

"Conner." Meera drew his attention. "You need to know something. Shazarack has gathered a great following of Necromancers—most of the order, it appears. I do not know how he holds sway over them. But with them comes a great army of undead—a necro-army. Shazarack plans to invade the realms, and to bring them under his rule. To do this, he plans on using another army awaiting his call, one even more powerful than a thousand undead soldiers."

"You believe he will succeed?" Conner asked doubtfully.

"Shazarack did not strike me as someone who boasts beyond his abilities. And if he created dragons, then yes, I fear he will. And when he has taken the realms, he will return to subjugate the Anarchic Lands. He wants to create a single social entity." She reached over and lightly touched Conner's shoulder. "I told you that I would repay you for letting me return home, and now I am at your service. Conner, you need to take command of this ... Army of the Dragonbonded. Whatever is coming, these people need to be ready. They need a leader."

"Leader? No, Meera. I have my own crusade. I could not possibly take on another responsibility right now. Besides, I know nothing about commanding"—he waved his hands at the campfires around them, not wanting to even say the word—"an army."

Marcantos's chin sagged to his chest. He scratched his bond's back, receiving a contented groan from the bear for his efforts.

"I will take this news of Shazarack to the queen of Griffinrock," Conner offered. "She will know what to do. She should at least consider this before signing a declaration of war."

"That won't work," Marcantos snapped. "Meera, what evidence do you possess to prove any of this? No one will accept the word of a freed Necromancer. And let us suppose that you did convince Veressa that a powerful Necromancer is preparing to invade the Harmonic Realms with a necro-army. You would still need the backing of the War Council." Marcantos shook his head. "They would see this as an Anarchic trick. Trust me, they won't believe any of this without hard proof."

Is it an Anarchic trick? Conner wondered. Was Meera a plant to sow discord or misdirection? Marcantos's argument sounded similar to Grimmley's the day Conner had revealed the conspiracy to make Marcantos Veressa's Champion. In the realms, secrets and lies took root like weeds in a garden. But he could not be distracted from his obligations. Grimmley's murderers were at large, Morgas was captive to a sadistic Assassin, and Wren needed guidance to find her powers. All of this while being crushed between protecting the queen from spies and trying to convince Wren that Harmonics were not out to kill her. Besides, what did he know about forging together Harmonics and Anarchists into a competent fighting force? And how would he use them?

Marcantos rose. "Conner, these men and women left everything behind—families, friends, fraternities, even their societies, because they have faith in you, or at least in what you represent. Meera has just given you a reason for the army's existence. You are the only person who has ever bested me on the field, so I say this with all honesty. You have everything you need to assume command ... except, it appears, confidence." He gave Conner a nod, then strode away.

"Conner," Meera said. "Marcantos is right."

Conner snorted. "Marcantos is mad."

"There is a thin line between madness and sanity. And that line is drawn purely from one's perspective of reality. If I told you half of what I have seen ... or what I have done ..." She glanced away. "You would surely declare me mad as well. What is more important than preparing for what clearly lies ahead of us?"

"Grimmley Rollingsworth was murdered."

"Oh." Meera dipped her head. "That is what you meant by secrets are getting good people killed. I recently saw a good man get killed before my eyes, so I understand. You want to find the killer."

"I am going to find them. They *will* be held accountable. The only clue I have is that he was killed over something called a Fettering Stone, so I have a lot of sleuthing ahead of me. I don't have time for Marcantos's army."

Meera inhaled sharply. "Did Grimmley tell you that he visited me the morning you retrieved me from the Shamans' prison?"

"No." So Grimmley refused to let me see Meera while he had a talk with her behind my back? He pushed the question away. I will not think ill of the reclaimed. Conner tilted closer. "What did he want to know?" he asked in a hushed tone.

"He wanted to know what I knew about the stones."

"And what did you tell him?"

"Not much. Certainly a lot less than I know now. Shazarack has two in his possession. He used one of the stones to get a new, youthful body. And the other he used to bring back his love." The color drained from Meera's face. Morgana sat up on her lap and squeaked. "Shazarack killed my preceptor for the stone used to give him a new body. I do not know where the other stone came from."

Conner sensed Meera was not telling him everything, but given how much she had shared so far, he was not about to demand more. A new body? So the half-rotted cadaver he had met in the caverns was no more. *Great.* "Are you suggesting that if he killed one person for a stone, why would he stop there?"

Meera shrugged. "I suppose it is possible. He could have dispatched someone to retrieve the stone. The second stone had to come from somewhere."

Possible, yes. But plausible? One of the killers had been either a Shaman or Necromancer. But there were too many unanswered questions. Was Shazarack connected to the network of spies Grimmley and Layna had been trying to expose? How could Shazarack convince a Paladin to participate in such a heinous crime? How did Shazarack know Grimmley had a stone? And how did he know where Grimmley would be and who would be with him?

"From what Layna told me," Conner finally said, "Shazarack had a very long obsession with these stones. Even if he did not kill Grimmley, maybe he knows who did, and why."

"If you are thinking of going to see to Shazarack, I would advise against it. He is incredibly powerful now, maybe the most powerful Necromancer that has ever lived."

"Well, I did figure out how to use my powers."

"Then you should be prepared to use them," Meera warned.

"I am hoping it doesn't come to that. Shazarack and I have some history."

"What do you mean?"

Conner was not sure he should tell Meera, but the opportunity to finally tell someone, anyone, of the first time he'd met Shazarack was too great to ignore. So, he told Meera of the quest had Grimmley sent him and Skye on. He explained how Skye helped him find a crescent-shaped cavern inside a mountain near the River Falmere gorge, just as Grimmley had described. He described ransacking the remains of several buildings and coming upon many semi-decayed cadavers, including one particular corpse sitting in a chair with thin, wispy hair flowing from under a gray hood and a gilded dagger protruding from its gray-robed chest. Conner told how he'd touched the red-gemmed dagger, which had sent off a bright white spark that had numbed his arm.

Through his tale, Meera sat and listened as she petted her mink bond, occasionally nodding. When he was through, she said, "Shazarack confided in me that a young man bonded with a dragon awoke him from his sleep. Even if I did not believe him, your description fits Shazarack when he arrived at Thanatos. As well as the dagger he wears at his waist. The jolt you felt was likely what awakened him."

"I was afraid of that," Conner said. "I'm responsible for reviving Shazarack."

"Do not be too hard on yourself, Conner. It was a mistake anyone could have made."

Conner doubted "anyone" had the power to resuscitate the undead. "Do you think this connection will have any sway with him? I don't just need to get to him. I need to talk to him."

"Possibly. Shazarack does have integrity, in a strangely skewed way. But there is something else in your favor. Shazarack believes he created dragons."

"As does my bond," Conner amended.

"So, it is true. Some part of me did not want to believe a person could be powerful enough to achieve such a feat. If he had the skill to create dragons, both lands have something to be terrified of."

Exhausted from the flight to Dragongarde, Conner thanked Meera for sharing her thoughts and said good night. He feared that anything more he might say to Marcantos would either anger or offend him, so he trudged south in search of Wren. He found her not far away, still chatting with Allisor. "We should head back. Skye and I need to rest."

Wren caught Conner's heavy expression and nodded. She hugged Allisor and followed Conner away from the camp. "Was Marcantos serious?" she asked. "He is really building an army?"

"Ignore the man. He has lost all grip on reality."

Flight Plan

Sleep was meager for Conner through the night, mostly restless naps nestled between long hours spent wrestling a nagging conscience over what he should do. Part of him knew the risk in going to see Shazarack. Meera had made that more than clear. But he also could not deny feeling at fault for Grimmley's death.

It was not just that he was the one who'd resuscitated the ancient Necromancer from his long sleep. It was also the warnings he'd refused to heed along the way. King Jonath's voice continued to torment him. *Unprecedented change is coming, Conner,* the king had said. *Your very existence is assurance enough for me. And you, young man—you will be in the middle of it, maybe even its very instigator.* There was also Wallis Arkman, the odd man Conner had met on Griffinrock's streets, who'd warned him that Grimmley and Layna were not capable of illuminating his path. And if that was not enough, Meera had said nearly the same thing, that he would have to learn to control his powers on his own. He had made Jonath a promise not to get too emotionally close to Veressa. He should have done the same for Grimmley. But his insecurities had kept him around ... until lightning struck. There was only one way to make this right, to redeem his spirit. No matter the risk, he was going to find whoever murdered Grimmley and bring them to swift justice.

Conner drew himself up from his bed and stumbled out of his chambers in search of Skye. He found his bond curled up in a dark corner of the main cavern. Sleeping, of course.

Conner roused his bond with a firm joggle, then waited for the dragon to go through his daily ritual of waking up. First came the blinking, followed by a series of yawns wide enough to walk into. Then there was the mouth smacking, which inevitably led to a litany of grunts and snorts, concluding in several laborious stretches. Once he was certain his bond was lucid enough for a conversation, Conner began. "How would you like to go meet your Shaman god?"

Skye craned his neck sideways, poking one eye up near Conner's face. "That is not something you should tease about."

Conner held his hands out wide in his defense. "No tease. If you don't believe I'm serious, search my feelings." If he was going to enlist the help of his bond, they needed to air some dirty laundry first. "By the way, I know why you behaved as you did in the moon-shaped cavern."

Skye stared back.

So now you're going to give me the silent treatment? Okay. "You know. When Grimmley sent us on a quest to recover the silver box. I was being pushed by a horde of undead toward a bottomless crevice. I screamed for you to help. But instead of swooping down to rescue me, you landed in front of one of those undead and bowed."

Skye's head swiveled away and gazed toward the opening at the far end of the chamber. Still he said nothing.

Just as that night by the campfire when Conner had confronted Skye for nearly letting him die at the hands of the undead mob, he sensed the swirling turbulence in Skye's emotions—embarrassment and regret. Conner placed his palm on the dragon's cheek. "Skye, it's okay. I know that was your Shaman god, Shazarack. I can only imagine what it must be like to drop in on one's creator."

Skye dropped his head. "You nearly died because I hesitated."

"But I didn't, did I?" Conner jabbed Skye in the snout with a finger. "Because you rescued me." Conner could sense his words were working their way into Skye. "I bring this up now because I need you to know something. There is no one I would rather have with me when things get rough than you." Conner knew Skye could feel his sincerity. "And lately, they've been plenty rough."

Skye blinked several times, then snort-sniffed. "So, you are suggesting that I should not go far."

"I'm saying don't get in your head that you are going to run off home again until the dust settles around us."

"But that may never happen."

"Exactly my point. Now, about Shazarack. I am thinking of flying to Thanatos and having a talk with the Nec— the Shaman. But there are a few things we need to discuss before we decide."

"We?" Skye twitched, his interest piqued. "Okay. Such as?"

"First, apparently, Shazarack has a new body. A young one. So don't be fooled by what you see."

Skye's eyes widened. "He *is* a god."

Conner sensed the flow of awe and adulation from his bond. "Yes, well, don't let that go to your head. I don't need you getting all reverent around him. I need you with me."

Skye squinted and rolled his head sideways, which was his sign for agreeing.

"Second, Grimmley's spirit was reclaimed. I wasn't sure of the right time to tell you. But he is gone. Murdered."

Skye's gaze returned to the opening of the chamber, and Conner sensed sorrow flowing through their connection. "I do not understand this compulsion your species has for killing your own kind."

"That makes two of us. Which is why I am going to talk to Shazarack. He may have information about who murdered Grimmley." Conner waited. This was the point he had debated through most of the night. But, in the end, he needed Skye to be all in on his plan. "It is also possible Shazarack was involved in Grimmley's death." Conner sensed the dragon's doubts, which was fine with him. He had his own. "Skye, I brought Shazarack back to life ... in that cave ... somehow. I am the reason Shazarack is here. That is why I need to know if Shazarack was involved."

"And if he wasn't?" Skye asked hopefully.

Conner shrugged. "Then there are other forces at work in the realms. Which means we had better unearth the disease before all the tomatoes rot on the vine." Conner blew out a long breath, ready for the quarrel he was sure was about to start. "So. You with me?"

"When do we leave?" Skye asked.

Conner's mouth dropped open. "What? No arguments? No negotiations? No demands?"

Skye snort-sniffed, delighted at shocking Conner. "I guess it will take time to get used to working together."

"For both us. Very well, then. Thanatos is very far from here. You should eat before we leave." Conner cast his gaze toward the hall leading to the other Dragongarde chambers. He could only hope the next conversation would be half as easy as this one had been. "And I need to tell Wren what we're doing."

Conner found Wren rummaging for food in the galley. He fixed her a large breakfast while summarizing what he and Meera had talked about the previous night: Shazarack's return and assuming control of Thanatos, an army of undead possibly invading the realms, and Grimmley's death. Wren was scraping her second helping of scrambled eggs from the bottom of her wooden bowl as he finished filling her in. "Skye and I are flying to Thanatos," he concluded.

"All right." Wren leaned over to see if there were any eggs left, her shoulders sagging when she noted the skillet was empty. "When are we leaving? I need to find Valkere."

"You're not coming with me."

Wren's face reddened. "You have no problem with me endangering myself by going to your Harmonic castle, but somehow my homelands are unsafe?"

"This is not the same. Graystone is not dangerous. Going to see a powerful, undead Necromancer will be."

"Tell that to your Shaman preceptor." Wren put her hand to her mouth. "I am sorry, Conner. That was insensitive of me. But you and I have quite different ideas of danger."

"It's okay. But Shazarack is not of this time, Wren. He is not an Anarchist. Nor is he bound to the principles of your people."

Wren's eyes hardened with sudden determination. "If it is not safe for me, then you should not go either."

"I need to find out what Shazarack knows of Grimmley's death. He may not perceive a person flying in on a dragon as a threat. But two?" Conner shook his head. "I don't need that." He gripped her hand tight. "I know you won't like hearing this, but if it comes to a fight, you're not ready to help."

Wren pulled away from him, her lower lip pushed out.

"I can access the powers I used to defeat Marcantos if I need to. I am willing to tempt fate for the chance to learn what Shazarack knows, but not if you are there."

"Conner." Tears pooled in her eyes. "Please. We must stay together. Either we both go or we both stay here."

"Why?" Conner fought to keep his frustration under control. First, she'd refused to go with him to Graystone, and now she did not want to be separated. Her stubbornness was not helping. Wren did not answer, so he tried again. "Why do you insist we stay together?"

"I am afraid," she mumbled, turning away from him. "Allisor told me last night that war is coming between our two lands, that there is no way to stop it. And when it comes, you will be forced to leave me ... and I will be alone. I will have no one."

"What? I will not leave you—"

Wren placed her fingers over his lips. "Be cautious of your oaths." Tears streamed down her cheeks. She slid her hand to his chest, pressing her palm over the Champion's amulet he kept hidden beneath his armor. "You cannot hide from the oath you took to protect your queen. When war comes, you will be called to carry out that oath." Slowly, she pulled her hand away. "It would break my heart if we found ourselves on opposite sides of this war. But it would break my heart more to sit by and let my people die. I cannot do nothing."

Conner swallowed hard. "Wren, I also made a promise to myself. I refuse to let myself be drawn into their war."

She smiled weakly. It was a sad smile. "You still have so much to learn about what it means to be Anarchic. You cannot make an oath that conflicts with one you have already taken."

"I will find a way through this, Wren. I don't know how. But I will not let the lands force us apart. And I will not fight you. On that, you have my oath."

She did not reply.

"Will you wait for me?" he asked, feeling pressed for time.

Wren stepped back. "It seems you give me no choice." She turned away, but then glanced back. "Where else do I have to go?" And she dashed from the galley.

A Path to Peace

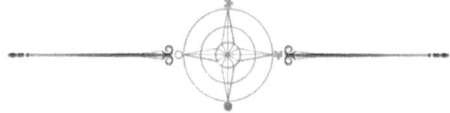

On the long flight to Thanatos, Conner had plenty of time to reconsider confronting Shazarack. Using what Layna and Annabelle had taught him, he played through some of the scenarios that might occur. But there were just too many ways it might go—and no shortage of outcomes that were not in Conner's favor. Still, he was driven to find Grimmley's murderers. So on Skye flew.

"It seems you've finally found something to be excited about," Conner shouted as they soared high above the Anarchic grasslands.

"I assume you mean the chance to meet the being that created my kind. Yes, the thought is exhilarating."

Conner considered warning Skye again that his creator might not be the benevolent fellow the dragon expected but doubted another warning would have any more effect on his bond's enthusiasm. He tried to imagine standing before whatever or whomever created people. But the only reference he knew about the creation of humans came from the *First Book of the Modei*, which only referenced in passing the splitting of the four planes and that spirits pushed into the Physical plane had been given bodies. He just could not conceive of having a conversation with the Cosmos.

ARMY OF THE DRAGONBONDED

The Dragon's Back Mountains gave way to autumn plains, the dry grasslands growing thicker and greener as they continued on their northeasterly path. Conner found Meera's landmarks along the way. After the immense oak forest around Xylor, they flew north, following the River Est as it meandered to the Antaric Sea. At the second sharp bend to the northwest, they banked hard to the right, Hemera sinking in the west behind them. The grasslands east of the river became rolling hills. Then, tinted in the gray twilight, the dark fortress of Thanatos loomed into view, perched high on a hill like a bejeweled black crown, just as Meera had described. Balls of elemental light, supplemented with lanterns and torches, brilliantly lit the buildings, fortress grounds, walkways, and parapets of the three tall stone walls ringing the city. Even at this distance, Conner sensed the massive draw of Fire and Earth.

With Conner's cue, Skye fanned his wings wide and glided in, coming to rest on the rooftop of the city's central tower, startling two black-cloaked women in an animated conversation on the far side of the roof.

"I am here to speak to Nartesis Shazarack," Conner declared.

The two women dashed down a flight of stairs.

Conner shuffled to the tower's edge, where he peered out over the jutting towers and crenellations of the city below. Necromancers in robes flitted about like black ants, carrying on with whatever abhorrent sorcery they did at night. As he waited, the stories he and Pauli had been fond of telling late at night when they were little, tales intended to scare each other, made the scene below all the more surreal. Meera's warning of Shazarack's powers kept playing over and over in his head. Whatever knowledge and power were required to give oneself a new body, it had to be extraordinary. A voice kept nagging Conner that he should leave, that he was nothing more than a hapless fly buzzing around the web of a cunning spider. But he fought the desire to flee.

Echoes of footfalls from the stairwell grew louder. A young man in necromantic robes appeared on the terrace, his gray eyes widening at the sight of the two of them. His pace slowed as he approached, as if wary or unsure of Conner's intent. An older man, thin and tall with a long gray beard and balding head, staggered through the passage at the young man's back, panting with his hand to his chest and looking quite vexed.

Conner tipped his head to the two robed men. "My name is Conner Stonefield. And this ... is Skye-Anyar-Bello of the family Cloudbender."

"I am Nartesis Shazarack, Supreme Lord of the Necromancers Order," replied the young man as he strode forward, examining Skye's dark scales, which reflected the bright lights of the city. "Cloudbender, eh?" he said in Dragon. "What a fine specimen of your family you are, my young friend."

"Powerful Shaman God Shazarack." Skye unfurled his wings and dipped into a low bow. "It is a great honor to meet you."

Shazarack rubbed his chin as he studied the dragon. "So, you are a descendant of Bello?"

Skye's head wriggled up with pride at the name of his Ancient ancestor. "Yes."

"I gave Bello his name, you know, because he was the most vocal of my dragons." Shazarack watched Skye's eyes grow wide. "I named all those I created." His gray eyes shifted to Conner. "But I suspect you are not here for a history lesson." Bowing to Skye, he said, "Offspring of Bello, would you mind terribly if I had a conversation with your human bond? My guards will attend to any needs you may have."

Skye dipped his head low. "You are most gracious."

Leading the way to the stairwell, Shazarack leaned toward one of the female Necromancers who had returned to the top of the tower. "Retrieve a goat from the farm and offer it to our winged guest. And I suggest you remain attentive. Let's keep our friend happy, yes?"

Conner followed Shazarack down the stairs. The thin old man, still huffing from the climb, shadowed behind. "You speak Dragon."

"In a way. My creations lacked the physical characteristics to speak our tongue, so I helped them devise their own language." In the better light, Shazarack studied Conner's Dragonbonded armor.

"So, you did create dragons?" Conner asked, though he could not help the incredulity from creeping into his tone.

"Of course, though 'forged' or 'designed' would be more accurate." Shazarack smiled warmly at Conner. "I did not start by mixing dirt and water, Conner. Though it took many years to find the right animal genus to use as the vessel for the beings I summoned into the Physical plane. I tried dozens of species—a horse, large cat, eagle, even a camel. You see, while the spirits I summoned had never possessed physical bodies, they brought with them"—the Necromancer moved his hands before him as if shaping a clay vase—"a self-image of sorts. Once summoned, the spirits directed elemental energy into the vessels, molding those bodies into their self-image. That was why my early attempts failed. None of the vessels I'd tried could withstand the force of the transformation." Shazarack stopped, poking his forefinger into the air. "Not until it occurred to me: What about snakes? They're highly adaptive, they shed their skins as they grow, and they originated from animals with legs. They turned out to be the perfect host."

Conner remembered: he'd retrieved the silver box from a cabinet in the back of a study. In the front, above the desk, several skeletons of snakes had hung from racks. And then Conner recalled Skye telling him that the Cloudbenders had come from pythons.

"I see you speak Dragon yourself," Shazarack continued, "which gives us a very special connection, don't you think? You are, after all, bonded to a descendant of one of my creations." He beamed at Conner and started down the stairs again. "Of course, that is not all that binds us."

"You are referring to our first encounter ... in the cavern in the southern mountains." Conner found it hard to connect this vital young man with the undead he had inadvertently resurrected.

Shazarack chuckled. "Yes. I am hardly the shriveled husk of a man I was then. Nearly a thousand years I spent in that cavern ... until you came along and revived me. How long might I have slept in that desolate cavern if not for you? I am extremely grateful for your assistance." He hung his arm over Conner's shoulder as if they were lifelong buddies. "You see? We are connected in ways neither of us could have foreseen. It seems the Cosmos is not without a waggish sense of humor."

With his arm still draped over Conner's shoulder, Shazarack directed him out of the stairwell and down a long, musty hall. Light from the lanterns' flames flickered and danced off the dark stone walls and floor.

Shazarack was being exceptionally friendly, possibly to get him to lower his guard.

"Here we are!" Shazarack proclaimed when they reached a large wooden door at the end of the hall. He turned to the thin man who had shadowed them from the roof. "Ousel, stay here and stand guard. I wish not to be disturbed."

"Of course, my lord." The old man bowed stiffly, his expression turning all the more troubled.

Shazarack led Conner into a large, dimly lit room. At the far end were nine massive wooden chairs arranged in a semicircle. The Necromancer took one of the chairs. To his right sat a young golden-haired woman dressed in a dark gray gown. She gazed ahead, her eyes unfocused, as if she were unaware that the two had entered the room. "This is my wife, Arna."

At the sound of her name, the woman turned toward her husband, her lips turned up at the ends.

"Arna, my love," Shazarack cooed, patting her arm. "Say hello to our guest."

The woman's head swiveled toward Conner, the smile frozen on her face. "Hello."

The hair on the back of Conner's neck rose. Something about her felt off. "Good evening, my lady."

"Now," Shazarack announced, gesturing to the chair at the hub of the semicircle. "For what purpose do you honor me with such a visit?" He took up a beaker of dark wine from a narrow oak table and filled a crystal glass.

"I am seeking information," Conner said as he slid into the offered chair.

"I see." Shazarack held out the glass to Conner. When Conner shook his head, the Necromancer sat back and took a deep gulp. "You do realize that I have been ... away for a long time. What could I possibly know that is of interest to you?"

"My preceptor, a Shaman named Grimmley Rollingsworth, was recently murdered."

"A Shaman?" Shazarack's eyes bored into Conner's as he drummed his fingers on the armrest. "And you think I know something of his death?"

"I know that he was murdered for a certain black onyx he had in his possession."

Shazarack looked genuinely surprised. "So, you think I had him killed. For a stone?"

"Not just *any* stone. And yes, that is the premise I am pursuing." Conner knew he was on thin ice coming to Thanatos and accusing a very powerful Necromancer of murdering Grimmley. But Shazarack had suggested they were connected. Conner wanted to test just how far he could stretch that connection.

To Conner's surprise, Shazarack burst into a hearty laugh. "I did not kill this Grimmley Rollingsworth. But I would be willing to share a few clues that might lead you to who did."

Conner leaned forward, then drew back, not wanting to look too eager.

"Let us trade," Shazarack offered after a brief pause. "I need you to do something for me first."

"Me?" Conner asked.

"Well, more precisely, your bond."

Conner leaned back, feigning disappointment. "That will depend greatly on what you need of him. I can tell you he is the most obstinate beast imaginable. And he's not very good at sticking to agreements. Besides, it would not be proper to make any arrangements without knowing what you need from him."

Shazarack slid his fingers over the armrest's velvet padding as if he had never experienced the sensation before. "News has reached my ear that war is brewing between the Harmonics and Anarchists. Both sides are gathering and consolidating their forces. It is a matter of time before someone lights a match and"—Shazarack put his hands together, as if holding a small ball, then slowly drew them apart—"boom." He dropped his arms. "But conflict is not inevitable. I want you and your bond to help me stop it before it starts."

"Stop the war?" Conner blinked. Since the founding of the War Council, Conner had hoped there might be a path other than an all-out war. After his visit to the Anarchic Lands, and with his need to resolve the tension with Wren, that hope had grown even stronger. Could there be a way out? "How?" he asked softly.

"By disrupting the paths both sides now tread ... before they reach the point of no return."

Moments of silence passed. Conner grew dizzy as Shazarack's vision of peace filled his mental sight. His tongue felt leaden.

Shazarack set his glass down. "Conner, you and I have a chance to create a world so much better, so much richer, than what either the Harmonics or Anarchists can offer. The two sides are fighting for all the wrong reasons. If they go to war, no matter who comes out the victor, we all lose."

It was hard for Conner to disagree with this logic. Still, he needed more. "What do you mean, fighting for the wrong reasons?"

"For starters, those who manipulate elementals have been taught wrongly. There are no Harmonic and Anarchic Sights. There is just *one* Sight. It is the weave that unites us all." Shazarack scrutinized Conner. "The world of the orders has been artificially manufactured to keep them from coming together. This is why their elemental powers are weak. Victory, by either side, would mean everyone would be forced to accept and live in a dysfunctional world. No one would ever achieve their full potential."

Shazarack held out his hand, palm up. "Imagine a world united in peace, where everyone has access to the powers that the orders have amassed over the centuries, then hoarded for greed and control." His fingers folded in until his hand was a tight fist. "Help me reunite them. Think of it. No more wars. No more class system. Just everyone living together in peace and harmony."

A world united in peace, Conner repeated to himself. Veressa believed war with the Anarchists would lead to destruction far greater than the Anarchic War. During that war, most of the Eastland towns had been ransacked and burned. Few of the farming communities had been left untouched. Famine and disease followed. Morgas had told him how that war had altered Elmsdorf. How many would die or suffer in a new war? Who would be left to rebuild from what remained? Would anything remain?

Taking a deep breath, Conner pulled his thoughts back from the edge of the horrors of war. "You can do this? You know how to reunite them?"

"With your help, I do. Without you ..." Shazarack shrugged.

"True peace." Conner swallowed hard. "If only." He had resolved not to be drawn into their war, but as Veressa's Champion, would he have a choice? And what would war do to his relationship with Wren? Could either of them stand by and watch their two worlds be ground to dust? He was filled with sudden excitement. Why shouldn't he believe there was another way? "How can Skye and I help?"

Shazarack leaned back with a warm smile. "When I created dragons, I endowed them with certain qualities—skills that would come in handy for their survival, like the ability to carve through dense granite." Shazarack rocked forward and rested his elbows on his knees. "And to find cavities in rock."

"Sounds like what Skye calls 'mountain breathing.'" Conner noted Shazarack's expression of confusion. "It is how Skye found the cavern you were in."

"Ah, yes. Precisely. I need your dragon ... Skye ... to locate a tunnel for me, a shaft that traverses beneath the mountain range."

Conner failed to see how a tunnel beneath the mountain range could prevent a war. "A tunnel?"

"The Modei excavated the tunnel long before our ancestors arrived in these lands, likely several thousand years ago."

"What do you need with such a tunnel?"

"It's for a pilgrimage of sorts." Shazarack picked up his glass of wine and held it to the candlelight nearby. He took a sip and closed his eyes. "The Modei were very spiritual people. So much so that they built a sacred city in the western mountains."

"You speak of Shan-Grail."

Shazarack's eyes popped open. "You know of this city."

Conner shrugged. "I grew up in Creeg's Point. The story of how Tatem Creeg found the ancient Modeic city is ingrained in us from our earliest days."

Shazarack beamed with joy. "Yet another connection, my young friend. Yes. Shan-Grail. The Modei built a series of tunnels beneath the mountains for Modeic pilgrims to reach the city. Unfortunately, the entrances to these tunnels have never been unearthed."

A surge of pride flowed through Conner at the thought he and the great Shazarack were connected. "And you want to find one of them."

Shazarack swirled the wine in his glass and downed it. "I have heard tell of one somewhere along the Dragon's Back Mountains' eastern rim."

"And that is what you want Skye to do? Just find the entrance?"

"I am hoping this ... exchange ... is the first of several, along the way to peace. But for now, that is all. Help me find this entrance, and I will tell you what I know about those in possession of your preceptor's stone."

Such an easy task to avert a war that would destroy everything. Conner leaned in, eager to accept Shazarack's offer. What had Layna and Annabelle told him about negotiations? It took a moment to recall. Yes. *Never be too quick to take bait just because it is dangled under your nose,* they'd said. "You mentioned a pilgrimage. You want to travel to Shan-Grail, to visit the Modei's holy city?"

A flash of impatience blew across Shazarack's face and then was gone. "I do. Of course, I would like you to come with me."

Conner stared back, unsure how to respond to such a magnanimous offer. He had always found the legend of Tatem Creeg alluring.

Shazarack went on. "My grandfather was a Bremenn priest. When I was very young, he confided in me that Shan-Grail was more than the Modei's holy city. He told me that it holds a very special power. You and I could work together to discover that power."

The ancient city's power, Conner thought. Not only had Creeg found the once-lost city of Shan-Grail, folklore also told of how the man had been transformed by it. Conner had never thought those tales of Creeg's transformation could be anything but myths. But what if they were true?

"You cannot deny that the Cosmos has brought us together, Conner. We both seek a world free of war, a world at peace, united in a common purpose, living in equality for all. Neither Harmonic nor Anarchic. Let us work together to make that world a reality."

Conner felt dizzy and dull, like being swept along in an exalted dream. *Why did I come here?* He shook his head, trying to clear away the fuzziness. "You mentioned disrupting the two sides' plans for war," he slurred. "Shan-Grail has the power to do this?"

Shazarack inhaled deep. "In a way, yes. So, are you with me?"

Conner could hear the tension in Shazarack's voice, a bite of eagerness Conner had not noticed before. The question clutched at Conner's throat, shaking him to answer. *Am I with him?* A pilgrimage to the ancient Modeic city, to walk the sacred streets that Tatem Creeg protected, to prevent a war of monumental scale? It was all so fantastical, and at the same time, so attainable.

The vision of peace dangled like a bright jewel before him. He only had to persuade Skye to find the entrance to a tunnel. In return, he would not be forced to fight in a war as Veressa's Champion. He and Wren could patch up their differences. He would even get one step closer to finding Grimmley's murderers.

Conner opened his mouth, but something trapped the words in his throat. But he was incapable of discerning what that might be, as if a haze swaddled his mind like a thick comforter. He blinked, trying to shake off his stupor. He had never forgotten anything before. Something about the tunnels. About how they might be used. *Couldn't it have something to do with Shazarack's plan to invade the Harmonic Lands?*

Conner regarded how placidly Arna sat at Shazarack's side with the same awkward smile painted across her face. A rot seeped from within her, as if her spirit were befouled, contaminated. He looked over at Shazarack, relaxing comfortably, smiling smugly next to her. And Conner saw the same blight. They were like two spoiled fruits, rotting in Hemera's summer light. There was a reek about them he had not noticed before—not an odor, but a stench all the same. And it made him ill.

There was something Meera had said to Conner, something about how Shazarack held sway over the Necromancers, defiling what the order had once been. Was Conner now being drawn into this same spell? Instinctively, he reached out and stepped into the conduit that connected him to Skye, and he was immediately wrapped in its comfort, energy coursing through him, the veil before his eyes lifted. And with sudden clarity, he saw Shazarack's sham for what it was. The underground passage Shazarack sought would help him get to Shan-Grail to harness its power, yes, but he would use that power to invade the realms.

Conner brought his focus back to Shazarack. "I think not," he said. "I will find Grimmley's killers another way." He rose stiffly.

Shazarack blinked in surprise. "What?"

"I will find another way," Conner repeated, and started for the door.

Shazarack trailed after him, past the old man and undead guards outside, and up the hall.

Relieved that Shazarack was making no effort to stop him, Conner entered the spiral stairwell they had taken down from the tower.

"Have you forgotten about the Omen of the Dragonbonded, Conner?" Shazarack called out from the base of the stairs.

Conner froze, his foot hovering over the next step. There it was again, the Omen. Clenching his teeth, he pressed on.

"How can I prove my sincerity to you?" Shazarack called in a wheedling tone.

Conner stopped and looked down. "I don't doubt your sincerity. What concerns me is what you are not telling me." At the top of the stairwell, he passed the two female Necromancers standing guard. Conner crossed the roof quickly to Skye.

When he was halfway across the terrace, the two Necromancers chanted, *"Hemea ousia fragizotholos."* A black dome descended over the entire roof. The sky went dark. The glow of the city dimmed, then even those lights were snuffed out. One point of brilliance near the stairwell was all that remained.

Conner spun back to Shazarack. Skye crouched, a low rumbling coming from within his chest.

"I cannot let you leave," Shazarack declared as he strolled forward, unaffected by Skye's truculent stance. "I had hoped you would assist me of your own volition. But, as I said, I need your dragon."

Conner shuffled backward. "You cannot keep us here."

"You are free to do as you wish. Stay or go. But I *will* take your dragon."
Conner stiffened. "I think not." He drew upon the four elementals and directed them between his open palms. As he pushed his hands closer, the weave drew tighter. The elementals resisted, sparking and flaring, fighting his attempt to compress them. Still, he squeezed until a white sphere of energy blossomed. A searing pain spiked up his arms. He labored against the growing pressure until he could no longer contain the force. The bright orb shot upward, exploding against the elemental dome. The roof rumbled and quaked as the ball of light shattered, sending brilliant, sparkling streams outward like rolling lightning across the night sky. And when the glittery display ended, the dome remained unmarked, undisturbed.

Conner's mind reeled. He had defeated the greatest Warrior to become the queen's Champion, turned away pixie spirits from another plane and sewn up a tear in the Cosmic wall, even outsmarted the powerful Assassin Lacerus and successfully brought Wren to Dragongarde. He had thought himself all powerful. How could this incantation have been so ... ineffective?

He remembered the feeling when Meera shackled him to the antechamber wall at Dragongarde, the loss of control. The same helplessness churned inside him now.

Shazarack approached, step by step.

Conner stumbled backward, bumping into Skye, still crouching, the dragon's eyes menacing blue orbs. *Maybe Skye knows how to break through this dome.* He looked hopefully at his bond.

"There is something you should know, Conner." Shazarack froze Conner with his words. "You are too late. The wheels to set Gaia free from its manacles are already in motion. You cannot stop the chain of events I have put into play."

Conner pressed his hand to Skye's shoulder to steady himself, gripping the conduit of power he would need to free them. Then he stopped and stared at Shazarack, elementals once more surging through him. "What have you done?"

"What I said I would do," Shazarack answered, shifting ever closer. "The queen of Griffinrock is the key. The only way to disrupt the Harmonics' plans for war is for her to die. She must be assassinated."

"Assassinated?" Conner shouted incredulously. *Chain of events already in play? Veressa!* "Killing the queen will only incite the people to war, not stop it!" Conner sensed the shifting turmoil inside his bond, sensed Skye's hesitation over what to do, how to help. The dragon did not want to believe his god could do this. *Help me, Skye!*

Five paces away, Shazarack shook his head. "Such a naive boy. I may be wearing a young body, but you forget I lived a full lifetime before the sleep from which you awakened me. I have experienced war and destruction you could not imagine." He raised his hands, fingers spread wide. "With the queen gone, I will extend to the Harmonics an alternative to war. Most cannot stomach conflict. Only those who hunger for control see conflict as a means to more power. With an undead assassin dispatched to Griffinrock, the Harmonic threat will be defused, and the Anarchists will fall in line."

"Death is never the path to peace!" Conner screamed. He glanced at his feet. Maybe he could blast a hole through the roof and they could escape that way.

Shazarack laughed, the same haughty cackle Conner had heard the day they met in the cavern. "No, Conner. Not death. *Sacrifice* is the path to peace. All of us must make an oblation to the great Cosmos if peace is to be achieved. I have given my entire life to see this vision become reality. What are you willing to sacrifice? There will come a day, a reckoning, very soon, when you will be called upon for your offering."

Everything was happening too fast. *What can I do? I must warn Veressa.*

Conner sensed when Skye's dithering snapped to a close, and the avalanche of decisions that followed. The dragon drew a deep breath. A deep resonating rattle rumbled from his chest.

Shazarack looked unconcerned at the red glow growing brighter in Skye's throat. "Conner. Come now. Aren't you tired of being the victim in a world you did not create? Isn't it time you grew up and took command of the destiny before you?"

The rattle in Skye's chest stopped. The dragon's mouth gaped wide and steam rolled from the sides of his mouth.

"*Hemea psychi elenchozorizo,*" the Necromancer invoked quickly. Bright jets of reds and greens sprouted like roots from Shazarack's hands, fingering outward like runners, striking Skye squarely in the chest.

Skye's head jerked forward, his flame extinguished. The dragon's body spasmed and he shrieked as blazing streams of rainbow energy enveloped him.

Conner staggered in unison with his dragon. A searing agony flowed through their link. Overwhelmed by the pain, he dropped to his knees. He was not supposed to feel his bond's pain! Skye was in unimaginable agony. "Stop!" he shouted, pressing his hand to the side of his head. Then, a rage he had never felt before erupted from within, and he bellowed. An elemental blade appeared in his hand. He lashed out, slicing downward with one clean stroke, severing the colored roots spiking through Skye's chest.

Shazarack cried out and shrank back, shaking his blackened and smoldering fingers.

Desperate, Conner recalled one of Grimmley's incantations. Placing his hand on Skye, he drew upon Fire and Earth. Summoning as much energy as he could, he threaded the elementals into a weave as Grimmley had done the morning of the Champion's tourney.

Shazarack stepped forward again. Scowling in the dim light from the stairwell, he raised his hands once more.

Enough, Conner thought and let the elemental threads rip free. The world around him spun wildly out of control. In the wake of a thunderous boom, Conner and Skye were sucked into a spiraling vortex.

After a moment of disbelief, Nartesis crept forward to the spot where the boy and dragon had disappeared. He closed his eyes in concentration.

"My lord?" Ousel asked at his back.

Nartesis flicked his arm up for silence. He leaned forward, sensing the residual effects of Conner's casting. Light warped as it passed through a small sphere, like crystal, the shrinking remnant of a portal to another plane. He reached for the sphere just as it faded away. He had heard of such incantations. Necromancers and Shamans used them to transport across distances. But those conjurations required a Transit Stone, such as the one in Thanatos. Conner had not used a Stone.

Shazarack sucked in a sharp breath. "Very impressive."

"My lord," Ousel interrupted. "It would seem reports that the young boy living among the Harmonics as the queen's Champion are true. But why did you lie to the boy about the queen's peril?"

Nartesis pressed his lips tight. He was growing annoyed at Ousel's incessant, nagging questions and his constant shadowing. "It was a test, Ousel. Merely a test. I needed to know where the lad's loyalties lie."

"It seems he takes the responsibility to protect his queen seriously."

"It would seem that way." Nartesis strolled to the railing, looking out over his majestic city. "Leave me," he commanded.

Shazarack pondered what he had learned from his encounter with the boy, and what he was dealing with. Foremost was Conner's ability to control elementals. As if his ability to transport to another place without a Transit Stone were not enough, the boy had thwarted Nartesis's attempt to ensnare the dragon. Then there was the way he had summoned the elementals. Unlike everyone else, Conner did not draw elementals from the matter around him. He drew them straight from his dragon. It was as if, when he touched the creature, he tapped into a great reservoir of elemental power. Shazarack's creations were very powerful indeed!

But that was not all Conner had demonstrated. Unbeknown to Ousel and Meera, Shazarack had included a special, insidious enchantment in the series of incantations they'd used to give him his new body, one that employed a distinct facet of the Fettering Stone. The enchantment that allowed him to charm those around him with his words had worked on Conner—right up until the boy refused him. Meera Asheborne had been the only other person immune to his charm.

Conner's surprise arrival at Thanatos had revealed Meera's whereabouts and intentions. She was the only one who could have told Conner where to find him, and that he might know who'd killed his preceptor—for a Fettering Stone. So Meera was working with Conner now. How unfortunate. He'd had such high hopes for her. Maybe he could still use that to his advantage.

He rubbed the stubble along his chin and cheek. He had miscalculated Conner's resourcefulness and overplayed his hand. He would not make that mistake again.

Enough ruminating, he admonished himself. If nothing else, the evening had convinced Shazarack it was time to marshal his army of Necromancers and undead for the long journey ahead.

He just needed a dragon.

The Champion's Return

There was little warning for those near the Transit Stone at the far end of the Graystone castle's bailey, just a low rumble that shook the grounds. The thin patch of trees around the Stone shivered nervously at the sound. A pair of guards unsheathed their swords and crouched at the ready. The rumbling stopped. The guards exchanged uneasy glances.

When the blast struck, it was sudden and intense. The two guards were blown off their feet. The trunks of several trees nearby snapped, scattering debris fifty paces and more across the bailey. Even the elementally enhanced gray stones of the castle wall cracked and buckled under the force of the explosion. As the dust settled, Conner staggered from what remained of the Transit Stone, which was mostly rubble mixed with fist-sized chunks of glowing granite. He stumbled to his knees.

The guards started forward to aid him. But Skye appeared from the cloud of dust to stand over Conner. With wings fanned wide, the dragon roared. Flames and sparks of electricity sprouted from Skye's mouth, sending the guards back on their heels.

Conner looked up to steady the horizon in his vision. He placed a palm on Skye's chest to keep the dragon back. His bond was livid, and the anger flowed like a raging river into his own mind. They had been betrayed by the dragon's god. "It's okay, Skye. We're in Graystone," Conner said softly, fighting to block out the ire burning through him. Conner needed to get the dragon away or he would certainly harm someone. "Please go to the dungeon and wait for me there."

Skye snorted at the guards, smoke rising from his nostrils.

The guards took another unsteady step back.

"Skye, please. I promise I won't be long." Conner tried to get his feet beneath him, but he fell again. "Take me to the queen. Quick!" he shouted at the flat-footed guards.

Conner was so dazed from casting his transit incantation that he was only slightly aware of the guards half lugging, half dragging him across the castle grounds. By the time they reached the reception hall, his head had cleared, though his bond's rage made it feel like someone was hammering an iron spike into the side of his head.

One of the royal guardsmen at the door stepped in front of them. "I am sorry, Conner. The War Council is in session. No one is allowed in unannounced."

"Then announce me. This is urgent!" Conner shouted, then grunted at the spasm tracing a line down his neck. He slid his feet under him and pushed up, slowly putting weight on his weak legs. He pulled his arms free of the guards who had helped him, then wobbled for a moment. *I am the queen's Champion,* he reminded himself. *I will not be carried before the queen.* When the doors swung wide, he lurched forward, focused on keeping an even stride. He was only partially aware of the dozen ordermen staring up at him from chairs assembled on either side of the aisle. Veressa was sitting on her throne with a tension he had not seen in her before. Even through Skye's anger, he could sense her displeasure—hopefully not at him. A tall, middle-aged woman with dark hair and a commanding presence waited at her side, a red fox at her heel. From Veressa's coronation, he recognized her as Veressa's aunt Mariette, the Duchess of Kallzwall. He tilted forward at the waist. "Queen Veressa."

Mariette glared at Veressa, her face filled with shock. "What is this?" she asked, turning back to Conner. "Where have you been, Champion?"

Conner realized his dust-coated Dragonbonded armor and disheveled appearance was anything but courtly. He was not sure exactly what Veressa had shared with the others in attendance about his recent disappearance ... or his mission. He waited for a cue from the queen.

One of the guards stepped forward. "My apologies for the interruption, Majesty, but I thought you should know. Graystone's Transit Stone has been destroyed."

Tara, the Shaman Don who had handed Meera over to Conner, leaped from her chair. "What? Destroyed?"

Conner flinched, then cleared his throat. "I am afraid I destroyed it. It was not my intention to do so. But I needed to return here quickly."

"You *used* our Stone?" Tara asked incredulously, her jaw slack. "You are not a Shaman. You had no right!"

Our Stone. Conner balked at the words. *Ours, yours, theirs, mine!* His fingers curled tight into his palms. *The precious words of Harmonics.* How foul they felt after his time at Xylor, where everything was openly shared.

Tara went on. "That Stone is central to the three realms and has been the Shamans' lifeblood for traversing our lands. We sit at the edge of war. It will take years to rebuild!" The Don's face reddened, and she shook her fist toward Conner. "You have been nothing but trouble to our order since the day you appeared at Grimmley's doorstep. I am glad he is not here today to see just what you have become."

Conner's throat constricted, a low growl issuing forth. *How dare she invoke Grimmley's name in this?*

"What purpose did you have for using the Stone?" the duchess asked.

"Aunt Mariette, Conner was on a personal assignment for me. That charge gave him the authority to use the Transit Stone."

"A personal assignment? You have a hundred ordermen at your disposal for such matters. The oath this boy took was to protect our queen. I would have thought he understood that simple fact, especially considering we are about to go to war."

Several members of the War Council mumbled to each other.

"What assignment could be deemed so important that only the queen's Champion could perform it?" Mariette asked.

Veressa bristled. "As I said, it was a *personal* assignment."

Conner took a moment to look around, his mind shifting to potential undead assassins in the room. The reanimated Shaman seer sent to the Shamans' temple to dispatch Meera had escaped notice by numerous guards. What if one of the council members was such an assassin? Any delay in conveying news to Veressa only put her in greater peril. "Majesty, if I may," he interrupted the two women staring each other down. "I need to speak to you privately regarding an urgent matter."

Mariette huffed. "More urgent than planning a war? Any matters for the queen can be shared before the War Council. They have all been sworn to secrecy under the Orderman's Code. Besides, they should be kept aware of all matters of state potentially impacting preparations."

Veressa bit at her lower lip, then signaled for Conner to continue.

"Your life is in danger," Conner declared.

"Her life is always in danger, young man!" Mariette shouted over the noise that erupted in the chamber. "She is the queen of the greatest realm! Have you no sense in that skull of yours?"

"That is enough, Mariette." Veressa stood, rising over everyone in the room. "Have you forgotten that Conner was the one who protected me from the Anarchic spies?" Veressa glanced at Conner with a troubled expression. "Continue, Conner."

"It is likely ... an undead assassin has been sent to kill you."

Mayhem broke out in the room, and several minutes passed before Veressa could restore order. "Go on, Conner. Who has sent an undead assassin?"

Conner started. He was not cut out for court affairs, and he lacked training in how to broach such topics as assassination attempts on a crown. If only Layna had been there to advise him how to handle this situation. When Veressa offered no further guidance, Conner took a deep breath. "Nartesis Shazarack."

Tara jumped from her chair again. "Preposterous! The boy's brain is addled!"

"Who?" Mariette asked Tara, her face pruned in confusion.

"Nartesis Shazarack is the paragon of the Necromancers Order. The man lived a thousand years ago!"

"He is alive now," Conner clarified. "I know it is hard to believe, but he is back."

"And you know this how?" Tara asked.

"Because I just spoke to him." Half the council sat in stunned silence while the other half started shouting questions at Conner. He raised his arms to silence them. "I received news that Shazarack had returned to Thanatos and taken control of the Necromancers Order. So I flew to Thanatos to confront him." Conner did not mention that he'd suspected Shazarack of murdering Grimmley, which would only incite another squabble since everyone here believed Herid had killed him. "Before Skye and I departed, he told me that he'd sent an undead assassin for Veressa.

He is plotting to disrupt both Harmonics' and Anarchists' plans for war. But I believe his real intention is to invade the realms with the necro-army he has at his command."

"This is insane," Tara sputtered. "A long-dead Necromancer back from the grave in charge of the dark order and commanding an army of undead? Tell us, Champion, what does a thousand-year-old man look like?"

Conner cleared his throat. "Actually, he has taken a new body, the body of a young man."

Several council members chuckled.

"And you actually expect us to believe this?" Mariette asked.

"I give you my oath that it is the truth."

Muffled laughter echoed again through the chamber.

"Do you have any evidence to this claim?" the duchess asked.

Conner bristled at the duchess hinting that he would lie about something as critical as this. If he were in the Anarchic Lands, he would have given her his oath, and that would have sufficed. He took in the doubting faces about him, saw the accusations behind their eyes. Oaths meant nothing here. However, recalling his oath to Jonath, he reached beneath his Dragonbonded armor and pulled the Champion's medallion out. Holding the ruby-studded pendant before them all, he announced, "I give you my solemn oath on this medallion that it is completely true."

Mariette sniffed, unimpressed by his theatrics. "You will have to do better than that. Did this Shazarack tell you he was invading the realms?"

Conner blinked. "Not exactly."

"Did you see this ... necro-army he supposed has?" Mariette asked.

"No," Conner mumbled.

"Then why would this man share such information with you?"

"Because he asked me to join him in his cause."

A few council members gasped.

Conner took them all in with a sweeping glance. "I would never betray our queen or this realm. I came back to warn the queen."

"Majesty, if I may?" Tara cut in, then waited for Veressa to give a hesitant nod. "Are you saying you transited from Thanatos to Graystone?" She gawked in disbelief. "That is impossible. Every trained Shaman knows the limit is several hundred miles."

Conner shrugged. "I am not a Shaman."

"No, you're not," Tara barked. "And you said that you received news that Shazarack had returned to Thanatos. Who told you this?"

The blood ran from Conner's face. This was why he needed Layna. *Well, too late now. You stepped in the middle of that cow patty.* He took a deep breath. "Meera Asheborne."

"The Necromancer? You let her go?" The Don fought to keep from exploding.

"At the Borderlands," Conner clarified. The room was quiet enough to hear an ant walking. "She was my prisoner to do with as I saw fit."

"So, let me see if I understand your claims," Mariette said. "After receiving news from a powerful Anarchist spy, whom you had released, you flew to Thanatos and met a young man claiming to be the long-dead Necromantic paragon, who voluntarily told you that he now rules over the order and is in possession of an army of undead that he plans to use to invade the realms. Then you destroyed the central Transit Stone to travel instantaneously across the known lands?" She looked around at several who were nodding at her summary. "I think I have heard quite enough ..." The duchess faltered, her brow slowly furrowing as she stepped closer. "Wait. Was that the mission Veressa sent you on? To Thanatos?"

"Absolutely not," Veressa interjected.

"Then where? The War Council has the right to know. Was it to the Anarchic Lands?"

Conner's eyes flicked to Veressa. He watched the blood drain from her face.

Mariette caught their glances. "It was," she hissed sharply. "For what purpose? Were you on some mission to forge a treaty with the Anarchists? Is that why the queen has held back from declaring war? In hopes of sealing some arrangement?"

"Of course not," Veressa cut in.

Mariette rounded on the queen. "Then give the council a reason why you sent your Champion to the Anarchic Lands."

The silence dragged on, awkwardness in the moment growing. Conner wanted to answer the duchess. But the queen had given specific instructions. The morning Conner departed for Xylor, the queen had sworn the entire group to secrecy. Only she could answer. Why Veressa was refusing to tell the War Council that there was another dragon bonding, Conner could not fathom.

Mariette leaned toward Veressa and whispered so only Conner could hear. "Veressa, what have you done?"

Veressa's eyes shifted from Conner to her aunt. "Neither my Champion nor I have done anything wrong. And when *I* think it is time to share the reason, and all this is cleared up, you and I will have a most unpleasant conversation." The words came out like a feral growl.

The queen's fiery stare and taut body did not go unnoticed. Mariette straightened and stepped back, then sniffed as if to bolster her defenses against the queen's threat. "I see. Then I have no choice but to call for a royal inquiry."

"What?" Veressa shouted. "You cannot!"

Mariette rounded on the council. "You give me no other choice, Veressa. If you had listened to your mother, you would realize that a queen's power is only as great as the trust her subjects place in her. Lose their trust, and your power vanishes. And with no power, you cannot rule them effectively. A royal inquiry is the only tool we have to instill the sense of trust a queen needs to rule."

"I will not be subjected to such a humiliation," Veressa hissed, her hands gripping the throne arms.

Antilles crouched slightly and growled at Mariette.

"If you have nothing to hide, then you should not mind an inquiry." The duchess's eyes shifted to the white leopard beside the throne. "Do you have something to hide, my queen?"

Veressa fought to control her anger under her aunt's scrutiny. "Of course not."

"Very well, then. Under our laws, only a member of the royal family can administer a royal inquiry, which must be conducted under the watchful eye of a tribunal comprised of members from the six orders. Since we already have assembled these high-ranking members of the orders, I see no reason to waste time assembling a new tribunal. Are there any objections from the council?"

Mariette raised her eyebrows as if daring any member of the council to challenge her authority. "Very well, then. I hereby declare the royal inquiry of Queen Veressa of Griffinrock underway, to determine whether her actions have hindered the welfare or security of our great realm."

Stunned, Veressa opened her mouth to object, but before she could get a word out, Mariette began.

"Majesty, you may ask questions to shed further truth, and you may elaborate on answers. But you may not direct or influence the investigation due to your position of power. Is that clear?"

Conner sensed Veressa's irritation growing. Any objection the queen might raise regarding Mariette's suggestion, like declaring the council's lack of objectivity, would only serve to raise suspicion of her guilt and undermine the authority she had worked so hard to obtain.

Veressa leaned back in her throne, her mouth drawn into a tight line. "I am fully aware of the rules regarding a royal inquiry," she growled.

"Good." Mariette turned her attention back on Conner. "To begin, I believe we have more than enough information about your Champion's conduct of late." The duchess pulled on the rope dangling near the throne, then gestured the two guards who entered to come forward. "Take this boy away from us. He shall be held under house arrest—"

"You cannot do this!" Veressa shouted.

Mariette turned stonily, wagging a finger at her niece. "The rules, my dear," she warned, and Veressa crossed her arms as her face flushed with rage.

Mariette returned her focus to Conner. "This young man shall be held under house arrest until he can stand trial for treason against the realm."

Hands gripped Conner's arms and shoulders, pulling him back forcefully.

"Wait," Mariette said. "On second thought, take him to the castle dungeons. There's no reason he should not be with his dear bond."

Conner sought to meet Veressa's eyes only to find them turned toward the floor, threatening to flood with angry tears. He did not fight the guards as they dragged him toward the door.

Part IV

Anyone can be loved, hated, and ignored, all at the same time. The same kind word comforts the depressed, angers the miserable, and is lost on those who refuse to hear.

—The Modei Book of Air (Second Book)

A Journey's First Step

Veressa jumped at the resounding clack of the chamber doors slamming shut. She had not seen Conner since his departure on his mission. She desperately needed to talk to him, to learn what he had done. Had he found another Dragonbonded? Had he convinced them to leave the Anarchic Lands? At least Conner had returned, alive. But what was she to make of the report he brought? Conner would never lie to her, but she found it hard to believe an undead assassin was coming for her. And a necro-army invasion? Now? A cold chill ran through her. It seemed too absurd to believe. More than ever, she needed to talk to Conner alone, to find out everything he knew about this powerful Necromancer. But Conner—her Champion—had been hauled away like a common criminal, and now she had to face the humiliation of this ridiculous royal inquiry.

Mariette pulled on the rope, then waited for the two guards outside to enter. "Bring in the captain of the royal guard," Mariette commanded. A few moments later, Ballett proceeded forward, stopping before the dais, his eyes studying the carpet at his feet.

Veressa's eyes narrowed at her aunt. What could Mariette possibly want to hear from Ballett?

"Ballett Wrighter. Is that right?" Mariette asked with a sweet smile.

"Yes, Duchess," Ballett answered, his gray possum bond peeking over his shoulder.

"How well do you know the queen, Captain?"

Ballett puffed out his chest and rotated his shoulders back. "It has been my honor to be assigned to protect her for more than eight years, Duchess."

"Half her life," Mariette nodded as she paced before the throne, her red fox bond, Corsazia, at her side. "So, you can say you know the queen quite well. Is that correct?"

"Quite well, Duchess."

Mariette strode forward to examine the captain up close with pursed lips. "You are quite young to be appointed as captain of the royal guard. Who assigned you to this rank?"

"As I am sure you are aware, Duchess, it is the king's duty. But with King Jonath's ... preoccupation of late, it was the queen who assigned me."

Mariette sniffed. "How unusual."

Veressa cut in. "It is not unusual, Mariette, when the king is unable to perform his assigned functions that those responsibilities pass to the matriarch. You know this."

"Of course, Majesty, you are right." Turning back to Ballett, Mariette continued. "And as captain of the royal guard, your responsibilities include receiving reports on all activities within and about the castle grounds, and then assessing those reports to determine which may be of interest for the safety of the queen and castle—is that correct?"

"I receive reports daily, Duchess."

"And tell us, Captain, have you received any reports of late regarding any peculiarities in the queen's behavior?"

"Peculiarities, Duchess? I fail to understand what that has to do with the queen's safe—"

"Changes in queen's behavior, captain. Or conduct one might consider odd for someone in her station."

Ballett shifted his weight and wrung his hands. "Uh."

Veressa's fingers constricted around the armrests of the throne. Her chest tightened. "Where are you going with this, Mariette?"

"That will become clear in due time, Majesty." Mariette returned her gaze to Ballett. "I remind you of your duty, Captain."

"Yes, Duchess." Ballett sighed. "Some of my men have mentioned in passing that the queen's behavior has changed of late. Others near the queen have also noted changes."

Veressa's breath caught. She had not been aware others had been observant enough to see through her struggles! "Must I remind this tribunal that I have been dealing with my mother's murder, my father's illness, and adapting to my new bond, all while navigating demands for plans of war? Surely, *changes* are expected."

Mariette put up a hand to silence Veressa, keeping her eyes on Ballett. "Changes, Captain? Such as what?"

Ballett was back to studying the carpet. "Loss of attentiveness and mood swings mostly. And a desire to be away from the castle."

"Yet you failed to report these," Mariette noted.

"Duchess, as Majesty just mentioned, the queen takes rides along the river nearly every day to improve her mood. It was my assessment that these shifts were due to the considerable stress she is under."

"*Your* assessment. And you are an expert in such matters?" Mariette stepped even closer to Ballett, until he visibly cowed before her. "Go on. What else?"

"Else, Duchess?" Ballett asked nervously.

"Have you received any reports regarding the queen's"—Mariette waved her arms—"use of elementals?"

Veressa choked back a gasp. Her body shuddered. *No!* Her mind raced to interject an answer, but she was not prepared for this line of questioning. How could Mariette even know to ask this?

Ballett cleared his throat. "Several of my guards have made mention that they observed her casting incantations."

"Made mention," Mariette repeated to be sure everyone had heard. "I see. And again, you failed to mention these incantations in any of your summaries. The royal guard is comprised of many guilds, so I suspect they would make note of which elemental she has been manipulating?"

"Air and Earth have been mentioned, Duchess," Ballett mumbled.

"*Combined* elementals?" Mariette studied Veressa with raised brow. Murmurs broke out around the chamber. "So not just the simple use of a guildsman's single elemental, but the more powerful merging of two. In fact, not just any two, but the elementals of a Ranger ... and their dark cousins, the Assassins." The duchess's head drooped forward a bit melodramatically. She raised her arm and flicked her hand toward the door. "You may go, Captain. Please send in the colonel of the Queen's Defenders; she should be waiting outside."

Ballett bowed low before the queen, tears pooling in his eyes. "Yes, Duchess."

Veressa clenched the armrest. *Ballett. My dear Ballett,* Veressa thought. *What have I put you through?* She felt shame tempering her ire.

As the captain drew the chamber doors wide, a young woman in a Defender's uniform stepped through. Veressa recognized her as the colonel in charge of the small force of Defenders that had accompanied her back from Cravenrock after her bonding—after Evinfaire had been assigned as her personal protector.

The colonel marched forward and bowed. "Majesty," she said with a snap of her head.

"Colonel"—Mariette drew the colonel's eye—"please explain to the council how you have served Queen Veressa."

The woman cleared her throat, though her eyes remained steady on Veressa. "While I was stationed at Cravenrock, the Countess Garlander assigned my patrol to provide armed escort for the princess—apologies, Majesty—the *queen* and her newly assigned protector back to Graystone."

"So, you attended closely to the queen from Cravenrock to Kallzwall. Is that correct?"

"It is, Duchess. Eight days, if I am not mistaken. No greater honor could be bestowed upon a Queen's Defender than to be of such service to the crown. Unfortunately, our service was cut short with the news of"—the colonel's lip quivered, then she breathed deep—"of Queen Izadora's assassination shortly after reaching Kallzwall."

"And explain what you conveyed to me after you arrived at Kallzwall regarding your observations of the present queen."

The colonel looked troubled, her eyes glancing toward the throne.

Mariette lightly touched her arm. "It's all right, Colonel. Just tell the tribunal what you observed."

"At first, the queen was resigned to returning to Graystone. But as we drew nearer, the queen became more aloof, more irritable, as if she were struggling with something intractable."

"And is it not true that later, you saw the queen interacting with Marcantos Evinfaire's preceptor? The man who called himself Blake Friarwood, the man we later learned to be an Anarchic spy?"

"Don't be absurd, Mariette!" Veressa scoffed.

"Does the council not deserve to know whether our queen has consorted with an Anarchic spy?" Immune to Veressa's glare, Mariette gestured for the colonel to continue.

The colonel steadied herself. "By chance, I observed Friarwood ... the spy ... speaking to the queen the night we arrived at the River Aradorm, near Bell's Ferry."

"Alone?" Mariette asked with brow raised.

"Yes, Duchess."

"And after that?"

"In the two days before we reached Kallzwall, I observed the two speaking in hushed tones alone several times, usually at night near the edge of camp. More precisely, it appeared that the man was giving the queen ... instructions on some matter of interest to her."

Members of the council whispered to one another, a few becoming quite agitated at the news.

Veressa recalled those days right after bonding with Antilles as she struggled to control her urges to run free in the wilderness. The nights had been torturous until Friarwood, the man she would only later learn to be an Anarchist spy, helped her bridle those urges. After arriving in Graystone, she'd confided in Annabelle everything that had happened, and the two had worked secretively to ensure there had been nothing insidious in the man's guidance. Neither of them could determine his true motive in assisting her. Still, the thought that she had allowed an Anarchist to instruct her made her violently ill. What could she possibly say in her own defense that would not lead to more questions that made the situation worse?

"Thank you for your service, Colonel," Mariette said. "You may return to your patrol."

The colonel snapped a salute, then spun on her heel and marched out.

Veressa sat staring at her hands. The walls were closing in around her. She had failed at keeping any of her "inappropriate" activities secret.

"As you can imagine," Mariette continued, "many things are a blur for me in the days following my sister's assassination. But I will make note of one important fact. Despite my best efforts, Veressa ignored my counsel and rode out of Kallzwall with no more protection than Evinfaire and his Assassin spy. It is a wonder she was not taken from us in those days before she arrived at Graystone." Several council members squirmed at such a thought. "I mention this only because, per the laws scripted into the Armistice of the Orders, a queen imminent is not allowed to be with more than one member of any order. Veressa knew this, and still she rode from Kallzwall to Graystone with two whom we all believed to be Warriors, who would later be indicted as Anarchic spies and conspirators of the most heinous acts imaginable."

"This is ridiculous." Veressa snapped up from her throne, unable to restrain herself further. "My father was lying gravely ill. I needed to be at his side. How was I to know at the time that Friarwood was an Assassin? You, Auntie, seemed to have no qualms about welcoming him to stay in your castle proper. He was with us in the breakfast hall the morning we received news of my mother's death, watching us like some ... spider lurking in a dark corner."

"Yes," Mariette's eyes floated toward General Grimwaldt, who was sitting quietly near the back of the assembly. "It seems many of us were duped into believing the man was a powerful Warrior."

The general bristled but said nothing.

"However," the duchess went on, "only Evinfaire and *you* were positioned to receive private instructions from this Assassin spy. And then, you arrive home, capable of enchanting powerful elemental spells—spells that are supposed to be secret incantations of the Rangers Order ... and *Assassins*."

Veressa trembled with sudden rage. There was that word again: *spells*. She wanted to shout at her aunt, to explain that she had been tutored not by an Assassin, but by her protector, the Ranger Annabelle. But her hands were tied. She had made a pact with Lady Kyles of the Rangers Order to never divulge the sovereign leader's approval for Veressa's advanced Ranger training. If the other orders found out, it would erode long-standing structures and balance of power among them. And that would threaten any chances of winning a protracted war with the Anarchists. *Oh, what have I done? Why didn't I heed Annabelle's warnings?*

Mariette removed a letter from a pocket on the side of her dress. "I would like to present to this inquiry a letter I received from the king of Elvenstein, a letter that precipitated my journey here to Graystone." She rattled the folded letter before the council. "In this letter, King Friedrick shared with me his anger over our queen's conduct during her recent visit to Charmwell, where she flagrantly used elemental spells!" Brandishing the letter at Veressa, she went on. "Do you have anything to say about this?"

"Of course I do! My use of elementals saved Prince Camion's life. I was not going to stand by and let a boar rip Camion into strips of cloth, though I doubt *that* is in King Friedrick's letter."

"I am sure King Friedrick and Prince Camion are most grateful for your gallant assistance. However, you did not learn to manipulate elementals so that you could go about saving princes in distress. You are the *queen* of Griffinrock."

Mariette was not finished. She turned to the tribunal. "To summarize, first we have the queen's erratic behavior, a sudden and unexplained lack of attentiveness, and the blatant display of elemental powers through *spells* known only by certain ordermen. Then her choice of a man endeared to her as captain of the royal guard, a man who has demonstrated a willingness to keep quiet about any of her ... improprieties." Mariette dropped her hands and shook her head in disapproval. "If that were not enough, she's been holding secret meetings with members of certain orders."

The duchess nodded at Veressa's wide-eyed stare. "Oh yes, my dear, I know of your meetings with that Ranger Loris, your Champion's so-called preceptors, and General Grimwaldt. Add to that your continued resistance to sign a declaration of war, a proclamation that needs no further deliberation, and anyone with a sane mind would ask: why?" Mariette was watching the council members now. "*Why* would a queen need private instructions from an Anarchist? Why would she send her Champion on a secret mission into the Anarchic lands? Why would she need to use elemental powers that just so happen to match those of the Assassins Order?"

Veressa could barely contain herself. "Are you calling me a *spy*, Auntie? Are you insinuating that I am—that *your queen* is an ... an *Anarchist*?"

"Oh my, goodness no, Majesty." Mariette looked aghast. "I would never." The duchess waved at the council members behind her, their accusations and doubts painted on faces. "And yet, when all of these facts are viewed together, what other conclusion can one draw—at least, one who does not know you as well as I? Majesty, you do see how this looks?"

The chamber was quiet for a long moment. Awkward tension was thick like fog settling in on an early spring morn.

Mariette looked at Veressa with an expression of concern the queen knew to be entirely false. "Oh, my dear, I can see that this is upsetting." She turned back to the council. "I believe we should take a break. Can the council please give me a moment to speak privately with the queen?"

The duchess studied Veressa as the council members filed out. After the room had cleared and the doors sealed, she continued. "Your mother would be crestfallen if she were here to see what has become of you."

Veressa took in her aunt's long, dark hair cascading down bare shoulders, her radiant complexion, her regal stance. Mariette looked so much like her mother that Veressa felt a sharp pain in her chest. Only now did Veressa realize how much she had relied on Izadora to always be there, pointing out to her when she was careless, and despite Veressa's determined ways, patiently guiding her back on the path to becoming a great queen. She had lost more than a caring mother. She had also lost her mentor.

"You asked me yesterday why I am here." Mariette moved closer. "Veressa, you have the potential to be nearly as great a queen as your mother. But I fear you have lost your way. And I know Iza would agree." Mariette lightly touched Veressa's shoulders as Izadora often had when she'd had something important to convey. "There is a path out of this. There is still time to salvage your legacy."

Veressa's eyes swept across the reception hall, recalling a day not that long ago when her mother had reprimanded her for being inattentive: *These people deserve a matriarch they can believe in, someone they can turn to with confidence for steadfast guidance in times of need.* Veressa had told her that she would try harder. But had she? She took a deep breath. "And how do I do that, Auntie?"

"I fear exhuming these exploits of yours any further will destroy whatever trust the War Council still has in you. Untended, your actions will reinforce the orders' continued infighting and vying for position and power, which is already tearing the orders apart. And if the orders fail, we all fail. Is that what you want? A war is what we need to distract everyone from this whole ordeal. A proclamation of war will unite the orders and the people in a common cause."

Veressa studied the intricate wood carvings of roses adorning the tall back, the red griffin finely embroidered into the back cushion, the armrests carved into clawed griffin's feet. The throne had fit her mother perfectly.

"And what of Conner?"

"The boy?" Mariette's voice rose an octave. "I honestly don't know what anyone sees in that country bumpkin. The people look up to him not because of who he is, but for what he is bonded with. He is uncouth, Veressa, and ill-suited for a life around nobility. After today's theatrics, that should be clear even through your rose-colored vision. An inappropriate word spoken here, an untoward gesture there, and everything you work hard to build will unravel around you." She shook her head. "No. The boy needs to go. For all our sakes. His destiny will be determined according to Harmonic Law." Mariette started to go, then scowled disapprovingly at Veressa, as Izadora often would when she heard of Veressa's behavior. "Sign the proclamation of war, and we can put all of this behind us." With chin held high, the duchess swept out of the chamber.

Veressa stood motionless, fingers combing through Antilles's thick ruff. In the deafening silence, the words of Ourel, vessel and spirit bearer of Earth elemental, echoed from her dream vision the moment she had bonded with the huge white cat. *Everything you hold dear is but desert sand, Veressa. Soon you must choose among many difficult paths. Some would bring you joy, but only at great sorrow to your world. Others you would take alone, bringing great sacrifice and suffering to those you hold dear, but the choice would heal your world from seeds of travesty yet to be sown. You must prepare for the journey ahead.*

She could sense that her time for preparation was over. She was about to take her journey's first step.

Imprisoned

The hours of silent darkness were marked by the rhythmic drip of water in the far corner of Conner's cell while the dank, earthy smells of dampness chewed at his soul. Finally, he spoke. "I'm still not seeing what you find so alluring about dungeons and caves."

"Did you spend the first ten years of your life in a place like this?" came the dragon's deep voice from the next room.

"No."

"I was eleven before my wings were strong enough to fly through the tall shafts to reach the upper surface of my home. And though I can still recall the first time my wings dried in the warm rays of Hemera, caves are the closest I have found to feeling at home."

"Home." Conner repeated the word, letting his head drop back against the cold stone. The smells and sounds of his parents' farm and Creeg's Point flooded back—the aroma of freshly cooked food, the warmth of summer on his face, the sounds of the town square market. He closed his eyes. How he would love to sleep in his bed again, waking to the smell of his mother's breakfast. But he needed to focus on more urgent matters.

"I am sorry for what happened at Thanatos." Conner waited, but when Skye did not reply, he pressed further. "I know how much you revered your god." Conner sensed the slow shift of emotions through his bonding. Skye did not let go of his anger easily, but he could sense the dragon's rage dissipating.

"Shazarack is only mentioned in the first few verses of our dragonsongs. Now that I think about it, nothing there describes why the Ancients flew away. Maybe there was some reason they did not wish to share it with the family."

"Yeah. It's hard to imagine anyone would be happy to discover their creator was a cold-hearted brute. And what kind of incantation was Shazarack trying to use on you?"

There was a long moment of silence before Skye answered. "I could feel him taking control of my body ... and my mind."

Conner inhaled sharply. "That was what happened that day we went on Grimmley's quest to recover the silver box, wasn't it? He was taking control of you. That is why you wouldn't tell me what happened." Skye was uncharacteristically quiet. Conner turned his thoughts inward and sensed the same flow of emotions he had the last time he broached the topic—embarrassment and regret.

"What are you going to do about your queen?" Skye asked.

Skye clearly did not want to talk more about Shazarack, so Conner took the dragon's cue, even though he did not want to talk about Veressa. "There's not much I can do here ... or anywhere for that matter. Defying house arrest, even on the excuse of protecting the queen, would only get me in deeper trouble. I'm pretty useless as her protector."

Conner heard Skye's scales scraping across the stone floor. Sea-blue eyes appeared through the cell bars. "You are being especially hard on yourself."

"Am I?" Conner rubbed his hands together. "The day I exposed the Anarchic plot at Graystone, Grimmley told me that without hard evidence it was foolhardy to accuse an orderman of being a spy. You should have seen him that morning, Skye. Grimmley handled the situation masterfully. And me? I pretty much made a mess of things up there in the reception hall. It seems I learned nothing from all his instruction."

The dragon's hard sniff reverberated off the thick walls. "You are angry because you are not like your Shaman guide? Angry for telling the truth? You told me not that long ago that you did not like playing Harmonic games of lies and deception."

"Well, since you put it that way ..." Conner loved Grimmley dearly, but he had to admit that his preceptor had been a master at twisting the truth to fit his needs. Those skills may have helped them save the queen from Anarchic spies. But if everyone could be trusted to tell the truth, they would not have been necessary. He felt the value of Anarchic life strengthen inside of him.

"Did you ever consider the possibility that you were not created to be a Harmonic?" Skye offered.

Conner was stunned by Skye's question. Was one created to be one or the other? Was it embedded in his makeup? Groegan had told him that Eastlanders had fought with the Anarchists during the Anarchic War. If that was true ...

Skye interrupted Conner from taking that thought further. "You did the right thing."

Conner's self-contempt slowly abated. "Thanks, Skye. I suggest you get some rest. We are late getting back to Wren and Valkere. No doubt, they are worried. First chance we get, we fly to Dragongarde."

Conner woke from a fitful sleep and sat up. The cell was just as dark as it had been when he'd fallen asleep—by his best estimate, just a few hours before. He became aware of someone's presence outside the cell. He had not heard any footsteps. No doubt due to Ranger prowess, masked by frequent snorts and grunts coming from a dragon sleeping in the next room. "This is not a place for you."

"My place is where I wish it to be," a commanding feminine voice spoke back.

Conner chuckled. He formed a fine weave of Fire and Air, and a small flame appeared before him. He pushed it away with his mind, and the flame floated to the middle of the cell like a raft cast out on a gentle lake. He squinted toward the rusty bars at the front of his cell. "Your father was right," he said.

"This is not your fault," came Veressa's voice.

"Isn't it?" Conner shivered in the dampness, rubbing his palms briskly across his cold arms. Whatever incantation he had used to transport back to Graystone had sucked most of the energy from his body. "The king warned me this might happen, and I did not listen. Grimmley warned me as well. Even that strange Wallis Arkman warned me."

"Who?"

Conner started to answer, then bit the words back. He was not sure he knew himself. "It doesn't matter. I wasn't smart enough to see this coming." He squinted toward the door. "Why didn't you tell the duchess and War Council about my mission? Why let them believe I had some ... nefarious purpose? You can't keep this second bonding a secret forever."

"No. And I am sorry for putting you through this, but I will straighten it all out quickly enough. I will have to inform the council before I sign a proclamation of war. But the timing must be right. Despite their vows of silence, nothing will contain the revelation that there has been a dragon bonding in the Anarchic Lands. Once news escapes, it will spread quickly across the realms. Within days, everything will be thrown into turmoil. Can you imagine the fear and panic that will ensue? I need to control this so the orders don't do something irrational, like running headlong into an ill-planned assault."

Veressa reached to grip the bars. But the door gave way to her touch and groaned as it swung wide. "What ...?" she asked. Her hands hovered where the bars had been.

Conner snorted. "Mariette did not see the need to lock me in. I'm sure she would like me to try to escape—then she'd be rid of me." A Champion's duty to the queen was lifelong. Death was the only way out of that responsibility. A rat, flushed out by the noise, scurried across the cell floor. "Besides, where would I go?"

"She wants the war proclamation signed," Veressa whispered, her vocal cords too constricted to speak louder. "She's using you to get my attention. It is an approach mother often used."

Conner could sense Veressa's emotions shifting like sand, doubts swirling inside her. Whatever pressures Mariette was applying, they were having an effect. It was not like Veressa to succumb to pressure from her elders, yet what could he do? He held his hands before him. With just a thought, flames danced along his fingertips. "Finally, I have access to my powers, yet there is nothing I can do to protect you." A mental vision of Grimmley appeared before him in the dark, and he heard the old Shaman's voice in his head. *Don't rattle your brains over your inability to find your powers, boy. You'll find the most formidable challenges you face in life can't be beaten down or snuffed out.* No matter how bleak the situation, his old mentor always had a way of finding a little humor. Conner felt a sharp twist of pain in his gut. How he missed Grimmley's comforting, sometimes whimsical, sayings.

Veressa stepped into the cell, moving toward the light. "I assume you were successful in your mission to find this other dragon-bonded."

"I was. She is at Dragongarde."

Veressa jerked to a stop. "She?"

"Her name is Wren." Conner sensed a sudden shift in Veressa's emotions. She was ... Conner jerked to his feet. "You're jealous?"

Veressa drew her body up taut. Her eyes darted around the room, looking anywhere except at Conner. "Well."

Conner rubbed his head. "But *you* went to Elvenstein to meet a suitor."

"No, Conner. I went to Charmwell to get away from the War Council and their incessant pressure. A parley for a marriage with the Elvenstein prince was a pretense, a ruse. The last thing I wanted was to go to war against the Anarchists while you were there."

Conner felt a flush rising in his face. "Oh."

Veressa stepping closer. "I talked to my father about your promise to him."

Conner swallowed hard. "Was he angry that you knew?"

"No. In fact, he agreed with me. He relinquishes you from your vow."

"Then I have a lot more I need to share with you."

"Like your encounter with a long-dead Necromancer?" Veressa probed.

"It is the truth," Conner said.

"I know it is. I told you before, no matter what, I trust you." She took another step closer. "What else do you need to share?"

"I lived among a band of Anarchists for several days. Veressa, they are a peace-loving people. We should not be going to war with them. For some reason I do not understand, the Anarchic order councils are pushing the lands toward war."

Veressa pressed her palm to his chest. "I wish I knew why. But I am running short on time to discover their reason."

Just as it had in the queen's reception hall before he'd departed on his mission, Conner's heart raced. It was hard to focus on what he needed to say. "Shazarack is the greater threat. He is very powerful, the most powerful orderman I have ever encountered."

Veressa gazed into Conner's eyes. "So what can you do? Fly to Thanatos and singlehandedly take on an entire order along with an army of undead?"

"No," Conner answered. "I know how that would turn out." *Me dead and Skye under his control,* he thought. "It would only help ensure Shazarack's success."

"Then we will address Shazarack and his army if and when they arrive."

Conner shook his head. "That will be too late. He's not the type to rely on any Anarchic forces to come to his aid. So, whatever he's scheming, he's doing it on his own. He would not invade the realms if he wasn't certain he could defeat whatever you send against him. And he won't stop at toppled the Harmonic crowns. Once he has done that, he will return to the Anarchic Lands and subjugate those orders as well."

"For what purpose?"

"To unify the peoples. He envisions creating one nation." Conner saw the confusion in Veressa's eyes and shrugged. "Shazarack believes that the separation of lands is artificial. He told me that there is no Harmonic or Anarchic Sight, that this belief in there being a difference is why the orders are so weak."

"Do you think he can pull it off?"

"I do. He told me that Shan-Grail has some kind of incredible powers. If he gets there, he will use that force to call upon another, more powerful, army than the one he already has."

Veressa pulled her shoulders in, drawing closer in the chill air. "An army more powerful than a thousand undead? What could that be?" She chewed on her lip for a moment, then offered, "I know very little about necromancy, but what if he knows a way to make undead invincible? Or to prolong their life in this plane?"

"Maybe. But that wouldn't be another army. Though it is possible Meera and I misinterpreted his intent." Then Conner had another thought, one more gruesome, more vile than even what Veressa suggested.

Veressa caught his expression of disgust. "What?"

"What if Shazarack can somehow create another army of undead? What if he is able to animate the dead right here in the realms from Shan-Grail?" Conner envisioned the dead digging their way up out of the slime and muck in graveyards all across the Harmonic Realms, and laying siege to castles, descending upon towns, villages, and farming communities. He imagined mothers cradling their babies, running, screaming in terror. "With sufficient power, it's possible Shazarack could summon such a ghastly horde."

"Oh, Conner," Veressa said breathlessly. "I need to take this up with the council. I need to convince them this threat is real."

"And if they don't listen to you?" Conner asked. "I need to go find proof."

Veressa shook her head. "Mariette has already cast suspicions about your mission. My Champion can't just pop in, announce a threat upon my life, and then fly away again. I am sorry, Conner. Until I am certain the council … the tribunal … won't panic when they learn of the true intent of your quest, you are going to have to wait here."

It was well past when Conner had said he would return to Dragongarde. Wren was no doubt beginning to worry. "Every day we wait is a day lost. There has to be another way."

"Let me talk to the council first."

"All right. But if you cannot convince the council, then *I* must do something to stop him."

Veressa lay her hand on the painted image of a dragon on Conner's breastplate. "I understand how important this is. If I don't make any headway, then we will come up with a way to break you out of here." She exhaled hard. "Now, was there anything else you wished to tell me?"

Conner took a deep breath. He felt light-headed and giddy with Veressa so close to him. "That I love you." He waited for what felt like eons, expecting some kind of reaction. But the moments ticked by, and fear seeped into his veins. Had he overstepped his bounds? Had he stirred things into yet a bigger mess?

When Veressa moved, it was sudden. Her hands clutched the hair at the back of his head, and she pulled his face to hers, pressing her mouth to his with a hard groan. The kiss was worlds different from anything Conner had ever imagined possible. There was an eagerness to Veressa's arms, a soft warmth to her lips, a sweetness to the taste of her mouth on his.

Conner's arms snaked around Veressa's waist as the kiss lingered. He pressed his palms to the small of her back, his hunger for her rising as he felt her body respond. At last, Veressa pulled away, leaving him quivering with unspent energy. He recalled that night in Pennington Point, the moment he'd held her, protecting her from the Sorcerer's spell. He'd had to force himself to let her go. He wanted to say something but feared any words would ruin the moment.

"Finally!" thundered a deep dragon voice in the next room.

Veressa jumped at Skye's sudden bellow. Antilles at her side hissed at the dragon.

"It is time you two kissed," Skye rumbled with delight.

Talk about ruining the moment! Conner thought. "Skye, shush and go away." At least Veressa did not know what the dragon had said.

"Okay, but I told you she wants to be your mate." Skye thudded off to a dark recess of the adjoining chamber.

Veressa pressed the back of her shaking hand to her forehead. "I should go. As it is, I won't sleep tonight. And I need to be ready to confront Mariette at first light."

Conner could not find his voice, so he just nodded. He goggled as Veressa floated through the iron portal and vanished into the darkness beyond.

Conner adjusted his armor and, in the morning light, wiped away bits of dirt and grime he had collected in the dungeon. He smelled of sweat, dirt, and worse, but there was nothing he could do about that. His eyes were red and swollen. He had not slept a wink. All he could think about was Veressa's kiss, replaying the glorious moment over and over in his mind.

He had been summoned back to the queen's reception hall, and he would present himself the best he could. The doors swung wide and he strode forward. Veressa was on the dais in a brilliant blue dress, looking as beautiful as he had ever seen her. Her arms were bare; her golden hair gleamed in Hemera's light. Nothing about her presence matched the sense of discouragement he had sensed in her all morning. Conner braced himself for disappointing news.

To her right sat the Duchess Mariette, her hands clasped together before her, chin regally high. Duke Regiboldt, whom Conner recognized from Veressa's coronation as the duchess's husband, stood stiffly nearby. Most of the War Council was missing. In their stead, a number of elder men and women watched him parade in. Tara, the Shaman Don, glared at him from beneath furrowed brow. From their formal dress, Conner surmised they comprised members of the six orders' councils. Now he felt like a man walking to the gallows.

"Majesty," Conner bowed to Veressa after arriving before the dais.

"Highness," Mariette snapped back.

Conner's eyes shifted between Veressa and the duchess, unsure of her meaning.

Mariette moved to stand in front of the throne. "You will address *Princess* Veressa from now on as 'Highness.'" Watching Conner smugly, the duchess sat on the edge of the great oak throne, her forearms on the edges of the armrests. "*I* am the new queen imminent."

Conner glanced up at Veressa. His mouth fell open. "What—" *What have you done, Veressa?* He searched their connection. What he had interpreted as discouragement was something different: fortitude and resolve.

Veressa was unwilling to meet his gaze.

"Kneel before me," Mariette commanded.

Conner took a knee, though his eyes remained on Veressa.

Mariette nodded with smug satisfaction. "Your services as the queen's protector and Champion are no longer needed, young man." She gestured to the female royal guardsman standing to the side.

The guardsman stepped closer and slipped the Champion's amulet from Conner's neck, then handed it to Mariette.

Mariette held the amulet high, letting the morning light sparkle off the ruby. Then she rose. "Gentlemen and ladies, the Tournament of the Realm will be held tomorrow morning. Your advocates must be ready by then."

Grandmaster Ranger Lendfeather rose from his seat. "But Queen Imminent, some of our advocates are not at Graystone. My order will need time—"

"We cannot wait for those you have been training to travel here. Every day puts our realm in further peril. I cannot be crowned queen without a Champion. You have today to choose your advocates. Any order that does not present an advocate on the Field of Contest at Hemera's rise will forfeit our consideration. I hope I have made myself clear on this matter."

"Yes, Queen Imminent." Lendfeather bowed low.

Mariette started to turn, but hesitated. "Grandmaster Lendfeather, it has come to our attention that a certain debt is owed to you regarding some support you provided to the crown. In recognition of your service, once I have signed the proclamation of war, I shall deed to you a hefty portion of the Eastlands."

The Ranger looked as shocked as everyone else in the chamber. He bowed low before Mariette. "Thank you, Queen Imminent. Your recompense is most generous."

Conner rose to his feet. "What?" he shouted. "Eastlanders have lived free of central realm laws for centuries. You cannot do this!"

"I can and I will!" Mariette shouted back, her hands clenched at her side. "The Eastlands have been doing as they please for far too long. In a time of war, they need our royal protection. And we surely don't want a repeat of what happened during the Anarchic War. Grandmaster Ranger Lendfeather will be the region's new baron."

"This is insane!" Conner leered at the stunned faces in the hall. Veressa shook her head at him, and he felt waves of warnings coming through to him. But he was too incensed to heed them. "You cannot use my homeland as a bargaining chip to garner support for your war. The Anarchists are not your enemy! It is Shazarack you must prepare for."

"That is *enough*!" Mariette was livid. "How dare you talk to me so? I will have no heresy in my court! Young man, you are hereby banished from Griffinrock!"

Veressa shifted forward. "What? Auntie, you promised—"

"I promised the boy would be released unharmed. I said nothing about him continuing to live within our lands. I will not have him speaking to me in that way!" Mariette turned to Conner. "If you are ever found within this realm, you will be summarily arrested. Is that clear?" She flicked her hands at the guards. "See that he leaves Graystone immediately!"

Conner glanced over at Veressa and saw her face filled with anguish. Before he could say anything more, two guards gripped him by his arms. He did not fight them. But he did twist his head to glance over his shoulder, unable to tear his eyes from Veressa until the doors slammed behind him.

As the guards shepherded him across the main yard, Conner caught a glimpse of Ballett heading toward the main gate. "Ballett!" he called out. With some effort, he convinced the guards to let him speak to the captain, though they refused to leave his side.

"Conner? What is this?" Ballett asked.

"Mariette has banished me from the realm."

"I am sorry to hear that," Ballett said. "I too have been disgracefully removed from my duties and have been told to leave. I don't know what to do. I have no way to care for my family."

"Then maybe it is time you got away from Graystone and saw the realms. It is what you always wanted to do, right?" Conner leaned close so the guards could not hear him. "Go to my bedchamber. In the closet is an old medicine box. Inside, you'll find a small sack of coins. It's not much, but it's enough to keep you and your family in good health for several years."

"Conner, I could not."

"Please, Ballett." Conner gripped the man's shoulder. "I have no need for coin where I am going."

Ballett chewed on his lip, then nodded. "Thank you, Conner. I will never forget what you have done for me."

"There is one thing. Have you seen Kriston?"

"I've been looking for the boy ever since I received news of your arrest. But no one has seen him."

"If you do—" Conner started.

"I will look after him like he is my own," Ballett promised. "He is a good lad. You have done right by him."

"Conner." One of the guards gripped his arm again. "I'm sorry, but we cannot lose our positions as well."

Conner waved farewell to Ballett and let the guards march him to the stairwell that led to the castle dungeon.

"It's time to go, Skye. I hope you're ready," Conner growled when he reached the dragon's chamber.

"More than ready," Skye snorted. "I sense a lot of anger in you. I take it your gathering of bipedal aristocrats did not go well."

"You could say that." The duchess had manipulated Conner into anger. Once again, he'd stepped into a steaming pile. Groegan was right—everything the Barbarian had said would happen was coming true.

But Conner had no time to consider what it meant for the Eastlands to be under baron rule. He needed to focus on stopping Shazarack from invading the realms. Like so many times before, he just needed to figure out how to make it happen.

This Is No Game

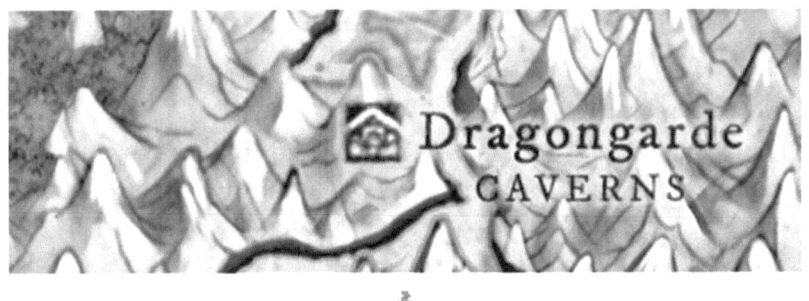

"**W**ren?" Conner called as he hopped from the saddle. But the fortress felt empty and hollow.

"I do not sense Valkere either," Skye added.

Conner walked to Dragongarde's main entrance and placed his fists on his hips. Squinting to shade his face, he stared off into the midday light. Light shimmered off Lake Arastone. If Valkere had been in the fortress, Skye would have heard him. "Maybe they went down to visit Allisor. Let's go see."

A few minutes later, Skye fluttered to a rest in the middle of the army camp.

Conner found Marcantos. "Have you seen Wren?"

Marcantos slapped his palm over his heart, then bowed to Conner. "She was here this morning talking to Allisor. But I have not seen her since."

Conner wished Marcantos would stop saluting him. It was unsettling to have the man he'd defeated hold some kind of deep-seated reverence for him now.

Allisor stepped into the clearing. "Where is Wren?" she asked.

"Just what I wanted to know," Conner replied.

"She should be with you."

"How so?" Conner asked.

"This morning, she mentioned being concerned that you had not returned from Thanatos as expected last night. She said she was going looking for you."

"She said she would wait for me! Surely, she wouldn't be rash enough to fly to Thanatos."

Allisor shrugged. "Then you do not know her well. Wren seldom does what she says. Besides, she seemed certain she would find you somewhere on the way there."

Conner searched the cloudy sky overhead, hoping beyond hope to glimpse Valkere's black form. *Nothing.* Hemera was already starting its descent. If they left now, they might reach Thanatos before dark. "Let's fly, Skye."

"Conner, wait." Meera came forward and shoved a bowl of steaming stew at him. "You do not need to be falling off your dragon before you get there." She gave him a concerned smile.

"Thanks." With his first bite, he realized he had not eaten in more than a day. Chewing was a luxury he could not afford, so he shoveled the chunks of elk and vegetables into his mouth as fast as possible. Someone came up behind him and slipped a flask of water over his shoulder. With his mouth still full, he mumbled thanks, climbed into the saddle, and waved good-bye as Skye climbed into the afternoon sky.

The flight to Thanatos seemed twice as long as the first. Conner spent a great deal of the time chewing on his lip and conceiving of ways he might help Skye fly faster, but the only sensible idea he devised was to hunker low on the dragon's back. Before them, along the eastern horizon, ominous black clouds billowed, accentuated by occasional flickers of lightning. Behind, Hemera sank into the west. As the hours slipped past, glowing white clouds turned yellow, then orange, and finally to deep reds, a stark contrast to the blackness ahead. Still, there was no sign of Wren.

It was deep into dusk when Skye drew Conner from his worried thoughts. "There!" the dragon shouted.

Conner squinted, but gloom of night kept him from seeing much more than the round hill where Thanatos sat like an ebony crown, dark and still. His anticipation churned into impatience as Skye glided toward the city. As they neared, Conner noted that the gates of the fortress were swung wide. No lights, no movement, no life. His eyes traced along the dirt road before them. A flash of lightning revealed a motionless form lying a hundred yards from the gates. Conner tensed.

Skye settled near the figure, rocking to the side as a blast of wind whipped around them.

"Wren!" Conner leaped off and ran to her.

Wren lay supine beside the dirt road. Her arms and legs were spread wide, wrists and ankles bound and staked to the ground. Her eyes were closed.

Conner glanced about. "Skye, do you see Valkere?" A bolt of lightning to the west was followed by a deep crackle of thunder rolling across the valley.

"No, but I will look." The dragon vanished into the black, churning sky.

"Wren," Conner whispered. He leaned closer, and felt a pulse in her wrist, faint and fast.

She moaned, barely audible over the trees groaning in the wind.

"Wren!" Conner nearly shouted with joy. He fumbled nervously with a knife he removed from his belt and worked at sawing through the thick leather straps that held her down.

"Conner?" Wren rasped. She tried to lift her head, but it bobbed like a cork in the water.

Reaching down, he gently scooped her into his arms just as the first large raindrops pelted his back.

Wren wrapped her arms tight about his neck and began to tremble. "Valkere," she wept.

"Where is Valkere, Wren?"

"Gone."

"Gone where? Is Shazarack inside Thanatos?"

"No." Wren's body spasmed. "He has gone. Shazarack took him. I cannot feel him anymore."

Skye fluttered to a rest near Conner. "Valkere is nowhere nearby."

"I am sorry to ask this of you, my friend, but I need to get Wren back to Dragongarde. She's in pain and I don't know how to help. I am hoping someone there will."

Skye's eyes burned bright, lighting the ground around them. "And Valkere?" A streak of lightning coursed over their heads.

Conner's eyes cast west, toward the eastern fringes of the mountain range. "I have a pretty good idea where Shazarack is going. But I don't want to risk another encounter with him just yet. Not like this."

Skye roared, underscored by a boom of thunder that shook the ground. Anger seared through Conner's mind. "We can take him!"

"If he has taken control of Valkere, he could force the dragon to defend him." Conner looked down at Wren. "We would both hate for you to be forced to kill her bond. We are going to need a different plan."

"Fine!" Skye bawled. "But Shazarack is no longer my god!"

Conner chewed on his fingernails as he paced before the tent entrance for more than an hour. Several had gathered around a campfire nearby, huddled in the cool, predawn air and speaking in hushed tones. Conner could make out Marcantos standing with arms folded, staring into the dancing flames. Allisor sat on a log nearby crying, as she had been since he'd returned with Wren. Others gathered at the fringes of the fire's light, including a rugged-looking Alpslander Conner had not met, who sat scratching the back of his grizzly bond.

Despite their incessant questions, especially regarding where Valkere was and why Wren had arrived unconscious though there was nothing physically wrong with her, Conner refused to say anything until he knew more about Wren's condition.

At last, Meera emerged from the tent, looking as exhausted as Conner felt, her mink bond trotting by her side.

"Is there anything you can do for her?" Conner asked impatiently.

"Keep her comfortable is all." Meera waved her hands in frustration and hopelessness. "Conner, I am a Necromancer, not a Shaman. We concern ourselves with the afterlife, not the living. You say her bond is not dead, but I know the symptoms of the Yearning when I see them. Even a wounded bond would not cause such dire manifestations as Wren has. And Valkere is already a drake, so he is not molting. When are you going to tell us what is going on?"

Conner pressed his lips together. "Let's return to the fire. It's time I shared a few things with all of you." As he and Meera neared, Marcantos, Allisor, and the hulky Alpslander gathered about, concern reflected in their eyes.

Conner squared his shoulders at the Alpslander and pressed his palm to his heart. "May the mountains always be the bedrock of your strength."

"May the snow be your blood," the Alpslander responded with a gleaming smile. "I am Gertrum Smelterman of the Gilstadt region, and

Harmonic guildmaster Scouter ... well, once I was. And that is Targon." Gertrum waved his arm at the huge grizzly at his side.

"Smelterman," Conner repeated. "I know that name. You traveled with the Ranger Loris on her mission through the Dragon's Back Mountains."

Gertrum puffed out his chest with pride. "I was leader of the patrol that arrived in time to help secure your release from those heathen Anarchic ..." The Scouter cleared his throat, his eyes darting toward Meera. Annabelle had narrated to Conner how Smelterman and his band of Scouters had fought the Barbarians that had taken Conner and Skye captive, and had helped Annabelle apprehend Meera. "Well, times are changing, as they say. When I arrived, Marcantos asked me why I left my post and responsibilities scouting for Dreadcreek. Just to be clear, I never did much like the commander, Grandmaster Ranger Lendfeather. It was bad enough when he was around, but things *really* went south at the outpost once he left to be on the queen's War Council. Anyway, as an Alpslander, it is an honor to be of service to the great Dragonbonded. My patrol and I have come to offer whatever assistance we might to this unruly band of misfits and deserters."

Marcantos spoke softly. "Meera, Allisor, and Gertrum have agreed to be my aides, so they should hear whatever you have to share."

Conner turned his attention to the group. "Very well. Most of you know that I flew to Thanatos and spoke to the Necromancer Shazarack. I will tell you more about what he and I discussed. But first, I want to fill you in on what happened afterward. When I departed Thanatos, I traveled to Graystone, where I tried to convince the queen that Shazarack is planning to invade the realms."

Marcantos's eyes widened. "I assume that without hard proof, that did not go so well."

"No." Conner waited for the swell of anger to pass. "But there is more. Veressa is no longer queen of Griffinrock."

Marcantos flinched, his hands clenched into fists. "What?" he exploded, drawing the attention of others around the camp.

"Mariette has assumed the throne," Conner went on in a hushed tone. "And as soon as she has her new Champion and is crowned, she will declare war on the Anarchists."

Marcantos leaned closer. "I feel the need to understand how this could happen, but that is for another time. This is more troubling than just a war."

Gertrum scratched at his chin. "A powerful Necromancer poised to attack the realms while the crowns and Harmonic orders put all their resources into a war with the Anarchic Lands—that isn't troubling enough?"

Marcantos's glare was intense. "Not for us." He gestured at the tents and fires burning about them. "Meera and I have had our hands full keeping this band together. We can't just dispel five hundred years of loathing into smoke. News that war between our lands is now imminent could cleave us in two. It is one thing to believe war is possible; another to know it is on the way. Some may decide to return and fight for their homelands."

"Hmm." Gertrum ran his fingers through his grizzly bond's pelt. "Then I suggest we keep this a secret until we are certain the rest can handle it."

Conner glanced away. More secrets. Still, he was forced to agree with the Scouter's suggestion. "Now, about Wren." He gestured toward Meera.

"Wren is suffering from the initial stages of the Yearning."

Allisor stifled back a sniffle. "Valkere is dead?"

"No," Conner answered. "Valkere was kidnapped ... by Shazarack."

"Kidnapped?" Marcantos asked. "How exactly does one go about kidnapping a dragon?"

"Not sure how to describe it." Conner rubbed at the back of his head. "When I attempted to leave Thanatos, Shazarack used some kind of powerful incantation to get Skye to submit to his will. I don't know exactly how he did it, but he has taken control of Wren's dragon." He looked over at Meera, hoping she might offer some explanation.

"Shazarack is very powerful," Meera offered with a shrug. "I do not know the bounds of his abilities."

"What does he need with a dragon?" Gertrum asked.

"Shazarack will use Valkere to find an entrance to a tunnel built by the Modei that runs beneath the mountain range. The shaft leads to the ancient city of Shan-Grail."

"How do you know what he plans?" Marcantos asked.

"Because Shazarack wanted to use Skye for just that task."

Marcantos's gaze shifted to the tent where Wren slept. "And why would he leave Wren alive?"

"He expected Conner to find her," Meera interjected. "I suspect he wants Conner to know just where he is going."

Conner nodded. "When I met him at Thanatos, he mentioned repeatedly that he and I were connected. He looked … surprised when I refused to help him attack the realms."

Meera huffed. "He has a powerful sway over those around him. Maybe he thought you would be equally spellbound. It is likely he still holds hope that you will assist him in dismantling the three realms."

The dark cloud of anger rolled across Conner's mind again. He might well be banished from his home, family, and the woman he loved. But he would never help someone destroy it all. "Either that or he's baiting me to come to Shan-Grail to try and stop him."

"Maybe he wants Skye as well," Meera offered. "Two dragons under his command could do a lot of damage."

"How are you going to stop him?" Allisor asked after a long silence.

Conner shook his head. "I don't know yet."

Marcantos leaned in, an eager gleam in his eye. "The army is the only way to stop him," he suggested.

Conner shook his head. "No, Marcantos. I will do this alone."

Marcantos started to argue, but Meera stepped between them. "Marcantos, look at Conner."

Marcantos blinked and stepped back. "What?"

Meera gestured at Conner. "Look how gaunt he looks. He has not slept in several days. He needs to rest before any of us can offer up a plan for how to get Wren's dragon back … or how to stop Shazarack."

"Yes. Of course, you are right," Marcantos said. "Thank you."

Meera turned to Conner. "Conner, the sedative I gave Wren will help her sleep until this afternoon, if not later. She needs to be part of any plan, but first she needs rest for her mind to mend. Go to Dragongarde and sleep. We will prepare a great meal. This evening, we will sit together and come up with a way to stop Shazarack and get Valkere back. Okay?"

Conner wanted to argue that time was critical, but he was not sure he had the energy. He nodded instead. "Skye is exhausted as well."

Conner slept restlessly through the morning. By noon, he was up. He returned to Dragongarde's main entrance, where, with Skye stretched out at his side, they watched the flow of life along the Valley of Souls. He was worried about Wren. What if he could not get Valkere back? He recalled the story of how Karlana Landcraft had lost her bond, a powerful eagle, and how the Yearning had taken her mind. Karlana was sweet, but the town could trust her with no more responsibility than to care for injured animals. Would that happen to Wren? *No. I will not allow it,* he vowed to himself.

His eyes shifted to where smoke rose from Marcantos's camp. The number of tents and campfires had nearly doubled since he and Wren had first flown down there—just a few days ago. By his best estimate, more than sixty ordermen and guildsmen now filled the ranks. And while most were Anarchic, Harmonics made up a growing minority. Conner had watched them milling in the predawn light while Meera cared for Wren. They did not intermingle much, though they all were friendly, even talking and laughing occasionally. Harmonics and Anarchists living and sleeping in the same camp. Conner shook his head in disbelief. If he had not seen it himself, he would not have believed it possible. What was Marcantos teaching them that would overcome five hundred years of hatred, mistrust, and differences? Could it be that the ex-Warrior was not as mad as Conner had first thought?

No. Conner still caught the madness reflected in the man's wild stare. The same stare as the day Conner had stepped onto the tourney field to stop him from becoming Veressa's Champion.

Veressa. Conner closed his eyes and swallowed hard. The gentle passion of her mouth on his, the smell of lavender in her hair, the taste of her warm lips lingered in his mind. Relinquished from his promise to King Jonath, he could finally unchain his feelings for her. *I love her,* he thought. It was a freeing thought that made his spirit soar. *And I know she loves me too. But will I ever see her again?*

So why had she capitulated to her aunt? Why would she ever surrender the crown of Griffinrock to that black-hearted woman? No threat the duchess might have exacted on Veressa would have broken her. There had to be something else. It had been *her* choice. He relived the meager moments they'd spent together in the dungeon, trying to look beyond the exhilaration of having her in his arms. With a clinical eye that would have made Grimmley proud, he searched for clues. But she had given him no hint of her decision then. That meant she had made it after she'd left. He recalled something she'd said when he was hauled before the new queen that morning. *Auntie, you promised—*

"Promised?" Conner asked himself aloud. "Veressa, what did your aunt promise you?"

As soon as he voiced the question, he knew the answer. A cold numbness flooded over him. Veressa had given up the throne for *him*, to release him from his duties as her Champion, to set him free from the detention that his own actions had put him in, all so he could stop Shazarack. *No!* he shouted to himself. Conner pressed the heels of his palms to his eyes as the tears surged forth.

"Conner?" Skye's worried voice came at his side.

"All of this is my fault." Conner explained. "I was the one who revived Shazarack, the one who caused Grimmley's death, the one responsible for Morgas's capture ... and now, the one who brought down the one who might have become the greatest queen in Griffinrock's long and illustrious history."

"Of course, you are right," Skye agreed, a little quicker than Conner expected. Skye tilted his head back and snort-sniffed. "You were also the one who stopped the Assassin from sitting at your queen's side, the one who released the Necromancer Asheborne, the one who found the second dragon-bonded, and the one who is now bringing together bipedal combatants from both sides." Skye's head swiveled to be in front of Conner. "Just as you will be the one who stops the Necromancer and reunites Valkere with Wren."

Conner reached out and patted Skye's neck. He slowed his breathing, focusing on the dragon's words. "You are right, Skye. I will not let Veressa's sacrifice be in vain." He wiped the tears away. "I need to focus on Shazarack and Valkere."

"Then let us find a way to do that. Knowing you, I am sure you have a plan."

Conner adjusted his armor. "Surprisingly not. However, Grimmley told me once that sometimes when you run out of ideas, you just need to go back to the basics—that they are the true seeds to solving a perplexing problem." He slapped Skye on the side as he headed across the main chamber. "Come with me."

Skye poked his head into the small chamber Conner led him to. Then he looked at his bond sitting in a chair behind a table. "Conner, now is not the time for games."

Conner waved his hand over the golden wheel atop the table. "This is no game, Skye. It is a training tool. I used this wheel to practice drawing upon the elementals before I faced Marcantos—" Conner's voice caught, his eyes frozen on the far wall.

"What?"

Conner moved to the wall. "I can read these hieroglyphs! Well, some of them." He ran his hand in a slow spiral over a few dozen symbols. "These describe how to draw upon and use the elementals. And I think this details what I did to defeat Marcantos." He backed away and waved his hand before the wall. "It's all here, Skye. If I had known then how to read Modeic, I could have saved myself a lot of frustration trying to find my powers." Something caught his attention on the side wall. He moved closer. Placing his forefinger over one of the glyphs, he looked at Skye. "This symbol. It means 'ascension.'" His eyes flittered over the glyphs surrounding it. "This is some kind of instruction for ascending."

"What does that mean?"

"Do you remember shortly after we bonded when I asked you what you knew of the Dragonbonded? You told me bonding didn't make one a Dragonbonded. You said your dragonsongs described how the Dragonbonded had to complete some kind of test before they were accepted into their order. And those who failed were exiled."

Skye tilted his head and peered at the squiggly figures and symbols. "And you think this tells you how to do this test?"

"I do." Conner skimmed the glyphs, decoding aloud what he could. "Cosmic Star ... cradle ... great powers." *Great powers? What if this will help me defeat Shazarack?* Excited, he started over, bringing his full attention to bear. "'A spiritual journey of great power can only be taken cradled in the tender bosom of the Cosmos.'" *Bosom of the Cosmos?* "'What you take will be lost. What you leave behind will be found.' Okay. This is about as helpful as those crazy sayings Layna had me translating at Grimmley's cottage."

Conner moved farther along the wall to stand before a scene depicting two knights in full body armor standing guard before a massive gate. The walls of the fortress were solid, as if they had been cut from granite. In the background rose a tall tower amid a number of shorter buildings, all made from the same granite. The image looked familiar, reminding him of stories he heard growing up about Tatem Creeg. "Shan-Grail," he whispered. Beneath the image were more Modeic glyphs. He bent his mind on them.

"What does it say?" Skye asked with more interest than Conner was used to.

Conner continued to squint in deep concentration at the hieroglyphs, then shook his head. "Something about truths and lies being beliefs." He pointed at one image with wavy lines. "And freedom." He examined the symbols a few minutes longer. "I'm not sure what it says."

He walked over to Skye and patted the dragon's snout. "We had better head down to the camp and see how Wren is."

An Army Is Born

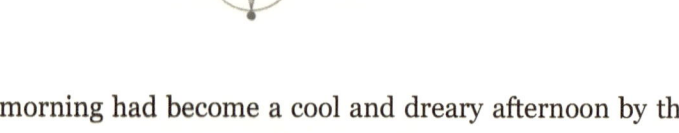

The cloudless morning had become a cool and dreary afternoon by the time Conner and Skye arrived back at the camp, an autumn chill settling in and rustling the browning leaves in the canopy of trees about them.

"How is Wren?" Conner asked Meera, who had taken up a makeshift chair outside Wren's tent.

Meera squinted up, examining the haggard young man before her with hands on her hips. Morgana was asleep next to her. "Sleep has helped. As expected, she has moments of lucidity between bouts of confusion. And she is still exhausted." She leaned forward, then sniffed. "Conner, you smell like an ancient tomb. Might I suggest while Wren sleeps that you take some time to freshen up? It just might help your temperament."

Conner raised his arm and took a whiff. "Oh," he winced. "I think you're right." With a promise to return, he lumbered to the edge of the lake, where he shed all his armor. A breeze had picked up, nipping him to the bone, so he ran naked into the water, then dove in headfirst. The cold, clear water took his breath. He swam to keep the chill away, but slowly, his body acclimated to the cold and he relaxed, floating, his mind wandering freely over his troubles. Suddenly, Skye's head burst from the water next to him. Conner screamed, then splashed the dragon in the face with a swift kick. "Don't scare me like that!"

Skye snort-sniffed, then splashed the surface with his tail, sending a wave over Conner that made him turn somersaults.

Conner came up coughing and choking, but it quickly became a fit of laughter. "Oh, you're going to get it now." He chased the dragon around in the water, trying to come up with ways to pay Skye back. It took nearly an hour for Conner to concede defeat to the dragon's better aquatic agility and speed. Then he washed all the previous night's slime and dungeon muck from the armor and donned the suit, surprised at how quickly it dried. Reinvigorated, with Skye at his side, he went back to the camp whistling and singing "The Sweetest Smelling Roses Grow in Manure."

"You were right, Meera," Conner said. "Thank you for the suggestion." His eyes locked on the tent flaps. "While I was swimming, I thought about this more. And there's something I don't understand."

"What is that?" Meera asked, stifling back a wide yawn. Morgana rose and bounded off into the woods.

"I spent a week away from Skye when I went looking for Wren. I missed him, yes. But I never felt the Yearning."

"So why is Wren so inflicted?" Meera pulled her shoulders up. "It is clearly more than distance. Whatever Shazarack used to take control of her bond, it had to be very powerful." She rose, arching her back with a low groan. "But I have to hope that if you get Valkere back, Wren will recover."

Conner did not move as he thought back to the night Shazarack had tried taking Skye from him, and the intense pain he'd felt. He thought of mentioning it to Meera. But then he noted her gaunt eyes and disheveled hair, so he took the conversation in a different direction. "Why are you here?"

Meera blinked, her head snapping back at his question.

"I hope it was not out of some sense of obligation to me for letting you go."

"No, Conner." She took a slow breath, rubbing her palms together. "After Skye took me to the Borderlands, as I said before, I returned to Thanatos as promised. But it was not the same city I had left. Everyone wanted to use me for their own gain. Shazarack had transformed the city in ways I had not imagined were possible. Everyone near him has been drawn into his ... dream. He has a power to persuade. I felt his influence sucking me into it. Even though I hated what I saw, I hated more what he wanted me to become, what I was being transformed into. I heard voices in my head, judging me, criticizing my every thought. I was being influenced, used. And that frightened me more than the vision he wants to create." Meera dropped her head. "So I ran."

"But that doesn't explain why you are *here*. Why not go home?"

Meera shook her head. "When an Anarchist is adopted into an order, the village they come from must forsake them. An orderman has no parents, has no home. Like life, there is no returning to what once was, no matter which place you call home."

Banished, orphaned, Conner could not agree more.

Meera placed her hand lightly on his arm. "Conner, I do not want you to think I came here because I had nowhere else to go. Shazarack is unimaginably powerful, and nothing will deter him from making his dream a reality. I came here to warn you of his scheme; I stay because I believe in your cause."

Satisfied, he gestured toward the tent. "Then I thank you, Meera, for all you have done for us."

Meera pointed at the tent. "She needs to be part of any talks involving getting Valkere back, so do not stress her, and keep your conversation short." With that, she headed toward the camp.

Conner took a deep breath. Bending low, he slipped into the canvas tent. The room was dark and cramped, with little more than a cot made from furs stretched between two oak branches. A rough-cut hickory bole served as the pillar for the center. Wren was awake on the cot, rocking, her knees pulled to her chin. Conner crept forward. He eased onto the cot next to her; she did not seem to notice. He reached out and touched her arm. "Wren?" he whispered.

Slowly, her eyes focused on him. Leaning forward, she clutched him around the shoulders. "Conner, it is good to know you are well."

"How are you feeling?" he asked, lightly hugging her back.

"I had such a horrible dream." Wren's arms constricted around his shoulders, and she placed her cheek on his chest. "I was looking for you when a mob came out of the night. They grabbed me, held me. Their faces were a blur. And the smell ... I scuffled with them, but others in gray cloaks appeared and they held me down. They wanted to take something from me. I fought to break free, but ..." Her body quivered.

"It's okay, Wren," Conner soothed, not wanting to excite her. "I am here. I won't let anyone hurt you."

Wren relaxed. Her breathing slowed, though she continued to hold him tight. "Thank you, Conner. I could not ask for a better companion."

As Conner continued to hold her, he realized how much they had in common. They had both lost so much—their family, their home, their friends. *Companion*, he thought. Yes. "No matter what happens, we will stick together." Still, she had lost so much more. "We will get through this, Wren."

"What of your queen?" she asked, not letting go of him. "Will you go back to her?"

In the rush of so much happening, Conner had nearly forgotten that when he'd left Wren to see Shazarack, they had fought. Wren was still worried he would leave her. "I am no longer the queen's Champion. I am free from that oath."

"So, you will not fight with the Harmonics?"

"No. Veressa and I were trying to keep war at bay." He wanted to tell her that Griffinrock had a new queen who hungered for revenge for her sister's death, that war was inevitable. But he feared that would upset her.

"And what of us? I know your heart lies with your homeland. If there is war, can you and I still be friends?"

Conner gently pulled her away and searched her hazel eyes, wide with uncertainty. He would need a strong relationship with Wren if they were to stop Shazarack and get Valkere back. "We will always be friends, Wren. Let's make an oath right now. We will not take part in their war. We stay out of it. I am no longer Harmonic. Will you agree to no longer be Anarchic?"

Wren grinned. "Yes. We will both remain free of their conflict."

Conner recalled hearing that it had taken years for the first Dragonbonded to be drawn into the Anarchic War. Had they had similar conversations? Had they made promises too? And if so, what had happened to change their minds? He reached out and placed his hands on her arms. "Now that we agree to that, let's get Valkere back."

"Valkere?" Wren looked confused, as if she had never heard the name before. Then her face softened. "Yes. Valkere."

"Wren, we will get him back. I will stop Shazarack and force him to release Valkere."

"How will you do that?" Her lower lip quivered.

"I have an idea, but I should share that with the others as well."

That evening, after supper, Conner, Wren, Meera, Marcantos, Allisor, and Gertrum huddled close around the fire to stave off an autumn chill. Conner leaned even closer and spoke in a hushed tone. "Skye and I are going to fly to Shan-Grail. With Skye standing guard, I will enter the ancient city and wait. Then I'll use my powers to stop Shazarack when he arrives."

Marcantos stared back at him like he had just spoken in Dragon. Lips pressed together, he snapped the twig he had been holding in half and threw the pieces on the fire. "That is so vague and ill-conceived, I don't even know where to begin to argue."

"Let me explain," Conner said. Unfortunately, he had to agree with Marcantos's assessment, which was why he needed their expertise to help him fill it in. "When I met with Shazarack, he said the ancient city held some kind of great power. He plans to use that power to invade the realms. If I can reach the city before he does and access those powers first, I believe I can stop him." Images painted on the wall at Dragongarde, of Dragonbonded ascending, filled his mind. He had to believe that ascension would give him access. "If these powers are potent enough for Shazarack to invade the realms, then maybe they're enough for me to stop him."

"And if you fail?" Meera asked. "What happens if you cannot get into the city or figure out how to use Shan-Grail's powers in time?" Conner did not answer, so she went on. "Not only will Shazarack move forward with his invasion, Wren will not get her dragon back. Maybe he will take Skye as well."

Conner knew he was taking a big risk, but having Meera state it so clearly ...

"Do I have to be the one to say it?" Marcantos interrupted Conner's thoughts, glaring fiercely at him. "There is no way you can defeat an army of undead *and* half the Necromancers Order, not to mention a reanimated ancient Necromancer, *alone*. Why are you being so stubborn?"

"Marcantos, I know what you're thinking. But—"

Marcantos jumped from his stump. "Then do not make me beg!" he shouted.

Conner saw a number of people at nearby campfires looking their way. "I know nothing about leading an army," he said softly. He turned to Meera and Gertrum, hoping to garner support, but they glared back at him expectantly. *They want me to take command too! Marcantos's madness is contagious!* Conner shook his head. He leaned forward to say more, but Wren's pleading expression caught his eye.

She reached over and gripped his hand tight. "I believe in you, Conner."

"Conner," Meera said. "Since I arrived here, I have been working with Marcantos on something important. He has uncovered a new way of sight, neither Anarchic nor Harmonic, but *both*. And he has been training everyone here how to ..." She glanced over at Marcantos. "What did you call it?"

"Being Aware."

Meera went on. "Once I understood what Marcantos was suggesting, I realized something. This is why Shazarack is so powerful. It is consistent with how he trained me on improving my own skills. It may explain how those in the orders before the Great War were so powerful. The ancient ordermen may have accessed their powers through being Aware. That is why I have been working with Marcantos, supplementing what Shazarack taught me with his approach. With enough time, this can be taught to anyone who manipulates elementals—ordermen and guildsmen alike."

Having met Shazarack, Conner could not refute Meera's supposition. In fact, Shazarack had made a similar reference to Sight.

Conner took in each hopeful gaze. Each was here for a different reason. Wren needed Valkere back. Gertrum needed to atone for his Alpslander ancestors. Meera was running from a home that was no more. And Marcantos ... Conner still was not quite sure of his story. And the truth was that he needed them as much as they needed him. "Okay. But this is only until Shazarack is defeated. And I'm expecting a lot from all of you if we're ever going to manage this disorderly gaggle of rebels."

Beaming smiles broke out around the fire.

Marcantos nearly knocked Conner from his stump with a cheery slap to his back. "That's the spirit!"

"Celebration is a bit premature, *General*. It seems we suddenly have the problem of getting nearly a hundred people to Shan-Grail before Shazarack arrives."

Marcantos popped from his stump. "Then let us retire to my tent, where we can strategize our next step in privacy."

After shooing Targon out of the tent to make room for everyone, Gertrum squinted at the map sprawled across the table in Marcantos's tent. It was an ancient one that showed the seven great realms before the Anarchic War. "Does anyone even know where Shan-Grail is? It was called the Lost City for a reason."

"I know about where it is." Conner offered. Calling up the map image painted on the wall in Dragongarde, he placed his forefinger on a point marking the highest peak in the mountain range. "The River Tresdan starts here, south of Dragongarde." He traced the river southwest until he reached a place where the river turned sharp to the south, then back to the northwest. "Somewhere in here," he said, tapping a spot by a crook in the river.

Marcantos grunted, then made a mark with a quill pen. He looked at Meera across from him. "How long will it take for Shazarack to reach Shan-Grail?"

Meera chewed at her lip. "I will have to make some assumptions. Let us assume that Shazarack does not lose any time finding the entrance once he reaches the mountains, and that the tunnels running beneath the mountains are straight ... and that he will not lose his way while in there. The Necromancers will ride at night to the entrance. Let us assume they will continue on foot from there, since horses would be useless underground." Her eyes skimmed the length of the map. "That is about two hundred miles on horse from Thanatos to the mountains, then another three hundred on foot through the tunnels."

Marcantos rubbed his chin. "The best an army can do at a forced march pace is thirty miles a day. That's a week just getting to the entrance."

Meera shook her head. "Except this army is undead. They are not so encumbered, do not eat, and can run at speeds of a galloping horse for hours without tiring. They will travel at night when their strength is greatest. That will put them at the tunnel entrance by tomorrow morning."

Gertrum whistled. "I personally have never crossed paths with such a fierce adversary. Now I am glad I have not. And you say Shazarack commands more than a thousand of these creatures?" His face slackened. "There is no way the realms could assemble a force fast enough to withstand such an invasion."

Marcantos studied the others with pursed lips, his arms folded tight across his chest. "Even if they could marshal the necessary forces, an army of undead would outmaneuver them. Undead could ransack entire cities and be gone before troops could be dispatched."

Conner tensed. He recalled the night he had broken into the Shamans' temple to see Meera, and his encounter with just one of these undead. *Fierce* did not seem adequate to describe what the undead assassin could do. And, according to Grimmley, it had been near the end of its existence.

For the first time, he understood just what was at stake. This was not just about getting Valkere back or getting information about Grimmley's killers. The entire Harmonic Realms and Anarchic Lands were in serious danger.

As if Meera could read Conner's mind, she added, "That is why Conner cannot face Shazarack alone."

In the lantern light, Conner scanned the expressions of his compatriots. The realization of what they were about to confront was overwhelming. No matter how great their skill was, a hundred of them just might not be enough.

"Without horses," Meera continued, "the Necromancers will slow the necro-army. Also, every four or five days, they will need to replenish the incantations binding the spirits to their bodies. Once they enter the tunnels, they will need ... another ten days to reach Shan-Grail. Maybe twelve."

Gertrum stroked his beard. "So, we need to reach Shan-Grail in less than ten days. And we are, what, a hundred miles away?"

"Our problem isn't distance," Marcantos answered. "It's speed."

Gertrum nodded. "What is the quickest route to Shan-Grail?"

"What if we travel east and use Skye to find the entrance Shazarack is looking for?" Conner asked.

Gertrum shook his head. "That would put us several days behind him with no easy way to catch up. Besides, I don't like the idea of battling an army of undead in a tunnel with incantations that could bring the mountains down on top of us all. That's a suicide mission."

"Not to mention," Marcantos added, "Farlorde is between us and the eastern end of the mountains. The Barbarians in our army would not take kindly to being forced to fight their way through their ex-comrades."

"Then that will be our route of last resort," Meera said.

"What about a forced march west?" Gertrum suggested. "Then use Conner's dragon to find another entrance along the northern fringes of the mountain range."

"How do you know there's one there?" Meera asked.

Gertrum jabbed a finger at a point north of Shan-Grail. "If the Modei could excavate a tunnel three hundred miles to the eastern rim, it stands to reason they would have done the same to the north and south."

"That makes sense," Marcantos agreed. "But there is a problem with that as well. News of Griffinrock's new queen signing the proclamation of war will have reached the outposts along the Borderlands in a few days. Ember's Keep will be on heightened alert. That means more patrols scouting the region. You can't just sneak a hundred people over the border without someone noticing."

"Let me be clear on this." Conner stared intently at each person there. "I will take no action that puts anyone else's lives in jeopardy. We will not march east *or* west if that means getting into a battle with Harmonic or Anarchic forces."

Wren reached over and squeezed Conner's hand.

Gertrum snorted in frustration. "Then that leaves just one way to the ancient city—over the mountains." After a moment of silence, he went on. "My knowledge of the trails gets fuzzy as we go west from here. Even if there were trails lined with flowers and merry signs guiding us to the doorstep of the ancient city, and we had bright, warm days and rainbows to light our path, we would be hard-pressed to make it there in ten days. Fall is on us, and that means snow will be falling in the higher altitudes." He ran a thick finger along a line of peaks between them and Shan-Grail. "And these granite beasties can be nasty when that happens."

A forced march through severe weather to fight a force that might kill them all anyway? Conner wanted to tell them he'd changed his mind, that he would fly to Shan-Grail alone and do what he could, that him reaching the city before Shazarack was better than none of them getting there in time. But no matter the angle, he would not succeed without their help.

Gertrum proceeded after the brief silence. "It should not be difficult to find the trail Ranger Loris and my band of Scouters took to Dragongarde. Once we reach the gorge that feeds Arastone, we turn west and follow it to the wellspring that feeds the rivers Aradorm, Falmere, and Tresdan to the south." He pointed at the map, the tallest point in the mountain range. "Skirting those formidable giants will add some distance, but should increase our chance of arriving within ten days."

Marcantos rapped his knuckles on the tabletop, a tradition common among Warriors for good luck. He reached into his satchel and unfurled the black flag he kept with him, then attached one side to a long wooden pole he removed from the corner of his tent. He held the makeshift flag out with an exuberant smile. "Tonight, the Army of the Dragonbonded is born! I will give the command that we march at first light."

Wallis Arkman

It was hours past nightfall before Conner left the army camp. The last hour had been spent arguing with Marcantos, who wanted to announce to everyone Conner's decision to assume command of the army. At last, he convinced the "general" to wait until morning, when they would leave for Shan-Grail.

As the dragon lifted above the tree line, Conner gazed skyward. The blackness was awash with stars. Erebus was rising full in the east, casting eerie shades of gray across the mountain peaks.

As Skye set his glide path for Dragongarde's main entrance, Skye pointed to a small fire burning just to the east with his snout. "Who is that?" he asked.

Conner leaned forward, squinting to make out a tall figure hunched near the glowing flames. It was a man in townsman clothing and wearing a broad-brimmed hat. Conner let out an audible groan.

"What?" Skye asked.

"Best drop me off by the fire, Skye. Then head on in. I'll join you shortly."

Skye peered back at him.

"No need to worry," he said. "The man is harmless enough. Well, I think he is."

As Skye alighted on the ridge, the man stepped forward, tipping his hat Conner's way and giving a toothy grin.

"Wallis Arkman," Conner announced with a bit of annoyance, stepping from Skye's back. "Why am I not surprised?"

"I did say we would meet again soon," Wallis replied while inspecting Conner in the firelight.

"As I recall, you feared it would be far too soon. Am I ready now for your esteemed tutelage?" Conner didn't mean to be rude, but the man did have a way of inserting himself into Conner's affairs. "Are you here to give me another lesson?"

"I would have preferred delaying this encounter, but with things as they are ..." Wallis shrugged. "As to your question, knowledge not heard, no matter how wise the student, is not a lesson. And we see where my previous attempt led." Wallis wagged his head.

"Yes, you tried to warn me that my two preceptors could not illuminate my path. Did you travel all this way to gloat?"

Wallis guffawed. "I gave up gloating a *very* long time ago."

Conner was exhausted. "Then maybe it is time you tell me who you really are ... and why you have such an interest in me."

Wallis returned to a large rock next to his fire, then tapped on a twin rock with the tip of his walking cane. After Conner sat, he said, "I have an interest in everyone. It is just that some people impact the future more than others."

"How about we start with who you are?" Conner grumbled.

Wallis gestured to the north. "Very well. I grew up in a village along the shore near what is now Ember's Keep. I was twelve when the first Cronoan settlers landed near my home, following the destruction of their civilization across the sea to the north. It was the first of many ships that would appear on the water's horizon in the years that were to follow."

Conner snorted a brief laugh. "That was over thirteen hundred years ago."

"Over fourteen hundred," Wallis corrected.

Conner rocked back and blinked. "But that would make you ... Modei. How ...?"

Wallis tipped his cane toward him. He pressed his thumb to the side of the handle, and the metallic top flipped back. Wallis gently removed something small within and handed it to Conner to examine.

Conner thumbed the black stone in his palm, watching the blue light swirl within. Questions stirred in him. But only one floated to the surface. What did Wallis know of Grimmley's murderers?

Wallis motioned to his squirrel bond chewing on a hickory nut nearby. "After bonding with Maestro here, I was accepted into the Modeic priesthood. We Modei were very spiritual people, so no greater honor could be bestowed upon someone. I devoted my life to helping all those in spiritual need. Upon turning forty, I was asked to lead the Fellowship of Priests. And while someone in this illustrious position has many responsibilities, the greatest of these was to be one of forty-six keepers of our great spiritual city."

"Shan-Grail."

"Yes. We took care of the city, assisting pilgrims on their celestial quest and protecting our most sacred artifacts. After my people were gone, Tatem Creeg found Shan-Grail. The relics that remained were gathered up and transported to Aldemeer, where today they reside under Paladin control." Wallis pointed at the stone in Conner's hand. "That included our greatest treasures—most of the forty-six Resolute Gems known to exist, what the Bremenn later called Fettering Stones. That stone is why I have lived this long."

Conner started to laugh until he realized Wallis was not joking. He carefully handed the stone back. "That is incredible—to live so long."

Wallis chuckled lightheartedly, as if just been told a joke. "I know you have not had much time to consider all the aspects of the bonding you have with your dragon. But I am sure you know that an animal bond's lifespan is that of its human."

"Of course," Conner responded, unsure where Wallis was going with the comment.

"The same is true if the lifespan of a bond is greater than its human's." Wallis leaned forward, his eyes widening. "And a dragon can live practically forever."

Conner's head snapped back. Skye had mentioned that some of those Shazarack had created, what Skye called the Ancients, were still alive … nearly a thousand years. But it hadn't occurred to him … He shook the thought away. He needed a few answers before he could ponder the thought of living forever. "All this time roaming around. To what end?"

"Mostly to offer spiritual aid, as I did for all those pilgrimaging to our city. You have to understand, Conner. I do not meddle in the affairs of others. I just offer ... opportunities along a different path."

Conner wanted to argue that one man's aid was another's meddling, but doubted that would lead him anywhere. "But my ancestors wiped out the Modei. Why would you help them?"

"The Fellowship of Priests helped all those on their spiritual quests, even while Cronoans were carrying out terrible atrocities on my people, which was when they needed it the most." Wallis placed his hand lightly on Conner's shoulder, staring directly into his eyes. "There is nothing sacred in retribution."

Conner looked into the dancing flames. He could not help but feel that Wallis was referencing his search for Grimmley's killers. But he had a more immediate problem. "A very powerful Necromancer named Shazarack believes the ancient city has some kind of power he can use, that will help him invade the realms."

"How could a Necromancer come to believe such a thing?" Wallis asked.

"He mentioned that his grandfather was a Bremenn priest."

"Ah." Wallis looked troubled as he fidgeted with his cane. "That explains why I am here." After several minutes, Wallis went on. "The early Bremenn priests, led by Tatem Creeg, were the first protectors of the city, back before they became Paladins. This makes it quite conceivable that Shazarack knows of the city's powers."

"So, the city does have powers? If Shazarack can tap into those forces ..." Conner could see Wallis struggling with whether to say more. He waited.

Finally, Wallis leaned against his cane. "When the Cosmos created the planes of existence—Astral, Psychic, Mental, and Physical—it needed something to keep them asunder. The energy you know as elementals is more than just the energy that creates Physical light and matter. It also shapes the barriers that prevent spirits residing in one plane from crossing over into another. The incantations Necromancers use to summon spirits from other planes open temporary gateways through which the spirits are called. As the enchantment wears off, the door weakens, and the spirit is drawn back through."

"In the Anarchic Lands," Conner interrupted, "in the middle of what used to be Dristonia, near a town called Xylor, there is a . . . a rip in the fabric separating our plane from the next."

"Yes. I know the place. A long time ago, before the Anarchic War, a great necromantic force of energy was used to summon spirits from far beyond our plane. The force was so powerful that the tear has never fully healed. All matter near that tear is affected. Prolonged exposure can be deadly."

No wonder Azarah had told Wren to stay away from there. "Plants and animals grow incredibly large there, and at night, they glow."

Wallis cleared his throat. "Maybe a brief explanation will help you understand the power at Shan-Grail. When the Cosmos created the planes, it needed an outlet through which the energy could flow, like a wellspring, or maybe like a grounding point, the cornerstone for a massive building. Shan-Grail was built atop Gaia's wellspring. The city was quite literally constructed on the foundation from which the four elementals surge forth into the Physical plane. The elementals extend in a great arc outward from Shan-Grail, each in a different direction, aligned like the Cosmic Star. A network of columns was built along the grid where these energies run, conduits that could be used to draw great quantities of the elementals."

Conner was starting to get a very bad feeling about where this was going. "Columns?"

With his cane, Wallis drew the shape of the Cosmic Star in the dirt, two perpendicular lines intersecting in the middle, then a series of three concentric circles. He jabbed the tip of his cane into the center. "This is Shan-Grail." He tapped the points along one line where the circles crossed. "My ancestors built stone columns fanning out from Shan-Grail across Gaia, even over the sea to the north."

"There is an obelisk along the northern fringe of the mountains at Elmsdorf—"

"That is one of the Earth columns," Wallis filled in with a nod.

"And Skye mentioned there is another on his island home."

"Yes, a Water column. Now. Back to Shan-Grail. The powers are not in the city, but in its location. The elementals emerge from this spot, like a geyser. And it is here that the walls separating the planes are their weakest. In the center of the city is a tall tower. At the top of that tower is the juncture of these forces. There, it is possible to tap into that vast wellspring of energy."

Wallis's description matched the image painted on the chamber wall in Dragongarde, with tall walls and a tall tower rising above a number of shorter buildings. "If this place is so powerful, why didn't the Modei use it? Why didn't you defend your lands against my ancestors? Or defend your people when they were being slaughtered?" Conner had never understood why the Modei had let the Cronoans massacre them.

"Shan-Grail was not built as a weapon. It was a sanctuary for those on a spiritual quest. Besides, we chose a path of peace long before the Cronoans arrived. That cannot be too hard to grasp. Isn't that the reason you refuse to be part of the upcoming war?"

Conner rubbed his hands together. The Modeic writing on the wall in the chamber with the golden wheel came to him. *A spiritual journey of great power can only be taken cradled in the tender bosom of the Cosmos.* "Yes," he answered meekly. So Shazarack was planning to use the wellspring of elemental energy. With sufficient power, could Shazarack summon his ghastly horde?

"Conner," Wallis interrupted Conner from his nightmare. "I know that you are going to Shan-Grail to stop the Necromancer."

"If you know what I'm planning, then you know why."

"I do now," Wallis said with a hint of sadness. "That is why it is time you gained a greater perspective of just what is at stake."

"If you are here to convince me not to go, you are wasting your time." Conner waited for Wallis to argue, but the man only stared back at him. "*I* started this," he went on. The moment he'd touched Shazarack's dagger kept playing over and over in his mind. "Once Shazarack gets into the city, there may be no way to stop his invasion. I cannot wait to see whether the realms can do anything."

Wallis still did not respond.

Conner furrowed his brow at the man. "I suppose if you agreed with my plan, you wouldn't be here."

"Good point," Wallis replied flatly. "But I am not sure you understand what will be required of you to stop this Necromancer."

"I know about the test the Dragonbonded took, if that is what you mean. I know about ... *ascension.*"

Wallis started to say something but pressed his lips tight. "If you *really* knew about it, you would not be so enthusiastic to go there. You are not in the right mental state to attempt this," Wallis went on. "In fact, you have not been in a right state since you defeated the Warrior Evinfaire on

Graystone's Field of Contest. Which is why you blocked yourself from remembering what happened that day."

Conner clenched his hands, his ire stoked. Wallis could not possibly know what he was going through.

Wallis raised his hand to calm Conner. "I know you are angry. But that rage is bleeding over into your bond. If you attempt ascension now, especially under the duress of needing to defeat this Necromancer and without the support your dragon could provide, you may not be ready to do what is needed of you later. As generals in your armies are fond of saying, 'There is no value winning the battle if it leads to losing the war.'"

"Then tell me how I can stop Shazarack without ascension."

Wallis chewed on his lip for a moment. "I know of no other way."

"Then I have no choice, do I? I must go."

Wallis's face hardened; creases Conner had not noticed before darkened his face. "Such headstrong independence. How much you are like Rissa."

"Rissa?"

"Rissa Elmcutter was the first dragon-bonded. Like you in many ways. She bonded with your dragon bond's father. For years, she toiled with learning how to adapt to their strong link. By the time more started bonding with dragons, the portent became clear to me. I elected to aid them with instructions." Wallis glanced down, grinding the base of his cane into the gravel. "Nothing worked. So I took Rissa to Shan-Grail, thinking ascension would help guide her. I should have foreseen she would not handle the trial well."

Would not handle the trial well? Conner repeated to himself. Images of the old Dragonbonded living in secluded caves in squalid conditions came to him. Madness among the Dragonbonded was legendary. Did ascension have something to do with that? The question frightened him. "But I thought ascension was a test used to accept those who bonded with dragons into the Order of the Dragonbonded."

"That was not Rissa's original intention, but she learned painfully that she could not trust those who failed. She was pressed to make a hard call. But let's not digress." Wallis cleared his throat. "My people took many years to complete their ascension—some an entire lifetime. And for good reason. Ascension was never intended to be done in one pilgrimage. But, like you, Rissa was under intense pressure and felt compelled to try. That was her mistake. Everyone's ascension is unique. My point is that, for varied reasons, none of the Dragonbonded were prepared."

"Yet most completed the test and became Dragonbonded, right?"

"Perhaps it is better to think of ascension as a series of trials rather than an exam to be passed." Wallis glanced up at the stars that had gradually appeared. "Let me put this in more personal terms. What is your first memory of what you wanted to become after bonding?"

Conner stared into the flames of the fire, recalling the day his parents told him he had been accepted as an Apothecary apprentice. He could still feel the excitement and pride that had coursed through him. "As long as I can remember, I wanted to be an Apothecary guildsman."

"A healer, yes? Did you ever wonder if there was a reason the Cosmos chose you for this bonding? Did you ever consider why you ended up being tutored by a Shaman? Or did you ever think that maybe your vocation never *really* changed, that you just needed to apply it on a different scale?"

Conner chewed on his lip, trying to understand Wallis's point. He recalled what Pattria said to him when she had called off their betrothal. *You are astute, valiant, and unyielding in your commitment to help others when in need. Those are your strengths. Your Eastlander upbringing will take you far.* Were these the qualities the Cosmos needed? He pushed the question away. "Different scale?"

"Maybe not the kind of healer you expected to become. But, like any living entity, Gaia needs to be healed from a wound, a wound that has hemorrhaged for far too long. And with the planetary alignment behind us, on the day you bonded, Gaia is running out of time."

Conner had no idea what Wallis meant by him healing Gaia, or her wound, or a planetary alignment. "I don't know what you expect of me. How am I to heal Gaia if I allow the lands to be ravaged by Shazarack and his powerful necro-army?"

"Well, that loops us back to how some people impact the future more than others. Despite what you may think, becoming Dragonbonded will not help bring about the change that is needed. You do not need to be fearless or strong or authoritarian to guide those around you. Nor will your dragon bond's strength and ferocity mend Gaia's lesion. Subjugation never leads to healing. Nor will your ability to call down lightning or make the earth quake or rain down the fury of fire. In time, you will know how to do these things, but fear and suffering never lead to a cure."

Wallis tapped the rock Conner was sitting on. "The Cosmos works in much more subtle ways. Any farmer knows the seeds you plant determine the crops you harvest. Have faith, Conner. You have all the tools you need. Let the knowledge bestowed by your Shaman preceptor, your training as an Apothecary, your raising on a farm be your guide. That is why you were chosen."

A thought brushed across Conner's mind, of the morning standing at Grimmley's back door, wrestling with the decision to either save his bond or warn King Jonath of the Assassin Lacerus's conspiracy. Grimmley had told him that he was like a stone skipping over a lake, leaving ripples, changing everything he touched. But what ripples had he left behind of late? He shook his head hard. His hands tightened on his knees. He wanted to scream. "No, Wallis. My actions forced Veressa to abdicate her throne, leaving it to a woman who wants nothing more than retribution for her sister's death. I was the one who brought Shazarack back from the dead so that he could threaten the realms. Wren's dragon would not have been captured if I had not gone to see Shazarack. I have been disgraced and banished from my homeland. And I was the one who brought about Grimmley's murder!"

"And when did all this start? Hmm? It did not start the moment you touched that dragon, did it? No. It began the moment you decided that *you* knew better what was needed, when you got it in your head that *you* were in control rather than trusting in your own inner compass."

Conner tried to imagine letting go as Wallis suggested he do, waiting to get in touch with his inner self. But when he did, visions filled his mind— of Graystone and Cravenrock and Creeg's Point in smoldering ruins, black smoke billowing from crumbled buildings, armies of undead shuffling across the lands, mangled bodies scattered like dust across the realms. *Wouldn't that make a great epitaph for my tombstone?* "I have to go through with this, whatever the cost. I have to stop the Necromancer and get Valkere back."

Wallis pressed his lips tight. "Sometimes the only way to best an adversary is to let them win."

Conner was not sure whether he or Shazarack was the adversary.

Slowly, Wallis stood, his eyes turning to the south. Suddenly, he looked much older in the campfire glow. "Well, I must go. Another long journey awaits. I cannot offer any more advice, especially since you will not listen. So I doubt we will meet again. I have done my best to warn you. Just remember one more thing. Truth, like falsehood, is merely a belief. Only those ready to shed their beliefs can be set free."

Truth, like falsehood, is merely a belief. More wisdom from the walls of Dragongarde. What did that mean?

"I wish you good life, young man." With a quick tip of his hat, Wallis trudged along the narrow trail that wound around the mountain and was gone.

Summit

Dragongarde CAVERNS

By the time Conner arrived at daybreak the next morning, Marcantos had gathered the band of nearly seventy ordermen and a dozen guildsmen to announce, to the cheer of the group, that Conner had assumed command of the new army. Marcantos then singled out a bright-eyed young mute named Staeffan from Gertrum's team of Scouters as the army's new standard-bearer. Before Hemera had risen fully above the mountains to the east, the small army had broken camp, mustered into two platoons— one of Anarchists, the other of Harmonics—and began their procession southwest across the Valley of Souls. As they marched, several Anarchists broke into a snappy ditty to help keep the pace strong. This was followed by playful whoops and shouts from the Harmonics at the front, who then returned with their own exuberant air. Soon, the two platoons were engaged in a high-spirited game of lighthearted one-upmanship, each side encouraging the other to best them for the snappiest tune and liveliest step. Keeping pace near the front with Wren on Skye's back, Conner occasionally heard Marcantos and Gertrum join in to help the smaller platoon of Harmonics.

Within several hours, they reached the foot of the Dragon's Back Mountains west of Dragongarde, where they reassembled into single-line formation and picked their way up the steep, rocky incline. By late morning, Gertrum and Targon found the trail that his band had taken to

Dragongarde, and sent several of his Scouters on ahead. With Staeffan proudly taking the lead, the black flag with red dragon hoisted overhead and fluttering in the cool mountain air, they marched south. By early afternoon, under a cloudless azure sky, they reached the crystal waters that formed the wellsprings for the three rivers flowing south of the mountains. The army turned west, skirting the western bank of the river that would become the River Tresdan farther to the southwest. By dusk, they had cleared another mountain. Having made such good progress, Marcantos called the army to a halt.

By dark, Conner, Wren, Marcantos, Meera, Allisor, and Gertrum sat huddled about their fire, listening to the laughter and singing from the fires burning around them. It had been a good first day.

Gertrum leaned back and scratched at his beard while he studied the mountain the army had conquered that afternoon. "If we can maintain this pace, we should reach Shan-Grail in plenty of time to be rested and prepared for whatever the Necromancer brings at us."

Marcantos peered about the camp. "Even more than our progress, I am pleased with how the Anarchists and Harmonics are coming together. We should take advantage of this energy and work them on developing their skills further."

Meera draped a thick wool blanket over Wren's hunched shoulders, then sat. She rubbed Morgana's ear while the mink tried to playfully bite her finger. "I agree fully. As soon as they have food in their bellies."

"How are they progressing?" Conner probed.

"Slow," Marcantos answered. "But I don't have any concerns quite yet." His eyes lost focused as he stared into the fire. "My first pupil took a number of days before she broke through her training in using Anarchic Sight. It isn't easy to change how you think after years of being trained a certain way."

"Marcantos and I have come up with a strategy to help with that," Meera added. "He works with one platoon on teaching them being Aware, while I work with the other on how to improve their elemental powers. In the next session, we switch off. So far, it seems to be working."

"Yes," Marcantos agreed. "But at some point, we need to mix in some training on how to work together in small groups. Hopefully, we will have time before we reach Shan-Grail."

Gertrum scooched closer to the fire. "The real test comes when you mix Harmonics up with Anarchists into teams. That's when we find out if they've got any real mettle."

Conner had wondered about Marcantos's tactic to keep the Harmonics separated from the Anarchists. "Why separate them if you're going to mix them up later? Wouldn't it be better to mix them now while their spirits are high so they learn to work together?"

"Keeping them segregated for now will help us train them in being Aware," Marcantos answered. "I need to work with those using Anarchic Sight apart from those using Harmonic Sight. And that has to be our first step. Besides, I want to keep some space between them until they have developed more trust."

Conner was not sure how keeping them apart would help bring them together later, especially since they only had a week to be ready. But he would gladly leave such decisions to his general.

Later that night, Conner sat next to Skye curled up near a large boulder, watching as Marcantos and Meera worked with the two platoons.

"How is Wren?" Skye asked.

Conner had sensed his bond's growing concern through the day, and knew it was for Wren. The dragon seldom left her side. "The same as yesterday. At least she's not worse." He glanced up at Skye, noting several new horns growing from under his jawline. "Thank you for giving her a ride."

"Thank-yous are not necessary. I cannot imagine the loss she must feel." Skye gave a brief snort-sniff. "In an absurd kind of way, I miss Valkere's exuberance. We could all use that right now."

Conner pressed his back to Skye's side. He had not slept well in several nights, so the day's long hours of mountain climbing lulled him further toward the sleep he fancied. The dragon's slow rhythmic breathing edged him even closer. As he drifted off, Skye's deep voice drew him back.

"Several times, I tried to strike up a chat with Wren. But she would become distracted and forget we were conversing. Occasionally, I tried to assure her that Valkere was okay and that you would get him back. But she did not remember him. I think to forget one's bond may be the greatest of tragedies."

Conner rolled to his side, wiggling into a comfortable position against the dragon and drawing his blanket up. "I don't even want to consider the thought of forgetting you, Skye." No longer able to fight the urge, he let sleep take him away.

With the army fully rested and the promise of cooler weather, the second day began with spirits high, and they maintained a vigorous pace. With Marcantos's direction, they settled into a stable formation, with Gertrum directing his band of Scouters in front, followed by Conner and Marcantos, then Staeffan proudly flourishing their flag at the end of his long pike. The smaller platoon of Harmonics and bonds trailed after the standard bearer, followed by the Anarchists and bonds, with Meera and Morgana, then Wren on Skye's back bringing up the rear. Talk was light and often full of banter.

By the fifth day, Conner reconsidered his reservations in Marcantos's strategy as he noted the two platoons mingling more and more, volunteering and sharing more of the responsibilities for setting up and breaking down camp, hunting, cooking, and cleaning up. He also noticed that they were casting more powerful incantations. Success fed their hunger to learn more, and soon, they were practicing their newfound powers at every opportunity. Even Gertrum, who'd started their journey brooding and grumbling about the long trail ahead, could be seen occasionally smiling and joking, though he still kept a sizeable distance from the Anarchists. While all of this was promising, Conner could not help but notice Wren's periods of lucidity were occurring less often with each day's passing.

"There's nothing more you can do for Wren?" Conner pressed Meera the evening of their fourth day as they huddled about the campfire, his eyebrows arched in concern.

Meera peered over at the sleeping form nestled beneath several blankets near Skye. "As I say each evening, I have done all that I can for her." She exhaled slowly. "I am sorry, Conner. I too worry for her, and of possible long-term effects this might have on her, even if you get her dragon back. All I can say is that I will stay with her, watch over her, and do what I can."

"Of course. Thank you, Meera."

On the other side of the fire, Gertrum motioned toward the huge summit of snow-capped rock blocking out much of the western sky. Only small portions of the horizon to the north and south of the peak were visible. "That is the highest point of the entire mountain range. The trail will take us to a pass along the southern section. From there, we will stay on the western side of the river until we reach Shan-Grail."

"Which puts us a full day ahead of schedule," Marcantos added with a beaming smile. "No more rocky ascents or steep climbs. It is all downhill from there."

As Conner said his good nights and headed over to join Skye and Wren, he could not believe their good fortune. He thought back to the events since he left home on his Calling—his misadventures and many struggles. This moment seemed a little too convenient to be real.

The next morning, Conner discovered just how accurate that feeling was. He awoke to a hard jostle and squinted up at a dark form hunched over him. He sat up, blinking sleep from his eyes. The air was crisp. With just a hint of light on the eastern horizon and no campfires lit, it had to be an hour before dawn. "What is it?"

The form leaned closer. It was Gertrum, who'd lost all semblance of humor sometime during the night. The Scouter pressed a forefinger to his lips, waved for Conner to follow, then stalked away. Conner followed Gertrum to where Meera was working to start a fire, while Morgana brought small twigs from the woods. Marcantos was there next to Copious, bowed forward, rubbing his hands over his face. "What is it?" Conner asked again softly.

Gertrum gestured to the west. In the first gleam of Hemera, Conner could distinguish a line of dark clouds on either side of the great mountain's peak. "What does that mean?"

"Bad weather," Gertrum groaned as he plopped down beside Targon. "Really bad."

Marcantos kicked a stone near his foot into the fire. "I knew it was too much to expect good weather the entire way."

Gertrum snorted. "We are past the fall equinox now, General. It would be foolhardy to expect good weather in the mountains on any given day."

"Just how bad will it be?" Conner asked.

"From the altitude and color of them clouds?" Gertrum asked, scratching his beard while his bushy brow sank over his eyes. "Dead-of-winter bad. Even worse, it is going to be here before we clear the summit." The Scouter squinted, mumbling to himself. "We may have until late afternoon before the brunt of it strikes. It would seem we are about to pay back with interest the last four days of pleasant weather."

Meera looked to where the others were staring. "You are the Alpslander, Gertrum. What do you suggest we do?"

"We should spend the time before the storm arrives fortifying our current position," Marcantos interjected. "We wait out the storm here and proceed once the weather clears."

Gertrum wagged his head, jabbing his finger toward the mountain. "We are in the open here, General. I would suggest we get as many steps as we can toward that beastie before the storm hits. We might even find some shelter along this side of the ridge that will offer protection from the wind." Marcantos was about to argue, so Gertrum added, "Every minute we spend debating this further is a minute we will have to spend traipsing through snow and ice after the storm passes."

Conner stepped forward. "Rouse the army, Marcantos. I want to be on the move in half an hour. We can distribute rations to eat on the way. Gertrum, I want two Scouters ahead of us at all times with regular reports back. I will send Skye on ahead as well. Maybe he'll get lucky and find a cave we can hole up in." He caught Meera's toothy smile in the faint light. "What?" he asked her.

She shook her head. Reaching down, she cradled Morgana in her arms. "Nothing. I will get Wren up and help her pack."

"Thank you." Conner squinted over at the large, black form snorting and twitching near the edge of camp. "And I'll commence to waking the dragon. The higher we climb in these mountains, the more sleep he thinks he needs. We'll be blessed if his eyes are open by the time we decamp."

Several hours out of camp, Skye descended from the misty gray sky to report he had found a large cavern not far off the trail about three miles ahead. Conner conveyed this to Gertrum and Marcantos. Cheers broke out along the line as the news was passed along. With the encouraging report, the army picked up the pace. However, they had not gone a mile up the trail before the wind picked up. Staeffan refused to stow the flag, insisting to Gertrum with animated gestures that he could keep the standard flying high. But when a gust blew him backward into Conner, he succumbed to Gertrum's demands and reverently packed it away.

Two miles from the cave, they were in a full gale. The temperature plummeted. Soon after, snow began to fall, clinging to their clothes in thick clumps. With the Scouters returned, the army paused long enough to string together their climbing ropes, which they used to ensure no one would be left behind. Skye did not seem affected by the cold, so Conner asked him to lead the way to the cave. With one end of the rope tied around his waist, Conner took guard position behind the dragon, and on they trudged.

Swirling snow blinded him, and his face felt like it was being pricked by a hundred needles. His feet vanished in snowdrifts that grew deeper with each passing minute, and he fought to keep his footing along the slippery trail. Progress ground to the pace of a turtle.

The last mile felt like an eternity. But at last, Conner staggered into pitch darkness and deafening stillness. He sensed the draw of Fire and Air behind. Someone rasped an incantation, flooding the cave with brilliant orange light. One by one, the army of men and bonds stumbled into the cave and collapsed in a heap. Soon, the chamber was filled with the echoes of groans and sharp breathing.

"Is everyone okay?" Conner shouted, trying to keep his teeth from clacking. Those with any remaining strength nodded or waved. He peered down at the big man huddled and shivering against his bear bond. "Gertrum, have your Scouters fan out around the cave. I want every nook and crevice of this place inspected within the next half hour. I don't want to be surprised by some creature angry we stumbled in on uninvited." He pointed at Marcantos. "General, get everyone up and assembled. I want to know that everyone made it in. Then come up with a way to heat this chamber ... and get us more light! I will work on a protective shield over the entrance to keep the wind out. And where's Meera?" He found her wrapping a blanket over Wren's back. "Meera, do what you can to offer aid to those who need it."

With everyone scrambling to carry out his orders, Conner went to stem the tide of frigid air and snow entering the entrance. After a handful of unsuccessful tries, he was able to create a barrier across the narrow mouth of the cave, involving several layers of woven elementals modeled from the rings that had been used to bind Meera when she was a prisoner in the Shamans' temple. He started with a weave of Earth and Water to cover the mouth, then followed it with a layer of Water and Air, and finally, one of Air and Fire. Once he was sure the barrier would withstand the wintry elements, he returned to thank Skye for his help and to offer assistance where he could be of some use.

By early afternoon, Conner gathered Marcantos, Gertrum, Meera, Allisor, and Wren for an assessment of their situation and to discuss next steps.

Meera began, speaking in a hushed tone, as conversations easily carried throughout the hollow chamber. "We have about a dozen men, along with several bonds, suffering from hypothermia. Another hour in that storm and we would be having a different conversation. Still, I think they will all recover. But it means we need to keep them warm until this storm passes."

"Gertrum?" Conner asked.

Gertrum puffed out his cheeks. "This is worse than anything we get in the eastern regions, so I have no idea how much longer it will last. Even if it stopped now, it would be midday tomorrow before we could dig our way free of the drifts."

Wren stared at the entrance, where the snowdrift was taller than Conner. And snow was still falling in heavy flakes.

Conner placed his hand lightly on Wren's shoulder, and the tension left her body.

Wren smiled at him.

"My concern right now is morale," Marcantos said. "Some of the troops have never seen snow before. I can see the fear in the young ones' eyes. I heard a few wondering what we will do if we get sealed in here. And there are whispers of wanting to go back to the valley, that they don't see a reason to risk their lives to defend the realms. Some warm weather would help their spirits."

"Actually, General," Gertrum said, "warm weather might not be a good thing. If the snow melted this afternoon and the temperature dropped below freezing tonight, we would be forced to traverse icy, dangerous trails tomorrow."

Marcantos's eyes narrowed at Gertrum.

"That discussion seems to be premature," Conner intervened, sensing the tension rising. "Since we can't predict what is going to happen, I suggest we take advantage of the time we have today and work with the troops, then let them stop early for the evening. We'll revisit this at first light tomorrow. Besides, keeping them busy might just be the medicine we need to improve *all* our moods."

Conner went looking for Skye. He found his bond taking a nap. Far beyond exhaustion, he joined in.

Fire in the Belly

Shan-Grail

Conner had not slept more than half an hour before he was awakened by the harsh sounds of shouting. Near the center of the cavern, where Meera had set up a site to distribute rations, a young Sorcerer pushed a Barbarian in the chest. The Barbarian bellowed and drew his sword while the Sorcerer took a ready stance, Fire licking his palms.

"What is this?" Marcantos bellowed, stepping between them. He shoved them apart. "What are you two doing?"

The Sorcerer poked a finger at the Barbarian. "He stole my dinner ration!"

"I did not!" the Barbarian growled, testing the grip of his blade.

"You—" the Sorcerer started.

"Stop it!" Marcantos shouted at the Sorcerer. He drew his own sword. That had their attention. Stepping forward, Marcantos jabbed the tip of his sword into the dirt, then lifted a skewered ration into the face of the Sorcerer. "Is this your ration?" After a prolonged silence, Marcantos flicked his wrist, sending the ration soaring to the back of the cave. "If you have enough energy to fight, then you have enough for an extra lesson."

"But my dinner—"

"Is forfeited," Marcantos roared, sheathing his sword. "Now go!" Rounding on the troops, he shouted, "Do not let me see any more fighting. Is that understood?" A few nodded, and he stalked away.

The troops went back to busying themselves, but Conner noted they clustered in their platoons, huddled closer. *Great, Marcantos. That will break everyone together,* Conner thought. He felt a hand on his back.

"Conner," Gertrum said with a troubled expression, "don't you think it is time you addressed the troops?"

"Me?"

"Aye, lad. You."

"What could I possibly say that would help this situation?"

"I don't know, but they wouldn't give a warm elk turd for anything I might come up with. And while they'll follow the general's orders, even listen to his instructions on how to gain power and control over elementals, he's not what motivates them to want to learn. Nor is Meera. If anything, I think those intrepid Barbarians are a tad bid afraid of her." Gertrum chuckled softly and shook his head. He jabbed Conner in the chest with a thick finger. "You're the reason all these people are here. You're their commander. They'll listen to you. You're the only one that can bring them together. You're the glue. That is, if the Cosmos wills it."

Conner's mouth hung open as he tried to think of how to respond.

"Everyone!" Gertrum shouted, raising his arms toward the cavern ceiling. "Conner has something important he wants to share with us. Gather around and listen!"

The troops plodded forward, the Harmonics gathering to Conner's left, the Anarchists to his right. The gap between them was wide enough for Skye to walk through. Conner made a note to kick Gertrum really hard when he had a moment in private with him. "General Evinfaire and I . . . Well . . . We've decided to wait out the rest of the day here, and leave first thing in the morning."

A cheer rang out among the troops. Still, no one moved.

Great start, Conner. But that's not going to be enough to mend this problem. He took a deep breath and dug deep inside, looking for something that might help. What had Wallis said? You have all the tools you need.

"I grew up in the Eastlands in a small farming town a day's ride from the Borderlands," he started, then gazed at the Anarchists to his right. "For those who don't know the place, it is in the central plains of Griffinrock." He realized he was fidgeting with his hands, so he swept them to his side. "We Eastlanders are a proud and hardy people, freemen with a long history of not meddling in the affairs of Harmonic life. We are self-reliant and learned centuries ago to stick to ourselves. I never really much thought about why that is so."

Conner swallowed hard. *Where are you going with this?* He took a step forward. "Until recently. You see, not long ago, I learned that my ancestors fought alongside the Anarchists in the Anarchic War—or as you Anarchists call it, the Great War. Like some of your ancestors, mine fought for the right of self-determination, to live free from the rule of other men. But when the treaty ending the war was signed, the Anarchists ceded the Eastland territories to the Harmonics."

Out of the corner of his eye, he saw some Harmonics shift and look down. "You have to understand, I was raised to fear Anarchists. Generations of tales and songs handed down, told to frighten children. We were taught to believe Anarchists were madmen and savages bent on destroying our towns and burning our homes. So, at first, I did not want to believe my forefathers had been Anarchists."

Conner reached out and gripped Wren's hand, searching her eyes. "I suspect all of you were raised to believe the same about those standing across from you here. It *is* hard to trust those we fear ... and those we have been taught to hate." He stepped forward, walking down the gulf splitting the two platoons, and turned to the Harmonics. "But, you see, I was lucky. The Cosmos gifted me with the most wonderful opportunity—the chance to travel to the Anarchic Lands, to see for myself whether what I had been told was true. I lived among Anarchists, in the town of Xylor. And through the guidance of several dear friends I met along the way, like Wren, her grandparents, Morgas, and Little Robin, I learned of the Anarchic ways. And my eyes were opened to the truth about the goodness and beauty in the Anarchic way of life."

Conner held his arms out. "Since we left the Valley of Souls, my eyes have been opened to an even greater truth. I have seen it every time one of you reaches a helping hand to another, every time you offer a word of kindness or jest, every time you nod your appreciation. General Evinfaire is giving you instructions on how to be Aware. You are finding that when Sight is taken, a Sight not viewed from a label of Anarchic or Harmonic ways, you are much stronger. *We* are much stronger together.

"I know you worry about the war that is brewing, one that threatens *both* our lands. But I cannot think on that right now, nor about what I may need to do when war comes. I have a mission to accomplish first. The

Necromancer Shazarack is on his way to Shan-Grail. In a few days, I must face him at Shan-Grail. I must get Wren's dragon back.

"If Shazarack succeeds in unlocking the power of the ancient Modeic city, he will invade the realms and topple the crowns and Harmonic orders. I know this because he told me so himself." A murmur flowed about the chamber. "But you need to know something else. Once he has laid waste to the realms, he will not stop. He will turn his sights back toward the Anarchic Lands. He will keep going until he has taken control of every homeland, dismantled every order, torched every institution. And when everything is gone, he will mold our societies into one—into what he wants it to be. He speaks of setting people free, yet no one will be given a choice. He will decide who has access to the powers that belong to the orders.

"We must stop him. But Skye and I cannot accomplish this alone. I need you for this mission. Each of you brings a special gift, without which we would be less than what we could be. But we can only reach our full potential if we are united."

Conner took a slow breath. He could not tell whether he was getting through to them. "If you believe in the Omen of the Dragonbonded, if that is what called you to be here this moment, then you know what is needed. What we do at Shan-Grail will determine how we are judged, not by those in this cavern, but by all those who need proof that we can live together in peace. If we succeed, then we can show both sides that war is not inevitable.

"This is your chance to make a difference. Just like me, the Cosmos is offering you a chance to break with the old, to create a new pattern, built on the strengths the Anarchic and Harmonic ways have to offer. I ask you now to join me. Do not waste this opportunity to have your eyes opened."

There was a long silence, and Conner felt an ache in his chest. He had tried, but he had failed to reach them. He needed them to come together if his plan to defeat Shazarack was to succeed. He looked at Wren. It seemed he would have to find another way to get Valkere back.

One of the Barbarians stepped forward and lifted his sword over his head. "The Dragonbonded need our help to end this Necromancer and his vile army. There are still a few hours of Hemera's light." He glanced at Marcantos. "I suggest we make haste and get this done!"

Marcantos shared a look with Conner then gave a nod, and a piercing shout rang out as troops raised their swords and staves high. Then, just as quickly, the troops dispersed. And for the first time since their arrival at the cave, Harmonics and Anarchists mingled as they gathered their gear and prepared to decamp. Even the young Sorcerer and Barbarian who had been arguing were chatting like old friends.

Gertrum slapped Conner briskly on the back. "Well done, lad. The fire is in their belly now! What you say we put some distance between us and this infernal cave?"

Within an hour of departing the cave, the army reached the high point of the pass and began their long descent down the western slope. A Scouter returned to report that the pass was unobstructed for at least several miles ahead. With the blizzard past, the scenic view at this elevation, with the smaller mountains blanketed in thick snow spread out before them, was breathtaking. The air was clear and crisp, Hemera's rays warm on their faces. Small crystals swirled and sparkled in the gentle breeze. To their right, the giant mountain jutted into the cloudless afternoon sky. And to their left, water rushed down a wide, limpid river. As they hiked, the troops sang sprightly songs. It seemed to Conner that they had once again been handed good fortune.

Soon, they came upon a thundering waterfall. There, the trail descended into a deep ravine. While Skye flew on ahead with Wren, the troops and their bonds picked their way along the steep, rugged path, slippery from a cool mist that drifted up from the ravine. Once the army had collected at the bottom of the basin, Conner took the lead and they continued west along a slick and level narrow path. Staeffan fished a branch from the river and attached the flag to the end, then proudly took the lead. To their right, water dripped from green moss and air plants hanging from strata of wet rock ascending vertically a hundred paces, while on their left, the river continued its gentle westerly journey. Overhead, a rainbow reflected off light from Hemera sinking toward the horizon.

It was nearly dusk before the army exited the mouth of the ravine, where Skye and Wren waited. Not more than three hundred paces ahead, the trail came to an abrupt end; a snowdrift, running continuously from the mountain peak to the flowing river, loomed like a great wall. Beyond the wall, everything was blanketed with a thick layer of fresh snow.

"I took the time to fly on ahead. This snow extends along the river for several of your miles," Skye said.

Gertrum slipped up beside Conner and folded his arms. "Good thing I was expecting something to go wrong. I hate being disappointed."

Marcantos appeared at Conner's other side, then grumbled under his breath while surveying the scene. "I suppose we could use incantations to melt the snow, but even switching off, it will be slow going."

Gertrum stroked his beard. "I'd be the first to say I know almost nothing about Fire elemental, but that is two paces thick."

"And Skye says we have several miles of this."

"Maybe your dragon can melt the snow over the path?" Marcantos asked.

"I can ask him, but ... several miles?" Conner shook his head in doubt.

"Then—" Gertrum started, but Staeffan came running forward, gesturing excitedly at the guildmaster Scouter.

"What is it?" Conner asked, thinking they might be in danger.

"Slow down, Staeffan," Gertrum commanded. "Now, repeat that."

Staeffan stuffed his flagpole against his chest so he could use both hands. He wound one hand around the wrist of his other, then pointed to the forest north of them, and made a chopping motion. Holding two fingers up like hooks, he held his open hand out, palm down toward the river. He beamed a big smile at his guildmaster.

Gertrum chuckled, then slapped Staeffan on the shoulder. "Great idea, lad! I knew there was a reason I brought you along." Turning to Conner and Marcantos, he translated. "Our young standard bearing here is suggesting we cut a hundred or so logs from the trees over there and build a score of rafts, then float downstream until we reach the other side of this snowdrift."

"I don't know," Marcantos shook his head. "What if there's another waterfall, or rapids?"

"I could ask Skye to scout on ahead to check." Conner shrugged. "And we can elementally strengthen the rafts so they will survive rough waters."

Marcantos started to say something, but Gertrum hooked his arm over his shoulder and dragged him back toward where the troops had gathered. "Come along, General. It may take some serious head scratching to get these chaps organized. And I would like to get some sleep tonight."

Nearing midnight, the troops collapsed beside their constructed and elementally enhanced rafts. Most slept where they dropped. A hearty few, invigorated by their labors, sat chatting as a waning Erebus rose in the east.

Conner found Skye watching over Wren, who had fallen asleep in a patch of grass on the bank. He slipped a blanket over her, then added his own when he noticed her still shaking from the chill.

"And what will you use to keep yourself warm?" Skye asked.

"Don't need a blanket when I have something better," Conner replied through a yawn. Then he slid up under Skye's wing and fell fast asleep.

Truths, Lies, and Beliefs

Skye settled on an icy ridge that he said was just east of the Shan-Grail. Conner clambered down to study what was visible, which was very little. The ridge line vanished to their left and right. Below was a vast valley enveloped in late-afternoon fog. "And you're sure Shan-Grail is down there."

Skye snort-sniffed. "Unless someone moved it last night, I am."

Conner grunted, his eyes searching the haze to the southeast. Somewhere back there, the army was setting up camp for the night. Too exhausted from four straight days of battling rapids, freezing waters, and thick fog to finish the last few miles, Marcantos had promised to have the troops at Shan-Grail by dawn. Conner didn't particularly like leaving them, but Meera had promised to look after Wren, and his time was better served finding a way into the ancient city than getting in the way while Marcantos planned how to defend the city against Shazarack's undead. "I know you're not going to like what I have to say, but I want you to stay up here until I signal you."

"Conner—" Skye gazed back, his eyes flaring brilliant blue.

"No, Skye." Conner shook his head. "If you get in Shazarack's line of sight, he will ensnare you just as he did Valkere. And I will be way too busy contending with him to fight you too."

Skye wagged his head. "I am your bond. It is impossible for me to hurt you."

Conner placed his palm on Skye's muzzle. "The laws of bonding are not something I want to test right now. Besides"—Conner chewed on his lip, recalling a comment Wallis had made about Conner needing his bond—"I will need you ... but only when the time is right. Which is why I need you to wait here. Okay?"

Skye surveyed the fog below, then tilted his head sideways. "Okay."

Conner could feel Skye's hesitation, knew he wanted to argue. But something was different about Skye, something Conner could not quite touch. Maybe his time at home had done some good after all. But Conner needed to be sure. Grabbing a thorny spike on the dragon's nostril, he pulled Skye's head down close to his. "And this time, we stick to the plan," Conner urged, giving his bond a good pat on the forehead. "See you soon." He started down the steep western slope of the rocky ridge. At the bottom, he continued in what he hoped was a westerly direction. But the fog was as thick as soup, the landscape nothing more than a half dozen shades of muddled gray. He was beginning to wonder if he was walking in circles when he stumbled upon an ancient road, made from slabs of stone the size of Skye. With a slight turn to his left, he let the road direct him.

He had gone no more than a hundred paces when a tall, dark structure emerged from the mist ahead, resembling the image of Shan-Grail painted on the wall in Dragongarde. As he neared, he could discern a wall rising over fifty paces above the stone road. And unlike city or castle walls, this wall was smooth, the color of the gray-brown rock base, as if the walls had been carved right out of the mountain it rested upon. Closer still, and triangular roofs of buildings appeared behind the city's great wall. And out of the mist, at what must be the city's center, a cylindrical tower stretched high above all the other structures. After a momentary pause, Conner pushed on.

The road led Conner to an enormous oaken gate, rising nearly the height of the walls, hung from granite posts with several rusted metal hinges thicker than Conner was tall. At the foot of the gate, two armored figures stood at rigid attention. *Why would anyone stand guard over an ancient city in such a desolate place?* They were dressed in full battle armor, each holding a long pike and a shield bearing the emblem of the Cosmic Star. The armor of the guard to his right was a dazzling silver. Even in the fog, Conner thought the plate metal sparkled, catching the few

ARMY OF THE DRAGONBONDED

random rays that found their way through the mist. To his left, the guard's armor was dull and black as night. Not far away, near the city wall, several dozen more men and women were gathered about a number of tents.

These were not guards. They were ordermen—to his right, a Paladin; the other a Black Knight, the Anarchic version of a Paladin. And then it made sense. Tatem Creeg's disciples, those who called themselves Bremenn, had been charged with protecting the Modei's spiritual city. With the creation of the orders following the War of the Orders, that responsibility was passed down to the Paladins Order. Spiritual fanatics when it came to protecting the Modei's most sacred treasures, not even the splitting of the order could negate that duty.

Conner shuffled to a stop before them and cleared his throat. "I need to get into the city."

Neither spoke nor moved.

Conner was wasting time. "You need to know," he tried one more time, "that there is a very powerful Necromancer on his way here with an army of undead. Shan-Grail is in danger." He puffed out his chest and cleared his throat. "I need to get into the city so that I can stop him."

Still no response.

Maybe there wasn't anyone inside the armor. Maybe they were propped up there like scarecrows to frighten away unwanted visitors. He started to step between them.

The ordermen snapped their arms to the side, their pikes crossing at the tips in front of him.

"Okay." Conner stepped back, then looked at the Paladin. "If this Necromancer succeeds in getting into your city, he will use the power inside to invade the realms and destroy them."

Still the Paladin did not move or speak.

Conner turned to the one in ebony plate. "Once he has destroyed the realms, he will turn his sights on the Anarchic Lands. He won't stop until everything is decimated."

"Shan-Grail is under the protection of the Black Knights and Paladins Orders," came the muffled feminine voice from the helm of the Black Knight. "Only those sanctioned may enter the city."

"All that is well and good, but how are you two going to protect the city against a thousand undead?"

No reply.

Conner tapped the red dragon emblem on the front of his armor. "Do you know this symbol?" he asked, trying to muster as much conviction as possible. "*This* is my authorization to enter."

The Paladin's helm swiveled toward him. "We know who you are, Conner of the Griffinrock Eastlands. Still, you may not enter without the proper sign."

"Sign?" Conner blinked at the Paladin. "I know of no ..." His mind stuttered to a stop. The painted image of Shan-Grail in the room with the device. Something scripted on the wall in Modeic. He had attempted to read it but failed. Something to do with truth and lies and beliefs. *Wait,* he thought. *Wallis said something about that. What was it?* Conner spoke the words aloud as he called them up. "Truth, like falsehood, is merely a belief. Only those ready to shed their beliefs can be set free."

The two guards peered at each other, then snapped back to attention. "You may enter," the Black Knight stated.

Conner hesitated. If Wallis did not want him to take the test, to ascend, then why had he given him the key he needed to enter? Well, no use burning energy or time trying to understand Wallis Arkman. For whatever reason the ancient Modei had, it would likely remain a mystery. Conner slipped cautiously between the two ordermen, then proceeded to the enormous gate, which swung wide, creaking and popping on the enormous hinges.

He proceeded cautiously down a long, narrow street, then crossed into what appeared to be a large and empty antechamber. Colorful, swirling images were painted over the walls and ceiling. More hieroglyphs. Conner's eyes skimmed over the writings, but he could not translate more than a few words—*journeyman, spiritual, wandering*. What if, unknowingly, he walked right past the glyphs he needed most? How would he find the source of the city's power? He could not afford the time it would take to try to decipher every hieroglyph he came across. He chewed on his lip for a moment. Proceeding to the only other doorway in the chamber, he examined the images overhead of people walking, then stepped through.

The next chamber was larger and just as empty, except for a spindly, triangular granite obelisk protruding from the middle and stretching nearly to the ceiling. A simple ring, the Modeic symbol for the Fire, the first elemental, was etched deep on each side of the column. The shining, golden image of Hemera filled the dome. The chamber had to be a temple of sorts—a temple to the Fire elemental. To his left was the only other doorway, which took Conner out into a long empty street, bending slowly out of sight to the right.

With growing urgency and dimming of light, he started up the road. On either side, he passed many buildings, buildings of different sizes and shapes and heights, as if they had been built as an afterthought or to give shape to the circular street. Along the building walls were more brightly painted hieroglyphs. And while he could not read them all, it was not hard to discern that they were about the Fire spirit—of births and beginnings, the creations of things new, of babies and Hemera rising, of seeds and sparks of energy. On Conner walked the street angling to his right.

After a while, the street led him to a building not unlike the temple that had expelled him onto this street. Bending low, he crept inside. As in the Fire temple, a thin, triangular granite obelisk protruded from the center, nearly touching the dome ceiling. This pillar was marked with three undulating vertical lines, the symbol for Air. Conner took a little more time touring this chamber. From the markings, he discerned it was, indeed, a temple. First Fire and now Air marked along a circular road. As Wallis had described it, the city was constructed in the shape of the Cosmic Star. He stepped to the center of the room and pressed his palm to the obelisk. It reminded him of the obelisk at Elmsdorf, just without all the grimacing, painted faces.

Wallis had mentioned a series of stone columns fanning out from Shan-Grail. Conner scanned the hieroglyphs again for a hint, but nothing caught his attention. Frustrated with the lack of progress, he crossed the temple and exited the other side. Just as before, the city street continued its slow bend. "Well, I have a pretty good idea where this goes," he told himself. "Water next." More buildings, more tall walls filled with painted images of the Air spirit—of families, bonds, and communities living in harmony with nature, of fields peppered with green shoots, of relationships and smiling faces, of children playing with puppies.

By the time he passed through the Water temple, it was dusk. *"Ora energi anakafanos."* He invoked the Night Vision incantation he had learned in Cravenrock's Thieves Guild, which gave the symbols and images sprawled across the walls of the buildings he passed an eerie glow—images of fields of flowers growing, of rivers flowing, of people standing at crossroads contemplating which direction to take, of thunderstorms on the horizon. These were images of the Water spirit, of evolution and change.

Conner wanted to stop and translate more, but his sight incantation would be waning soon.

He hardly slowed as he passed through the Earth temple and down the street on the other side. Here, the walls were painted with images of Hemera setting in brilliant reds and oranges, of withered crops in snowy fields, of decomposing trees, of reclamations and destruction, of Modeic funeral pyres and Midsummer's Night, of faces downturned with mourning and grief. Death and the endings of cycles. This was the Earth spirit. Conner did not like the feelings the pictured invoked, so he moved on quickly.

It was well past nightfall when he came to the end of the street. He had completed the entire outer loop of the city, bringing him to the rear of the Fire temple he had started in earlier that day. Except rather than arriving at another building, a wall loomed before him. To his left was a doorway. On the door frame were several symbols which Conner took for *departure* or maybe *retreat*. That had to lead back out of the city. To his right, another doorway led to a dark, narrow alleyway. But before he could read the symbols along its frame, his Night Vision expired, and he was left standing in the dark.

Conner plopped down where he was, pressing his back against the cold wall at the end of the street and wishing for a fire to stave off a night chill that was sapping him of his remaining energy. He exhaled warm air into his hands, then rubbed them together. He had hoped to learn about the power the city possessed, or at least more about the city. Instead, his journey seemed to simply have been about the four elementals, about the cycle of life, from birth to death.

He leaned his head back. Thoughts of the army crowded around a dozen fires along the riverbank came to him, and he felt a pang of loneliness. Would they make it to the city before the Necromancers and their undead arrived? Would he find what he needed to stop Shazarack? His confidence was waning. And into the void rushed doubt and dread. He studied the alleyway that would take him deeper inside the city. He had to believe he would find something tomorrow. If not ... He closed his eyes and slipped into a restive sleep.

Splitting Forces

Marcantos splashed across the rocky riverbed, exhausted, unable even to lift his feet above the three inches of freezing waters. At the stony shoreline, he dropped to his hands and knees, head hanging, gulping air, shivering. At last, he rose, swaying on trembling legs. Troops and their bonds were scattered along the bank, soaked and battered, many just crawling and stumbling from the river. Behind them, the remains of their empty makeshift rafts bobbed playfully along, only to vanish around the next bend. The final leg of their journey to Shan-Grail had been short—a few miles at most—but it had been brutal in near total darkness, fraught with rapids and navigation past huge boulders over a swift-running river. At least he saw no bodies floating downstream. Men and women glistened in the predawn light, littering the banks like drenched debris after a bad storm. "Did we lose anyone?" he shouted over the sound of the raging current, then reached back to help several others crawl to the higher embankment.

"It does not appear so," Gertrum responded before bending forward and placing his palms on shaking knees. Targon growled his displeasure and shook his bear coat dry.

"Gather the troops," Marcantos commanded. "I want a tally before we march. We will rest once we reach the city."

Gertrum's eyes turned toward where the city should be. "At least the fog has lifted."

Marcantos shivered in the cold, wrapping his arms tight across his chest. "Right now, being alive is a blessing."

Once everyone had been accounted for, Gertrum marshaled the troops into their platoons. Marcantos signaled them to advance, and Gertrum sent two of his Scouters on ahead. By the time they returned to say they had found Shan-Grail, the army was halfway there.

Several hundred paces farther, Marcantos called the two platoons to a halt. After a brief discussion with his aides, Marcantos led a small entourage—Gertrum, three Barbarians, a Conjuror, a Mystic, and two Sorcerers—on ahead. The nine of them had more combat experience than the rest of the troops combined. Just as Skye had described, Shan-Grail stood at the center of a large bowl-like valley. A small garrison of men and women milled about a cluster of tents near the eastern wall, while two sentries guarded the gate. "What are your thoughts?" he asked the group after they had gathered along a ridge south of Shan-Grail. He was already formulating a few ideas on setting up a defensive perimeter around the city. But he had learned years before that many eyes on a problem reduced the chances that something important was overlooked.

Saven, one of the Barbarians, squinted into the morning light. "I heard tell Shan-Grail has been guarded by Black Knights and Paladins since before the War of Breaking. It would help tremendously if we could secure their support."

Marcantos slapped Saven on the back. "Good. We need everyone we can muster. That will be your charge when we get there."

Saven rolled his eyes.

"Our first problem"—the Conjuror Breda made a sweeping gesture with her arm—"is that we have no clue where Shazarack will pop out of his hole. It could be anywhere." After a moment of silence passed, she added. "It is possible the tunnels lead right into the city."

Marcantos shook his head. "Somehow, I doubt that. Look at the height on those walls. Why would the Modei build such a structure if people could enter easily through tunnels?" He gestured toward the massive wooden gates near the southern side, and the road leading off to the east. "But it would make sense to put the tunnel entrance near the gate."

Saven nodded. "That seems to be the only road into the city."

But the Mystic Hendrake grunted her dissent. "That road was likely used by Creeg and his Bremenn apostles to cart their spoils back to Aldemeer for safekeeping. Any other roads the Modei built for the pilgrims would be long buried by the weather."

Marcantos scratched Copious's ear, his eyes tracing the mountain ridges ringing the city. Nothing about the situation looked promising. "So, we must defend a city we cannot enter, out in the open, from the weaker position, outnumbered, against an army of undead that might appear at any moment from anywhere?"

Gertrum gripped the hilt of his sword. "The walls are too high and smooth to scale, even for undead. It seems our only advantage is that they will have to enter through the gate. Protect the gate, and we protect the city."

The Mystic huffed. "You're forgetting that the Necromancer has control of a dragon. He can fly over the walls while his brutes keep us busy on the ground."

"Which is why we will split our forces," Marcantos said. "The main force will assemble near the gate. Each of you will command a squad of about eight to ten troops. Your task is to protect that portal at all costs." He pointed to a position immediately south of the city. "I will command a contingency of a dozen ordermen there—Barbarians-Warriors and Mystics-Conjurors. Our task will be to protect the main force's flank. But if Shazarack decides it is more expedient to just fly over the wall, we will rain down a missile assault to keep him back. Agreed?" He waited for their endorsement before stepping back. "One last thing. Pass the word to everyone—Wren's dragon is not to be harmed unless as a last resort. Is that clear?"

Gertrum scratched at his bearded chin through the prolonged silence. "Let us find out if all our training has paid off."

Guiltless Dreams and Innocence

C onner woke with a pain spiking down his spine and a gnawing hunger in his belly. He chided himself for not having had enough foresight to bring food with him. He had always been that way, forgetting about his stomach when his mind busied itself wrestling with a challenging problem. His mother had been fond of fussing about how he would likely die of starvation before he completed his Apothecary Guild's apprenticeship ... right before she shoved a plate of delicious food under his nose. *Yeah, an Apothecary apprentice.* That was a lifetime ago. He inspected the narrow alley leading deeper into the city and the numerous glyph warnings sprawled across the walls. *Only those prepared should journey forth,* one cautioned. There was nothing there to help bolster his waning confidence. He took a deep breath and pushed through the doorway. Just as on the tourney field and in the glade with the pixies, all his senses tangled, as sight became tastes, smells became sounds. Confused, he stumbled and fell.

Conner's eyes fluttered open to the merry sound of a nightingale through a window. Motion drew his attention—tan chiffon curtains twitching in an early autumn breeze. He blinked several times, but it did not change the fact that he was home. Hemera, rising in a cloudless sky, shimmered through the wind-blown pine tree. He squinted in the bright light, feeling confused by the scene but not knowing why. He sat up and yawned, catching the wonderful smells of his mother's cooking. With stomach grumbling, he padded out his bedroom door and down the narrow stairs, then stepped into the kitchen. He shuffled to a stop. "Mom?"

Oshan turned, wearing a broad smile and the apron he had bought her when he was ten. She waved a spatula his way. "Don't just stand there. It takes a lot of effort to have all this food ready at the same time, so sit down and eat before it grows cold."

With tongue pressed to his upper lip, Conner slipped into the seat near the doorway and swallowed down saliva flooding his mouth. He leaned forward and closed his eyes. The aromas of buttered eggs, fresh-ground flour, and mint rushed at him as if in an old memory. "You always knew when to have my breakfast ready." He picked up a hot biscuit and split it open. Steam swirled upward. Before he could bite into it, Ignatius, Oshan's chipmunk bond, scurried across the table to wait patiently beside his plate. Conner pinched off a piece of biscuit and held it out.

Oshan worked on scrubbing the stove as she spoke over her shoulder. "I ran into Master Merich Cleaverbrook the other day. He said he still hasn't found an apprentice. He had such high hopes for you in the Apothecaries Guild. He is so disappointed."

Conner lifted the biscuit to his mouth but froze. The Apothecaries Guild, he thought. Yes, I was going to be an Apothecary. That was very important to me once. Why did I forget that?

His mother went on. "When you are done, you and Pauli can do whatever boys do to get into trouble."

Pauli? Conner thought. I thought he was on his Calling. Wasn't he about to enter the Warriors Order? Something felt off. But before he could work out what it was, he noticed his father sitting at the far end of the table, just as Conner had seen him a hundred times before, staring out the window in quiet contemplation, Notorius curled contently in his lap. Conner nearly jumped. He had not seen him there when he entered the room. But Anton looked different. Yes, years working in the fields had made his father lean and the color of tanned leather. But he looked much older now, frailer, his calloused hands gnarled and wrinkled like an old oak tree root. "What's wrong with father?" Conner asked breathlessly.

Oshan lost her smile. "Anton is tired, dear. Since you left on your Calling, it has been up to him to harvest the fields. He is too old to do that alone. And your sisters are too young to help. Anders Whiterock assisted for a while, but he died of pneumonia shortly after we returned from

Graystone." She stepped forward and placed her hand lightly on Conner's arm. "You should stay and help."

"I— I can't, Mom. I shouldn't be here. I've been banished from Griffinrock." The words felt strange to his tongue, like describing a dream in the morning. *Did I just dream all that?*

Conner caught the sadness in Oshan's eyes before she glanced away. "We heard. Anton was so proud of you. He hasn't been the same since. Now he fears he will not see you again before—" She turned back to the stove, doubling her efforts to scour away the stubborn rust blotches on the iron top.

"The coins you saved for my apprenticeship. Use them to hire help to get you through the fall," Conner suggested. "I'll find a way to get you more money before winter sets in."

Oshan put down the brush. Hunching forward, she shook her head. "The coins are gone, Conner."

"Gone?" Conner asked, the buttered biscuit still steaming between his fingers.

"Soldiers came through the area a few days back—Baron Lendfeather's men. They demanded money for back taxes to secure the funds needed to build a castle for the baron between here and Lincolnton Point. Once his men learned we were parents of … an exile, they returned several times. They were especially harsh on your father."

Conner looked more closely at his father. Anton's eyes and cheeks were bruised, as if he had been in a brawl.

Conner put the uneaten biscuit back on the plate. The baron's men did that? "I should have been here," he rasped between clenched teeth.

Oshan's eyes went wide with sudden hope. "Yes," she said eagerly. "You could hide here. No one in Creeg's Point would dare say anything. You know how they all love having you around—Karlana Landcraft, Estora and Minch Elflander. Always so helpful, you are. Even Pattria misses you."

Conner stiffened. He'd had such great hopes—an Apothecary guildsman, raising a family in town, helping those sick, seeing all the people he grew up with. It was an innocent age, of laughter and playing, of songs and dances, of an honest day's work.

"Stay, Conner," Oshan implored. "You still can. We will find a way to make it work. Everyone would be so happy."

Conner's hands were shaking as he gripped the edges of the table, his body growing taut. *No*, he thought, *this is wrong*. He pushed the hot plate away, ignoring the gnawing pain in his stomach, then rose. The rickety old chair rumbled across the stone floor.

"Conner?" Oshan asked with an inquisitive look.

He forced his legs to carry him to the kitchen doorway, then he stopped. Oshan was trembling, the edges of her mouth arcing low. From fear, sadness, both? "I can't, Mom. There is something I must do."

"Conner, wait," his mother called out, stopping his legs from moving. "You won't get a second chance. You will never see us again—me, your father, Miyra, Sayra, Pattria, all those in town." Oshan sniffed, tears streaming down her cheeks. "Please."

Another chance, Conner thought. "No," he shook his head. He was bonded now. He had to grow up sometime, to let go of guiltless dreams and innocence, of guileless games and waggish play, of naivete. "I know I won't get a second chance. Sometimes we just need to be content that we are given a first."

He stepped through the doorway and found himself back in the quiet, narrow alley, alone. He waited until he had adjusted to the new sensations—the delicious taste of Hemera's morning rays, the colorful sight of his feet crunching over the gravel dirt passage, the melodic sound of the earthy-colored walls. It occurred to him that he had been clinging to remnants of hope that he might someday return to the future he'd wanted before bonding with Skye. With that realization, those hopes melted away, taking with them whatever had been left of his anger and frustration toward Skye.

He wiped away tears, and with a ragged breath, pressed on. If Wallis's map of the city was correct, the second Fire temple was ahead.

Black Knights and Paladins

Marcantos turned slowly around, his experienced eye tracing the line of ridges west, south, then east. "Form up!" he shouted to the troops huddled about several fires where they crowded drying their clothes and armor.

"And what am I to do?" Meera asked. She had been watching silently with arms folded while the general picked out the dozen Barbarians, Warriors, Mystics, and Conjurors he would gather around him to stop Shazarack from flying into the city. Morgana peeked out from beneath Meera's damp hair scattered across her narrow shoulders.

"You, Meera, are going to lead the main force," Marcantos answered.

"Me? I know nothing of war."

"And everything about Shazarack. Besides, you are our only Necromancer. If there is anyone here who can anticipate what this orderman might do, it is you."

Meera took a step back and shook her head. "I will not kill those I have spent most of my life calling friends. They have done nothing to deserve death."

Marcantos squeezed his eyes shut. "Then focus your attention on protecting the troops and sending the undead back to where they came from. My team will put its attention on dealing with the Necromancers commanding them."

Meera swept her eyes across the open terrain, no doubt searching for another way, another path to resolution.

Marcantos's impatience was growing. "I need to know, Meera. Are you with us?"

Meera chewed on her lip for a moment, then nodded.

"Good."

Gertrum prodded Marcantos, then motioned toward the city where Saven escorted a small band of Paladins and Black Knights their way.

As the band drew near, the Black Knight in the lead swept her eye over the gathering of Anarchic and Harmonic troops, then at the fluttering black-and-blood-red flag Staeffan held proudly over the ranks. "I am Commander Roshesh." She tipped her head toward the Paladin next to her. "This is Commander Prei Cartwrighter. You are here with the young Dragonbonded?"

"We are," Marcantos answered. "You talked to him?"

"I did," Roshesh answered. "He mentioned there is an army that seeks to occupy our holy city. Saven here says the attack is imminent." She swept her arm toward the mountain ridges. "So where is this invading army?"

Meera stepped forward. "There is a very powerful Necromancer on his way here now in command of an army of a thousand undead, maybe more ... and a dragon. We believe he has gained access to tunnels created by the Modei that run beneath the mountains. If that is true, we expect him to arrive at any time."

Roshesh signaled a young Black Knight behind her, who sprinted back toward the small crop of tents. "There is little wealth remaining in Shan-Grail. Everything of value was moved to Aldemeer. Do you know what this Necromancer seeks?"

"Power," Meera answered. "He believes he can access extraordinary elemental forces from within the city. He plans to use that power to create another army, a very powerful one, and then to use them and his necro-army to invade and destroy the realms."

Meera caught Cartwrighter's troubled expression. "So, there is truth to this? The city does possess powers?"

Cartwrighter pressed his lips tight, then asked, "How did he come by such knowledge of the city and the underground tunnels?"

"His grandfather was a Bremenn priest," Meera answered.

"But the Bremenn priesthood ended a millennium ago when the Paladins Order was created."

Meera glanced at Marcantos, and likely sensed his growing agitation. "It is a long story that does not help us prepare for what is coming our way." She looked at Commander Roshesh with a sense of urgency. "We could use your help."

Roshesh shook her head. "Our duty is to protect Shan-Grail, not to assist you in your fight."

Marcantos could tell this discussion was shaping up to be one to decide who was in charge of the situation. And he was not about to relinquish his army to this or any other commander. "Somehow I doubt your instructions foresaw having to defend the city against an invading army."

The Mystic Hendrake stepped forward. "Wasn't the city built to defend against an invasion?"

"No. It was a site for Modeic pilgrims. Peace was the way of the Modei. The walls you see were purely symbolic."

"The city would offer us at least some protection," Hendrake suggested.

Roshesh shook her head again. "I am sorry. The edict we follow came from Tatem Creeg himself. None of us may enter."

"We are here to protect your precious city," Gertrum railed.

Roshesh took a rigid stance before Marcantos. "As I see it, you are here to stop someone from invading *your* homelands. No one may enter the city without the permission of the Paladins and Black Knights Councils."

Gertrum started to argue with the woman, but Marcantos placed a hand on his shoulder. It would be a waste of energy trying to convince a Black Knight or Paladin to let them use the city as a defensive position. The orders' focus was spiritual; everything else was irrelevant. The general took in the solemn faces of his troops gathered behind him. "We need a strategy to stop Shazarack from out here."

The Great Waters of a Benevolent Cosmos

Shan-Grail
RUINS

Conner squinted up at the bright sky as he stepped through the second Fire temple. His senses were still scrambled, but if his bearings were correct, hardly any time had passed since he'd stepped into the alley that had taken him back home, what felt like an hour. Relieved, he pressed on.

He spent the remainder of that morning traversing the second ringed street. Concerned he might miss a vital clue, he stopped frequently along the way to examine the many hieroglyphs painted on the walls. But none he was capable of translating helped. Many of the glyphs were similar to the ones he had passed along his way down first ring, but with subtle differences. Instead of images of people and families, these were of beings that looked much different—some like the pixie-like creatures that had attacked him in the glade near Xylor, some tall light-skinned people with pointed ears and high brows, some squat muscular people with gnarled faces. He passed images of worlds unimaginably different from Gaia. In his altered perception, his mind was filled with images of seeds of ideas sprouting, smells of the formation of theories, sounds of great flowing streams of impressions, taste of rainbows of reasoning, of clouds raining logic, of solitary beings immersed in unscented introspection.

Some part of him could not fathom their meaning, and yet he also sensed something new awakening within him, sprouting in the fertile soil of his freshly tilled mind. He recalled the morning just two fortnights before when he'd argued with Skye about returning home. *I'm frustrated. I'm upset. I'm annoyed. This morning, Pattria ended our relationship and is returning home with my parents. I too would like to return home, Skye. But some of us don't get what we want.* It was as if someone else had said those words.

He saw now how that hope of someday returning to the life he'd known before had altered him, how it had driven his decisions. On he walked, and the heavy weight of his past was lifted from him.

He was barely aware of his arrival at the end of the second ring, though when he stopped, he could recall passing through its four elemental temples. Just as at the end of the outer ring, a wall loomed before him. To his left was a doorway that would lead him out of the city. Again, he directed his body to his right, to another alleyway much like the one at the end of the outer ring. Around him were painted warnings and suggestions to turn away. *No more, Conner,* a part of him complained.

He recalled Wallis's words that Modeic pilgrims took many trips to complete this maze. Now he understood why. He was exhausted, his mind weary and laden with thoughts he did not yet fully comprehend. It would take time to process them all. Would he be given another trial? Would he be transported home again, to be challenged once more to stay? Would he have the fortitude to leave this time? But the urgency of the moment called his legs into motion. Hesitantly, he stepped into the alley. And all his senses folded back on themselves. Blind and numb, he fell into the darkness that engulfed him.

Conner was standing at the bank of the lake near Grimmley's home. Grimmley had just told him something important. What was it? Yes, that he should let his inner voice guide him in what to do. Do? He gazed at the sparkling water. Ripples cascaded across the lake, each wave mixing and mingling with the others. Conner had a choice to make—to save his dragon or warn the king of Evinfaire's conspiracy.

Conner squeezed his eyes shut. No, that was not right. It was something different. He looked out again. Light glistened off the lake waters stirred up by the breeze. The leaves of the oaks and birch beyond the water, spotted with yellow and orange, trembled from a sudden gust. Their reflection shimmered across the lake. It was fall, not mid-summer. Where had time gone? He pressed his palm to his forehead.

Grimmley's voice pulled Conner from his reflection. "Where are we heading?"

Conner smiled at his old preceptor. He was not sure why, but he was ecstatic to see Grimmley again, even though he looked quite disgruntled.

"Stop grinning like Stomper caught stealing toast from my table!"

At the sound of his name, the raccoon appeared by the kitchen windowsill and chortled at the old Shaman.

Conner focused his attention, wanting nothing more than to burn this moment into his mind, to never forget. "I'm sorry, Grimmley."

"Sorry?" Grimmley's head snapped up. His face softened before bolstering his defenses. "As well you should be! Not paying attention to what you're doing, not listening to my instructions, sleeping well past Hemera's first rays." Grimmley threw up his hands, his lips puffed out. "Baa!" He stepped closer to examine his pupil over the tops of his wire-rimmed glasses. "I honestly don't know why I have kept you around so long!"

Barthox gave a supportive hoot from her perch inside the cottage.

Grimmley's complaining only made Conner beam all the brighter at the two. Why *was* he sorry anyway? "You were always there for me, Grimmley. I should have been here when you needed me most." The words came out of Conner before he could stop them.

For an instant, Conner caught a reflection of sadness in Grimmley's eyes. But he blinked it away. "Then you haven't heard a word I've ever said, have you? If I had to contend with you always underfoot ... Well, Barthox and I would never get anything done!"

There was more Conner wanted to say, so he let it out, like water gushing up from an underground stream. "I am sorry for defying you and breaking in to the Shamans' temple. And I am sorry for not telling you about letting Meera go free. I wanted to tell you that I didn't kill her, but I—I thought I would always have the chance. I never thought I wouldn't see you again."

He was still not clear where all this was coming from. As the words bubbled forth, he sobbed, his heart caught in a vise. And still there was more. "And I should not have told you I learned Shazarack was a Necromancer from research at Graystone. That was a lie. Skye heard it from Meera. I should have been more open with you. I should have trusted you more."

He could no longer look at his preceptor. Grimmley would be disappointed in him.

"That is all well and good, boy, but why are you telling me all this now? You want me to sleep better at night?" Grimmley chuckled. "Conner, I'm gone."

Gone? Yes, Grimmley's spirit had been reclaimed by the Cosmos. How could he have forgotten that? He had been so consumed with preventing Shazarack from invading the realms, with the coming war, with being banished from Griffinrock, with worrying about his parents under baron rule, that he'd never given himself time to grieve Grimmley's death. He had refused to let his feelings of loss overwhelm him. But they would not be denied any longer. Conner wept.

"Regret," he said, sniffling. "I regret what I did, Grimmley."

"Why are you telling me this?" Grimmley asked softly.

"Because I am disappointed in myself." *There it is!*

"Conner." Grimmley gripped his shoulders, staring up at him over his wire-rimmed glasses. "This disappointment, this sorrow feeds your anger, and that is why you lash out. Seeking vengeance for my death will not release you from the past any more than it will release you from your sorrow. And you will not be able to do what is needed if you don't let go of it." Grimmley's hands tightened. "You cannot change the past any more than you can control the future. You can either focus on the present or be dragged down by regret."

Conner recalled the words Grimmley had told him that morning when they were here. Grimmley had said he was like a rock skimming over the lake. Each time he made contact with someone, he left behind a ripple flowing outward, a wake of change in his passing. "Someday, my boy," Grimmley had said, "you will have to realize that even the stone succumbs to the will of the water." And he felt himself being drawn under, slowly immersed into the great waters of a benevolent Cosmos.

Suddenly bolstered, Conner started up the boardwalk leading to Grimmley's gazebo. But he stopped, looking back to take in the tranquil scene one last time—of Grimmley standing in his manicured garden, a pipe in his mouth. Gray smoke curled gently from his chimney. Sara pranced sprily in the field beyond, her tail high in the air as she tossed her head. He wanted to burn the image into his mind.

"I will find who killed you," he promised, not out of a desire for revenge, but based on his own solid conviction. Turning away one last time, he took his next step.

Conner pressed his palm against the wall, forcing his mind to focus, to adjust once more to his new perceptions. All his normal senses were gone. Yet he sensed an awareness of his environment—of the impressions of matter and intuitions of light as they ebbed and flowed, shifting in a constant stream of consciousness. He knew his body was there, breathing and wondering, but that too was simply an impression. He could neither see nor hear nor smell. Once the dizziness faded away, he found himself back in Shan-Grail, in the narrow alley he had just entered.

Conner floated onward, slipping into the third Fire temple.

The Battle at Shan-Grail

While Marcantos and several aides discussed how to use the open terrain to their advantage, Meera strolled before the marshaled troops. Many stood nervously, rubbing their palms along their staves or fingering the edges of their swords, shuffling their feet with an anxious restlessness. Most had never been in battle before. And though she had not either, she was determined not to show any signs of fear or doubt.

"You must not think of undead as soldiers," Meera shouted as she strode before the ranks. "A spear in the chest, a severed arm or leg, even eviscerating their bowels will only slow them down. The only way to stop them is to remove their heads with your sword or burn them to cinders with fire and lightning. Is that clear?" She shuffled to a stop while the troops mumbled their understanding. She was not infusing them with courage. Still, bravery was irrelevant if they did not know how to take these ghouls down.

"And remember what the general and I taught you about being Aware," Meera went on. "Stay focused. And work together. You will succeed if—" A deep rumble cut her off. The ground beneath her feet undulated. Pebbles danced for a moment, then everything went deadly still. Dust across the valley drifted upward, covering the wide expanse in a brownish haze.

"Where did that come from?" Marcantos called out Near the southern wall. "Gertrum, locate the source of that. Quickly now!"

Several Scouters gathered around Gertrum. Together, they squatted in a tight circle. Pressing their palms to the dirt, they called upon Earth. But before they could utter a chant, a sonorous groan reverberated throughout the vale, making it impossible to know the direction of its source. The ground quivered and moaned. Boulders and rocks along the ridges east and west of the city clattered down the steep inclines.

Gertrum pointed to the west. "It sounds like—" He never finished the sentence.

The blast that followed was so intense that nearly everyone was blown back by its force. The slope along the west ridge of the valley vanished in an ever-expanding puff of dust and rock. Several Sorcerers and Warlocks hastily constructed a dome over the huddled troops to shield them from the boulders and stones that, moments later, hailed down over them. At last, the rocks stopped falling. The dust drifted to the south, exposing a cavity as massive as the city's gates. And through that gaping hole, like ants scurrying from their bed after a rainstorm, swarmed a seething horde of undead.

Meera swallowed hard as the undead boiled forth. When at last they stopped swarming, she surveyed a necro-army much greater than she had thought possible. She estimated the count to be at least three thousand.

Marcantos glowered at Meera. "You said a thousand!"

"I had no clue!" she gaped back. How could I have been so mistaken? We are all going to die.

Assembled into several masses, the necro-army fractured to create a rent down the middle of their lines. And out of the mouth of the hole emerged Valkere, with Shazarack and Arna astride his shoulders. The dragon did not pause but strolled down the chasm created by the necro-army and out onto the valley.

Marcantos growled at Meera, then pointed to the northwest. "Move the army to a more protected position!" Then, summoning his small band of ordermen about him, he took a position behind the main force nearer the city wall.

Valkere traipsed forward, moving as if he had all day.

Meera pulled her hood forward to hide her face, lest Shazarack see her. She moved to Wren's side and drew her behind the front line of Barbarians standing at the ready. She gently hugged Wren against her shoulder, trying to soothe the girl, who at the sight of her dragon bond, had begun to sob.

Valkere came to a halt twenty paces before the assembly.

"Are you in charge of these forces?" Shazarack asked the Paladin and Black Knight standing at the front.

Roshesh stepped forward. "I am commander of the Black Knight forces charged with protecting our holy city." She gestured to the man dressed in bright armor beside her. "Prei commands the Paladin forces."

"Ah, then you are the two I need to speak to. I would like permission to enter Shan-Grail," Shazarack declared, as if giving an edict.

Roshesh shook her head. "We cannot give you permission."

"Surely, I can appeal to your sensibilities," Shazarack suggested smoothly. "The great Cosmos itself has brought me to your sacred city." Neither responded, so Shazarack went on. "I am not interested in any of the venerated relics that might reside within. And I do not wish to disturb your hallowed ground." Still, they did not respond. "I am on a pilgrimage, just as the august Modei did before. I have come seeking guidance from our Cosmic creator and wish nothing more than to learn what it has to teach me of our Gaia."

After a few moments, Roshesh turned toward Prei, and the two commanders began to debate in a hushed tone.

Surely, they are not seriously considering Shazarack's request! After several minutes of the commanders' hushed deliberation, Meera threw her hood back and slipped forward through the lines. Grabbing the shoulders of the two commanders, she shook them hard. "You are being beguiled by this man. Do not listen to him!"

Roshesh blinked at her as if she were half asleep but said nothing.

Meera pushed between them, stepping forward to glare at the man astride Wren's dragon.

"Ah, Meera. I wondered where you'd scurried off to," Shazarack said.

"I did as you suggested. I sought out my purpose."

Shazarack chuckled. "It seems you found one." His eyes swept across the small army at the ready, then smirked. "You think stopping me is your purpose?"

"I do."

"You cannot keep me from the city." Shazarack glanced up at the flag tied to the end of Staeffan's long crooked branch, then scanned the strained faces assembled before him. "Interesting flag. Now where is that meddlesome boy? And his wayward dragon?"

Meera looked around as if she had misplaced something irrelevant, then shrugged. "What boy?"

Shazarack laughed. "I believe you know who I mean—the Harmonic, Conner Stonefield. The lad is quite talented at sticking his nose into places it does not belong. No doubt he is around here somewhere."

"Oh, *that* boy. Yes, well, he's with the main force of our army at the river just south of here. They should be arriving very soon now." Meera found it hard to keep a confident pose under Shazarack's intense scrutiny.

Shazarack lost his smile, his gaze turning to the city and the gray-brown stone wall towering before him. "Somehow, I think not. In fact, I think *this* is your main force." He straightened his shoulders. "I believe the boy is looking for a way in, if he is not already inside. If the boy can enter, then so can I."

"You will not be given permission to enter our holy city," Roshesh declared over Meera's shoulder.

Shazarack gestured toward the undead gathered near the cavernous opening, then leaned forward. "Oh, it will happen. The only question we have to debate is how."

"Do not step onto these hallowed grounds and threaten the Paladins and Black Knight Orders," Roshesh responded. "You have lost your right for sanction and must leave. Now. There will be no parley."

"Very well. Then let us see on which side of this conflict the Cosmos stands." Shazarack's eyes were full on Meera. "It would seem the only purpose you have found is to die on this desolate scrap of mountain dirt." With a slight nudge from Shazarack's heel, Valkere ambled back to the necro-army.

Meera spun to face her people. "Prepare for the assault!" While the main force tightened their ranks, Meera went to Wren. "I need you to go stand with Marcantos and his band." Wren started to argue, but Meera glared back. "No arguing. Go!" While Meera watched Wren retreat back to Marcantos's position, Roshesh and Prei mustered their guards of nearly two dozen to supplement the line behind the Barbarians and Warriors.

Roshesh pressed up beside Meera and drew her sword. She looked over at Shazarack as she ran her thumb across the blade. "Thank you. I have no idea what happened back there, but I was compelled to do as he requested."

"I understand. I was also nearly caught in his web."

"Commander!" one of the Black Knights shouted, pointing across the valley. Valkere was taking flight, spiraling ever higher above the necro-army. At a height of several hundred paces, the dragon twisted and angled toward the city. As Valkere neared, Marcantos and his band began their aerial defense. The Conjurors and Mystics chanted, and the bright clouds overhead darkened. Thunder rumbled through the valley. Several bolts of lightning streaked down from a black cloud and struck Valkere before he was halfway to the city. The dragon reeled.

Wren cried out as she watched, her hand to her mouth.

Valkere circled back and landed on the western ridge above the necro-army. Shazarack gave a signal to his Necromancers.

"Shazarack knows he must stop the aerial assault if he is to get into the city," Meera shouted to the troops. She could see the fear in their wide stares, smell it on the wind. "Our task is to keep the necro-army from reaching Marcantos's band. Do you understand? Hold the line—at all costs!" She did not have time to say anything more as she heard a thundering sound like stampeding horses. The army of undead was surging forward, chewing up the space between them at an alarming rate.

"Shields!" Meera shouted. She closed her eyes, letting the feeling of being Aware take her and ignoring the flares of elementals being drawn from those around her. Driving her staff into the ground, she beckoned to Earth and Fire, and they answered her call. She imagined herself as nothing but a receptacle, as Earth and Fire sprang from ground beneath her feet and surged through her body. Her legs trembled and shuddered. Still, she drew upon the elementals. Her arms trembled. She fought against the force that wanted to shatter her bones like glass. Her mouth gaped and a deep bellow ushered forth. *More, Meera!* Her spine spasmed and arched with the exertion of holding so much energy. When she could stand the pain no longer, and she thought her entire body would explode, she released the energy all in one great incantation. *"Hemea ousia fragiaspida!"*

Meera's shield descended around the army just as the lead undead struck. The shield buckled with the force of their mass slamming into it, but Meera bent her mind to fortify it further. Less than a pace away, undead screamed their rage, scratching and clawing in a chaotic frenzy of arms and teeth, fighting for a chance to rip apart the living flesh of those just beyond their reach.

Other ordermen and guildsmen behind the front line added their own shields to hold back the swarm, while Barbarians, Black Knights, and Paladins along the front began the grisly task of destroying the snarling, seething mass of undead with their elementally enhanced blades. The Warlock next to Meera sent an undead spiraling away, then slammed his battlestaff down on the top of an enraged undead's head, spraying his bone, hair, and gray matter over the bodies of the undead about him. To her other side, an elderly undead woman's arm broke through Meera's shield, clawing at Meera's cloak. A Barbarian severed the limb with a quick flick of his sword, maddening the woman further as she bit and clawed at the shield with her remaining arm.

Another undead, a man old enough to be Meera's grandfather, pounded on the shield before her, his pallid face frozen in a horrific snarl. Meera raised her hand, palm out. *"Ourera psychi apostelpsychi."* He crumbled to the ground, only to be replaced by a young woman who climbed on top of the old man's body, screaming and scratching on the shield.

I Am Dragonbonded

Conner's perception was awash with sensations he did not understand, which made time seem to grind by slowly. Exiting the Fire temple, he became aware that the noon sky had turned black, an angry froth of boiling dark clouds and flashes of lightning. Though he could no longer discern up from down, the patterned Weave waved across his mindscape. It was as if he were walking across the fabric of space itself. And everywhere around him, brilliant rainbow funnels of Anarchic life twisted and churned, feeding off the Harmonic Weave's rippling colored patterns, which twitched in response to the funnels. Captured on the city's walls, he beheld the ignition of gas coalescing into stars and the birth of planets swirling around bright, flaming orbs.

Conner kept his body moving forward along the street. After the Air temple, he encountered images of even more exotic creatures than those in the previous ring. Some were far more hideous, with bug-like eyes, bloated bodies, tails, or bulky legs, while the beauty and wonder of others were beyond description. After the Water temple, he watched the colors and brightness in the Weave undulate and morph into amazing shapes that extended in every direction. Scenes of great battles between ships in the skies preceded spiraling clusters of stars flying through brightly-lit gaseous clouds. As much as he wanted to stay, he pressed on. And finally, when he had passed beyond the Earth temple, he witnessed stars exploding, sending their matter and energy back out into the universe to become the seeds for other stars. He beheld planets colliding or being consumed by their stars, entire populations of living things snuffed out in an instant.

As in the previous ring, Conner could sense the images altering him, shifting his consciousness, molding his thought in subtle ways. As he walked, he came to see that his belief that he'd caused Grimmley's death was the source of his hunger for revenge. Regret had blinded him to seeing the world clearly. And as he let go, he understood the meaning of the glyphs in the room with the golden wheel: *What you take will be lost. What you leave behind will be found.*

Hemera had crossed its zenith when he came to a stop, the back wall to the Fire temple ahead of him. As before, a portal to his left led out of the city. And to his right ... Beyond the shimmering entrance that would take him to the very core of the city was a flight of spiraling stairs. Again, he hesitated. Before he could reach the stairs, he would be given his third trial. His first two had dredged up a lot of emotional agitation in him. Where would this next trial take him? What if he did not come out again? He was weary and hungry. Did he have the strength to do what was needed? The strength to leave?

He closed his eyes. This time, he would fight to hold on to the present, cling to the now, and not be pulled deep into whatever dream he stepped into. With clenched jaw, he stepped into the portal. And all his senses flew away like autumn leaves in a winter gale. What remained was but a single perception. Not sight. Not sound. But an awareness that cleared away all delusions manifested by his senses. And with its forging, he staggered and pitched to the side, falling into a wild darkness.

Conner held his hands before him. With just a thought, flames danced along his fingertips. "Finally, I have access to my powers and there is nothing I can do to protect you." He stiffened, confused but not sure why. The sounds of dripping water echoed from the next dark chamber. He was in the Graystone castle dungeon. He heard a noise. Making a quick fist, he snuffed out the flames. Veressa was stepping into the dank cell, moving toward the light he had summoned in the middle of the room. They had been talking about something. What was it? Yes. Something about Mariette taunting him, forcing him to remain in a clammy, unlocked dungeon cell.

"Why are you down here alone in this underground fortress?" Veressa asked gruffly, her eyes furrowed. "I would have expected that from your dragon, not you."

Conner cringed at the suggestion that he was hiding. He wanted to defend his actions, but deep inside, he knew she had struck a chord.

Veressa strode closer. "You are my Champion, Conner. You are endowed with the powers of the great Dragonbonded. Yet you play handmaiden to a duchess?"

Conner stood there, his jaw hanging slack. His cheeks burned at her candidness. After all, he had, just moments before, told Skye that he was useless as Veressa's protector.

Veressa shifted forward, moving so near that Conner felt the heat from her supple body in the dank cell, smelled the lavender in her shining blond hair.

Yes. Why are you down here, Conner? Why are you playing handmaiden to a duchess? Conner's eyes flitted about the empty chamber, looking for any way to avoid facing the answer. But the dungeon offered no means of escape. Finally, he settled on Veressa's steady stare, her blue eyes reflecting fierce self-confidence and intense poise. He drew upon her strength, then took a long, slow breath. "I could not believe the Cosmos would entrust *me* of all people with the onerous responsibility of being Dragonbonded. I fought against it." He shrugged. "It was easier to cling to my timidity and believe the Cosmos had made a mistake choosing me than it was to accept that I had the mettle needed for the work at hand."

Veressa slipped her arms around his waist. "Timidity?" she chortled. "Timidity did not save me from the Sorcerer in Pennington Point. Nor did timidity disrupt the Anarchic plans to place an Assassin at the royal table. Nor did it guide you to confront Shazarack at Thanatos. It takes considerable courage to let go and let the Cosmos guide you. When are you going to accept that you have everything you need?"

With Veressa so close, Conner found it hard to focus. "Yes. I did not believe in myself, nor did I have faith the Cosmos would guide me. I see that now." He considered how vehemently he had resisted accepting help from Marcantos and his army. Morgas had taught him that strength could become a weakness. "I needed to prove that I could stand on my own. And my desire for independence became my weakness." As he spoke the words, he felt the strength of their meaning flow through him, washing clean all his doubt. And with it came a sudden urgency. He had something to do, though he could not remember what it was. He started toward the entrance of the cell, but Veressa's words made him waver.

"What are you going to do?" she asked.

"There is a reason the Cosmos chose me. Now I must discover what it is. But I will no longer be a duchess's handmaiden. I *am* Dragonbonded."

Conner propped his body against the wall, trembling as if he had sprinted a mile. He felt stripped bare and raw. Wallis's warnings that he was not ready for ascension haunted him. Stories of Dragonbonded madness floated across his mind. He needed time to think through what was happening to him, to understand the changes he could feel moving inside him, altering him, redefining who he was. He just wanted to lie down and sleep.

Far beyond exhausted—physically, mentally, emotionally—he pushed away from the wall and shambled toward the stairwell ahead.

Everything You Need

Marcantos stood with his Conjurors and Mystics, watching helplessly as the struggle played out before them. With the necro-army so close to his troops, he would not risk collateral damage with any missile strikes. The undead horde refused to relent. Maddened beyond anything human or animal, the undead beat against the shields while those on the front line diced them into chunks of inanimate flesh. And still the undead came in a manic frenzy, clambering over those piling ever higher at the base of the army's shields, surging up Meera's elemental dome.

Motion drew Marcantos's attention, and he pointed to the middle of the valley, where a hundred or so black-cloaked figures were charging forward in a tight cluster. "Look!" he shouted with delight to the master Mystic beside him.

The Mystic smiled. The Necromancers had made a tactical error, leaving themselves exposed. The Mystic directed the others to begin another missile assault. Within moments, streaks of lightning, explosive projectiles, and blazing fireballs churned the central area of the valley into a billowing cloud of gray dust and debris. With the deaths of several Necromancers, some of the mob of undead collapsed near the shield, while others stopped their attacks and began wandering aimlessly.

Marcantos's attack must have been the signal Shazarack had been waiting for. Valkere took flight once more, winging over the undead forces and toward the city.

Again, Marcantos's band was forced to shift their focus back to the dragon. To the general's frustration, by the time they had compelled Shazarack to retreat to his ridge, the Necromancers had crossed the valley and were mingling with their undead near the shield.

Much of the last fortnight had been like a bad dream for Wren. But seeing Valkere being blasted with bolts of lightning and balls of fire snapped her out of her doldrums. She could not watch Marcantos's band of ordermen turn their assault on Valkere again, so she slipped away along the city wall, then sprinted toward the main force. Those in the rear of the formation, having rotated off the front line, were sapped of both physical and psychic energy. Several Barbarians did not even have the strength to lift their swords. She had to do her part, to help in whatever way she could.

Wren studied the shielding overhead, sensing Meera's weave of Earth and Fire. The shield was weakening under the undead's perpetual assault. It would not last much longer. And once it was gone, the Army of the Dragonbonded would be overwhelmed within a matter of moments. She closed her eyes, trying to recall the exact pattern of elemental weave used to protect Dragongarde, but it was far too elaborate for her to attempt to recreate. Instead, her thoughts turned to the shield Conner had created near Valkere's cave the night they'd escaped Xylor.

Once she had the image of the pattern in her mind, she zigzagged forward, getting slammed from all sides by men and women in the thrall of battle. The odor of sweat and urine was intense. The sounds of jarring grunts, of shouted orders, of pleas for help, of screams and crying, of steel slicing through gristle and bone pricked at her ears. The force of elementals being cast made her head throb. A battlestaff struck her in the back of the head, and she fell forward. But she clawed her way back to her feet and staggered on.

Near the front line, she closed her eyes, driving away the sounds of fierce battle, the inhuman snarls and howls of the undead. And she drew on the four elementals. As she wove them together, the shield sprouted from her hands. But before she could mingle her weave with Meera's, something metallic struck her in the temple. She went down hard. Dazed, she tried to get up. But Meera's shield faltered, then, sparking, collapsed. And Wren was trampled beneath the undead horde.

Marcantos watched in horror as Meera's shield collapsed. The great necro-army wave flooded over the troops, pounding and biting, howling with glee of no longer being constrained. Immediately, the front line folded, many of them buried beneath the sea of undead like raging water over a ruptured dam. "Shift your attack back on the Necromancers and their undead! We cannot leave our army to die at the hands of those fiends!"

"But Shazarack!" The master Mystic shouted, pointing at the dragon winging toward them. "He will get into the city."

"We have done what we can for Conner. It is up to him now to stop the Necromancer."

Through his melded senses, Conner felt the rumble of explosions outside the city, the clash of steel, the shouts of men, the inhuman screams of rage. Even here, in the middle of the vast uninhabited city, he knew his army was fighting and dying to prevent Shazarack from reaching Shan-Grail. That could only mean they had not been able to stop him yet.

With no other choice, Conner staggered forward and found himself at the base of a spiraling staircase. About him were more painted images of beings. Some had spiraling horns and magnificent leathery wings like bats, while other had great feathered wings like birds. Others had four or six arms, and still others sported an array of legs. He was not sure how, but he knew these to be images of Astral Beings.

As Conner ascended the long spiral stairwell, he drew his body along behind him, his leaden legs trudging slowly up, up, up. Outside the bounds of space and time, his senses melded into a single perception, he heard nothing, saw nothing, felt nothing. And yet it seemed the entire universe opened to his consciousness. He knew that insects scurried over flowers growing along the walls of the tower, that troops struggled as they battled undead just beyond the city, even that Gaia around him thrummed with a gentle aliveness. He had never felt so sentient.

At last, he stepped out onto the tower's roof. The sky was a churning caldron of blackness, blocking out the remnants of Hemera high overhead. Rain fell in small droplets while lightning flickered. Immediately, Conner knew he was not alone. Shazarack was there, examining a Cosmic Star built in the center of the floor, marked with thick, dark stones. The Necromancer's spirit was a glorious, shining fount of perpetual energy. The amulet around his neck flared and pulsed as if it were Shazarack's heart. Nearby, Valkere hung from the side of the tower, his talons deep in the hard stone, his wings spread wide to sustain his balance. Yet Conner sensed the dragon was in great anguish, as if his anchored spirit were imprisoned within unbreakable chains and heavy locks. Arna stood rigidly near the tower's ledge.

"Conner!" Shazarack shouted over a clap of thunder at the sight of the boy. "There you are!" He strolled closer. "I was wondering when you would arrive. Impeccable timing, as expected."

"You were expecting me?"

"Of course!" Shazarack laughed. "I told you before—we are connected, you and I. The Cosmos meant for us to come together. Surely, you see that now? It was not fate that bonded you to one of my very own creations or gifted you with the ability to speak a language I devised. Fate did not send you to my cavern to awaken me from my long slumber. Fate did not bring the woman's dragon to me so that I could find the tunnel. Nor was it fate that brought you to Thanatos so we could meet. Look around you." Shazarack raised his arms and spun slowly. "Purpose, not coincidence, brought us both to the ancient city at this moment. I, the bringer of balance to all things; and you, the instrument of the transformation."

As Shazarack spoke, Conner sensed the Necromancer's stone thrumming, and he was awestruck with the realization that Shazarack was right. *Why did I not see it the first time we met?* he wondered. Everyone had been trying to tell him that he could not deny the Cosmos's will. He could not draw his thoughts away from Shazarack. Spellbound by the young man's wonderous brilliance, Conner felt compelled to listen to him, to savor everything the great creator of dragons said.

"Do you know why Necromancers have always been rejected by society? Why people, even Anarchists, consider our work so repulsive?" Shazarack asked.

Conner shook his head. Eagerness grew inside him. He wanted to know the answer. Surely Shazarack would not torment him by not giving him the answer!

"It is because we scare them, because we have keys for locked doors to realities they prefer remain unopened. They fear the truth that lies on the other side."

"And what truth is that?" Conner wanted to know, though he was not sure why it was important.

"That the universe is much greater than they could ever conceive. They don't want us to discover what lies beyond, because then we would see through their small-minded sham, and they would no longer have control over us."

"Yes," Conner agreed, his own heart pulsing with the rhythm of the stone in Nartesis's amulet.

"Don't you think it is time we change that, Conner? Together, we have that power. Let us draw back the curtains and force them to see the universe in all its glory and complexity. And once they have seen beyond their veil, we can move forward to build the most incredible society. Is that not what was ordained in the Omen of the Dragonbonded?"

"Yes," Conner whispered. He could see it now. He could almost feel it, taste it. If everyone saw the interconnectedness of everything as he did now, there would be no need for war. Conner recalled Wallis's words. *Sometimes the only way to best an adversary is to let them win.* Suddenly, he wanted more than anything to help Nartesis. "What do you need me to do?"

"Call upon the elemental powers of the city. Let us usher in a new age for all men, a new dawn of peace and prosperity, the likes of which has never been seen before."

"And then what?" Conner needed to know what was expected of him.

"As I mentioned before, I endowed my creations with certain qualities. I imbued them to heed my call. Draw upon the four elementals, and I will show you how to call them here. Think of it—thousands of dragons at our command. No one will dare stand against us. In one decisive move, we will subjugate them all."

Yes. Conner could see it now. He envisioned them coming—drakes, wyverns, even amphitheres—all flocking in droves, blackening the skies in every direction. *Of course! This is my purpose!* The Cosmos had brought him here to summon the dragons.

"I know how to call them!" he whooped. Eager to begin, he stepped over the center of the Cosmic Star and reached his arm to the south. The Fire obelisks along the three rings of city streets below responded to his call, and Fire surged through him. He swung his arm to the west. And the three obelisks in the Air temples responded. Filled with Air, he looked to the north and drew deep on Water. Then finally he pulled Earth to him from the east. The elementals surged and flowed through him. His body shuddered and shook with the forces. He had never felt so alive.

Shazarack laughed with glee. "More, Conner! You will need much more!"

Conner threw both arms out to the south. Reaching his consciousness out, he traveled along a flowing vein of Fire. In a flash, he was standing high on top of a great mountain. Far below, the River Tresdan flowed to his west, and Lake Donogal sparkled in the brilliant light to the south. He knew this place. It was the dormant volcano along the northern border of Elvenstein. Next to him rose an obelisk with grimacing, painted faces like the one at Elmsdorf. Fire blazed around it. He reached out and touched the stone monolith with his mind. Immediately, Fire burned through him and he screamed out in agony. But the pain lasted only a moment, then was gone.

He looked around. He was no longer on the volcano, but on a small island in the middle of a large, crystal-clear lake. Beside him, Air swirled around another obelisk, again with grimacing faces. As with the Fire obelisk, he pressed his palm against it.

In a blazing flash of light, Conner was standing on the top of a great island structure surrounded by a vast ocean. He felt mist on his face, tasted salt on his lips. Against billowing, white clouds in an azure sky, a hundred black wyverns spun and dove in a playful game of tag. He did not know how he knew, but this was Skye's home. He reached out and touched the obelisk.

The ground quivered beneath him, and Conner was standing beside the obelisk in Elmsdorf. Alpslanders were all around him, at work and play, though none seemed aware he was there. He touched the obelisk's growling faces and was immediately back on top of Shan-Grail's tower, the four elementals raging through the marrow in his bones. It had begun to drizzle. To the north, a twister churned over a mountain peak.

"Yes!" Nartesis shouted in the growing rain. "Now call upon my creations! When they arrive, I will use the city to bind them to my will. It is time we build our new future!"

Conner nodded. The thought of helping Nartesis thrilled him. Slowly, he turned his consciousness inward. He drew the elemental threads together. Mud and dust whirled around his legs. Streaks of lightning arced from his palms up into the dark clouds. Spiraling columns of fire spun around his outstretched arms, emitting waves of steam and heat. He had never imagined he could control so much elemental energy. And the power made him giddy.

A sleek form streaked across the sky, but Conner would not be distracted from his purpose. He felt along the spiraling rings of elemental force, and the obelisks with their angry faces responded. The roar of a maddened beast rang in his ears. He jerked his arms out wide, the words of his summoning on his lips, ready to create the weave that would call the dragons to Nartesis.

A massive shockwave of light and air nearly blew Conner off his feet, disrupting his spell. He stumbled forward. Suddenly, his awareness was fully back in his body.

"Conner!" Skye bellowed next to him.

Conner shook his head hard, then turned his gaze to his bond. Beneath the shell of the dragon's scaly skin, Conner beheld a nearly blinding radiant being of energy, reminding him of the paintings in the stairwell below. Skye's crown of spiraling horns and magnificent, leathery wings fanned wide in regal display brought tears to Conner's eyes. A stream of energy ran between him and his bond.

"Finish what you started!" Shazarack shrieked.

Conner glanced back at Shazarack. But the Necromancer's beautiful spirit had become shriveled and ravaged with blight, reminding Conner of the tainted and befouled spirit he had seen at Thanatos. Arna looked the same. Their images had been illusions manifested by Shazarack's stone. Exasperation gnawed at Conner. He had been duped yet again. "No. I will not do this."

"Look down there." Shazarack pointed past the city gates. "Finish calling the dragons and I will save your friends from the deaths they now face."

Conner gazed down. A mass of raving undead had washed over the front line of men and women. The second and third lines of troops had also buckled under the weight of the bodies crashing over them, sending the army into total mayhem.

"If you do not finish what you started, everyone down there will die needlessly. Whether you help me or not, my creatures will come. I shall not be denied my vision."

Conner watched as Staeffan was buried beneath a mob of undead, clawing, beating, shrieking. In defiance of their concerted efforts, Staeffan kept his arm extended high above the pile of undulating bodies, gripping his makeshift flagpole. The black Dragonbonded flag whipped about, but did not fall.

"Finish it!" Shazarack shook his fist at Conner.

Conner saw Meera enchanting something. The heap of undead smothering Staeffan crumbled to the ground, and the flag rose higher from the pile of bodies, still fluttering in the wind. Conner considered sending bolts of lightning or balls of fire, but knew he would likely kill more troops than undead. Rage boiled in him. He felt helpless, defeated.

But Veressa's voice broke through the clamor in his head. *When are you going to accept that you have everything you need?*

Conner closed his eyes, blocking out Shazarack and the destruction far below. Something Wallis had said to him drew his thoughts, about how Necromancers summoned spirits from other planes through temporary gateways. Suddenly, he could see strings of energy stretched from the undead, as if they were marionettes suspended from the Mental plane.

Conner harkened back to the night in the Shamans' temple, to the weave Meera had used on the undead assassin. He interlaced Fire and Earth as she had, then drew the threads together. Conner felt the gateways to the Mental plane weaken, then clamp shut. The strings of energy dangling from the Mental plane snapped, and far below, the great mass of undead shuddered, stiffened, and collapsed.

Everything fell still and silent.

"No!" Nartesis shouted, his eyes wide as they swept over the fallen undead littering the valley. His vision, his dreams, everything he had spent his life's energy on—gone in a flash. "What have you done?" he asked, numb.

"What was needed," Conner answered.

Nartesis had barely heard Conner's answer. "Why did the Cosmos forsake me?" He scanned the city horizon, searching for an answer, something that would bring meaning to his shattered existence.

"Nartesis, the Cosmos did not forsake you. You forsook the Cosmos. We were never meant to live forever in the Physical plane. Look at Arna. Her spirit has been too long in this plane. She needs to be renewed, as do you. Reclamation has a purpose."

Nartesis had never considered the idea. Yet he could feel some force, like gravity, pulling on his spirit. It had been there ever since Conner had awakened him in his cave. But he had walled his mind off from it, and from the part of himself that hungered to be reclaimed. Now, with his purpose gone, he could hardly deny its siren call. "Yes." *Nothing ever lasts. But neither is anything lost.* It was something his mother used to tell him when he was little.

Still, something was holding him back, anchoring him to the Physical plane. One misdeed that had to be rectified first. He slipped his arm gently around Arna, who gazed back into his eyes. "But Arna's spirit is trapped in this plane. I will not leave her here to spend eternity alone."

"Her spirit is not trapped. She has just lost her way." Conner held out his open hand. "I can guide her spirit back."

"You would do that? After all that I have done?"

"I will. If you answer a question. Were you involved in taking the stone from my preceptor?"

Nartesis nearly cried with joy. Conner's request was a simple payment for his help. He clung to Arna's body even tighter. "I was not involved in your preceptor's death. But here is what I do know. Long ago, I summoned a spirit to assist me in acquiring the Fettering Stones I needed. It is my belief that, since before the Great War, someone has been calling that spirit back to the Physical plane, giving her living, breathing flesh much as I am now, working within the Necromancers Order. This spirit's last incarnation was as Breanen Sagamore, wife to the Necromancers' sovereign prince, Galan Martesian. She was also Meera Asheborne's preceptor."

"Meera?"

"Yes." Nartesis lifted his amulet. "I took this stone from Breanen Sagamore, the stone that gave her life. For her to return to this plane again, she would need another stone. It would seem your preceptor was murdered for his stone. I do not know the purpose of her summonings, who summons her, or how they acquired the skills to use these stones to give her life." Nartesis shrugged. "This spirit prefers to go by names similar to BrieAnn. Find her, and your preceptor's killers will not be far away."

"All the stones you stole long ago. Where are they now?"

Shazarack smiled. "I used all I could get my hands on, all but this stone, thirty-two in all. I placed them into the beating hearts of my creations. The stones were what gave my dragons life."

Conner glanced at Skye and then back again.

"Conner." Nartesis felt compelled to share one last point. "There is something else for you to consider. I may have tricked you into helping me, and for that I am sorry. But the charm I used on you would never have worked unless some part of you wished my vision to come true."

Conner stared back at him.

"Do you understand, boy?" Nartesis waited until Conner met his eye. "The Cosmos did not bring you here to be my assistant; I was brought here to be *yours*."

The pull on Nartesis's spirit was growing ever stronger, reminding him of the day he received the Calling, the day he found his mouse bond, Peeps. Now, at the end of this cycle of life, when he felt the weight of so many regrets, one shining light beamed through. He kissed Arna softly on the lips. "Let us go home, my love."

Nartesis nodded his gratitude to Conner, then he and Arna gripped each other's amulets and slipped the thick chains from their necks.

With a flash of brilliant blue light, the force that fettered the two spirits to their vessels broke and the bodies collapsed to the floor.

Conner sensed the two spirits breaking free from their Physical bindings, and with a gentle nudge, he guided them toward the Cosmic pool of energy, completing their reclamations. Then he reached down to retrieve the two amulets and slipped them into a pouch at his waist.

Valkere roared and fluttered away from the ledge.

"Valkere has gone to find Wren. I will stay with him," Skye said. "No doubt, he is burning with rage over what our god did."

Conner felt consumed by thoughts and feelings, a web of unanswered questions and burgeoning beliefs, a frayed network of prickling wonderment and raw impressions. Unable to speak, he nodded, then stepped to the edge of the roof, looking out at the vast patchwork of buildings below. He heard Skye take flight. With the elementals still swirling about him, Conner stepped from the ledge.

"Look!" Marcantos shouted, pointing up as Conner drifted out from the tower and over the city. "Do you see? It is true!" the general proclaimed.

Nearby, Valkere fluttered to the ground and began picking through a jumbled heap, tossing bodies aside. With a roar and eyes a vivid brown, the dragon reached in and plucked a thin body from the bottom of the pile. Wren flung her arms around her bond's neck. Her shoulders shook as she began to weep.

Marcantos threw his arms out wide in exultation, eyes cast to the breaking clouds overhead. And he recited to the small army gathered around him:

> *"The dragon shall rise with its alliance from the east,*
> *And the fall of a great order shall be the presage of the times.*
> *Ascended, the sacrificial gift shall return to the bloodied earth.*
> *These are the signs that the time is nigh. Prepare yourself!"*

"It is the preamble to the Omen of the Dragonbonded!" Marcantos shouted. "The time of the omen is upon us, just as the prophecy foretold!"

As Conner floated over the city wall and descended among the ragged troops and the littering of bodies, Skye settled nearby. Marcantos stepped forward, then dropped to one knee. He lifted his sword to Conner. "It is time, young Dragonbonded, to avow your title as commander of the army."

Just as Hemera broke through the clouds, Conner reached down and, gripping the hilt of the blade, lifted the bloody sword before the gathered crowd. "The Army of the Dragonbonded is born!" he shouted.

The troops roared, brandishing their gleaming weapons high into the air.

Secrets Shared

Conner stood alone, listening to the sounds of the river and nightlife, of crickets and tree frogs and owls. The dense fog that had plagued them for days had lifted, and warm, dry air had settled like a comforting quilt. A number of fires burned near the river, where the army had set up camp, their mood somber, their spirits beleaguered. Conversations were kept to whispers. Conner understood why. Through the afternoon, they had completed the messy, grueling task of burying the friends and comrades who'd died that day, as well as the many undead bodies. A form appeared out of the dark next to him, and he nearly jumped from his skin. "Marcantos," Conner said, his voice shaky. Even in leisure, his general was stealthy.

Marcantos said nothing, seeming to savor the tranquil moment as well.

Conner's eyes traced the jagged edges of Shan-Grail in the distance, silhouetted against the bright night sky. When Conner could stand the silence no longer, he spoke. "It is unfortunate."

"What?" Marcantos asked.

"Having to bury good men and women." Conner had come to know some of those who died, like Staeffan. He could not get the vision of the young man's bright blue eyes, beaming smile, and tenacious spirit from his mind. Nothing had made the Scouter prouder than the honor of being the army's standard bearer. Conner felt responsible for these good people's reclamations. "They fought and died for me."

"They fought for a cause they believed in. There is no better manner in which to die." After a few moments, he added, "Conner, I have fought in numerous battles. Good people always die. Some good did come of this day."

Conner rocked back. "What good ever comes from war, General?"

Marcantos gestured toward the camp. "They knew what they were confronting. When we began this journey, they were Harmonics and Anarchists. Now ..." He pointed to where a few from both platoons congregated, chatting and laughing.

"You think one battle will overcome five hundred years of hostility and distrust?"

"No." Marcantos's gaze never wavered from the huddled groups. "But it is the first small step. Those who have experienced the rite of passage in battle knew what was at stake. Of course, coming out of battle victorious helps. But if we are going to turn them into an army, a *real* army, we need a lot more progress."

Conner was still not sure what he would do with an army now that the threat of Shazarack was gone. Shazarack's offer for a path to peace might have been a sham, but some part of Conner still hoped there was a way to resolve the tension between the two sides that did not bring more needless deaths.

Something Shazarack had said to him at Thanatos kept echoing in his head. Sacrifice is the path to peace. ... There will come a day, a reckoning, very soon, when you will be called upon for your offering. Sacrifice.

Then he recalled the words of Tatem Creeg. War is never glorious, though those who sacrificed life or limb or spirit should be glorified, for they are worthy of our praise. And with our praise, let us hope for the day such sacrifices are no longer needed.

Shazarack had been onto something, just from the wrong perspective. Healing did not come through sacrifice, but through giving. Maybe it was time Conner gave something back, something to help move the troops along the path. He walked toward the large bonfire at the center of the camp. "Wren!" Conner called out.

Talk dwindled as everyone's eyes turned to Conner. Beyond the edge of the firelight, Conner noted Valkere's glowing brown eyes next to Skye's blue; the two had been conspicuously friendly ever since darkness had set in.

Wren parted from the field of silent faces, stepping forward. She lowered her head, her face red. She had defied Conner's command to stay out of the battle.

A murmur broke among the Anarchists, who were unsure what would happen next.

"Meera, is there a name used among the Anarchists that means *audacious*?" Conner could see in the flickering firelight the confused expression on Meera's face.

"Someone who is audacious ... or as we say, plucky"—laughter broke out among the camp—"we call *baelic*."

Conner cleared his throat. "I know that I do not come from Xylor. But in the short time I have known Wren, she has become family to me. And as someone bonded with a dragon, she is my sister. So it is with this declaration, and according to the customs of the Anarchic people, that I name this woman ... *Baela*."

"Baela!" rang up in a great cheer around the fire in Dristonian tradition.

Baela ran to him and threw her arms around his shoulders. Her cheek was warm and wet against his. "Thank you!" she whispered in his ear over the continued chant of her new name. Then turning, she thrust her arms out wide, tossed her head back, and bayed a wolf-like cry over the Anarchic clamor.

The Anarchists erupted as one, a seething tide washing forward. Lifting her on high, they carried her back to the fire where others gathered around, shouting in joyous celebration.

Conner walked back to Marcantos as the jubilant Anarchists grabbed the Harmonics around them and dragged them into the chaotic merrymaking. Within minutes, everyone was singing and dancing. He winked at Marcantos with a smile. "Small steps."

Marcantos chuckled, shaking his head. Then his face clouded over. With everyone distracted, he drew Conner to the edge of camp. "Conner, I have been withholding something important for far too long. I cannot keep this to myself any longer. And I believe you are the right person to share this with."

"What is it?" Conner asked.

"When I was in the Barbarians camp at Farlorde, I had an opportunity to view the camp commander's campaign map of the lands to the north of the Dragon's Back Mountains. I know this map to be authentic because it contained the marks of the Anarchists' equivalent of the Harmonics' Cartographers guild. Also, the corner marks on the map showed that it was only fourth generation from the original maps created five hundred years ago."

"Okay. And?" Conner asked.

"As a member of the Warriors Order, I was involved in many skirmishes along the Griffinrock Borderlands. I know that strip of land incredibly well. However, except for the region near Lake Arastone, there are significant variations in the locations of the Borderlands between the commander's map and those drawn by the Harmonic cartographers."

"You're saying there was an error in the map?"

"No, I don't believe so," Marcantos answered. "The chance the map was drawn with such significant errors is incredibly small." He studied Conner's confused expression. "The commander's map would have been checked and rechecked by several experienced mapmakers before it was ever put to use. Therefore, I am confident that the map at Farlorde is an exact replica of the one handed to the Anarchists at the signing of the Treaty of Alignment at the end of the Anarchic War. And since all campaign maps are made from the same master, that means all Anarchic maps are the same." Marcantos rubbed at his chin. "This could only mean that the maps given to the Anarchists at the signing of the treaty were different from those handed to the Harmonics. That could only have been by design."

"To what end?"

"I have had time to think long about that, and the only answer I came up with is to perpetuate distrust and hatred between the two sides. Think of it. It is the perfect ruse to ensure that Harmonics and Anarchists never reached any amiable resolution to this long-term stalemate."

"No wonder there's never been any lasting peace."

"For five hundred years, both sides have believed the other responsible for flagrant violations of the treaty by crossing into what they thought to be the Borderlands. Who would seriously contemplate proposing a truce under such circumstances?" Marcantos squared himself before Conner. "I would like to learn more about how this happened, and who might have been part of this. But I am an outlaw in both lands."

"Stealing a map from the Anarchists and giving it to the Harmonics won't help. Anyone still in the good graces of the realms would be challenged to explain how they came upon the map." Conner considered asking Layna, but as Conner's preceptor, she would be guarded closely for some time.

"It will require further conversation. Others must be brought in before a plan is devised. But one thing is certain." Marcantos's brow bent low. "Once war breaks out between the two lands, we cannot pick a side. To do so would fragment our fledgling army."

Marcantos's mention of war drove Conner's thoughts to Veressa. He could not help thinking about the three fortnights he had been her Champion, and of the day on their ride along the River Tresdan that she had opened up to him. Now he wished he had acted sooner, told her how much he loved her. Would he ever see her again? Where was she? Was she safe? He closed his eyes, searching through his feelings. It took but a moment before he sensed her—safe, though tormented. He stretched out with his mind, and she reached back. A gentle caress, reminding him of how she made him feel. Veressa would always be there, with him, a part of him, like a pleasant dream he would hold on to. But a dream was all she would ever be.

Conner opened his eyes, grounding himself in the smells of fire, the flickering rhythmic motion and merry songs of his army in celebration. In the morning, they would repair the damage Shazarack's forces had caused along the western ridge, then the army would use the tunnels to return to the Valley of Souls. As news of the necro-army's defeat at Shan-Grail spread, more would assuredly come to join the ranks. He had the Omen of the Dragonbonded to thank for that.

He gave Marcantos his gratitude and went to have a talk with Skye. He found the dragon alone. Valkere had moved closer to Wren—Baela. "How is Valkere?" he asked.

"He will live," Skye stated. "He is surprisingly tough ... for a Mountainshaker. And Baela?"

Conner watched Baela dance by the fire, mingling and laughing with the troops. "She is going to be just fine."

"So, what are we going to do next?"

"I think the first priority is for me to train Baela. She needs to improve her skills in using elementals if we are going to get Morgas back from

Lacerus. She's a quick study, but I need to trust that she has my back before I go poking at hornet nests."

"And I will work with Valkere."

Conner thought Skye was volunteering just a little too quickly, but no need bringing that up. If Skye and Valkere wanted to make a big show of pretending to not like each other, then who was he to get in their way? As long as they were both ready when they went to retrieve Morgas. But Conner had another quick mission before he tackled training Baela: a quick trip into Griffinrock, one he would have to take in the cloak of darkness. "You have a lot of explaining to do."

"About what?"

"About what happened on the top of the tower. Shazarack had some kind of power over me. I could feel him influencing me, but I couldn't do anything about it. Then you showed up. How did you stop him?"

Skye looked away. "I will tell you how. But not now. Not yet."

"What do you mean? When are you going to tell me?"

"When it becomes important."

Conner sensed his bond's stubbornness setting in like clay baking in Hemera's summer rays. "Oh, we are not done with this."

Skye snort-sniffed in response.

"It seems you have spent too much time around all us bipedal Harmonic bores."

Still, no response from the dragon.

"Fine, then. Keep your secrets."

Getting more from his bond would be like pulling teeth, so Conner found a quiet, secluded spot to set out his bedroll and get some well-deserved sleep, though it did not come swiftly. He tried to quiet the thoughts, to silence the questions. But they would not leave him be. Images of hieroglyphs and painted pictures, of people and creatures unimaginable. A picture of Nartesis blew across his mind. Nartesis had suggested he was there for Conner's benefit, not the other way around. Could that be? Was Nartesis just another trial for his ascension? And there was the spirit of Skye, shining and glorious, blasting away Nartesis's falsehoods. Conner rolled on his side and gently shooed all his musings to the dark corners of his mind.

Conner woke later than he'd expected. He sat up with a groan and squinted to the east. Hemera had already crested the mountains, bringing some much-needed warmth to the valley. The camp was mostly quiet, likely from the celebrations that lasted until early in the morning. The smell of smoke, carrying a hint of rations cooking, wafted his way. Rubbing his grumbling belly, he stumbled forward in search of something to eat. By the main fire, Meera sat with someone wearing deep-blue Sorcerer robes. The two were huddled close, intensely animated though speaking quietly. When Meera saw Conner, she waved, rose, and strode away.

The Sorcerer turned his way, and Conner stopped and stared. "Layna?"

Layna smiled up at him, her face haggard, the stem of her pipe between her teeth. "Good morning, Conner."

"How—? What—?"

"That is a longer story than you would want to hear standing up." The Sorceress tapped the log next to her.

Conner dropped onto the log, eager to hear what she had to say.

"Shortly after you ... left Graystone, I talked to Veressa, who conveyed what you told her about Shazarack and his plan." She shrugged. "I came to lend a hand. Alas, Horasius and I got caught in a snowstorm, so it took much longer than I had expected. It seems I am a day late for everything recently." She leaned closer. "But since I am here and we have the camp to ourselves, maybe we can finish that conversation we started when last we met."

"I agree. I've had a lot on my mind lately." Unsure where to begin, he waited for her to break the ice.

"You know I cannot be your preceptor any longer," she said.

Conner dipped his head slightly. "Because I have been banned from Griffinrock?"

"That is a factor. If my order were to find out ..." She shook her head. "But that's not the main reason." She refilled her pipe before going on. "When you left on your mission into the Anarchic Lands, Grimmley and I took advantage of your ... departure to take on our own missions of sorts. I told you about Grimmley's—to investigate the stones."

"Yes."

"My mission was along a different path. Like everyone who ever researched the first Dragonbonded, I had reached the conclusion that little information remained about them because they were mysterious and aloof. However, all that changed when you came along."

"I don't understand. How did I change that?"

"Within days of your arrival at Graystone, stories of your heroism were being shared, put to pen, stage, and song. That is when it occurred to me—that is what *should* have happened with the first Dragonbonded. So why aren't there any books about those who brought about the end of the Anarchic War? Dragonbonded fanned out across the Harmonic Realms to protect the greater castles. There should be dozens, if not hundreds of books filled with stories and accounts of the days of the first Dragonbonded. Instead, all we have are … misleading folklore and a few fairy tales."

"So maybe the old stories of the Dragonbonded going mad living like hermits at Dragongarde were all just … fables?" It was almost too much to hope for.

"I think so. The morning following your departure, I rode to Darmascus to see if I could uncover something more about the first Dragonbonded." Layna sighed her frustration. "I won't go into the many sordid details, but with some groveling before the king, and a little perseverance and ingenuity, I struck gold in the most unlikely of places—in the personal diary belonging to Grenetia's young Prince Elliot. In 693, some forty years following the agreement between the realms and the Dragonbonded that created the Order of the Dragonbonded, Prince Elliot wrote extensively about one of the Dragonbonded who spent several years safeguarding the city of Darmascus. Her name was Rissa Elmcutter."

Conner leaned back, recalling Wallis Arkman's story of Elmcutter, the first dragon-bonded, the one who'd bonded with Skye's father. He recalled several paintings and tapestries hanging in Dragongarde in which groups of Dragonbonded were depicted. In most of them, a young woman was always featured in the foreground, with short-cropped blond hair and blue eyes. What stood out about her was the same sad expression. Finally, he could put a name to that face.

"We have love to thank for this revelation," Layna went on. "It seems Prince Elliot developed quite a fondness for Rissa. And because he was so enamored, he was observant of everything she did. And he wrote much of it down. Several hundred pages, in fact."

That piqued Conner's interest. "What did you learn?"

"We will save a good bit for when we have the energy to pick through and find the nuggets. However, there are two details I want to share. First, the Dragonbonded did not use the same form of magic as the other orders. They had mastery over all four elementals. And they did not use incantations or focuses. They just"—Layna shrugged bewilderment—"did it. And *that* is why I cannot be your preceptor."

Conner felt a sudden relief. "Yes, that pretty much describes what I've learned—I just *do* it." Layna's confirmation of this meant he could feel confident teaching Baela this way. "I know you would like to know more, but I don't think I could describe it. At least, not yet."

Layna smiled. "That's fine. It brings me joy to know you have figured it out."

"And the other detail?" Conner asked.

"Through Prince Elliot's writings, it was evident that their relationship was becoming romantic. And during the blossoming intimacy, the prince asked Rissa how she could wield so much elemental power. She confided in him that it was through her link with her dragon. Her dragon *was* her focus."

Conner recollected the times he had been forced to use elementals—in Pennington Point when he'd saved Veressa from being captured, when he'd faced Marcantos on the Field of Contest, at Thanatos when he was challenged by Shazarack, and at the pinnacle of Shan-Grail's structure that morning. Each time, he'd tapped into a conduit in his mind, like a running stream of light. Just recalling those memories made his heart race, sent energy coursing through him. Skye was his focus.

After some time, Layna asked, "Does that make sense?"

Conner glanced away. "It does. And it will come in handy helping Baela learn how to use elementals. But why do you think *this* document is the only record to survive?"

Layna raised her eyebrows, giving him time to answer his own question.

"You believe someone deliberately destroyed all the books and scrolls about the Dragonbonded."

Layna nodded, seeming somewhat surprised. "I do."

"Wouldn't that take years to accomplish?"

"To expunge all traces, or to morph them into misshapen tales of fantasy?" Layna chuckled. "Decades, if not centuries. Want to share how you reached the conclusion I did with only a fraction of the effort?"

Conner rubbed the pouch at his side containing the two amulets he had taken from Shazarack and Arna. "Right now, it's just a hunch I'm working on." He took a deep breath. "When do you head back?"

"With Hemera's first light. It occurred to me that our network of Anarchic spies may have played a role in getting you banished from Griffinrock. If so, they are alive and well. More work is needed if we are to smoke them out."

"Which means these spies have wormed their way into Queen Mariette's graces."

Layna only nodded, unable to loosen her jaw.

"It will be dangerous."

Layna laughed. "I am an orderman, Conner. *Life* is dangerous."

Conner nodded with pursed lips, his thoughts turning to Grimmley.

"I tried to warn Grimmley not to kick a hornet's nest," Layna said, as if reading his thoughts.

"None of this makes any sense, Layna. I have to believe the majority of Anarchists would prefer a peaceful resolution. So if the Anarchists have enough influence over the new queen to get me out of the way, why wouldn't they stop her from declaring war, or at least slow her down? If these spies don't want to stop the war, what do they want?" Conner remembered something Shazarack had said to him at Thanatos. "Someone I met once said, 'Only those who hunger for power and control truly desire war.' Maybe all of this is for power." As he said the words, he knew he was onto something. What if the differences in the maps and the proclamation of war were meant to inflame hostilities between the two sides? In fact, what if Queen Izadora had been assassinated for that very same reason? Conner felt dizzy at the notion someone had designs to rekindle the Great War. Numbness gripped him.

"Power can make people to do irrational things," Layna said. "Meera told me how you defeated Shazarack and saved the army. And she told me about last night, giving Baela her name." Layna smiled warmly as she squeezed his wrist. "Grimmley would be very proud of how you have changed."

Conner dipped his eyes, his cheeks flushing at Layna's compliment. "I did not do it alone." He thought back to the previous night, watching as Wren—Baela—whooped and danced about the bonfire that had grown to nearly twice its previous size, while a chorus of men and women clapped in time. The only way to tell the Anarchists from the Harmonics had been by who knew the words to the songs.

Layna broke out in sudden laughter. "Maybe you haven't changed so much after all."

Conner cracked a huge grin. "I don't feel any different either." Especially since I ascended, he thought. What changes did you expect, Conner? To grow a tail? Sprout dragon horns?

"What I mean is that while the world is being ripped asunder, you have found a way to stitch a few pieces of it together."

"At least for now," Conner responded.

"Yes, well, Meera is another good example. Your act of kindness to let her go led her to Thanatos, where she learned of Shazarack's scheme, so that she could return to Dragongarde and warn you. Without her help, we would be on the verge of a necro invasion."

Conner bobbed his head. "Marcantos says the Omen of the Dragonbonded is upon us. He believes the preamble has already been fulfilled."

"And what did I tell you about prophecies?" she grumbled.

"I recall. We make of them what we want." He considered saying more. But his thoughts were a jumble of confusing emotions and unanswered questions. He wanted Layna to be right about the Omen, but for the first time, he was unsure. She, like Grimmley, knew how to twist the meaning of words into pretzels. And if the Omen was true? Well ... life was about to get a whole lot more dangerous.

The crunching of boots nearing drew the pair's attention. Meera squatted next to Conner and prodded the flames with a long stick, kicking up sparks that flicked off to the west. Morgana appeared next to her, staring at the fire.

Meera peered at Layna from beneath furrowed brow. "You think we should tell him now?" she asked as she heated her palms near the flame.

Layna narrowed her eyes, sizing Conner up across the flames. "I still am not sure he is ready for the news."

"News? What news?" Conner prodded as the women exchanged glances.

Layna winked. "Well, I just heard myself, so I think you should tell him."

"Tell me what? Out with it," he growled.

"Is he always this impatient?" Meera asked.

"You have no idea," Layna shook her head.

Conner stifled a cheeky remark. *Let them have their fun, Conner.*

Meera looked over at him. "The day before we broke camp north of Dragongarde, two new recruits arrived bearing news from their lands. One was from near Cleft Castle in Grenetia; the other from the Anarchic desert far to the southeast." She bit her lower lip, then shrugged. "Conner, it seems there have been two more human-dragon bondings."

An Unannounced Visitor

Wallis Arkman strolled up the dirt street, whistling an ancient tune, spinning his walking cane and making the occasional comment to Maestro, his squirrel bond riding on his shoulder. The town crier had already turned down the lamps lining the wide street, so it was nearing midnight. After Wallis reached the town square, he shuffled to a stop outside a pub. Overhead, the large marquee for Estora's Tavern, featuring a colorfully painted farming cart being pulled by a prancing pony, swayed in the pleasant autumn breeze. The sounds of laughter and singing inside pulsed through the two broad wooden doors.

Pangs from fortnights of solitude made Wallis pause long enough to have a peep inside. Through two colored-crystal panes in the shape of frothing mugs, he discerned the animated motion of those within. A fortnight hiking from Dragongarde, he was hungry, dirty, and weary, so he contemplated stepping inside. But alas, he had something important yet to accomplish this night. Besides, Eastlander townsfolk were not fond of visitors dropping in unannounced, especially late at night. With a sigh, he shambled on until he came to the large, granite fountain in the center of town. There, extending into the starlit sky, rose the sizable statue of Tatem Creeg, the Paladins Order paragon and the town's namesake. In the lamplight, Wallis examined the effigy. Of what he could still recall of Tatem Creeg, this figure did not much resemble the man he had met. Creeg was a simple man, a guildsman of the Modeic clergy. This statue had the same solemn expression, the same compassionate eyes ... well, even the same crooked nose. But the real Tatem Creeg had never shaved his head. And Creeg would certainly never have worn armor or carried a sword! He would have thought the great Bremenn priests who sculpted this effigy more reliable in creating images of their idol. At least they'd gotten the round disk he held in his other hand right. He leaned closer, squinting to read the epitaph beneath the statue, but the granite plate was so worn that *Legend* was the only word he could make out.

"Legend," Wallis snorted, then straightened his back. "Hmm!" He proceeded across the square, then headed up the western street until he came to a place where the road ended abruptly with a line of dense trees and brush. He entered an open structure to his right and wove his way stealthily across the hardwood floor littered with a patchwork of furniture. He evaded numerous animals, mostly asleep, covering the surfaces and filling cages that hung like tropical moss from ancient oaks.

At the back of the building, he came to a set of stairs, which he took, leading to an enclosed sleeping loft above. In the bed slept a thin, middle-aged woman with frizzled brown hair. He sat on the bed next to her and closed his eyes. He drew on the four elementals and placed the tips of his fingers behind her left ear. Sending out gentle waves of energy, he probed for the gulf in her mind, the hole that brought about the Yearning. When he found the spot, he threaded the four elementals together in a delicate weave, and, with surgical precision, gently connected the surfaces of the gap. When he was done, he sat back with an exhausted sigh and waited. The operation was not permanent, just a makeshift measure that would dissolve in a few hours. But it would be enough for what was needed.

After a moment, the woman's eyes fluttered open.

Wallis smiled down at her. "Hello, Karlana."

Karlana Landcraft blinked several times, her face looking like she'd just bit into a lime. "Wallis?" she finally asked.

Wallis swirled his hands upward in a grand gesture. "In the flesh."

Karlana pressed her palm to her forehead. "I— I was having a bad dream." She looked about. "Am I still in Striker's Keep?"

"I am afraid not. You are in Creeg's Point."

Karlana squeezed her eyes shut. "So it was not a dream. Or am I still dreaming?"

Wallis squeezed her hand in his. "You are very much awake." He leaned close. "Karlana, I need you to listen to me." He waited for her eyes to settle on him.

"Of course, Wallis. Anything I can do to repay your generosity."

"When Conner Stonefield comes to see you, there is something I need you to do." Wallis moved his lips to her ear and whispered his request, then sat back. "Can you do that for me?"

Karlana appeared puzzled for a moment. "Are you sure Conner will come to see me?"

Wallis studied his hands. "I cannot say for sure. The lad is beyond my viewing now. If he does, then we all may still have a chance. If not ..." He shrugged.

Then they sat and talked about Karlana's troubled youth growing up orphaned, retracing the day Wallis showed up in her town and offered her a different future. They chatted about how he'd taught her to manipulate Fire and Water at an early age, and laughed about the time she'd caught his clothes on fire. They chatted about her wonder and joy when Wallis had told her that someday, she would find a very special bond.

"I have not thought of those days in a very long time," Karlana said. "I never understood, the day you took me to Brightmead Estate, how you knew they would look after me, that I would be accepted in the Sorcerers Order. I was only twelve. How did you know I would become a powerful Sorceress? Why did you even care?"

"I care about everyone, Karlana. It is just that some impact the future more than others."

On they chatted of her days at Brightmead, of her commission into the Queen's Defenders, of her days at Striker's Keep. But soon Karlana lost her focus, misplacing her thread of thought mid-sentence. Then she forgot where she was.

Still, Wallis stayed with her, holding her soft hand in his, telling her that it would be all right, that she would always be looked after.

Karlana smiled kindly at him. "Who are you?" she asked.

He patted the back of her hand. "Just a friend stopping by to say hi. But I see you need your rest. It is time for you to sleep. Tomorrow, you have animals to care for."

"Yes." She nodded with pride. "They need me."

Maestro climbed on his shoulder as Wallis rose. "We all do, Karlana. We all do." He waited until Karlana drifted back to sleep, then departed.

Cravenrock

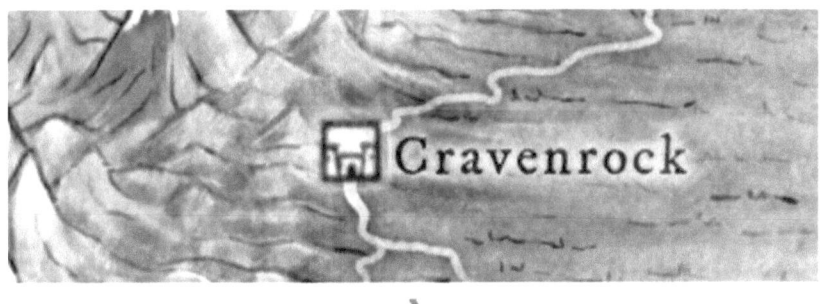

Jarvus pulled his Warlock cape and hood forward to stave off the bone-chilling wind gusting down from the mountains to the north. It was the kind of cold late-autumn air that seeped into the bones and sapped one of all energy. It was shaping up to be a harsh winter. His eyes moved across the open plains before him, then farther northwest, where the pale orange glow of the enemy's Dreadcreek outpost fires shimmered in the distance. A horse's footfalls drew him from his brooding thoughts. He hoped the rendezvous would be quick. "Brother," he said with a bite of irritability.

"Brother," Sarmenion responded, reining in beside Jarvus.

"I doubt I will sleep a wink tonight," Jarvus said. Centuries of planning had led the Kindred to this point. Everything hinged on the next few days. He examined the Anarchic oracle beside him. "Have you had any new divinations regarding the Dragonbonded?"

Sarmenion huffed. "Do not let the boy or his dragon distract you, Brother. Their efforts have played right into our hands, as I said they would. And now, not only is the meddlesome Shaman Rollingsworth out of the way, but the boy is banished from Griffinrock. He is no longer a threat." Sarmenion laughed at Jarvus. "My sight may be hampered by their bonding, but since the Cosmic alignment on Midsummer's Night, I see clearly enough. Have a little faith in our plan. It will succeed. You need to focus on the coming battle."

"My mind is clear, Brother." Jarvus's brow bent low. He did not like the oracle reminding him what was needed.

"Everything is coming together perfectly, Brother," Sarmenion said soothingly. "Once the Anarchic orders received news that the new queen signed the proclamation of war, and that the Necromancers' army has been destroyed, they understood the full gravity of the situation. Our report that a dragon-bonded Anarchist has joined forces with Conner was just the nudge they needed to see they had no choice but to go on the offensive. Now"—Sarmenion leaned closer—"what of the army?"

"The Anarchic forces are amassed along the Borderlands behind us. We begin the invasion of Griffinrock at first light."

"Just as I have foretold," Sarmenion said with intense pleasure, then pointed at the fire glow of the outpost ahead. "Dreadcreek will fall before first snow. With supply lines across the Borderlands secure, the Anarchic army will march on Cravenrock before the plains freeze."

Jarvus grunted skeptically. He was not so easily swayed by the oracle's predictions. Sarmenion's divinations five hundred years before had resulted in the Great War. And with the meddlesome first Dragonbonded's interference, that venture nearly became a debacle. The Kindred were only now recovering. "And you are confident that Griffinrock does not see this coming?"

Sarmenion guffawed. "They are ill prepared for what is ahead for them. The Harmonic spies hiding out in our army have all been hunted down and expunged. All while Brothers Karmenian and Eladon work to mislead the Harmonic orders into preparing for a spring invasion. Neither crowns nor Harmonic orders will expect this bold move. And with winter setting in, the crowns will be helpless to assist the city before spring. With the fall of Cravenrock, Griffinrock's demise will follow."

Jarvus nodded, eager to return to his warm fire. "Cravenrock will be in our hands within a month." Turning his mare, Jarvus rode back to camp.

Kriston waited in the shadows outside the gates of Cravenrock, watching two guards let the last stragglers into the city before they closed the gates for the night. When it came to Cravenrock guardsmen, the best policy was always to remain unnoticed, especially this late at night. Though city guardsmen had a very short memory, it had not been that long since he and Conner had broken out of the stockade, not to mention nearly getting caught attempting to steal a scroll from a Sorcerer passing through. None of this dampened Kriston's confidence. If he seriously thought he would be stopped, he would have used the secret underground passage north of the city. As it turned out, his faith in the guards' ineptitude was well justified.

As the two guards frisked a drunk staggering toward the gate, he slipped behind them and on into the city. Just past the gates, he skirted the city's large dirt courtyard and then headed up a narrow street. Soon, the sounds and smells of Cravenrock's marketplace with its usual bustling nightlife filled the air.

Kriston checked the purse he had lifted from a merchant he passed near Bell's Ferry. Five coins remaining. If he rationed his spending and took advantage of opportunities that presented themselves, he had more than enough to get by … until the appropriate job opening came his way. He started forward, but a familiar deep voice drew his eye from across the open square. Three Warrior apprentices in a fit of laughter were approaching his concealed location. There, in the middle, was … *Pauli!* Smiling, Kriston started to step out of the shadows, but then shrank back. *What are you thinking? A good thief always remains unnoticed!*

"I'm telling you," Pauli beseeched his two comrades. A young grizzly waddled along beside Pauli. "As honest as wheat grows in fields! I was the Dragonbonded's best friend. We grew up in Creeg's Point together. Heck, I used to beat Conner up when we were young."

Pauli's words only drew further guffaws and jeers of skepticism from the other two.

Conner, Kriston thought as Pauli disappeared into the darkness on the other side of the market. When news of Conner's arrest had reached his ear, Kriston had contemplated going to see him in the dungeon. But he had been afraid the royal guard were looking for him. So he hid out the night in the city. The next morning, he saw Conner fly away on Skye and heard that Conner had been banished from Griffinrock. Kriston had been abandoned yet again, tossed to the side of the street like trash. He had allowed himself to believe that someone had actually cared for him, someone would look after him. He would never be that stupid again.

After pilfering some food from the market, Kriston snaked north along dark alleys. At last, he entered an abandoned building. Lifting the side of a fake crate in the back, he peered down at the black hole, a vertical shaft that would take him to the underbelly of the city, to the Cravenrock Thieves Guild. He knew that the guild's patron saint, the Assassin Lacerus, was gone—a wanted fugitive of the realms. But Kriston had faith in the guild's resourcefulness and powerful people's greed. They would have a new sponsor. And with a little luck, maybe they had a new leader, someone more inspirational than that cruel Pirate.

Only one way to find out, Kriston … no, Bandit thought as he attacked the ladder with enthusiasm. Finally, he was home.

Epilogue—Monastery at Stonewell

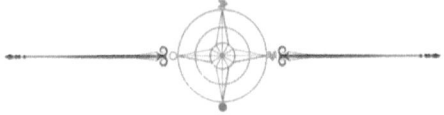

Veressa leaned forward in her saddle and flipped back her green hood to get a better look at the monastery. Though it was anything but what she'd expected, the sight still made her shiver with excitement. The cloister was rugged and old, with walls constructed of thick oak logs aligned vertically and sharpened to points at the top. Its single stone building, capped with a bell tower, made it appear more like a remote outpost near the Borderlands than a secluded fortress deep in the Griffinrock forest, a mere eighty miles south of Graystone. A splattering of winter's first snow covered the grounds outside the gate that appeared near the rutted road they had taken from nearby Stonewell Castle. A handful of people gathered near the gate waited patiently.

"I cannot believe you are going through with this, Veressa," Annabelle admonished, for what little good it would do. "But then again, you've never listened to my advice when you get some crazy notion stuck in that dense head of yours." In the silence that followed, the Ranger chewed on her lip and fidgeted with the reins. "You were the only one successfully holding back the tide of war. With your aunt as queen, the War Council is moving quickly in planning their invasion. And this is when you choose to stick your head in the sand?"

Veressa furrowed her brow, eyes narrowing at Annabelle, who just two days prior, had completed her grandmaster studies in a near-record thirty days, only to appear at Graystone to discover Mariette had assumed the throne. And since then, Annabelle had been unrelenting in telling Veressa just what she thought of her decision to step aside. "I would not call my efforts to stem the push for war a success. I was merely delaying the inevitable. You know that. Father used to say, 'If you can't lead, get out of the way so someone else can.'" She crossed her forearms over the saddle horn. "And I am not sticking my head anywhere it doesn't belong. Must I remind you of my dream vision?"

On the day Veressa had bonded with Antilles, she'd fallen and struck her head. In her unconscious state, the Djinn Ourea came to her. *I am Ourea, vessel and spirit bearer of Earth elemental. Everything you hold dear is but desert sand, Veressa. Soon you must choose among many difficult paths. Some would bring you joy, but only at great sorrow to your world. Others you would take alone, bringing great sacrifice and suffering to those you hold dear, but the choice would heal your world from seeds of travesty yet to be sown. You must prepare for the journey ahead.* Since then, Veressa had struggled to make sense of the Djinn's words. *In time, all will be clear,* the voice had said. She had to believe she was making the right choices.

"I could also remind you," Veressa went on, "that *you* were the one who said I had been chosen to play a vital role in the future of the realms."

"I would have thought by 'vital role' you knew I meant as Queen of Griffinrock. Maybe I should have been more specific," Annabelle grumbled. "I suppose delaying the proclamation for war did have some effect. No general worth his weight in hay would want an army stranded on the Dristonian plains during the dead of winter. Queen Mariette cannot begin the invasion of the Anarchic Lands until spring."

Veressa felt compelled to remind Annabelle about a key factor in her decision to secede the throne. "Don't forget: Conner was right. Shazarack *had* returned from the dead. And if I hadn't done what was necessary to set him free, Conner wouldn't have stopped him," she added with pride. Just saying her Champion's name made her heart ache. She wondered if she would ever see him again. Unfortunately, neither his heroism nor her pleas had moved Mariette to rescind his banishment. "Think where we might be if I had not stepped aside."

"Okay, Veressa." Annabelle tilted her head toward the monastery. "But are you sure *this* is what you want?"

Veressa chewed on her lip for a moment, then peered down at Antilles. The large white cat perked his ears forward and took a step, then looked up at her. Veressa sensed the flow of feelings from her bond, ones she had never sensed before—anticipation and excitement. And she recalled other words Ourea had said to her. *I am to send you my young brother Antilles so that he may bring you strength and aid you along your path.* Veressa did not answer Annabelle.

"You do realize that once you enter those gates, your life will no longer be yours. You will come out as a Ranger student rank. You could be commissioned as an officer in the Queen's Defenders, doing your aunt's bidding. Or maybe you'll be commanding a platoon of archers on the front lines of this war. Or an officer in the Elvenstein royal guard, protecting one of King Friedrick's darling princes."

Veressa shot flaming arrows at Annabelle with her eyes. "When has my life ever been my own, Annabelle?"

Still, Veressa refused to keep secrets from her best friend, the woman she thought of as her sister and closest confidant. "There is something I did not tell you about my trip to Elvenstein. King Friedrick said something that actually helped guide my decision."

Annabelle took a deep breath and rolled her eyes. "Anytime you consider using something that bumbling old fool says, you should have your head examined. What did old King Friedrick say?"

"That one must choose between royalty and the orders, that one cannot do both."

Annabelle blinked. "Maybe there is something left in that old misogynist after all."

Veressa's stomach churned over the idea that her choices always seemed to be between only two options. "Enough on that. How about sharing some secrets about what I can expect inside?"

Annabelle tilted her head forward and furrowed her brow at Veressa, lips pressed tight.

Veressa chortled at the Ranger's unusual silence. "No harm trying."

"Just remember what I taught you. Don't let your self-confidence get in the way of listening, and you will do fine. Just keep in mind that a Ranger's strength is not just about how to use elementals. It is about deception, patience, stealth, and cunning. And do not trust everything you see and hear."

"Okay." Veressa drew the word out slowly. "That sounds ominous."

"And do not mention your dream vision to *anyone*. Most would write it off as the rantings of royalty attempting to get attention, or some such nonsense. But a few might take notice and consider its validity. In either case, it does you no justice."

"I know better than to draw attention to myself."

Annabelle huffed. "If that is true, then you *have* changed."

The deep sound of an iron bell preceded the gate swinging wide. The half dozen people waiting outside filed in.

Annabelle drew her shoulders back and nodded proudly at Veressa. "Well, off with you, then."

Veressa heeled Toran forward and cantered the last hundred paces to the monastery. Already, she could sense this was not just going to be a new chapter in her life. She was starting a whole new story.

– THE END –

BOOK 4: OMEN OF THE DRAGONBONDED
Available in late 2021

Conner has ascended, though he is still not sure precisely what that means. Banished from his homeland, he turns his attention toward training a burgeoning cadre of dragon-bonded youths gathered from across the two lands, and an army growing from news of his victory over the ancient Necromancer, Nartesis Shazarack, and the declaration that the Omen of the Dragonbonded has begun.

Having relinquished the throne to her aunt Mariette, Veressa begins a new journey as a Ranger apprentice, to find her path as the elemental Djinn Ourea, vessel and spirit bearer of Earth elemental, had foretold. But first, she must face deep-seated demons that she has worked hard to suppress.

While Conner and Veressa wonder if they will ever see each other again, the Kindred have pushed their plans to the final stage, convincing the Anarchic orders to take the offensive. And the invasion of Griffinrock has begun.

Be sure to visit the Dragonbonded website to find out more about upcoming books or to sign up for the monthly newsletter:

https://www.thedragonbonded.com

ABOUT THE AUTHOR

JD (Jim) Hart's own fantasy adventure began when, during college, *The Hobbit* was literally dropped in his lap. With the turn of that book's first page, he was forever bound to worlds of magic, dragons, and epic adventures. After many years working as a software manager, engineer, and organizational change consultant, he has decided to leave the fast-paced, high-tech world behind. His new adventure is writing imaginary tales that explore humanity's immense diversity in philosophy, and our connections to each other and to the natural world. Jim lives in North Carolina.

His debut series, **The Dragonbonded Return**, introduces readers to the distant lands of the Harmonics and the Anarchists, home to Shamans and Necromancers, Rangers and Assassins, Warriors and Barbarians, Sorcerers and Warlocks—and, of course, those who bond with dragons.

www.ingramcontent.com/pod-product-compliance
Lightning Source LLC
Chambersburg PA
CBHW030842030726
47495CB00005B/1333